# THE
# LOST
# BOOKS

teddekker.com

# DEKKER FANTASY

*Immanuel's Veins*
*House* (WITH FRANK PERETTI)

## BOOKS OF HISTORY CHRONICLES

### THE LOST BOOKS (YOUNG ADULT)
*Chosen*
*Infidel*
*Renegade*
*Chaos*
*Lunatic* (WITH KACI HILL)
*Elyon* (WITH KACI HILL)
*The Lost Books Visual Edition*

### THE CIRCLE SERIES
*Black*
*Red*
*White*
*Green*
*The Circle Series Visual Edition*

### THE PARADISE BOOKS
*Showdown*
*Saint*
*Sinner*

# DEKKER MYSTERY

*Kiss* (WITH ERIN HEALY)
*Burn* (WITH ERIN HEALY)

### THE HEAVEN TRILOGY
*Heaven's Wager*
*When Heaven Weeps*
*Thunder of Heaven*

*The Martyr's Song*

### THE CALEB BOOKS
*Blessed Child*
*A Man Called Blessed*

# DEKKER THRILLER

*THR3E*
*Obsessed*
*Adam*
*Skin*
*Blink of an Eye*

# THE
# LOST
# BOOKS

## TED DEKKER

**THOMAS NELSON**
*Since 1798*

NASHVILLE   DALLAS   MEXICO CITY   RIO DE JANEIRO

Published in Nashville, Tennessee, by Thomas Nelson. Thomas Nelson is a registered trademark of Thomas Nelson, Inc.

Published in association with Thomas Nelson and Creative Trust, 5141 Virginia Way, Suite 320, Brentwood, TN, 37027.

Thomas Nelson, Inc. books may be purchased in bulk for educational, business, fund-raising, or sales promotional use. For information, please e-mail SpecialMarkets@ThomasNelson.com.

Publisher's Note: This novel is a work of fiction. Names, characters, places, and incidents are either products of the author's imagination or used fictitiously. All characters are fictional, and any similarity to people living or dead is purely coincidental.

Cover Design by The DesignWorks Group, Inc.
Page Design by Casey Hooper
Map Design by Chris Ward

**Library of Congress Cataloging-in-Publication Data is Available**

ISBN: 978-1-40168-754-0

*Printed in the United States of America*

12 13 14 15 16 QG 5 4 3 2 1

# CONTENTS

# CHOSEN

## LOST BOOK 1

# BEGINNINGS

O ur story begins in a world totally like our own, yet completely different. What once happened here in our own history seems to be repeating itself thousands of years from now, some time beyond the year 4000 AD.

But this time the future belongs to those who see opportunity before it becomes obvious. To the young, to the warriors, to the lovers. To those who can follow hidden clues and find a great treasure that will unlock the mysteries of life and wealth.

Thirteen years have passed since the lush, colored forests were turned to desert by Teeleh, the enemy of Elyon and the vilest of all creatures. Evil now rules the land and shows itself as a painful, scaly disease that covers the flesh of the Horde, a people who live in the desert.

The powerful green waters, once precious to Elyon, have vanished from the earth except in seven small forests surrounding seven small lakes. Those few who have chosen to follow the ways of Elyon now live in these forests, bathing once daily in the powerful waters to cleanse their skin of the disease.

The number of their sworn enemy, the Horde, has grown in thirteen years and, fearing the green waters above all else, these desert dwellers have sworn to wipe all traces of the forests from the earth.

Only the Forest Guard stands in their way. Ten thousand elite fighters against an army of nearly four hundred thousand Horde.

But the Forest Guard is starting to crumble.

# ONE

## DAY ONE

Qurong, general of the Horde, stood on the tall dune five miles west of the green forest, ignoring the fly that buzzed around his left eye.

His flesh was nearly white, covered with a paste that kept his skin from itching too badly. His long hair was pulled back and woven into dreadlocks, then tucked beneath the leather body armor cinched tightly around his massive chest.

"Do you think they know?" the young major beside him asked.

Qurong's milky white horse, chosen for its ability to blend with the desert, stamped and snorted.

The general spit to one side. "They know what we want them

to know," he said. "That we are gathering for war. And that we will march from the east in four days."

"It seems risky," the major said. His right cheek twitched, sending three flies to flight.

"Their forces are half what they once were. As long as they think we are coming from the east, we will smother them from the west."

"The traitor insists that they are building their forces," the major said.

"With young pups!" Qurong scoffed.

"The young can be crafty."

"And I'm not? They know nothing about the traitor. This time we will kill them all."

Qurong turned back to the valley behind him. The tents of his third division, the largest of all Horde armies, which numbered well over three hundred thousand of the most experienced warriors, stretched out nearly as far as he could see.

"We march in four days," Qurong said. "We will slaughter them from the west."

# TWO

Twelve of the forest's strongest and bravest young fighters crouched in their brown battle leathers at each end of the grassy stadium field, waiting for the command to stand and fight for the hairy ball sitting at center field. Five thousand spectators stood in the stands carved from the earth, holding their collective breath. Four squad leaders were to be chosen today, and each one given a house to own, the choice of any horse, and an emerald-handled sword—making them the envy of every man, woman, and child in the village.

All of this would be decided by one man: Thomas Hunter, supreme commander of the Forest Guard.

Johnis stood next to his father, Ramos, shivering a little. It wasn't cold, but the breeze dried the sweat on his neck and made him cool. So he told himself, anyway.

He had dark hair to his shoulders and, according to his father, a strong jaw that was sometimes best kept closed. His nose was sharp and his lips full, giving him the appearance that he was fourteen, not sixteen.

He stared at the hairy Horde ball at center field. His mother, Rosa, had been responsible for that lump of Scab hair. Three months had passed since she'd been killed by the Horde at the forest's edge while searching for a special plant, the catalina cactus, whose herbal power might've healed a fever that had come over Johnis. The Forest Guard had been to the north in battle, but she'd refused to wait for an escort while her boy suffered.

His mother had always been like that, dropping everything on his account. Sweet Mother, with her long, dark hair and ruby lips.

*Mother, why did you go? Please forgive me, dear Mother.*

Johnis had thrown himself on the ground and wailed for the whole village to hear. His father had left the forest in a rage and returned with the long, tangled hair from ten Horde he'd killed that very afternoon—the makings of that hairy Horde ball on the field now.

But nothing eased the pain in Johnis's chest.

Two weeks ago Thomas Hunter had announced the decision to lower the Forest Guard's recruitment age from eighteen to sixteen. He was looking to boost the fighting force by one thousand. The forests had erupted in debate.

Those who had protested had cried in fear at the thought of their sons and daughters entering battle against the Horde. They all knew that the Forest Guard was outnumbered ten to one. They knew that every time the Guard went to battle, many died. They knew that the weakest, their sons and daughters, would die first.

But the people of the forest also knew that the Horde had sworn to kill them all. All living followers of Elyon knew, whether or not they admitted it publicly, that the fate of the Forest Dwellers rested squarely on the shoulders of the youngest fighters now joining the Forest Guard.

All sixteen- and seventeen-year-olds worth their salt had then signed up to be considered. With his mother's death fresh in his mind, Johnis had been one of the first in line. The Guard had dismissed all but two thousand, from which they would select the final thousand fighters.

Johnis was one of those who'd been dismissed. Too small, they said. He was just barely sixteen and still too wounded from his mother's death. Maybe next time, if there was a next time.

"What do you say, Johnis?" his father whispered. "Who is the strongest?"

Johnis scanned the players in this game Thomas Hunter called *football*—a name that supposedly came from his dreams of another land. All twenty-four were already mighty fighters, even though none was older than seventeen. Roughly half were women, and of those Johnis thought maybe Darsal was the strongest. Not the largest, but the strongest. And very quick.

She crouched fewer than fifty feet from where Johnis stood on the sidelines. Her fingers were wrapped tightly around the same three-foot fighting stick they had all been given. Muscles rippled up her arm, glistening with sweat. The side of her sleeveless tunic was stained with a little blood—it was, after all, a full-contact sport. Within thirty days the recruits would be swinging razor-sharp swords in full battle against the Horde. No one dared enter the Forest Guard fearful of a little blood when so much more was at stake.

Her long, brown hair was tucked under a leather helmet and had been pulled back into a ponytail, showing a strong, smooth jawline to her ear on the right side of her face. A terrible scar marked her left—a burn that forced Johnis to stare and wonder what had put it there. It made her more fearsome than ugly. Whatever had caused the wound had also gotten her left shoulder, although her leather armor covered most of the scar there.

The Horde had killed her father. Johnis could practically see the thirst for revenge in her squinting eyes. But something else had happened to make her stick close to Billos, another fighter in contention for the top spot today. They were from the same forest and were clearly very close. At first Johnis had assumed they were brother and sister, but no.

"What do you say, lad?" his father asked again.

"Darsal," he said, in a whisper that sounded hoarse.

His father grunted. "Now *there's* a choice. She'd make any man a fine wife." He glanced down at Johnis. "A little more muscle on those bones and you could make a play for her yet, boy. Though she seems a bit stuck on the other youngster."

His father nudged him, and Johnis gave him a weak smile.

Father could not know that his frequent comparisons with those who'd been selected to try out for the Forest Guard bothered him. The honor of wearing the hardened leather breastplates, wielding the Guard swords and whips, riding the best horses, being watched by everyone else as you walked down the path on your way to battle—who wouldn't trade his life for a chance to be called one of the Forest Guard?

Who, besides Johnis? Truly, he wasn't sure he would make a good fighter in bloody battle. In fact, he was quite sure he wouldn't.

Still, Father's small comments made Johnis feel weak, reminding him that he stood on the sidelines because he wasn't worthy. He shifted on his feet and crossed his arms over his chest, hugging himself.

Thomas Hunter paced across the field. There wasn't a man or woman among them who wouldn't be honored to kiss the commander's hand. The Forest Guard had saved the forests many times, and Thomas Hunter was the reason for it all.

He slid his emerald-handled sword from its metal sheath, filling the stadium with the sound of steel scraping steel. Perfect silence settled on the crowd.

Thomas swung the sword absently, neatly cutting the grass at his feet in an arc.

"Is this all I can expect from you?" his voice rang out. He jabbed the air with his sword. "I'm looking for four leaders to step forward and show they are worthy to stand by my side."

No one responded. What Thomas could be looking for that he hadn't already seen was beyond Johnis.

"Take a look around," Thomas shouted. He slowly swung his sword across the stadium. "The fate of every man, woman, and child in this arena will be in the hands of the Forest Guard. And you say you want to *lead* that Guard? You are all either mad or complete fools, because I don't see a leader in the lot."

He paced back to the sideline, studying the line of twelve on his right, then the line on his left. Behind him the ball of hair lay undisturbed.

To win, one team had to run to the middle, pick up the ball, and cross the other team's goal line. What seemed simple enough was made very difficult by the fact that the other team was armed with fighting sticks.

The day had started with a hundred of the most promising recruits. Seventy-six had been dismissed, seventeen of them on stretchers.

It was down to these two teams of twelve each.

Thomas raised his sword high, then swung it down hard. "Go!"

The two lines of recruits silently bolted from where they crouched and raced toward the ball on a collision course.

# THREE

For a count of five, the only sound Johnis could hear was the thudding of feet as the two lines sprinted for each other. Silvie, the wiry fireball with short blond hair, was the first to reach the ball.

She'd just scooped it up when the lines collided with a tremendous thud. Then the sound of sticks smashing filled the stadium with bone-jarring cracks.

The crowd erupted in a roar of support that smothered the grunts of the contestants. The leafy trees surrounding the oval amphitheater seemed to shake on all sides, sending birds scattering for cover. Possums, lizards, rodents, and smaller animals of all shapes and sizes ran into their holes as if they knew that their future, too, was at stake in this game.

Silvie ducked under a vicious swing from a fighter named Jackov, the largest and clearly the strongest one on the field. She came up under his extended arm with her own stick, but Jackov was too skilled to be fooled so easily. He deflected her weapon with the shield on his left arm and knocked the ball loose with his knee. The football flew high, then landed in the tangle of bodies, lost from sight.

"Think!" Thomas screamed. "Use your heads! For the sake of Elyon, use your heads!"

*If the players on the field were not all highly skilled at deflecting blows with their leather-wrapped forearms, they would undoubtedly all be dead,* Johnis thought. *They would at least be a pile of broken bones.*

"Better to break an arm here among friends than have your head cut off in the desert," Thomas cried to all who protested the brutal fighting. These were desperate times, and they called for desperate measures.

Billos, the seventeen-year-old snake-quick fighter who was known as "the bulldog," slid out of the mess and ran around the sparring teams, searching for the ball.

He darted in, snatched something near Darsal's feet, took two steps toward the opposite goal, and came face-to-face with Jackov. The big boy swung his stick at Billos's chest. The wood landed with a blow that rose over the crowd noise.

*Thud!*

Johnis winced. The stadium fell silent except for a few clacking sticks.

Billos stood his ground, stunned, ball gripped in his left fist.

Seeing Billos hurt, Jackov dove in for the kill.

"Head butt!" Darsal screamed.

Instead of dodging, as Johnis expected him to, Billos tossed the football in Darsal's direction, lowered his head, and stepped into the onrushing opponent.

But Jackov sidestepped Billos's helmeted head and snatched the flying ball from the air before it reached Darsal.

Billos flew past him, hit the ground, and rolled to his feet.

Before Jackov could head for the goal line, Silvie grabbed his right ear from behind. She yanked back, slamming the boy on his back.

Then twenty-four bodies dove at the loose ball. They were all so bunched up, so tangled and intertwined, that no one had room to swing, much less take the time required to think through any strategy.

And the ball was lost in that pile.

Thomas paced like a lion and let them fight, but he wasn't happy. And no wonder: a fight like this with the Horde would get them all killed.

Some said the only way the Forest Dwellers could survive would be to make peace with the Horde, but they said it in a whisper because such cowardly talk could get a person killed. Only traitors would dare say it publicly.

But watching the mess on the field, Johnis wasn't sure a battle led by any of these sixteen- or seventeen-year-old fawns would be better than surrender. They looked like one huge ball of hair themselves.

Something shot out from the pile and bounced across the grass toward the sideline. It was the ball of Horde hair, the football.

All would have been fine if the ball had stopped on the field. But it didn't. It kept rolling. Toward Johnis.

He was sure it would stop as it passed Thomas, but it kept rolling.

Still toward Johnis.

Every eye in the stadium followed the lumpy brown sphere. Johnis glanced up at Thomas and saw that his eyes, too, were on the ball. When he looked back down, the football had stopped. At his feet.

One look at the field and Johnis saw that the fighting had only intensified.

"Fools will get us all killed," his father said, bending to pick up the ball. He grabbed it with a thick, cracked fist, lifted it, then stopped.

"Throw it out," Johnis said. "Hurry!"

Instead, his father dropped the ball. It bounced once and landed on Johnis's left foot, where it rested.

"What are you doing?" Johnis asked, glancing up at his father. But Ramos's eyes were on Thomas.

Johnis looked down at the ball. A picture that had haunted his dreams flashed through his mind: an image of ten huge Horde warriors—"Scabs," as the Forest Guard called them— killing his mother. This was their hair! It made him suddenly sick. He froze.

"Stop!" Thomas Hunter's voice roared above the sounds of fighting. "On your feet!"

Jackov was already standing, storming toward the crowd at Johnis's right. He was hunting for the ball, Johnis realized. The boy's face was red from fighting, and his eyes glared with anger.

"Give it up," Jackov growled, eyes scanning the crowd.

Whether it was the image of his mother or the sight of the furious Jackov, Johnis didn't know, but he moved without thinking. He slipped his foot around the ball and eased it behind his heels so that it was hidden from view.

"Give it up!" Jackov thundered, pacing along the sideline closer to Johnis. The other fighters had stood and were watching.

"You've lost the ball and you think a few words will bring it back?" Thomas called.

Johnis's heart thumped. He almost kicked it out then. But he didn't.

"Use your head!" Thomas said, facing the others. "All of you, listen to me. How many times have I told you that you must defeat the Horde with what's in your head and your heart before you defeat them with your muscle? They outnumber us! They outmuscle us! They are stronger, but we have more heart. So think with your heart!"

His voice rang out with enough force to bring a tremble to Johnis's legs.

"Let them see the confidence in your eyes. Let them know that your heart cannot be stopped! I need leaders who will stand in the face of terror and laugh. I need a few who will throw their heads back and roar at the sun because they know that Elyon is on their side, and no one, not even the smelly Horde, can defeat the followers of Elyon!"

Encouraged by Thomas's speech, Jackov screamed at the crowd. "Give up the Horde hair or I swear I will slit your throat where you stand!"

*Is this what Thomas meant?* Johnis wondered.

"Use your head, Jackov!" Thomas shouted, egging the fighter on. "Find me my football!"

Jackov began to run along the sideline, joined now by three others from his team.

"An extra horse to the one who finds my ball!" Thomas challenged.

Now ten of the twenty-four ran to the sidelines, slapping their palms with sticks.

Johnis felt sweat running down his neck. Why was the crowd so silent? He'd done a foolish thing, hiding the ball. Why wasn't his father scooping the ball up and throwing it out before any of the fighters discovered that it had been him, Johnis, who'd hidden it from them?

Then Thomas winked at him, and he knew what was happening. The commander was using him to make a point. *Even a weak boy, rejected from consideration to join the Guard, can hide a ball from you.*

"Stop!"

They stopped. All but Jackov, who required more urging.

"Stop or take the back of my hand, boy."

Now Jackov stopped.

"Use your heads," Thomas said, pacing again. "I said I want you to find my Horde football. It was a special gift, and I have no intention of losing it."

He faced Darsal. "Darsal, do you think the football has vanished? Plucked from us by a beast in the sky?"

"No, sir. It's being hidden by someone along the side."

"Then why are you standing in the middle of the field?" Thomas asked.

"Because as soon as your football is found, there will be another fight," she said. "I'm resting."

Thomas hesitated, then nodded. He looked at Billos. "And you?"

"I plan to retrieve the football for you, sir," Billos replied.

"Is that so? By standing there in the middle with Darsal, resting?"

Billos glanced at Darsal but said nothing.

Thomas shifted his attention to Silvie, the short blond who'd reached the ball first. They said she was an intelligent one, given to schooling before she lost her mother and took up fighting. All Johnis could see was speed and power and a firm jaw. She was a quiet girl.

"And you, Silvie?" Thomas asked.

"If I thought stomping around the field like a spoiled child would get me the ball, I still wouldn't bother," she said.

"Then you don't care about my football? I, your supreme leader, have offered you an extra horse if you can find it, and you stand as if you don't care?"

"Begging your pardon, sir," Silvie said, dipping her head. "But you're right, I *don't* care about your Horde football. In fact, I find it a bit disgusting. And I think there are a thousand boys who will offer me their horses after today."

This was the most Johnis had heard her say in all the days he'd watched them spar. She was the loner on the field, like him in some ways.

"You're not married yet?" Thomas asked.

"No." Even though sixteen was an acceptable marrying age, marriage was discouraged among new recruits.

"Sixteen or seventeen?"

"Sixteen, sir," Silvie said.

They all knew Thomas would make his selection as much on how they answered his questions as on how well they fought. He was obsessed with this thinking stuff. Head and heart, head and heart, head and heart, it was more head and heart than strength, he often said.

Thomas turned to Jackov, who was still scanning the sidelines and hunting for the ball. The only reason he hadn't spotted the sphere of hair behind Johnis was because of Ramos's larger boot blocking part of the view.

"Jackov?" Thomas demanded.

*It has come down to these four,* Johnis thought. Thomas had chosen two men and two women.

"I would have found your football, sir, but you stopped me," Jackov said.

"I don't remember stopping you," Thomas said.

"You ordered me to stop," Jackov protested.

"I also ordered you to find my football, which you failed to do in a timely manner," Thomas said. "Then I suggested you come to your senses or take the back of my hand. But you know the rules: there *are* no rules in matters of wit and mind. Yet you blame me for your not having the ball in your hands at this very moment?"

"Then let me resume my search," Jackov said as he bowed.

"I intend to. As soon as I give Billos a chance."

Thomas turned in a slow circle and spoke loudly so that the thousands gathered heard every word. "And when you do find my Horde football, Jackov or Billos or whoever manages the task by might or mind, I want you to beat that single soul who has hidden my Horde football to a pulp."

Silence echoed.

"Do you hear me?"

"Yes, sir," Jackov said.

"Just enough to teach them a lesson," Thomas said. "Enough to break a bone or two."

"Yes, sir."

"And if they try to squirm out of it now, I will personally break a bone or two," Thomas said.

Johnis's heart pounded with panic.

# FOUR

The day had taken a terrible turn for the worse, and Johnis was out of options. He had always been known for two things: his love of words and his impulsiveness. What so many thought of as an odd combination seemed perfectly natural to Johnis. But at the moment, he doubted running impulsively from the stadium in blind panic would make his day any better.

That left words, and the only words Johnis could think of at the moment were, *The Horde ball is a trick.*

Johnis didn't have time to think through the reason or likelihood these words might help him out; he just spoke them on instinct, knowing that something in his head thought it was a good idea, if a bit juvenile.

So he pulled his father down by his sleeve and whispered into his ear, "The Horde ball is a trick. Pass it on to save my life."

"What?"

"Pass it on to save my life—the Horde ball is a trick."

His father gave him a short, strange look, then leaned to his neighbor, Thelma, a seamstress who made leather goods for the Guard, and whispered into her ear. She in turn whispered into her neighbor's ear. And around it went.

"So, Billos," Thomas was saying, "will you agree to beat the one who's hiding the Horde ball to a pulp if you uncover him?"

"Consider it done," Billos said.

"Then have at it."

By now the whispering had gone a quarter of the way around the stadium and had gathered some attention. Five or six people sharing a secret was easy to hide, but this secret was passed on and on, gathering more and more looks from those around. Even some of the fighters had noticed.

Billos scanned the crowd and called out for all to hear. "My friends, as you can see here, I will soon be serving in the Guard, which means I will be offering my life to protect yours."

Johnis guessed that Billos meant to ask the crowd to turn him in.

Billos noticed the whispering and glanced to his right, by the far goal, where a man was bending to a shorter woman, passing on the secret. Most of the fighters had followed Billos's eyes and were watching with some curiosity.

"In exchange for my life, I would like to ask one thing only," Billos continued.

Johnis moved quickly, while their attention was diverted. He slipped the knife from his father's belt, squatted down over the ball, and quickly sawed at the main cord that held the long strands of hair tight. Sweat streamed down his cheeks.

The cord around the ball snapped easily, thank Elyon.

Johnis dropped the knife, turned so that his back was toward the field, and stood, holding the Horde ball in his hands.

Horde warriors never cut their hair, preferring instead to weave it into long, nasty dreadlocks. The hair was greasy in his hands as he fumbled with one of the knots. It smelled like sulfur.

Still, considering the predicament he was in, he might have swallowed the whole ball of hair if it would save him from a beating.

Then again, who was to say that Billos could really beat him in a fight? Johnis was no stranger to swinging a sword.

Then yet again, Billos was stronger.

The knot loosed, and the hair unraveled. Johnis wrapped it around his hips, slid it up to his waist, tucked each end under his belt, and pulled his shirt over it. He slowly turned around.

"I pledge my life," Billos was saying. "Offer me the ball, my friend, and I'll go easy on the beating I've been ordered to give you. It's the least you can do."

No one on the field appeared to have noticed Johnis. Who could resist a whispered secret? No one. A mild but effective distraction. Now he had the Horde hair hidden around his belly.

The murmurs and chuckling of those around him might give him away. His father had already thought of that. "Shut up!" he snapped at those behind.

They quieted.

Billos called to an old man who'd just been whispered to by a girl. "You there, old man. Step out."

He did.

"What did she tell you?" Billos asked.

"She told me, 'I'm bored and sick.'"

"Bored and sick?" Billos repeated.

"This talk is making us all bored and sick," the old man said. "Get on with the fight, boy!"

"The Horde ball is a trick" had become "I'm bored and sick," Johnis realized. Laughter rippled softly through the crowd, and his tension eased a little. Maybe this would all work out.

Then again, there was that "beat him to a pulp" thing.

*Elyon, by the mercy of the Roush, save me,* he pleaded, referring to the stories of the white bats that had once protected them from Teeleh and the evil Shataiki bats. None had been seen in thirteen years, but some said the shrieks of the black bats could be heard in the desert night.

The legends didn't matter at the moment, but Johnis could use a miracle. Some of the power of old.

A little magic, maybe.

But there was no magic. Not here, not now. There was just him with smelly Horde hair wrapped around his bare, sweating belly.

How had he managed to get into such an absurd situation? Quick thinking could save your life or end it, Thomas was known to say.

Johnis was the king of quick thinkers.

Billos swung around, gazing at the crowd and wearing a grin. "I must say, I have to agree. It's all become a bit boring and sick to me as well. Some fool has gone off and hidden the ball and won't give it back. Fine, let's try something else. All those who think that the fool who is hiding Thomas's Horde hair ball should give himself up, step forward and be counted."

Without pausing to consider precisely why it made perfect sense, Johnis stepped out. It did make sense, of course. Perfect sense. The best defense was always an aggressive offense. So said Thomas Hunter.

Billos faced him. "Good, one boy who knows the meaning of honor. A small boy without much meat on his bones, but more courage than the rest. Is he the only one?"

Almost as one the entire first row of onlookers stepped out to form a ring around the stadium.

Billos glanced at Darsal. "Check behind them."

Darsal took off in a jog, running behind the row that had stepped out, scanning the ground and bleachers for the ball.

"This is absurd!" Jackov cried out. "Give me my way and I'll find you your Horde football, sir."

Darsal finished her loop and rejoined Billos, shaking her head. No ball.

Thomas studied his fledgling Guard recruits. "I still don't think any of you are using enough of the muscle between your ears to be counted as leaders. The objective of this entire game was a simple one. You started well, Billos, but have still failed at the objective. Which is what?"

Billos, the seventeen-year-old with dark hair, returned Thomas Hunter's stare. "To cross the opponent's goal with the ball."

"Rules?"

"No killing or intentionally maiming," Billos said.

"Yet the ball has yet to cross the line. You have all failed to satisfy this objective." Thomas walked around them, swinging his sword angrily. "You've all stood here like idiots engaging me. The opportunities for victory have been countless in these last few minutes!"

Silence.

"I do think I could take any sixteen-year-old from the crowd and show them stronger than any of you."

"Then do it!" Jackov screamed.

Thomas swung to him. "There are no rules in matters of wit and mind, Jackov, but I still haven't made my final selection. You should watch your emotion."

Jackov saw his mistake and bowed his head. "Forgive me."

"I will. And I will agree to your insistence that I . . . *do it*."

He faced Johnis. "You there, who stepped out first. What is your name?"

At first Johnis wasn't sure he was speaking to him, but there could be no mistake. All eyes were on him.

"Johnis," he said.

"Johnis. How old are you?"

"Sixteen."

"Are you married, Johnis?"

"No," Johnis said.

"Well then, I think we have our new player." Thomas faced his fighters. "I do think that this boy, who was either too cowardly to try out for the Guard or was dismissed early, could run circles around the lot of you."

Jackov spit to one side.

Rather than consider his options in slow deliberation, Johnis once again reacted on impulse, trusting his heart. He simply did what he knew he must do if he wanted to avoid a terrible end to this day.

"Should I invite him to show you all a lesson?" Thomas demanded of his fighters.

Without any further invitation, Johnis left his spot by the side and walked toward Jackov.

Quick thinking.

Deadly thinking.

# FIVE

Johnis was halfway across the field before he'd fully decided on what he would do. He'd committed himself to either being beaten to a pulp, as Thomas had put it, or teaching them all that a smaller boy with a love for books wasn't as useless as they thought.

A slight grin settled on Thomas Hunter's face. "You've come out for your whipping so eagerly, lad?"

"No, sir," Johnis said, striding faster now. Straight for Jackov. "I've come out to show the big thug that mind is greater than muscle." He wasn't entirely sure where all of this courage was coming from.

Courage or stupidity?

Jackov grunted and took a step in Johnis's direction.

At this point Johnis could do one of two things. He could continue on—into the jaws of this monster, so to speak—or he could turn tail and sprint for the end with the ball safely around his belly.

He supposed that Thomas wanted him to do the latter, to show them all that mind was greater than muscle. But Johnis suddenly wanted to do more.

So he started to jog, arms pumping loosely, hoping that the Horde hair around his waist would stay put.

There were twenty-four fighters on the field, grouped at the center. There were five thousand onlookers in the stadium. There was one supreme commander, Thomas Hunter, standing to one side.

And every last eyeball was pinned to him. To Johnis. Heading straight into terrible trouble.

"I want you to put this cheeky lad on the ground, Jackov," Thomas growled in a low voice heard by all on the field. "Don't maim or kill him, but I want you to hurt him."

Jackov needed no encouragement. He was moving forward already.

So then, perhaps Johnis's plan wasn't quite so smart after all. Why had Thomas Hunter turned against him? The Horde had killed his mother, the Forest Guard had dismissed him from service, and now the supreme commander himself, leader of all the forests, had ordered the strongest young fighter to beat him to a pulp.

Why?

Johnis set the question aside and breathed deeply. They were twenty yards from a head-on collision when he suddenly pulled up and slid to a stop.

Johnis reached under his shirt, grabbed one end of the Horde hair, and yanked it free. It hung from his hand like a knotted whip.

Those in the crowd who didn't know he had the football gasped. Jackov blinked. He missed a step. They were no more than ten feet apart.

"My mother paid for this Horde hair with her life," Johnis screamed. "Now it's yours!"

He flung the cords of hair high in the air, toward Jackov. The larger boy shifted his attention from Johnis to the ball.

Johnis launched himself up and into Jackov then. His years of running had made him fast, and he was light. His body left the ground like a battering ram, fists forward.

But he didn't strike the other fighter with his fists. One measly blow with his knuckles would do nothing but daze Jackov. Instead, he jerked his arms wide at the last moment, pulling apart Jackov's hands to make way for his flying body.

Johnis felt the top of his head thud squarely against Jackov's unprotected face.

Pain flashed down his spine, then was gone. Johnis landed hard, rolled to his feet, and spun back. The Horde hair was still airborne, sailing straight toward him.

Jackov, on the other hand, was on both knees, shaking the cobwebs out of his head.

Johnis snatched the Horde hair from the air and stood in a

crouch, feeling confident and ready for a counter. But he decided quickly that another attack wouldn't go nearly so smoothly for him, so he made a show of bravado by spinning to face Thomas.

"Is that what you had in mind?" he demanded.

The supreme commander had lost his smile. He stared hard, and Johnis wasn't sure what to make of that. Hadn't he done well?

Without waiting for Jackov to fully recover, Johnis turned his back on the group of stunned fighters, jogged to the end zone, dropped the Horde hair football unceremoniously on the ground, and faced the stadium.

For a moment the silence was so thick Johnis wondered if he was in a dream. Jackov was standing beside the other fighters, looking at him.

Darsal was grinning, but Johnis couldn't tell if it was a wicked grin or one of satisfaction.

Silvie frowned, her jaw muscles bunched.

Billos had crossed his arms and was pretending to be interested in something in the trees. A company of parrots squawked and took flight over the stadium. Okay, so maybe he had seen something.

Milic, a friend to Johnis, was the only fighter on the field who was clearly pleased with this turn of events.

Johnis started to walk for the sidelines, unsure how he was supposed to feel. Or what he was supposed to do, for that matter. He wasn't even sure what had happened.

His father suddenly thrust both fists above his head and

screamed his approval in a terrifying, raspy wail. Cheering erupted like a huge wave, thundering cries of approval.

Johnis stopped. For the first time the significance of his feat became clear. He might not be eligible for the Forest Guard—in all honesty he wasn't even sure he *wanted* to be eligible. But in his mind he'd honored the memory of his mother, Rosa, by crossing the line for all to see, with the very Horde hair harvested by his father.

He'd followed his instincts, and he'd done it for love of his mother. He had thought with his heart, as Thomas himself had insisted the others do.

Thomas Hunter strode toward him, face sullen. He stopped and took a bow. "Well done, lad."

He stepped forward and touched the top of Johnis's head, the tips of his fingers bloody as he retracted his hand. He gripped Johnis's jaw and turned his head gently as if examining him for something, then lowered his arm. "You have won the horse that I was going to give to Jackov." Thomas bowed again. "Thank you. You may join your father."

Johnis walked off the field to another roar from the crowd, still unsure how he felt about all of this.

His father dipped his head. "Elyon's strength, boy."

"Elyon's strength."

Thomas raised his hand at the center of the field and the throng quieted.

"I've made my decision," the supreme commander said, pacing

around the group of fighters. "These are dangerous times we live in. We have received word from our scouts that the Horde is gathering to the east"—he pointed his sword toward his left, eastward—"and will march on this forest in four days with an army over two hundred thousand strong."

Johnis caught his breath. Such a large army against their much smaller Guard? A parrot squawked far away.

"Normally our recruits would prepare for months before being thrust into battle, but those days are gone," Thomas said. "The thousand new recruits will fight by our sides in four days' time."

A mother cried out. But only one. Somewhere a child was crying, oblivious to all.

Four days. It was too soon for sixteen- and seventeen-year-old fighters! They would be slaughtered. True, on a good day one guardsman could handle ten Scabs, but these new recruits would be lucky to handle one.

This was grave news indeed. Johnis felt a terrible pity for the twenty-four young fighters on the field, not to mention the other 976 pups who would rush out to face the Horde in four days.

Thomas continued. "I know they are young, but they are strong. We have no choice. The ten-thousand-member Guard we now have in this forest needs every advantage."

The somberness of his decision to throw the young recruits into battle so soon began to sink in. Johnis felt a knot rise in his throat.

"I need four strong leaders under my seasoned commanders,

and today I have found them," Thomas said. "As agreed, each will be given a house, a choice of horse, and an emerald-handled sword. In addition, as soon as they have finished one final test this very day, each will be promoted to the rank of lieutenant."

Johnis watched the four who would receive the honor. He couldn't quite imagine Darsal or Billos, or even Jackov, swinging a sword into the chests of the beasts called the Horde. They'd be shredded like taro root.

Thomas faced the recruits. "Take a knee, all of you."

They all knelt.

"If you are willing to give your life for the forests and for Elyon, and to lead others to that same end, stand and step forward as I speak your name."

As was customary for special selection, the twenty-four fighters lowered their heads.

Thomas pointed his sword at the witty, dark-haired boy with high cheekbones who was well known as Billos. "Billos of the Southern Forest, step forward if you will."

Billos rose, stepped forward, and kissed Thomas's sword, signifying his acceptance to die if his service required it. The silence was thick.

Thomas pointed to Silvie, the spicy blond with brilliant eyes and as-of-yet unscarred skin. "Silvie of Northern, step forward if you will."

She rose, kissed the sword, and took her place next to Billos.

"Darsal of the Southern Forest, step forward if you will."

She did.

Still no cheering. The moment was too sacred, for this was a moment in which each was choosing to die as much as live.

Thomas pointed his sword at Jackov of the Northern Forest. Johnis felt gratitude flood his chest. It had been one thing to beat Jackov in the game, but he didn't want the boy to miss such an opportunity on account of him.

He sighed softly and lowered his head. For the first time since he dumped the Horde football in the end zone, Johnis smiled. The day had turned out well.

"And for the fourth I choose you," Thomas's voice rang out. "Step forward if you will."

Johnis wasn't watching. He was thinking of that one final test Thomas had said these four must face. Customarily it would be a task that would force the new leaders to work as a team. More than once a chosen leader had failed the final test and been sent back to the squad to be replaced.

"Are you refusing my commission?" Thomas asked.

What was this? Johnis lifted his head, wondering what had gotten into Jackov to refuse the commission. But he didn't see Jackov refusing the commission.

He saw Thomas pointing his sword in his direction.

At *him.*

Johnis's heart stopped. A shiver passed down his neck.

*Him?*

But that was impossible. He didn't want to be the *him* this sword was pointing at. Didn't want to go out battling the Horde in four days' time. Didn't want a new house or a new horse.

In fact, staring at Thomas's sword, Johnis was terrified to be counted as one of the Forest Guard, much less lead a swarm of fighters into bloody battle.

It occurred to him that everyone was silent. Waiting for him.

"I can't," he said.

"You can't? Or you won't?" Thomas said, sword unwavering.

"I was dismissed," Johnis said.

"Consider yourself *un*dismissed."

"I'm too young."

"Have you ever given your heart to a woman?" Thomas asked.

He hesitated. "Yes."

"Then you're old enough to fight for love and for the Great Romance," the commander said, speaking of their religion, which revolved around love.

"I'm too small," Johnis said. "I'm a lover, not a fighter."

Thomas angrily thrust his sword into the dirt. "Any lover of Elyon or any of his creatures is a fighter for Elyon and his creatures! I will decide if you are too young or too small or too slow or too cheeky for your own good! Do you understand?"

"Yes."

"And I have decided that you are more worthy than all of these!" Thomas pointed to the fighters he'd rejected as leaders. "Are you questioning my judgment? I, who have crossed the worlds, who have hung my life out to be swatted at by the Horde in every battle since the blasted Shataiki ravaged the land! You think your fresh little mind can match my judgment?"

"No, sir."

A woman stepped out from the bleachers on Johnis's left. Rachelle, wife to Thomas, wore a short fighting tunic and leather sandals with straps that crisscrossed up her calves to her knees. A knife was secured to her thigh.

Legend had it that Rachelle had taught Thomas everything he knew of fighting—and of love—when he'd fallen into this world from another long before the Great Deception. Watching her slink toward him, Johnis thought the legends had to be right.

She seemed to rob the breath from even Thomas.

Rachelle stepped up to Johnis and studied him, smiling gently. She took his chin in her hand and turned his face, as Thomas had done.

"He's right, you know," she said. "You're a born leader. The world will turn on you. You are chosen."

Johnis was about to step forward and accept when she continued.

"You do realize that the girls will fall in line to marry you now, don't you?" She winked. "I recommend you trust my husband. Everything he's done, he's done for your good. There is no one I know who has better judgment than Thomas."

Johnis felt short of breath. He stepped forward on legs that felt not entirely there.

"Will you?" Thomas asked again.

Johnis walked out to the supreme leader, kissed the handle of the sword that still jutted from the earth, and bowed. "I will."

Again it was Johnis's father who cried out first, but this time with a hoarse voice from all of his yelling earlier. Five thousand strong stood to their feet and roared at the sky, then began to stomp the earth so that it shook.

Thomas let them roar for a full minute, while Johnis stood quietly, head bowed, unsure of what they expected from him or what the other three thought of him.

When the cheers quieted, he lifted his head and saw that Thomas had raised his sword. Eyes on him.

"To receive your commission, you will arm yourselves and ride on four of our fastest horses directly west to the Igal point. There you will retrieve a group of four marked catalina cacti at the forest's edge and return them by nightfall without breaking a single needle."

"Four?" Billos said. "They're too large."

Thomas shot him a glare. "That, lad, is the point. You'll have to use your heads and work as a team."

"What about the Horde?" Johnis asked.

"Well, you can't very well love them to death, can you, Johnis?" Thomas grinned. "I wouldn't be too concerned—our reports have them to the east. You're headed west, young man. If you're lucky enough to run into a straggler or two, bring me more hair for my football."

The fighters chuckled, but Johnis found no reason to join them.

"The sun is sinking. I suggest you get your bruised bodies to

the stables and fly like the wind. It's a two-hour ride from here."
Thomas spread his arms and turned in a circle, addressing the
crowd. "Send them off, lovers of Elyon. Tell them they will not
give their lives in vain!"

And they did, though Johnis couldn't actually understand the
jumbled cries of encouragement beating against his ears.

No one noticed the hooded man slipping discreetly from the
stadium's southern entrance. He hurried into the forest, mounted a
black steed that was awaiting him, and pounded into the shadows.

Toward the desert.

Toward the Horde.

# SIX

Seen from high above, Johnis's world was mostly pale desert sand. No oceans, no islands, no continents. Canyons and valleys were filled with sand and rock, not trees or ponds.

But if one looked closely, he would find seven forests, each roughly a day's walk across. And at the center of each forest, a green lake. And around each lake, a large village inhabited by the Forest Dwellers. Each forest was simply designated by its position relative to the Middle Forest. Thomas's Forest.

The Middle Forest village—which was more of a city than a village, judging by size alone—was built in large circles with the lake at the center, the lake that contained the powerful cleansing waters they all depended on for their health. Flowering vines blossomed on most of the wood houses—a garden splashed in reds and blues and yellows.

Bathing in the lake once each day kept the Forest Dwellers' skin free of the painful, scaly disease that turned the Horde gray. Miss a day of bathing and the pain would begin at the joints, spreading outward.

Miss two days and the skin would begin to crack.

Miss three days and you were pretty much a Scab, one of the Horde, covered from head to foot in the flaking disease. Worse, your mind would succumb to the delusion the Horde had regarding the dangers of water.

The lake, first found by Thomas Hunter, was Elyon's gift to them, an escape from the evil that had latched itself onto the Scabs. Each evening the village celebrated the Great Romance at the lake's shores at what was called the Gathering. There they danced and sang of Elyon's love, retelling the legends of a time only thirteen years earlier when they could breathe the intoxicating waters and laugh with Elyon himself if they so desired.

According to the legends, before the disease had come, large white bats with furry bodies—known as Roush—had guarded their paradise. Back then, the evil black Shataiki vampire bats were confined to the Black Forest, behind a green river they could not cross.

But the river had been crossed by a human, and the Shataiki had been set free to ravage the land. The evil once confined to the Black Forest now clung to the skin and minds of all who refused to follow the single escape that Elyon had left them all. Seven lakes in seven forests.

This all according to legend, of course.

But since that day, not one Roush had been seen. Not a single Shataiki vampire bat. Well over a million Horde now waged war on a hundred thousand followers of Elyon. Because of legend.

Indeed, although they bathed daily and defended their way of life against the Horde, most Forest Dwellers at least questioned the truth of the legends (although it had been only thirteen years). Had there ever really been a magical lake whose waters you could breathe? Did Roush and Shataiki bats ever really roam the land? Had Teeleh actually brought the disease on the Horde? For that matter, did the lakes really come from some unknown god called Elyon?

Or were all of these simply religious explanations to describe a natural disease that was healed by the medicines contained in the lakes? Only thirteen years had passed since the whole planet had been ravaged by the disease, true, but who was to say that these memories had not been caused by the disease itself? There was no real evidence to the contrary today.

Eager to complete their final quest before the day was gone, Billos, Darsal, Silvie, and Johnis prepared for the journey in the same way all Forest Guard did before undertaking any mission: they equipped themselves with leather battle-dress, thin horns to blow to warn of danger, knives, and their new emerald-handled swords. They'd loaded enough bathing water and food for two days—those were the requirements.

Johnis was assigned the task of gathering food. With help from his father and younger sister, he grabbed what he could from their kitchen: taro root and some soft sago cakes, both good for starch. Fruit, of course. Nanka, blingblings, rhambutan.

"You want the plum pudding?" Kiella asked. "I'll put it in a shoe so it won't smoosh."

"Now, what would I do with plum pudding?" Johnis demanded, feeling both frustrated and admittedly a little proud that he had been selected. "You think the Forest Guard takes desserts with them when they fight the Scabs?"

"I would," she said. "It'll keep you sweet."

"That'll just make me better for the Horde to eat," he said, knowing the Horde didn't really eat human flesh.

Kiella's eyes went wide, and she said nothing more.

"Hurry, lad," his father urged, bursting into the kitchen, face bright with pride. "They've gathered to send you off!" He waved him forward with a thick, gnarled hand. "Come, hurry, come!"

Johnis got his finer frame and features from his mother, she'd always told him: His pronounced cheekbones and dark hair. His brown eyes, too often covered by bangs for her liking. His fingers, better for the pen than for the sword, his father had once said. Mother disagreed. He was perfect for both!

Johnis loved his father, but he'd cherished his mother, Rosa, with every living fiber.

Johnis met the other three new leaders at the square fifteen minutes later and galloped out of the village with Thomas's last words ringing in his ears.

"Think with your hearts. Elyon's strength!"

JOHNIS RODE AT THE REAR OF THE PARTY, JUST BEHIND Silvie. For the first hour not a word was spoken.

The entire business was wrong, he thought. Completely and absurdly wrong! He'd stumbled along behind the others, out of the stadium, into the lake, into the battle-dress, dumbly doing what was expected of him.

*You're in the Forest Guard now, Johnis!*

His childhood fantasy of slaying the Horde at the end of the wooden sword his father had given him when he'd turned three had been laced with glory, not this vow to lead others into death. And in four days' time! A Horde army of several hundred thousand strong would leave plenty of dead under hoof.

The muscles of the huge black steed under him rippled, sweaty. If they kept up this pace, they would kill their horses. Ahead, Silvie's short, wavy hair rose and fell. It occurred to him that he had no clue who these three people were apart from the bits he'd heard. They hadn't even spoken to him since leaving the stadium.

Darsal and Billos both came from the Southern Forest, and they shared an uncommon bond that came from years of knowing secrets, he thought. All he knew about Darsal was that her father had died in battle when she was young.

Billos, who had been so talkative on the field, led them in stern silence. He rode as if the mission was his alone to finish.

They all did.

Johnis reined in his horse and came to a stomping halt. The other three galloped on without a glance backward, uncaring. They disappeared through the trees. Any lingering hope that they might include him vanished. He was alone and—

A *screech* from the trees cut his self-pity short. Johnis jerked his head and scanned the branches, but nothing looked out of the ordinary. No parrots or possums that he could see. Only leafy green branches swaying in the wind.

*Eeeaaaak!*

Johnis shifted his sight to his right. A shadow perched at the top of a mango tree.

A shadow with red eyes.

A shadow with red eyes and large black wings that now spread slowly to a span of three feet.

Johnis caught his breath. The bird or bat or whatever this beast was stared at him for several long seconds, then leaped straight up, leaving nothing but rustling leaves behind.

He'd heard a thousand stories of the Shataiki beasts, and in his mind's eye they had always looked exactly like that. But that was impossible. No one had seen a Shataiki since the Great Deception.

Johnis kicked his horse hard. It bolted forward and galloped full tilt through the trees. In the space of ten breaths he'd caught the others.

"Stop!"

They ignored him and sped on.

"Stop, I said!" he yelled, angry now.

Billos pulled up hard, spun his horse around, and kneed past Johnis. "Shut your flap, boy!" he rasped. "Every Scab in ten miles will hear you. You want us all dead?"

Darsal and Silvie had come to a stop twenty yards farther and were staring back without expression. Johnis had intended to tell them about the Shataiki, but he knew immediately by Billos's tone of voice and the looks on their faces that they would only scoff. He switched tactics.

"No, I don't want us dead, which is why I suggest we stop running the horses," Johnis said. "We'll kill them, and without horses we *could* be dead."

Billos's mount snorted heavily, flesh quivering. Sweat wet its shoulders and rump.

"Was I born yesterday?" Billos demanded. "I'd take a dead horse over a Horde scouting party any day."

"I don't know; I think you could handle a few Scabs pretty easily," Johnis said, in an attempt to win some favor back.

Billos jerked his new sword free of its scabbard and whipped its blade up to Johnis's neck. The boy was fast. Very fast.

"You're right," Billos said. "But that's *my* call, not yours."

"Then what's your call? Do we walk the horses, or do we ride them to death?"

Billos hesitated.

"Watch your cheek, boy," Darsal said sternly, walking her horse back. "That may have been a cute trick you played in the stadium, but you have no right to fight by my side. You aren't a true soldier. If you want to live long enough to marry, you should turn back now. Give it up."

*She is beautiful despite the terrible scar,* Johnis thought. *And cruel.* Separating Darsal and Billos would be like separating the ironwood bark from its tree.

"You're suggesting that I defy Thomas," Johnis said. "Believe me, this wasn't my idea."

"You're a reject," Billos said. "There's not enough muscle on you to swing a sword, much less kill a Scab."

"Tell that to Jackov," Johnis said. "Tell it to the supreme commander. But for now, make your call. Do we run the horses or walk them?"

Three sets of eyes drilled him. If Johnis wasn't mistaken, Silvie didn't share Billos and Darsal's hatred of him. But he wasn't sure. She sat small on the huge mount, looking back at him with lost blue eyes and that flawless tanned face. He held her gaze there. Intelligent, they said, but how intelligent?

Darsal grunted and jerked her horse around.

"We should walk our mounts," Silvie said.

Billos gave Johnis a parting glare, trotted to the front, and slowed his horse to a walk. "We walk."

A shriek pierced the air to the west. Johnis looked to the sky and nudged his horse forward, thoughts of their cruelty suddenly gone.

No sign of the black bat. But now the same far cry came from his left, above the trees. A flight of black flickered through the branches.

They passed into a clearing, and Johnis pulled up right next to Silvie. He scanned the perimeter for bats. No flying beasts that he could see, but they rustled through the treetops on both sides now.

He spun his head to Silvie and saw that she was studying him with that same soft look that seemed frozen on her face.

"Did you hear that?" Johnis asked.

She just stared at him. Obviously not.

"None of you can hear that?"

"Shut your flap, Scrapper," Billos snapped without turning.

They walked on. The horses' hooves clumped softly. The trees rustled.

The sky shrieked softly on both sides.

Johnis shivered. Something very wrong was happening, and he seemed to be the only one who knew or cared.

"What do you hear?" Silvie asked.

Johnis wasn't sure she could handle the truth. He gave it to her anyway. "We're being followed by Shataiki bats on both sides. They're crying out. You don't hear them?"

"We hear your fear," Billos said, looking at him. "The Shataiki are the stuff of legends; they don't exist. Evil is everywhere you look and wears the face of a Scab, not some ghost in the sky. Everyone knows that."

No one disagreed.

"You do realize that you and I will be leading campaigns together one day," Johnis said. "We should work together, but you're so bitter about nothing that you're exposing your flank to the vilest creatures at this very moment. Thomas would be proud."

"He's exposing his flank to a ghost," Darsal answered. "Look, maybe we will lead campaigns together if we survive the month. Only Elyon knows. But our objective today is to retrieve the cacti and return them to the village in one piece. That would have been much easier if Jackov were sitting on that horse instead of you. Do you disagree?"

She had a point. "You may be right. But if you do want to return to the village in one piece, you'd better at least listen. They're following us this very minute."

As if to agree, a long cry cut through the air on their right. Johnis spun and pointed. "There!"

The black bat rose from the treetops slowly, banked, and soared overhead, pupilless eyes staring down like two shiny red tomatoes.

*Eeeaaaak . . .*

"There, you see it, right above? Don't tell me you can't see it!"

They all looked up. "No, we can't see it," Silvie said. "And if you want us to take you seriously, I suggest you set this nonsense aside."

Johnis decided he had no alternative but to bide his time. His eyes were not fooling him—he knew that much. Something was very wrong—he knew that as well. But for the moment he could only follow these insolent thugs.

"I heard about your mother," Silvie said, casting him that same frozen look. "The Horde ball. Losing someone so close can do terrible things to a person."

"I appreciate your concern," Johnis said.

"I don't mean it in a cruel way. It's just that my father and mother were both killed by the Horde. I understand how it feels. I left a life of study, destined for the priesthood, on account of it."

Johnis felt a pang of empathy for her. The brightest from each forest were selected for special training to teach others the ways of life. Science, arts, religion, history—everything but war. She'd taken up fighting only after her parents were killed.

"How did it happen?"

"My mother was taken in battle four years ago," Silvie said. "My father went after her and they killed him as well. Now they'll take me, but not before I take a hundred of them."

"Only four years? You look like you were born with a knife in your hand."

She looked at him, unsure.

"I mean that in a good way, of course," Johnis said. "You learn fast."

She shrugged. "Be the best at what you do, my father used to say. Billos lost his mother and Darsal her father. Both to the Horde. In this way we're all the same."

"Losing someone to the Horde doesn't make you worthy to lead," Billos said.

Darsal's jaw flexed. "What good is a father if he's off to war his whole life?"

"I'm sorry you feel no respect for the dead," Silvie said. "But I do."

Darsal spit to one side. *There is indeed a story here,* Johnis thought. Darsal drew her motivation from hate, Silvie from revenge. Either way, they were finally talking, and for that Johnis was grateful.

They were halfway across the large clearing and the shrieks on each side now came from dozens of Shataiki, assuming that's what they really were. For this, Johnis was far less grateful.

But he couldn't return to the subject, not yet. He had to prod them with something else if he wanted to keep them talking.

"I realize that my being here is a complete fluke," Johnis said, "and I respect your frustration. I'm a lover and a poet, not a fighter, although I'm better with a sword than you might think. Either way, I want to thank each of you for being selected. I know it means you'll all probably be dead within the month. But you're the best in the forests."

"Shut your yapper, Scrapper," Billos said.

The boy's rudeness was too much for Johnis. "It's comforting to ride with such strong company when you're surrounded by Shataiki, even though you're all too blind to see them. Speaking of which, I really do think—"

"Silence, boy!" Darsal snarled. "I swear, I'll cut your tongue out and shove it so far down your throat you won't need to eat for a month!"

Her voice echoed through the clearing, but the sound was quickly muted by dozens of black bats suddenly taking flight on each side. They screamed and flapped into the sky, spreading wide leathery wings like kites.

It struck Johnis that Darsal wasn't the one they'd reacted to. He stopped his horse and scanned the perimeter. "Silvie! You have to listen to me."

"It's okay, Johnis," she interrupted. "Some people think I'm a little crazy—"

Four beige stallions bred for the desert stepped out of the forest thirty paces ahead. On each sat a Horde, dressed in black leathers known to be worn by the Horde's assassins, Qurong's elite guard. The Scabs were tall and stately despite the rotting skin that fell from their bones.

Johnis smelled them at the same time he saw them. He'd heard thousands of stories, he'd felt the pain they brought, he'd even seen a dead Scab or two, but this was the first time he had seen a Horde warrior face-to-face.

These four had come for a purpose.

They'd come to kill the young.

# SEVEN

For a long moment the four new recruits stood frozen like desert rocks. A hundred thoughts flew through their minds. Johnis was aware only of his own.

*I'm too young to die.*

*This is all a mistake; I'm too young to die.*

Then his impulsiveness took over. Even as the other three slipped their swords from their leather scabbards without so much as budging their horses, Johnis kicked his mount hard and bolted to the right at a full gallop, to the edge of the clearing.

He was running. He was tucking tail and fleeing in terror.

Or so he desperately hoped the Scabs would think.

From the corner of his eye, he saw two of them break off and thunder after him, leaving two to fight Billos, Darsal, and Silvie. Three against two. That was a good thing.

Then again, there were now two Scabs pounding down his one backside. This was a bad thing.

Johnis had just passed into the trees when he heard the first cries of battle from behind. Billos and Darsal as one, screaming in rage as they took swords either from or to the elite Horde fighters. Silvie would fight in silence, he guessed. It was her way.

Now Johnis had two options: He could turn and fight—his younger, inexperienced body swinging his as-yet-undrawn sword against two older, battle-hardened beasts. An absurd proposition to say the least.

Or he could dance his way around these trees, hoping one or both of the Scabs would collide with a branch and be knocked silly so that he could then dismount and behead them before they woke.

An even more absurd proposition.

Fighting was out of the question, he decided. He wasn't here to kill Scabs. He was here to retrieve the catalina cacti with the others, return to the village, and then explain to Thomas Hunter that he'd made a dreadful mistake. When Johnis had said "I will" in the stadium, he'd really meant "I won't," but the beauty of Thomas's wife, Rachelle, had messed with his thinking.

Johnis ducked his way around trees and caught sight of the two black wraiths hounding him like shadows. They rode in silence, but their horses pounded and snorted. He could practically feel the hot air from their nostrils blasting against his neck.

Forest Guard horses were said to be faster than the Horde's, but the tight trees took away this advantage. They were actually gaining!

Johnis veered to his right, cutting back toward the clearing. He had to get back into the open to give his horse a chance. And if he couldn't break away, he would draw his sword and try to kill at least one before they chopped him.

But there was a chance that his very first instinct would prove right. In which case he wouldn't run *or* turn and fight. He would lead these two beasts into a trap.

He galloped free of the trees several hundred yards down from where he'd first entered them. To his far right, three horses stood where there should have been five.

Two had fled. The two desert horses were gone.

Billos, Darsal, and Silvie sat on their stamping mounts, swords still drawn.

Johnis jerked his horse right and thundered toward them. Behind him the two dense thugs followed. Hope swelled in his chest.

He was fewer than fifty yards from the other three when one of the horses in pursuit whinnied. He glanced back and saw that the Scabs had smelled the trap and were reining back.

"Go!" Johnis yelled. "Go, go!"

Billos, Darsal, and Silvie went. They flew past Johnis, headed straight toward the two stunned Scabs behind him, who by now had surely seen their fallen comrades in heaps on the grass, dead.

Johnis turned his mount and kneed him forward. But the

three new Forest Guard fighters didn't appear to need his help. Darsal and Billos split wide left and right, forcing the two Scabs to cover their flanks while Silvie drove straight up the middle toward them.

Johnis watched in fascination as the battle unfolded like a choreographed dance. Even though the three recruits had been in training only two weeks, they worked together flawlessly.

Seeing Silvie bearing down on them, the Scabs both shifted their attention to her. She dropped her sword and whipped out a knife.

At the same moment Billos screamed, bearing down from the right, and Darsal from the left. For a split moment, both Scabs diverted their attention to the two fighters at their sides.

Silvie threw her knife. And then a second knife Johnis hadn't seen her draw. But she hadn't thrown the knives at the Scabs. Rather at their horses, much larger targets.

The blades glanced off the strong shoulder of one horse and clipped the side of the other, enough to make both jerk and snort in pain.

Billos and Darsal swung their swords when the Scabs were off balance.

For the first time, Johnis watched diseased Scabs fall in battle. And it was a gruesome sight. The earth shook when they landed. Then they lay still, and their horses bolted into the forest.

A lone Shataiki screeched and took flight, soaring away over the canopy toward the west.

Quiet settled on the field. Billos walked his horse back to where Johnis waited in his saddle.

"So you are a coward," he said.

Johnis said nothing. He'd risked his neck to give them a chance.

"You do that again, boy, and I'll help the Horde chase you down," Darsal said.

"It was us four against those four," Johnis said. "I made it you three against two."

Billos scoffed.

"And when you three killed the first two, I led the other two into the same fate," Johnis continued.

"In my mind you are no Guard at all," Billos said, biting off the words. "I will never fight by your side."

"Easy, Billos," Silvie said, kicking her horse into a trot. "Coward or not, we're alive and the Horde are dead." She loped past them toward the west. "We have a mission, and the sun isn't standing still."

"They were waiting for us," Johnis pointed out. "Doesn't that bother you?"

"The mind of a coward always sees the worst," Billos snapped. He slapped his horse and brushed past Johnis.

It took them another half hour to reach the Igal point at the forest's edge. Johnis once again rode at the rear. The Shataiki began showing up after ten minutes, but apart from their red stares and wicked cries they made no attempt to stop the fighters, so Johnis avoided another verbal lashing by keeping this observation to himself.

Still, two thoughts beat through his mind. First, he alone saw the bats, which he guessed had always been there, unseen by the Forest Dwellers. And second, they probably *were* being led into a trap. But he was powerless to change their course.

Darsal was leading when they reached the last line of trees, and she lifted her hand to stop them. They pulled up beside her, four abreast.

Beyond the tree trunks lay the canyons with their flat shale tops that fell away to the desert sands. And beyond the canyons, sand dunes as far as the eye could see. The sun was already halfway down to the horizon. Soon the sky would turn bloodred, as it did every evening.

"Do you see anything?" Billos asked.

They scanned the desert for sign of Scabs. And cacti. Just beyond the forest a tall rock jutted fifty yards into the sky. This was the Igal point. Climb its peak and they said you could see for a day's ride.

"Should we scale the point?" Darsal asked no one in particular.

"We don't have time," Silvie said. "Do you see the cacti?"

Billos guided his horse out of the trees and stopped for them to join him.

"Do you see it?" Darsal asked again.

"There's no clump of four that I can see. That one to the left there is small and by itself. Maybe he meant for us to find four separate ones."

"No, he said a group of four," Johnis said, coaxing his ride to the right where the rock shelf hung over a ravine.

"But there's no saying what he meant by 'group,'" Billos persisted.

"Even so, I don't see four," Silvie said. "The catalina cactus likes sand. We'd have to go deeper into these canyons to find more."

"Either way, I think two of us should make the stretcher we'll need to carry them back unharmed," Darsal said. They'd already decided to return the large cacti home safely by strapping them to two long poles with branches between to form a stretcher.

"Fine," Billos said, "the coward could manage that task, I would think."

But Johnis hardly heard him, because he'd come to the edge of the ravine and could now see that they were in more than a little bit of trouble. The shelf fell off ten feet to a bed of sand that stretched into a widening canyon.

Their catalina cacti were at the base of this shelf, growing from the sandy bottom. He'd found them, and that was good.

But so had someone else.

Found them and smashed them to bits.

"I found them," Johnis said.

"Where?" They hurried over and stared into the ravine with him.

Each cactus had to have been as tall as a horse, judging by the size of the green chunks that littered the floor. For a moment they were all too stunned to speak.

"Elyon help us!"

"Now what?" Johnis said.

Billos forced his horse in a tight circle, studying the terrain.

"You know now what," he said. "We have no choice. There have to be four more, deeper in."

Silvie studied the desert. "Deeper? Do you think that's wise?"

"What choice do we have?"

"Ride along the forest edge," she said.

"The large ones don't grow in rocks!" Darsal said. "Billos is right: we have to go deeper where we know they are, or we could spend hours looking for nothing."

Johnis took his eyes off the shattered cacti and looked farther into the canyon. Didn't these recruits, the best of all the young fighters, see what was so obvious to him? The Horde had done this. It was a trap!

Johnis turned back, thinking how he should drop this little jewel into their minds, when movement at the treetops stopped him cold.

He hadn't noticed them because they weren't squawking, but the Shataiki had come. By the hundreds. Even more—too many to count, perched on the branches, staring at them with their beady eyes.

His horse shifted and snorted, as if it, too, had noticed.

Silvie followed his stare, then looked into his eyes, searching him.

Johnis spoke quietly for her to hear. "The Horde know we're here. They obviously smashed the plants and are waiting for us to enter the canyons. Surely you can see that."

"Of course the Horde smashed them," Silvie said. "They eat the smelly flesh at the center. That doesn't mean it's a trap."

"The coward is seeing ghosts again." Billos smirked. "I suppose the Shataiki are swarming the trees again—isn't that right, Scrapper?"

"The Horde were waiting for us in the clearing, and if we head into the desert they'll be waiting for us again," Johnis insisted. "We know the Horde is gathering. This doesn't seem to be the time to go into the desert alone."

Billos blew some air and rolled his eyes. "Please. The Horde is on the other side of the forest, in the east. We're on the western side. Does logic escape you completely?"

Johnis studied the canyons, not sure how he felt any longer. It wasn't fear that cautioned him. It was, in fact, common sense.

"We have a mission," Billos snapped, growing impatient. "Are you refusing to come?"

"No. I'm just telling you what I know."

"Save your knowledge for children, poet. We're wasting time."

Billos nudged his horse to the edge, then slapped it hard. It plunged over the lip, rode a small landslide of tumbling stones, and landed by the cacti far below.

One by one they followed his lead. The moment they headed down the canyon, the Shataiki bats left the trees and lined the cliff edges on either side of them. A foul stench drifted into the stuffy ravine, smothering Johnis.

He'd bided his time with these fools, but now his patience was growing thin. Even his younger sister, Kiella, wouldn't have had any trouble believing that if you added everything up, it amounted to a hellish mess. The fires were reaching up and licking at their backsides. That was the advantage of a young mind—believing was easier.

Perhaps that was part of this "thinking with your heart" business that Thomas seemed so taken by. Either way, they were headed toward trouble. He could see it, smell it, even feel it.

But instead of trouble, they found large cacti. Two of them. Near the mouth of a deep canyon that branched off to the right a hundred yards from where they'd started.

"There!" Billos pulled out his sword, swung his leg over the saddle, and dropped to the ground. "What did I say?"

An obvious question ran through Johnis's mind. "How do we carry them out?"

Billos cocked his sword back and jerked his head toward Johnis. "You're still with us? I thought I ordered you to cut the saplings for a stretcher."

"I—"

"Hightail it, Scrapper. We're not playing ghost any longer."

Silvie turned her horse around. "I'll go with him."

Johnis ignored Billos's insults and headed back out of the deep canyon with Silvie. Behind them, Billos began to hack at the base of the cactus.

"Don't listen to him," Silvie said.

"I'm not."

She nodded. "But Billos is right. The Horde couldn't have

known we were coming to the Igal point. And even if they did, we have no choice. We have our mission."

"My mother had her mission as well," he said. "I had a fever, and she came to the desert for the healing power of this same cactus. Mistakes in the desert kill people, mission or no mission."

That gave her pause. "Point taken," she said. "And for what it's worth, I don't think you're a coward."

Silvie's horse whinnied nervously as they started the turn into the first ravine. Johnis lifted his eyes and saw why immediately.

The animal had smelled Horde.

Not just one or four, but at least twenty this time, headed down the canyon straight toward them.

"I may not be a coward," Johnis said, "but I think I may be dead. Run!"

# EIGHT

R un!" Johnis screamed again, whirling back.

"Run!" Silvie cried in support. She galloped back into the ravine in which Billos and Darsal were cutting the cacti. "There's twenty of them on horses! Mount up and run!"

Johnis held up for a moment, undecided. It did no good for all of them to race down the canyon that Silvie, Billos, and Darsal were now in. Twenty Scabs cut off the ravine that led back up to the forest. That left the ravine straight ahead, which was clear as far as he could see.

He'd risked his neck to divide Horde forces once today and gotten his throat cut by Billos.

So be it.

Johnis sped straight ahead, away from the Horde, away from Billos, Darsal, and Silvie.

Across the canyon floor, without trees to dodge, their steeds were faster than the Scabs' horses, but the canyon would eventually give out, maybe box them in.

A glance behind told him that the party of Scabs had indeed split, half after him, half after the others.

Once again the Shataiki shrieked along the tops of the cliffs.

Once again he'd fled his comrades to split the Horde.

Once again he faced death.

What happened now was beyond his control. The canyon would either give him a way back up to the desert floor or end in a box.

He could hear the thudding of hooves behind him. They didn't seem to be falling behind quickly.

*Lover of my soul, save this tiny ant from the beasts.* He whispered the common prayer in his mind. Then repeated it.

*Elyon, lover of my soul, save this creature from the beasts.*

The rock walls on each side rose higher, steeper. A box-end was coming—he could sense it.

Without warning, the cliff on his right suddenly gaped into a second smaller ravine. Johnis veered and thundered in. But he'd gone only fifty yards and turned a slight bend before realizing he'd made a mistake.

This smaller canyon ended here! Large boulders twice the size of his horse were piled at the end, blocking any passage. The walls on both sides were vertical, a hundred feet high. One particularly massive stone towered to his right, fifty feet high, but not high enough to reach the top of the cliff.

*Dear Elyon, save this scrapper!*

The muted sound of hooves on sand boomed just beyond the bend behind him. For the first time in his life, Johnis withdrew his sword with the intent to kill or be killed.

He spun his horse back and swallowed the fist stuck in his throat. "You are not forgotten, Mother," he said in a soft shaky voice.

*"Psst."*

An animal was scurrying behind the huge boulder beside him, but Johnis cared more about the ten animals that were about to tear around the corner.

What would Father do in this situation? He'd always wanted Johnis to join the Guard. Well, he had—for about half a day, before being cut down by the Scabs. It would be the shortest time served in the short history of the Forest Guard.

*"Psst. Pssssssst."*

Johnis turned to the *psst*. A creature, maybe two or three feet tall, white and furry with bat wings and a cute face, stared at him with green eyes, beckoning him with a spindly finger.

Johnis was so startled that for a moment he forgot about the Horde.

"Hurry, boy!" the fuzzy white bat creature cried. "Are you wanting to be steak?"

"What?"

"This way if you want to live!"

The creature ducked behind the rock. Johnis wheeled his horse and hurried forward. A wide gap led into darkness, hidden from the canyon by the boulder. Large enough for a horse.

Johnis could barely see the furry white body of the bat waddling into the darkness. He held his breath and plunged forward into the crevice.

His head hit the stone ceiling once, but the pain was washed away by a dozen thoughts swirling through his mind. Starting with who this creature ahead of him was.

A Roush. His eyes had been opened to the evil Shataiki, and now he'd met a Roush, those wise protectors spoken about in the legends.

Out in the sunlit canyon behind him, one of the Scabs was swearing in confusion. Would they find the opening?

Then he was through the dark passage into what appeared to be a huge hole in the rock, maybe a hundred yards wide. The bowl he was in had two possible exits that he could see. Blue sky above.

No Shataiki.

The Roush had stopped on the sand, twenty paces out, and was looking at him with an impish grin on its face. A cute, cuddly koala bear-looking thing. White as the clouds.

The air whooshed behind him, and Johnis watched in amazement as a second Roush swooped in with wings spread wide, landed on the sand, and waddled over to the other one, eyeing Johnis as it walked.

They faced him in silence, as if he was an unusual thing that had dropped out of the sky. He supposed he was giving them the same look.

"Well, well, well," the second Roush said in a voice that purred softly. "So it begins."

"Uhhh . . ." was all Johnis managed. He glanced back at the gap through which he'd been rescued. No sign of the Horde.

"Forgive us. It's been thirteen years since any human has seen us. You have to understand that this is quite an ordeal, being seen again by such a noble creature."

"You . . . you can speak," Johnis said.

"And so can you," the Roush said. "My name is Michal. This is Gabil. We've rescued you from death."

And so they had.

"Thank you. Thank you, I just . . ." Johnis wasn't sure what "he just." He was grateful to be alive and stunned into amazement all at once.

"It's okay, lad," Michal said. "We—"

"It's fine, fine by us," the first one, Gabil, interrupted. "I'd be stunned by such a daring rescue myself. And I was quite clever, wasn't I? Pulling you out at the last minute."

"Gabil, please, no need to overdo it," Michal said without looking at his comrade. "As we agreed, I'll carry the conversation."

"Of course."

Michal took a short breath. "We don't have as much time as my friend would like. They'll eventually find a way in."

Michal folded his wings behind his back. "We're here, my friend, because you've been chosen for something special."

"Do you mind stepping down?" Gabil asked. "You're just a bit"—he stretched his wing and spindly fingers up— "tall for my tastes. On the horse, that is."

Johnis dropped to the ground, walked several feet closer, and stopped. "So this isn't a dream," he said. "I mean . . . you're really real. I wasn't killed by the Horde back there and am now in another world, speaking to ghosts."

Gabil laughed and wiggled a little jig, delighted.

"Gabil? We talked about this," Michal warned.

"Sorry. He's just so . . . cute."

"He's a man," Michal said. "Sixteen years old. 'Cute' is the wrong word."

"I'll bet the women line up for a chance to get close to you, don't they?" Gabil asked.

Johnis just stared at him, dumb.

"I knew it!" Gabil thrust his fist in the air and threw back his head. "He's *sooooo* . . . cute!"

"Gabil!"

"Sorry."

The silly Roush pulled his right wing over his face and peeked over it with emerald green eyes. "So sorry," he said in a muffled voice.

"Have you ever noticed the mark behind your right ear?" Michal asked.

Johnis touched his neck. He'd never seen it himself, except dimly reflected in water, but he knew he had a birthmark behind his ear—a circle split with two hash marks like an *X*. "Yes."

"The circle mark," Michael said. "A similar tattoo marked humans' foreheads to show they'd been united with a man or woman before the Great Deception wiped out all such markings through the skin disease. It was the symbol of marriage. But on you it means you've been chosen by Elyon."

"Chosen? Aren't we all?" Johnis was still having a hard time accepting the fact that he was talking to two fuzzy white bats.

"All humans are chosen—yes, of course," Michal said. "But you are special."

Johnis didn't know what to say to that, so he said nothing.

"You are chosen to save the humans, lad," Michal continued. "'A chosen child marked by Elyon will prove his worth and destroy the Dark One.' This was the second prophecy given to Thomas Hunter. He's guarded the secret closely to protect the young from coming under attack from anyone wanting to upset the balance. Something similar happened once in history."

This was all quite ridiculous, of course, but Johnis didn't bother stating the obvious. They all knew the original prophecy: that a way would come when things were at their worst. But this bit about it coming from a boy seemed preposterous to him.

"How's that tied to saving us humans?" he asked.

Gabil pulled his leathery wing from his face and blurted the answer. "By dealing with the slimy, black, flea-infested, snaky, beady-eyed bat vermin one final time, lad!"

"No, actually, that's not it, Gabil," Michal said.

"Or something like that," the shorter Roush insisted. "In the end, anyway."

Michal reached behind him and pulled out a leather-bound book he'd kept hidden until now. Two straps of red twine were wrapped around the ancient black cover—one at the top, one at the bottom—binding it shut. It looked like a small journal.

The Roush held the book out for a moment, then dropped it into the sand, where it landed with a soft thump. "Your task is to find the six lost Books of History."

The book looked magical, sitting still in the sand, staring up at him, halfway between his booted feet and the Roush's thin, bare toes.

"I don't think you understand," Johnis said, searching for something intelligent to say. "I'm actually just a new recruit in the Forest Guard. We're here to take four cacti back to the village. In fact, I should probably get out of here and help my friends."

"Cute," Gabil whispered, grinning again.

"Yes, we know all about your friends and the Horde," Michal said, "and if you'll just listen to me, you'll have your opportunity to save them. They're needed as well. But you have to listen to me. It is very important that the six lost books be found by you before they land in the hands of the Dark One."

Johnis paced, confused by the sudden turn of events. "I'm not even a real fighter—this can't be right. I don't even know what these books are."

"The Books of History, lad! Everything written in them is perfect history. The first seven books crafted by Elyon, each in a different color, were bound by red twine, never to be opened except in the most terrible circumstance, because they hold a very great power. Which is why you must find them before the Dark One does."

"Do you accept?" Gabil asked, eyes bright.

"This can't be right—"

"Now you listen to me, lad." Michal walked forward, around the book, and stopped three feet from Johnis. "Why you humans fell for that beast Teeleh the first time, I'll never understand. But this is a chance for you to find yourselves again. Not only you, all of you! You're not just some random sixteen-year-old boy—you've been chosen from birth, even before the Great Deception! I expect you to accept your destiny."

For the second time this day, Johnis found himself being asked to be someone he didn't think he was. First by Thomas, now this.

He felt his face flush with frustration. What would Father say to this? He knew what Mother would say. "Run, boy. You know that anyone who goes on missions that make no sense always ends up dead."

"Will I be killed?" Johnis asked.

"Of course."

He stopped pacing, stunned. "You *know* that?"

"All humans are killed at some point," Michal said.

"And is my 'point' soon?"

Michal eyed him, then sauntered back to Gabil's side and turned around. But he didn't answer the question. "There are a few other details you will need to know. We can tell you that one of the books hides in the west."

"There aren't any forests west of here," Johnis protested. "We'd turn to Scabs without water."

"You'll *find* water," Gabil, the odder of the two, said. "Do you think we'd let such a cute face shrivel into Scab flesh?"

"Where to the west are these books?"

"We don't know," Michal said. "If we did, we wouldn't be here talking to you."

"This is impossible! We can't just head west and find six missing books in the desert! The *Horde* lives out there, for Elyon's sake."

"The Horde is the least of your worries," Michal said. "You don't believe me? Have you lost the simple belief you once had as a child?"

"I'm not saying that. I'm—"

"Yes, you are. Go west! Find your destiny. Find the books. And if you die, so be it. You've been chosen!"

A long stretch of silence separated them.

"I knew it, I knew it," Gabil whispered. "What did I tell you, Michal? He's going to accept!"

"He hasn't accepted yet," Michal mumbled.

Johnis tried to stall them. "What are the other details?"

"You'll need the other three."

"The other three hate me. I may need them, but they don't need me."

"If you can't convince them to follow you, you will pay a terrible and immediate price."

"They call me Scrapper."

"Shut your yapper, Scrapper," Gabil said, chuckling. He saw the insensitivity of his comment right away and covered his mouth with a wing. "Oh, sorry! Sorry, that wasn't nice, was it?"

So the Roush had been near enough to overhear Billos on the trail. That gave Johnis some confidence. And there was this book on the sand. And the Roush themselves, not to mention the fact that Gabil had rescued him.

"Furthermore," Michal said, "you can't breathe a word of this to anyone else, only the four of you. Do you understand? Under no circumstances will you tell any living person in this world anything you learn on your quest."

Johnis thought about it all. A faraway cry carried into the bowl.

He faced the Roush, still hot in the face. "So it's as simple as that, is it? 'Just go west and find the six missing Books of History filled with enough power to destroy all humanity, lad. Never mind that you aren't a fighter. Never mind that you're out here by mistake. Never mind that the others hate you. You've got the mark. You were chosen.'"

"Yes," Michal said.

"And how do we escape these Horde?"

Gabil leaped into the air, soared to one of the crevices that Johnis had first thought might be a way out of the bowl, landed in a somersault, and sprang to his feet. He swept his wing toward the small gap. "Here!" he cried, as if unveiling a grand prize.

Johnis walked over, gave the Roush a wide berth, and stepped up to the gap. Beyond lay the deep desert's rolling dunes. The sun was sinking directly ahead, to the west. A butterfly beat in his belly.

"And as for your friends," Gabil said, flying to the bowl's opposite end, "they're trapped in a canyon beyond this wall, through here." He pointed to a third small gap.

"This is their only escape," Michal said. "Take the book and show them this escape—surely that will be enough to convince them that you know what you're talking about."

"Then you don't know Billos or Darsal," Johnis said.

"I know humans. It's enough."

"You accept?" Gabil asked again, waddling back.

Johnis walked over to the book and picked it up, turning it in his hands. The title *Stories of History* was etched into the black leather cover, between the two straps of red twine.

"Careful, you may not want your blood to touch that book," Michal said, taking a step forward. He was staring at Johnis's finger, stained with blood from when he'd last touched his head to feel how his cut was doing. Striking Jackov head-on had left a deep wound that matted his dark hair with blood.

Without thinking Johnis touched the book with his bloodied finger. "Why not? I—"

An image slammed into his mind. A black strobe that ignited his world with darkness, even though it was still light.

The twisted image of a man or beast shrouded in a black cape. Or wings. A hat perhaps. Striding straight for him, featureless except for the capewings and an outstretched arm with long spiked fingers grasping at him, as if it wanted the book.

A loud moan, like that of a man in the throes of death, wrenched through the air. *Mmmmwwwwaaaaa . . .*

Johnis gasped and yanked his hand from the book. The image was gone. But his fingers were shaking like a rattler's tail.

"That's why," Michal said. "And don't ask what just happened because I can't tell you. It's beyond me. Beyond you. Just keep the books from blood."

Johnis was too stunned to speak.

"It's real," Michal said softly. "Will you accept this task?"

"I will," Johnis said softly. He wanted to ask about the book, but he wasn't sure what to ask.

"Good," Michal said, waddling away. "You'll see us again, don't worry. Remember, no one but you four may know of us— or the books or anything else that happens to you."

"But the Horde is going to attack," Johnis said, still feeling a bit numb. "We have to get back and report what we've seen."

For a few beats the white bat just eyed him. "Yes, the Horde. Is it better for ten thousand to die now or a hundred thousand in a month?"

Johnis blinked. "Ten thousand now, I suppose."

"Then find the books."

He asked the one question that came from his heart of hearts. "Will I live?"

"That should be none of your concern. If you die, you die for Elyon."

"But being chosen doesn't mean I'll die. Or does it?"

Gabil looked at him with sober eyes. When he spoke, his voice was soft. "Most who are chosen die, Johnis. But when the time comes, you won't care. Just try to stay alive long enough to find as many of the books as you can. Promise me that."

Johnis swallowed. "I promise."

*What an absurd promise,* he thought.

# NINE

O ur assassins are dead?" Qurong roared. "Then these four saplings had an escort?"

"No," the priest of the Horde said in his low, gravelly voice. "I don't think so."

The general stood from the table. His head brushed one of the serpent statues this cursed priest himself had hung from the tent to protect them. Four others stood in each corner of the lavish tent, gazing at him with their beady ruby eyes. Underfoot, mats dyed purple covered the smooth sand.

They were at the heart of the Horde camp, a massive field of tents hidden deep in a long desert valley to the west of the Middle Forest. The sound of clanking metal rang through the air as it always did—swords and sickles and spears being hammered back into shape by the blacksmiths, a task made necessary because of the soft bronze they used to fashion their weapons. It was no secret that the Forest Guard used better materials in their swords, but that would soon end. The traitor was teaching them well.

In three more days they would march on the forests from the west. The spy had reported that Thomas expected them in the east. All was according to plan.

All except these four runts.

"Then how could four of our most experienced warriors fall to children?"

"They aren't children." The priest picked a fly off his arm and crushed it between his thumb and forefinger. He didn't bother wiping the innards from his skin. "But you're right, we should have had them. They were as green as seedlings."

"That's no answer. Are you telling me that they are a match for our forces?"

"No," the priest said. "They used their black magic, I would say. Trickery was involved."

"Bah! I don't care about your spells and magic. We know from the traitor that none of their attempts at magic work." Qurong clubbed his chair, breaking the spindles that had been crudely fixed as a backrest.

The priest was a sly, wicked snake. His days would end with the swing of a sword.

"I wouldn't dismiss Teeleh's power so easily," the priest said.

"Your whole point is to capture the marked one because he can lead us to the missing books."

"I want the boy only because of *their* superstitions, not mine. Thomas Hunter believes the boy will save them. Do you think he called up so many young to send them off to die? No, he was looking for the promised one, and now he thinks he's found him. Killing the boy will crush Thomas."

The high priest drilled him with a dark stare and held his gaze the way he often did. "Then you don't believe finding the seven lost Books of History will give us an advantage?"

"Did I say that?" Qurong turned from the man's crushing glare. "Show me Teeleh and I will give him my soul and find the rest of the books. But for now we fight with flesh and blood, not spells and magic."

"If I'm not mistaken, you *have* given him your soul," the priest said softly.

Qurong turned away. "It doesn't matter; we'll have these four saplings in the canyons. Send another five hundred men. If the recruits escape now, they will inform the forests that we have elite fighters on the west side. That devil Thomas will know we've fooled them with this show of force on the east."

FOUR HOURS' RIDE DUE WEST FROM WHERE QURONG'S LARGE camp hid in the desert valley, Thomas paced in one of the gazebos that overlooked the lake. Mikil, the woman he'd promoted after

Justin's recent defection, stood by the railing, watching several hundred who'd already gathered at the lake for the night's celebration.

"We should have sent spies at least," she said. "Someone to watch over them and report back."

"I have my reasons for sending them alone," Thomas shot back. "They're meant to be tested, not pampered."

"Those four are bound to tear each other apart. Or at least tear Johnis apart." She shook her head. "They're a wounded lot. I hope you know who you picked."

"I picked the four strongest candidates. You have Billos, the tempestuous bulldog who swings first and asks later; Darsal, battered and insecure inside but covers it with enough boldness to take on a whole squad on the outside; Silvie, who is the smartest recruit in the field with a burning revenge that will drive her to the end."

"Those sound like weaknesses," Mikil said.

"They are. But these fighters use their weaknesses to fuel excellence. They will be warriors because they must. The only question that remains is whether they can lead. Together."

"And the fourth? You didn't mention Johnis. Or is his weakness that he's simply not qualified?"

"He's the one who will bring the rest together or die trying."

Only he and Rachelle knew about the prophecy concerning the chosen child who would prove himself and save them all.

Today Thomas had found the child. His name was Johnis.

"You're probably right," Mikil said with a sigh. "The sun sets in two hours. They still have plenty of time."

"It's dark in three hours," Thomas said. "They have enough time to take a nap along the way."

"Unless—"

"Enough." Thomas lifted his hand. "There won't be an *unless*. How many of the Guard are pitched in the Eastern Forest?"

"All ten thousand. Leaving the rest of the forests unprotected, including the western flank, where you've sent the four new recruits."

"You're saying that we have a reason to doubt our scouts? There are enough tents out in the east to house an army of two hundred thousand Horde. That's an illusion?"

"Not my point, sir." Mikil said. "I'm just worried about the four you sent off alone. We hardly have enough Guard to mount a rescue if they did run into trouble."

Thomas nodded but held his jaw firm. He knew that sending them off so close to a major battle wasn't entirely sane. But he also knew that one of those four had been chosen. Perhaps he had to know. Perhaps he'd intentionally sent Johnis off with three scrappers, knowing that he would be tested.

"As I said, I have my reasons," he said. "What worries me more is the battle we will throw them into when they return." He sighed. "I want you to take the thousand new recruits to the eastern flank at first light with all the resin from our reserves. They can help finish the trenches and pour the resin. When the battle comes, they will man the torches and spring the traps. I don't want them in battle this time. It's too early."

He'd come up with the notion of digging deep trenches in the sand and filling them with flammable resin from the nanka tree. The Horde would ride their horses into a firestorm, if it worked as well as he hoped.

Mikil's eyes twinkled. "That's"—she hesitated—"a good idea, sir. The recruits are too raw to fight."

"No, you're wrong," he said, walking out of the gazebo. "They're not too young. But I can't bear the thought of any dying so soon."

# TEN

Johnis was forced to lift his legs up by the saddle so his horse could make it through the narrow gap the two Roush had directed him to before flying off in a rush. He expected the sounds of fighting but could hear only the hollow whistle of wind through the canyons.

The blue sky above was turning red, as it did every evening over the desert. Johnis's palms were slimy with sweat, and he couldn't shake the chills that spread down from his neck.

He still couldn't truly believe all that he'd heard. Or the flash he'd felt when he touched the book. Alone here in the rocks, with the sky turning red and the Horde scouring the canyons, the idea of heading out into the desert in search of six lost books seemed like suicide.

And the notion that he was chosen by Elyon to undertake this quest was the most ridiculous thing he'd ever heard.

He wasn't brave.

He wasn't strong.

He wasn't crafty.

He wasn't even very smart.

Even if he was one of those things, he wasn't ready to die, which was the only thing Michal had said that made sense.

If he went into the desert, he would die sooner or later, probably sooner. If the Horde didn't get him first, he would die from the disease. Without the lake to bathe in, his skin would crack open, his eyes would turn gray, and he would writhe in pain on the hot desert sand.

Johnis stopped the horse at the end of the crevice, held his breath, and listened for any sign of Horde or the others. Something knocked a few pebbles off a ledge to his right. His pulse spiked, then eased when he saw a blue lizard scamper into a crack. Nothing else.

He let his breath out slowly.

He wasn't sure where he was in these canyons, but he could probably find a way back to the forest to tell Thomas everything. That's what he would do.

Of course that's what he'd do. He had no choice. Anything else would be irresponsible. He couldn't go looking for the others only to get himself killed. He had to warn Thomas. There were elite Scab fighters on the west who knew more than they should.

There was a spy in the forest. Someone who bathed in the lakes but was really a Scab at heart. That was the meaning of what he'd seen when he had touched book. An evil omen, if it had happened at all.

Johnis leaned over the black stallion and rubbed its neck. "Shh, shh, shh. Stay quiet, boy." He nudged its flanks and walked out into the canyon, guiding the animal over the areas of thickest sand.

The canyon came to a T, but the left channel was blocked by fallen boulders. Johnis guided the stallion to his right around a large boulder, sweating now, begging Elyon that no Scabs would be  waiting so he could make his way out, back to the forests, back home.

There was no Horde.

Instead, there were three Forest Guard fighters: Billos, Darsal, and Silvie. They had dismounted and were holed up behind a rock, keeping their horses muzzled.

Johnis pulled up. This was the worst of all possible developments, he realized. If Billos and the others were hunkered down in hiding, then there was no escape. There were obviously Scabs in the canyon beyond the boulders.

The moment Billos saw Johnis coming up from behind, his eyes widened, and he frantically motioned for him to get along the cliff wall.

Johnis instinctively ducked and moved his horse to the cliff. He slipped off and led the beast forward. Silvie's bright eyes followed him in. Darsal looked stern but not frightened. Billos, on the other hand, looked furious. And no wonder—in his mind, Johnis had run off to save his own skin again.

Johnis was tempted to leave them and hurry back the way he'd come, through the crevice into the bowl and out into the desert by himself. He would find another way back to the forest.

But then something happened that changed Johnis's heart in the space of one breath. Silvie, the short, beautiful fighter with blond hair and bright blue eyes, winked at him.

She'd winked at him. Why, he had no clue. They were in a canyon, trapped by Horde, and she'd drilled him with her blue eyes and winked.

He was so startled by her wink that he stopped five feet from them. Her flawless face glistened with sweat, and her cheekbones were smudged. She lifted a single finger to her lips, signaling silence.

Johnis acted spontaneously then, letting his instincts take over, thinking, he told himself, with his heart. He waved Silvie forward with his hand. Then more urgently when she hesitated.

She left her horse and stepped up to him, keeping her blue eyes on his. He motioned her closer, and she came near enough for him to smell the gardenia blossoms that many of the women in the village used to scent their necks.

He leaned forward so that his mouth brushed the hair over her right ear. "Tell the others to follow me," he whispered. "If they want to live, follow me."

Then, without looking to see what her response was, he turned and led his horse back the way he'd come.

No matter how tempted he was to look back, he refused. Either they would follow, or he would go alone. Into the bowl, into the desert, then back around to the forest and home. Maybe even run into a few catalina cacti along the way.

He turned the corner, walked another fifty feet, and pulled up. Now he looked back. No sign of Billos and company scurrying after him.

Another ten seconds and still no sign. They probably hadn't budged. He thought about going back for at least Silvie. If he explained . . .

She suddenly came around the bend, leading her horse. And behind her Billos, then Darsal.

"This is a dead end; we've been here!" Billos whispered as they came close. "We'll be rats in a crate if the Scabs come this way. Our position at the rock at least gave us a fighting chance."

"Then go back," Johnis said. He looked at Silvie. "I've found a hidden passage out of this canyon. You can join me if you want, but we have to hurry."

Without waiting for any response, he turned away and continued down the canyon.

"The scrapper's lying," Billos whispered.

"Then go back," Silvie returned.

Darsal searched Billos's eyes. "Maybe he's onto something, Billos."

Johnis felt his heart lighten. Darsal had sided with him? She was no fool; he'd known that from the beginning. None of them were, but facing death had a way of slowing your thinking. Maybe that was the difference between him and Billos. When faced with death, Johnis's mind worked better, faster. Billos's, like most, slowed.

Then again, maybe not.

He led them into the crevice, feeling as strong as he had all day. *There is now true hope,* he thought. They were going to get home tonight, alive and well.

Billos and the others sat on their horses and scanned the large, empty bowl. No Shataiki, no Roush, just a hiding spot in the middle of the canyons. Now that Johnis thought about it, he hadn't seen the black Shataiki bats on the cliffs since the Roush had left.

"How did you find this place?" Darsal asked.

"A gap in the rocks over there." Johnis pointed back to the entrance through which he'd first come. "But I think there are Scabs on the other side."

"Then they'll find the same hole you did," Billos said. "This could be a trap."

"Better than being trapped behind a rock," Silvie said. "If they come after us, we can kill them one by one as they squeeze through the opening."

"The Horde won't find the hole easily," Johnis said. "But we can't stay here. Follow me."

"Just hold up, Scrapper," Billos snapped. "How do you know the Horde won't find the hole if you did?"

Johnis threw caution to the wind and told them then. "I didn't find it. A Roush named Gabil led me to it."

They looked at him as if he'd just suggested that the Horde were figments of their imagination and that the Forest Guard had been mistakenly fighting sand all these years. Even Silvie showed no belief. But she did give him some benefit of doubt. "Really? How so?"

He told them the whole story, everything except the fact that he was marked with a circle with two slash marks and chosen for this mission—because he didn't believe that himself. That and the bit about the book's reaction to blood.

When he finished, they just looked at him with eyes that made it clear they were convinced they were looking at a lunatic.

"I know, it sounds crazy. But I think there might be something to it." As he said it, he realized he was arguing for something that just minutes ago had sounded as absurd to him.

"You're trying to tell us that a fuzzy white bat told you to take us all on a quest to find the six lost Books of History?" Billos demanded. "Do you realize how absolutely mad that sounds?"

He looked at Silvie, but she wasn't defending him now.

"Yes, I realize that. And do you realize that I've just rescued you?"

"Have you, now?"

"We're standing in a bowl carved from the canyons, for the sake of Elyon!" Johnis said. "How else could I have found it?"

"You stumbled on it, obviously. The Horde is gathering on the east, you fool! You think we should desert the Guard on account of this nonsense? It would be treasonous!"

Johnis tossed open his saddlebag and pulled out the bound Book of History, careful not to touch it with his bloodstained finger. He shoved it at them. "And what about this?"

Their eyes settled on the black leather book.

"Tell me where I found this," Johnis demanded.

Silvie stepped up and took the book gingerly. Her finger traced the title etched in leather. "*Stories of History,*" she said softly. "I think this is real."

"It could be one of his books," Billos said. "A book of poetry. Open it."

Johnis took the book back. "You can't. The book has too much power. They warned me against opening it. They also claimed that if I wasn't able to convince you to follow me, something terrible would happen. Immediately." He wrapped the book in a cloth and set it back in his saddlebag.

"This is all fine and well," Darsal said, "but are you ready to take off into the desert, directly west, without water for your skin, to take on the Horde because two fuzzy white bats told you to?"

"Do we have a choice?"

"There *are* no fuzzy white bats!" Billos cried.

A distant horn moaned through the desert. They glanced west.

"There you have it," Darsal said. "Going west is suicide."

"Johnis is right about one thing," Silvie said. "The Horde knows we're here, and they're not taking it lightly."

"The only way they could know . . ." Darsal's voice trailed off.

"Is through a spy in the forest," Silvie finished.

Not even Billos argued this point.

"Say what you want, Billos," Silvie continued, "coward or not, Johnis hasn't been wrong yet."

The seventeen-year-old scowled. "So you're ready to abandon Thomas and run after these supposedly lost books?"

"No, but you need to use your head a little more."

With that, they plunged into a round of argument that Johnis was content to watch in silence. Silvie defended him but still didn't seem to actually believe his story. Darsal defended Billos but didn't seem too comfortable with his suggestion that they turn back immediately and finish their mission.

After a good ten minutes of bickering, Darsal settled the matter.

"Listen to me, you young Guard pups!" She was saying it to all of them, but she was looking at Johnis. "We can't abandon our supreme commander for a story of two fuzzy white bats that we all know don't exist. We have to get back and report this clear danger. For all we know, the Horde is preparing to attack from this side of the forest. And if they do that, with all of our forces on the east, the Middle Forest will be annihilated! As the oldest, I'm taking charge. We go back!"

Without waiting for consensus, Billos leaped into his saddle and started toward the gap in the far wall where Johnis had first come in. "Follow me."

In his confusion, Johnis was the last to mount. "Remember what Michal warned," he said, taking up the rear.

"Yes, we know," Billos said, "a terrible thing immediately. What this bat forgot to tell you is that the terrible thing happened three hours ago when Thomas chose you to be one of the Guard."

They followed Billos through the narrow passage and out into the canyon where Johnis had been trapped. No Horde.

"This is the canyon you came down, Johnis?" Darsal whispered.

"Yes."

"We go to the left ahead," Billos said.

*Eeeaaaaouuu . . .*

Johnis jerked his head up at the screech. The cliffs were lined with Shataiki again. Watching them with red eyes like vultures waiting for the kill.

"I don't think this is a good idea," Johnis whispered, trying not to sound frantic.

"Maybe he's right," Silvie said.

"We can't abandon Thomas!" Darsal snapped.

So they walked on. Toward the mouth of the canyon.

They all heard the distant thundering of hooves at the same time, but Darsal was the first to throw up a hand. "Stop!"

Johnis stood in his saddle and looked around the corner into the main canyon. The black Horde stormed toward them from two hundred yards out. Not just a dozen or two, but hundreds.

"Back! Back!" Darsal cried.

"Follow me!" Johnis cried, whipping his horse around. They had to get back into the bowl. Silvie was already riding hard beside him, and just to her rear, Darsal.

But Billos had hesitated.

They took the corner into the smaller canyon at a full sprint, horse hooves sliding on the sandy floor. But the sure-footed animals would not fall.

Billos was last, and the Horde were close, far too close for comfort.

"Hurry!" Johnis screamed. He slapped the stallion's rump with the flat of his hand until his palm stung. The huge black beast pounded toward the dead end ahead.

Johnis pulled up sharply and jerked the reins to the right, forcing the animal around the boulder and into the crevice that appeared out of nowhere.

The clacking of his horse's hooves echoed off the narrow walls. "Did they make it?" he asked, twisting back.

"Did Billos make it?" Silvie asked Darsal.

"Not yet, he's still—"

Billos's roar carried into the passage, cutting her short. Then a grunt. Then nothing.

All three of them stopped in the narrow passage, panting. Horde yells carried past them. Then one last muted yell from Billos.

Johnis urged his horse forward, into the bowl. He pulled to one side and waited for Silvie and Darsal to squeeze through. The moment Darsal had cleared the passage, she spun her horse around and headed back in.

"No!" Silvie snapped. "There are too many!"

Darsal pulled up short, her horse stamping. Silvie was right, of course. There had to be a hundred of the Horde stuffed into the small canyon, searching for the three Forest Guard who'd vanished by magic.

But it wasn't magic, and the Scabs would eventually find the opening.

Movement at the bowl's rim caught Johnis's eye. Michal sat there watching them, looking stately. And beside him, Gabil, bouncing a little.

Silvie followed Johnis's eyes, saw nothing, and faced him.

"Are you with me?" Johnis asked.

Darsal spit to one side, pulling her horse in a tight circle. Her eyes were on the passage that led to Billos, or what was left of him.

"He's alive," she said. "He's not easily killed. We can't leave him!"

"If he's alive, the Horde will take him to their camp," Johnis said. "That camp is out in the desert. West."

Darsal eyed him angrily, as if Billos's fate was in his hands. "I will not abandon him!"

"What do you suggest?" he asked.

"We go after him! We rescue him! For the love of Elyon, we don't abandon him!"

"Then we may all die. These are impossible odds. You went against me once, and look what it cost. You're wanting to try again?"

"You cocky little runt!"

"I . . . Forgive me, I don't know what else to tell you."

Silvie was looking west. "You're sure about this, Johnis?"

"You said the book looked real, didn't you? I found this bowl, didn't I? We've paid terribly for your not listening the first time, haven't we? If I wasn't sure before, I am now."

Darsal grunted. Clearly every last fiber of her being wanted to race back after Billos.

"They'll find the opening," Johnis said. "Then we'll all be dead."

"Billos is not dead!" Darsal yelled. Her voice echoed.

"And now the Horde knows that we're nearby," Johnis said. He slapped his horse and shot toward the passageway leading to the red desert. "But you're right, Darsal—Billos isn't dead."

"Is that so?" she said angrily, still unmoving behind Silvie, who had started her horse after Johnis.

"Yes, that is so. I know it is so because the fuzzy white bats that don't exist told me that all four of us were needed."

Silence.

Johnis peered into the passage and saw the desert sand waiting. A dozen black Shataiki winged their way through the red sky.

He turned back. "We need Billos, and now Billos needs us."

With that Johnis headed into the passage.

# ELEVEN

It's dark," Rachelle said, speaking the obvious to her husband. "You can't keep this up forever."

"That will be my judgment, not yours."

She smiled gently in the darkness, unbothered by his stubbornness. Annoying at times, but one of the qualities that made him the great leader he'd become over the last ten years.

Three of his officers—Mikil, William, and Suzan—stood with crossed arms on his right, as he paced impatiently in the war room, housed in the barracks to the south of the great amphitheater. From here they could see hundreds of flaming torches around the lake. A ring of gazebos circled the upper shores of the large body of water, seven of which were reserved for council, all now empty.

Dancers twirled around the fires, moving to music from wood flutes and drums. They all knew the beating drums carried far into the forest to the ears of any Scab scouts sneaking through the darkness, but this only encouraged them. The Horde should know that the Forest Dwellers danced in the face of their threat.

Though thousands gathered for this show of celebration, as they did every evening, a sense of defeat hung over the village, Rachelle thought. Death was coming in three days. Four at the most. If the Horde broke past the eastern defenses and the wall of fire that Thomas intended to ignite, they would sweep into the village, forcing every man, woman, and child to take up a sword.

Something had to change. They couldn't keep the Horde back forever. In the last major battle, more than two thousand had fallen, forcing Thomas to call up the younger ones as he had. But surely they couldn't pin their hopes on a thousand sixteen- and seventeen-year-olds.

"They've been held up," Thomas said. "Probably dropped a cactus and had to go back for more."

"The army is expecting you on the eastern front," Mikil said, standing. "I told you we should have sent an escort!"

Marie, Thomas's twelve-year-old daughter, ran up to the outlook and took the steps two at a time. Her cotton tunic flapped around thin tanned legs. Her hair was drawn back in a ponytail, and she wore a leather fighting helmet, too large for her head. She and her friends had been recounting the football game played by the recruits earlier, no doubt.

"Are they back, Father?" she cried.

"Not yet, dear," Rachelle answered.

From the darkness flew another child, and Thomas's heart fell when he saw who she was. Johnis's younger sister, Kiella, a friend to Marie.

"Tell her it's not true," Kiella said, running up.

"What's not true?" Rachelle asked.

Marie answered in a loud voice. "Samuel says they are dead. Tell me it's not true."

At ten years old, Thomas's son, Samuel, was full of vinegar like his father, Rachelle thought. "Don't be ridiculous," she said, brushing dirt from her daughter's chin.

"That's what I told him. No Forest Guard would let the Scabs kill them on their first day! But he says Johnis isn't really a Forest Guard and likely got them in trouble. Now they're being eaten for stew."

"He said that?" Thomas asked. "Tell him that I say who the Forest Guard is, not him. Tell him Johnis will one day save his skinny neck!"

"Easy, dear," Rachelle whispered.

"And then tell him I love him more than I love my own life. I would never put him in danger by choosing the wrong fighter to protect our home."

"It's dark," a man said, walking in. It was Ramos, Johnis's father. And he looked worried.

Rachelle exchanged a glance with Thomas and saved the

children from hearing what might be exchanged by taking Kiella's chin in her fingers. "Your brother is a hero, Kiella. And he'll return to a hero's welcome."

Kiella's eyes widened. She brushed past her father, flew down the steps, and ran into the darkness, Marie hard on her heels.

"Where are they?" Ramos asked. "It's dark."

Thomas bit the inside of his cheek, then said what he always said when faced with the families of his fighters: the truth. "We don't know where they are."

Ramos's eyes bugged. "Don't know. You mean they're lost?"

"We don't know."

Ramos's face reddened as the implications settled in. "Lost" meant hurt or wounded or dead. There was no such thing as lost in the forest. They all knew it like the knots in a Horde ball.

He shoved his large hand toward the west. "Then find him!"

"Easy, Ramos," Rachelle said. "We will find him."

"Now! Find my son! You sent him out, you bring him back. For Elyon's sake, don't just stand here!"

"Please remember who you're talking to," Mikil snapped.

Ramos caught himself, took a deep breath, and settled down. "Forgive me. I lost myself. But they will be okay, you think."

"I think they're probably struggling with four large catalina cacti right now, arguing over whose fault it is that they dropped one," Thomas said.

A crooked grin split the man's face. "That would be them. Not Johnis, but the others. Thank you, sir." He dipped his head. "And forgive my indiscretion." He took Thomas's hand, bowed to it, then hurried off into the night. "It's okay," Thomas could hear Ramos say to someone. "They're on the way back."

He turned away and faced the dark lake.

"What do we do?" Mikil asked.

"We go after them."

Mikil stepped up and lowered her arms. "The Horde is gathered and ready to march on the east. We can't compromise our defenses on account of four recruits."

"We go after them!" Thomas whispered harshly. "These are not just any four recruits."

*Surely Mikil knows there is no sense arguing with Thomas when it comes to matters of loyalty,* Rachelle thought. *Then again, she is fairly new in her promotion.*

"I remember rescuing you once, when you were left with a spear in your side," Thomas said to Mikil in a low voice.

That stopped her short. She dipped her head. "Forgive me. I'm indebted to you always."

"Gather one hundred of our best fighters," Thomas said. "We leave within the hour."

# TWELVE

S top!" Darsal cried. Her voice rang out over the desert dunes. "For Elyon's mad love, stop this!"

Johnis eased the reins back and faced her. A round, red moon that gave little light hung large over her head. Silvie pulled up just in front of her.

Darsal lowered her voice. "For the last time, I really do think we should reconsider this," she said, glancing around at the empty dunes.

The desert air was quiet. No Horde, no Shataiki, no lizards, nothing but them and their horses. But they all knew nothing could be farther from the truth. The forests had disappeared from sight an hour ago, and Johnis's courage had begun to fade as well.

"You can't possibly think that this makes any sense," Darsal said. She seemed to have changed without Billos by her side. Her eyes moved nervously, and she repeatedly scanned the dark desert, not for Horde but for Billos, if Johnis guessed correctly. It made him wonder what had created this bond they shared.

"You chose to follow me," he said. "And if you like, you can choose to turn back now."

"I came because the Horde were climbing up our backside and Billos was taken," Darsal snapped. "What did you expect from me under such pressure?"

"To go after Billos with me," Johnis said.

"We're not going after Billos! We're headed to the end of the world. No one's ever crossed this desert and returned alive."

"Michal was quite clear," Johnis insisted. "He said directly west, so we go directly west."

She pulled her horse up next to his. "Then look directly west. What do you see?"

He scanned the black horizon. In all honesty, he hardly felt more confident than she did. It was so dark he couldn't tell where the sand stopped and the sky began.

"If it's any comfort, I'm not enjoying this either," he said quietly. He took a deep breath and let it out slowly, thinking that maybe now was a good time to tell them the rest of what the Roush had said.

But Darsal spoke first. "I don't care whether or not you're enjoying this. The question is whether or not you've lost the few peanuts contained in that container above your shoulders. I think we should turn back and report Billos's fate now before it's too late."

Johnis clenched his jaw and headed down the dune. "And abandon Billos?"

She muttered a curse and plunged down after him.

He had to stop this bickering of hers. The path they were on was frightening enough without her throwing doubt at them at every step. The image that had crashed through him when he touched the book filled his mind. Maybe he should cut Darsal's finger and force her to touch the book and then see what he had seen. Silvie too. They would surely agree then.

But the Roush had said it was dangerous to touch blood to the books. Had warned him not to, which just as surely meant not to make it common knowledge. That's why he'd decided not to share this experience.

But he had to try something to get Darsal off his back. If not for the fact that Michal had insisted he would need all of them, he would send her away rather than try to convince her to stay with him.

Reason was the only way. Reason *with* heart. Perhaps he could force her to think with her heart if he matched her insistence with his own. He should be stronger, not more understanding. In honesty, he was already being nearly as strong as he dared, but it clearly wasn't enough.

"You will follow me, Darsal," Johnis said as she pulled up.

Then he said something that sounded offensive even to him—he had to; he saw no other choice. "You will follow me to hell itself if that's where I lead you."

Even Silvie seemed taken aback by his boldness. "She may have a point, Johnis. You know we could still cut back and make it to the forests in the darkness."

"But we won't," he said, holding firm. "We can't. Our destiny is out here in the desert of death where the Horde lie in wait, desperate to feed on our flesh."

"Of all the . . ." Darsal was fuming. "You're speaking like an idiot, Scrapper! We came this far because . . ." She paused, searching for words to make her case. "Okay, you *did* say a few things that made sense, I'll admit that. And Billos *was* taken. But that doesn't mean you have to lord it over us, for the love of . . ." She spit to one side.

"You'll follow me to the moon and back, Darsal," Johnis said in a soft voice. "You might as well get used to it."

He knew he sounded like a jerk, but he had his reasons.

They rode in silence for a few minutes, perhaps only because Darsal was so taken aback by his sudden change in tone. The sandy dunes gave way to hard, flat ground that had been baked by the sun.

Then Darsal started up again. "Okay, I really think—"

"If I tell you to march off the end of the earth, you will, Darsal," Johnis interrupted.

"Of all the—"

"If I tell you to dig a hole and bury yourself in the hot sand, you will, and you'll do it singing my praise," Johnis said.

Darsal stopped. "I will not!" she screamed.

Johnis spun back. "Of course you won't!" he said. "But the question you have to ask yourself is, what *will* you do?"

Silvie reached out a hand. "Johnis . . ."

"You too, Silvie. What will you do? Ask yourselves now, once and for all, what you will do, because I can't live with this bickering for days on end."

They looked at him, dumbstruck, not understanding.

He sighed. "I was rescued by two Roush who told me that I was chosen, along with you, to find the six lost Books of History. And believe me, I didn't like what they told me one bit. What they asked me to do was the same as jumping off the end of the earth, as far as I was concerned. Like burying my head in the sand, ignoring reason. But I had to make a choice."

Now did they get it? Darsal blinked. Silvie held his gaze.

"They said you should follow me off this cliff, and I'm staking my life on the hope that you will," he continued. "But you have to decide. Will you follow me, Darsal? Will you, Silvie? Will you both follow me to hell and back because two fuzzy white bats told me you should?"

The desert rang with his demand. He'd shocked them into a new frame of mind, he thought. A brilliant piece of manipulation. This was why he was their leader now instead of Billos—or Darsal or Silvie, for that matter.

"Go bury your head in the sand and light your backside on fire for all I care," Darsal said.

But she didn't turn and ride for the forests. She rode her horse forward, deeper into the night, deeper into the desert.

Johnis could see the smirk on Silvie's face despite the darkness. She, at least, found some pleasure in his quick thinking.

They rode in silence for another two hours, and Johnis was content to let Darsal lead them. It gave her a sense of purpose apart from finding Billos, something she desperately needed. Silvie came next, and once more he took up the rear.

When Darsal held up her hand to stop them, announcing that they had to get some sleep, he simply plopped off his horse, unrolled his blanket, and lay down before either of them had a chance to dismount.

"Tie your horse's reins to your ankle so it won't abandon us," Silvie told him, throwing her blanket near him. "Do you want to walk home?"

"We're not going home," he said.

Darsal humphed. "If we don't find water at first light, we are."

Johnis did as Silvie instructed and lay back down, using his arms as a pillow. "We will find water."

"How do you know?"

"Because Michal said we would."

"The fuzzy white bat speaks again," Darsal quipped.

"And was there anything else the Roush told you that you haven't bothered to mention?" Silvie asked, lying three feet from him. To preserve body heat, the Forest Guard normally slept side by side if caught out in the desert, but she didn't seem eager to follow the practice.

"They told me two things," Johnis said.

Darsal grunted and slumped to the ground on his other side. "Wonderful."

He was now flanked by two beautiful, grumpy women. Wonderful indeed.

"Well?" Silvie pressed. "What did they tell you?"

Johnis cleared his throat. "The first thing they told me was that I was chosen at birth to save all of you."

Silence.

"The second was that I will die."

# THIRTEEN

There had been that time when his younger brother had broken six ostrich eggs into a bowl and forgotten about them in the woodshed. A week later the smell had raised cries of outrage from three houses down, so foul was the stench. It was the same year that Billos had first met Darsal.

The year when both of their lives had changed one very ugly afternoon.

This was the odor that filled Billos's nostrils now. The smell of sulfur and rotten eggs and maggots, all rolled into one terrible perfume.

Horde breath.

His left arm was hurt, maybe broken. A lucky sword thrust by their captain had knocked him from his horse as he'd been riding after Darsal in the canyon.

His first thought upon landing in the sand was one of gratefulness at being alive—the sword could have taken his head off.

His second thought was one of doom—they were on him, and his horse was bucking ten feet away. Worse, his sword was on that bucking horse.

Still, he'd put up a courageous fight, charging the onrushing Horde on foot, dodging the first Scab before taking a club to the side of his head from out of nowhere.

His world had gone black then. Even when he awoke much later, he wasn't sure if he really was awake. There was no light, and it took him a good minute or two to realize that there was a bag over his head.

Slowly his senses came to him. And so did the smell.

He was in a Horde camp. By the sounds of the widespread laughter and the distant baying of dogs, it was a sizable camp, maybe even a city.

He was on his back, and his hands and legs were bound around a pole, like a pig being carried to the slaughter.

With his senses now intact, the meaning of his position began to settle on him. Billos was a captive of the Horde, alive for now but soon to be dead. The Horde never let captives live. They took what information they could from them through torture, then cut off their heads with a broadsword.

Thomas Hunter's stern warning to the thousand gathered

recruits still rang in his ears. "Never be taken alive," he'd roared. "Never! They'll skin you alive and you'll wish you'd never been born. Fight to the death."

Fighting a sudden bout of panic, Billos tested the ropes that bound his wrists around the pole.

He was rewarded with a boot to his ribs, and he grunted in pain.

"The worm is trying to wriggle free," a gruff voice laughed. "I say we bleed it now."

"Qurong wants it alive," said another with more authority.

"They say you can bleed it alive and it won't die," the first voice said, kicking Billos again. "It isn't human."

Something touched his hand. "Not even human," the Scab breathed.

The warrior was rubbing Billos's fist with his scaly, diseased paw. It had never occurred to him that Scab palms were cracked and rough like the rest of their skin. Nausea washed over him.

"Leave it be," a third Scab ordered. "Qurong wants to question it."

Qurong! He'd heard the name of the Horde general many times. Elyon help him, he was being taken to the monster himself!

Billos felt true fear for the first time that day. Seeing so much fighting as a boy destined for the Guard he'd found it was easy to become hardened to the threat of death. They were all destined to die anyway, it was said. It was only a question of how many Horde you managed to kill before you died.

But lying here on his back, with a bag over his head and Horde breath choking him, Billos realized that he didn't want to die. He was far too young to die! Only seventeen.

He hadn't even married yet. He hadn't owned his own house. He hadn't fought in his first battle, not really, unless you counted the encounter with the four Scabs in the forest earlier.

Billos regretted not accepting the proposal of marriage from Sebrina, an eighteen-year-old looker who'd taken a mighty fancy to him last summer when he was only sixteen. His father had discouraged him, saying that it wasn't wise for a boy destined for the Forest Guard to marry too young, before he became skillful enough in battle to survive a few years. The forests had far too many widows left by overeager young fighters, he'd said.

Now Billos cursed the Forest Guard and all that had put him in this predicament in which he was about to die unmarried!

"Then let's take it to Qurong and be done with it," the second voice said. "Its smell is making me sick."

The flap of a canvas curtain silenced them. Boots shuffled forward. *We must be in a tent,* Billos thought.

"Take a look, sir," a new voice said.

Someone scoffed, as if offended by the presence of this new *sir.* The scoff was immediately followed by a hard slap.

"Show respect," the new voice said.

Someone pulled the bag up to expose Billos's head. They *were* in a tent. Dirt floor, flaming torches. Several Scabs staring at him, close enough for him to smell every breath.

A man dressed in a black robe stepped up to him. Orange

torchlight lit the face of a Scab who stared down at Billos. The robed man wore a hood over his head, his diseased face hidden in shadows. But even so, Billos was struck by a sense of familiarity.

He'd seen this man.

But that was impossible. He'd never seen a live Scab before today, and this wasn't one of the Scab warriors from the canyons.

"Teeleh's breath, I cannot stand the sight of that traitor," one of the original Scabs hissed.

Billos had seen enough Scab meat today to fill a dozen nightmares, but here in the confines of a closed tent, their appearance made him ill. Flaking skin, yellowed by the torches. This one had a large nose, plastered with the powdery "morst" they used to ease the pain of their cracked skin, but blood or some other fluid seeped through the white powder. His muscles bulged, hardened by countless battles, no doubt, slaying the Guard. The man's imposing form sent a chill through Billos's bones.

Another Scab stepped up, jerked the sack back over his head, and spit. "If you hope to live out the year, you'd better hold your tongue. He's one of us now."

*A defector from the Forest Guard,* Billos thought. *No wonder the Horde has made so many advances lately. A traitorous Forest Guard fighter is feeding them information!*

"We take it to Qurong at first light," someone said.

And then it sounded as though they left the tent, leaving Billos alone, hog-tied to a pole with a bag over his head.

He lay shivering in the night air, further chilled by the cooling of his sweat. A hundred thoughts worked their way through Billos's mind, and not a single one brought him any comfort.

For a while he tried to conjure up what the others might try for a rescue, but he soon dismissed any hope in his comrades. They would be fools to head into the desert to find him, and the only true fool among them was the runt, Johnis, who was also a coward.

He tried to imagine that this business about Johnis meeting the Roush was true, but he couldn't manage it. Even children knew that Roush were myths created by the council elder, Ciphus, to promote the Great Romance, this religion that had the Forest Dwellers eating out of the palm of his hand.

Billos lay exhausted and trembling late into the night and finally, after many hours, slipped into sleep.

He'd been in the land of nightmares for just a short time when a soft ripping sound woke him. He caught his breath and jerked his head to the right.

A soft giggle sounded far off, then the howl of desert wolves. Nothing else. He was just starting to relax when the sound came again, very slowly, as if a knife was stuck in the canvas and was snapping threads one by one.

*Riiiiiiiiippppp . . .*

Billos froze like a skewered pig. Darsal! She'd come for him!

*Riiiiiiiipppppp . . .*

The sound hissed in the night. But, no, that hissing wasn't coming from inside the tent, he realized. The hiss came from beyond the tent wall, made by whoever was cutting the canvas.

Or *what*ever was cutting it.

"Hello?" Billos managed in a whisper.

The sound stopped. But the cutting resumed within seconds. There could be no doubt about it—someone was cutting through the canvas.

Billos heard them cut the tent. Heard them slide inside. Heard their deep, deep breathing as not one but several *someones* walked about him, feet slowly padding on the ground.

He held his breath until stars began to pop in his eyes, and then he sucked in air as quietly as he could. The moment he did, the putrid stench of Horde drove up his nostrils and lodged itself in his sinuses. He gasped and tried to breathe the smell out, but he also needed wind, so he was forced to suck it deep into his lungs.

Evidently unbothered by his sucking and fussing, whoever had come slowly lifted the pole he was bound to off the ground. He hung from his wrists and ankles, like a sack of taro root.

And then they were moving. Through the tent wall.

Through the Horde camp.

Into the desert.

Into the night.

# FOURTEEN

## DAY TWO

Johnis woke to a buzzing fly near his ear and the blazing sun in his eye. Without moving from his back, he gazed slowly about the camp.

His stallion stood black against the pale desert, still tied to his ankle. *The horse will need water, and soon,* he thought. But Billos's horse had been carrying the extra water jug. They each had a large canteen of lake water to either drink or bathe with, but that wouldn't last the day.

It was said that the skin disease came on so quickly in part because of the dry desert heat.

Silvie stood by her brown stallion, cinching up her saddle. The sun shone through her short blond hair, giving her a glow that reminded Johnis of a gardenia blossom. As he looked at Silvie now, working with strong arms, her smooth jaw flexing—she was stunning.

"You'll want a kind woman with spirit," his father had often advised him. "Beauty is in a woman's words as much as in her skin." Johnis moved his eyes to Darsal's horse. But Darsal's horse wasn't where it had been last night. He sat up and looked about.

"Where's Darsal?" he demanded, seeing no sign of her.

Silvie gave her saddle cinch one last tug. "I don't know. She was gone when I woke."

"Gone?" Johnis jumped to his feet. "What do you mean, gone?"

"I mean, as in not here. Her tracks lead that way." She nodded at the rising sun. East. Home.

"She just left us?"

"Evidently. What did you expect, kisses in the morning?"

"No, but she can't just up and leave."

"But she can and did," Silvie said, drilling him with her bright blue eyes. "And don't think I'm not considering the same."

Johnis felt his heart fall into the pit of his stomach. "Then everything will be lost. You can't!"

"Why, because we have to save the world? Find these lost books of yours?"

"Forget saving the world," Johnis snapped. "I don't care about saving the world either, believe me. And they're not *my* books. But by leaving us, Darsal has put herself in terrible trouble. You heard what the Roush said about Billos. And he was taken. You don't think the Horde are waiting back there for Darsal?"

"I heard what *you* said the Roush said about us," Silvie said. "And it's the only reason I haven't left you myself. But I don't see how going further into the desert is any better than facing the Horde in the canyons. I'd rather die fighting Horde than baking to a crisp in the sun."

"We'll *find* water!" Johnis yelled.

Silvie blinked at his outburst.

Darsal's voice rang out behind them. "We'd better, Scrapper!" She drove her horse down the dune from the south. "Because there's a line of Horde marching toward us from the east."

Silvie flung herself into her saddle, rode up the rise facing east, and studied the horizon. "You're sure?"

"Would I be here if I wasn't sure? I don't think they saw me, but we'd better be gone when they get here." She frowned at Johnis. "You satisfied?"

"About the Roush being right about the terrible trouble we would be in if you didn't all follow me, or about the Horde coming our way?"

She held his stare long enough for Johnis to wish he hadn't been so clever, then kneed her horse on, heading west.

They traveled deeper into the desert, three abreast for two hours, before drinking and giving the horses some water from their canteens. Twice Darsal had doubled back to see if the Horde was still following. Twice she'd returned saying they were. They should cut north or south, she insisted.

"No, the desert ahead is safer," Johnis argued. "If there were

Horde ahead of us, the ones behind wouldn't bring such a large force to drive us forward into a trap—certainly not for just three scrappers. Clearly the desert ahead is free of the beasts."

"Free of beasts and any other living thing," Darsal returned. "Including us soon. It's not surprising that no one's crossed this blasted dust bowl and survived."

"You had your chance to turn back," Silvie snapped. "Don't make it worse on us by griping all the way."

Darsal grunted and plowed reluctantly on. But Silvie seemed to be coming his way, Johnis thought. Or at the very least she wasn't set against him.

"I'm sorry for yelling at you this morning," Johnis told her, encouraged by her support. "I had no business being so rude."

"Don't think I like this," she said. "I'll head back and kill some of those Scabs before I die."

She seemed adamant about avenging her mother's death. He felt pity for her but understood the sentiment. "You must have loved your mother and father very much," he said.

Silvie frowned and turned her head away from him. "Both were lieutenants in the Guard when I was twelve, but they couldn't bear to be without me, so they both stepped into the reserves and took time guiding me through my special studies. My mother wasn't supposed to be on duty the day she was killed. It was my fault."

"Yours? You were only twelve."

"You don't understand. The other children mocked me, calling my mother and father cowards for leaving the Guard. I went home and yelled at my mother. I told her I was ashamed of her for deserting the Guard. We argued, and she agreed to take up her sword that very afternoon to prove she was no coward."

"And the Horde killed your mother and then your father when he went after her," Johnis said.

"I haven't stepped into a classroom since."

"I'm sorry. I'd hate to be one of the children who mocked you."

She nodded. "There were a few broken noses the next week; we'll leave it at that."

He left her alone then, not wanting to risk losing her friendship.

The first sign of pain crept into Johnis's bones when the sun was halfway down the western sky. He pulled up and flexed his fingers, surprised by how suddenly the stiffness had set in.

"The disease?" Darsal demanded, looking back at him.

"I don't know."

She lifted her arm and studied her skin. "Teeleh's teeth! So soon?"

Silvie jerked her arm up and gazed at her flesh. The tiny cracks in the skin just beneath the hair were unmistakable. Like the beginnings of a riverbed gone dry.

Johnis's heart thumped with dread. He whipped out his canteen, popped the cork, and splashed water on his forearm, eager to be free of the disease. He frantically rubbed his skin, as if washing off mulberry juice before it stained. The cracks faded.

He started to tip the canteen for more water.

"Ho, Johnis, slow down!" Silvie cried. "The horses will die before we do at this rate. Save the water for them."

He looked at her face and saw the faint cracks on her cheeks as well. But she was right—they didn't have enough water. Not bathing would make them Scabs, but not drinking would kill them and their horses. Better Horde than dead. Or was it?

"The disease affects your mind," Darsal said. "They say it turns you into an idiot. When that happens, we'll just wait for the Horde to catch us. We'll probably celebrate our defection with them!"

"I'm not willing to assume they're as foolish as we say they are," Johnis said. "They trapped us in the canyons, didn't they? Either way, we'd better hurry."

"Hurry where?" Silvie asked.

"Just hurry!"

As it turned out, hurrying didn't do them much good. It only tired the horses faster and drove them to greater desperation. The sky had turned red, the desert had flattened again, the horses were down to limping, and there was still no sign of water.

Worse, there was no longer any sign of the Horde behind them. Even the desert dwellers had given up the pursuit, probably convinced that the recruits would be doomed this deep in the desert.

Slowly, like the inching of a slug, they settled into plodding hopelessness.

Johnis stopped them when the sun dipped past the horizon. His mind was starting to go, he thought. The pain had set in so strongly that he had trouble dismounting. When he was ten he'd fallen from a mango tree, landed on his back, and rolled down a hill, over a bed of rocks, and into a stream. He'd suffered a broken collarbone and a badly bruised body. The next morning he hadn't been able to move.

This felt like that, only with fire on the skin.

"We have to rest," he said, grimacing with each step.

"If we lie down, we might never get up," Darsal said. "Maybe we should use the last of the water for a spit bath."

Silvie sat in her saddle, looking miserable. Her once-flawless face was gray and cracking already. But worse, her blue eyes had dulled and were turning white.

Johnis walked back to his horse and pulled down his blanket, shaking. "We have to rest."

Thinking that his arms hurt too much to be used as a pillow, he turned back, flipped open his saddlebag, withdrew the leather-bound Book of History that was wrapped in cloth, and dropped it at the head of his blanket.

He was happy to see that Darsal had dismounted, and now Silvie eased herself out of the saddle. They moved without speaking, plopping their blankets next to his.

*One good thing,* he thought, *is that we are past our bickering.* Fighting this much pain, none of them had the energy to stand, much less argue with one another.

"We should tie the horses," Silvie said.

But none of them got up to do it. One by one the three horses lay down. There was nowhere for them to go anyway.

Johnis stared out at the flat white desert, suddenly feeling like a complete fool. Or worse, a monster who'd mistaken himself for a prophet. Roush or no Roush, the very idea that they should set off into the desert to save the world was about as naive as you could get.

He lay on his blanket and stared at the flat sand. Beneath his head lay that book. There was something about that book. Oh yes, the thing about blood. Maybe using it for a pillow wasn't so brilliant, with a cut on his head and all. But it was wrapped, wasn't it? And his cut had probably stopped bleeding by now.

"Fellows—" he started, but then realized they weren't fellows. They were both girls. But they would understand. He had to set the record straight, and he didn't care whether they were fellows or girls. So he just told them what he felt.

"I've been an idiot," he said in a dry voice.

Neither disagreed, and that hurt a little. They could have said something nice, like "Don't be silly, Johnis." But they were right not to disagree. He *had* been an idiot, hadn't he?

"I don't know what got into me. Trapped in the canyon like that, with the Horde coming down on us, what did you expect? I was probably fantasizing. And now we're going to die because I fantasized two fuzzy white bats who told me to go off and save the world. I'm sorry, really. I was an idiot."

They didn't even look at him. They could at least look at him.

"Will you forgive me?" he asked, trying to ignore his self-pity.

But Silvie and Darsal just lay down on their backs and stared at the first stars, twinkling in the red sky. *It is too early to sleep,* Johnis thought, resting like a lump.

"What happens if we're Scabs when we wake?" Darsal asked.

It took a while for Silvie to answer. "Then I'll kill my first Scab," she said. "You won't mind, will you, Johnis?"

"You'll kill me?"

"I'm sworn to kill Scabs, and you'll be a Scab. I won't have a choice."

"Even if you're a Scab?"

"Does that change my vow?" she asked.

Johnis thought about that. "I suppose if I'm a Scab, I'd prefer to be dead. Go ahead, kill me."

Darsal faced him, wearing a scowl. "You see why all but the foolish understand that the legends are nothing more than ghost stories? Because pretending to see white and black bats when they don't exist can get you killed. If I live through this, I'm going to remember that."

"I'm sorry, Darsal," Johnis said, and he really was. He wasn't so sure he really had seen the Roush, or for that matter, the Shataiki bats. He had, after all, been accused of daydreaming more than once. What if it was all a mistake?

"I'm really sorry, guys."

Johnis shifted his body on the blanket. Resting his head on the book in its cloth, he closed his eyes and let his mind fade. Darsal began to snore softly.

WHAT JOHNIS DIDN'T NOTICE THROUGH THE FOG CLOUD-ing his mind was that the cloth had fallen free from one corner of the book.

That and the fact that he'd used his head to level Jackov two days ago. The cut on his scalp had scabbed but then broken open when he'd scratched it as his skin became diseased.

There was blood on his head.

And the book of terrible power beneath.

# FIFTEEN

The valley of the Horde, deep in the western desert, lay silent
in the morning light. Qurong dipped his fingers in a bowl
of porridge, sucked the slop from his hand, and wiped the residue
on his white bed-robe. Purple drapes divided his eating chamber
from the cooking tent. Bronze statues of the winged bats called
Shataiki occupied every corner—at the priest's insistence. This religion of his gave Qurong a chill, and truthfully, he didn't know why.

"Take this away," he growled. He took a swig of beer—the
only drink he trusted anymore.

The cook came in with his head bowed, took the bowl off the
table, and shuffled off into the adjoining room. Qurong had left
Barok, his regular cook, back in the city and brought this slug, who
was better fit to feed horses than humans.

The traitor had made good on his word, beginning with the insertion of spies into the forests: Horde who were forced to bathe in the lakes so that they looked like the Forest Dwellers until their mission was over and they could turn back to a more agreeable Horde state. And if they had any doubts about returning to the Horde, they would have to contend with the deaths of their families. This insurance had been the traitor's idea, and it worked well. Evidently a man's appetite for his family strengthened after bathing in the cursed lakes. Weakness, but weakness that played to Qurong's favor.

One such spy had watched the game Thomas had forced on his people—something called "football," played with a Horde-hair ball. The spy had informed them that four recruits had been sent on a mission. But he was interested only in the marked one, and then only because the traitor and that cursed priest had insisted that this one runt could play an important role in the war against the forests.

A rap sounded on the frame of his tent.

"Come."

The traitor stepped in first, followed by Tulong, the colonel he'd placed in charge of the prisoner who'd escaped during the night. The traitor preferred to wear his hood over his head at all times, in part because he was still growing his hair long enough for locks.

"You called us," Tulong said.

"What is this? You have no respect for authority?"

"Forgive me. This new order is just . . . new."

The new order he was speaking of was something the traitor had suggested, putting the army under a system not so different from the way the Forest Guard ran things.

"Yes, well, get used to it." Qurong spit. "I was told you lost our prisoner in the middle of the night. Tell me I've heard wrong."

Tulong hesitated.

"One simpleton in your grasp and he's gone?"

"Yes."

*"Sir."*

"Yes, sir," Tulong said.

"And have you discovered who took this young fighter?"

"Not yet."

"And why not? There's no trail?"

"They dragged the body. But then the marks vanished."

"Just vanished? I would guess it's your investigative skill that has vanished."

Tulong didn't react. *His heartless demeanor makes him a good officer,* Qurong thought. *No reason to expect any feeling from him.*

"Some are saying it was magic," Tulong said.

"Bah! Magic. There is no such thing. The other three?"

"Gone into the desert. Deep."

Qurong faced the traitor, who'd remained silent. There was a mystery about him that was nearly irresistible.

"But this changes nothing," Qurong said. It came out more like a question.

"The prisoner is Horde by now," the traitor said. "But the marked one is with the others. They should never have been allowed to escape."

"They are deep in the desert. Horde as well. This means nothing."

"And why haven't they turned back to join us?"

A good question. The traitor only asked good questions. "They will," Qurong said.

"Then let's wait until they do," the traitor said. "If for no other reason than to satisfy the priest. He insists that black magic is underfoot, and the word is spreading through the army."

"What do you suggest?"

"We tell the forces that we will delay our attack until we have them. We don't need tales of black magic haunting our men when they attack the forest."

*This is what makes the traitor so special,* Qurong thought. *Whereas before, the Horde army has relied solely on brute force, he brings trickery and planning and double-talk to the war. A good thing.*

"How long?" he asked. "You yourself have said that we depend on surprise, which we now have on our side. If we delay, we risk the campaign."

"The Guard has massed on the eastern front, and they are digging in," the traitor said. "We attack from the opposite side as planned in two days, when they are fully entrenched."

"Good. Pass the word."

THOMAS HUNTER STOOD ON THE LEDGE, SCANNING THE canyons to his right and left. They'd come with a hundred fighters and spent the night searching with dogs, but they had found no sign that the four had reentered the forests after arriving at the Igal point.

Now, in daylight, the fighters were searching from the cliffs for any sign of the recruits.

"Anything, Mikil?" he asked.

Mikil stood atop the Igal point, using the eyeglass Thomas had formed from melted-sand glass and a hollowed gourd. "Nothing." She lowered the glass. "If they are out there, they're either Scabs or dead."

"Impossible. I'm telling you right now that we haven't found their bodies because they *escaped* the Horde."

"They might have," she said. "Or were taken prisoner. Either way, they don't have enough water to bathe. We found Billos's horse with the extra water."

"Then we go after them," Thomas said.

None of the others knew about the prophecy or the fact that Johnis was marked. Then again, there was always the possibility that the birthmark on Johnis just resembled a circle without any connection to the prophecy. If so, he'd sent a boy to his death for no good reason, an innocent boy who had no business in the Forest Guard.

William spoke on his left. "We can't risk it, not so close to a battle on the other side of the forests. Besides, you have to know that if the four recruits escaped, they would have headed back into the forests. We'd have found them by now."

"They could have gone out into the desert," Thomas said.

"Only fools would do something like that. Were they chosen for their foolishness? And if they did head out into the desert, they're dead."

William sighed and turned toward the desert. "Face it, Thomas, these four are lost to the Horde. If they're still alive, we'll fight them in battle one day. But for now we should get on with the Horde at hand. We have to return to Middle and coordinate preparations."

"I could stay with fifty men," Thomas said.

"Please, sir. The men need their commander to show strength. Their lives are at risk as much as these four. You have to go back."

Thomas knew his officer was right. Admitting it aloud wasn't so easy. If it weren't for the disease, he would mount an extended search for Johnis, Billos, Darsal, and Silvie. But by the time they organized, the four would be Scabs.

"I don't like it," Thomas said.

"There's little to like these days," William said.

A thudding of hooves crashed in from behind, and Thomas turned to see a large brown stallion bursting from the forest. In its saddle sat Ramos, Johnis's father, in full battle dress. He reined up on his horse's frothy bit.

He drilled Thomas with a hard stare.

"Dropped a cactus, is that it?"

William put his hand on the handle of his sword, but Thomas immediately motioned him back.

"I had hoped so. But wasn't willing to take the chance."

Ramos studied him, then dismounted his horse and stepped forward. "And?"

They locked stares. Thomas's heart broke for the man. "We don't know, Ramos."

"But no sign?"

"No sign."

Ramos marched to the edge and stared out at the desert canyons. "Then we go after them. We mount an expedition this moment."

"There's nothing I would like better," Thomas said. "Their water was found on a horse." He walked up and looked at the pale desert with Ramos. "Even if we left now, we wouldn't find them before the disease—"

"No!" Ramos roared, knocking Thomas's hand aside. "No! We go now. He's out there, you hear me? My boy is out there, and I will not allow him to die or turn into one of those filthy beasts!"

William walked forward. "Ramos, we are gathering for battle."

Ramos broke then, standing on the cliff next to Thomas. His red face twisted in rage, and spittle flew from his mouth with each word. "Are you all cowards?" he screamed at Thomas. "You sent him to his death! He's a boy, just a boy with a Horde ball who felt compelled by his mother's death to cross your foolish line! He doesn't deserve to be deserted!"

Thomas gently motioned William back and let the man have his emotions. "I'm sorry, Ramos. My heart breaks with yours. But the forests are at stake."

"So is my son!"

He snatched his sword in panic and started for his horse, but Thomas grabbed him by the shoulder.

"You can't go after him, Ramos."

He spun back, tears wet in his eyes. "They killed my wife! Now you say I should let them take my son?"

"And if you go after Johnis, your daughter will be without a father."

His words stopped the man cold. They all knew there was nothing one man or ten men or a hundred men could do to save one who'd gone into the desert without water. The number of men who'd lost their lives trying could hardly be counted.

Ramos's lips began to tremble. Tears leaked silently down his cheek.

"You can't find him, Ramos," Thomas said gently. "But don't give up hope. Johnis is a very special boy. This is not over, I promise you."

The man whirled around, leaped onto his horse, and spurred it toward the forest. Without a word he thundered away.

"He's a sergeant?" Thomas asked.

"Yes, sir."

"Now he's a captain," he said. "See that he gets his honors."

# SIXTEEN

The three lost recruits lay in the cool desert night, snoring and occasionally groaning as disease overtook body and mind.

The body would still function well enough, but with pain and revolting smells obvious to all but those who were afflicted by it.

The mind would also function well enough, but with a limited capacity to appreciate a disease-free state of living.

Five hours into sleep, the disease had sufficiently worked its way through Johnis's skin to stretch it ever so slightly, a condition that often resulted in cracking. Fresh blood seeped from his head wound and began to snake down his hair toward the book.

All would have been fine if Johnis hadn't grunted and turned his head in the throes of some disturbing dream. But as fate would have it, when he did, his bloody locks made contact with the only part of the Book of History that wasn't covered by the cloth.

And in that moment, Johnis's world changed.


JOHNIS WAS LYING IN A FITFUL SLEEP WHEN HIS MIND exploded with black light that seared his nerves. He jerked and screamed out in pain.

He wasn't sure if the pain came from the blackness itself or from his sudden movement in the diseased state. The man-beast shrouded in black was there again, striding forward from a surreal world, reaching for him.

A moan shattered his ears, and he threw both hands over them, screaming once again.

Then the pain was gone. And the man-beast in black vanished.

Johnis wanted it all to be gone, wanted to wake up, maybe even wanted to be dead, but darkness still fogged the corners of his vision.

He could hear his breathing, long and heavy, echoing in the fuzzy tunnel ahead of him. Another image slowly came into view at the center of the foggy hole.

A desert dune. In daylight. And in fact, Johnis himself was standing at the face of the hole, part of the darkness behind him, part of the day-lit desert ahead.

He reached his hands out to feel the air, and he could swear that the air in front of him was warmer than the darkness behind. Crazy—yes, of course—but so real.

At least in his mind. Or was it more than his mind?

His horse suddenly ran down the dune directly in front of him, stepped to the right, and looked back up the dune he'd come from. To Johnis's amazement, a man stumbled over the crest of the dune, stared at him hard, and walked toward him.

The image was a bit distorted, as if heat was rising between them, but that didn't make it any less real.

This wasn't the threatening man-beast, nor Horde, but Johnis couldn't breathe anyway. Something was very wrong. The man wore a shirt made from a thin fabric, with writing across the breast, and fitted blue pants. Leather boots—but not the dress of a warrior.

More than his dress, the man's demeanor was out of place. Rather than walking like a skeleton in the desert, this man looked healthy. As if he'd had all the water he needed.

Johnis stepped back, frightened by the sight.

"Hey," the man said in a very strange accent. "What's . . ." He looked around. "What's going on?"

Johnis was too stunned to speak.

"You from Summerville?" the man demanded.

"I'm from the Middle Forest," Johnis said. "We need water."

The man eyed him carefully. "Show me the town, and I'll show you water."

"But I don't know a town out here," Johnis stammered. Perhaps the man was mad from the desert heat after all.

"The town, Summerville." The man motioned to the dune

behind him to the right. "There's a killer forcing us to play a game. I need you to help me find the cops. Tell them to get to the library. It's all about the library, tell them."

Heat shimmering off the sand distorted both the man and his words for a moment, then passed.

"Cop?" Johnis had never heard the word. It could be a code word for Horde. The Horde were in the library? "Have you seen my two friends, Silvie and Darsal?"

The man looked completely flat-footed. Maybe he'd been bitten by the desert heat, turned stupid. Johnis looked in the direction of the supposed place called Summerville. When he turned back, the man was gone.

Gone!

Johnis scanned the distorted dune, but nothing changed. He stepped back, just one step, and the hole suddenly closed in front of him, as if drawn by a noose.

Blackness filled his vision.

And the black man-beast was back, reaching—reaching and moaning. This time Johnis saw that he had more books with him, under his arm, but he couldn't tell how many because the long fingers reached for his throat, and he had to jump back or die. Yes, he knew he would die if he let those fingers/claws touch him.

Johnis screamed and opened his eyes.

Daylight blinded him, and he snapped his eyes shut. When he opened them again, he saw that he was back in the desert.

His horse was lying at his feet. Two bodies lay against him, one on each side, snoring softly. He turned his head and stared at Silvie's graying face inches from his own.

Silvie lay dead to the world, mouth parted slightly, breathing through some mucus that had gathered in her throat. He fought a sudden fit of empathy for her. Her skin was cracking and puffy. And she smelled.

Something nudged his other shoulder, and he turned to see that Darsal was nestled against his arm, faring no better. And if he could see himself in the reflection of water, he would undoubtedly see that his own skin was hanging from his bones.

"Johnis?"

Silvie had opened her eyes and was staring at him.

"Are we dead?" she asked.

Johnis pushed himself up, grimacing with pain. The horses were still alive; that was good. The Book of History lay where he'd placed it for a pillow, smudged now with a small circle of blood. He'd made a terrible mistake. *Never again,* he thought.

He picked up the book, wrapped it tightly, and shoved it back into his saddlebag. Whatever happened, he knew now that he had to protect this book at all costs.

"We have to give the stallions water," he said. "They won't make it long."

He watched Silvie struggle to her feet, amazed at the disease's progression through the night. *What have I done? I'm the supreme commander of utter fools, and now we will all pay.*

The desert rose with small dunes to the north, he saw. "Maybe they've sent out a search party." But he knew this was only more fool's talk. Better to head north, into those dunes he'd dreamed about.

Johnis was slipping the book into his saddlebag when suddenly the dots connected in his mind. Dunes to the north? Just as he'd dreamed!

His pulse suddenly pounded in his ears. "Fellows?"

They didn't even look at him.

"Girls, I think I may know where we can find water," he said.

"I hope you *drown* in your fantasies of water," Darsal rasped.

"But you see those dunes?" He pointed north. "I dreamed that those dunes were there, and I met a man who told me Summerville was there. There's water in Summerville."

Silvie moved painfully, watering her horse from her canteen, still refusing to look at him. "Fine, Johnis," she said. "Lead us to our deaths. Why stop now?"

"You'll follow me?"

"Into hell, remember?"

He gave his horse the rest of his water, then managed to mount despite his hurting flesh. "Okay, follow me."

In reality he had no clue what they'd find. Dunes, he could see that much. But the idea of water being there did seem like a fantasy.

They trudged through the desert, over the dunes. Nothing. So maybe he had been wrong.

They crested the fifth dune and pulled up.

There, in the valley below, a pond of sweet blue water shone in the rising sun, bordered by several tall palm trees and some large cacti. Catalina cacti.

"Water," Silvie said, staring dumbly.

A painful grin split Johnis's face. "Water."

# SEVENTEEN

They took off, leaving Darsal gaping in their dust, then flogging her horse to catch them.

Ahead a white head poked up from the bush, then dove into the pond and disappeared.

"Did you see that?" Johnis cried. "A Roush."

"See what?"

So they still weren't seeing. But they *had* found water.

Darsal caught them before they reached the pond, and all three rolled from their horses in pain, landed on the sandy shore, and flung themselves into the glistening water.

The question now was, what kind of water? There was the drinking variety found in many streams throughout the forests, and the lake variety found in only the one lake at the center of each forest.

Was this water Elyon's?

Johnis knew the moment his skin hit the cool liquid that they had found gold. The waters of Elyon reached into his flesh, burning it like a hot iron for one terrible moment. It was no wonder the Horde feared water. He thought he could actually hear a hiss as the power spread through his skin, vaporizing the disease until the pain was gone entirely.

He sank below the surface, hardly able to contain his joy. And there, under the water, he trembled with relief.

Johnis burst from the pond, fist raised high. "Ha! What did I tell you? What did I tell you?"

"Ha!" a white Roush cried on the shore, wing jutting high like Johnis's fist.

"Gabil!"

"Johnis!"

"You're here!"

"*You're* here!"

The white bat shook its fur, spraying him with water.

The water parted as first Silvie, then Darsal, emerged facing Johnis with glowing, tanned skin and wearing impossibly wide smiles. They stared at him for a moment, then all three began to speak at once.

Johnis: "I'm sorry this happened like . . ."

Darsal: "You were right, Scrapper . . ."

Silvie: "You've yet to be wrong . . ."

They laughed like children, lost in relief and life, and for the moment they were ecstatic. Above them the sun shone in a blue sky. Below, in this oasis of living water, leafy palms swayed in a gentle breeze. Even the cacti bristling with thorns looked at peace among the gray boulders. They'd found a pocket of Elyon's power in the desert of death.

"I guess this settles it," Silvie said.

"The Horde must not get this far out," Darsal said. "If they knew this pond existed, they would have filled it in long ago."

Silvie scooped up a palmful of the water and let it dribble through her fingers. "I thought Elyon's water could only be found in the forests."

Behind her Gabil was rocking back and forth, grinning from ear to ear, bursting at the seams with an eagerness to be noticed.

"You believe me now," Johnis said. "That's what's important."

Darsal frowned, but her eyes were bright. "Do we have a choice?"

"I believe you, Johnis," Silvie said. "We're the fools, not you."

"Then maybe you should turn around and tell me what you see."

They looked over their shoulders, then jumped back as one.

Gabil crossed one wing over his chest and snapped his spindly legs together like a soldier reporting for duty. "Master Roush— defeater of the slimy, snake-eyed, putrid-breathed beasts—reporting. Otherwise known as Gabil."

"You . . . you're a Roush," Silvie stammered. Then to Johnis, "They really do exist?"

Darsal blinked. "You're a ghost?"

"Do I look like a ghost to you?" Gabil demanded.

"No. Well, you are as white as a ghost."

"But ghosts don't know karate." The white bat kicked his thin leg out from under a round torso, tried to steady himself with a flutter of wings, and toppled backward. He hopped back up, frowning. "Sorry, sorry. Not used to the air out here in this hot, very hot desert. Normally that goes much better. Do you know karate? That's what Thomas Hunter calls it in his dreams."

"You mean this?" Darsal lunged from the pond dripping wet, snapped the air with a perfect roundhouse kick above her head, and dropped into a crouch, ready to defend.

Gabil stood as tall as he could, which was just over two feet, stuck out his chest, and eyed Darsal as if trying to decide whether he approved or not. "Close enough, I guess. Although that's not perfect. One day I'll show you the finer forms of karate."

"Show me now if you—"

"No." Gabil halted her with an extended wing. "Not enough time now. Too much to do. I have a message for you."

Johnis and Silvie exchanged suppressed smiles as they stepped from the pond.

"He's so cute," Silvie whispered.

Gabil's ears perked immediately. "What's that? Am I?"

She knelt on one knee and kissed him on the forehead. "The cutest creature I've ever dreamed to meet."

Johnis couldn't tell if Gabil turned red under his white fur, but he was clearly smitten by Silvie's generous praise. Or perhaps more by her. He paced unsteadily and stroked his chin, acting the part of importance.

"Well, I've never been called cute. A mighty fighter, an expert flyer, a defender of the land, the greatest Roush who ever did terrify Teeleh, but never cute. I'll take it as a compliment." He bowed.

But Johnis knew that Gabil would rather be cute, as Silvie put it, than anything. She'd won his loyalty for life.

The Roush cleared his throat. "Now the message Michal sent me to deliver is this: This water"—he pointed at the pond—"is the water you were looking for."

They stood dripping around him. "That's it?" Darsal said.

"That's not important?"

"We already know this is water."

"Well, it's not my fault that I waited two days here, baking in this blasted heat while you bickered away the hours in the desert. But you've made it. You're the first humans to ever lay eyes on this pool."

Gabil glanced at the horizon. "I really should be going. I wasn't technically supposed to . . . you know . . . swim with you. Just keeping an eye out. That's all I'm doing." He sauntered away from the pool.

"Now what?" Darsal asked.

Gabil looked back at her. "He didn't tell you?"

"Well, he said something about the six lost Books of—"

"Then you know. Did he also tell you that he would die?"

She glanced at Johnis.

"Then again, all humans die," Gabil said. "Sooner or later. Sooner if you make mistakes."

He stared at them, then suddenly jumped up, swung one spindly leg around in a roundhouse kick similar to the one executed by Darsal, and landed with a *Hayaa!*

A sly smile split his face. "You like that? That's how a real karate kick is done. And next time I'll show you even more."

He waited, expecting an encouraging response, so Silvie gave him one. "That's good, Gabil. We look forward to it."

"I knew it," he said. "I told Michal you would need my help!"

He leaped into the air and swooped over the sand. He'd gone a hundred yards before circling back and yelling down at them, "The rock, look at the rock!"

And then he was gone.

Johnis looked around. "Rock?"

"Rock," Silvie said, walking to a large, angular stone with a flat top jutting from the sand beside the pond. "This rock."

They stood over it together, staring at words that looked as if they'd been etched into the surface a hundred years ago.

Beyond the blue another world is opened.
Enter if you dare.
In the west, the Dark One seeks seven
To destroy the world.

A shiver passed through Johnis as he read the words. "'Beyond the blue'?"

"A path," Silvie said. "To the Dark One."

Darsal stepped around the rock, studying the words. "I don't like it."

"I don't think it really matters if you like it," Johnis said. "We're not here by accident."

Silvie was still contemplating the riddle. "'Beyond the blue?' The sky's blue."

"So is the water," Johnis said.

"It also says 'Enter if you dare,'" Darsal said. "That doesn't sound like an order to me. We have a choice."

Johnis walked to the edge of the water, knelt down, and stared into the mirrored surface. His face looked back at him, smooth and tanned again. He impulsively closed his eyes and lowered his head into the pool. With no disease to heal, the cool water felt like nothing more than a pool of water, so he pulled himself out.

"Anything?" Silvie asked.

"Nothing."

She knelt beside him, watching her reflection as the pool stilled again. "Did you open your eyes?"

"No."

She stuck her face into the water, was still for a moment, then suddenly jerked it out, gasping.

"What?"

"Eyes of Elyon, it's . . . There's something inside!"

Without waiting to hear any further explanation, Johnis and Darsal both plunged their heads underwater.

The deep pool below exploded with light. The light vanished as quickly as it had appeared, but now something else filled Johnis's vision: a black void, and at the center of that void a single Book of History, crackling with light, as if the light was trying to get out.

The book was now joined by another and another and four more until there were seven—one black, one brown, one blue, one green, one purple, one red, and one more Johnis couldn't make out because it was covered by the others. All seven became one book, and the red twine vanished, absorbed by the covers.

The shrouded black man-beast with long claws suddenly stepped in and sank his nails into the book. He tried to pry it open. Arcs of lightning shot from the pages, struck Johnis in the face, and shook him to his bones.

He jerked his head out of the water, gasping. Silvie and Darsal both had their heads in the pool, but they came up, too, hollering in pain.

For a few moments they just stared at one another. Then back at the water, stunned by the power.

"It's like another world," Silvie breathed.

"'In the west, the Dark One seeks Seven,'" Johnis said. "The seven Books of History."

Darsal stood and wiped at the water on her face. "I don't like it."

"We have to go west," Johnis cried. "We have to keep the seven books from the Dark One."

"And do we even know who the Dark One is?"

"Teeleh. It has to be."

"The Roush are one thing," Darsal said. "Maybe even Shataiki. But are you sure this mythical creature named Teeleh truly exists? Besides, the Roush saved us from death. Surely you're not suggesting we continue on west, further into this blasted desert that not even the Horde will inhabit."

"I am."

"We can't!"

Silvie walked to her horse, who'd filled its belly with water. She pulled out her canteen and returned to the pond.

"What are you doing?" Darsal demanded.

"Preparing for the journey," she said.

Darsal drilled Johnis with a hard stare. "That's right. We have plenty of water for the journey home, Scrapper. I suggest you fill your canteen as well."

"The journey west," Silvie said. She stood and plugged the leather bottle she'd filled with a cork. "I'm with Johnis. It's true, Darsal. Everything he's told us is true."

"And I'll tell you what else is true. Billos is gone, captured by the Horde. The disease has probably turned him into a Scab. We have to find him, and that means a rescue mission with veteran fighters. Now that we have water, we have to go back for help— for Billos's sake if for no other reason!"

"Even if we did go back," Johnis said, "we couldn't tell Thomas what we've learned."

"Why not?"

"Because the Roush ordered us not to."

"You're putting too much stock in a white bat who thinks he knows how to fight. I could never break my vow to the supreme commander by keeping all this hidden."

"For the love of Elyon," Johnis said, "you've just learned that the legends are all real and you still question this calling?"

Darsal looked to the desert, frowning. "I don't know what I'm questioning. None of this feels right. And they have Billos! He should be here, bathing in this water."

Johnis stared at her for a long time, trying to think of how to help her see the light. But perhaps there were secrets in her heart that were making her as stubborn as a log. And he didn't think Michal had intended for him to be her parent.

"Then we should split up," he finally said. "We go on, you head back. Is that what you want?"

Darsal marched to her horse, face red. "That's fine by me. But don't say I didn't warn you. I know what I saw in the pool."

"What did you see?" Silvie asked.

She turned back. "I saw death." Then she added as an afterthought, "Both of you are going straight down into hell."

# EIGHTEEN

Freshly watered and fed, the horses struck out with surprising willingness. But the desert heat quickly reminded Johnis and Silvie that their water would only last so long. They made note of the oasis's location between distant dunes and the sun. Looking at the white flats stretching west, Silvie suggested that maybe Darsal had been right in suggesting they were headed straight down to hell.

But both agreed that Darsal would eventually come to her senses and realize that going back alone presented just as many challenges as going on did. For one thing, the Horde was behind them—reaching the forests wouldn't be an easy thing. And she could just as easily get lost as be taken by the Horde. Silvie said she expected Darsal to gallop up behind them at any moment.

But that moment never came.

They headed due west, and except for the sun rising and falling over their heads, nothing changed. The desert remained flat and hot. The horses plodded forward, always forward.

Silvie and Johnis talked as their horses walked. It was all they could do. And for Johnis it was more than enough, learning what Silvie loved and hated about life—slowly uncovering the heart that hid beneath layers of skin.

She loved peanuts, which she scolded him for not bringing. The sago palm cakes he'd brought weren't fit for horses, much less humans, she claimed. Although when he gave her one he'd salted with black rock salt from the Southern Forest, she ate the whole thing without complaining.

She preferred wearing red flowers in her hair because her mother wore red. Elisa, her mother, had been nothing short of a miraculous woman, she said. And then she spent an hour explaining exactly why.

When it came to weapons, Silvie preferred a knife to a sword because she'd learned how to throw them from a good distance. With a sword you had to get in close, she said. She showed Johnis how to throw one of the four she carried and was impressed by his quick learning. A natural, she said. Unusual.

They talked about a hundred things, and all the while Johnis became more and more aware that they were slowly but surely abandoning themselves to this unexplored desert. An afternoon wind scattered their tracks, making it impossible to retrace them.

"Have you ever fallen in love?" Johnis asked as the afternoon turned red.

Silvie looked at him and winked. "Once. When I was fifteen. You?"

Talk of love was common and encouraged among the Forest Dwellers. Their religion, the Great Romance, had started when Tanis, the firstborn, had given his love to Teeleh, they said. Now the greatest reminder of Elyon's love was found between a man and a woman, though a father or mother's love for a child came a close second.

"Yes," Johnis said. "I loved a girl named Mirim last year. She was a very . . . nice girl."

"Was she? But you no longer love her?"

"My father says that I'm too young to really know love. Maybe he's right."

"Bah! Don't you believe it," she said. "If you're old enough to die in battle, you're old enough to understand the love you die for."

Johnis nodded. "The love of Elyon. But that's not the same."

"No? That's not what the elders teach. It may not have always been like this, but when we fight for our lives, we should also be allowed to love for our lives."

"So then, do you love this boy of yours?" he asked.

"I do."

Johnis felt his heart sink. She was in love with another boy? He realized then how much hope he'd unconsciously put in her.

"Well, that's nice."

"It is and it isn't," she said. Then she winked at him again, and Johnis cursed his heart for its impulsive leap. He didn't have the time or the mind or the heart to love a woman at this moment. He was committing himself to death, for the sake of Elyon.

"You're disappointed?" she asked with a smile.

"Why should I be? He must be a very happy boy."

"Hmmm."

"Hmmm?" he repeated. "What does that mean?"

"I was rather hoping you'd be disappointed. It's always nice to be loved."

Johnis didn't know what to make of that. Women could be quite crafty, he knew that much. His father said it often. Smarter than men, too, most of the time. You had to know your way around if you wanted to fall in love with a woman. *"Best to wait, lad. Just take your time. No rush."*

"It is nice, isn't it?" he said. Their eyes met, and he blushed a little.

The sun dipped over the horizon an hour later, and all notions of love vanished with it. Johnis pulled up. For a long while they stared at the growing darkness in silence.

"What if the desert never ends?" Silvie wondered aloud. She sounded as if she was doubting again.

"We should keep moving while the sun is down," he said. "The disease will begin again tomorrow."

"I agree," she said. "It's so"—she looked around and shivered—"quiet out here."

"We can talk," Johnis said.

Silvie started her horse forward again. "I would like that."

But they went for ten minutes without talking.

"Johnis?"

"Yes?"

"I'm scared."

"I know. I am too."

DARSAL SAT ON THE DUNE, FACING EAST, TRYING TO DECIDE if that really was dead east or just sort of east. Because if it wasn't dead east, she could easily miss the entire forest, and that would guarantee her death.

She knew the stars well enough, but she'd never had to navigate by them. A few inches one way or the other could mean many miles farther on. She knew the sun better, and she thought it might be smarter to wait until morning. The last thing she wanted to do was run into a Horde camp.

On the other hand, she still had an awful long way to go, and the disease wouldn't wait. The sooner she got to the forest, the greater the likelihood of her survival.

And the sooner she could apply herself to finding Billos. Thoughts of what might have happened to him sent shivers of fear down her spine.

Her horse gave off a terrified bray behind her, and she spun around to see that it was forty yards off, lying on the ground. And it wasn't just a matter of being tired.

There was blood on the sand by its belly.

Blood?

Darsal's heart slammed into her throat. The animal's skin quivered for several long seconds, then stilled. Someone had just killed her horse!

She stood frozen to the sand. Her sword was under the beast, pinned to the ground. Without a horse, without a sword, she was lost.

Something made a soft brushing sound behind her where she knew nothing but dunes lay. Slowly, terrified of what she might find, Darsal turned around.

There on the sand, in a wide half-circle starting to her right and extending all the way around to her left, stood a throng of black bats, staring at her with beady red eyes. Hundreds, maybe thousands.

Their wings hung to the sand—this was the brushing sound she'd heard. Their jaws were open, all of them, revealing dirty fangs and mucus. And then they stepped toward her, like a slow tide, eyes unmoving.

Darsal ripped her feet from the ground, whirled around, and tore into the night, screaming in mindless terror. She knew it was hopeless, but she didn't expect what came next.

One of them, maybe more, slammed into her back and sent her flying onto her face. They were on her before she could even scramble to her knees. Fangs sank into her forearms and calves.

Her hair and clothing were jerked up, and she was lifted from the desert floor, still facedown. Wind from their wings beat against her face. They were airborne.

Or she was dead and drifting to the skies—she didn't know which. A fuzzy snout nuzzled her neck and cheek, breathing hot, foul breath over her skin.

A long scream from her own throat cut through the sounds of a thousand beating wings.

It was the last thing she remembered.

# NINETEEN

Johnis and Silvie had gone for another six hours in the darkness until they were practically falling from their horses, and then they'd crashed on the sand, side by side.

Johnis dreamed of the fuzzy white bat swinging his leg in a karate kick and toppling backward in the sand. And of the blue waters in the pond, soothing his burning skin. And of Silvie kissing him. He wasn't sure why he was letting her kiss him, but he was. And he wasn't minding it.

"Johnissssss," she whispered in his ear. He liked the sound of that. "Johnisssss." Her hand shook him. "Johnis!"

His eyes snapped open. It was still dark, and Silvie was leaning over him. Her eyes were staring into the dark past his feet.

"Wake up!" she whispered.

Johnis sat up and followed her stare. A line of red swept the horizon from north to south, like a long string.

"What is it?" she asked. "What's making that red light?"

He pushed himself to his knees. "Shataiki."

Her fingers dug into his shoulder. "Shataiki?"

Johnis hadn't seen any since leaving the canyons. Well, they were back. They sat on the ground unmoving, unblinking, far away. Just staring in perfect silence.

"Shataiki," he said again.

"What are they doing?"

"I don't know."

"What are we doing?"

"I don't know."

"Stop sounding so casual about it!"

"I . . ." But he didn't know what to say. He was terrified, sure he was. But what could he say? They had arrived.

"Where are we?" Silvie asked.

That was the question, wasn't it? Why weren't the bats attacking, or at least making a fuss? They looked as though they were guarding something rather than massing for an assault.

Johnis slowly stood to his feet. "I have this feeling."

"This doesn't look good," she said in a thin voice. "What are we supposed to do? They know we're here!"

"Yes, they do."

Silvie looked at him. "Don't tell me you're thinking what I think you're thinking."

"I have this feeling that we've made it," he said. "This is it."

"You can't be serious, Johnis. There's way too many. There's no way we came here to be killed by Shataiki bats."

The horizon had started to gray. Dawn was coming.

"I don't think we'll have to kill any of them."

Johnis walked to his horse, took a drink of water, his eyes still fixed on the beasts, and then mounted. "Drink, Silvie. We're going to need it."

"What are you doing?"

"Thinking with my heart," he said. "Thomas insisted."

"Nonsense." But she already had her canteen out. "I don't like this, Johnis. Please don't tell me you're going up there."

"Do you want to wait here?"

"No! I'm not staying alone."

"Then mount up."

She did, but not without more objections, all of which he ignored. They turned the horses due west toward the line of Shataiki. The dull morning light now revealed something else. The ground beyond the line of black bats was dark. There was more to this than met their eyes at the moment.

"Ready?"

"No," she said.

But Johnis was already moving. Forward. Toward whatever destiny awaited him two hundred yards ahead.

Slowly the shapes of the Shataiki came into focus. Vampire bats half Johnis's height, wings draping, jaws open, drooling. Like hounds fixed on their prey, unconcerned. Squatting in a line on the sand.

But Johnis was now more concerned with what lay beyond the bats than the Shataiki themselves. If they wanted to kill him and Silvie, they could have done it while they slept. Something else was happening here.

"That's a valley," Silvie whispered. "It's black."

She was right. The desert floor fell away into some kind of valley beyond the Shataiki. The bats were actually perched on the lip of a huge black bowl, extending as far as Johnis could see.

"What do you think it is?"

Surprisingly, Johnis knew what it was. "It's where the Dark One lives."

"Then it's where we'll die," Silvie said. "I wasn't quite this serious when I said I'd follow you to hell."

Johnis stopped twenty paces from the line of bats. They still stared at him, making no threats. But the fact that they sat unblinking while flies crawled on their faces seemed to be its own kind of threat.

Gray dawn now showed them what lay in the valley behind. It was a forest. Black trees. A black forest.

The legends of old crashed through Johnis's mind. How Teeleh had led the Shataiki from the Black Forest into the unspoiled colored forest, turning it to ash as he passed. That was how the desert had been formed, how evil had ravaged the land and turned a once loving, peaceful people into the Horde.

This valley was the original Black Forest?

"If we go in there, we'll never get out," Silvie said.

"Do you have any other suggestions?"

She thought about it for a long time. "No. But we can't go into that valley. Are you sure the books are in there?"

"I sure hope so." Johnis nudged his horse. It snorted and tried to turn back, but he forced it forward.

Still the Shataiki did not move.

He slapped the horse's hide. "Move!"

A single Shataiki leaped to the air thirty yards down the line and swept into the valley on black, leathery wings. But none of the others moved.

"Please, let's go back and talk this through, Johnis," Silvie said. "It doesn't feel right to me. You're not the only one committing yourself to this madness. We have to go back!"

"We can't. We came for this."

"Curse your impulsiveness, Johnis!"

He faced her, holding his jittery horse firm. "You have to trust me, Silvie. I can't blame you for not wanting to, but I need you to trust me. I was *born* for this!"

"I wasn't."

"You do know that it was these Shataiki that killed your mother and father, don't you? They probably control the Horde. I promise you, if you follow me you'll have your chance to kill more Shataiki bats than you thought possible."

She looked at the beasts. "They don't look like they would be easy to kill."

"You're magic with the knives and quick with the sword. Trust me. Please."

"Look at their claws. This is just absurd—it's two against a thousand!"

"They won't fight us. Trust me."

Her jaw flexed, but she didn't object. "They aren't going to let us pass," she said.

Johnis reached behind, withdrew the Book of History from his saddlebag, and faced the Shataiki.

Their response was immediate. First shuffling and hissing as the book came out. Then they parted in front of him, dragging their wings behind, red eyes never leaving the book.

"They are now," Johnis said.

He looked past them and saw that a bridge made from a patchwork of wood planks and poles stretched between the lip of this depression all the way to the floor, at least a hundred yards down. It was as if a giant had put his massive boot into the earth here, shoving the ground down deep. Black trees had found a way to grow at the bottom.

But there was more than trees down there. Much more. The question was, what?

He nudged his horse. It refused to budge, so he kicked it hard. With a snort of protest, the black stallion took its first step toward the Black Forest.

# TWENTY

The narrow bridge creaked and groaned as Johnis and Silvie guided their horses down into the abyss. There was no railing, and the drop on either side fell a hundred yards down to bare slate rock. A fall would kill them.

Johnis glanced back at Silvie, who gripped her reins with white knuckles. Her face glistened with sweat despite the cool morning air.

"You okay?"

She shot him a frightened look, then glanced over his shoulder at the trees below. "Neither of us is okay," she said.

Behind her the Shataiki had turned around and were staring at them from the top of the cliff, content to let them descend into their world.

Johnis turned back and studied the Black Forest, searching for anything that might give him a clue as to what he was meant to do. Find the missing books, but how? For that matter, what made him think he was meant to enter this forest? Even if he did survive long enough to find the books, getting out looked to be impossible.

He gripped the book in one hand and moved his horse farther down.

It took them five minutes to reach the bottom, but those few minutes felt like an hour. Charcoal gray stone led from the bridge up to lumpy black ground from which the trees grew. Tall black angular trees without leaves. Black moss hung from the bare branches, and what looked like nests made from this moss were nestled in the crooks of the branches.

The nests undoubtedly belonged to the Shataiki watching them from the bowl's lip. A suffocating stench filled the air, so thick Johnis thought he could feel it. He shivered as they stepped off the bridge to the forest floor.

"Now what?" Silvie asked in barely more than a whisper.

"We go in," he said, nodding at the trail that cut into the forest ahead of them.

"You've lost your peanuts."

"I know. I'm following my heart, not my mind," he said. "Isn't that what Thomas told us to do?"

"I doubt he had suicide in mind. And why do you suppose there's a trail on the ground? These bat-beasts fly, right?" She paused. "Do you have *any* idea what you're doing, or are you just leading us into the jaws of death for the joy of it?"

"I don't know," he said.

"That's a problem, Johnis. This isn't a time not to know."

"All I know is that we were meant to go directly west, and this is directly west. And I know that I can't pretend I wasn't told to go directly west. I thought you agreed."

"I did agree to go directly west. But not to enter this pit of misery when we got there."

"Yet you're still following me," he said.

They walked their horses right to the forest's edge. Then under the first few moss-covered branches. Then deep into the shadows. The cliffs behind them disappeared. The Shataiki let them march ahead, content to watch from the cliff. There was evidently no need to guard trespassers who'd already committed themselves to the pit of death.

Johnis put his hand up to stop them, dropped from his mount, and handed Silvie his reins. "Wait here."

"Where are you going?"

"We're not the only ones who want this," he said, tucking the Book of History under his arm.

He hurried into the forest, counting trees. One, two, three, four, five, six, seven. He scanned the trees above him—no Shataiki that he could see—then he kicked at the ground, which was covered in ash and moss. He set the book in the hole he'd made and quickly covered it with moss. Satisfied that it looked pretty much untouched, he hurried back to where Silvie waited.

"Forty-nine trees in, seven trees south," he said, swinging back into his saddle. "You and I are the only ones who know."

Johnis wondered if he'd made a mistake telling her where he'd hidden the book. But if he couldn't trust Silvie, he could trust no one.

The first Shataiki didn't show up in the trees for another half hour; then they made themselves known with flapping and hissing high above. If Johnis wasn't mistaken, some whispering was mixed in with that hissing. These beasts could speak.

The farther in they went, the thicker the trees grew and the darker it became. They'd grown accustomed to the smell, but the thought of this putrid air working its way into their lungs made Johnis nauseated.

"How far are we going?" Silvie asked in a thin voice.

He looked at her and saw that she'd resigned herself to following him. Truth be told, *he* wasn't sure he could be trusted, but they were committed now. From the beginning of this whole mess, since battling over the Horde football, he'd trusted his instincts, moving when and where his gut told him to move. So he would continue doing the same.

But look where it had gotten him! Elyon help him. They could use Billos and Darsal now.

"'In the west, the Dark One seeks Seven to destroy the world,'" Johnis said, recalling the inscription on the stone. He looked up at a bat that swooped down and then shot back into the canopy, screeching. "We're here because the Dark One lives here."

"And he's seeking the six missing books," Silvie said. "So we go until we find this Dark One."

"Teeleh."

She set her jaw and stared ahead. "The worst he can do is kill us, right?"

"No, the worst he can do is get his claws on the seven books." He raised his voice. "That's why we're here, and that's why I hid the other book in the desert."

She blinked.

If the bats could whisper, they could listen, which was why he'd been careful not to say much. Thinking about it, he wished he *had* hidden the book in the desert, but it was too late for that now.

A long lonely scream drifted through air, and Johnis pulled up. The Shataiki scattered like a flock of parrots, squawking noisily.

"That sounded like . . ." But Silvie didn't finish.

"Like what?"

She moved ahead of him, ears tuned, and Johnis followed. Her sudden display of courage made him proud. She was, after all, the better fighter here, without contest. Silvie was his protector.

They'd gone another fifty paces when the scream came again, long and forlorn, like a thin horn blown for a funeral. The path forked in front of them, one trail veering left and one veering right, toward the sound of the cry.

"Which way?" Silvie asked.

"To the right," he said.

So she steered her horse right. The next time the scream came, it was so loud that Silvie gasped. The sound of a whip split the air. *Crack!*

Silvie twisted in her saddle, her face white with panic. "That's human!"

She suddenly kneed her horse and took off, galloping through the trees.

"Silvie!"

But she was gone, and Johnis slapped his horse into a full run after her.

The scream echoed through the forest again. And not just any scream, but one that sounded amplified and inhuman. Johnis's heart hammered with the pounding of his horse's hooves.

It was one thing to be leading, forcing himself to be confident. But following Silvie, Johnis was suddenly terrified. *We're galloping into hell,* he thought. *We've lost our minds!*

Their trip into the Black Forest stopped when the path abruptly ended at the edge of a huge hole that fell fifty feet, flattened at the bottom, then rose on the far side.

Johnis had seen this before. It was an amphitheater, nearly identical to the stadium they'd played Horde football in several days ago in the forest.

Black trees rimmed the stadium but had been cleared from the field at the bottom of the bowl. Bleachers cut from darkened slabs of rock stepped up from the field, a hundred rows at least. The field itself was made of lump ash.

At the center of the field was a pond. And next to the pond, a platform made of the black wood from these dark, angular trees.

And on the platform, a large circular wheel standing tall.

Two humans were strapped to the wheel, arms and legs spread like an X.

"Billos!" Silvie whispered.

"And Darsal," Johnis said.

Not another creature in sight.

For a few moments Johnis and Silvie were so shocked at finding their comrades alive, here in this vile forest, that they could only stare.

Darsal sagged in her ropes, limp or dead to the world. Billos's head hung to one side, but his legs twitched now and then as if they were being pricked by some unseen needle. They were stripped to the tunics they wore under their battle dress to keep the armor from chafing their skin.

Without any obvious cause, Billos suddenly arched his back, jerked his head up, and screamed with terrible pain. The sound echoed in the stadium, which amplified it and sent the scream skyward like a warning to all who could hear.

*Or like an invitation to the foolish,* Johnis thought.

*Come and die with us, you fools. Come and join us in our pain that you cannot see.*

# TWENTY-ONE

Silvie jerked her horse left and right, searching for a way down to the floor of the amphitheater. "He's alive!"

Johnis wanted to stop her, wanted to tell her that Billos and Darsal surely weren't alone down there. But now she was moving by impulse, just as he had for days.

There was no path leading down to the field, only these benches cut from the black rock. Silvie slapped her horse on the rump and took it over the edge, leaning back to keep her balance. The stallion was sure-footed and trained for battle—it might shy from the stench of the Black Forest, but it didn't hesitate now.

Johnis clenched his jaw and followed, bucking with the horse as it went.

Billos was whimpering as they raced across the stadium flat

toward the pond. The wheel on which their friends were strapped stood on the platform ahead.

Shadows moved on the ground as if a cloud were moving overhead. But it wasn't a cloud, Johnis saw.

It was Shataiki bats. Thousands and thousands, flowing into the bleachers from the sky on all sides. The sight was so strange, so frightening, that he almost overshot the pond. He slid to a stop next to Silvie, and they dropped to the ground together.

In three long bounds they reached the platform, which stood three feet from the ground, like a dock on the pond's edge. One more leap and they both landed on the wood floor, crouched.

Billos and Darsal hung like rags on the large solid wheel. Their chests rose and fell in ragged breathing. Alive, but beaten and bloody from a dozen cuts or bites. The Scab disease covered their flesh. If Johnis didn't know that only Billos and Darsal could possibly be here, strapped up to die, he might not have recognized them for all the cracking and graying of their skin.

Around them the Shataiki bats continued to fill the stadium, like a wall of black fur with red beads sewn on, hissing and clicking like a million insects.

Johnis felt his heart slamming against his ribs, but he couldn't hear it for the sound of the bats. Silvie gripped her sword tightly. Johnis had forgotten his in the scabbard.

"Billos!" Silvie whispered. She started forward.

"Wait," Johnis breathed. Then louder so she could hear. "Silvie, it's a trap."

No surprise on her face. She knew already. But she was too fixated on easing their pain.

A thin, flea-bitten rag of a bat flapped up from his hiding place behind the wheel and streaked to the sky. He had been hurting Billos's back with the needle in his claw.

Furious at this obscene torture, Silvie screamed after the Shataiki and drew back her blade to slash the ropes that bound Billos and Darsal to the wheel. With a grunt she swung and cut one thick cord.

Billos's left arm dropped free, and his shoulder slumped forward. But he was unconscious now and made no effort to right himself.

Silvie drew back for a second swing, and the stadium suddenly hushed, as if she herself had signaled immediate silence. She glanced at Johnis, shifted her eyes over his shoulder, and froze, eyes wide.

Johnis felt the Dark One's presence before he saw him. An oppressive, thick blanket that robbed him of breath was approaching from behind.

Johnis fought a bout of panic and turned slowly. A large vampire beast floated in on oily black wings, huge talons extending down twice the length of his torso, which was three times the size of the other Shataiki. His mouth was a cross between a bat's snout and a wolf's jaws. Bloodred eyes bulged below a jutting brow.

This was Teeleh.

Johnis felt his stomach tighten in protest, and for a moment he thought he might throw up. He clenched his fists and stepped back, but inside he felt like water.

The beast landed on the wood with a clacking of talons. He folded his leathery wings, extended his chin, opened his jaws wide so that Johnis could see the back of his throat, and swallowed a small rodent lodged in his teeth.

"Thank you for coming," he said, his voice low and raspy.

For a long time he just stared at them, but it was hard to see where he was looking because his red eyes had no pupils.

"I can see that you're both ill," he said. "We could help you."

"They're ill," Johnis said, looking at Billos and Darsal.

"No, they're perfectly fine now. But you . . . You have a skin disease. The smell is sickening."

The beasts thought *humans* smelled? Their minds were a twisted mess.

"It's not I who see things wrong, my friend," Teeleh said. "It's you."

*If the beast can read my thoughts, we're dead,* Johnis thought.

Teeleh took three slow steps toward Darsal and drew a finger gently down her side, tearing the sleeve of her tunic with his razor-sharp claw.

"The human is so sickening, you know," he said, facing Johnis and Silvie. "But it won't last long. The Horde will end this madness." The Shataiki twisted his head. "The Horde. They've embraced the new world. They listen to reason."

"They wage war on the Forest Dwellers who love Elyon," Johnis said.

The creature's jaws snapped impossibly wide, and he roared with enough power to shake the platform. Hot, rancid breath blasted over Johnis, who found he couldn't move, much less jerk back, at the bat's sudden roar. Teeleh was reacting to the name Elyon?

As quickly as the roar began, it ended with a snapping of the bat's jaws. Saliva dripped over his lips and strung to the ground.

"Elyon," Johnis said.

The bat's furry, flea-bitten skin quivered. But this time he just stared.

"Do you have my book?" Teeleh asked in a grating voice.

"What book?"

"The book that makes everything right."

"The question is, do you have *my* books?" Johnis asked.

The throngs of Shataiki bats were glued to the scene. They hissed, bickered, screeched. Silvie glanced at him with questioning eyes.

Teeleh whipped his head toward his legions and snarled. Like a crackling rifle shot, the sound from his mouth echoed around the stadium, silencing them immediately.

Teeleh gathered himself. "Do you doubt my intent to have the books?"

Johnis felt his knees quake, and he tried to still them. "No."

"Do you think you can stop me?" Teeleh asked.

He answered honestly. "No."

"But you're sick with delusions about your destiny, so you can't tell me where the book is. Let me put your mind at ease. Look at your hand."

Johnis lifted his arm and saw that the flaking of his skin had already begun. So soon? It must be the Black Forest.

Teeleh's voice was low. "Humans all have the same destiny: to become Horde and to serve me. It can come easily, or it can come with great suffering. The choice is yours. In the end you will never stop me."

"Why do you need the Books of History?" Silvie asked, her voice thin.

At first Johnis wasn't sure Teeleh would answer. "To heal me," the beast said.

"You're sick?"

"I'm . . . incomplete. But I can be beautiful again." He swept his sinewy arm wide. "This can all be beautiful—if I have the books."

"I'm sorry," Johnis said. "You'll have to find another way. Maybe the Horde can help you."

Again the throng hissed their shock at his courage.

Teeleh kept his eyes fixed on Johnis and curled a single claw as a sign. Two mangy bats *whooshed* to where the horses sat, dumped the saddlebag contents unceremoniously on the ground, and began to search for the Book of History.

Eight more Shataiki flew in from behind the platform, settled to the floor around the wheel that held Billos and Darsal, and began to push the contraption forward as if it were an upended table being scooted on edge, rather than rolling it on its side.

Johnis watched in amazement as the wheel slid along the platform and out over the water on a railing system connected to a frame behind it. There was a hole in the back. The Shataiki had been stabbing Billos and Darsal with needles through that hole.

The bats spun the wheel back so that Billos and Darsal faced them again, then slapped them both until they stirred to consciousness.

They looked around with gray eyes. Darsal was the first to recognize them.

"Silvie?"

"Where?" Billos asked. "You see Silvie?"

Darsal's face wrinkled in anguish. "Oh, Silvie. I'm sorry. I'm so sorry. I shouldn't have left you."

"Is that you, Scrapper?" Billos asked, staring at Johnis. "You've come to die with us, is that it?"

"It's okay, Billos," Johnis said. "Everything will be okay."

The Shataiki cranked the wheel, turning it so that Billos and Darsal were both held parallel to the lake below them. What were they doing? They cranked again until Billos and Darsal were upside down, heads pointed at the water.

It all clicked for Johnis then. "This is a mockery of Elyon's water," he said. "He's going to drown them!"

As if on cue, one of the bats turned a large wooden handle, and the entire wheel began to descend toward the water. Their heads would go under first, Johnis realized. They would drown!

"You can't do this!" Silvie cried.

Teeleh didn't flinch.

The bottom of the wheel broke the surface and continued its descent.

"You can't kill them!" Silvie screamed, springing toward Teeleh with her sword lifted.

Moving faster than Johnis thought possible, the large vampire bat reached out with one wing and swatted Silvie to the ground as if she were nothing more than a fly. Her sword clattered on the wood planks.

Johnis stared at Billos terrified that he might actually be drowned here on account of him!

Darsal's hair slipped into the water. Then her forehead. Then Billos's hair. They didn't realize until that moment what was happening, but when they did, they both began to struggle. Their wails of desperation cut Johnis as if they were blades.

Then they were under and drowning.

Johnis threw out his arm to stop them. "Stop it!"

"Let them drown," Teeleh snarled.

"No!" Johnis scrambled for reason. "I'll give you my book! Pull them up!"

"Where is the book?" Teeleh asked, unconcerned.

"I'll tell you. Just pull them up, for the sake of Elyon!"

Teeleh might have roared with rage at the use of the name, but he seemed beyond that at the moment. He stared at Johnis, snout quivering.

"If you kill them you might as well kill me too," Johnis said, biting off each word with conviction.

Teeleh studied him as if trying to determine his true intention. If Johnis was willing to die rather than tell Teeleh the book's location, Teeleh would be lost. And Johnis was now certain he would do just that—if the beast killed Billos and Darsal, he would refuse to give up the location, no matter what else happened.

Teeleh steadied himself and nodded. The Shataiki immediately cranked the wheel, pulling Billos and Darsal from the water. The two recruits sputtered and gasped for breath.

"Well?" Teeleh said.

Johnis shook his head. "No, turn them right side up."

The black bats looked at Teeleh, saw some signal that Johnis missed, and turned the wheel right side up. Water drained from Billos and Darsal's tattered tunics and splashed into the water at their feet.

"Now let them go," Johnis said.

"Am I a fool?" Teeleh growled.

"I don't know, are you? Let these three go, and you'll have me."

"I already have you."

"And you'll get nothing from me," he cried. "It was me who got them in this mess. I'll get them out by giving you the book, but they get out first. All the way out, into the desert."

The stadium echoed with his last words, then fell quiet.

"Are you going to die with us, Scrapper?" Billos asked. He'd lost his mind to the disease, Johnis realized.

Darsal wasn't so far gone. She looked at Silvie and started to cry. "I'm sorry, Silvie. I'm so sorry."

Silvie hurried to Johnis's side, eyes flashing with fear. "You can't do this," she breathed. "Once you tell him, he'll kill you. What do you think you're doing?"

"Thinking with my heart," he said. "Is it better for all of us to die?"

Her eyes brimmed with tears. Blue eyes, just starting to gray. He leaned forward and kissed her lightly on the cheek. "Take the book with you," he whispered in her ear. "And when you reach the top of the cliff, blow your horn."

All Forest Guard carried thin horns made from the gourd reed, which, when blown, carried for miles on the still air. Silvie's was still under her belt.

Then he pulled back and faced Teeleh. "Do we have a deal?"

"Even if we do," the beast said, "how do I know you'll keep your end?"

"You don't have a choice. If you don't let them go, you'll never see the book. Kill us all, and the location of the book will die with us."

Teeleh thought about the proposal for a few seconds, then faced the eight Shataiki who stood around Billos and Darsal. "Let them go," he growled. "Today we will kill only one, not four."

# TWENTY-TWO

J ohnis watched as Silvie pushed Billos into her horse's saddle, then Darsal onto Johnis's horse. Silvie looked back at him, apprehension cut into her face. "Don't let him kill you, Johnis. Promise me."

What could he say to that?

"Please, just say it."

"I promise," he said. Then to Teeleh, "Give them their swords."

Another hesitation. Another nod. Two bats tossed the blades to Silvie and Billos, who dropped his. The bat hissed and shoved the sword at Darsal, who handled it well enough.

The Shataiki parted to form a path through the stadium seats, and Silvie led the way, straight up the same trail they'd arrived on.

At the top she whirled and her horse reared back, nearly dumping Billos off his back.

"Promise me, Johnis!" she cried.

"I promise!" His voice echoed through the stadium with determination. But in reality, he had no clue how to keep a promise that might also give Teeleh the book. His mind was on another promise: Teeleh had just promised to kill him, and Michal had said that when it was his time to die, he wouldn't care. But that sounded hollow in his ears. He did care, very much.

Then the two horses galloped from sight. All was quiet again except for the sounds of whispering from the thousands of Shataiki in the stands. A sea of red eyes watching, waiting. And on the platform, Johnis stood completely lost, ten feet from the huge vampire beast with draping black wings.

"Where is the book?" Teeleh finally asked.

"My deal was to tell you once they are safe in the desert. It'll take them at least half an hour."

"Why delay the inevitable?"

"When Silvie arrives safely at the desert, she'll blow her horn," Johnis said. "And if you think one of your bats can counterfeit the call, don't kid yourself. If I don't hear her horn within the hour, our deal is off."

Teeleh regarded him with his blank red eyes, standing perfectly still, like a lizard waiting for a fly to happen by. Looking at his mangy, flea-infested fur, Johnis wondered how old his carcass was. The legends had it that Teeleh had once been the most beautiful creature made by Elyon, and it had all gone to his head. Now look at him. His black skin looked like the rotting hide cut from a dead horse.

Skirmishes broke out among the bats as time slipped by. A huge battle over some disagreement in a far corner filled the stadium with such a ruckus that Johnis wondered whether the whole arena might erupt in fighting. Teeleh ignored it as if this sort of thing was to be expected among his subjects. Even welcomed.

Ten of the Shataiki ended up on the stadium floor in bloody heaps. The rest fixed their eyes back on Johnis and paid the dead bats no mind.

All the while Johnis tried to think of a way out alive. He couldn't give away the location of the book, he decided that much. As soon as Teeleh had the book in his claws, he wouldn't need Johnis. The book would keep him alive, for a while at least.

Until the disease took him.

There was always the possibility that Silvie would find a way to save him. Silvie and the book, these were his only hope of living.

Another question crossed his mind: why didn't the Roush just destroy this forest?

But the answer was found in the legends: the Roush were the subjects of men, not their masters. The Roush needed him as much as Teeleh needed him. Much more than he could imagine depended upon him, Johnis of the Middle Forest, doing the right thing at this moment.

A long, high-pitched tone floated over the stadium, and the

bats hushed. Silvie's horn. Then another long note. She'd blown the horn twice.

"They're out," Teeleh said. "Now tell me where the book is."

Johnis felt a sudden surge of desperation, which was followed immediately by sorrow. His hopes faded. Silvie hadn't doubled back to save him.

He would die alone with his secret.

"I can't tell you where the book is," he said.

"Don't try my patience!"

"You don't understand. I can't tell—"

Teeleh roared, a crackling thunderous bellow that shook the stadium and made Johnis cower. His fangs jutted down like knives from gaping, bared gums.

If Teeleh's intent had been to silence him, he'd succeeded. He'd stolen the breath of every living creature in the stadium.

The beast snapped his jaws shut with a bone-jarring crack. "Give it to me!"

"I can't."

Teeleh walked over, claws scraping on the wood planks. He leaned forward, breathing with long, noisy pulls of air. "You will," he said softly.

"I can't," Johnis said breathlessly.

The beast moved faster than Johnis could. His paw flashed up and struck him on the side of his head like a hammer. Johnis felt himself fall. Felt himself land in a heap on the wooden platform.

Then his world faded.

# TWENTY-THREE

Silvie lay on her back in the darkness, not sure exactly why she was here, or, for that matter, where *here* was. It was night—or was it?

Her skin stung. Her bones ached. The disease was overtaking her body quickly.

"Darsal?"

Someone grunted nearby, and she faced the sound. Whispering and hissing filled her ears. "Let's kill her now," the snakelike voice wheezed. "He'll never know."

"Billos!" Silvie cried.

"She's awake, you coward! Make up your mind!"

She hadn't heard the voice of the smaller Shataiki until now, but she couldn't possibly mistake the similarity to Teeleh's own voice.

Silvie remembered now. She remembered all of it, from the moment they left the stadium until . . .

Until now.

SILVIE HAD LED BILLOS AND DARSAL THROUGH THE BLACK Forest while the black bats crowded, staring and whispering their treachery on all sides. But for all their snickering and bickering, the Shataiki had let them pass.

The cliffs appeared ahead without warning, and she realized that she'd missed the section where Johnis had hidden the book. But there were more than a hundred of the beasts pressing in— she couldn't double back and show them the location now!

To be honest, she wasn't sure she wanted the book anyway. It had brought them here, to this blasted black hole. Johnis was back in the stadium, giving his life for them and for the book, but no matter how hard Silvie thought about it, she couldn't think of any way to help him.

The only way to get the book, as Johnis had said, was to come back for it later. How, she didn't know.

She stopped at the edge of the Black Forest and stared at the long bridge stretching out of the bowl. The Shataiki fanned out, flying in circles, watching, always watching with those beady eyes that refused to blink.

An image of Johnis standing brave and alone on the platform with Teeleh waiting nearby filled her mind. Was she really just going to leave him? Her throat tightened, and she swallowed hard to clear it. She could never leave him. He'd given them all a chance at living by offering himself—how could she desert him?

But what choice did she have? There was no way she could take on the bats by herself. Billos and Darsal were hardly in a state to fight.

Silvie bowed her head and nudged her horse forward, allowing tears to slip down her cheeks. Elyon have mercy on them all.

They clacked up the bridge, teetering dangerously. Then they reached the top and faced the desert sands. One thing for certain, as long as the book was hidden, Teeleh would not kill Johnis. She had to attempt some kind of rescue, not only because she liked him very much, but because he was special, she realized. This boy, who had gone off into the desert because two Roush had told him to, wasn't just any ordinary boy.

Silvie grabbed the horn from her belt, faced the Black Forest below, and raised the instrument to her mouth. But before she could blow it, one of the Shataiki shrieked on her right.

She spun around in time to see its furry black body flying in, fangs bared. She had her sword in her hand, and she instinctively swung up, severing the beast's head in one smooth motion.

"Hey," Billos said. "Why'd you do that?"

Then the Shataiki descended on them, spewing hot breath and shrieks of terror. Silvie dropped the horn to the ground and spun her sword in a wide circle, scattering some of them, slicing into the flesh of others.

Darsal swung her sword as well, keeping the bats at bay. Billos cried out in protest, but she wasn't sure who he protested, them or the bats.

There were too many—she saw that almost immediately. Billos was deadweight, Darsal was slow, and Silvie couldn't hold them back on her own. Even if all three were at their best, the bats would surely overrun them.

"Run!" Silvie cried to Darsal, rolling off the horse. She slapped the stallion on the rump with the broad side of her sword. "Take Billos. Save yourselves!"

They took off without hesitation, one on each horse, galloping out to the desert. It was the only way, Silvie knew. All three of them would end up dead if they tried to take on the Shataiki in this diseased state.

The bats let Billos and Darsal go. And then they smothered Silvie. One of them must have picked up the horn and blown it, because she heard the mournful tone over the bats' shrieks. The last thing Silvie remembered was a hot mouth stretched over her face.

Until now.

"Hey!" she cried, struggling against the ropes that bound her tight. A bag was pulled off her head, and Silvie saw that it was still day. For all she knew, only minutes had passed since they'd taken her at the cliff top.

Black, angular trees rose up all around. The Shataiki that had pulled the bag up had a deep gash in its right wing, and Silvie knew her own sword had put it there.

The bat spit on her, a vile glob of yellow goo, then jerked the bag back down.

"Make it go to sleep," a Shataiki said. "Make it still."

They put her to sleep with a club.

SILVIE DREAMED OF FLYING BATS AND WHITE DESERT AND A silly Roush trying to do backflips but landing on its head instead.

A claw pinching her cheek woke her. It took her a moment to see that she was in the stadium again, with a sea of red eyes staring at her.

How . . .

"Silvie?"

Johnis's faint voice whispered her name on the right, and she tried to turn to him, only to discover that her body was bound spread-eagle to the same wheel that Billos and Darsal had been strapped to.

Beside Silvie, Johnis was tied like a spider to the web.

He was graying with the disease and bruised from more than one cuff to his face, and his eyes drooped with exhaustion. Still, he was such a handsome boy, even now. Dark hair to his shoulders and a strong jaw. Sharp nose and full lips, younger in appearance than in age. But he had the muscles of a strapping sixteen-year-old, defined by forest living.

"Johnis?" she croaked.

"Did you get it?" he asked in a barely audible whisper.

*The book.*

Terrible sorrow swept through her chest. "No. I'm sorry . . . They were watching."

"Billos? I heard the horn . . ."

"The bats must have blown it. Billos is free," she said. Then she started to cry because she knew what a horrible failure she was. And still this boy beside her didn't think about himself, but Billos. Billos, who'd mocked him at every turn!

Like a million insects, the Shataiki began to flitter and click their nasty tongues. Teeleh stepped into Silvie's view from behind the wheel, red eyes unchanged.

Without explaining himself, he clumped slowly over to Silvie, wings dragging behind like a tattered black wedding dress. He brought his snout close to her face and licked her cheek with his long pink tongue. The sick smell of decayed meat from his mouth made her tremble.

"Human," he breathed. "Do you love this human?"

"Get back," Johnis cried, but the sound came out in a hoarse rasp.

Teeleh ignored him and spoke to Silvie. "The kind of pain you are about to feel cannot be described," he said. "It's a pain reserved for the Horde when they die. But if you let your mind go, I think you could grow to like it."

Silvie's bones began to shake. She sagged in her ropes and begged Elyon to allow her to die.

Sobbing sounded on her right. Beside her, Johnis was crying.

His head lolled to one side, and his face was twisted in anguish, tears streaming down his cheeks. Their rock, this boy who didn't seem to know fear, was breaking.

"I'm sorry, Silvie," he whispered. Then louder, moaning with a breaking heart: "Forgive me! I'm so sorry! Please, please don't hurt her!"

Teeleh struck him in the face without looking his way.

Then his claw was on Silvie's cheek, tracing her jaw. "It's a new kind of pain," he said. "One that starts in the soul and works its way to the bones, setting them on fire. It can be done in the spine, but I prefer to do it through the neck." He drew his fingernail down past her ear.

"Stop it," Johnis whispered. "Stop it."

"Only you can stop it, boy," Teeleh said. His fingernail pressed into Silvie's skin, and she felt fire burn down her spine.

Silvie screamed.

And so did Johnis. Only his scream came with words.

"I'll tell you!" he cried. "I'll tell you. Along the path, forty-nine trees from the edge, seven trees to the left! At the base of a tree!"

Teeleh froze. Silvie's world was swimming already, but she clung to consciousness, realizing that something terrible had just happened.

The beast stepped back. Nodded. A hundred bats took flight in search of the book. And they would find it, Silvie knew.

Beside her Johnis hung his head and sobbed.

# TWENTY-FOUR

Johnis couldn't seem to stop the waves of regret and sorrow that kept washing over him. He'd failed on every level, and he'd done it in such short order. Just a few days ago he was watching the Horde football game with his father, feeling sorry for himself but safe. A nobody who made no trouble.

In four short days he'd managed to lead the three most promising new leaders of the Forest Guard into the desert where they would now die. Worse, he'd played into the hands of this beast and given him a book that contained only Elyon knew what kind of power to destroy the world.

And even worse, he'd let Silvie down. He didn't understand why, but this seemed like the greatest of his sins. Maybe because it was so personal.

"It's okay, Johnis," Silvie whispered. She'd been trying to comfort him, and even that didn't seem right to him. He should be comforting her, not the other way around.

Teeleh stood on the platform's edge, facing away from them, perhaps waiting to possess the book before killing them.

"Johnis, do you know when I told you I loved the other boy?" Silvie said.

He looked at her. What did that have to do with any of this?

"I do love him, but not more than any other boy," she said.

She paused, and he still wasn't understanding why she would discuss this while they faced their deaths.

"Do you understand what I'm trying to say?" she asked.

He studied her eyes, brimming with tears, and fought another wave of guilt. To have done this to such a beautiful, kind girl was a horrible thing.

"I think you're the kind of boy I would love," she said. "If I had known you better. You're a very good person. I want you to know that."

But he didn't feel that way at all. Still, he didn't want to discourage her by arguing at a time like this. "It's okay, Silvie. I think I love you too."

She blinked. Had he really said that? It was not what he'd meant to say, not so openly. But what difference did it make now?

Shrieking from the west signaled the Shataiki's return. They flew in a haphazard formation, two dozen of them, sweeping over the trees and into the stadium.

A particularly mangy-looking bat carried the Book of History against his chest. He settled on the platform, shot Johnis a red stare, then snaked over to Teeleh, bowed, and handed him the book.

Johnis couldn't read Teeleh's expression because his eyes were fixed and his jaw shut, but the beast's claws were trembling as he reached out for the book. He held it between his talons and traced the title, *Stories of History*, with his nail.

Not one snicker, not one cough, not one hiss or one breath could be heard from the throngs of Shataiki. Whatever was in that book was even more valuable than Johnis imagined possible.

For a long time Teeleh stared at his new treasure. Then he flung out one winged arm, eyes unmoving from the book. A tall, skinny Shataiki with drooping cheeks stepped out from behind the wheel.

Johnis hadn't noticed him flying in from the sky. Then where had he been hiding? He was taller than the others, halfway between Teeleh and the other bats, and somehow more wicked looking, if that was possible. Blue blobs of flesh hung like sacks under his eyes, and his skin was nearly bare of fur. He looked like a plucked rodent.

But it was the Book of History in his claws that sent a shiver through Johnis's bones. A second book, which he carefully handed to Teeleh. Only a single length of red twine bound this one, unlike the two bands of twine that bound the book the Roush had given Johnis.

Teeleh took the book. He now held one book in each hand,

like two counterweights. His sinewy arms quivered, and he held each delicately, as if they were eggs.

He suddenly faced the throng, lifted both books high over his head, tilted his head back, and roared at the sky. The gathering broke into earsplitting shrieks, a hundred thousand strong.

Johnis thought his eardrums might burst. He looked at Silvie, whose eyes were wide with fear.

Teeleh lowered the books and let the cries of approval wash over him. He walked to the far edge of the platform, holding the books like a mother clinging to a precious newborn child. Then he tucked them under one wing and twisted back.

"I want them to become Horde first," he snarled. "When they've both become Scabs, kill them."

Then he leaped off the platform and shot for the sky on wide leathery wings.

# TWENTY-FIVE

Gabil flew fast and furiously just ten feet above the western desert sand. He'd known it could all go bad, but he'd never really expected it. Not so soon, anyway. Not so terribly bad.

He'd watched from the clouds with seven other Roush and reported to Michal as soon as Johnis had offered his life for the others. But the elder Roush knew already and was preparing for the worst.

The Roush lived in the green forests, building their nests high in the canopy, where they could raise their young without fear of any human or horse stepping on them accidentally. They were blind, these humans. They couldn't see a Roush if they were punched in the nose by one. They would assume they'd hit themselves before believing a Roush from the legends, as they called history, actually existed and had just bopped them on the nose.

Lovely things, these daughters and sons of Elyon, but so pigheaded at times. Thought they knew everything. Even after changing their minds five times on the same matter, they didn't pause to consider the fact that they might be wrong this sixth time as well. Heaven forbid! They would fight for the sixth opinion with as much conviction as the first!

"It's red, I say. *Red!*" one would cry.

"No, it's blue," another would respond.

"Red, you fool. Red, red, red."

"Blue for certain. Look at it from this angle and you see it's blue. Or maybe a bit green, if you think about it."

"Say what? Not green. Only an idiot would see green. More like purple, if you must. But not blue and not green."

"I say green. Definitely green. If you can't see green, you're not fit to hold a rank in the Guard."

"Purple! For the sake of Elyon, open your eyes! Any half-wit can see it's purple."

Only the arguments weren't usually about colors but something more interesting, such as whether this tunic or that face marking would be appropriate to wear.

Gabil saw Billos and Darsal ahead now, slumped on the two horses, hopelessly lost. Both had grayed and lost their minds to the disease, a condition that would quickly change from the stupidity they currently displayed to plain deceit. The Horde could be as sharp as Teeleh's claws once their minds grew accustomed to the disease's influence, but their deception would only strengthen. He clucked with shame for them and sped up with wide sweeps of his wings.

He dove for Darsal's horse, slapping it hard on the rump with his right wing as he screamed past. The horse jumped to the right, plowing into the other horse.

"Watch it!" Billos snapped. "What are you doing?"

"It's . . . it's this blasted horse."

Gabil had to get them headed to the north, and fast. The fact that they could no longer see him in their diseased state meant he would do it the old-fashioned way, which had often proved to be disastrous in his rather extensive scope of experience. Other Roush seemed to boast of more success, but Gabil often succeeded in doing nothing more than upsetting all involved.

If they still had canteens strapped to the horses, he would have dumped the water on them to bring them out of their stupor. But the bottles had evidently been stripped off by the Shataiki.

He grabbed the reins of Billos's horse and tugged to the right. "This way, you black stallion beast!" Gabil flapped his wings hard, blowing up dust, tugging the stubborn horse.

"Hey!" Billos mumbled at no one in particular. "What are you doing? Where'd that wind come from?" His horse veered to its right, north, and Darsal's followed.

"Where're you going?" she asked dumbly.

"Where're *you* going?" he returned. "Isn't this the way?"

"Yeah, well, where are we going?"

"You don't know?"

"I thought you did."

Gabil used his claws on both of the horses' rumps this time, swiping both feet together like a double karate kick. *"Hayaa!"*

The horses bolted forward at a full gallop, with Billos and Darsal flailing and yelling. How they managed to stay on, Gabil didn't know, but he figured it served them right for not believing Johnis sooner.

He took off after the spooked horses and kept them moving with an occasional swat to the rump. "Move it, you dumb beasts! Fly, fly like the wind. *Hayaa!"*

Billos and Darsal shouted all kinds of orders at their mounts, but all were ignored. Gabil, master of the sky and now the desert, was in control.

*"Hayaa!"*

He kept the horses running for a full fifteen minutes before thinking that perhaps he was overdoing it. They were sweating and wheezing. What if they fell over dead from this terrified sprint of theirs? Michal had said "as quickly as possible," but Gabil wasn't completely sure how far he could push these snorting beasts.

Then an image of Johnis flashed through his mind, and he slapped the horses again. Johnis might not be able to be saved, but there was a slim chance that one or both of the books could be recovered.

They pounded over a hill, and the oasis suddenly dawned into view, a hundred yards ahead. Two fresh horses grazed by the water, ready to ride.

"Don't let them run for the water!" Billos cried. "They might drown us! Stay clear of the water!"

They were that far gone? Horde feared water. Despised it. Billos was deceived to the core.

"No, the water could be good!" Darsal said. "I think we need it."

"No! Stay clear. Only fools think water won't drown them."

"No, Billos, I need water!" She veered for the pond and, without Gabil prodding her horse from behind, managed to wrestle control back.

Billos's horse followed despite his curses. "This way, you stupid beast!" He tugged on the reins to no avail.

The horses headed straight to the water, reared to a stop, thrust their muzzles into the clear blue liquid, and began to drink. Darsal stared at the water in wonder, somewhat unsure but perhaps remembering.

Billos, on the other hand, drew his legs up and scooted to the rear of his horse, cowering. "Have you lost your mind?"

"It's blue," she said.

"It's brown! Any fool can see that."

"Blue," she said, staring.

"Brown, brown, brown, you imbecile! And what's more, it will kill you!"

Gabil flew toward the recruit, rolled into a ball at the last moment to avoid hurting him, and slammed into his back with enough force to launch the terrified Billos off his horse and into the pond with a great splash.

His cries were swallowed by the water. Darsal dropped to the sand and peered in. "Billos?"

But there was no Billos.

"Billos, are you drowning?" she cried.

Only rising bubbles answered.

Now she became truly worried. "Billos!"

He came out of the water like a rocket, gasping and grinning at once. His skin was again pink. Gabil thrust a wing at the sky and cried with delight. "Yes!"

"What are you waiting for?" Billos demanded.

Darsal smiled dumbly and fell forward like a log. The pond accepted her, then swallowed her dusty, graying body. Then she was under with Billos, who dunked himself for a second bath. Gabil paced on wobbling legs, eager to jump in himself. But he had a mission to finish. Mustn't forget the mission.

When they rose from the water moments later, Darsal threw her arms around Billos and squeezed him tight. "I could kill you!"

"For what?" he demanded, but he was laughing.

"For leaving me! Don't you ever do that again. Swear it!"

Gabil could hold himself no longer. "Hey, you two."

They whirled around, eyes like full moons. "Where did you come from?" Darsal asked.

"I've been around since the legends," he said. "Question is, where did you come from?"

Billos looked as though he'd seen a ghost. Gabil was the first Roush he'd seen. "What . . . what's that?"

"A Roush," Darsal said.

They looked at him, dripping wet, minds spinning.

"Do the words 'Black Forest' conjure up any images?" Gabil asked. "How about nasty black vampire bats with rotting breath and slimy noses? Run into any of those lately, by chance?"

"Johnis," Darsal said.

"Now you're getting the picture," Gabil said. He waddled back and forth in front of them. "It seems the sight we granted you is easily compromised. Thanks to the cleansing pool, it's back. We don't have much time, so I need you to listen to me very carefully." He wagged his finger at them. "No nonsense this time. Just trust me and listen."

They slopped out of the water, and he jumped back to avoid being splashed. Not that he minded the water, but they were still smeared with stubborn dirt and could use a proper bath.

"Now, Darsal, do you remember me showing you a karate move or two?" he said. "You'll need that when you go back in."

"Back in where?" Billos asked.

"The Black Forest, of course. The one thing these black beasts do is come at you with their teeth and claws first. So I suggest you perfect the dodge-duck-kick routine that I am best known for. I'll show—"

"We're not headed back in!" Billos cried. "We should take these catalina cacti and head back." He pointed to a group of seven large cacti on the other side of the pond. "The Horde is marching by now! Or soon. And they are coming from this side, not the other. We have to tell Thomas!"

"This book is more important than Thomas," Gabil said.

"What? How can you say that? And going back to the Black Forest would be—"

"Don't be a coward, boy. You're going back."

"Two of us against all those . . . those black beasts! It's suicide."

"Well, no one said it would be easy," Gabil snapped, feeling just a bit put off by the boy.

"Easy? We would be marching to our deaths!"

Gabil decided he'd had enough of this. They were out of time, and he hadn't yet demonstrated this move of his. "Now you listen to me, human. You were dead already. Your life isn't yours to decide any longer. You were saved by Johnis, for Elyon's love! Are you so thickheaded?"

Billos stood shivering as the water cooled on his skin.

Gabil pushed while he had the boy on his heels. "And let me tell you something else. If you hadn't been so stubborn in the beginning, none of you would be in this mess right now. Both of you should be ashamed."

"He's right!" Darsal cried, running for her horse. "We have to save Johnis and Silvie!"

Billos stood flat-footed, unsure.

Gabil hurried toward Darsal, nearly tripping over his own feet. "Wait, I haven't shown you what you'll need." He slid to a stop and threw out his wings for balance. "Watch." He ducked an imaginary punch, rolled right, and simultaneously threw his leg out in a kick.

But at the last moment he lost his balance and crashed on his rear end.

"Keep your tricks, white bat," she said. "Just tell me where the Black Forest is."

He jumped up, stunned by her audacity. "Keep my . . . ? You have almost no chance of surviving, and you still stick your nose in the air like you're the master of it? My karate could save your skinny neck, thank you very much!"

"I've seen your karate. It's cute. But—"

"I don't fight on the ground, you fool." He jumped into the air and executed the same move, ducking and rolling and kicking with perfect precision this time. *"Hayaa!"* he yelled, and dropped onto the ground, crouched for another attack.

Darsal's jaw gaped. "Wow."

"Yes, wow. They don't call me the king of the skies for nothing. Now I suggest you learn that move. As I was saying, the Shataiki attack the same way every time: fangs and claws first. Dodge those and you'll have an easy angle for their soft underbellies."

"I still don't see how we can fight off a hundred, much less ten thousand," Billos said, walking up.

"You can't," Gabil said.

"We can't? Then what's the point?"

"The point is, Johnis saved us," Darsal said. "Mount up, Billos."

"You can't defeat them," Gabil said. "But I have something

that will give you a fighting chance." He pulled out the bag he'd strung under his wing, held it out with great fanfare, and dropped it on the sand.

"What's that?"

"That," Gabil said, "is the one thing those bats fear the most."

# TWENTY-SIX

Qurong, leader of the Horde, sat on his stallion and gazed eastward. It would take them nearly a day to move the large army to the canyons along the forest's edge. It would be another half day through the canyons and into the forest, provided the Guard hadn't been alerted. The cliffs gave their enemy a natural barrier that made his task difficult.

But the last report had sounded an all-clear. Thomas's Guard was still camped on the east, where a smaller Horde force made daily raids to keep them busy.

Still no sign of the missing recruits. Dead, the word was. Killed by the desert. Even the priest had proclaimed it, though with some coercion from Qurong. He would kill that snake of a priest yet. All his talk of Teeleh and these blasted missing books was enough to drive him mad, especially in the wake of losing the boy from his own custody.

He looked back at the horses, more than a hundred thousand of them, all mounted and awaiting his command. And behind, three hundred thousand foot soldiers, armed to the necks with sickles and hammers and spears, as well as a sword for each.

"We're ready?" he asked the traitor, who sat astride a horse beside him.

The man looked eastward for a long time, making Qurong wonder if he'd ever consider going back to the forests. He was fully Horde, but then again, so were their spies, who bathed and became Forest Dwellers for the cause. Even so, what could this man tell Thomas that he didn't already know? The Forest Guard already knew all too well how to kill Horde.

"As ready as we will ever be," the traitor finally said.

Qurong lifted his hand, then lowered it slowly. The massive army began to move, a sea of gray flesh, horse meat, and enough metal to sever the head of every living creature in the forests.

"So it begins," Qurong said.

"So it begins," the traitor breathed.

"LET ME GIVE YOU MY NAME," THE TALLER SHATAIKI SAID, plodding slowly across the platform in front of Johnis, arms clasped behind his back. "My name is Alucard. Let me tell you what it means. Demon. Do you know what a demon is?"

Johnis hardly heard him. His mind was fogged by
though he desperately tried to hold on to reason. He
think about the book that Teeleh had taken such delight in. He
didn't know why the beast had trembled with joy when he'd taken
possession of the second book, but it couldn't mean anything
good for humans.

Several delirious hours had passed, and the sun blazed bright
and hot overhead. Except for a few Shataiki that flapped about the
bleachers, the amphitheater had emptied when Teeleh had soared
skyward. Four of the Shataiki stood guard on the stage with this
demon wretch, waiting for Johnis and Silvie to finish their transformation into Scabs.

Beside him, Silvie was crying again. But in his own foggy thinking he was having difficulty determining *why* he should comfort
her, much less *how* he could comfort her. He began to think that
she sounded a bit like a bat.

"You don't even know why the books are so powerful, do you?"
something said. Oh yes—Alucard, the Shataiki bat, was speaking
again. "I could torture you with needles, but the full knowledge
of your failure will cause more pain."

"What's that smell?" Johnis heard himself mumble.

The bat stopped pacing. "I would think that's your flesh rotting," he said.

*But it is more,* Johnis thought. *Something smells vaguely familiar.*

"The books have the full creative power of will," the Shataiki
said. "They can influence the power of human decisions. They

can make the word become flesh. They can make a moon red with blood or a soul black with lies."

"'Destroy the world,'" Johnis whispered, remembering the inscription on the rock. *In the west, the Dark One seeks Seven to destroy the world.*

"Yes. Something like that. The seven original books are the keys to heaven and hell. Teeleh is the rightful prince of both. He holds two in his library below." The Shataiki gave a hissing cackle. "So close, yet so very far."

"Smoke," Johnis breathed, barely aware of his own voice.

"The smoke of hell is what you'll soon be . . ."

The bat stopped midsentence. As a matter of fact, Johnis *did* smell smoke. The old bat was smoldering like a trampled fire, perhaps. Dust to dust, fire to fire, ash to ash.

A chorus of high-pitched shrieks carried across the hot wind from the east. Probably just more Shataiki squawking over a piece of rotten fruit or a rat they'd found.

Alucard whirled around and faced eastward.

Johnis lifted his eyes to clouds that boiled on the horizon. *Odd,* he thought. *Those clouds weren't there a few minutes ago. Is rain coming? It never rains in the desert, but what about here?*

He didn't want it to rain. Rain would mean water, and water was a dreadful thing. Wasn't it? Water would kill you if you let it. Drown you. Which was why he'd rather walk through the fires of hell than drown in a lake.

"Fire!" one of the guarding bats cried. "It's fire!"

Alucard seemed to have frozen into a tree. But his trance didn't last long. His wings snapped wide like a black kite, and he leaped off the platform with surprising strength. "Fire!" he screeched.

Fire?

"ENOUGH!" DARSAL YELLED ABOVE THE HUGE CRACKLING flames that licked at the black trees. "We're out of time!"

Billos was standing in his stirrups, swinging his sword in wide circles with both hands as if it were a club. No fewer than ten Shataiki came at him from all sides, screaming in death-defying dives.

His blade connected with the lead bat, cutting its cry off at the neck. He dodged another, knocking it wide with his forearm, then drove down on the beast's back.

His horse trampled the bat and reared. Billos was now in his element, showing why he'd been selected by Thomas as one of the four greatest fighters to join the Forest Guard.

Darsal threw her flaming torch into a pile of dried moss and snatched her sword up just in time to defend against the jaws of another bat who, seeing her let loose of her fire, dove in expecting an easy prey. Not so. Darsal was nearly as efficient with her blade as Billos was. She ducked in the way Gabil had suggested and thrust the blade up through the bat's jaw, pinning its mouth shut. Then she flung it behind her and screamed at another bat soaring in.

This Shataiki thought better of it and broke off its attack just short of her blade's reach.

The black bats were terrified of fire—this alone had given Darsal and Billos the advantage. Gabil had sworn nothing less when he'd given them the resin and flint.

"Set the forest on fire!" he'd said. "As long as you're near fire, the bats will hesitate. Burn the whole forest and ride the edge of the flames all the way to Teeleh's lair."

"How do we get out?"

"That's Michal's part," the Roush had said. "Go. Hurry! And don't forget about the karate!"

They'd lit the torches before reaching the cliff's edge, then approached at a full gallop, with such speed that the few Shataiki on the bowl's lip had been thrown into confusion. By the time the bats realized what was happening, Darsal and Billos had their horses running down the unsteady bridge and were warding off the bats with fire.

At the edge of the black trees, they had taken off in opposite directions, as planned. Billos went north, Darsal south, thrusting fire into the foliage as they galloped.

As Gabil had promised, the undergrowth and the black trees rising from it went up like a tinderbox. It was almost as if they were soaked in resin, begging to be burned.

Fires of hell.

They'd gone a mile in each direction, then doubled back and met at the path that led into the forest.

Already huge flames rose to the height of the tallest trees, blasting Darsal with heat. Only the bravest Shataiki endured the smoke now, again as Gabil had promised. The winds carried the fire toward them. Toward the center of the forest. Toward the stadium.

Toward Johnis and Silvie.

"Hurry!" Darsal cried.

Billos screamed at three fleeing bats. At the moment she could not think of a man she would rather have by her side than Billos. He was better with a sword than most of the seasoned fighters who defended the forests.

"Go, go!"

They went at a full gallop. The fire behind them was making its own wind now, crackling like thunderclaps as the black trees exploded with heat. What if it was too big? What if they couldn't outrun the flames?

Darsal glanced back and saw that the flames were leaping high above the trees, licking at the sky hungrily. Heat rode their backsides, pushing the horses faster. Even the bravest Shataiki had now fled the fire.

"We're going too slow!" Billos cried, echoing her concern.

They pounded through the Black Forest, twisting and turning with the trail. Here nothing was straight, not even a path that could have easily been laid down in an orderly fashion, right through the trees. But the Shataiki obviously didn't know the meaning of straight.

The flames roared to the rear, gaining, now only fifty yards back.

Darsal cursed the crooked path and drove harder, slapping her horse's rump with the broad side of her sword. "Faster!"

The stallion needed no encouragement, and she gave it up, holding tight to the reins in one hand and her sword in the other.

"Which way?" Billos screamed from behind as they approached the split in the trail.

Darsal veered right. "Hurry!"

The fire was gaining. Her hair might go up in flames at any moment.

Billos pulled up beside her, though there was hardly enough room for two horses abreast on this trail. She saw why—his horse's tail was singed! Billos was hunkered down, trying to keep the heat from burning his neck. She let him surge ahead.

The stadium suddenly opened up before them, a huge oblong hole in the ground. Now they had two options: they could slow and risk being burned from behind, or they could plunge into the bleachers and risk a bad fall.

Billos chose the latter, urging his horse even faster. He launched the stallion over the lip, trusting the mount to find its own footing. It sailed into the air, over the stepped risers, dropped ten feet, and crashed into the stone steps just ahead of Darsal's own horse, which launched itself into the air just behind.

This was why picking the horses was such an honor for the best fighters. Both steeds landed at a full run and descended into the stadium without slowing, sure-footedly placing their hooves in precisely the right spot.

The fire reached the edge of the stadium above them and shot out with searing orange heat. But without more fuel the flames collapsed back on themselves and swept to the right and left, ringing the stadium.

Billos and Darsal reached the field and raced across the flat ground toward the platform where Johnis and Silvie slumped in their ropes. They looked to be unconscious on the great wheel. Grayed with disease and lost to the world.

"The water, quickly," Darsal yelled, searching the perimeter for signs of Shataiki. There were none that she could see. For the moment.

They slid from their horses, pulled out the bags of blue water they had filled at the pond, and bounded onto the platform.

"Just dump it?" Billos asked.

Without answering, Darsal yanked out the cork, lifted the leather bag over Johnis's head, and began to splash the water over his face and shoulders. It ran down his chest like a river.

The transformation wasn't unlike watching cool water wash over parched, dusty skin, or rain falling upon a dried riverbed. Each flake of flesh touched was restored to fresh skin on contact.

Johnis jerked his head up and gasped, just as Billos dumped his water over Silvie. Darsal continued to pour, eager for every square inch of Johnis's body to be rid of the disease. More water, over his head now, flooding his eyes and nose with the healing water.

Johnis sputtered and coughed, and Darsal drained the last of it over him.

"My face," he said. "Wipe my face!"

He was practically drowning in the water, she realized. Beside them, Silvie began to sputter as well. Billos was showing no more restraint.

Darsal reached up and wiped the water from his face. Johnis blinked the last of the moisture away.

"Darsal?"

"Who did you expect? Teeleh?" She gave him a grin.

His eyes scanned the fire sweeping on each side. He locked his gaze back on her. "You came back . . ."

"Forgive me."

"You . . ." Johnis seemed too surprised to think clearly. "You came back."

"I was a fool to leave you. I'm so sorry."

"But you came back!" he cried.

"You can kiss her later," Silvie said sharply. "For the sake of Elyon, get us off of here!"

"You were right, Scrapper," Billos said. "I owe you an—"

"Cut us down!" Silvie cried.

"The fire won't keep them away for long," Darsal said, yanking out her knife. "We have to get out of here."

"Not until we have the books," Johnis said.

"That's ridiculous," Billos snapped. "We're in the middle of the Black Forest, if you hadn't noticed."

"We came for the books," Johnis said.

Billos wouldn't let go. "The Shataiki will be swarming—"

"Enough, Billos!" Johnis shouted. "I will not leave without the Books of History!"

That shut the boy down as if he'd been forced to swallow a cork.

"Books, as in more than one?" Darsal asked.

"Books. He has two. We can't leave without them."

"And do you have any clue where these books are?"

Johnis took a deep breath and swallowed. "Yes, I think I do."

# TWENTY-SEVEN

Are you sure it's a fire?" Thomas demanded, marching with Mikil down the main path toward the barracks. "In the west, you say?"

"Have you ever seen a black cloud rise from the earth?" Mikil said. "It's a fire, and it's farther out than we've ever ventured."

"Horde, then," Thomas said.

"Maybe."

"To the west, not the east."

"The question is, how many?" Mikil said. "First our four recruits go missing in the west, and now we see a large fire on the western horizon. I don't like it."

Thomas frowned. "Neither do I." He looked to the east, where the main body of their forces was entrenched. "We've had no significant Horde activity except for these persistent raids on the east for three days now."

"No."

"Then maybe the camp on the east is a ruse," Thomas said. "They could be attacking from the west. Is that possible?"

Her eyes were wide, and sweat beaded her forehead. "It could be. But if we move our forces from our defensive positions in the east, we'll leave that flank exposed."

"We have the high ground on the west because of the cliffs. How many fighters could hold the cliffs? Five thousand?"

"Ten," Mikil said. "At the very least."

Thomas closed his eyes and tried to settle his frayed nerves. It was like this often now, flirting with death at every turn.

"Take half our forces, five thousand. And the thousand new recruits. Stand them on the cliffs. Make them look like ten. Do whatever you have to—just show force. If they are planning on a surprise, even a smaller force will throw them. Then send a scouting party one day out into the western desert. We hold the other five thousand in their positions in the east for now, but have them ready to move if word comes that we've been tricked."

"Yes, sir," Mikil said. "You'll stay here in the village?"

"Yes, until I know for sure. No more word on the recruits?"

"None. They're lost, Thomas. I'm sorry, but there's no way they could have survived this long in the desert."

"I don't know. I'm still not convinced."

"Then let me go," Mikil said.

"Out into the desert?"

"I'll lead the scouting party. For you, sir."

He thought about her suggestion, then nodded. "Take ten of our best—and extra water. Head directly toward this smoke. One day out, no more. Let's see what secrets the desert is hiding from us."

IT WAS MORE OF A HUNCH THAN SPECIFIC KNOWLEDGE, BUT Alucard's statement that Teeleh's lair was below and not very far had gnawed at Johnis's subconscious from the moment he'd heard it. He couldn't shake the suspicion that there was more to this stadium than met the eye.

He dropped to the ground and ran behind the platform.

Actually, the single greatest tip-off had been Alucard's sudden appearance with Teeleh's Book of History. He'd come from the back, Johnis remembered. And he hadn't seen the beast fly in.

Rough-hewn planks formed a wall around the platform, like a skirt that hid whatever lay below. Johnis ran the perimeter and pulled up hard at the very back.

There, almost exactly as he'd pictured it in his mind's eye, was a gate made from the same planks. He pulled it open and peered in. Stairs cut from wet, mossy stone descended into the ground. The putrid smell of death that rose around him made him blanch involuntarily.

This was it! He knew to the core of his bones. The Dark One's lair awaited below.

Johnis returned to the front. "Wait here. Watch the horses. And if you have any trouble, blow the horn."

"Where are you going?" Silvie demanded. "I'm going with you!"

"No, you're not. Teeleh's either down there or he's out because of the fire. If he's still in the lair, it's finished; you have to accept that. Not one of us stands a chance against that beast. No use in all of us risking our necks."

"I was under the impression that we were already doing that," Billos said.

They ignored him. Darsal threw Johnis an unlit torch. "Take this with you. One strike and it will burn."

Johnis looked at it. This was what they must've started the fire with. Who'd given it to them was anyone's guess, but an image of a fuzzy white Roush came to his mind.

The moist, mossy stone steps leading down were best gripped with claws, not boots. They twisted to the left, forming a circular staircase, darker with each step down. He lit the torch and stared downward. Yellow light touched the rock walls, but even this seemed to be absorbed by the blankness below.

Johnis forced his way down twenty, maybe even thirty, steps, then stepped off the last worn stone into a circular atrium. Same dark mossy walls; same putrid, sulfuric odor. The floor had been worn smooth by countless padding feet. The ceiling was low, and the black smoke from his torch fanned out directly over his head.

Straight ahead of him the curving wall was broken by a large, glistening black door with a corroded handle. Staring at that tarred door was like staring into the heart of Teeleh. Johnis suddenly hoped it was locked so that he could turn and run.

He stood shivering, knowing that time was too short. Billos was right—the Shataiki might be fleeing the fire, but with so many of them in the forest, they would be swarming back soon enough.

He stepped up to the black door, reached for the rusty handle, and hesitated. He watched his trembling fingers for a long ten seconds, then touched it.

He'd half expected a flash of darkness. Another vision of the dark man-beast reaching for his throat. But nothing happened. The handle was cold.

He turned the latch and pushed the door gently. It opened with a soft squeal of metal. A puff of warm, musty air brushed his face and blew the flame, which wavered and crackled. His heart thumped in his ears, but he detected no sign of Teeleh.

Then he stepped in. Into Teeleh's lair that had surely been carved from the pit of the earth hundreds, maybe thousands, of years ago.

He faced six smaller, arched doors set in stone, forming a twenty-foot semicircle. Water dripped somewhere deep behind these walls. The doors presented him with another decision, and at the moment he was hating decisions, particularly ones that all seemed to lead deeper into trouble.

But time was going. Maybe already gone.

He quickly tried the door on his right.

Locked. Thank Elyon.

The next door, also locked. And the next, and the next, and the next.

Thank Elyon. He didn't want to be down here any longer.

Johnis grabbed the last handle and pushed, expecting to be given the liberty of fleeing back through the main door, up the circular stairwell, and out into fresher air to announce that Billos was right. All was lost; they would have to go back.

But the door swung in silently. He jumped back, startled.

Now he had no choice. He had to go in. And so he did, just two steps.

The door opened to a tunnel carved out of stone, tall enough for a man to walk easily. Or a beast. The walls glistened with a moist gel or resin. Standing so close to them, Johnis was sure the terrible rotten odor that plugged his nostrils came from this gel.

Here and there his torchlight showed huge pink roots that ran along the slimy walls. The cobblestoned tunnel floor ran wet into the earth. The passageway was terrifying in itself, but still no sign of the Shataiki bat.

Johnis started to walk down the tunnel, holding the crackling torch in front of him.

Farther into the earth. Farther from his comrades. The tunnel seemed to stretch into darkness forever. He stopped and considered returning. Thinking with his heart was one thing; madness was another.

And this was the latter.

He stared at one of the pink roots to his right. It was a good

six inches in diameter, moist and smooth except for round rings
every few inches. Like a huge earthworm.

The root suddenly bunched up slightly and slid forward.
Johnis's heart skipped a beat. Two beats.

It *was* a worm. And the worm was sliding forward through the
thin layer of worm gel coating the wall.

Panicked, he tore his feet from the ground and bolted forward,
deeper, screaming to himself that he was going the wrong direction.

He should be going back! That's what his mind cried. *Back,
back, back, you fool!*

But he wasn't thinking with his mind. He knew that he
couldn't go back, so he ran on. The worms lined the tunnel walls,
leaving long trails of slime in their wake.

For a brief moment he wondered what that stuff would taste
like, because although it made no sense to him, he did feel an odd
attraction to it.

*You're in Teeleh's lair, Johnis. This must be where the disease was
first born. This is where the worms feed on the souls of humans and
leave sludge behind. You have no business being in this place.*

A room suddenly gaped on his right, and he slid to a stop.
Beyond a large wrought-iron gate sat a wooden desk, and in front
of the desk, an old stone stool. Three candlesticks stood on the
desk, along with an inkwell, closed at the moment. Bookcases lined
the walls, filled with dozens of dusty, leather-bound volumes.

Teeleh's library? Or lair? Perhaps both.

The vision he'd seen in the desert, when the man had told him

it was all about the library—"The Horde is in the library," he'd
said, or something similar—came to mind. It was all connected.
Books, visions, power, lairs, libraries, killers, Horde.

Teeleh.

The dark man-beast he'd seen when touching the book with his
blood. *But more than Teeleh,* he thought. It still didn't all add up.

Johnis reached for the latch, found it unlocked, and pulled the
gate open, wincing at the loud screeching of metal against metal. He
glanced both ways down the tunnel and heard no sounds of pursuit,
only the continued dripping of water on stone. *Drip, drip, drip.*

He walked in slowly, trying not to breathe too loudly. Looking
around the room, he couldn't help thinking he'd been here before,
in this very room.

Several volumes sat on a table at the center. Their titles had
been rubbed away. A green book, a black book, and a red book.
In contrast, the books on the shelves were shades of dark brown
and bound in leather.

Words had been drawn on one wall. Strange scribblings that
meant nothing to him:

Welcome to Paradise.
Born of Black and White
Eaten with worms
I'm a Saint. a Sinner. a Siren of the word
[Some words had been smudged here.]
Showdown at midnight.

*Born of Black and White.* Could that mean writing? Or Teeleh? Or a skunk, for all he knew.

*Eaten with worms.* Surely the worms in the tunnel.

*Saint, Sinner, Siren.* Only Elyon knew. As with the last line, *Showdown at midnight.* A coming confrontation of epic proportions, waged at night.

Johnis turned his eyes to the desk. He'd almost missed them because there was a dirty rag draped over them, but there in the light of his torch he saw the edges of two books bound in red twine.

Two Books of History. The black one from Michal, and a dark brown one.

For a moment Johnis couldn't move. Then he couldn't stop moving.

He dashed to the desk, snatched up both books, whirled around, and ran from the room, mind fixed on one thing and one thing only.

Out. He had to get out.

Still no sign of Teeleh.

He raced back down the tunnel, slipping twice and very nearly sprawling on his backside. The door to this tunnel was still open, and he flew through, gripping the corner of the wall as he exited. His fingers sank into the gel that coated the stone, and for one crazy moment he thought about sucking the gel from his hand. The tunnels were making him mad.

Flinging the stuff off with a snap of his wrist, he bounded out of the atrium, up the steps, and into the open air, letting the gate smack shut behind him.

He'd made it. He stood in a crouch for several quick breaths, grappling with the accomplishment. Then he stifled a whoop of victory and raced around the platform.

"I have them!" he cried, unable to contain himself any longer. "I have them both!"

No response. Did they hear him?

"I have them! Silvie, I have both of them." He rounded the corner and saw Silvie, Darsal, and Billos by the horses, backs to him.

"I have . . ."

He pulled up hard when he saw what they were looking at. The sky was still filled with smoke, a good thing.

But now the bleachers were filled with Shataiki, who'd come either to escape the fire or to butcher the thieves who would take their books.

A bad thing.

For a while Johnis just stared, refusing to accept the meaning of this sudden turn of events. They were trapped. There was no way out from here, was there?

He set his jaw and strode past the others, suddenly furious at how it was all ending. He'd believed the Roush and crossed the desert and risked his life and found Teeleh's lair. All for this?

Johnis faced the black beasts, thrust both books into the air as Teeleh had done, and screamed at the sky.

"I have them!"

The words filled him with courage.

"These books belong to Elyon, not to Teeleh! I have them. Go ahead, you filthy beasts, try to take them. Step forward and see what Elyon makes of his books."

As one, the Shataiki crept forward onto the field, like a thick carpet of oil. They pressed toward the platform, one step, then two, then on, plodding slowly, silent and deliberate.

"Now you've done it, Scrapper," Billos said softly.

Johnis walked calmly to his horse, stuffed both books into the saddlebag, and withdrew his sword. He'd yet to swing it, he realized. Now was as good a time as any to baptize the blade with blood.

Shataiki blood.

He raised it and pointed at the bats who were still approaching like a slow-moving tide.

"For Elyon, you filthy beasts. When you take up against us, you take up against Elyon!"

First Silvie, then Billos and Darsal, stepped up beside him, blades by their sides.

"This is it," Darsal said.

"Yes, this is it." Silvie breathed out. "This is definitely it."

Billos swished his sword once. "Duck, dodge, kick."

"Karate," Darsal said. "Watch their fangs and claws. Go for their soft underbellies."

Silvie nodded. "You do realize there are too many. Way too many."

"Yes, too many," Darsal agreed.

"They'll kill us," Silvie said.

"Yes, they will," Billos said.

The black throng stopped no more than thirty paces off, red eyes glowing, waiting for what, Johnis didn't know.

"The books are mine," a gravelly voice growled from high on their right. Johnis saw Teeleh for the first time, perched on the stadium's lip. "Rip them limb from limb!"

The Shataiki threw themselves forward with a chorus of shrieks. Johnis braced himself, ready to cut through.

As if drawn by the onrushing Shataiki, white smoke began to pour over the eastern lip of the stadium, where black trees had stood tall just an hour ago. It spilled in silently, a blanket of fluff, coursing over the rings of seats carved from stone, flying low and fast and boiling with power.

Johnis caught his breath and nearly forgot about the front line of rushing black bats—because this wasn't white smoke flooding the stadium.

This was white Roush.

Thousands of them, so thick you could swear they were a flood of cotton balls, so silent you'd guess a drifting cloud.

And at the head of them were two he recognized immediately: Michal and Gabil.

"Roush!" Johnis screamed.

That one word pierced the din and reached the ears of the mangy black bats, only because they all were listening warily for it.

The Shataiki spun their thin necks as one, saw the wall of white, and took off straight up, streaking for the sky.

Johnis did manage to take one swing, and he felt his sword strike flesh. A black rag of a bat plopped dead on the field in front of him.

Then the sky was dark with Roush and Shataiki locked in ferocious battle. They tore into each other, and from what Johnis could see, the Roush didn't have the advantage. Perhaps a little, but not in the way he expected.

"This way!" a thin voice cried. Johnis spun and saw Gabil pulling two horses forward. "Hurry, you must take the books out!"

Johnis and Silvie threw themselves on one of the horses. Darsal and Billos climbed onto the other.

"Out, out!"

"What about you? You have to come!"

"I have some karate to deliver, boy!" A dead Roush slammed into the platform to their left. Gabil looked at his fallen comrade, made a terrible face Johnis didn't know he was capable of, and whirled back.

"Stop at the pool," Gabil cried, leaping into the air. "Then back to the forests on the horses you find there! Do not stop until you are safe!"

Johnis glanced up to his right and saw that Teeleh was gone. A Shataiki and a Roush locked in each other's claws hurled past them, smashed into the ground, and rolled to a stop. Neither got up.

How many would die for them today?

"Let's go!" Darsal cried. She bolted up the stadium seats, with Johnis close behind.

The forest was burned to a crisp and still smoldered hot. The horses ran at a gallop, over fallen logs and smoking branches. It wasn't an easy ride, but the path to the desert was free of Shataiki.

The Shataiki were behind them, killing the Roush.

# TWENTY-EIGHT

Qurong paced on the sand in front of his horse, feeling heat rise from the blasted desert, but more so from his own skin.

"Well?" he snapped.

The traitor tossed him the eyeglass he'd introduced to the Horde just months earlier. A device for farseeing that Thomas Hunter had come up with.

Qurong caught the gourd, lifted it to one eye, and peered at the distant cliffs. The line of Forest Guard started as far north as he could see and stretched south, past the device's limits.

"It's the smoke," the priest hissed behind him. "Didn't I tell you there was black magic in the air?"

"Smoke is not magic, you fool."

"This smoke is. There *is* no forest behind us!"

"What lies *ahead* of us is the issue now," the traitor said. "We can deal with this fire soon enough. But looking ahead I see a slaughter."

Qurong flung the glass at him. "*Their* slaughter, you mean. I won't let this string of fighters perched like proud cockatoos foil my plan! We go in!" He swung onto his horse. He'd become so accustomed to the pain of sudden movement that he gave it no mind.

"Then you'll lose your army," the traitor said. "You can't keep going back—"

"Don't talk to me of our old ways!" Qurong roared.

"Then be my guest. Commit your men to their deaths."

Qurong breathed heavily through his nose. There would come a day when he'd leave the fighting to his generals. Perhaps to the traitor himself. But today he commanded.

"You can see it, can't you?" the traitor asked softly. "They have the upper hand. Their archers will kill most of our horses in the canyons from their positions above. Like fish in a barrel."

"Fish in a barrel?"

The traitor hesitated. "A saying Thomas uses. The point is, this plan has been compromised. We'd be better off attacking from the east, where there are no cliffs."

"But our forces are here! Because of you, I will add."

"Better to fight another day," the traitor said.

And Qurong knew he was right.

"We've been foiled by black magic," the priest of Teeleh said behind them.

"Curse your black magic!" Qurong snapped.

The priest didn't flinch. There was something to this whole mess, this business of Teeleh and missing books, that Qurong thought might end up playing into his hands.

"Your decision?" the traitor asked.

"We fight another day," Qurong said and spit to one side.

The traitor dipped his head. "Wise. And that day will be sooner than you think."

Then he did something that Qurong found very strange indeed. He withdrew a silver ring from his pocket, rode to a boulder jutting from the sand—the only such rock for a thousand paces—and placed the ring on top.

"What's the meaning of this?" Qurong demanded.

"Do you want your battle?"

"I don't see what a ring has to do with battle."

"But I do." He took out his knife, cut his finger, and soaked a small piece of cloth with the blood. Then he placed the cloth under the ring.

"Enough with your secrets," Qurong said.

The priest spoke confidently. "It's the language of black magic!"

The traitor returned to their sides. "No. But it's a language that is as strong. They will know. Believe me, they will know."

# TWENTY-NINE

Father! Father!" screamed Thomas's daughter, Marie, running like the wind through the front door. "They've been found!"

Thomas bolted up from the table, spilling his beetroot soup. He snatched his sword from the wall and took a step toward her before he'd had time to process her claim.

Waiting here in the village while his officers tried to determine where the battle would come from had driven sleep from him for the past two days. Now his daughter was informing him that the Horde had been found. He had to get to his men!

But this was Marie crying at him. Why would his young daughter bring news of the Horde?

"The Horde?" he demanded. "Who? What're you talking about?"

"Johnis! Billos, Silvie, Darsal! Your recruits are back!"

Thomas closed his eyes, stilled the tremor in his tired limbs, and stepped back to his chair. "Don't be silly, child." He sat again, surveying the mess he'd made. The children had turned the four dead recruits into heroes and played games around the clock, pretending to be them. Now they actually believed their games. It was going too far.

"This is nothing to play with!"

His son, Samuel, sprinted in, face white as a pastry puff. "Father, they're entering the stadium now!"

Rachelle stood from the end of the table. "Thomas?" Her voice made it clear that she saw truth here. At the very least, Marie and Samuel believed their story to be true.

Could it be?

"They're in the stadium now? With Mikil?"

"All four," Samuel said, "with Mikil and another ten of the Guard. The village is coming out to see them." He whirled and was gone in a blur of arms and legs, followed by Marie.

"I told you!" Marie cried. "I told you!"

Thomas tore from the house, vaulted one of the rosebushes at the end of his walk, and ran toward the wide path that split the circular village like a spoke of a wheel.

He heard them before he found them, only because at least a thousand others had already found them and were ushering them into the stadium. Dusk was falling; the daily Gathering would begin soon. If Marie and Samuel were right about the recruits, these four would be the talk of the forest for a week.

He ran past a few hundred villagers hurrying to the amphitheater, spun into the passage that led to the field, and ran toward the cries and whistles of approval.

He could see them now. A group of roughly fifteen Forest Guard led by Mikil had stopped in the middle, facing the field entrance in expectation of his arrival. This was Mikil's idea, no doubt. She was making a spectacle of this turn of events, knowing it would bring courage to them all.

The stadium was filling as word spread. Thomas slowed to a walk and stepped onto the field. Almost immediately the crowd saw him and hushed.

Four stallions were in the center of the group, and on these horses sat Johnis, Billos, Darsal, and Silvie. But he saw something else now. Two long poles were strapped to their saddles, making a stretcher.

Only this stretcher didn't carry the wounded. It carried four large catalina cacti.

Thomas hid his smile and stopped twenty paces from them. For a long moment no one moved. What he saw next struck a chord of pride in his heart.

Johnis, the youngest of the four, dismounted, walked up to him, and knelt on one knee. "Your cacti, sir. Forgive our tardiness."

So, whatever had happened, Johnis had emerged as the leader. The other three were on the ground now, kneeling.

"Stand up." Thomas waved them to their feet. "Stand up and be counted."

They stood.

"You're alive," Thomas said.

No response.

"How did it happen?"

Johnis hesitated. "We got lost and were taken captive," he said. "A large Horde army marched in from the west but turned back when they saw the Guard on the cliffs. We were afraid you'd been fooled by their forces on the east, sir."

Thomas glanced at Mikil, who nodded. "Four hundred thousand strong, by our estimates. They were turned back."

So it was true! Qurong was becoming wiser in his ways of war. A year ago he never would have thought to try such trickery. The Horde was learning fast, much too fast.

"And the smoke we saw?" Thomas asked.

Again Johnis hesitated as if unsure how to answer. "There was a fire?" he asked. "Then I would assume it came from the Horde or their allies, the Shataiki."

"Shataiki?"

"Figure of speech, sir."

Billos and Darsal had been beaten and cut, he saw. Johnis and Silvie had bruises, but not like their comrades. All of them wore tattered tunics, stripped of armor. The poor souls had endured far more than he could guess. But they were alive, and at the moment he took more pride in these four than in any other members of the Forest Guard.

Regardless of what Johnis said, Thomas knew the smoke that

had warned them had more to do with these four than they let on. There was too much coincidence to assume otherwise.

The crowd continued to swell, staring, eagerly listening for what Thomas, their supreme commander, would say to these four.

"Send word to the army," Thomas said to Mikil. "Hold on both fronts, and let the Horde know that we aren't fooled. I'll join you in the morning."

"Yes, sir." She kicked her horse and galloped past him, headed for the barracks.

Thomas paced before them. "Your time to bring the cacti back has passed," he said.

Johnis bowed. "And you would be remiss to instate us in the Forest Guard after such a dismal failure."

Thomas could not hold back a small grin. "Is that so?"

"I think so, sir."

"On the other hand, you have done what no other Forest Guard could do by warning us of the Horde in the west. We would have faced wholesale slaughter if you had brought the catalina cacti back on time."

None of them spoke.

"How about you, Darsal? What say you?"

"I say I would give my life for the Guard. But the choice is yours."

"I see. And you, Silvie?"

"I say that Johnis should not only serve in the army, but command an army. The rest of us, I'm not so sure of."

"Really? And why should Johnis command an army? He's only sixteen."

"Because he thinks with his heart."

There was more to this story. Thomas would get to the bottom of it sooner or later. But none of that mattered at the moment. Johnis had the circle mark on his neck. That alone qualified him.

"And you, Billos?"

"We killed our first Horde, sir. And we escaped their clutches. I think that should qualify us for service, if nothing more."

"Johnis!" someone cried behind Thomas. He turned and saw that his father, Ramos, stood in the same entrance Thomas had used, panting from a long run. His face beamed, wet with sweat. "You're . . ." He stumbled forward, spreading his arms. "You're alive!"

A slight smile crossed Johnis's face.

Ramos turned in a circle, screaming out to those gathered now. "My son is found! My son! What did I tell you?"

He'd "told" the crowd nothing, of course. This comment was directed at Thomas.

He rushed up to Johnis, collided with him roughly, lifted him in a great bear hug, and spun him around. "My son is home!"

Then he kissed his son on one cheek, then the other, and ended on his nose—a great bearded rub that no one in any other circumstance could possibly appreciate.

Poor Johnis hung like a straw doll. But he was grinning when his father plopped him back down and ruffled his hair.

"I knew it!"

Thomas faced the crowd. He knew what they wanted. It was the same thing he wanted.

He lifted both arms. "I say this day that Johnis, Billos, Silvie, and Darsal have proven their worth!" he cried. "I say they have fulfilled the mission and can serve by my side as squad leaders. And I say that on this day, each shall be given the rank of sergeant."

The stadium erupted in a roar of approval.

"Welcome home your Guard!" Thomas thundered. "Give them your blessing. Tonight the celebration is for them!"

The dancing began then, in the stands, as thousands shouted with fists raised in salute.

Johnis stared around, dumbstruck. Thomas took his jaw and turned his head. The mark was still there. "Blessing, lad. Don't resist your calling. And let's keep it to ourselves, shall we?"

The boy simply stared at him with wide eyes.

*Someday Johnis will be a king,* Thomas thought.

*A king who listens to his heart.*

# THIRTY

The night went long, and the celebration was far more than Johnis could handle. The line of proud well-wishers who came by to shake their hands and speak words of encouragement seemed to never end.

And he was pulled into more than a few dances with young women who suddenly thought he was the moon itself. Billos ate it all up. Even Darsal took it all in stride. But Johnis and Silvie were the quiet ones, and the attention was overwhelming for them.

Still, he was rather proud, he supposed. They had done good, never mind that they'd stumbled into it all.

The celebration had finally wound down and the fires had been put out. Soon dawn would gray the eastern sky. But there was still business to be done. As agreed, the four stole away and met in one of the gazebos by the lake to get their story straight.

"Well, what do you think of that?" Billos beamed. "We're heroes, by the stars."

"This will only make things more difficult," Johnis said.

"Have you lost your mind, Scrapper?" Billos snorted. Then he clapped him on the back. "You know I don't mean that in a bad way."

"What?"

"Scrapper. It's just an endearing term that will help keep you humble. Though Elyon knows you deserve more respect than any one of us."

"Then don't call him Scrapper," Silvie said.

"It's okay," Johnis said. "I rather like it." He pulled out the two books he'd stashed under the bench and set them on the table.

For a moment, they just stared at the Books of History. Red twine still bound the black and the brown covers. It was the first time any of the others had laid eyes on the books since Johnis had retrieved them from Teeleh's lair.

"This . . . is what it's all about," Johnis said. His words fell like stones, heavy after the night's celebration.

Silvie stepped forward and touched the leather cover of the book that had come from Teeleh. "All of what we went through, for these books? We nearly gave our lives for them. What would happen if we opened one?"

"We can't!" Johnis said. He still hadn't told them of his horrific visions. Too dangerous. And he wasn't convinced they were just visions. "The power is terrible. You saw the look on Teeleh's face."

"There are five more books," Darsal said.

"I don't see how we can find five more books, if the last few days is any measure," Billos said.

Johnis looked up at him. "Do we have a choice?"

"You always have a choice," a voice said on their right. There on the railing perched Michal, the Roush. Gabil floated in on wide white wings and landed delicately on the rail beside Michal.

"Hello, kids," he said. "Care for a karate lesson?"

"Ho, Johnis!" a man cried, walking by. He raised his fist in a salute. "Billos, Darsal, Silvie. Fine job. You can fight by my side anytime. Anytime, I say!"

Johnis dipped his head. "Thank you."

"Yes, thank you, fierce warrior," Gabil cried. "And don't forget that I was there, too, putting the black beasts through this blender called my feet!"

"Gabil . . ." Michal started but then gave up.

The man walked off, grinning, showing no sign that he'd heard Gabil.

"They can't hear you?" Silvie asked.

"Or see us," Michal said. "You're the only four who can. We've always been around. One of these days we'll show you our village."

"You have villages? What about babies?"

"Of course. In the trees." He pointed up.

A lone shriek pierced the air. A Shataiki cry.

"Them too?" Billos asked.

"Your eyes have been opened, lad," Michal said. "Just because most people can't see a reality doesn't mean it doesn't exist. The legends are true. I hope I don't have to remind you that you can't speak of this to anyone. Not even Thomas."

"Then what, pray tell, are we supposed to tell them?" Darsal asked. "You want us to lie?"

"Be creative. But you cannot speak of the Black Forests, of the Books of History, or for that matter, of your mission, which is all that matters now."

"You said Black Forests," Johnis said. "As in more than one. We burned the forest to the ground!"

"That you did. It was the smallest forest. It will soon be covered by sand as though it never existed. But there are five more, all much larger. Seven green forests and six black forests."

"And each contains a book?"

"I wish it were that easy," Michal said, sighing. "Unfortunately, I don't have a clue where to send you next."

Gabil sprang from the railing and settled on the table with the books. "Which is just fine—more time for training!"

"Honestly, Gabil," Billos said, grinning, "your moves are made for flying bats. Unless you can teach us to fly, we're at a loss."

"Really? Well, maybe I *can* teach you to fly. It might cause a few bumps and bruises, though. And I can't promise you that you will ever actually fly, but you must learn my karate. If that's the only way . . ."

"Please forgive my friend's eagerness," Michal said. But this time he was smiling. "Now, I suggest you get your story straight and prepare to go after the next book. Gabil, we should get back. We still have wounded to care for."

Gabil fluttered off. "Practice your moves!" he cried. "I'll test you soon."

"Oh," Michal said, turning back. He withdrew something from his belt and set it on the railing. A silver ring. "I almost forgot this. We found it in the desert with a piece of cloth. It was placed there today."

Then he whooshed into the night.

Johnis stepped forward and lifted the ring. He recognized it immediately. "My mother's ring!"

"Your mother's ring?" Silvie said. "Michal wanted you to know that the Horde took it?"

But Johnis didn't think that was what Michal had meant by leaving the ring. His heart pounded, and sweat beaded his forehead. "She's alive."

"I thought she was killed," Billos said.

"They never recovered her body. This means she's alive!"

"You . . . you mean she's a Scab now?"

The possibilities swirled through Johnis's mind. Scab or not, she was his mother, and the thought that she was at this moment alive was almost too much to bear.

He pocketed the ring and faced the other three, jaw set. "I say we make a vow." He placed one Book of History on top of the other and placed his right hand on both. "The balance of power is on our shoulders. This is all that matters now. We take a vow now—all of us or none of us."

"To find the other five books," Silvie said, placing her hand on his.

Darsal walked over and slid her hand over Silvie's. "To fulfill our destiny."

They looked at Billos, but Billos was walking already, eyes on the books. He put his hand on the top and looked Johnis in the eye. "To kill the Horde, slaughter the Shataiki, and find the missing Books of History if it's the last thing we ever do. I vow it."

"I vow it," Darsal said.

"I vow it," Silvie said.

Johnis took a deep breath. "And I vow it."

Their eyes met again, and they nodded at each other in the cool morning darkness.

"Then we live or we die for the Books of History," Johnis said. "Let the quest begin."

# INFIDEL

LOST BOOK 2

# BEGINNINGS

Our story begins in a world totally like our own, yet completely different. What once happened here in our own history seems to be repeating itself thousands of years from now some time beyond the year 4000 AD.

But this time the future belongs to the young, to the warriors, to the lovers. To those who can follow hidden clues and find a great treasure that will unlock the mysteries of life and wealth.

Thirteen years have passed since the lush, colored forests were turned to desert by Teeleh, the enemy of Elyon and the vilest of all creatures. Evil now rules the land and shows itself as a painful, scaly disease that covers the flesh of the Horde who live in the wasteland.

The powerful green waters, once precious to Elyon, have vanished from the earth except in seven small forests surrounding seven small lakes. Those few who have chosen to follow the ways of Elyon are now called Forest Dwellers, bathing once daily in the powerful waters to cleanse their skin of the disease.

The number of their sworn enemy, the Horde, has grown, and the Forest Guard has been severely diminished by war, forcing Thomas, supreme commander, to lower the army's recruitment age to sixteen. A thousand young recruits have shown themselves worthy and now serve in the Forest Guard.

From among the thousand, four young fighters—Johnis, Silvie, Billos, and Darsal—have been handpicked by Thomas to lead. Sent into the desert, they faced terrible danger and returned celebrated heroes.

Unbeknownst to Thomas and the forests, our four heroes have also been chosen by the legendary white Roush, guardians of all that is good, for a far greater mission, and they are forbidden to tell a soul.

Their quest is to find the seven original Books of History, which together hold the power to destroy humankind. They were given the one book in the Roush's possession and have recovered a second. They must now find the other five books before the Dark One finds them and unleashes their power to enslave humanity.

We find our four heroes at the center of attention, celebrating their recent victory. But only they know the whole story.

Only they know that the quest is just beginning.

# ONE

The night went long, and the celebration was far more than Johnis could handle. The line of proud well-wishers who came by to shake their hands and speak words of encouragement seemed to never end.

And he was pulled into more than a few dances with young women who suddenly thought he was the moon itself. Billos ate it all up. Darsal took it all in stride. But Johnis and Silvie were the quiet ones, and the attention was overwhelming for them.

Still, he was rather proud, he supposed. They had done well.

The celebration had finally wound down, and the fires were put out. Soon dawn would gray the eastern sky. But there was still business to be done. As agreed, the four stole away and met in one of the gazebos by the lake—to get their story straight.

Johnis pulled out the two books he'd stashed under the bench and set them on the table.

For a moment, they just stared at the Books of History. Red twine still bound their leather covers. It was the first time any of the others had laid eyes on the books since Johnis had retrieved them from Teeleh's lair.

"This . . . is what it's all about," Johnis said. His words fell like stones, heavy after the night's celebration.

Silvie stepped forward and touched the leather cover of the book that had come from Teeleh. "All of what we went through, for these books? We nearly gave our lives for them. What would happen if we opened one?"

"We can't!" Johnis said. He still hadn't told them of his horrific visions—too dangerous. He wasn't convinced they were just visions. "The power is terrible."

"There are five more books," Darsal said.

"I don't see how we can find five more books, if the last few days are any measure," Billos said.

Johnis looked up at him. "Do we have a choice?"

"You always have a choice," a voice said on their right.

There on the railing perched Michal, the leader of the large, fuzzy, batlike creatures they called Roush. Gabil, his humorous friend, floated in on wide, white wings and landed delicately on the rail beside Michal.

"Hello, friends," he said. "Care for a karate lesson?"

"Honestly, Gabil," Billos said, grinning. "Your moves are

made for flying bats. Unless you can teach us to fly, we're at a loss."

"Really? Well, maybe I *can* teach you to fly. It might cause a few bumps and bruises, though. And I can't promise you that you ever will actually fly, but you must learn my karate. If that's the only way—"

"Please, forgive my friend's eagerness," Michal said. "Now, I suggest you get your story straight and prepare to go after the next book. Gabil, we should get back. We still have wounded to care for."

Gabil fluttered off. "Practice your moves!" he cried. "I'll test you soon."

"Oh," Michal said turning back. He withdrew something from his belt and set it on the railing. A silver ring. "I almost forgot this. We found it in the desert with a piece of cloth. It was placed there today."

Then he whooshed into the darkness.

Johnis stepped forward and lifted the ring. He recognized it immediately. "My mother's ring!"

"Your mother's?" Silvie asked. "Michal wanted you to know that the Horde took it?"

But Johnis didn't think that was what Michal had meant by leaving the ring. Sweat beaded on his forehead. "She's alive."

"I thought she was killed months ago," Billos said.

"They never recovered her body."

"You . . . you mean she's a Scab now?"

The possibilities swirled through Johnis's mind. Scab or not, she was his mother, and the thought that she was, at this moment, alive was almost too much to bear.

Mother was alive . . .

JOHNIS LAY ON HIS BED, NEAR DAWN, UNABLE TO SLEEP FOR the voice that haunted his mind. His mother's voice.

*I love you, Johnis. You are my life, Johnis.*

He opened his eyes and stared at the reed thatchwork in the ceiling. The house was built out of timbers and had carved planks. The inside was mostly flattened reed walls that flexed easily when pushed. A wood dresser and the bed he lay on made up the room's furniture. Simple, but perfectly functional.

His fingers rubbed the silver ring in his tunic pocket. Mother's ring. Rosa's ring. She'd been killed by the Horde months ago, leaving him in utter despair; his father, Ramos, a widower; and his sister, Kiella, motherless. Or so he'd come to believe.

His mother was alive.

Johnis stared at the soft dawn light that filtered through the window and rehearsed the events that had led up to this moment, still not sure if he could truly believe it all.

It had started with the Council's decision to invite all sixteen- and seventeen-year-olds worth their salt to join the Forest Guard. A thousand had been chosen. And by some impossible turn of events, Johnis had found himself leading a band of three other unlikely heroes who were sent on a final test: Billos, who was seventeen; Darsal, also seventeen; and Silvie, who was sixteen like Johnis.

Together they had struck out to the forest's edge to recover four Catalina cacti and return by nightfall as ordered by the supreme commander. But it was not to be. Disaster had changed their course. They'd been to hell and survived, and then returned to a great many cheers and a celebration that had ended just a few hours ago.

But they had also returned with a terrible secret that had to stay among the four. Not a word to anyone else, Michal had said. The eyes of the chosen four had been opened to see the unseen forests and deserts as they really were, populated by beings from the legends—the evil Shataiki bats from the deep desert and the furry white Roush who lived in the trees.

Not a word to anyone, Michal had said. Not a word about the Shataiki or the Roush or their mission to find the seven Books of History.

And now this business of his mother's ring.

Someone from the Horde army had left it after they'd been foiled and retreated into the desert, which could mean that his mother hadn't been killed by the Horde as Johnis had thought. Why else had Michal brought him the ring? No, she'd been captured, and now she had succumbed to the disease and was Horde!

A distant rooster crowed.

Johnis flung his blanket off and threw his feet to the bare floor.

His mother was alive, but a Scab, covered by the scaly disease that the Horde lived with. Her mind was steeped in deception without a care to return to the forests.

Johnis felt panic boil through his blood.

The two Books of History they'd recovered only days ago were wrapped in cloth and under his bed. He pulled them out. Carefully, in case there was any blood on his fingers to trigger the power of the books, he peeled back the cloth and stared at them.

Ancient, dark, leather-bound volumes, tied shut by red twine with the same title etched in each: *The Stories of History.*

He suppressed an awful temptation to pull back just the corner of one cover to see what lay inside, but Michal had been clear: never open the books. Judging by the dark visions he'd had when his blood had come in contact with the skin of the book in his hand, he wouldn't be surprised if actually opening one would kill whoever held it.

None of the other three knew of the books' power yet. He wasn't sure he could trust them with this secret. If there was any hope in finding his mother, the power of these books would lead him, wouldn't it?

He quickly wrapped the books in the cloth and shoved them back into hiding under his bed. His mother had been captured by the Horde because she'd gone to the desert to find medicine for him. He owed her his life.

Johnis stood, pulled on his boots, suddenly sure of what he would do. What he must do. His mother was with the Horde army, he was certain. And at this very moment the Horde army had been spotted heading into the western desert. Away from the forest.

Time wasn't on his side.

He grabbed his sword and sneaked down the hall, wincing with the house's creaking.

"Where you going?" a voice whispered.

His sister, Kiella, stood at the door to her bedroom, nightgown flowing around her ankles. She was short even for her ten years. Delicate, like a flower, Mother had always said.

Johnis lifted his finger to his mouth. "Don't wake Father."

"Where you going?" she repeated.

"I'm a Forest Guard now," he said. "I have things to do that no one else knows about."

She stared at him without blinking. "You're going to kill more Horde?"

"No! Shhh. Stay here with Father. Tell him I'm on an errand. Don't worry."

He turned to leave, but she hurried over to him, put her arms around his waist, and hugged him close. "I'm so proud of you, Johnis. I always knew you were a hero."

"I'm not."

"Everyone says you are."

"They're wrong." He bent and kissed her blonde head. "Be good."

He hurried into the cool morning air before she could stall him further.

The village, at the center of the middle forest, arched around the front side of the lake in which they all bathed daily to keep the disease away. Elyon's gift, everyone said, though secretly many thought the water simply had medicinal qualities that healed the skin. But Johnis knew the truth: the waters were beyond the natural.

He hurried down the side path that ran behind the main village, eager to find Silvie at the barracks without meeting too many people on the way. Blossoming flowers spilled from vines around most of the rock pathways that led up to the houses. Thomas of Hunter, or Thomas Hunter as he preferred to be called, had brought some fantastic ideas to them—supposedly from his dreams of another world as rumor had it. From the histories themselves.

Whether or not their leader's special knowledge came from another place or from Elyon or by whatever means, Johnis, like the rest of the Forest Dwellers, had no problem making good use of the metals they used for their weapons or the hinges on their doors or the many other innovations that bettered their lives.

"Johnis," a woman on his left, whom he didn't know, said. "Thank you, son. Thank you for your heroism."

He dipped his head. He didn't feel like a hero. If they only knew what had really happened in the desert, they might not be so sure of his worth.

Overhead, forest larks chirped. They could be Shataiki for all he cared. Nothing that had happened in the last week measured up to the terrible desperation that continued to build in his heart.

Silvie had said that he was worthy to lead because he thought with his heart. At the moment his heart was too bound up to think at all.

Johnis ran into the barracks, past the main hall, and took two steps into the women's wing before stopping to reconsider.

He couldn't just barge into a room full of sleeping women. As was customary, Silvie, Darsal, Billos, and Johnis would be given their own homes to honor their promotions, but having traveled from the southern forest, Silvie and the others would stay in the barracks until they decided which forest they would serve in.

He slipped into her room, passed several double bunks, and found her sleeping soundly in full battle dress. He reached out to shake her.

Silvie grabbed his wrist and pulled him down, knife at his neck. They were nose to nose, nearly mouth to mouth.

"Johnis?"

"Morning, Silvie."

She held him for a moment, longer than she needed to, he thought, then pushed him back. "What on earth has gotten into you?"

"I need you to come with me, Silvie. Quiet. Hurry." Then he turned and walked out, knowing that she would follow.

She emerged from the barracks, short blonde hair tangled; but otherwise she looked flawless. Even with the marks where strong claws had held her neck too tight, she looked stunning in the graying dawn.

Her eyes sparkled like jewels. "What time is it? I've hardly slept a wink."

"We have to hurry," he said, running toward the lake. "Bathe."

"Hurry where? What's going on?"

"My mother," he said. "I have an idea."

"But—"

"Bathe," he said, pointing to the right, where large boulders hid a bathhouse reserved for the female fighters. Johnis broke left without waiting for her to respond and ran into another bathhouse.

Kicking off his boots and dropping his tunic to the ground, he splashed water from a large basin on his torso, quickly wetting his skin. Three days without this water and any Forest Dweller would be consumed by the graying Scab disease, which cracked and grayed the skin.

Both emerged from the lake houses with damp clothes. Johnis veered toward the forest before she could speak.

"Hold on, for the sake of Elyon!" she cried.

"Please, Silvie. Time is running out. Please, follow me."

He ran into the trees, crossed one well-worn path that led to a stream of drinking water, and headed deeper into the forest. The last time he'd asked her to follow him, they'd nearly lost their lives.

"Johnis . . ."

"Run!" he cried. Deeper, still deeper he led her. Then, when he thought they'd gone sufficiently far so as not to be heard, he pulled up, catching his breath.

"What is it?" she demanded, bending over her knees.

"We have to speak to the Roush." He stood tall, cupped his hands around his mouth, and screamed at the top of his lungs.

"Michaaaaal!" Then again. "Michaaaaal!"

"What are you doing? They can't hear you."

He ignored her and cried again. "Michal! Any Roush! Please . . ."

A flap in the foliage to their right answered, followed by the beating wings of a white Roush that Johnis hadn't yet met. Then again, he'd only met two: Michal, the stately one, and Gabil, the spirited one.

"You'll look like a fool screaming to the sky," the Roush said, settling on the ground. He stood two feet tall, with spindly chicken legs, a furry white body, and wide batlike wings. Face like a possum crossed with an owl.

"Hunter at your service. You called?"

"Hunter?"

"That's what I said. Hunter. You like it?"

"Never mind. I need to talk to Michal," Johnis said. "Immediately."

"That's delightful," the Roush said. "Unfortunately, Michal isn't here."

"Then take me to him."

"Do you fly?"

"Do I look like I can fly?" Johnis asked.

The Roush raised its brow. "Touché. You really can see me, can't you?"

"You're a fuzzy white bat-creature standing right in front of me," Johnis said.

"Amazing. It's strange to be seen by a human after all this time. And why only you four can see us, only Elyon knows." He turned away. "You'd better get your horses. It's a long run to the Roush trees."

# TWO

It took them an hour to retrieve their stallions and follow Hunter to the Roush trees. As one of the many sentries posted around the middle village, he'd taken the name of the supreme commander, Thomas Hunter, he said.

They came to a valley filled with very tall Bonran trees, branchless for fifty feet, then spreading out like leafy sunflowers at the top. Johnis remembered the valley well because the flowers were a bright purple and were harvested when they fell to the ground. Their scent was used in many perfumes favored by the women.

What he hadn't seen the last time he'd passed through this valley were the hundreds of huge, round nests scattered throughout the upper branches. Nor the thousands of fluffy white bats that perched on the branches around those straw nests.

"Roush trees," Silvie said, gazing upward as Hunter winged up to join the others high above. "They . . . they're expecting us."

"Looks that way," Johnis said.

The Roush lined the branches and hopped about, staring down. Large ones, small ones, babies even, bouncing on thin twigs that didn't look strong enough to support their fat little bodies. The valley was filled with a cooing that made Johnis want to smile. For a moment he was too awestruck to remember why he'd come. These Roush had been here all along, unseen by any of the Forest Dwellers until now.

"Do you want to climb a tree?" a voice said behind them.

Johnis spun to see Gabil squatting on the forest floor, smirking.

"Can we?" Silvie asked. "I mean, will the branches support our weight?"

"I don't see why not; they hold twenty of us. Of course, they have been known to break. That's why we build so high. First, so we're not stepped on by any beast or human, and second, so that if the branches break, we have time to swoop under the little ones before they smash to the ground. Pretty smart, don't you think?"

Johnis stared up at the nests—more like small huts with wood platforms that encircled them. Four tiny Roush were jumping with such enthusiasm on a branch directly above them that Johnis thought they might fall.

"You'll have to forgive them," Gabil said. "They've all heard that you can see them. I also told them that I taught you a few karate moves."

One of the chicks suddenly jumped from the branch. Then another, apparently not to be outdone by the first. Then two more, screeching as they fell, like four stones.

A large Roush swept in from the left, another from the right, and two more from behind them. As if this was something they did frequently, they effortlessly caught the youngsters on their backs and soared down to a landing next to Johnis and Silvie's horses.

The six-inch Roushes tumbled from their backs and rolled to their feet.

"Are you Johnis?" one cried.

Johnis was too dumbstruck to answer.

"Johnis, say it, I know you're Johnis."

"And Darsal!" another offered, eyes too big for its tiny face.

"Silvie," she said, grinning wide.

"I told you!" a third chided his friend. "Billos and Silvie, that's what I said."

"You're both wrong," Gabil corrected. "Johnis and Silvie. The two lovebirds."

A moment of awkwardness hushed the forest. Johnis felt his face flush, and he briefly wondered if Silvie was watching him, but he felt too bashful to look.

More of the Roush settled to the ground, some carrying those too small to fly, some pacing in excitement. The forest floor began to resemble a cotton field.

It all felt very magical and wonderful to him, but Johnis was stung by an eagerness to get to the Horde army before they retreated too far into the desert. Sweat ran down his cheeks although he'd ridden here, not run, and the morning was still cool.

"We can't help you," a familiar voice said on his right. There, perched on boulder, waited Michal, the very Roush who'd given them the task of finding all seven missing books before the Dark One did.

The same one who'd also given Johnis his mother's silver ring.

"You gave me her ring!"

"*I* can help you!" one of the small Roush chirped.

"Take them to the trees," Michal ordered. And without delay the young ones were scooped onto backs and whisked skyward.

"I love you, Johnis!" one cried in a high-pitched voice.

"I love you, Johnis," another called down.

Silvie chuckled. "They're so adorable! How many—"

"That's not why we're here!" Johnis snapped. He regretted the outburst immediately but didn't bother apologizing. His mount shifted under him.

"I said we can't help you," Michal said. "You're on your own this time."

"That doesn't make any sense. You have to at least tell me if she is alive."

"Why?"

"So I can—"

"Rescue her?" Michal interrupted. The trees above had stilled to little more than the occasional squeals from chicks and the hushes from mothers trying to control them. "I gave you the ring so that you would know she's alive. Having said that, assuming it was her, and I do believe it was, she is most definitely Horde."

Johnis felt a surge of anger swell from his belly. "She's my mother. Not just some Horde."

"Easy, lad. Her mind is gone. Her skin and eyes are gray. She has no desire to return to the forests."

"And she left the ring for you to find. Why?"

Michal looked away. "I can't tell you everything. I sought the ring from her. If you win this war, then maybe one day you'll find her."

"Not *one* day," Johnis said, suddenly furious at the Roush. "Now!"

"I can promise you one thing, Johnis," Michal said very sternly. "If you think you can find her now, then you'd better be prepared for far worse than anything you've dreamed of. I wanted you to have hope; I didn't expect you to lose your mind. Patience."

"Take it easy, Johnis," Silvie whispered. "He's right."

"Yes, take it easy, Johnis," Gabil said. "Michal is right."

One of the young ones above cried down before his mother could muffle him. "That's right, take it easy, Johnis!"

But Johnis couldn't get his mind to take it easy. He fixed his jaw and tried to remain at least outwardly calm.

"In the meantime," Michal said, "put your mind on finding the books. The worlds are at stake, my friend. If you fail there, nothing else will matter."

"You can't just tell us to go looking for the books without giving us a clue where to look," Silvie said.

"Well, yes, that is the challenge, isn't it?"

"Do you suggest we start looking under all the logs in the forest? Without any ideas, we're stuck."

She was right, of course, but Johnis was more focused on the dismissal he'd been given regarding his mother. *There's still a way*, he thought. *One small way that just might work.*

"We should go," he said.

"Hold up." Silvie looked at the elder Roush. "Well? What do you suggest we do? You know that Billos and Darsal will ask the same thing. We stumbled on two books, but what now?"

"You didn't stumble on anything," Michal said. "Follow your hearts."

"That's what I'm trying to do," Johnis said.

"And try not to be stupid about it."

Johnis suddenly wanted out of the valley, out of this fluffy white sea of Roush. When the time was right he would come back, but right now the time was definitely wrong.

Whoever in the Horde army had left his mother's ring on the rock was retreating even now. Time was running short!

"If you have anything more that will help, you know where to find us," he said, turning his horse away.

"You are not as strong as you might think, Johnis," the Roush said very softly. "Don't think you can withstand the greatest test."

"What's that supposed to mean?" Silvie shot back, defending him.

"Pray you never find out."

Johnis dipped his head in farewell, unable to find any words. Then he spurred his horse into the forest.

Behind him Silvie said something to the Roush, then took after him. "Wait!" She pulled alongside. "What's gotten into you?"

He didn't know. Wasn't he only doing what he had always done? Wasn't he thinking with his heart?

"Where are you going?"

He thought about it for a moment, then answered frankly. "To use the books."

# THREE

The four fighters stood around the boulder in the middle of the clearing, staring at the Books of History that Johnis had placed side by side on the cloth.

Silvie glanced up at Billos, who was distracted by the tree line. A Shataiki bat was up there somewhere, having shown itself once before retreating into hiding. There was nothing they could do about the black bats. Surely the Roush would chase them off.

A tussle and a shriek high to their right was evidence of precisely this. Darsal and Johnis looked up with Billos.

"Chased off," Billos said.

They returned their attention to the books.

"So, there they are," Billos said. "What about it?"

"My mother's alive," Johnis said.

"You don't know—"

"I have no choice but to assume I am right! And these books may help us find her."

"Us?" Darsal asked. "No offense, Johnis, and Elyon knows that I was a fool not to trust you before, but our task is to find the missing books."

"He's lost his mother," Silvie said. "Go easy."

"And I'm sorry for that. But we can't forget our mission to find the other five missing books. We should stay on point."

She'd become a true believer in their quest, Silvie saw. Billos, on the other hand, was still more interested in the trees than the books.

"We've only been home a day," he said. "Heroes aren't meant to rush off the moment they receive their glory." He grinned and winked.

"We aren't heroes," Johnis snapped. "This isn't about us; it's about . . ." He stopped.

"The books," Darsal said. "That's my point; it's all about the books."

Johnis stepped closer to the two books and studied them. "Then we should see what the books say," he said softly.

Billos was suddenly interested. "Open them?"

"I thought that was forbidden," Silvie said.

Johnis leaned closer to the boulder. "No, we can't risk opening the books. Only Elyon knows what would be unleashed. But there is something else we can do."

He reached out and touched one of the leather covers with his fingertips, tracing the grooves made by the etched titles. *Stories of History.*

He looked up at them. "We made a vow last night, right?"

"Yes," Silvie said, and the others dipped their heads in agreement.

"So then we have to trust each other with everything we know."

"You've held out on us, Johnis?" Billos demanded.

"Before the vow, yes. But I have your word to stay true to the books now. Correct?"

"Do we have yours?" Darsal asked. "True to the books, that is," she said. *As opposed to your mother*, she was probably thinking.

"Of course."

*Such a true heart*, Silvie thought. She didn't doubt that he meant it, even though he was clearly distracted by the discovery that his mother was alive. An idealist to the core.

"Of course," Billos said.

Johnis looked back at the books. "When I was in the canyon, I touched this book with my finger. My finger had blood on it. Before Michal could warn me, a dark world opened up in front of me. Like a nightmare. Only real."

"You had a vision?"

"Michal said it was real. He couldn't explain it, but believe me, it didn't feel like a vision. It happened again in the desert, when I slept on one of the books with a cut on my head. That's how I knew how to find Summerville, the pond."

"Now you think you can use the book to find your mother?" Silvie asked.

"Why not?"

"Because Michal warned you not to go after your mother."

"He did? When?" Darsal asked.

Silvie looked at Johnis. "This morning we went to the Roush trees."

Darsal looked at him with wide eyes that wondered why he hadn't invited her along. Or Billos, for that matter.

Johnis laid his eyes on the books, ignoring their stares. "If the books don't mean for me to go after my mother, they won't show me, will they?"

Billos stood over the rock. "You're saying we could have this vision right now?"

"I think so, yes."

"How?" Billos touched one of the books, eyes lost in mystery.

Johnis pulled out his knife. "By cutting our fingers and touching the books."

"Really? What's it like?"

"I told you, a dark world. Enough to stop your heart, trust me."

"Michal said it was dangerous," Darsal said. "I don't think this is wise."

Johnis's jaw was fixed with determination. Looking at him now, with his high cheekbones and soft brown eyes, hair falling over his brow, Silvie felt her heart tighten. This man whom she'd followed to hell once before would not be easily turned back. An idealist with resolve.

In answer, Johnis lifted his left hand and drew the blade over his index finger. Blood seeped from the skin. He stared at them. "Who's with me?"

Billos withdrew his knife and cut his finger without a word.

Silvie touched Johnis's shoulder gently. "Are you sure—"

"Did we need water in the desert?"

"Yes."

"Did I find you water?"

"Yes."

"I used the book and we're alive, aren't we?"

A drop of blood ran around his finger. Silvie exchanged a nervous glance with Darsal, then cut her finger as the men had. Darsal grunted in protest and followed their example. Now all four stood around the books, each looking at a line of blood on a finger.

"Brace yourselves," Johnis said, then lowered his hand and touched a book.

The moment his blood came in contact with the leather cover, he gasped. His body went rigid, and his mouth stretched in a silent cry. Silvie stared in amazement. Did he really expect all of them to subject themselves to whatever horrors waited in this dark world?

Billos shoved his finger down onto the book and gasped. Then Darsal. Now all three of them were trembling, eyes closed.

Silvie followed their example impulsively, refusing to consider the consequences any longer. She lowered her finger next to Johnis's and touched a book.

The darkness came at her like a blast of heat and swallowed her. She'd expected something, but not this flash of blackness.

A dark being stood in front of her, reaching out with fingers that looked too long. She couldn't tell if this was a man or a woman or a beast because he-she-it wore a hood and cape. Or was it wings? Enshrouded in shadow and distorted by heat waves.

A loud moan filled Silvie's ears, and she instinctively cowered. Such a sound of trembling agony that she thought she might be dying. But there was another sound, a woman's cry, behind the moan, echoing softly.

"Johnis . . . Johnisssss."

The dark man-beast's arm reached for Silvie slowly, and she felt herself panic. Just beyond the darkness the horizon faded to light. A desert fogged by black streaks.

This was the other world?

But the Dark One was trying to kill her. She stepped back, and only then managed to remember that her finger was on the book, making the contact. She yanked it off.

The dark world blinked off. Forest light blinded her.

Silvie jumped back and stared at the others who'd already come out as well. Billos had his eyes on the books, captured by a frightful fascination. Darsal trembled slightly. Johnis's face had gone white, like a Roush.

No one could speak.

"Did you see him?" Billos finally whispered.

"The Dark One," Darsal said. "The books are evil?"

"The Dark One is evil," Silvie breathed. "The books reveal the truth. They're Books of History, after all. Absolutely true history."

Billos wiped his bloody finger on his pants. "They do more than reveal truth, clearly. What was that behind the Dark One? The desert?"

Johnis spun from them and paced three steps before whirling back. "Did you hear her?" he cried.

The woman . . .

"Did you hear my mother?"

Silvie had heard a woman, but not a voice she recognized. Then again, she hadn't known Johnis's mother. "Are you sure?"

"Yes! She's alive."

"But I didn't see anything that would help us find her," Darsal said.

"You heard her, though! She's out there! In the desert!"

His eyes were wide and pooled with tears. Silvie had never seen him so frenzied. Contact with the book had pushed him even further over the edge.

"Please, Johnis, we don't know that." She closed the gap between them. "What I saw was evil, and the intentions weren't good. I don't think there's anything we can do."

Johnis closed his mouth and drilled her with a stare, nostrils flaring.

"The books have more power than anyone could have imagined," Billos said. He slowly reached for one of them.

Johnis marched up to the rock, shoved Billos aside, covered both books with the cloth, and carried them back to his stallion. He had that look, Silvie saw. The one he always had before jumping off a cliff.

"Where are you going?" Billos demanded. "They aren't your books, you egotistical, slimy snake!"

"They are for now." Johnis flung himself into his saddle, whipped the reins around the horse's head, and glared at them. "We have a mission to find the other five books. Until we have them all and they are in safe keeping with Elyon himself, I'll guard them with my life."

"You can't just take over!" Billos shouted, red-faced.

Johnis gave Billos one parting glare, then spun his horse and was off.

Silvie, Billos, and Darsal stood empty-handed around the boulder, listening to the sound of fading hooves.

"So *he's* the leader then?" Billos asked in a bitter voice.

Darsal nodded. "So it seems. Let it be, Billos. Until he's proven wrong, we follow him."

"To the ends of the world," Silvie said.

Billos glared with dark eyes. "We can't just keep trotting off cliffs on one boy's whim."

*He is right*, Silvie thought. On the other hand, so was Darsal.

But if they'd listened to Billos or Darsal when this all started, they would likely be dead.

"Give him space," she said. "He needs time to clear his head."

Billos spat to one side. "His head needs to be more than cleared."

# FOUR

Johnis spent the morning in the forest, fleeing himself as much as any villagers who were unlikely to leave him alone. He found a large mango tree under which he buried the books for safekeeping. The look in Billos's eyes had unnerved him to the spine.

He wasn't sure what the others had experienced, but contact with the book had revealed more than one thing to him. The power of the books, yes. And his mother's cry—he could never mistake her voice. But if he was right, the books had revealed Billos's heart. He wasn't quite sure how, and he wasn't sure he wanted to find out.

Either way, the books had to stay hidden from Billos.

And perhaps from him. From Johnis, who couldn't put the fear and the anger and the anguish of his mother's cry behind him.

*Johnis . . .* Her voice, as clear as the last time she'd spoken to him while he lay sick in bed with a fever, just a few months ago.

He could still feel her cool hand on his burning cheek, see the wrinkle of her brow. "I'm so sorry, Johnis."

"It's okay, Mother, you don't have to baby me. I'll be fine."

"Baby you? You're only sixteen. I'll baby you if I want."

"Sixteen is old enough to be married," he'd said.

"Maybe, but until the day some other woman takes you into her house, I'll make the decision on whether or not to baby you." She stood and paced.

"Please, Mother, you're making me nervous with all this walking. I'm fine!"

"You're burning up, Johnis. I can't find a scrap of Catalina cactus in the village. I can't just stand here and let you burn to a crisp!"

He'd tried to convince her to wait until she had a proper escort, but she reminded him that she did know how to swing a sword well enough. And his fever was getting worse.

The last time he saw her was in his door frame, giving him parting instructions: "If your fever gets too hot, put the wet cloth on your forehead."

"I know, Mother."

"I'll be back in two hours. No longer."

"You're sure about this?"

"I love you, Johnis."

And then she was gone. It was the last time he'd seen her, because they hadn't recovered her body. They found the blood on the sand and her boots, but her body had been hauled off by beasts or Horde.

Ramos, his father, had gone on a rampage and killed ten Scabs, the hair from whom he'd formed a Horde ball which he'd presented to Thomas, the supreme commander of the Forest Guard.

Johnis had recovered from the fever, but not from his mother's death. And then last night he'd learned that she wasn't dead at all. She was, instead, a Horde.

The thoughts buzzed through his mind like a mammoth Mazumbi hornet. Had he ever been so helpless? There was nothing he could do, was there? Nothing at all.

Johnis pulled the reins tight and stared through the branches at the village outskirts. Nothing at all, except . . .

But the thought bordered on lunacy.

He loosened the reins and let the horse have its head while his own head spun with this new thought.

The truth was Michal had found evidence of his mother, presumably alive.

The truth was Johnis had heard her voice in the books.

The truth was the books had saved him once before.

The truth was there could be a way, however insane, to go after his mother, who at this moment was with the Horde army, retreating to the south, a step farther with every breath he took. He could still hear his mother's voice from the books.

*Bring me back to life . . .*

Did he have a choice?

But this thought now burrowing itself deep into his mind was impossible. And if not impossible—if by some trick or power he made it happen—it was the stuff of blithering foolishness.

Then again, wasn't this entire quest foolish in its own way? Being forbidden to tell, for whatever reason he could not hope to guess. And what if he managed to recover his mother?

Nonsense! Absurd! Utterly, completely.

And so began the war in Johnis's soul as his horse wandered into the forest, stopping at patches of grass to feed on the sweet Wiklis flowers. Johnis hardly noticed. With each passing minute his mind sank deeper into the details of a plan he knew was as wrong as it was right.

In the end it was his mother's voice that won him over.

*Johniss . . . bring me back.*

He'd heard that, right? He'd heard her precious voice crying to be heard in the desert. The Dark One hadn't plotted for him to hear the voice as a lure; no, that wasn't it. No, the Dark One had tried to smother her cry! But Johnis had heard the order from his mother.

And now he would go do it.

As suddenly as the thought had first presented itself to him, it now became one with him. He was meant to execute this plan or die trying. He was chosen for this day as much as he was chosen to recover the missing Books of History.

Johnis lifted his head, saw that he was deep in the forest, jerked the horse around, and spurred it into a gallop.

The trees gave way to the outskirts of the village ten minutes later. The Forest Dwellers numbered over a hundred thousand among all seven forests, and of those, twenty thousand lived here in Middle Forest. But the houses were woven through trees except at the center, giving the city a village feel, which was why they still called it a village.

Johnis bore down on the wide road that split the village in two, and galloped through the main gate. He ignored the few calls from well-wishers crying out to their newly appointed hero and thundered past. Time was running low, so very low now—the Horde was retreating deeper into the desert with each passing hour!

The barracks, please let her be in the barracks, he prayed.

He slid from his horse while he was still moving, landed in a run, and barged into the barracks Silvie was holed up in, one of twenty similar buildings on the edge of the village.

The barracks were constructed of wood planks, ten simple rooms per barracks, with five bunks in each room. One blanket per bed. Most of the Guard lived in their own homes, which provided more comfort, but the temporary accommodations were all a fighter who'd come from another forest needed.

Johnis had rehearsed the role he would play from this point forward, and he adopted the correct attitude as he banged through the barracks door. The smell of sweat filled his nostrils.

*Sergeant. I'm a sergeant, and I'm a well-known hero, fresh from saving the village!*

He grabbed the first fighter he saw in the common area, a corporal who watched him stride in with lazy eyes.

"Do you know who I am?"

"You're in the wrong place, pup," the man said, sneering.

Johnis considered several options at this unexpected response, and chose the last one that popped into his mind.

"I have an urgent message for Silvie of Southern, the girl who was returned from the desert a hero. Do you know her?"

The warrior sat up, suddenly serious. "Of course I know her. What red-blooded soul wouldn't know her?"

The man's reaction gave Johnis pause. If he wasn't mistaken, this corporal was attracted to Silvie. The whole blasted barracks was likely attracted to her.

"Fine, red-blooded soul. Where is she?"

"Not here. If she was here, she'd be with me, now wouldn't she?"

"Somehow I doubt that."

"You insult me?" The man stood to his feet, a full foot taller that Johnis. Perhaps a different approach would have been wiser. He didn't have time for this!

"She's at the archery range, Johnis of Ramos," a voice said.

Johnis glanced back to the new fighter who'd entered the barracks. "Thank you."

He ran out the front, only mildly amused by the sounds of argument behind the shut door. Red-blood was getting his ears cuffed, maybe. It didn't matter. He had to find Silvie.

He found her at the grass-covered archery range, shooting arrows into a stuffed gunnysack thirty paces off. Dressed in brown battle leathers, firm muscles flexing the bow string, short blonde hair loose and twisting around her face. The desire of any red-blood indeed. He watched her for a beat, thinking that he might be able to execute this plan of his without Silvie. She didn't deserve what was coming her way.

Johnis discarded the thought and called out. "Silvie of Southern, will you come with me?"

She let her last arrow fly with perfect precision, watched it thud into the mark, and then answered without turning. "And why should I come with you, Johnis of Ramos?" She turned, eyes twinkling.

"Because I need you to help me save the world."

"Really?" Her smile faded and concern crossed her face. "Are you okay?"

*No, I'm not okay, Silvie. Can't you see that?*

He walked over to her and stared into her eyes. "Silvie . . ." Words suddenly failed him.

"No, Johnis, I will not ride with you out into the desert to find your mother," Silvie said. "That's what you're planning; I can see it in your eyes. And it's suicide."

"It's not that simple!" He took her hand in both of his. "Was I right about the Books of History? Was I right about Teeleh? Was I right about the water? Was I right about everything I've said these last few days? Then trust me, I'm right about this."

"About what, Johnis? Precisely what are you right about this time?"

He fought through a wave of frustration. "About my mother. About why we heard her."

"And why did we?"

"Because I'm meant to go to her."

"Unless that's what the Dark One wants you to believe."

Johnis released her and ran both hands through his hair. "That's not it! You can either choose for or against me. But I have to be at the forest's edge by nightfall. Make your decision."

He spun and walked away, frantic that she might not follow, but resolved to continue on his own regardless.

"Johnis." She caught up to him. "Did I follow you into hell?"

"Yes."

"Then I'll do it again. But I don't like it. Michal warned us."

"Michal doesn't know everything. The books' powers are beyond him—he confessed that much. He doesn't know what will happen next. He can only warn of danger. I say, 'Warn, little bird; there's not a breath I will ever take again that isn't laced with danger, thanks to this cursed quest!'"

That set her back long enough for both of them to catch their breath.

"Okay. I'm with you. What's the plan?"

"The plan is to bathe in the lake again."

"Because we aren't going to be bathing again so soon," she guessed.

"Fill canteens with lake water."

She sighed. "We should tell Thomas."

"No! Not this time."

Silvie eyed him. "What are you planning, Johnis? What has you sweating like a cold bottle of water in the hot sun?"

"I'll tell you on the way," he said.

But he knew he couldn't tell her. Not yet, not on the way, not until it was too late for her to turn back. If she knew what was in his mind at the moment, she wouldn't follow so easily.

# FIVE

It took Johnis and Silvie two hours to don appropriate battle dress with the sergeant hash marks, refresh their supplies, retrieve the two Books of History that Johnis insisted stay with him, if only because he didn't trust anyone else in his frayed state of mind, and race to the Western Forest edge.

He told Silvie the plan on the way. Most of it. And the plan she heard was simple enough: a scouting mission out into the desert.

But Johnis had no interest in a scouting trip. In fact, the closer they came to the desert, the more he knew that a scouting trip was pure folly. He already knew what they would find. The Horde army would be moving south from where they'd been turned back just yesterday. But Johnis didn't care about the Horde army.

He only wanted his mother back. And to his way of thinking, there was only one way to accomplish that here and now.

As they neared the desert, they began to pass fighters returning home from the western front. Five thousand had been posted here just yesterday, and their supply of lake water was undoubtedly low.

Every Guard fighter was required to carry enough lake water to bathe at least once every three days to fend off the graying Horde disease, but when a whole army traveled, they often carried extra water in large canvas bags thrown over mules and horses.

Johnis was looking for one of these. Or more if he could find them. And he found them as the fighters left the forest behind. One of the Guard was towing a train of three mules, each laden with two five-gallon canvas water bags.

Johnis veered for the mules. "You there, with the mules. Are you headed back to the village?"

"I am."

"Then I'll take these off you. You won't need them where you're going."

The man eyed him. "And you will? Sir?"

"I may. It's none of your concern. How many are left on the cliffs?"

"Most have gone. The Third Fighting Group is holding back till morning."

"Carry on."

The man hesitated, then tossed the lead rope to Johnis, who caught it and led the animals back the way they'd come.

"And you need the water for what?" Silvie asked. "We just bathed."

"The last time we went out, we nearly lost our lives because we ran out of water. Never too safe. Here, take them." He handed her the rope and kicked his horse. "Wait by the Igal point."

"Where are you going?"

He pushed his horse to a trot, refusing to answer.

The Forest Guard had positioned itself along a line of cliffs overlooking the canyon lands that petered out into sand dunes a mile to the west. From there the desert stretched as far west as anyone had traveled. The last of the fighters was slipping into the forest, but common strategy required a rear guard to hold a front long enough to ensure that no attack could be mounted from behind.

It was this rear guard that Johnis wanted. Needed.

He found them camped with open fires along the edge of the cliff three hundred yards north of the Igal point, the lookout that saw far into the desert. The Third Fighting Group, five hundred fighters strong. Their fires would be seen deep into the desert by any Horde.

A group of three officers stood to their feet as he galloped toward them on his black stallion. Johnis wiped the sweat from his brow and fixed his jaw.

"Who commands?" Johnis demanded, pulling his horse up hard.

"Who comes?" a fighter with the slash marks of a captain asked.

"Johnis," he said. "With urgent business. Are you in charge?"

"You have a script?"

"There wasn't time for formal orders. My word carries the authority of the supreme commander, Thomas Hunter. And the longer we talk, the greater the danger. Who commands?"

"What is the word of a sergeant? What's the business?"

"I can't speak to anyone but the commander. Hurry, man, tell me!"

"Mind your rank!" the captain snapped.

The second of the three, another captain by his marks, stepped forward and placed his hand on the first captain's arm. "Johnis, you say. Johnis of Ramos?"

"It is."

The man's eyes brightened, and he dipped his head. "Johnis of Ramos, Captain Hilgard of Middle. We've all heard of your victory. The word of any fighter who single-handedly turned back the Horde is an honor to hear."

The third soldier, a sergeant, hurried forward and took a knee. "It's an honor, sir. We are indebted."

"But the captain isn't sure?" Johnis drilled the first officer with the hardest look he could muster.

For a long moment the captain he'd first offended held his eyes. A grin slowly crossed his face. "You're the runt who survived the desert, then."

"I'm the appointee of Thomas who can only follow his orders before it's too late."

"Forgive me, then, lad. I'm in charge. Boris of Eastern. What are the orders?"

"To give me temporary command of your group," Johnis said. He covered any hesitation in his voice by using more volume and glancing over their shoulders at the five hundred men sitting or standing around their fires. "I need the men ready to move out in five minutes."

He started to turn his horse as if the matter was settled. Standard operating procedure required that all front guard units be always ready to break camp in under five minutes, but such an order would come only in times of immediate threat.

"Thomas ordered this?" Captain Boris demanded.

Johnis faced him again, flexing his jaw. "The middle village celebrated me late into the night because I offered my life to save yours, Captain," he bit off. "Now if you want to undo all that I've done, then hesitate. But every minute you stand there and question the supreme commander's authority will cost more lives. Choose now, or let me find a more worthy captain!"

"Easy, lad! I've offered my life in a hundred battles; don't speak to me as if I'm a horse! Now, for the sake of Elyon, tell me what the orders are."

"To rescue a fighter taken by the Horde before they get too deep into the desert."

Boris's face flattened. "Into the desert? That's unusual."

"Then let me tell Thomas of your decision and find someone willing to follow orders before it's too late."

"I didn't say I was refusing orders. But you have no script, and you're talking about considerable danger. I have the right to question a pup half my rank, don't you agree?"

"Fine, question fast. The Horde already has a day's start. It'll take a night of hard riding on fast horses to catch them. I want to be in and out before daybreak."

Crickets sang in the forest to their right. Johnis continued. "Leave the fires burning, and gather the men. We have to run, but as Thomas said, your horses are rested, and we have water to bathe on the way. Can you be ready in five minutes?"

Again the captain hesitated.

Johnis knew that in the Guard, special missions were common— as unusual as this order was coming from a sergeant who was hardly sixteen years old. He was counting on the fact that it wasn't beyond the realm of schemes Thomas had cooked up on a dozen occasions before.

"Why rescue this one fighter?" Boris pressed.

"For the love of . . ." The captain known as Hilgard faced his peer. "We're letting time slip, man!"

"This one fighter is the mother of the Chosen One and the hope of the forest!" Johnis cried. "And no one can know that. Not a soul, or I'll know it came from one of you! If that means nothing to you, then accept it on blind faith. I have Silvie of Southern with water mules. Meet us at the bottom of the pass. But for the love of all the forests, hurry!"

He reared his horse around and slapped it into a full run.

*You've lost your mind, Johnis.* He swallowed hard. He was mad. *And your heart has been blackened by the Dark One. This time you're playing with the lives of five hundred fathers and mothers.*

He grunted and slapped the horse again. No, he had to follow his heart, no matter what the cost! He needed his mother back. That and nothing else was what his heart told him.

"Mount up, Silvie!" he cried, rushing in. "We're going down the pass into the desert! If we go all night, we'll—"

"Stop it!" she snapped.

What did she mean, *stop it*?

"You're not yourself! You're rushing off, and you aren't telling me everything."

"I *am* myself! I'm more myself than I have ever been. And you're going to have to decide if you like me this way, following my heart, doing what I know is the right thing to do."

She stared at him as if he'd slapped her, but he didn't have time for this. The plan was set in motion, and he wouldn't compromise it now. He had to count on Silvie's loyalty to him.

He grabbed one of the mules' ropes and tugged the beast behind. "If you decide I'm worthy, then bring the rest of the water with you. If not, then run back to the village."

"Johnis . . . please!"

He ignored her and headed for the gap that led down to the canyon floors. The stallion navigated the rocky ground easily, but Johnis slowed its pace, silently begging Silvie to run up behind him and swear her allegiance as she had once before.

And she did, trotting her own horse and the two mules down through the pass, sending stones rolling loudly as she rushed to catch up with him.

Silvie pulled up behind him and fell in line. "Fine, you have my decision; are you satisfied?"

He looked back and forced a grin, though he felt more like crying, swamped with desperation at what he was leading her into. "It's your call, Silvie. I'm only doing what I have to do, with or without you."

She waited a moment before speaking again. "Don't kid yourself. You need me."

"Do I?"

"You do."

"Then it's a good thing you're not letting me run off alone to get my head chopped off, isn't it?"

"You're not yourself, Johnis," she said quietly.

He hesitated, then spoke strongly, as much for his own benefit as hers. "You're wrong."

The setting sun was hidden by canyon walls when they reached the sandy floor and headed out toward the desert, where their course would turn south.

South . . . after the Horde.

"Permission to ask a question, your Almightiness," she said, her voice dripping with sarcasm.

He didn't answer.

"I understand your fear of running out of lake water, but these mules don't exactly run like the wind. We're on a scouting trip after the Horde. Don't we need to run like the wind?"

"We do. And we will. As soon as we get out of the canyons."

"Then why not stake the mules here and go?"

A clatter of rolling stones echoed through the canyon from the cliffs behind them. They looked back and saw the group of fighters hurrying down the pass to catch them.

"Because the water's for an army," Silvie said with more than a little wonder in her voice. "You're bringing an army."

"I am."

"How . . . ?" She didn't bother finishing the question. "You don't need an army to scout. What kind of impossible scheme have you thrown together?"

"Be at my side, or leave me now, Silvie," Johnis said, staring into her eyes. "But if you stay, promise not to undermine me."

Her face slowly softened. "I stay with you. Elyon knows you're going to need me."

# SIX

Voices carried in the desert, and for this reason they spoke only as necessary. The fighters who hadn't bathed yet that day took turns splashing water over their skin before catching the main group. When they'd all bathed enough to last them another twenty-four hours, they cut the mules loose and ran, as Silvie had put it, like the wind.

Silvie rode beside Johnis, who kept his face fixed forward into the night. She didn't say much, but with every passing stride, her regret swelled. The only reason she stayed by his side was because the last time she'd doubted him, he'd shown her wrong, so utterly wrong.

So then, this time he could be right as well. Hadn't she praised him in front of the whole village for his ability to think with this heart? And she'd cried for all to hear that he deserved to command an army, never mind that he was only sixteen.

Well, now he *was* commanding an army. And the thought unnerved her to the core.

Two hours into the night, one of the forward scouts found the deep marks left by the Horde's retreat. The fighters turned after them, headed south. Stars glittered in the cool sky high above. The red moon was down in the west. Pitch blackness ahead—it was only a matter of a few hours before they caught the army. And then what? Johnis didn't seem eager to answer that question, though she asked it twice.

The word had spread through the ranks: they were on a secret mission for Thomas. One of their own had been taken and must be recovered at all costs. The Horde would never expect a raid from the rear only a day after its massive army had been turned back.

And who was the fresh sergeant who led them? None other than Johnis of Ramos, the one who'd turned back the Horde in the first place. They owed their lives to him.

Onward! Into the desert! They would harvest enough Horde hair to fashion a hundred footballs!

But Silvie knew that the Guard always rode into battle with the expectations of giants taking on rodents. True, Scab warriors were slower than Forest fighters due to the disease that pained their flesh. And also true, Scab warriors didn't have bows yet, or metal blades as strong as the Guard's.

But Scab swords had no difficulty taking off a head or severing an arm. And the Horde army greatly outnumbered the Forest Guard. In this case, several *hundred thousand* to their paltry five hundred.

She pulled up next to Johnis and spoke quietly. "If I ask a question, will you at least give me the honor of answering?"

His head was low over his horse and his high cheekbones firm. She'd never seen him so determined. Stubborn was more like it. Like those mules they'd left behind in the desert. She wasn't even sure he'd heard her.

"Would you risk the lives of all these fighters for your mother?" she asked.

She knew he could hear her above the pounding hooves behind, but he wasn't answering. Only then did she see the wetness on his cheeks.

Tears, drying in the wind. Her heart felt sick for him.

She pressed the issue. "Tell me you're not going to go in with swords swinging."

Johnis spun, face hard, eyes wet. "Of course not!" he growled. "Do you really think I'm a fool?"

"I think that if you would jump off a cliff for a Roush named Michal, you'd go even further for your mother."

He faced the darkness ahead. "And you think that's a mistake?"

"No. But would you go there for me? For the rest of these fighters? You and your mother aren't the only ones in the world tonight."

Just this morning Silvie had wondered if she would like this sixteen-year-old man to ask for her hand in marriage. The notion had quickened her pulse. It had been a wild moment of impossible thoughts, but they were both of marrying age. Both fighters and lovers of Elyon. Both willing to die for the other.

Both beautiful in their own ways. She certainly thought he was.

She wouldn't necessarily accept his proposal, of course. The Guard discouraged fighters from wedding as young as civilians did, but the heart didn't always follow army regulations, did it? She relished the thought of being asked.

But the voice that came from him now was from an animal, not a lover. "Leave me, Silvie. If you're going to undermine me, leave me!"

The words cut like daggers. She knew he couldn't mean it. He was only reacting to the news of his mother. He'd been overcome by whatever he'd seen in the books.

Still, these words from him made her want to cry. They raced over a dune, then down a long slope that rose again across a wide valley of sand.

"Hold up!" Captain Hilgard whispered hoarsely. "We're there!"

So soon! They were only several hours out from the forest—surely the Horde had withdrawn much further.

Johnis pulled up and stared into the darkness ahead. The whole company stamped to a halt.

"You're sure?"

"I can smell a Scab at a thousand paces, lad. If we don't see the outskirts of their camp in minutes, I'll give you my sword."

On cue the lead scout galloped over the next dune, reined in his horse, and made a quick signal for contact.

The captain nodded. "Go slowly."

Hilgard motioned the fighters slowly forward on panting horses. Some leaned over, rubbing the mounts' noses or feeding them water from a canteen. Most held at least one weapon loosely in hand as naturally as a cook might hold a spoon. In the desert the Guard slept with a blade half-swung, so the saying went.

Silvie pulled out her sword and laid it across her lap. Eight-inch knives rested in sheaths, two on each calf. She could use a knife more effectively than most who'd fought a hundred battles, but in pitched combat arrows and swords fared better than knives.

The Third reached the scout, who waited in her saddle. She nodded at the crest. "In the valley ahead, as far as the eye can see."

Hilgard dismounted and ran forward, with Johnis and Silvie close behind. They dropped three abreast and were joined by Captain Boris.

Silvie didn't see them at first for lack of fires. But they weren't looking for fires—it was the dead of night, and the Horde would be asleep.

Slowly the faint outlines of the massive Horde camp separated themselves from the surrounding desert sands. The pale tents blended well, only slightly darker, like honey on bread. At the camp's center, far away, several much larger tents rose above the others. To the right, thousands of horses slept on their feet or gnawed on straw, their heads bent.

Silvie's pulse pounded in the silent night.

The single greatest advantage the Guard cavalry had over the Horde was the fact that Horde horses couldn't smell as well because of their own stench.

Guard, on the other hand, could smell perfectly well the horrible stench that rose from the camp ahead. A nauseating rotten-egg smell hit Silvie in her face like a blast of Shataiki breath. She spat into the sand.

"Perhaps now would be a good time to give us the plan," Captain Boris whispered.

Johnis just stared into the valley. It struck Silvie that he wasn't prepared for this. None of them were, really. Following idealistic whims, even throwing yourself in front of stampeding horses for a cause was one thing. But leading fighters into battle was another.

"The ring was left intentionally," Johnis said to no one in particular. "It's the only reason the Roush could have found it. We have to assume that they wanted us to come after her."

"Roush?" Hilgard said.

Except Johnis and Silvie, none of them had seen a Roush in many years. Johnis was prohibited from speaking of their experience. He'd slipped. So Silvie deflected the question.

"Figure of speech. He means *scout*. Unseen and silent."

Hilgard nodded. "You'd need to be Roush to get in there, I can tell you that much."

"Not if we create a distraction," Johnis said.

"And how can you be sure you know where this fighter is?" Boris demanded. "A distraction will only cause commotion for so long before it wakes the whole camp. Our horses are tired; remember that."

"Where would you keep the most valuable prisoner you possess?" Johnis asked.

"At the command center."

"Exactly. That's where they have her."

"But if you're wrong?"

"I'm not."

A small flame flared to life from a tall hill on their right, then faded and died. "What was that?" Silvie asked.

But she didn't need to ask again, because she now saw the dark outline of a rider, unmoving against the distant horizon where the flame had burned.

Had they been seen?

"So soon," Qurong, leader of the Horde, said. "Because of one ring. How could you know?"

"I have my ways. We are agreed then?"

They stood in the courtyard of the royal tent, gazing west toward the hill from which the signal had come. The Horde army was four hundred thousand strong, and although they left most of their women and dogs at home, they still moved slowly. It wouldn't have taken long for the Guard to catch them.

Most of the heavy equipment was loaded on carts dragged

behind horses and mules—carrying tents that each slept ten, cakes of sago bread and taro root, barrels of wheat wine, hay for the horses, and blacksmith's wares. Mounted warriors carried the rest.

They'd pitched the tents and bedded down so that all would appear to be business as usual, although the traitor had made it clear that the Forest Dwellers didn't really know what business as usual was among the Horde. They didn't send spies for fear of catching the skin disease. This was the one advantage the Horde held.

Qurong rolled his neck and felt it crack. A pain in his spine had kept him from sleep—so he'd spent the hours pacing and drinking. The Dark Priest had suggested he offer a prayer to the winged serpent they worshipped, to ease his pain, but Qurong didn't trust this black magic business. He was more interested in destroying the Forest Dwellers.

How leaving one ring on a boulder could have led the Guard into the desert, Qurong had no idea. But if the traitor could lure them so easily, he would command as one of their generals, as agreed.

"Of course, agreed."

"And I will be called Martyn," the traitor said.

"Fine, Martyn. How many are there?"

"Our scout says only a handful. A few hundred. We'll slaughter them. We have ten thousand on their flanks, closing on them as we speak. They have no escape. The battle I promised you will be over in minutes."

"If Thomas isn't with them, then it will be a shallow victory," Qurong said. "It's Thomas we need."

"And it's Thomas we will have," the traitor who would be called Martyn said. He took a long breath, then explained with soft confidence, "The ring I left for them to find belonged to the Chosen One's mother."

And then Qurong understood. They'd taken the woman months earlier and learned only recently that she was the mother of the young recruit whom Thomas believed had been chosen to deliver the Forest Dwellers: Johnis.

"You've lured Johnis with his mother?"

"Yes."

"And then you'll lure Thomas with Johnis."

No answer. Clearly, that was his intent.

"And if you fail?"

"I won't. The trap is sprung."

The traitor's brilliance made Qurong wonder if he himself should be concerned for his power.

"This is why we turned our army back at the western cliffs, because of this plan you'd hatched? It would have been better for you to tell me this sooner."

"No, we turned back because the Chosen One survived the desert and warned them with the fire—don't ask me how, but he did. The Guard had higher ground and would have cut us to ribbons at the cliffs. That's why I turned back. That and the fact that there is always more than one way to skin a cat."

"Skin a cat?"

The traitor who would be called Martyn shrugged. "An expression that Thomas brings from his dreams of the ancient time. You'll have Thomas within the week. Excuse me." He turned to go. "I have a battle to attend to."

"Bring me Thomas's head, Martyn. Just his head."

# SEVEN

"There, another!" Silvie whispered, pointing to a second torch on their left.

"It's a signal." Boris spun for his men. "They've seen us!" The fighters in the valley below immediately scrambled for the high ground on the dune behind them.

Silvie and Hilgard flew down the dune. "They knew we were coming! Get out. Back!"

Johnis heard all of it behind him as if in a dream. The captain snapping orders in hushed tones, the horses snorting as their riders kicked them into sudden motion, the creak of five hundred saddles as fighters twisted in retreat.

His own breathing was heavy in his nostrils as he lay on the dune's crest, staring at the huge Horde camp ahead. He couldn't understand why, but the sight of so many tents, filled with so many diseased Scabs, froze him.

Two thoughts crashed through his mind. The first was that, Scab or not, these beings lived in tents and had homes. Whenever he'd imagined the Horde, he'd thought of axes and battle and fire-breathing beasts bearing down on the forests. Not this sleeping camp made from canvas tents.

The second thought was that his mother, Rosa, was in there somewhere, maybe watching him now. And she was a Scab.

Then a third realization dismissed all other thoughts. The Horde was expecting them. He, Johnis of Ramos, the Chosen, had delivered them into Horde hands.

Michal's warning whispered through his heart. *You'd better be prepared for far worse than anything you've dreamed.*

"Johnis!" Silvie tugged on his sleeve. "Run!" She'd come back up the hill for him.

He tore down the dune with her, fully confused by panic. This wasn't just him and a few chosen ones following the Roush into hell, was it? No, it was him leading five hundred against the Roush's advice.

He slid to a stop by his horse, unsure how to proceed. They were running from his mother? Leaving her?

"Johnis!" Silvie slapped him upside his head. "Move, boy! You have to start using your head!"

He threw his leg over the stallion and allowed it, more than urged it, to bolt up the hill behind the others, the last of whom were already cresting the dune.

Silvie was beside him, bent low over her saddle. "Stay with me!" she said.

She was ten times the fighter he was; they both knew that. For the first time true fear settled over him. The Guard didn't frighten easily, and yet they seemed unnerved now.

They flew up the dune and pulled up hard. The rest of the Third Fighting Group had halted halfway down the other side in a bunch. Johnis lifted his eyes and saw what they saw.

The scabs wore black cloaks now, not the pale cloth that matched the desert sand, as though cut from the black sky behind them.

Thousands upon thousands of mounted Horde lined the next dune, stretching half a mile each direction, cutting off their escape. Behind them more came from the night, filling their ranks ten, perhaps twenty deep.

"Dear Elyon, help us," Silvie whispered.

Johnis's mind scrambled for some kind of meaning, some thread of hope, some logical solution to this impossible sight. It was as if the image of the Dark One that had reached out to them from the books in his saddlebag had come alive, many times over, here in the desert night.

"Take your sword out, Johnis!" Silvie snapped. "Keep your shield up. I know you don't have that much experience fighting, so remember one thing: they are slower. Wait for them to draw back, and cut quickly under their exposed sides."

He stared at the line of Horde.

"Johnis!" she whispered harshly. "Your sword!"

He turned to yank it out and froze with his fingers on the handle. Behind them, on the dune they'd just vacated, stood another Horde army, silent and black against the dark sky.

"Behind us!" Johnis cried. His voice echoed through the valley.

Boris was the first to move, rearing his horse around and back up the hill toward Johnis and Silvie. "To the high ground!"

Five hundred moved as one, scrambling to the crest beside them, swords drawn, horses stamping and snorting with the scent of Horde in their nostrils. The Third Fighting Group was sandwiched between two armies, each large enough to smother them with Scab flesh, never mind their swords.

Boris spoke low and hoarse, keeping his command firm. "Hold until I give the word. Archers first."

The fighters passed the order down the line, stilling their horses, never removing an eye from the black riders.

Johnis looked far right and left, but no escape route presented itself. No place to run.

From behind came a single voice, so confident, so forceful, yet so conversational that Johnis wondered if the Horde commander who spoke was Teeleh himself.

"Give us the one named Johnis, and the rest of you will live."

Johnis could hear the Scabs' horses breathing. He wasn't sure why Boris had commanded them to hold. Either way they were staring at death. Only he could save them.

"Give me up," he said, voice faint. Then louder, "I'll go; take me!"

"Never!" Boris screamed. "Never give in to the beasts!"

"No, I have—"

"Shut your hole, recruit!" Boris growled.

"Then you will all die," the commander of the Horde said. His understated tone left no doubt. A slaughter awaited them.

The Horde commander spoke his order. "Take them."

The army on the far side surged over the hill and down into the valley like a thick tar that would surely swallow anything in its path.

"Ready . . ." Boris said. "Ready . . ."

Two hundred of the Guard raised drawn bows, aimed down.

Johnis turned back, alarmed to see that the army behind them was spilling into the opposite valley. From two sides the enemy swarmed.

When the first full line of Scabs reached the lowest point in the sand, Boris cried his order.

"Now!"

Arrows flew silently, barely seen in the darkness. And they found a mark, each one. The Horde army stalled in its rush as hundreds fell or reared back on wounded horses.

Faster than Johnis could have imagined, the archers strung fresh arrows and shot into the black mass. Then they reversed their aim to the back side and sent shafts into the Scabs on the other side.

For the briefest of moments, Johnis embraced a thin hope.

But the Horde simply forced their horses over the dead and rushed up the dune toward the Guard.

"I'll go!" Johnis screamed. "Take me; I'll go!"

His voice was swallowed by a thousand roars as the two armies collided.

Johnis discovered immediately why Boris had driven them to the top of the dune where they held high ground. Striking down on a slower foe gave them a distinct advantage. A snorting horse ridden by a warrior twice Johnis's size clawed slowly up the sand toward him. The Horde's arm jerked back, spear in hand, and Johnis went stiff.

Silvie lunged between them, yelling with rage. She swung her sword into the Scab's side and plunged past him as he crashed to the ground, dead.

"Sword, Johnis!" she shrieked, swinging at two more Horde hard on the heels of the first.

Johnis felt more than he heard the battle cry from his own throat. He let the reins fall, gripped his sword with both hands, and swung at one of the Scabs.

Cutting into his first beast felt the same as cutting into a sack of grain, and he was surprised to see the Scab drop his mallet, grab his chest, and fall backward over his horse's rump.

"Stay on your horse!" Silvie shouted.

Johnis dug his heels into his stallion's flanks and swung again.

They said any Guard worth his spice could take down ten Horde without breaking a sweat. It was the kind of fireside boast that children believed. But Johnis now saw that there was less boast and more fact in the matter.

Fallen beasts clogged the hilltop within moments, making it difficult for the Horde to reach the high ground with their swords.

"Back to the top!" Silvie yelled. "Back, Johnis!"

She'd never fought a full-scale battle herself, Johnis knew, but she'd been through enough training and possessed enough natural skill to best many a fighter.

He grabbed the reins and clambered back up. But the moment he crested the dune, he met swarming Horde from the other side.

High ground or not, there were too many. The Third Fighting Group began to fall among the dead Horde.

Johnis closed his eyes and swung, screaming at the top of his lungs now. *Thud!* He snapped his eyes wide. This time his sword had bounced off leather armor.

The Scab he hit roared and bore down hard. A knife flashed past Johnis's ear and silenced the warrior with deadly accuracy.

"Don't stop, Johnis!" Silvie cried. "Swing!"

And he swung. Then again. And yet again.

Still the Horde came. A large rock thrown from a sling bounced off his shoulder and spun into the night. His right arm went numb. He grabbed his sword with his left hand and thrust the unwieldy weapon as best he could, blocking blows more than doing any real damage.

The desert valleys on either side were now filled with crowding Horde, like a lake of black oil on either side. All was lost. It was only a matter of how many Scabs they killed before every last fighter of the Third lay dead.

Still, Johnis swung his sword by Silvie's side.

THOMAS HUNTER KNEW THAT HIS WORST FEARS HAD become real when they were still too far away to save them, knew that the report from the corporal who'd seen Johnis and Silvie dressing for battle and galloping out of the village in a near frenzy had come too late.

The Third Fighting Group was headed for an ambush that would redden the sand with their blood.

The roar of battle carried over the desert dunes. He caught a glimpse of William, one of his lieutenants, on his right, bent over his horse in a full sprint.

"We're too late!" William said.

Suzan, another lieutenant, pulled ahead on the left, followed close by Mikil. Both rode loose, feet pulled up high like jockeys as he'd shown them from his memories of earth in another time.

"Ride!" Thomas screamed.

Behind him the Guard army of five thousand rode.

Any other horses not trained and hardened for battle would have dropped long ago. And even these sweating beasts, bunched with muscle and sinew, tempted death.

Dust boiled toward the sky in their wake. Thomas begged Elyon for more time. Just enough to save a few.

The Guard pounded over a large dune and saw the battle in its entirety with a single glance. The Horde had their backs to them, thousands strong, fixed on the next valley. They themselves hadn't yet been seen in darkness or heard over the battle din.

Thomas stood tall in his saddle, still in full gallop, and pointed to either side, then straight ahead, with both hands.

The army responded to the signal as if he'd pulled invisible strings that coordinated its movement. A thousand broke right; another thousand veered left; and the main force stormed ahead, right up the enemy's backside.

Clashing swords and cries of rage covered any sound of their approach. None in his army so much as breathed to betray their attack. Not a single horse slowed.

They slammed into the Horde at full speed, plowing hundreds into the earth with the sheer momentum of their first contact. Their cries ripped through the air, five thousand throats as one, tearing into mounted Scabs.

On either side a thousand swept wide, unseen.

Thomas hacked his way forward, leaping over fallen horses and dying Horde. "To the heart!" he yelled. "Find them; take them out!"

# EIGHT

Captain Boris cradled a wounded right arm in his lap while swinging his sword like a sling with his free hand. Johnis was transfixed by the sight, knowing even as he stared that at any moment a Horde mallet could take off his own head.

What did it matter? He deserved whatever fate awaited him on this dreadful hill.

"Johnis, for the love of me, don't just stand there!" Silvie cried.

A stone came flying up the hill, and he deflected it with his sword, an almost lucky bang of stone on metal.

The night air behind him suddenly swelled with shrill cries. Johnis spun around toward the desert. The Horde on the far dune was boiling in battle.

They were fighting themselves?

"The Guard!" Silvie yelled.

Johnis saw them then, a thousand or two thousand Forest Guard cutting through the Horde army from behind.

Shouts erupted from the right and the left, and he swiveled to see that two other groups were bearing down on the enemy from either side.

Silvie froze for just a moment, then charged the Horde. "Take them from behind!"

The Scab warriors had turned to the new enemy and bared their backs. Silvie tore into them, taking down one, then two, like straw puppets. Five spun back to defend their rear, but she retreated uphill before they could reach her.

She wheeled back for another attack the moment they re-focused their attention on the much larger Guard threat on the flanks. The Horde had killed both her mother and her father, and she'd sworn to avenge their deaths. Tonight she was making good on that promise.

Johnis joined her on this second attack, swinging his sword with his right arm, which was now regaining its feeling.

"Johnis!"

He jerked around and saw a horse cutting through scattering Scabs. And on that horse sat Thomas Hunter, supreme commander of the Forest Guard. Relief flooded him, immediately replaced by horror.

He'd been the cause of this slaughter, and Thomas's dark eyes spoke his disapproval with nail-pounding conviction.

Johnis averted his eyes. On the hill behind he could see the outline of a lone horse—the commander who'd known his name. And beyond the commander lay the Horde camp, now hidden by the dune. And in that Horde camp, his mother.

She had to be there.

"Now, Johnis!" Thomas shouted, smacking a Scab in the forehead with the butt of his sword. The beast dropped on his seat and toppled unconscious. "Silvie, now! Follow me!"

Thomas veered to the south, followed hard by Silvie and Johnis. They skirted the battle and ran back toward the open desert.

"Retreat!" Thomas screamed. "To the desert!"

"Retreat!" voices cried, carrying the order through the battlefield. "To the desert!"

Johnis glanced back at the dune on which the Third Fighting Group had taken its stand for him. The number of fallen bodies dressed in familiar Guard uniforms was too high to count.

He lost his head at the sight and pulled back on the reins. The emotions that rolled through his chest numbed him. Terror and fear and pain—the raw physical pain of death.

He couldn't leave them!

Silvie reared back just ahead. "Johnis! There's nothing you can do! Run! For the sake of Elyon, run!"

So he ran. But he didn't run with any forethought or direction. He let bitter regret wash over his chest and silent tears run down his cheeks.

Silvie was yelling something else at him, but he couldn't make out her words any longer. Ahead lay sandy dunes and night, and he wanted to vanish there where no one could find him.

Johnis wasn't sure how long his horse galloped, but when he finally pulled up, all was silent. He fell off his horse, lay facedown in the sand, and wept.

Thomas and Silvie were the first to reach him. And when Silvie helped him to his feet, he saw the Guard army was following behind, headed straight toward them, an army of accusers.

"It's okay, Johnis," Silvie whispered, brushing the sand from his face. "I know you want to die, but you have to live. If for nothing else, then for me."

He glanced at Thomas, but the supreme commander wouldn't return the courtesy. And Johnis wouldn't have either, had *he* just pulled a treasonous rat from the jaws of death.

"Get back to the forest," Thomas said, then turned toward his army.

Johnis mounted with some difficulty and let his horse head into the night. Silvie followed in silence.

They walked like that for an hour, not speaking a word, keeping the main army well to the rear so that Johnis wouldn't have to answer to their angry stares just yet.

"How many?" Johnis finally asked.

Silvie didn't respond immediately. "How many what?"

"How many did I kill?"

Again she hesitated. "Horde or Guard?"

He swallowed. "Guard."

"I don't know. Over a hundred. Where did you put the Books of History?"

"In the saddlebag."

"You don't have a saddlebag," she said.

"Of course I . . ." He caught the words in his throat. Both bags were missing! They'd been cut or torn off during the battle!

"Dear Elyon, help me," he whimpered. "I've lost the books."


MARTYN THE TRAITOR, AS THEY LIKED TO CALL HIM, SAT atop his horse and let conflicting emotions pass through him. He'd once held a high rank among the Forest Guard.

A Forest Dweller. Forest Guard. He still wasn't quite sure how he'd lost his faith in the battle for the forests, only that he'd woken one day and known that it was all wrong. The fight was useless.

More important, he'd lost his belief that there was any reason to fight for a truth that no longer compelled him. Who, after all, was this Elyon who'd hidden himself from them all for so many years? And who said that clean skin was better than scabbed skin?

From there it was only a matter of time before his curiosity had led him to the desert. So Martyn knew what it was like to turn from Guard to Horde. He knew any man could be led down this path.

He knew that one day every last forest-dwelling fool would be led down the very same path he'd walked.

The thought of Thomas and his wife, Rachelle, tugged at his

heart from time to time, if only in respect for their loyalty to a dying cause. In reality, there was no man alive that Martyn respected more than Thomas Hunter, but this made the man no less his enemy.

And now Martyn had found Thomas's underbelly. A new recruit named Johnis, who was more idealistic than Thomas himself.

Back in the tent, Qurong would be storming about the beating they'd taken tonight. Not that Martyn blamed him, but how could he explain the complexities of the matter to a mind as simple as Qurong's? Given a little training, the leader would soon outthink them all, but for the time he was—what was it Thomas had said?—all brawn, no brain.

The bodies below him were already nearly picked over. Looting was a pointless habit of the Horde, but he didn't see any reason to stop the scavengers after such a firm defeat.

"Black magic," a voice to his right said. The Dark Priest had slipped up on his blonde mare. Like Martyn, he wore a hooded black robe. "Their magic will be the undoing of us all."

"You're talking to a man who left them because he realized that they have no magic," Martyn said.

"I've been visited by the Shataiki," the religious man said without any hint that he was speaking impossibilities.

"And what did they tell you?"

"That the books are more important than the forests."

Martyn looked down at the dead. They would leave the bodies for vultures and desert jackals who would make quick work of the flesh before the blowing sand would swallow what was left in a natural grave.

"You'd like nothing more, wouldn't you? A few more relics for your temple? Your source of power is mystery, not magic."

The priest sat on his horse without offering a defense. It occurred to Martyn that this druid should not be underestimated. The power of belief alone could change the course of history.

"You'll have to forgive my skepticism," Martyn said. "But I did live among them, and I saw no magic."

"Because you were blind. Why else would you desert them?"

"You're saying I was wrong?"

"I'm saying that only a fool has no belief. The Shataiki who visited me was named Alucard, advisor to Teeleh himself, and I'll tell you that not to believe in this beast will be death for us all."

"Really? What else did this Alucard tell you?"

"There are seven original Books of History, each tied with red twine. They belong to him. The power that goes to him who finds them cannot be fathomed. The torment of failure to find them will be far greater than losing to the Forest Guard."

"Then search for your books," Martyn said. "In the meantime, I'll see that our swords don't grow dull. We stay out of each other's way."

"I think you'll *need* my books," the Dark Priest said. "And I'll undoubtedly need your sword. Perhaps a more reasonable union would be in order."

"You're saying that you have these books?"

"Did I say that?"

"Your Highness!" A warrior trotted in on a black steed. He was addressing the priest, Martyn realized. Calling him "Highness," the name reserved for Qurong? The power of religion never ceased to amaze him.

"One of the men found this." He tossed a saddlebag to the priest, who snatched it out of the air and then shot the man a glare that suggested throwing anything at him was inappropriate.

"What is it?"

"Books."

"Books," the priest repeated.

"The unreadable kind."

Martyn blinked, suddenly curious. The only books the Horde could not read were the Books of History. Their contents seemed to be written in code: gibberish that made no sense. What he didn't tell the Horde was that he was quite sure that the Forest Dwellers *could* read the books.

The druid opened the saddlebag and pulled out a cloth-wrapped bundle. He quickly peeled back the scarf and stared at a dark leather cover with three sets of markings that identified the book as a Book of History.

But it was the red twine wrapped tightly around the book that sent a chill down Martyn's back.

For a few beats both of them just stared.

"Thank you, soldier; you may leave," the priest finally said.

The warrior left with a grunt.

"This is one of the original seven books?" Martyn asked.

"Yet you doubt me," the priest said.

*These books could command an army,* Martyn thought. *Their power is mythical, but myth can bring any army to its knees.*

"It seems fortune is smiling on you tonight," Martyn said. "I'll give you my sword. In return I want your allegiance."

The priest turned his hooded head toward him. His deep-set eyes were hidden by black shadow. "We need all seven," he said. "Help me find all seven, and I'll give you the forests on the palm of my hand."

"What is your true name, priest?"

"No one knows my name."

"No one except the man you're swearing allegiance to."

The priest hesitated, then spoke softly. "Call me what you like. You can't accept the truth."

"I doubt that. But if you insist, I'll call you Witch."

"Witch?"

"A name Thomas used to call Teeleh."

A thin grin may have crossed the druid's face—Martyn couldn't tell for sure; it was too dark. "Then call me Witch."

"You help me kill Thomas and destroy the forests, Witch. For that we need Johnis. Do that and I will help you find the other five books."

"The other *four* books," Witch said. "I now have three."

# NINE

Silvie watched Johnis, who was seated beside her on the rock on which they'd just yesterday rested the two missing Books of History. In the space of twenty-four hours he'd gone from heroic fighter riding the praise of the forests to this hunched form of shame, elbows on knees, chin in palms, silent—so silent she thought that maybe he'd actually lost his voice.

Thomas paced across the clearing, staring at Johnis, Silvie, Billos, and Darsal. He'd said he wanted them all here to hear what he had to say, even though it was Johnis who'd betrayed his trust. Silvie had fallen from grace by following Johnis, she knew. And the other two by association. If one hero could fall so far and so hard in the space of one day, there was no way to trust the other three, they would say.

"One hundred and thirty-seven dead," Billos growled. "What were you thinking?"

"No need to pile it on. He has enough shame," Thomas snapped, but then he stopped and faced Johnis. "What *were* you thinking, boy?"

Johnis didn't budge.

Silvie had agreed to keep secret the fact that he'd lost the two books until he could sort things out. But she wasn't sure how he expected to sort out the deaths of 137 fighters. The mourners were already crying in the streets of Middle.

"Mother or not, you have no right to lead my men into battle!" Thomas yelled. "You listening to me, pup? I don't care if you *are* chosen, I have half a mind to *un*choose you."

"Please," Johnis whispered. "Do it."

"I will not!"

*So then this chosen business Johnis has told us about is true,* Silvie thought. Thomas, at least, believed him to be chosen.

Darsal frowned. "Excuse me, sir, but I don't think we quite understand what he's been chosen for."

"To kill 137 of our own?" Billos said.

"Shut it, lad!" Thomas put his hands on his hips and glared at Johnis. "There is a prophecy we've followed for years. A child marked by Elyon will prove his worth and destroy the Dark One. We believed that Johnis was that child, but after today's stunt I'm having serious doubts."

"No need for doubts, Thomas," a voice said from the woods. Rachelle stepped out, red tunic flowing around her calves.

Silvie watched her walk gracefully across the grass, eyes fixed on

Johnis, who still didn't budge. This woman, whom many claimed was responsible for Thomas's fighting skills, had been the stuff of legend to Silvie. Watching the woman now, Silvie couldn't suppress a tinge of jealousy.

"He may not be perfect," Rachelle said. "He may be a fool at times, but he's chosen."

"What makes you so sure?" Billos asked. "I've never heard of this prophecy."

"Only a handful of people ever knew of the prophecy," she said. "We couldn't afford exposing the identity of this child before he was ready. We ourselves didn't know who it was until a week ago. Too much danger for the child."

"He's undoubtedly still not ready," Thomas said.

"He's marked. He stepped forward. He saved us from the Horde. He's ready." Rachelle's tone was sweet but final.

"Speak, lad. Tell us what got into that mind of yours!"

Johnis still didn't blink, much less lift his eyes and give the supreme commander an answer. Silvie's heart broke for him.

"Tell him, Johnis," Rachelle said. "Tell him how such a purebred idealist thinks and feels. How the thought of your mother's harm makes your heart fracture into a hundred pieces. How you would cross the desert to defeat the Horde and cross ten deserts to find your mother."

Slowly Johnis looked up from the ground. Silvie watched tears well around his soft brown eyes, then slip down his cheeks.

His face didn't show any emotion, only his eyes, spilling tears as he stared at Rachelle. Silvie desperately wanted to reach out and put her hand on his shoulder, to give even the smallest gesture of comfort. But she couldn't. Not in front of these others.

Instead, Rachelle walked up to him and touched his cheek tenderly, and Silvie thought he was accepting her comfort, although he showed no sign of doing so. As absurd as it seemed to Silvie, she felt a pang of regret that she hadn't been the one to comfort him.

"You can never live down these lives on your head today," Rachelle said, lowering her hand. "Don't try to. Accept blame where blame is due, but don't let this thing distract you from what you are meant to do."

Johnis swallowed. "And what is that?" he breathed.

"Only you know."

"As long as it's not marching my men into madness!" Thomas said. "I know how an idealist thinks, and I know that most men on the battlefield die for misguided idealists. You've put me in a very difficult position."

Johnis looked at him and started to say something, but nothing came out.

"Tell us what happened in the desert this last week," Thomas demanded.

There it was, the question Silvie knew this would lead to. But they were sworn to secrecy about their mission and the desert they'd crossed to fulfill it.

The leafy canopy above suddenly rustled with the sound of

what could only be a dozen birds simultaneously taking flight. Silvie glanced up. A black Shataiki bat, four feet in length, flew directly over them, screeching wickedly in frantic flight, chased hard by a white Roush ten feet behind.

Billos and Darsal both jerked their eyes to the sky and followed the flight. The sight of the black beast flooded Silvie with ice-cold alarm. No person could grow used to those leathery wings, the mangy body and wolflike jaws, fangs dripping with saliva. Those talons that had, only days earlier, touched her own cheeks. Those red, pupil-less eyes.

Thomas looked up, searched the sky. "What is it?"

But of course, he could see neither Shataiki nor Roush.

"Johnis told you what happened in the desert," Silvie said. "We were taken captive. Beyond that none of us can speak; it is still too raw. You can't force us to tell you what horrors the beasts forced us to endure. We fought our way out and left the whole place burning. That's enough."

"That's not good enough," Thomas said. "Anything we can know about the Horde is to our advantage."

"Not now," Silvie said. "Please, sir. It's too fresh. And Johnis is our concern now."

"Let it go, Thomas," Rachelle said. "There is more going on here than any of us could piece together anyway." She looked Johnis in the eyes again. "Isn't that true, Johnis?"

"Yes," he whispered. Then to Thomas, "I'm sorry, sir. It won't happen again. Ever."

His tone was so remorseful that Silvie thought he meant it couldn't happen again because he planned to end it all here and now.

"I need to be alone," he said.

"What do you expect me to tell the Guard?" Thomas asked. "That I've decided to leave you alone without any repercussions because you are *sorry*? You've put me in an impossible situation!"

"Then strip me of my rank," Johnis said.

Rachelle faced her husband. "You know we can't do—"

"*I'll* decide here! This is *my* army, not yours!" He breathed hard for three long pulls of air. "I won't strip you of rank, but I expect you to give a full accounting to the Council by day's end. Pass their tests and I might let you be, but I wouldn't expect to do it with those puppy eyes."

Rachelle tsked and rolled her eyes. "Please, Thomas, quit being such a man! This isn't a battle, for Elyon's sake!"

"The rest of you stay nearby. No more heroics until we get this settled!" Thomas spun around, stormed to his horse, swung into the saddle, and disappeared into the trees.

"He's right, there will have to be an accounting," Rachelle said. "But don't lose heart. None of you." Then she, too, left, gliding more than walking into the forest, where her horse presumably waited.

"Now you've gone and done it," Billos said. "We're on a mission to find the books, not this."

"Unless you have some enlightened plan to find the books,

keep your hole shut," Silvie snapped, surprising even herself with her anger.

Darsal stepped up. "Easy, Silvie. I know you've been through a tough night—"

"Tough? We came within a bat's hide of having our heads taken from our bodies!"

"You satisfied your lust for killing a few beasts, didn't you?"

"I saw more death than I care to remember."

"Thanks to your—"

"Quiet!" Johnis yelled, standing. "Leave me! All of you."

"Please, Billos, you should use some tact," Darsal chided. "This is a fine start to our vow to find the books. Fine, Johnis, we'll give you space, but if the bat we just saw wasn't reminder enough, the books are our priority."

"Speaking of which, where are the books?" Billos asked.

"Safe," Johnis said. "Now, please—"

"Safe where?"

"He said, safe," Silvie said.

Billos eyed her and backed off. "We should use them to find the other black forests. As soon as this blows over."

*Strange to hear Billos so concerned with resuming the mission for the books,* Silvie thought. Johnis might have been justified in wanting to hide the books from him.

Darsal walked up to Johnis and offered him a supportive grin. "If it helps, you have my sympathies. I know your heart is gold, Johnis. And I admire your love for your mother."

"Me too," Billos said. "We'll leave you. But collect your thoughts, Scrapper. This isn't over."

They left Silvie and Johnis alone together.

"You too, Silvie," Johnis said.

She felt a dagger in her chest. "Johnis . . ."

He looked at her with sad eyes. "I owe you my life, Silvie. And I will pay up, I promise. But my head's falling apart here. I have to figure out what happened."

"We know what happened." She walked up to him and lifted his hand. "You're a lover, not a fighter, that's what happened. Although once you got the hang of it, you swung that sword pretty well."

Her attempt to lighten the mood failed.

She let her grin soften and continued. "Stick to loving and you'll be fine." She kissed the back of his hand.

Then against her better judgment, she left him standing alone in the clearing, knowing she could not leave him again. Not now, not ever.

# TEN

Johnis lay on the rock and wept.

He wept for the fighters who'd died. He wept for Thomas, whom he'd betrayed. He wept for Silvie, who had stood by his side when she knew better. He wept for his sister, Kiella, and his father, Ramos, who still didn't know the truth about Rosa.

And he wept for his mother.

But none of his weeping brought relief. Only more weeping. If the Roush depended on him to find the books, then all was hopeless, because his mind and heart were lost on his mother. Rachelle was right; his heart was fractured, and try as he might, he couldn't mend it.

The hours slipped by, and sleep finally gave him the relief he desperately needed. When he opened his eyes next, the sky was already darkening. Had it all been a dream?

"You planning on sleeping forever?" a voice to his right said.

He jerked his head, surprised. A large boy leaned against a tree, arms crossed. It was Jackov, the seventeen-year-old fighter whose nose he'd broken just last week in a most improbable fight that had given him the position he now held as an officer in the Guard.

Jackov tried to grin, but his blackened nose discouraged muscle movement. He lowered his arms and walked up to the rock. "I heard what happened."

Memories of his fateful attack on the Horde raged back, and Johnis closed his eyes. Not a dream. "What did you hear?"

"That you led five hundred Guard into a trap set by the Horde. That you've betrayed the forests. That if you show your face in the village, a thousand Guard will string you up by your ankles and lower you into water."

He faced the stronger fighter, wondering if all of what he said was true. Undoubtedly. Except for the method by which the Guard would execute him—drowning was the Horde way, not the forests'.

"You're in a predicament," Jackov said.

"I am."

"What will you do?"

Johnis looked around the clearing and saw that no one else was nearby. Pity. He'd hoped Silvie would come back for him.

"I was there, you know," Jackov said.

"Where?"

"In the desert, with the Third Fighting Group."

"You were? I didn't know you'd been assigned to the Third."

"I wasn't. Thomas had the new recruits preparing fires for the Horde. He didn't want us in battle so soon, so he came up with the crazy notion of filling trenches full of resin to light in case the Horde attacked. I was put in charge of a hundred worker bees." Jackov sneered. "Imagine that, from the best of the new recruits to a taskmaster. On account of one squat who threw one lucky blow."

"I'm sorry," Johnis said, knowing Jackov spoke of him. "You're right, it was lucky, and if I could take it back, I would. I didn't have this in mind. How did you end up in the desert with us?"

Jackov shrugged. "I saw you leave the forest and slipped into the group when they entered the desert."

"Then I'm glad you made it out." Johnis slipped from the rock and brushed dirt from his seat.

"I heard some things," Jackov said.

"The whole world is hearing things these days."

"About a woman," the large lad said.

Johnis eyed him. "What woman?"

"A woman they took from the forests when she was collecting the Catalina cacti for her sick boy. Now *she's* sick. A Scab who looks like a baboon for all the rotting—"

Johnis dove at the boy, knocked him backward to the ground, and straddled his chest with a raised fist before he fully realized what he was doing. He'd exploded at the mention of his mother's demise—he was hardly acting like a good candidate for leadership among the Guard. An impulsive hothead, more like it.

He paused, and that slight hesitation cost him the advantage. Jackov jerked his knee up into the small of Johnis's back, then twisted to one side.

What happened next couldn't be easily explained by Johnis, who'd never trained in the art of close-in fighting as Jackov had. All he knew was that the fighter proved why he, not Johnis, deserved to fight for the Guard. Jackov swung one leg high over their heads and spun on one shoulder so that his heels lined up with Johnis's head.

His boot crashed into Johnis's temple. The tables were so quickly reversed that Johnis forgot to defend himself.

Then Jackov was over him, with one knee in his throat and a knife in his hand.

"Is this what you want, squat? Don't think for a moment that your stunt in the stadium was anything more than a fluke. I could cut your tongue out now and be rewarded for—"

A body flew in from behind them, parallel to the ground, and crashed into Jackov's shoulder. The stronger lad was taken out like an apple being swatted off a stick by the broad side of a sword. As the attacker streaked over Johnis, he saw who'd saved him: Silvie.

Shorter than Jackov by a full head but as fast as a fireball, she had him flailing and landing hard on his buttocks before he knew what hit him. Then it was her knee in his throat and a knife in her hand.

They both knew how skilled she was with those knives. Jackov threw up both hands. "Easy! Get off me, for Elyon's sake, back off!"

"You tangle with him, you tangle with me," she snapped.

"He tangled with *me*!" Jackov hissed.

"And so would I if you insulted my mother," Silvie said.

"Fine, just back off. You'll want to hear what I have to say."

Johnis rolled to his feet and rubbed a lump on his left temple. "Let him up, Silvie."

"I don't trust him."

"I'm not asking you to trust him. Just let him up."

She did so, backing away slowly, knife still in hand. Jackov got his feet under his body and pushed himself up. "You're both loose in the head," he said.

"What is it that you think I should hear?" Johnis asked.

Jackov took a deep breath. "Your mother isn't with the Horde army."

"How do you know?" Johnis exchanged a glance with Silvie.

"I told you, I overheard one of them," Jackov said.

"The Scabs were fighting, not talking," Johnis said.

"You think I let myself get caught in the middle of that blood-bath? I trailed and dipped into a valley when they came up behind you. I heard them then."

A soldier who would duck a fight might be a coward, but in retrospect Jackov's actions could be seen as wise rather than cowardly.

"Where is she, then?" Silvie demanded.

Jackov circled them and leaned on the rock, lips twisted in a grin. "In the Horde city."

"The city . . . There's more than one city."

"There's only one large city. Three days' ride southwest."

"How do you know that?" Johnis asked.

"Everyone knows that," Jackov said. "But they said as much. Follow the course they were on and you'd come close. But it's hidden."

Johnis wasn't sure what to make of this admission. Jackov seemed sincere enough, but he also had confused motives. What if he was simply out to ruin Johnis for the trouble he'd caused him?

"You don't believe me?"

"Should I?" Johnis asked.

"He's right about the city," Silvie said.

Johnis frowned, his eyes holding Jackov, who looked more like a snake than the bearer of truth at the moment. "But should we believe him about overhearing the Horde?"

"Your mother's ring should convince you," Jackov said.

Only Billos, Darsal, and Silvie knew about the ring. So then Jackov was telling the truth—he must've heard about the ring from the Horde. Unless Billos had joined him in a plot to undermine Johnis, something he couldn't accept. Billos might be testy, even rude, but he wasn't a traitor.

"Who told you . . . ?"

"I told you, I *heard* them! How many times do you want me to repeat myself?"

"And what else did you overhear?"

Jackov looked toward the west, eyes lost in thought.

"Tell me!"

"She's a slave for someone they call the Dark Priest."

"You're lying!"

"I can show you how to find her."

And with those words, Johnis knew that he was going out into the desert again. He wouldn't show his face in the village or make any further explanation to the Council. Not until he knew the truth about his mother, and looking at Jackov now, he knew that the truth awaited him in the desert.

"Why would you risk your neck for my mother?" Johnis asked.

"To redeem myself," Jackov said. "To show the forests that I can lead men too."

The boy's logic made sense, in a desperate sort of way. If Jackov led the very fighter who'd taken his place as most favored young recruit on a successful rescue mission, the forests might reconsider his heroism. Good for Jackov.

And if they did find his mother . . . Johnis felt his hope swell.

There was also the matter of the missing books—now either in his saddlebag on the route they would take or in the possession of the Horde.

Johnis suddenly felt desperate to be gone, into the desert, to the Horde city. He ran for his horse, still tied to a tree at the clearing's edge.

"Where are you going?" Jackov asked. "Is this a yes?"

"Yes, Johnis, where are you going?" Silvie demanded. "You can't seriously think you're going with him."

He spun back. "You don't trust me?"

"Should I?" she asked.

It wasn't the first time these last two days she'd asked the question. The last time he'd answered immediately: yes. Now a beat passed before he responded.

"No. No, you shouldn't come with us. But you should also realize that I have no choice."

"Of course you do! He's doing this for his honor, not yours."

Jackov stepped up. "Would I do it if I wasn't certain? The desert's a dangerous place."

"And how do you know where she's being held?" Silvie demanded. "So you take us to this Horde city, which only leads us into a trap!"

The fact that she'd included herself wasn't lost on Johnis. A pang of guilt rode his spine. She, like he, surely knew there was more to this whole business than what Thomas or the Guard could possibly know. He was playing the fool, but in the absence of a better way, he would follow his heart—the stakes were much higher than any of them knew.

This was about more than his mother. It was about the forests' survival. He deserved the severest punishment. Or was it a hero's welcome yet? Silvie seemed to know even more than he did. Why else would she stay by him after how he'd treated her?

"Then don't take me up on it!" he challenged. "But she is

there, and she is alive, and she is a Scab. And I will take you at least that far; that's what I'm offering. Nothing more."

"Silvie . . ." Johnis covered the ground between them quickly and took her by the arm, turning her away from Jackov. He whispered so that the thug couldn't hear. "It's the books, Silvie. We have to go after the books!"

"This isn't about the books. It's about your mother."

"No, it's about both. Do I have a choice?"

*She liked it when I moved close to her*, he thought. So he pressed even closer, shielding her from Jackov. "If I go to the Council now, they'll have my head. Will that serve our mission to find the books? You know it won't!"

"This is crazy, Johnis! We just had our backsides handed to us!"

"Then they won't be expecting us. I have to do this."

For a long moment she considered their options, staring back at Jackov, then into Johnis's eyes. "Billos and Darsal?"

"No, we can't involve them."

She nodded slowly. "I still don't trust him."

"The books, Silvie! We took a vow!"

"And you're using that vow for something else."

"Can I help it that my mother is with them? Am I a fool?"

Her eyes searched his, and for a brief moment he thought about kissing her, but he knew that his motivation was mixed, so he let the moment pass.

"You are a fool," she said. "The kind I might die for. If we go, we do everything by agreement."

"Of course."

"We don't go off thoughtlessly. We stay cautious and move like snakes. No bulldogs."

"Do I look like a bulldog?"

"No, but he does." Silvie glanced back at Jackov.

"I'll let you put a muzzle on him if you want," Johnis said. "We'll have to take supplies and water. Enough to last a week."

"It's not the water I worry about."

"Then what?"

"It's you," she said. "I worry for your sanity."

# ELEVEN

The first day out of Middle Forest crawled by with all the speed of a snail, as any day filled with such raw nerves would pass.

They'd spent half the night laying plans and pulling together supplies, a task left mostly to Jackov because Johnis was certain that if he or Silvie were seen pulling water from the lake or loading up six horses or sorting through weapons at the armory, an alarm would be raised. But Jackov managed with surprising ease.

The plan was quite simple, Silvie thought. Six horses, three burdened with enough water and food to last three warriors a week in the desert. They would ride stallions, pale to blend with the desert and fast in the event they were forced to make a run for it. The route would run along the same course they'd taken after the Horde the previous night, then two more days deep into the southwest. If any Scabs presented themselves, they would take the freshest horses and run, which meant that they had to keep the animals watered at all times. Horde horses, like the Horde themselves, were far slower than those of the Forest Guard and would never stand a chance in a pursuit.

In the desert, speed was their greatest friend.

Jackov explained how he'd lain half-covered with sand that night, listening to three men discuss Johnis's mother, who was in the main city, Thrall, slaving for the Dark Priest, as they called their holy man. Jackov knew where this city was because the Scabs scoffed at the notion that anyone would go to such lengths to find his mother. They'd joked that such a fool would probably search until he found the city itself, hidden behind the large Kugie dunes to the southwest, two days' march from where they'd fought the night battle.

And what was Jackov's plan once they found this hidden Horde city named Thrall? Simple: find the Dark Priest; find the mother. They would have to dress as Horde, of course.

Silvie quit protesting the lack of a more detailed plan soon enough. Until they saw what they were dealing with, they could hardly plan with any confidence, Jackov insisted.

In the late afternoon they came upon the battlefield where 137 of the Third Fighting Group had been slaughtered.

Silvie raised her hand as she rode up the dune just north of the battle scene. The sun was hot, despite the wind. A single dead Scab lay half-buried by sand on the crest, just ahead. His black battle dress flapped lazily in a stiff breeze. A vulture hidden by the folds of the tunic squawked noisily into flight, beating wide wings.

"You sure you're up for this?" Silvie asked. "We should go around."

"We have to look for the saddlebags," Johnis said, but she could hear the dread in his voice.

They crested the dune, and the valley beyond came into view. Silvie stopped, stunned by the sight below them. The valley was perhaps seventy-five paces across at the bottom, filled now with hundreds of black-clad bodies. Fallen Guard speckled the field in brown leather armor.

Not until then did she see the other black beasts feeding on the dead bodies. At first she thought they were vultures, but then she saw their faces, and chills of terror washed through her chest.

"Shataiki!" Johnis whispered.

As one, hundreds of large black Shataiki bats swiveled their long snouts and red eyes toward them. The valley froze for a moment, and then the Shataiki bats sprang into the air, screeching shrilly.

The horses snorted, rearing back, and it was all Silvie could do to keep her mount from bolting. The Shataiki winged down the valley and swept toward the south. *To some undiscovered Black Forest.*

"Take it easy!" Jackov snapped. "You're spooking the horses. Haven't you seen vultures?"

Of course, he saw only the vultures, not the Shataiki bats.

"They're feeding on Guard!" Johnis bit off angrily. "Have some heart."

*The Roush have stayed conveniently out of sight,* Silvie thought. Michal had said they were on their own, but she'd half expected at least Gabil to make an appearance. Not a whisper, though. And if they'd consulted with the Roush before this expedition of theirs, the furry white bats would have undoubtedly warned them off.

Johnis led them down the valley, over the badly eaten bodies, and up the slope to the place where he and Silvie had fought off the Horde.

No sign of the saddlebags.

Traces of the Horde camp lay on the flats beyond the dunes, but the desert had already reclaimed most of what the Scab army had left. An odd tent stake here, some butchered goat carcasses in a pile over there, and a dozen large water barrels they'd left for some reason. The water stank like sewage.

They passed in silence and said nothing for the next hour.

The second day proved to them why so few Forest Dwellers ever ventured into the desert, and none so deep. The heat was unbearable, and the horses consumed more water than expected. Still, they had enough for the trip, Johnis insisted. As long as they didn't spend more than a day at the Horde city.

No pursuit followed them from the forests.

"Do you think they'll forgive me, Silvie?" Johnis asked soberly.

"For the slaughter or for this?" she asked.

"For the Third Group's loss." He still wasn't calling it a slaughter.

"You're forgetting that I followed you willingly that night. They'll need to forgive both of us."

"And will they?"

"Like you say, it depends on what happens next. Thomas isn't the kind who can be betrayed more than once."

"We left of our own accord, willingly, endangering no one's life," Jackov said on Johnis's right. "How's that a betrayal?"

"He's right. If we succeed here, then it will help."

Johnis stared into the horizon, where they could just see the line of huge dunes Jackov had promised. "Then we have to succeed," he said. "There's too much at stake to let one mistake, however terrible, undermine our mission."

"Keep things in perspective." Jackov said. "This is about each of us getting what we need, not the end of the world."

Jackov knew nothing about the missing Books of History. Still, the way he made his announcement struck Silvie as shallow and bothersome. She could see now why Thomas had passed him over.

They reached the dunes as the sun disappeared behind them. Now the tension returned, like a knife along their nerves. The Horde lived beyond these dunes—there was no mistaking the worn grooves in the sand from the army's recent passing.

"We sleep here tonight," Silvie said.

"We press on!" Johnis protested.

"No, we sleep. You've barely slept in a week. I'm not willing to barge in with our minds half-gone from exhaustion. Like snakes, not bulldogs, right?"

"But the sun—"

"We can bear the sun. We can't bear lack of sleep!"

"Fine. But I'm not the least bit tired."

Johnis was the first to snore fifteen minutes later. Silvie lay next to him and took his hand in hers. There was no telling what awaited them with the rising sun, but she was increasingly sure of one thing: wherever Johnis went, she would go. They were meant for each other, in more ways than one. The journey would lead them to some kind of bliss.

It was her new duty to keep him alive long enough to enjoy that bliss.

"MISSING?" THOMAS SNORTED. "AGAIN?"

"Well, no one's seen either of them for two days," Billos said. "I think that qualifies."

*And what's worse, the books are missing with them,* Billos thought. With each passing hour his realization that the quest for the ancient books was indeed not only a worthy pursuit, but one that demanded his complete devotion, grew. A week ago he'd scoffed at the idea; now he was desperate for it, for that power he'd felt but once when touching the book.

"He's hiding, then," Thomas said.

Darsal nodded. "Could be, but if so, they're hiding pretty well. The last they were seen was at your scolding."

"I wouldn't put it past him to hide for a week," Thomas said. "Are they in love?"

Love? Johnis and Silvie? Billos had never considered the possibility.

"Could be," Darsal said. "They are fond of each other, that's obvious."

"And what about you two?" Thomas asked, matter-of-factly.

Darsal looked away and blushed.

Neither could deny that there was an unspoken connection between them. This strange bonding that had evolved since he'd rescued her from certain death nine years earlier. Was it love? Maybe not, but looking at the side of Darsal's flushed face now, Billos guessed the bond between them was something as strong as love. Perhaps stronger, if that was possible. But what did he know of love?

"Not that I'm aware of," Billos said, facing Thomas. "At least not love, as in we're-to-be-married love."

Thomas studied him, perhaps wondering why Billos might try to hide the truth. It was that obvious, wasn't it?

"Keep it that way if you can," Thomas said. "I need officers who have their wits and priorities on the mission, not on each other. Follow?"

Yes sir," Billos said. He ignored a silent glance from Darsal and changed the subject. "What about Johnis and Silvie?" he asked.

"Give them time to heal, lad. You two put your minds to the squads we're forming. I want the lists of your twenty best by this afternoon. The next time we meet the Horde, I'll need these young recruits doing more than filling trenches with resin and hiding in the bushes."

Billos left feeling more anxious than he'd been when he'd approached the supreme commander. "Something's up, Darsal. I can smell it like a hint of smoke."

"You're right." She steamed, refusing to look at him. "Amazing you even notice."

"Why didn't they come for us?"

"Because some things are best done alone, Billos. There's more than war and lost books to think about. But you're too thick-headed to know anything about that, aren't you?"

"Don't be silly," he said.

Darsal strode on, jaw clenched. And Billos knew then that Darsal really was in love with him.

# TWELVE

The Horde city. *Thrall.*

Johnis stared through one of three gourds with ground-glass lenses that Jackov had taken from the armory. On the tall dune next to him, Silvie and Jackov lay on their bellies, breathing heavily and staring at the sprawling city through the other two.

For as far as the telescope could see, baked mud mixed with straw formed square buildings topped with canvas roofs. He'd heard the other Horde cities described, but none of his imaginations matched what he saw now. It was said that Qurong, the leader of the Horde, lived in all of the cities, but looking at the vast spread of structures below, Johnis knew this had to be his primary dwelling place. Maybe this was where all the Scabs lived—the rest of the cities being nothing more than way stations leading here.

"I thought they lived in tents," Silvie said breathily. "These . . . It all looks so permanent."

"The Horde is here to stay," Johnis said.

"This won't work, Johnis. It's massive! We'll never find her."

His own sentiments were as hopeless. They were three Forest Dwellers crouched at the top of a sand dune far from home, gazing into an endless spread of houses that stood between them and the taller structures at the center of the city. They were aliens in a foreign land that resembled nothing even remotely similar to what they knew.

A large gate with two square mortar towers marked the entrance to Thrall, but no barriers prevented coming or going from any other direction. Clearly, the Horde didn't expect an attack. And no wonder; the Forest Guard wouldn't stand a chance against such a massive enemy.

The roads that cut through the city ran crooked, jagging in haphazardly toward the center, like fractured spokes making a feeble attempt at finding their way to the hub. A large palace that looked to be a half day's walk away rose next to a dozen other larger buildings.

His mother was there, slaving for the Dark Priest.

"There are more people here than in all the forests combined," Silvie said. "Ten times more."

Jackov had remained quiet, but Johnis demanded he speak now. "So what do you suggest we do now? You said you could get us to my mother."

"I said I could get you here, not inside. We have to find some-one to help us."

"Please!" Silvie cried. "Why would anyone help us?"

"Because we can be persuasive. All we need is the right cloth-ing, and we can work our way inside."

"Easily said. You suggest we just kidnap the first Scab that hap-pens by and tell them we wish to convert to Horde? 'Give us some clothes and take us to your priest?'"

"That's one way."

Horses drew carts of straw and barrels down the roads. The Scabs ate desert wheat, Johnis knew that much. And they drank mostly wine made from the wheat. The barrels likely held either water, wine, or grain.

"We need to get closer," he said. "Jackov is right; we need the right clothing. Maybe then we can take over one of those carts and slip past the main gate."

"The main gate? Why not from the side?"

Johnis slid back and walked toward their horses in the valley behind. "Because the carts are faster and natural. And the barrels could provide a way in."

It took them half an hour to work their way to a large out-cropping of rock just outside the outskirts that Jackov insisted they use for cover. From here they could smell the awful sulfuric stench of a million Scabs. The city was nothing more than an open sewer.

They tied the horses off, shoved enough hay under their

muzzles to keep them fed, and climbed one of the rocks for a better view.

Streams of tan-clad merchants angled their carts through the gates several hundred paces off, perhaps back from the desert wheat fields Johnis had heard about. From here they could still mount the horses and flee the city faster than any ambush could take them. Once they stepped into the city, however, an escape wouldn't be so easy.

"We wait for dark, Johnis," Silvie said.

"Maybe."

"Not maybe, not bulldog. Snakes, remember. We slip in and slip out."

"At night the streets will be deserted," Jackov said. "I say the more people on the streets, the better."

"We don't have the clothing! Even if we did, they'd see our smooth hands and feet. And we smell to them, right? They'll smell us coming, even at night."

"What do you suggest?" Johnis asked. "Caking our faces with mud and rolling in horse droppings?"

She looked at him, and he knew immediately he'd struck upon something.

A giggle drifted on the air from their left. Johnis froze. He and Silvie jerked their heads and saw that Jackov already had his lens out, searching the nearby dunes against which the city butted.

Four Horde suddenly ran across the sand directly in front of them, three chasing one.

Children.

The sight of young sapling Scabs was so startling that Silvie actually gasped. And when the girl being chased pulled up at the sound, Jackov and Johnis forgot to duck. For a dreadful moment, their eyes locked. Hers were small and gray, and he knew that she was a girl by her brushed hair, which was completely different from the dreadlocks worn by the other three children.

All four stared up at the rocks, silenced by what must have been a very strange sight to them: three tanned humans with smooth skin peering over the rocks, an unlikely sight for four Scabs with scaly white skin.

The three boys turned and scrambled across the sand toward the city. "Run! Shataiki! Run!"

But the girl did not run. She stared at them with large, puppy eyes, hands by her sides, one holding a straw doll. Johnis wasn't sure whether to think of her as a beast or a human.

Her tunic hung straight down to sandaled feet, the thongs of which were softened with some kind of cloth so they wouldn't bite into the diseased skin between her toes.

"Hello," she said.

Johnis ducked down, confused by the utter humanity this child seemed to possess. She couldn't be a day over ten years of age. Her voice was soft and sweet, like a delicate chime.

Hello, she'd said.

"Hello," Jackov said.

Johnis tried to hush him with a *shhh,* but he knew it made no sense. It wasn't as if they could pretend not to have been discovered.

"What's your name?" Jackov asked.

"Karas," the girl said. "What's your name?"

"Jackov."

"What are you doing up there?"

Johnis lifted his head up and looked down on the girl. His anxiety eased, replaced by the mystery that this odd encounter brought.

"We're looking for someone to help us," Jackov said. The boys were already out of sight. With any luck their cries of seeing Shataiki would be met by dismissals.

"I can help you," the little girl named Karas said.

Her offer caught them flat-footed.

"You're not frightened by us?" Silvie asked.

"Yes." But she didn't run.

Jackov dropped to the sand and walked around the rock toward the girl, who seemed rooted to the desert floor. Johnis and Silvie followed quickly, stepping out into the open ten feet from her. *The road leading into the city is still far enough away to avoid any scrutiny,* Johnis thought, *but we can't risk even a casual glance that might raise an alarm.*

He backed behind one of the boulders. "Can you step over here?"

"Why?"

"Why? Because we don't want to be seen."

"Why?"

He exchanged a glance with Silvie, who rescued him. "Because we're afraid they won't like us. You can see we're . . . our skin has problems. Do we smell?"

"Yes."

"Well, that's why. We won't hurt you; we just need some help. Promise."

Karas appeared to consider Silvie's promise, then walked toward them. She looked at the road and stopped when the rock blocked a direct view.

"Are all girls like you so brave?" Silvie asked, offering a smile.

"No. Are you going to fix your skin?"

"Yes," Johnis said. "That's what we need help with. We need to get to the Dark Priest's home. Or maybe to the temple so we can find help. But we're afraid that if people see us like this, they'd throw us out. No one can know we have this . . . this problem."

"You mean 'disease,'" she said. "I may be small, but I'm not that stupid. You're Forest Dwellers, and you have the skin disease. You want to fix your disease? Then you should stay away from the water. Everyone knows that the forest water can kill you."

Johnis blinked. She reminded him so much of his sister, Kiella, in her manner of speaking that for a moment he wondered if he was dreaming and this was Kiella, but with the skin disease.

He'd been part-Horde once, so he knew how confusing the transition was. But watching this young, articulate girl, he knew that the Guard's assumption that Scabs were less intelligent because

379

of the disease was wrong. It affected their perception of moral truth, perhaps, but not their intellect.

"Will you take us to the priest?" Jackov asked.

"Yes, I can."

Silvie shot Jackov a questioning look. "No, wait, that's not what we want. What he means is, can you get us clothes so that we can sneak in without the whole city throwing mud at us?"

"I can, but if you want to see my father, I can take you. Is that what you want?"

"Your father?"

"The priest. He's the one you need to see, right?"

Johnis felt his pulse surge. "Your *father* is the Dark Priest?"

"Of course."

She said it so matter-of-factly that Johnis wondered if she understood their meaning. "You mean the priest who leads the— you know, the religion of the Horde."

"The priest who insists we all worship Teeleh, the brass snake, yes . . . that priest. The only priest."

"You only have one priest for the whole city, then?"

"One priest," she said. "If you want, I can take you now."

This girl might know his mother, Johnis realized. They had struck a gold mine. But if they didn't proceed with caution, that very mine could collapse around them.

"Yes, that would be good," Jackov said. "Take us directly to your father."

"Are you mad?" Silvie blurted. Then, for the girl's benefit: "I can't be seen like this. We have to have head coverings—robes that make us look at least somewhat normal."

"What about your mother?" Johnis asked. "Is she also a priest?"

"I don't have a mother. She was killed when I was a little girl. The servant takes care of me now."

"What servant?"

Karas studied him with her big gray eyes. "Why do you ask so many questions?"

"I just want to know, so I don't make a fool of myself in the city."

"I think you're lying," she said. "I think you have some trick up your sleeve."

"Don't be absurd! Look at me." He lifted his arm for her to see. "I'm diseased, what do you expect from me? Of course I'm nervous; we all are. What do you expect? For all we know, you're the one playing the trick."

He noticed now that her skin was covered in a white powdery substance that seemed to put off a flowery odor. He'd never heard that the Horde tried to disguise the cracking of their skin.

"Really? Do I look like the kind of little girl who would play a trick on you?"

He thought about that and answered together with Silvie. "No."

"Then believe me when I say can get you in without a commotion. Of course, I'll get you clothing, I'm not crazy. We'll go in on a cart, and you'll look like some peasants from the wheat farms who want to worship Teeleh."

"Perfect!" Jackov said. "We can't go wrong with that."

They had indeed stumbled on a gold mine, but the purpose of their journey wasn't to visit the priest. It was to find his mother. They couldn't follow the girl to the priest or let her know that they didn't want to meet him.

"We can't endanger you like this," Johnis said, casting a quick side-glance at Silvie. "If someone knew that you hid us, you could get into trouble. Maybe we shouldn't go straight to the priest. What about his servant? Maybe she could help us?"

"No one's supposed to see her," she said. "She's being punished now."

"She is?" It had to be his mother! "How . . ."

Johnis felt urgency storm up inside him, but Silvie squeezed his arm and addressed the girl before he could condemn them by blurting something incriminating.

"If you could just get us the clothing, I think we could manage. We would be so thankful for just that."

The little girl kept her eyes on Johnis. "What do you care about the servant? She'll likely be killed, you know. My father is a very powerful man who can squash those who cross the ways of Teeleh." Her voice trembled slightly.

Again Silvie pressed her fingers into Johnis's arm to keep him silent. He felt his face flush. They didn't have time to wait!

"You say that like you've been squashed a few times yourself,"

Silvie said, and by the girl's sudden stillness, Johnis knew immediately that a chord had been struck.

For a long time none of them moved.

"You've done well," Jackov said. "Bring us robes and tell us how to get to the temple, and we'll be fine. But you can't breathe a word. Can you do that for us?"

"Of course."

Without another word the girl turned on her heels, ran with a flapping of her sandals around the boulder, and was gone.

Their fate was now in the hands of a nine-year-old Horde girl who would undoubtedly be severely punished for helping them if caught. Johnis had no sense of her loyalty to the Dark Priest, but he hoped that if she suspected any foul play on their part, she would be smart enough to betray them, if only to protect herself.

But, as promised, Karas returned half an hour later, hauling three large, tan robes and a bowl of some white paste she called morst. If they covered their skin with it, they might pass as Horde.

Twenty minutes later, having donned the robes and spread the morst on their exposed flesh, Johnis, Silvie, and Jackov followed little Karas into the Horde city.

# THIRTEEN

Johnis walked through the main gate beside the little girl, sure that all eyes were on him. He kept his stare low, on the rear wheel of a cart they'd fallen in behind. Jackov and Silvie followed, silent and undoubtedly as nervous. If he wasn't careful, his sweat would wash off the morst paste and show his true colors.

In more ways than one, this was worse than the Black Forest. For starters, they weren't following the orders of the Roush. They had nothing like the books to strike fear in the enemy. They had no leverage, no plan, no power, no advantage of any kind. Even their secrecy was subject to the whim of this girl who led them.

He felt a hand take his and squeeze. Karas was looking up at him with her round eyes. "Be brave," she said quietly. "You're only doing what you have to, like the rest of us."

What did she mean by that?

"I like you, Johnis. I'm sorry about all of this."

She knew his name? Heat flashed through his face. Could it be a trap? Not if he was reading her right, but, until this point, they'd had an escape route. Now they were at the city's mercy.

"Some of these carts go straight to the Thrall temple, where my father lives. Be careful; he can be wicked. His servant, the woman, is in the cell below the serpent's chamber. I won't come with you because you either don't trust me or you want to protect me; I don't know which. But if you ride the cart, you'll reach the temple—some call it the Thrall—in less than an hour."

Why was she telling him about the woman? Did she know they'd come for Rosa? And if she did, was she sending them to their deaths? Johnis didn't know how to respond to this barrage of admissions on the girl's part.

Karas continued. "You can't miss the temple. It's the pointed building with a serpent on the roof. My house is the one with red mortar next to it. It's the most beautiful house in the city, according to my father." She released his hand after another squeeze, then hurried forward.

"You there!" Karas called.

The driver of a cart loaded with four large barrels looked lazily back.

"Take these peasants to the Thrall for worship." She patted the cart's flat planks.

This young girl wasn't like any he had ever met! Certainly

nothing like any Scab he could have imagined. He'd never seriously considered the idea of Horde children—had hardly been aware they existed, much less considered them human. Karas was unquestionably as human as any forest child.

He nodded at Silvie, and they hoisted themselves up next to Jackov, who'd gone oddly silent. Quiet since they'd found the Horde city. Perhaps he was second-guessing this plan of his after all.

Karas spoke to the driver again. "And don't speak to them, because they've been set aside for punishment." She looked up at Johnis and winked. "That's so he'll leave you alone," she whispered.

"How do you know my name?" he asked.

"Because you told me," she said.

Had he? He couldn't remember.

"I'm sorry," she said. "Maybe we can make it up to each other."

The cart lurched forward. They rolled deeper into the city.

"What did she mean?" Silvie whispered. "Did you tell her your name?"

"Of course he did," Jackov said.

"I guess I did. Keep it down."

They sat like the three peasants they were meant to be, legs dangling off the end of the cart as it wobbled forward on rough wheels.

The houses were rectangular with abrupt corners, but not squared by any stretch of imagination. Their architects were either sloppy or terribly inventive. The canvas roofs on most were at least partly torn at the edge, but with little or no rain in the desert, it wouldn't matter. They wanted to keep the sand and wind out, not water.

Johnis watched in fascination as children chased each other with straw swords, builders slopped mud into woven frames to form a wall, and Horde women beat the dust from rugs. Smoke rose from half the chimneys, mixing the scent of burned wheat cakes with the offensive Horde odor, which already smelled less offensive than when they had first entered the city.

"So, these are the infidels," he muttered, lost in wonder.

"Infidels?"

"It's what Ciphus sometimes calls the Horde: unbelievers."

Silvie just grunted softly.

For the first time Johnis considered what growing up Horde might be like: eating wheat cakes instead of sago cakes, drinking strained but still muddy desert water as he saw several youngsters doing from ladles. Did the Horde kiss? Did they laugh? Did they roll on the floor with their children? Did they dance?

The answer to this last question came a moment later as they passed a larger house with its door open. Thumping drums beat out a chaotic rhythm to which a boy was writhing awkwardly. It wasn't any dance that Johnis would be caught dead trying, but for all he knew he'd just seen someone celebrated for his dancing.

Johnis had been born to a mother who followed the traditions of the forests and worshipped Elyon, whom Teeleh, the god of these people, had sworn to destroy. But what if he'd been born to a Scab? Would he have raced through the huts with Karas, swinging straw swords? It was a deeply mysterious thought that left him confused as he bounced on the back of the cart.

And then the memory of his own descent into the disease flooded his mind, and he found some clarity. Their culture might be different only because of where they lived, but their worship of Teeleh and the terrible disease that gripped mind and body was death. He should know.

They passed a young child who wore no clothing, squatted on the side of the road, scratching his elbows where large sores bled. The boy lifted his eyes as the cart wobbled past, but then returned his attention to his cracking skin. He didn't cry, perhaps because he was so used to the condition that crying would do nothing for him. But he surely still felt the pain. His whole body was gray and flaking.

A strange thing happened to Johnis then. He began to feel pity for these poor souls trapped in such a pathetic state of disease. They feared water because their minds had been twisted against it. Rather than slaughtering them, the Forest Guard might be more successful if it flooded the desert with lake water, forcing them all to bathe!

Of course, that was impossible. There were only seven lakes, and the Horde despised each one. So much so that they sacrificed thousands of warriors in their attempt to destroy the forests.

But why? Why couldn't these diseased people leave the forests alone? Live and let live? The Guard never attacked the desert cities, so why should the Horde attack the forests?

"Off," the driver ordered roughly.

Johnis turned around and saw the towering steeple topped with a winged serpent. Beneath, a large square building made of mud. The Horde temple. The *Thrall,* some called it.

*Whoever designed that serpent has seen Shataiki,* Johnis thought. *Maybe Teeleh himself.*

He slipped off the cart with Silvie and Jackov and waited for the driver to pull away. Dusk had driven the majority of pedestrians from the hard-packed streets, but those who did remain glanced at them with questioning eyes.

"We have to get off the streets," Johnis said, eyeing the large temple doors. He'd been so distracted by the strange sights that he hadn't noticed how deep into the city they'd come. Besides the temple marked by the serpent, one other structure spread out, three times the size of any other.

This had to be the palace. Unlike the temple, its roof didn't rise in one large steeple but in a dozen smaller ones, like a tent on many poles. Large triangles that resembled spearheads had been dyed red and purple on the palace canvas.

The red mortar house that Karas claimed was hers sat to the right, next to a stable that presumably held the palace horses. *The Dark Priest lives in that house,* Johnis thought.

"This way," Jackov said, hurrying toward the temple doors.

"Hold up!" Silvie whispered harshly.

"Follow me." Jackov rushed down a broad path that led directly up wide steps and into the temple's wide brass doors.

"Jackov! Jackov, stop!" Silvie started after him, but stopped and spun to Johnis. "What's he thinking? We can't just walk inside!"

"No? Then what? It might be better to slip inside, see what we find, and then slip out before anyone but Karas even knows we're here."

"Sly like a snake," she reminded him yet again. "Not like a bulldog."

"And snakes are quick."

"Yes, well, so is that one." Silvie eyed the winged serpent with ruby eyes, drilling them with its red stare.

"Then let's get in and out before they lock the doors." Johnis hurried after Jackov, who was now motioning them from the door. "Think about having to find a way past the locks at night. We'd be noticed for sure."

"Not if it's done right." Silvie matched his stride, and together they rushed up the steps and past the door through which Jackov disappeared.


THE TEMPLE WAS DIMLY LIT BY A SKYLIGHT AND TWO LARGE flaming torches. The torches sat on either side of a huge, brass, winged serpent on one end of the room, identical to the one on the roof but larger. Smaller versions were mounted on the walls every ten feet. The serpents' ruby eyes glowed red in the wavering flames. Cooler here. Smelled of the morst paste Scabs used to cover their cracking skin, a musky floral scent.

Jackov stood in the middle of a large circular rug dyed purple, fixated on the large serpent. No one else was in the room. *This has to be the main worship hall,* Johnis thought, barely daring to breathe.

Two large columns rose on their left, and between them red curtains swept from ceiling to floor. He could just see the light between them. Another room.

"This way."

"Careful," Silvie whispered.

Johnis cautiously drew the drapes aside and looked into the second room. Tall bookcases lined the walls, filled with leather-bound books. It was a library. As far as he could see, vacant.

Johnis stepped in and stared at the spines. *The Stories of History.* These were similar to those he'd seen in the Black Forest! A staircase descended at the far end. His mother was at the bottom of those stairs. She had to be. He could nearly smell the gardenia perfume that usually wafted behind her as she busied herself around the house.

"I thought the Horde couldn't read," Silvie whispered. "Are these the missing books?"

"No, but they're Books of History. The Horde has them."

An obvious observation, but one that would interest Thomas and the Council. They were prohibited from telling the Council, because they'd sworn to tell no one anything they learned on their quest for the missing books. But Jackov could.

"Take one of them, Jackov," Johnis said, spinning back. He had to find out if his mother was here. "Just one so they . . ."

Jackov wasn't there.

"Where is he?"

Silvie ducked her head past the drapes and came back immediately. "Not there."

"You can read the books?" a woman's soft voice asked. Johnis jumped and jerked to his right. "Is that what you're saying?"

A woman stood from a chair hidden by the shadows in the corner and stepped toward them. Her long, flowing gown swept the floor as she walked. It was made of a silky white material, not the crude gunnysacks that passed for robes on most Horde. Her face was white with the morst paste.

"Answer me, albino," the woman said.

Albino? She knew they were Forest Dwellers! Johnis stood rooted to the floor. He thought about running before it was too late, but he knew that would only confirm guilt. He had to play along, to think with his heart, something he'd failed miserably at lately.

"Yes, I can read them," he said. "Why do you ask?"

Silvie stepped up next to him. "We're here to confess," she said.

"Confess what, that you're diseased?"

Silvie's response was rushed. "Confess our sins and offer our allegiance to Qurong, the supreme commander of the Horde."

"Of course you are," the young woman said. "But can you teach me to read these books?"

A scream cut through the Thrall. Johnis jerked his head around, then started for the stairs. They had to get below. No matter what else happened, he had to know if his mother was where Karas had claimed.

"Running will get you nowhere," the woman said.

The drapes flew back, and Jackov stumbled in before sprawling to the ground, bleeding from a gash in his ear.

A tall man dressed in a black robe with a pointed hood strode into the room. Several brass chains around his neck held a large serpent pendant. The Scab turned his hooded head and stared into Johnis with piercing gray eyes that stripped him of all hope.

This was the Dark Priest; there could be no doubt.

Jackov twisted back, face contorted with rage. "You promised me—"

"Silence!" the priest screamed. "We promised nothing yet!"

The room rang with these words of betrayal. From the beginning Jackov had been working with the Horde! Johnis was frozen, but his mind spun through desperate measures.

"Easy," Silvie whispered softly.

No one moved. There was no point.

A new voice, low and smooth, spoke from the opposite side of the room. "Please leave us, Chelise."

Johnis faced the newcomer who stood at the entrance to the staircase. An officer with the air of supremacy.

The woman in white, named Chelise, dipped her head. "Is there no sacred place any longer, *General* Martyn?" she asked with a biting note that highlighted his rank. "I'll speak to my father about this."

The priest answered for the officer. "Qurong is *part* of this. Leave us!"

Chelise, Qurong's daughter, glared at the priest, eyed Johnis with parting interest, and left the room.

"Welcome, Johnis," General Martyn said.

A trap had been set, and they'd walked directly into it.

"I believe you've come for love," the general said.

Johnis couldn't speak. The full breadth of this betrayal made him feel smaller than he could remember feeling.

Martyn, general to the Horde, stepped to one side and swept his hand toward the staircase. "Your mother is waiting."

# FOURTEEN

The circumstances they found themselves in didn't resemble those Johnis had wished for, except in this one significant detail: Mother was alive. If for nothing else, he would be grateful for her, assuming the general wasn't goading him on with false hopes.

Johnis strode forward, then rushed past Martyn and descended the stairs, two at a time. The dungeon he entered was lit by torches, taking his mind back to the Black Forest. But there were no tunnels down here, only a square cavern the size of his house, carved from the earth and reinforced by rock on all four sides.

In the middle of the cavern sat a cage roughly ten paces across, and in this cage a woman stood innocently in a simple dirty tunic. No hood.

Her hair was tangled and matted, her face and arms were

scabbed with the graying disease, her eyes were white, her lips cracked, but even so Johnis saw with his first glance that this was Rosa.

"Mother?"

She didn't show any reaction.

He ran up to the iron bars, grabbed two, and tugged with all of his might. But the bars didn't budge.

"Mother? It's me, Mother. It's Johnis!"

But Rosa didn't seem to recognize him. Her eyes watched, unblinking.

The priest shoved Silvie up next to him, opened the cage gate with a large key, pushed them both inside, and slammed the gate shut. He turned on his heel and strode for the door. "Enjoy a few precious moments together," he said and shut the door leading to the stairs.

Rosa stood unmoving, though she'd turned to face them. Johnis felt Silvie's hand on his elbow in support. "Johnis?"

He rushed up to his mother. "What did they do to you?"

Rosa backed up, eyes fired with fear. But her grayed retinas flittered back and forth over his face, digging for something that sparked recognition in her.

"Mother, please . . ." He reached out for her, and she took another step back.

The pain of her rejection was almost more than he could bear. He had to get her to see the truth about him! "It's me—your son, Johnis!" he cried. "You were taken by the Horde and forced to serve them. I don't know what they've convinced you of, but you're my mother. Please . . ."

She began to tremble, and he knew that his words were breaking through. He stepped up to her, slowly this time.

"It's me: Johnis." Tears flooded his eyes, and he let them leak down his cheeks unabashedly. "I'm your son. Kiella is your daughter. Ramos is your husband. We miss you terribly and want you to come home as soon as possible."

Her eyes welled with tears, and her lips quivered as she seemed to be trying to grasp his words.

Johnis reached for her, touched her sleeve. The smell of her rotting flesh filled his nostrils, but he paid it no mind. "I love you, Mother. I miss you so much."

Slowly, like a creeping tide, her right hand rose and moved closer to him. Her fingers were white with disease, cracked and bleeding from work. Johnis tried not to think of what kind of abuse had turned her—a woman who had marched around the house lovingly bossing them—into this shell of a human. But he failed and let his imagination run wild.

They'd tortured her! Beaten her! Forced her to work with bleeding fingers! The priest had done this; his own daughter had confirmed it. Punishment, Karas had said. A wicked man. Now Johnis saw just how wicked the man was.

"Johnis?" She spoke her first word, and it was his name.

He began to sob silently. His tears distorted her image, but he blinked them away and reached for her hand.

"Mother."

Then his hands touched rough Scab flesh.

"Mother, what did they do to you?" No, he didn't want her to think about her suffering. He spoke before she could answer. "Do you want to go home?"

"Kiella?"

"Yes, to Kiella. To the forest." He could hardly stand the pain in his chest.

"My . . . my husband. Is he still alive?" She was still whispering. The disease didn't do this to a Forest Dweller; he knew because he'd been there. The fact that his mother was in this state on his account tightened the noose cinched around his throat. He wasn't sure he could speak past the pain.

"Yes. And I'm going to take you home to him, Mother. I promise. I swear . . ."

The door flew open, and the priest strode in. Flung the gate wide. "Leave her if you want to see her alive tomorrow."

"I will *not* leave her!" Johnis cried. "What have you done, you monster?"

"She stays too," he said, pointing at Silvie.

"She will not! This isn't right or humane!" He was screaming incoherently, but his desperation didn't allow for anything else.

"Your mother has been preserved for this day. If you think she's in bad shape now, just refuse me, and you'll see what shape she'll be in tomorrow."

Silvie rushed to his side, eyes frantic. "Johnis . . ."

"Don't worry, Silvie; I won't let this happen!" But he knew they were just words. He was powerless.

She took his face in both hands and searched his eyes. "I love you, Johnis. Don't let me die here. Save your mother and me. Swear it."

"I swear it! I won't let them hurt you."

She kissed him on the lips and pulled back, teary eyed. "Don't forget me."

Johnis's mother approached them. "Who's this, Johnis? You have a woman?"

She was too far gone to feel the danger of the moment, being instead his mother for a moment again.

"Mother . . ." But Johnis couldn't finish any reasonable thought.

"Keep her safe, Silvie. Keep my mother safe."

"Enough, please," the priest said. "We all know there's no way anyone but me can keep anyone safe, so let's get on with this."

Johnis stopped at the door and stared back at the two women he'd put in this cage. He owed his life to both. "I swear it."

The priest locked the gate and the door into the stairwell behind. Then they were in the library again, facing Jackov, the traitor, and General Martyn.


THE FURY THAT RAGED THROUGH JOHNIS FOGGED HIS MIND.

"If it's any consolation," Martyn said, "I didn't approve of the way your mother's been treated. But sometimes the greater mission must be served."

Jackov stared at Johnis beside Martyn, eyes blank. And graying. He'd acted strange the last time they'd bathed; for all Johnis knew he hadn't actually washed his skin at all.

"You're wondering if your friend is Horde," Martyn said. "The answer is yes and no. Yes, he wants to be. No, he's not completely transformed yet. When he has fulfilled his promise, he will hold a place of honor among our warriors. It turns out that Guard members who defect make excellent leaders in the campaign."

"What do you want from me?" Johnis asked. He forced the anger back and cleared his mind.

The Horde general smiled. "Thomas."

Johnis felt his heart fall into the pit of his belly. He was going to be asked to betray Thomas.

"You and Jackov will return to the Middle Forest and meet Thomas. If he doesn't do exactly what you ask, your mother will have her limbs amputated. If anyone besides Thomas learns of your visit, the same. If we fail to take Thomas as planned, she will never walk again."

"What you're asking is impossible. If you know Thomas, you know that."

"Actually, I do know Thomas. Which is why I know he will come. Tell him that a mighty Horde general known as Justin demands to meet with him in the Valley of Bones, alone, in complete secrecy. None of the Council may know. Those are the conditions."

Justin? This was Justin, who'd defected from the Guard? Or was it a ploy?

"He won't come," Johnis said.

"He will. He'll come because he believes you are chosen to lead. There will be no other explanation for how you managed to bring this message from deep in the desert without being killed yourself. He'll come."

"Justin is the Guard officer who defected?"

The general hesitated. "Yes. And his message is one Thomas must hear if the world is ever to be at peace."

Johnis looked at Jackov again, disgusted with the fighter's cowardice. "I should have killed you in the clearing when you insulted my mother."

"You should have killed me at the Horde game, squat," Jackov said. "Before I planted your mother's ring where I knew it would be found."

"Jackov will make the journey with you, bathing once again before he enters the forests. You may not leave his side."

"How will you know . . ."

"We have our ways."

Spies? There was no way out, Johnis realized. He had no choice but to choose between Thomas and the two women below who meant life to him.

"What is your decision?" Martyn asked.

"Give me time! How do I know you'll release them?"

"You don't. But I will. Both of them. I have no interest in a misguided boy and his mother unless they can help me bring down the forests. Give me Thomas, and I'll give you your mother. It's the best I can do. Decide now."

"For Elyon's sake, give me a moment."

The Dark Priest walked up to him and slapped his mouth. "Watch your language, heathen. You're in the temple."

"One minute alone," Johnis shot back. "I doubt there are weapons stored here, so you have nothing to fear. Just let me clear my head."

Martyn considered his request and faced the priest. "I'll be back in five minutes. Give him his space, Witch." He turned, robe swirling, and disappeared through the drapes.

"Get out," the priest snapped at Jackov.

They left Johnis alone. He hurried to the desk where Chelise had been working and snatched up her pen. He couldn't write in the Horde way, and he wasn't sure how well Chelise could read his own writing, so he drew what he wanted to say on a piece of parchment and slid it into the book she had open.

He knew the attempt was hardly more than a gesture of blind hope, but he was out of options.

His mother was in the dungeon, mind lost to the world, and Silvie was beside her, weeping, waiting for him to fulfill his promise.

He would follow his heart now.

He would betray Thomas and save Rosa and Silvie.

# FIFTEEN

Jackov and Johnis loaded on two horses enough water to take them home in a two-day sprint, but Jackov refused to bathe until they were just outside the canyons on the western front of the Middle Forest. By then he was fully Horde.

"Easy, you stinking squat!" Jackov roared as Johnis dumped the water over his head.

There was enough left after his own bath to give the traitor a healthy soaking, and Johnis intended to use every drop. "Shut your hole and take it. Maybe some sense will find you."

Jackov had his shirt off, exposing his cracked flesh from head to waist. Johnis had seen Scab flesh revert to its natural smooth texture as fashioned by Elyon several times now, but the mechanics of such dramatic transformation remained a mystery. Parched gray skin mended like a dry lake bed under a rushing torrent.

"It's too late for sense," Jackov sputtered. "Easy!" He pushed Johnis away and wiped the extra water from his skin. "It's the switching back and forth that is the pain. This will be the last time for me, you can count on that."

"You make me sick," Johnis said, mounting his stallion.

They headed up the canyon pass, stopped for a moment at the Igal point, then turned into the forest. The sun was red in the west and would be down completely when they reached the village.

Lush green trees rose as thick as a carpet, and after so many days in the desert, Johnis wanted to weep. But he couldn't, at least not with any sense but dread. The journey with Jackov had been a terrifying ordeal. He'd spent the first day begging the thug to reconsider his defection to the Horde, but Jackov only turned more sour with each word. The second day had brought a deathly silence.

And now they were here to practice their betrayal. Johnis already knew what he would do, but no matter how hard he tried, he couldn't convince himself that the feeble plan had any hope of working.

Martyn, the Horde general who Johnis thought might have once been a member of the Guard himself, had planned this entire betrayal out with careful forethought.

He knew that Johnis was chosen.

That Thomas would follow the Chosen One.

That something as simple as his mother's ring would set everything in motion.

That Johnis would risk his life for his mother.

That the only way to be sure Thomas would be taken was to isolate him from his horse and lake water without any hope of help.

That a cloak and a dagger could sometimes do more harm than an entire Horde army.

He'd used Jackov as a matter of convenience, but Johnis, not Jackov, was the centerpiece of this plot to destroy Thomas.

He'd searched for a way to slip the word to Thomas that trickery was underfoot, but the risk to his mother and Silvie was too great. There were spies about, watching, ready to send word to kill Rosa and Silvie the moment anything changed from the plan. According to Martyn, that word could be sent by signals across the dunes, flashed on polished metal during the day and torches by night. They would know of any foul play within half a day.

Johnis took a deep breath and said what he'd waited a full day to say. "I've changed my mind. I'm not going to do it."

Jackov looked at him, unconcerned. "I don't care if you do or don't. If you don't, I will."

"Thomas won't follow you."

Jackov twisted angrily. "I'm not nothing!"

"No, you're a snake, and he knows it."

"You'll do it," Jackov said.

"No, I won't. You know as well as I that the wicked priest Witch will kill my mother either way."

Jackov remained fixed on the trees ahead, and Johnis knew he was right. A lump rose in his throat.

"And there's almost no chance I'm going to survive more than a few days."

Still no response. This was all part of their plan.

"So I won't do it unless you let me speak to Kiella, my sister. I would rather speak to my father because he's undoubtedly worried sick, but I know you'd never allow that. I have to tell Kiella that she will be okay and that her mother is alive. If you don't let me do that, I won't help you."

"Fine, I'll let you speak to Kiella. In my presence."

"Alone," Johnis said.

"You take me for an imbecile? Martyn was specific. We can't let you walk around the forests raising havoc or trying to slip a message in secretly."

Johnis nodded, knowing it was the best he could hope for. "Fine, with you, then. But before you bring out Thomas."

The cover of darkness made it easy for Johnis to remain hidden when they reached the village outskirts. As tempted as he was to rush in and spill his guts to Thomas, he remained still on his stallion, cursing the impossibility of the situation.

Jackov returned an hour later with Kiella on his horse. She slid off and ran up to him. "Johnis! What happened? The whole village is looking for you. Papa is worried sick!"

He dropped to one knee and embraced her. "I'm sorry, Kiella. It's okay."

"You had me so worried."

"I'm sorry. You don't have to be worried now. I'm just . . . Let's just say I'm trying to sort things out. Everything's been a bit crazy—I'm sure you've heard all the rumors."

"Are they right?"

"I don't know; I haven't heard them myself. What are they saying?"

Jackov hurried them. "Enough now, Johnis. We have some other business."

He eyed the large lad and stood, mind jerked back to the hopelessness of what he now had in mind.

"I've learned some good news, Kiella. Mother's still alive."

Kiella gasped. "What?"

"It's true. And someday we'll get her back. She's a Horde, but that's not as bad as you might think. Scabs can wash and become clean again, right?"

"A . . . a Horde?" She was reeling, eyes as round as the moon. "Mother's a Scab . . . but how's that?"

"I'll tell you how, but not now. Tell Papa and Darsal, so they—"

"Watch it!" Jackov hissed.

"It's harmless, Jackov!" Johnis snapped back. Then to Kiella again, "Tell them not to worry. I just have to fix a few things, and I'll be back to report to the Council. Okay?"

She didn't respond, maybe couldn't respond. It would take her more time than they had to deal with this sudden revelation. Johnis gave her a hug.

"Come on," Jackov ordered. "Your brother will be just fine. Let's go."

"Mother is a Scab? You're sure?"

"Yes. But she's alive, Kiella. There's hope. I'll get her, I promise you. If it's the last thing I do, I'll get her."

"It will be," Jackov said softly, wheeling his horse around and into the forest.

THE WAIT FOR THOMAS WAS SURPRISINGLY SHORT. THE supreme commander of the Forest Guard galloped with Jackov into the moonlit clearing; he was dressed for war despite the late hour. Whatever Jackov had said to make him come had clearly worked.

The commander pulled up, horse stamping, and drilled Johnis with a glare. "What's the meaning of this, recruit? Or should I say 'sergeant'? No, I think I should just say 'recruit' for all this foolishness."

"I'm sorry, sir," Johnis said. "I know it's all . . . unusual."

"That's not the word for it. I ordered you to make an accounting to the Council. Instead you vanish and sneak back in the middle of the night to beg forgiveness? That's not the way of the Forest Guard."

"I'm sorry. What did Jackov tell you?"

Thomas let a moment pass between then. "Don't speak to me like I'm your servant, boy. I'll do the asking."

"Yes, sir. Sorry, sir."

"So what is the critical information that Jackov insists only you can deliver?"

As agreed then, Jackov had told him nothing except that Johnis had to speak with him urgently.

"You know where the Red Valley is?"

"Over a day's ride south," Thomas said. "Why?"

"How long would it take to get there on the fastest horses?"

"A night and a day. What's this about?"

"Your General Justin of Southern, who is a general for the Horde now, wishes to meet with you in the Red Valley as soon as possible under the strictest confidence. Your meeting him will save or destroy the forests. That's my message."

Thomas's face remained unchanged. No surprise, no anger, no disbelief, nor belief. He'd seen more than any man alive, they said, and looking at him now, Johnis knew it must be true. The man was unshakable.

"We have to leave immediately," Johnis said. "No one, not even your wife, can know. Just you, Jackov, and myself. The fate of us all rests on your hands."

"Is that so, lad? Drop everything and rush out to an ambush because the boy who led another five hundred into an ambush said so?"

"He's speaking the truth," Jackov said, bringing his horse alongside.

"Shut up, boy. You're not helping him." Thomas's dismissal of the fighter was like using a mallet to slam a cork into a bottle, Johnis thought. The leader of all men, casually putting a stopper in the throat of the traitor of all men.

"I swear by my life that whatever happens in the next day will shift the balance of power forever," Johnis said.

"As would an ambush."

"Do you think anyone with half a wit would try to lure you into an ambush like this? You're not an army—you're the fastest fighter in all the forests. If you don't like what you see, turn tail and run. They can't stop you."

"Watch your tone. I don't turn tail. Don't mistake wisdom for cowardice."

"Sorry, sir," Johnis said. "I'm trying to appeal to your wisdom."

"Why the secrecy?"

"Because there are spies in the village. For all I know we're being watched now. If anyone were to know about this, Justin would be executed."

"A good thing."

"Or a terrible thing," Johnis said. "You'll have to decide."

Time was running short, and Silvie was growing gray next to Rosa. Johnis pulled out his trump card then, feeling as much a traitor as Jackov but knowing he had no choice.

"But what if you're right?" he asked.

"About what?"

"What if I am the Chosen One?"

It took Thomas another ten minutes to agree, but Johnis

thought he'd known he would the moment Johnis had laid out the request.

The supreme commander was back in fifteen minutes, sacks of water draped over his horse, two swords and a shield strapped to his saddle, and the steel will of a hardened man fixed on his face. "Move out! The sun won't wait."

This was the same Thomas they had all grown up practically worshipping.

This was the Thomas that Johnis, the supposed Chosen One, would now deliver unto death.

# SIXTEEN

They rode hard all night, south but east of where the terrible battle with the Horde had occurred five nights ago now. Thank Elyon they didn't have to face that mess again.

Thomas demanded more answers as they pounded through the desert, and Johnis gave him some. Lies, mostly, about how he'd wandered back to the battle scene with Jackov for company to mourn the dead. Jackov had been there, at the massacre. They'd met a lone rider in black who'd delivered the message about meeting in the Red Valley, a huge valley that provided no cover for any ambush.

Johnis whispered to Elyon his remorse for lying and gratefully whipped his horse faster over the dunes. He had only one thought, and that was to finish what he had started.

To save his mother no matter what the cost. To save Silvie if it cost him his own life. The rest he would have to put in the trust of great men like Thomas, assuming Thomas lived long enough to *be* trusted.

When the sun rose, they kept on, and for the first time Johnis succeeded in the common practice of strapping into a saddle, leaning forward, and sleeping while making a crossing. The less time one spent in the desert, the better, they said. So when forced to enter the deserts, as most were when they made the pilgrimage to the Middle Forest once every year for the Gathering, they did so without stopping.

Johnis slept out of pure exhaustion, dead to the world. But he didn't feel any relief from the nightmares that haunted him.

They reached the valley at dusk, after a night and a day of travel, exactly as Thomas had said.

He stopped them at the top of a massive sweeping dune that fell into the wide valley. It was known as Red Valley because it looked like a bath of blood in the setting sun.

He pulled out his gourd spyglass and scanned the valley.

"Okay . . . now what? I see nothing."

Thomas dismounted, then squatted on the sand to steady his arms for long-distance viewing. The slightest quiver shook the image to a blur.

Jackov nudged his horse next to Thomas's while the commander's scope was up. He began executing the foul play before Johnis fully realized what was happening.

"That's because there's nothing to see, old man," Jackov said, and slashed the bags of water draped over Thomas's horse. The contents crashed to the sand, wasted.

Johnis sat in his saddle like a slab of rock, incapable of moving. He'd known the moment would come, but this soon? Jackov didn't have the patience to bide his time!

"What on . . ." Thomas had his sword out of his mount's scabbard before he finished the last word, but Jackov was already away, grinning like a devil.

"You want water, old man?" He put a slit in his own bag of water. "You have to dig a well. I'll pass."

"You're Horde," Thomas said, understanding the situation immediately. Then his knife was out and in the air, flying like an arrow toward Jackov.

The fighter clearly hadn't expected such an outright attack on his life. He'd expected to prance away on his horse while Johnis executed his part of the plan. But it was this kind of reversal that Thomas was famous for. General of the Horde, Martyn or Justin or whoever he really was, knew Thomas well enough to know that the man couldn't be beaten by any normal means.

The long throwing blade turned three times, whistling with each rotation, and buried itself in Jackov's chest just as the fighter began to realize he was in danger.

The desert echoed with a *smack!*

But Jackov had the presence of mind to reached down with his own knife, and jerk the blade across his horse's thick neck: a gruesome sight that stopped even Thomas in his tracks. Slowly the horse's front legs buckled. Then he was in the sand, dying with Jackov, who was already dead beside the animal.

Johnis knew that he had a few moments at best, and although he'd planned his next move to the last detail, he executed it now only after almost throwing his hands up with pleas for forgiveness.

Instead he eased his horse up to Thomas's, took the reins, and walked them both away from the commander, who was still staring at Jackov and the dead animal beside him.

Johnis was fifteen feet away when Thomas turned back. "It's a trap! We're down to your water. It's not enough to wait around. We turn back now and take advantage of the night." He strode for his horse, obviously thinking that Johnis had simply pulled the animal away to keep it from spooking.

"How much left in your canteen?"

*Two canteens full,* Johnis thought. But he couldn't speak. He eased the horse farther, looking over at the commander from the corner of his eyes. Almost out of throwing range. And Thomas would, he knew. If he realized what was about to happen, he would.

But the fact that his Chosen One was about to betray him evidently wasn't in Thomas's mind. "Take his weapons . . ." he said, motioning back to Jackov with his head. "Bring me my horse."

Johnis kicked his horse then, when Thomas was flat-footed. Both animals, away from Thomas, carrying Johnis and the last of the water into the desert.

Behind him Thomas had stopped and was simply staring.

*Forgive me, sir!* Johnis wanted to cry. But he lowered his head and galloped into the dusk without a word. He couldn't risk leaving Thomas in any condition other than what he'd agreed to: on foot, without water.

Thomas was resourceful, he told himself again. It had been over a day since they'd bathed, but he would find a way to stay sane long enough to foil the Horde and make it back to the forests.

Of course, that wasn't very logical. Martyn had wanted precisely this, for Thomas to be stranded without horse or water. Logic told Johnis that Thomas was already as dead as Jackov. And he probably knew it.

For that matter, so were Silvie and Rosa.

And Johnis.

# SEVENTEEN

Report," Martyn ordered, striding from the command tent they'd set up just south of the Red Valley.

"They've reached the valley, sir," the colonel said.

"They've been seen?"

"Not in the valley, but short of it by ten miles."

"And why not in the valley? I demanded they be kept in sight at all times."

"You also ordered that we not be seen. There was no place to watch without tipping our hands. Now it's dark. And you didn't want men in the valley where they might be seen."

The colonel made a good point. One whiff of betrayal and Thomas would be gone. Unfortunately, they had to trust that

Johnis's love for his mother was greater than his sense of duty to Thomas. Everything depended on the heart of one fighter.

"Then it's either done by now or lost," Martyn said. "Sweep the valley."

"It's dark, sir. You mean in the morning."

"No, I mean now. Use all five hundred of your trackers. Find him. Then leave him to wander."

The colonel looked up, surprised by this last order. "Sir?"

"He's too dangerous to approach."

"He's on foot! You doubt my men on horseback against one man on foot?"

"All he needs is one horse, and he'll be gone to fight another day. Do you deny he could kill one of your men, take his horse, and flee?"

"But one man—"

"Not one man," Martyn said. "Thomas Hunter. You forget that I know him like a brother. Be patient. Find him and let the desert dry him up like a dead leaf."

"And then?"

Martyn looked at the dark, eastern sky. "Then I'll take him myself."

TIME WAS AGAINST JOHNIS. HE KNEW IT LIKE HE KNEW that the sun would rise again. If he couldn't reach the Horde city by daybreak, then all would surely be lost. Martyn's attention would now be on the Red Valley, but once light flooded the desert, they would see him crossing the flats that ran up to the dunes that hid the city.

Johnis bathed as the horse ran and kept the beast headed west toward Thrall. Toward Rosa and Silvie. He switched to Thomas's horse after the first hour because his was nearly dead from the exhausting days of running. Without a loyalty to Thomas, his horse would either follow him, or turn and find its way back to the forests.

Every hour he considered turning back and throwing himself at Thomas's feet for mercy. Surely Thomas would think of a way to save his mother. Was he risking too much for a desperate attempt to save two honorable women? Or was he serving his own selfish need to be loved?

Yes and yes. Still, he rode west, as hard as the tired stallion would take him.

The large sandy hills rose on the dark horizon when the stars were still in the sky, and Johnis surged forward, clinging to a thin line of hope. But reaching the city was only the beginning of his challenges. He had a plan, sure he did, but so much depended on his speed and boldness.

Speed, because the light would ruin everything.

Boldness, because only a fool would attempt a rescue. Perhaps *foolishness* was a better word. Speed, boldness, and foolishness. Of the three he had mostly the latter.

But he did make it over the hills before sunrise. And when the sprawling Horde city came into view, he spoke the first words he'd said all night.

"Elyon, help me."

THOMAS WASN'T SURE WHY JOHNIS HAD CHOSEN TO BETRAY him, only that he'd done it masterfully by playing on Thomas's greatest weakness—his belief in the lad.

Unless it was the Horde general who'd conceived the whole plot, which meant they were playing on Johnis, knowing that he was the way to Thomas because Thomas thought he was the Chosen One.

Either way, they knew too much. The forests were filled with spies!

He walked over to Jackov's dead horse and quickly stripped the knives and sword. He'd been stranded by design, which meant the Scabs would come for him. And when they did, he would take more than a few down in an attempt to take a horse.

Jackov's drinking canteen was half full, and he gave himself a spit bath hoping the water was lake water—but he doubted it. Fighters rarely put the healing lake water in their drinking canteens so as not to mistake it for ordinary water and waste it by drinking rather than bathing with it.

There was no way he could make it to the forest on foot in time. His only chance of survival was to find a Horde horse. But tomorrow would be his third day without a full bath, thanks to a decision encouraged by Jackov not to bathe earlier in the day.

Better to wait until the Red Valley so the effects of the healing water would last longer if they ran into trouble, he'd said.

Now, the disease would be setting in by morning. With each passing hour he would grow weaker and less capable of finding or taking a horse.

He used the spyglass to scan the valley again, but the light was completely gone and he couldn't make out the hills, much less Horde on the hills.

Thomas shoved the glass under his belt and turned west. There, low rolling hills led into several shallow canyons. He had to reach them, but not until he'd gotten their attention. Played their game. Shown himself. Let them know their plot had succeeded. He would draw them into a pursuit on his terms, so that he stood a chance of ambushing a stray group and taking a horse.

If their objective was to strand him in the valley until the disease took him, they wouldn't attack him until he was weak—his reputation would buy him at least that much time. That is, unless they were fools, and this general wasn't.

Thomas took a deep breath, looked left then right into the night, and headed down into the open valley to show himself to this general who called himself Justin of Southern.

THE SKY WAS JUST STARTING TO LIGHTEN WHEN JOHNIS reached the city's main gate. Within an hour the Horde would begin to stir. *One hour, or all is lost,* he thought.

Speed was his friend. Speed and boldness and more than a little bit of foolishness. For the moment, speed and stealth were impossible companions, so he went for speed alone, kicking the horse and forcing it into a full run straight up the city's main road.

The street was made from hard-packed dirt, not stone, so the hooves thudded rather than clacked, but the sound was still enough to wake those in the houses that lined the road. With any luck, those dead asleep would wake, but he would be past, and they would roll over for more sleep.

Sweat trickled down his temple, over his cheekbones, past the corners of his mouth. The morning was cool, but he was fever-ishly hot. He felt as if he was galloping into the throat of a dragon—the smell of sulfur that led straight to hell.

Johnis passed hundreds of houses, and each remained dark after he passed. As he thought, a warring people were accustomed to these kinds of disruptions.

The temple loomed ahead. "My house is the red mortar house on the right," Karas had said. Johnis slowed his horse to a walk as he approached the house he assumed was hers.

Moving now with stealth, he guided the animal around to the stable he'd seen. His horse shook its head with protest, so he knew there were Horde horses inside. A good thing.

He stripped the saddle, the bridle, and the water bag from his own horse and dumped the saddle and bridle in a barrel by the stable. Without the telltale Guard saddle, which was designed to be light for quick movement, the horse looked similar to any Horde horse.

Pushing the animal into the empty corral, he angled for the Dark Priest's house, water bag over his shoulder.

"Speed and boldness," he whispered to himself. "The light is coming."

He found the first window open, pushed in the twine-hinged window doors, and worked his way inside, knife in hand. He'd never been in a Horde home before, but it looked like he imagined it would, having been in the temple. It was made mostly from mortar with straw thatchwork covering the walls. Other than every conceivable use of desert wheat, the Horde relied on leather and stone or mortar for all of their construction, giving a very plain look to everything.

A half dozen large sacks of grain were piled in one corner of the small room. Barrels of wheat wine lined one wall. He had found his way into a pantry, it seemed.

The exit was covered by canvas—no swinging doors. Johnis slipped his head past the hanging drape, saw the hallway beyond was empty, and slipped into the heart of the Dark Priest's house.

Karas was his goal. Just let him find Karas quickly, and then he stood a chance.

His one saving grace was the fact that the Dark Priest snored. That sound was coming either from the Dark Priest or from Karas, and he doubted such a little girl could produce a sound so disturbing. There were four sets of drapes leading from the hall.

If he wasn't mistaken, the snoring came from the room on the far right.

He crept down the hall and checked the room opposite, saw that it was a large living area with brass hangings on the walls and large cushions on the floor, a table with eight chairs.

Eight. Why would a house for the Dark Priest who had only one daughter have a table with eight chairs? Unless there was more to this house than . . .

Something touched his elbow, and his heart climbed into his throat in a single beat.

Johnis whirled around. The girl Karas stood behind him, dressed in a white nightdress. White dress, white skin, white eyes—she looked like a spirit from the night.

She lifted a single finger to her lips, took his hand, and led him down the hall toward a fifth door he hadn't seen. A wooden door, this one. He didn't know if she was leading him to his death or not, but he did see that the sky outside was lighter.

Speed and boldness. They were running out of time!

He gave her a nudge, and she doubled her pace, down steps into a black space with several oil lamps on the walls to guide the way.

"You're a fool," she whispered, hurrying forward.

She was right. "And now I have a fool's company," he said.

"You think I'm helping you?"

"Are you?"

She didn't answer. The curtain at the end of the passage opened into a room lit by two torches that licked with orange flames at open holes above. Oily smoke rose into the exhausts and vented somewhere outside.

Reclining cushions covered in colored silk cloth ringed a thick table. On the table sat brass candlesticks fashioned to look like winged serpents. The far wall was covered with a dozen examples of Horde weaponry, some of which Johnis had never seen: maces with spiked balls at the end of chains, leather shields like the ones the Forest Guard used, swords of all kinds.

A hundred or more books of history lined shelves on the near wall. A trunk sat on the floor beneath the largest of several serpent idols. *A lavishly decorated room by Horde standards,* he thought.

"There are guards above next to my room," Karas said, stepping past him. "They will kill you this time."

"Have you ever seen books similar to these but with red twine binding them shut?"

She just looked at him, lost.

"Never mind. You have to help me, please. You yourself said that your father was wicked. He forced you to help Jackov trick me, right? Because of that, he's going to kill my mother."

She stared at him for a several long seconds. Her own mother was dead—he wondered how she felt about it.

"When the sun comes up, they'll know that I came here. Please, I beg you, Karas."

"Did you know the priest killed my mother? That's why I hate him. He cut her throat with a knife when I was a child."

*You're still a child,* he didn't say. He'd come to save his own mother and Silvie, but looking at her diseased face, flaking white, he felt a terrible pity for her. He could no more force her against her will than let his own mother die.

Desperation filled his throat like a fist. He swallowed. "Will you help me?"

"I saw you from my window and sneaked past the guards. If my father knew, he wouldn't be happy."

"But he's sleeping. All I need is the key to the dungeon below the temple. I brought water, see?" He held out the bag. "I can still get my mother and Silvie out."

"I doubt my father is sleeping."

"Where is he?"

"I don't know. He doesn't sleep in this house."

"I thought . . . Never mind, we're running out of time." Johnis paced frantically. "If you're not going to help me, just let me go. I have to go. Now!" He strode back toward the doorway.

"This way," she said, stepping toward what he'd taken as a huge leather shield on the far wall. She lifted the thick leather and stepped into a dark tunnel. "Hurry."

A passage to the temple! Johnis ran after her, nerves firing with tension. He could see his mother now, standing with gray eyes, stunned by months of abuse. And Silvie, now writhing with the disease.

Karas grabbed a ring of keys from the wall, rattled them noisily as her small hands struggled to open a rusted lock, then pushed a door that swung open on rope hinges. They stepped into a room lit by a single torch.

The dungeon.

The cage.

Rosa and Silvie stood in the middle, staring at them with eyes of death. They'd heard the clanking at the door and stood with fear, Johnis thought. Every other time the lock had been opened, they'd faced a new horror.

This time they faced Johnis, whose legs had turned to stone.

A door squealed above them.

"Hurry!" Karas cried, and ran for the cage door.

# EIGHTEEN

The night hours dragged by as Thomas Hunter walked the valley, cutting first one way, then another, making as much noise as he thought seemed natural without shouting his intentions for all the hidden Horde to hear.

He wanted them to know he was there, without their realizing he wanted them to follow. Although he hadn't seen so much as a hint of shifting shadows or smelled the slightest Horde scent, he knew they were there, watching in the night.

They would be wearing black, mounted on horses, because if the Scabs were slow on their horses, they were even slower on foot, fighting pain through long hours of forced march. The Forest Guard could outrun the Horde at twice their speed on foot.

The problem with horses was noise. A snorting beast could be heard for miles in the desert. Not to mention Scab odor, which the Horde had learned preceded them.

His mind wandered as he marched, mulling over this treachery Johnis had pulled. Could he and Rachelle both be wrong about the boy? Only they and a close circle of confidants knew of the prophecy about the Chosen One who would save them one day.

They'd often wondered why two prophecies had come, the first spoken by Elyon, the boy, before he dove into the lake waters and disappeared thirteen years ago. The second by Michal, the Roush, spoken to Thomas in his dreams a year later. *A chosen child marked by Elyon will prove his worth and destroy the Dark One.*

Johnis had the circle mark on his neck, and he'd proven himself by defeating the Horde once already. A most unlikely candidate, true. But Rachelle was sure. And before today, Thomas had been sure.

Now Johnis had betrayed him, Thomas Hunter, supreme commander of the Forest Guard. He'd led five hundred fighters into battle, three hundred men and two hundred women, all far more experienced in the ways of war than this young new recruit, who was lucky enough to escape the massacre unscathed except for a bruised shoulder.

He carried himself like a hero one day and an utter fool the next.

Rachelle saw it differently, of course. A hero one day, she'd said, and the kind of idealist who would save a world the next. *If he's chosen, he's chosen, Thomas.*

"But what if he's not?" Thomas whispered in the darkness.

*His task isn't to save us*, Rachelle had said. *His task is to destroy the Dark One.*

The Dark One. Teeleh? The Dark Priest? The Horde? For all Thomas knew, the Dark One was from another world entirely. He himself was. Wasn't he?

Thomas reached the smaller dunes with the first hints of dawn. He hurried in stealth now, eager to lose any pursuit. He had only one shot at this, and it all came down to the next half hour.

The dunes steepened and gave way to shallow canyons. Scanning the sand, he ran, keeping to the rocks that littered the ground.

It took him fifteen minutes to find the right lay of rock and sand. Balancing on two rocks, he dug the sand between them deeper, then lay back in the shallow grave. Already he could feel the onset of the Scab disease paining his joints. He looked at his skin, but the light was too dim to show any scabbing or cracking.

He took one last pull from Jackov's canteen, popped the lenses out of the hollow gourd that made his telescope, put one end into his mouth to form a breathing tube, and buried himself.

The wind was blowing already, as the sun's warmth pushed air from the east. The silt would cover his marks within an hour.

As far as the Horde would be concerned, Thomas Hunter had disappeared. For now.

Or so he desperately hoped.

"Hurry!" Karas spun back. For the first time since Johnis had met this young bundle of spice, she looked truly frightened. Her eyes shot to the stairs down which Johnis had come the last time he'd been here. Nothing.

"What's going on?" Silvie asked in a high, nervous voice. "Is that you, Johnis? What's happening?"

Karas finally got the cage latch to fall open and threw the door wide. Johnis had been here once and knew that talking to Silvie now, in this state of transition to full Horde, was nearly pointless. It took a very seasoned will to remain clear.

But this time Rosa recognized him without hesitation. She hurried over. "I've been waiting, Johnis! I knew you would come back. Silvie and I have been waiting. I wasn't sure, you know, that it was you before. But I've been waiting, Johnis. I've been here waiting for you . . ."

Johnis lifted his finger to her lips. Once-pink lips cracked gray with disease. He couldn't take her disorientation, her rambling, because he knew it came from the priest's abuse, not simply the disease.

"Shhh, Mother. We have to hurry."

The floor above them creaked.

"Lie down, both of you."

"Johnis, what's—"

"Lie down!" he snapped. "On your backs! Both of you."

"Not the water, please," Rosa begged. "Not the water, Johnis."

"You don't mean that. Lie down, please, Mother, hurry."

Silvie stepped back. "Johnis, maybe you should listen to her."

"Get down!" he yelled, realizing too late that anyone upstairs would surely hear.

They dropped down immediately this time, put their arms by their sides, and stared up at him with wide eyes.

"Close your eyes," he said, unwinding the twine on the bottled lake water.

They clenched them tight, and he threw, rather than poured, the water over them from above. Rosa gasped, whether from the cool water or from the healing he couldn't tell, but her transformation was immediate and staggering. Sweet, sweet relief, flushing her body from the crown of her head to the soles of her feet—Johnis had felt it twice before.

He splashed the healing waters over Silvie, soaking her clothes and hair, then moving back over his mother, then splashing even more on himself.

"What . . . what is that?" little Karas asked, voice wound tight. "What's happening to them?"

Johnis was about to splash the last of the water over Silvie when her voice stopped him.

"Do want to see?" Silvie asked. "We could wash you."

Karas backed up two steps, terrified. "No . . . no."

He suddenly wanted nothing more than to save little Karas from her own disease; never mind that she didn't even know she was diseased. The Forest Guard was sworn to kill the Horde, but at this moment Johnis wanted to save this frightened Scab.

But they didn't have time.

Silvie and Rosa were both up on their feet.

"Johnis? Dear Elyon, Johnis!" Rosa rushed forward and kissed him on his cheeks, then started on his hands, weeping with gratitude now.

"Mother, we don't have time. I love you desperately, and I'll tell you later, but right now I need you to run." He spun to Silvie. "Through the passage, up the stairs, there's a stable out the back. Mount and ride as hard as you can, out of the city."

"You?"

"I'm with you." Dropping the nearly empty bag of water, he rushed to the gate and pushed them ahead of him. "If we get separated, we meet at the rocks, follow?"

"Follow," she said.

"Then on into the desert, if the other party doesn't come within ten minutes. We'll have Horde horses, so we'll need a head start." The desert water that the Horde horses drank made them slower than Guard horses, it was said. None of them really knew if that was the real reason.

They ran toward the tunnel, first Rosa, then Silvie, then Johnis. They were going to make it. There was still the main road to navigate at full speed and the desert to cross, but armed with swords and free on horses, he and Silvie could manage easily enough.

A surge of hope and gratitude washed over him. There was Thomas, but they actually had a chance of recovering him from the Red Valley now. He'd hoped against the faintest hope that precisely this would be his outcome.

Speed, boldness, and more than a little bit of foolishness had become speed, boldness, and brilliant maneuvering.

Only the missing Books of History remained problematic. But his first priority had to be his mother. Then he would get back to his vow and start the quest for the books from scratch.

"Through the tunnel, all the way to the end!" His voice echoed softly in the long passage. "Come on, Karas!"

No response. He turned around. "Karas?"

But Karas was gone. The room was empty except for the limp bag of water in the cage. And deadly silent. She'd run into another passage, perhaps, unnerved by his water.

"Johnis!" Silvie whispered.

"Go, go!" He ran after them, down the tunnel, into the underground room with the large table and weapons.

"Follow me," he breathed, rushing past them. "It's a sprint out of the city now."

But his mother needed no encouragement. She wasn't in the same condition she'd been in before her captivity, but her training as a fighter and her eagerness to escape this hellhole didn't fail her entirely. She pressed hard at his heels, pushing Johnis faster.

They slipped through the upper house and into the storage room. Johnis searched the staircase one last time to see if Karas might have decided to follow them after all, but only darkness stared up at him.

When he stuck his head back into the pantry, Rosa was already out and Silvie halfway. He piled through the window after them.

"This way!" Johnis sprinted to the stables, ignored Thomas's horse which, though normally faster, was worn half-dead from the night ride, and chose three stallions in close stalls. These were undoubtedly among the best the Horde owned, picked from among the hundreds of thousands they bred for war.

A dog began to bark from one of the nearby houses. "Forget the saddles. Bridles only."

They slid the Scab-designed bits into the horses' mouths and threw their legs over bare backs.

"You came back, Johnis," Silvie said. "Thank you. You're a bold man."

"And a bit foolish," he said. "Okay, remember it's a full sprint. They may give chase, but we stand a good chance if we don't hesitate. You know the way, Silvie. Right down the middle of the city. If they have the city gate blocked, split two ways and join at the boulders. Ready?"

"Let's go." Silvie grabbed a sword off the wall, kicked her mount, and pushed past the doors, followed by Rosa, who snatched down her own blade.

"She's right," Rosa said, drilling Johnis with a bright stare. "You've grown into a bold man since I last saw you."

"I missed you, Mother."

"And I missed you, my son."

The sky was fully gray now. Roosters crowed here and there

about the city. The dog that had started to bark stilled, but now another answered it from across the way.

Thrall woke in the same way the Middle Forest woke, Johnis thought, and then spurred his horse forward. Silvie, then Rosa, then Johnis bringing up the rear.

He rounded the house, followed them into the street already at a full gallop, and glanced back at the temple. It was simply a parting look, perhaps because he knew he would be back for the books soon and wanted to imprint the lay of the land on his mind.

Instead the sight of a young child seared his mind, like a branding iron on a horse's hide.

Karas.

She stood in a large triangular window above the temple's main door, feet strapped tightly together, arms bound behind her back.

A hangman's noose hung around her neck.

The Dark Priest stood in the temple doors, hands clasped in front of his long black cloak. Even at this distance his white eyes shone in contrast to his dark clothing.

"Her life for yours, Chosen One," the Dark Priest said with just enough power for his voice to carry through the still dawn.

Johnis jerked the reins hard, and the horse snorted in protest.

"Johnis!" Silvie cried. "Run!"

He glanced toward them and saw that both had stopped. "Go!" he shouted. "Silvie, take her out! Promise me!"

"Johnis? No, Johnis—"

"Go! Go, Silvie. I'll be right behind! I promise!"

"Please . . ." Her voice was begging and desperate, and he knew then that she loved him.

"Go, go, go—or they'll kill us all!"

"Johnis!" his mother cried. "Johnis, you come right this instant! I'm not going to lose you."

"I'm coming, Mother. Just go. Ride, for the love of Elyon, ride!"

Silvie spun her horse, slapped its rump with her sword, and charged down the street with Rosa galloping behind.

Johnis would follow them, of course. Surely he would never jeopardize his mission to save Rosa by last-minute heroics. Leaving Rosa with a dead son would be worse than if she had never been rescued in the first place.

So he would go, now, as soon as he sorted this mess out in his mind: this absurdity of a father threatening to hang his sweet, nine-year-old daughter; never mind that she was a Scab whom the Forest Guard was sworn to kill in battle at every opportunity.

The sight of her in the window above him stopped his heart.

"If Qurong knew what was in his interest, he'd butcher you, Witch," Johnis said, using the name he'd heard used for the priest. He said it in a soft voice laced with bitterness, but the words carried unmistakably across the courtyard.

"And if you run, *I'll* butcher *her*," Witch said.

"She's your daughter!"

"And it seems you care for her more than I do," Witch said. "I, on the other hand, care for the other four books. You're going to tell me where to find them."

The Books of History. Witch was looking for the other four. There were seven in all. Which had to mean he had *three*, not just the two Johnis had lost!

Johnis knew he had to leave now, before guards rushed out on all sides. The sound of Rosa and Silvie's escape faded as they raced further on.

He gave his horse a slight nudge to turn. "You won't do it. She's your daughter."

"Then run, Chosen One. And look behind your shoulder to see the doll fall."

Johnis was going to turn and run then, for his mother's sake, for Silvie's sake, for the sake of Elyon and the forests and the Roush and his own oath to find the missing Books of History and to try to rescue Thomas. But then something happened that he never could have anticipated.

Karas began to cry. Softly at first, like a low flute hiccuping in the stillness. Choking back the terror that flooded her small lungs.

"He's going to kill me," she said, barely above a whisper. But it struck Johnis like a hammer.

The anguish in her voice. The agony of hopelessness. She didn't expect Johnis to exchange his life for hers, or she would have said, *He's going to kill me if you don't save me, Johnis.* But she wasn't the kind of girl who knew a hope that would expect anyone to save her.

"He's going to kill me."

The heavens might have opened then and dumped buckets of empathy on Johnis for all he knew. One moment he was chiding himself for delaying his own escape because of this fury he felt against the Dark Priest. And the next he didn't care about his escape or the priest's wickedness.

In that moment he cared for nothing but Karas, for this nine-year-old Horde who was crying with white eyes in the bell tower.

For this infidel.

The pain that slammed into his chest made him weak and limp. He wanted to rush up to her and save her, whatever the cost.

But he had to go. He knew that. He simply had to go, for Elyon's sake, for Mother's sake. Karas was only a Scab. His other obligations and loves were for his own, not for the Horde.

"He killed my mother," the little girl cried in a very soft voice.

Pain crashed around Johnis like a torrential rain. He couldn't move for the hammering of his heart. It was as if he felt every fiber of her pain, her panic, her terror, trembling up there in the bell tower one shove away from a cracked neck. He had to leave.

But he didn't.

Unable to withstand the absurdity before him for even a moment longer, Johnis threw his arms wide, tilted his head up, and screamed at the sky. A long, full-throated scream that shut down the pain in his heart for a few seconds.

He was shaking, he realized, resigned now to what he knew he must do. For all he knew, he'd followed his heart to the Horde city for Karas as much as for Rosa or Silvie.

His cry echoed around him, and he sucked in a long breath. When he lowered his head and opened his eyes, he saw that there were six guards in the courtyard, facing him with spears. He could still go, he knew that. The priest wouldn't kill him if he turned to flee even now—the man wanted the Chosen One alive.

But Karas would die. Witch wouldn't soil his reputation with anything less.

"Bring her down," Johnis said. "Set her free."

# NINETEEN

Silvie lay atop the tallest dune and gazed out at Thrall sprawling out under the blazing midday sun. Riding away, she thought she'd heard a long, piercing scream from far behind, but with the pounding of the horse's hooves and the crashing of her own heart filling her ears, she hadn't been sure.

Still, she'd almost turned back. If it weren't for Rosa, who was still weak from her captivity, she would have. But she'd promised Johnis to take his mother to safety, and that was one promise she would keep no matter the cost.

An hour had passed while they paced at the boulders where they'd first met Karas. The little Horde girl seemed to have bewitched Johnis.

When two hours had come and gone, Silvie knew he wasn't

coming out, but she refused to admit it. She'd moved them to the dune and wrestled with the decision of whether to continue on as promised, or go back and perhaps sneak into the city this very night to set Johnis free as he had done for them. Never mind that he'd told them to leave if he didn't join them in ten minutes.

But setting him free this time wouldn't be an easy task: they would be waiting. Whereas Martyn, the Horde general, seemed bent upon Thomas Hunter's destruction, the Dark Priest was more interested in Johnis, the Chosen One, as he called him.

He'd pressed Silvie for several hours for information on the Books of History, and she'd told him that Johnis knew it all. She'd done it for his sake. As long as the Dark Priest thought Johnis held valuable information, he wouldn't be killed.

Even so, the Dark One was playing them, she now saw. He'd told her that Johnis would return, though he clearly hadn't expected him so soon. Still, he had what he wanted.

He had the Chosen One.

"They have him," Rosa said. "We have to go back in after him."

"Do you know why the Horde aren't scouring these hills looking for us, Rosa?"

Rosa looked around as if wondering the same for the first time.

"Because they're commanded by the general, Martyn, and Martyn is far wiser than any Horde I've ever heard of. He knows that you and I have no chance of recovering Johnis, and having realized this, we've fled to Middle Forest."

"But I would never leave my son!"

"Obviously. Risking your neck for the Catalina cacti is what started this whole thing in the first place."

"And I think you would do the same, if I'm reading your eyes correctly."

Silvie looked at Johnis's mother and knew there was no hiding what both understood. "You're right. I love your son. So we have a problem." She looked back at the city. "We have to leave for the forest, but we can't leave without Johnis."

"And we don't have any more water," Rosa pointed out.

"Correct."

They rested on their elbows, staring in hopelessness.

"How old are you?" Rosa asked.

"Sixteen. Nearly seventeen."

"Then you're older than him."

"Not much."

"It's young to be married," Rosa said. "I know it's common, but still . . . very young."

"Do you really believe that, or are you more interested in keeping him?" Silvie asked. She felt free, after two days together in the cell, to say anything to Rosa.

"I suppose it's to keep him," Rosa said, sighing. "You'd be a very lucky girl, you know. He's stubborn, but he's a purebred."

"Then you know about the prophecy?"

Rosa blinked. "What prophecy?"

"'A chosen child marked by Elyon will prove his worth and destroy the Dark One,' the secret prophecy goes. Thomas and

Rachelle claim it was kept secret to protect whoever that Chosen One was. You know the mark on his neck?"

"Yes." Rosa's eyes were wide.

"The Roush, Michal, told us that Johnis is the Chosen One."

"You've . . . you're saying you've seen a Roush?"

Silvie remembered their vow to keep all they'd learned and seen in complete confidence. This was a dangerous track she was on, though seeing as how they'd lost the books and Johnis might be dead, the vow they'd made to the Roush seemed distant and irrelevant.

"Metaphorically speaking, in a dream. Thomas was given the prophecy in a dream. Do you doubt that your son is chosen?"

"No. But it's the first time I've heard anyone else say it."

"You knew? How?"

"I had a dream too. A Roush told me the prophecy, and I knew that Johnis bore the mark. So Thomas and Rachelle both know!"

Silvie felt her last lingering doubts disappear. Johnis was the Chosen One.

A flock of birds circled in from the west. *Black vultures*, Silvie thought. But then she saw that she was wrong. They were Shataiki.

They'd hardly seen any since returning to the forest, or for that matter, Roush. They seemed to be giving them space. But now more came in from the west, hundreds dotting the sky, like locusts.

She looked at Rosa. "Do you see them?"

Rosa stared at the city. "The Dark Priest? See who?"

No, she couldn't see the Shataiki. But they now numbered in

the thousands, flapping in and circling the Horde city, indeed like vultures preparing to prey on the dead.

Silvie watched, riveted by the sight. Seeing the Shataiki feeding on the dead Horde in the valley of massacre had been the first time she'd ever considered the possibility that these beasts from hell had an appetite for flesh or blood. But in a world where evil showed itself in physical form, it made perfect sense.

Silvie knew the Shataiki could see them—they clearly were more interested in something else: the Horde. Johnis.

A particularly large beast, like the one who called himself Alucard in the Black Forest, perhaps Alucard himself, led the Shataiki in a dive. The black bats tucked their huge wings and streaked toward the earth, toward the center of the Horde city.

Silvie jumped to her feet, thinking that they had to do something. Something was up. Johnis was in trouble.

"What?" Rosa asked, standing. "You see something?"

Silvie tried to see what the Shataiki were doing, but they were too far away. They were flooding the city, she could see that much. None of the traffic on the main road seemed to change—the Horde could see nothing of the Shataiki.

But Johnis would.

"What is it, Silvie? You're frightening me! Tell me!"

"Nothing."

"What do you mean, nothing? You jumped up!"

"I thought I saw something on the street." She sat down and drew her legs under her chin. "I was wrong."

Rosa lowered herself next to Silvie, and they were silent. The sky was empty except for a half dozen Shataiki circling—sentries.

"So, you intend to be my daughter-in-law?" Rosa asked.

"I didn't say anything about marriage. You're right, we're too young. I doubt he really knows I love him. *I* don't even know. We're both in the Guard! This is crazy. It's . . ."

Rosa's hand on her arm stopped her. "Of course you love him, dear. And of course he feels something for you. I can see it in his eyes when he looks at you. No use denying that. But it's good that you're cautious. We should see where this prophecy leads him."

"Maybe it leads him to me," Silvie said. She was sounding like a double-minded fool, perhaps because when it came to him, she was.

"We're talking nonsense!" she cried. "He's dead, for all we know!"

Rosa took her hand away, fingers now trembling. "So, what do we do?"

Silvie's vision distorted with a flood of tears. Her throat ached, and her chest felt hollowed by a Horde spear, but she refused to weep.

"We wait."

"Wait for what?"

"For something to present itself."

"We'll turn back to Horde. Maybe we should get some water." The prospect of turning back into a Scab unnerved Rosa more than she was letting on, Silvie guessed. Months of captivity had reached deep into her mind.

"I can't leave him," Silvie said, gazing ahead.

Rosa stared at the city. "No, of course we can't. But I'd rather die by a Horde blade, fighting for my son, than by the disease. Don't leave me here, promise me that."

"I promise."

THOMAS HUNTER LAY UNDER THE SAND. BARELY BREATHING through the makeshift snorkel, listening, listening, always listening. Though his ears were clogged with sand.

Most of the day had come and gone, and as of yet they hadn't discovered him. They'd passed over the two dunes on either side of the shallow canyon he was in, but judging by the soft thudding of their hooves, they hadn't come near enough for him to attempt anything.

He was now having serious doubts about the wisdom of the path he'd chosen. He needed a horse. The Horde had horses, but unless he lured them close enough, they would see him coming and simply run away, knowing that their greatest weapon against him was time, because with time would come the disease.

Thoughts of his skin slowly rotting elevated his pulse. He hadn't moved for hours. He was protected from the sun, but lying in this shallow grave, he was rotting, wasn't he?

His mind drifted back to the time when he used to dream, before he'd sworn to Rachelle that he would eat the Rhambutan fruit at least once each day to keep his mind from dreaming, a

453

promise he'd fulfilled faithfully for thirteen years. He couldn't remember what it felt like to dream of anything, much less another world.

Rumor had it that those in his dreams had told him that this reality was the dream. Ludicrous, of course. A hundred battles with the Horde had washed away any such fantasy.

He had three pieces of the fruit in his pocket now, but their flesh wouldn't hold him for long. He had to find a horse.

Thomas moved deliberately for the first time in hours. Pain sliced through his muscles. The disease?

Panicked by this sudden evidence, he sat up and let the sand fall from his face and chest. For a moment he was distracted from the pain by a need to see if any Scabs were in sight. But seeing none, he turned his attention to his arms.

They had turned gray and were cracking. Pain flashed through his skin with the slightest movement.

Thomas jumped from the grave and stared at his spread hands. He was a Scab! Or nearly one. He was stranded in the desert, turning to Horde as the sun sank to the horizon.

He turned around, saw the dunes on all sides empty, and made for the closest. It took him a few minutes to climb because of all the pain in his legs, which forced him to claw his way up with sore hands. A terrible thing, this turning to Scab.

His view at the top of the mound rewarded him with nothing but sand and rock.

Nothing! Not a single Horde warrior that he could see.

For a long time he stared around, dumbstruck by his bad luck. Why weren't they crawling over the hills looking for him? Surely they knew he was still here!

Then he remembered that being caught by the Horde in the open would only ensure his ruin. They would see him and stay away, leaving his flesh and mind to rot.

*And my mind is rotting,* he thought. He was careless already.

Thomas slid back down the hill, groaning with pain. Maybe they'd already seen him and were biding their time. No, they would have posted sentries on the hills. He'd hidden too well! He had consigned himself to death!

Thomas lay on the desert floor, overcome with desperation, and wept. He cursed the disease with bitter cries of protest. Then he ate two of the fruit in his pockets, finished the water from his canteen, and walked into the night.

# TWENTY

H e's not there," Martyn said. "The arrangement was that you'd leave him in the Red Valley, which you did, but this business about telling him to run for the forests immediately not only makes no sense; it's not what he did."

They had left Johnis in the same cage most of the day, then hauled him up into the temple library for this audience with the Dark Priest, who stood draped in black; Qurong, who was trying to make sense of Johnis; and General Martyn, who paced in front of Johnis, grilling him with questions about Thomas.

He was a prisoner.

Silvie hadn't returned to rescue him.

They had his legs bound to the chair.

But Karas had been freed. His little Horde girl was alive, and now he wasn't entirely sure he understood why he'd taken the chance on her. To save her, naturally, but at what cost? Not to him, but to his mother, to the forests, to the mission? It didn't matter, he'd done what he'd done for love, thinking with his heart. It was the only thing he knew to do.

"And what did he do?" Johnis asked.

"He went into the canyons just west and disappeared. We checked the way north to the forests and came up short. So tell me where he is."

"I told you hours ago: I don't know where he is. I told him to head back, so I can only assume he tricked you into thinking he was going west, then doubled back. You're not dealing with a child here."

"You don't need to tell me who I'm dealing with!" Martyn said. "We pulled our men to the north and came up empty. Where could he have gone? A man just doesn't fade into thin air."

"I don't know."

"Then you'll pay with your life."

The first thing he'd noticed upon entering the library was the empty side table where the book he'd slipped the map into had been. Gone. With any luck, Chelise, daughter of Qurong, had taken his bait.

"Karas will live, as long as I'm general." Martyn drilled Witch with a glare. "That stunt was inhuman."

Witch defended himself. "I have your Chosen One, haven't I?"

"Without Thomas, you've given me nothing," the general snapped.

"I have to agree with Martyn," Qurong said. "Our war isn't with any recruit who can barely hold a sword. It's with the forests and with Thomas, who stands in our way."

"You'll do well to remember that Thomas himself placed slightly more weight on this recruit, who can barely hold a sword."

"Watch your tone, Witch," the general said.

The door behind Qurong opened, and Chelise filled the frame. But not only Chelise.

First one, then a stream of twenty Shataiki slipped past the gaping door, into the library where they attached themselves to the shelves and stared at Johnis with pupil-less, red eyes. The one closest to him hissed, fangs dripping with saliva.

Johnis pulled back instinctively.

"What is it?" the Dark Priest glanced at the wall where Johnis stared.

The gaunt Shataiki called Alucard stepped around Chelise as she closed the door. He eyed Johnis, then walked over to the Dark Priest and leaped to his head, where he perched.

The priest scratched his head but otherwise made no attempt to remove the beast. He felt something, Johnis realized, just not the full extent of what was there.

"You," Johnis said to Alucard. "I thought we'd burned you in the Black Forest."

"Not me, you fool," the Shataiki hissed.

"Who are you talking to?" Qurong demanded. Then to Witch, "He's lost his mind."

"It's black magic," the priest said.

"He's lied to us. Kill him," Martyn said, burrowing into Johnis with a dark stare. He turned to go, and Qurong stood to join him. "Before sunset. This is a dangerous runt who's more use to us dead than alive. We begin a new sweep of the Red Valley at first light."

"Sir!" the Dark Priest protested. "I beg you! This is the Chosen One!"

"To them, Witch, not to us. His black magic is nothing more than foolishness, offering himself for a child he doesn't know and not caring if he lives or dies."

"I would say those are noble traits," Chelise said.

"And I would say they are the traits of an idiot," her father snapped. "What interests you with this young pup?"

"He can read the books," she said.

"He can lead us to the missing books," the Dark Priest said.

One of the bats fluttered over to Qurong and sank his claws in the man's shoulder. He grasped his muscle momentarily, then brushed it off as if only a fly had lighted there. There were dozens in the room now, lining the walls and ceiling like clusters of lumpy black grapes.

When Johnis looked back at the priest, Alucard had hopped down on his shoulder and was licking the man's ear with a long, pink tongue. He twisted his head and made to sink his jaws in the man's neck, all the while staring at Johnis.

"If Martyn says kill him, then I say kill him," Qurong said. "Before the sun sets." Alucard left with Qurong, and as they opened the door, more Shataiki entered. Apparently they didn't live among the Horde, but they did seem to come and go freely.

Johnis grasped for the slightest advantage. "You'd be a fool to kill me, Witch. The fact is I do have black magic. I can prove it."

"Tell me where the books are and I'll let you live," the priest retorted.

Johnis kept his eyes on Witch. "I can put marks on you from here. You'll feel a prick at your neck, and it comes from my mind."

"You don't scare me with this nonsense."

"Why do you like the taste of blood, Alucard?" Johnis said, watching the Shataiki beast on Witch's shoulder sniffing and licking his neck. "Why do you want to bite him?"

"Human blood gives me the life that was robbed," Alucard said, and sank his teeth into Witch's neck.

The man slapped at his neck as if a mosquito had landed and bit him there. Smack! The black beast flapped off his shoulder and landed with claws extended on the stone floor. It stepped awkwardly to one side, fangs still bared, licking a tiny drop of blood from its teeth.

"You see, Chelise?" Johnis drilled her with his most urgent look and spoke quickly. "I do know the magic of the books, and I can tell you I'm not the only one who can read these Books of History. There is a member of the Horde who can teach you to read. I know, because he was the one who taught me to read. He'll be masquerading as someone else, of course, but he can change your life if you give him your horse."

"Stop!" The Dark Priest threw his hand up. "Don't try to bewitch her; I won't have it!"

"She wants to read the books. Is that a crime?"

"No one can read the books!"

"*I* can!"

"You lie."

"Show me a book and I'll read," Johnis said.

"That's impossible. Who would know if your rambling matched the words?"

Eyes back on Chelise. "There's a Horde who knows how to read the books."

"I must ask you to leave us," Witch said, turning to Chelise.

Chelise looked from one to the other and back. "There is evil in this room," she said, then spun on her heels and strode through the door.

"Are you mad, trying to beguile Qurong's daughter?" Witch cried.

"I'm only trying to get someone in this impossible Horde city to realize that you've all missed the most important thing of all. It's no wonder you can't win any battles against armies a tenth your size."

Witch paced by him slowly, stroking his beard. "Is that so? And what would that be?"

"Black magic. You felt it, didn't you? The sting on your neck? Keep me alive, and I can teach you things you've only dreamed of."

"Trickery won't save you this time," Alucard hissed.

"Then kill me now," Johnis snapped. "You can't, can you? Not here, where you have your puppets to do your killing. You can't kill us unless we enter your black forests. Isn't that right?"

The beast recoiled, and Johnis knew he'd stumbled on the truth. The Shataiki couldn't destroy the Forest Dwellers unless they either became Horde or entered the Shataikis' domain.

"Who are you talking to?" Witch demanded.

"To the Shataiki beside you," Johnis said; then he shifted his eyes back to Alucard. "You've come to make sure they do what you failed to do in the Black Forest. You're here to watch my death."

"Knowing the truth won't save you, human!" the black bat said.

Witch had gone a shade paler. He glanced to his left and stepped away. "I'll ask you one last time, where are the missing books?"

"Keep me alive, and I'll tell you."

"Karassssss," Alucard hissed. "Kill Karassssss."

"Tell me or I'll kill Karas," Witch whispered.

"Then kill me, because I can't tell you where the books are. I can only open your mind to the black magic."

The Dark Priest glared at him for several long seconds that stretched into an endless minute. Then he spun and walked from the library.

Four Horde guards came in, pulled Johnis from his chair, hurried him down the steps, and locked him in the same cage that had imprisoned his mother and Silvie.

They snuffed out the oil lamp and slammed the door, leaving him in total darkness.

He was alive. He couldn't fool the Dark Priest for long with his talk of black magic, because beyond the trick he'd already played, he had none. But he was alive. Johnis sat in the corner and eventually slumped on one side. He'd hardly slept in a week, and exhaustion swallowed his mind.

The first pains of the disease hit him when he woke a day later. He knew a day had passed because it took the disease two days to deliver any pain, and he'd bathed a day before being locked in the cage.

It was so black in the dungeon that he couldn't see his hand in front of his face. Witch had left him to turn to Horde down here, as he'd done to Rosa.

He would become Horde for Karas.

# TWENTY-ONE

When Thomas Hunter awoke on the morning of the fourth day without having bathed in the lake's healing waters, the first thing he realized was that the pain didn't seem as bad as it had the day before.

But it was all moot. Unless he found water to drink in the next few hours, he would be dead by day's end. The sand felt better underfoot, but his cracked lips stung at the touch of his tongue.

He'd evidently discarded his boots somewhere back along the way, and which way that was, he had no idea. His armor and tunic, as well. He'd stumbled on for hours, nearly naked, as his flesh slowly grayed and cracked.

But looking at it today, his skin didn't look as bad as he'd been led to believe in his hallucinatory state yesterday. Who said smooth was better than scaly, anyway? Even the smell seemed more tolerable.

Thomas gazed about and finally decided that he was still in or near Red Valley. He'd likely walked the dunes in a great circle, for all he knew.

Honestly, he felt rather stupid. But surely the Horde weren't this dim-witted all the time. Maybe only during the transformation from Forest Dweller to Scab.

Thomas began to plod on, then stopped, wondering where he should go. Did he have the strength to actually go anywhere? No, not really. So he eased himself down on the sand and sat staring dumbly into the rising sun.

An hour or maybe two hours later, he fell backward, covered his eyes with his arms, and tried to die.

They found him about an hour after that.

"You there!"

His mind was playing tricks on him, speaking like Horde.

"You there!"

Thomas lifted his arm off his face and squinted in the sun. Two Horde sat on pale horses, staring down at him. One tossed him a robe that landed on his scaly chest.

"Put on some clothes."

"Why?" he croaked.

"Because you're naked. There's a woman in this group."

"Oh." He struggled to his feet and shrugged the long cloak on, lifting the hood to cover his head. They thought he was Horde.

Was he?

"Drink," one of them said, shoving a flask at him.

The water inside smelled brown. "Spit water," they called it in the forests. But today spit water went down surprisingly smoothly. He drank half the flask before the Scab pulled it away.

Almost immediately his head began to clear some.

Was he really Horde?

"She wants to talk to you," one of the men said. They led him to a small caravan with roughly twenty horses. The woman who came out to talk to him was dressed in a white tunic unlike any he'd seen, certainly nothing worn on the battlefield. She moved like swaying wheat.

Her eyes studied him from head to foot.

"Why do you wear your hair like this?" she asked. True, he didn't have the dreadlocks so typical among Horde. Long wavy hair dirtied by the desert, but no locks.

"Does every man need to be cut from the same mold?" he asked.

The answer seemed to amuse her. "Are you married?"

Thomas stood there, scalp burning under the hood, and stared at the desert dweller, taken aback by her question. If he said yes, she might ask who his wife was, which could cause problems.

"No."

She stepped up to him and searched his face. Her eyes were a dull gray, nearly white. Her cheeks were ashen.

She drew her hood back and exposed bleached hair. In that moment Thomas knew that this woman was propositioning him.

But more, he knew that she was beautiful. He wasn't sure if the sun had gotten to him or if the disease was eating his mind, but he found her attractive. Fascinating, at the very least. And no odor. In fact, he was sure that if he were somehow miraculously changed back into the Thomas with clear skin and green eyes, she would think *his* skin stank.

The sudden attraction caught him wholly off guard. Until this moment he'd never considered what a male Scab's attraction to a female Scab felt like.

The woman reached a hand to his cheek and touched it. "I am Chelise."

He was immobilized with indecision.

"I am . . . Roland."

"Would you like to come with me, Roland?"

"I would, yes. But I first must complete my mission, and for that I need a horse."

"Is that so? What is your mission?" She smiled seductively. "Are you a fierce warrior off to assassinate the murderer of men with all the other thugs?"

"As a matter of fact, I am an assassin." He thought it might earn him respect, but she acted as if meeting assassins in the desert was a common thing. Unless she was referring to the search for him that was underway at this very moment.

"Who is this murderer of men?" he asked.

Her eyes darkened, and he knew that he'd asked the wrong question.

"If you're an assassin, you would know, wouldn't you? There's only one man any assassin has taken an oath to kill."

"Yes, of course, but do *you* really know the business of an assassin?" he said, mentally scrambling for a way out. "If you are so eager to bear my children, perhaps you should know with whom you would make your home. So tell me, whom have we assassins sworn to kill?"

He could tell immediately that she liked his answer.

"Thomas Hunter," she said. "He is the murderer of men and women and children, and he is the one that my father, the great Qurong, has commanded his assassins to kill."

The daughter of Qurong! He was speaking to desert royalty. He dipped his head in a show of submission.

She laughed. "You don't need to bow to me."

The way her eyes had darkened when she spoke his name alarmed Thomas. He knew he was hated by the Horde, but to hear it coming from the lips of such a stunning enemy was unnerving.

"Come with me, Roland," Chelise said. "I'll give you more to do than run around making hopeless assassination attempts. Everyone knows that Thomas is far too swift with his sword to yield to this senseless strategy of my father's. Martyn, our bright new general, will have a place for you."

Martyn. He'd never heard the name. This was Justin, the traitor. Or a defector at the very least. Their new enemy had a name, and it was Martyn.

"I beg to differ," he said, "but I'm the one assassin who can find the murderer of men and kill him at will."

"Is that so? You're that intelligent, are you? And are you bright enough to read what no man can read?"

She was mocking him by suggesting that he couldn't read?

"Of course I can read."

She arched an eyebrow. "The Books of History?"

Thomas blinked at the reference. She was speaking about the ancient books? How was that possible?

"You have them?" he asked.

Chelise turned away. "No. But I've seen a few in my time. It would take a wise man to read that gibberish."

"Give me a horse. Let me finish my mission; then I will return," he said.

"Can you teach me to read the Books of History?" she asked directly.

"Will you give me a horse if I say no?"

"I'll give you a horse," she said, replacing her hood. "But don't bother returning to me. If killing another man is more important to you than serving a princess, I've misjudged you."

She ordered a man nearby to give him a horse and then walked away.

Thomas mounted stiffly, took a full canteen and a sword from one of Chelise's guards, and rode toward the sun.

Not until he was out of sight did he stop to realize his incredible fortune. He was going to live, he knew. He still had to reach

the forest and bathe in the lake without being killed by his own
Guard, but he was confident he could accomplish that much.

Then again, did he really want to return to the forests? Why
not turn west and find the Horde city? Or return to Chelise and
let her guide him to the city where a million others had embraced
the disease on his skin?

Then he thought of Rachelle and the prophecy and the Forest
Guard and the war with those who would slaughter his family.

Thomas took another long pull of the spit water, turned the
horse to the north, and rode for the Middle Forest.

# TWENTY-TWO

The sun was setting over the western dunes, and still Silvie couldn't make up her mind. She and Rosa sweltered in the hot sun overlooking the city through the day, discussing a hundred options, but each was riddled with impossibilities. Given the slightest hope for success, she would throw herself at whatever obstacles stood between her and Johnis.

But there was no such hope.

"Then let's just go in," Rosa said, standing. "The darkness will cover us, and we'll have a chance. If we don't try tonight, the disease will get us!"

But Rosa didn't know about the Shataiki. True, Witch would be waiting for some kind of rescue attempt and would surely catch them. True, the temple was surely locked up like a chest, prohibiting any entry by one and a half fighters—Rosa was only half in her weakened condition.

But truer than either of these were the Shataiki bats who'd descended into the city and not emerged.

"If we die, then he'll die in vain," Silvie said.

"Then what are you waiting for?" Rosa snapped. "That's my son down there!"

"And that's the man I love!" She continued quickly to cover her frank admission. "But we can't rush into death blindly!"

Rosa suddenly reached for her arm, eyes fixed on the boulders below them. "Someone's there!"

Silvie dropped to her knees and spun. Four horses stood behind the boulders that had hid them when they'd first found the city, two with riders, two tied behind. Guard horses.

Even in the dimming light she recognized the two riders. "Billos and Darsal!" she cried. "They've . . . they've found out!"

"Guard?" Rosa ran for her horse. "Then we have a chance!"

Silvie stared at the two fighters, then at the city. Her heart soared for an instant. Then settled. *No, we still don't have a chance*, she thought. Two or four, it hardly matters. They might kill more of the beasts, last a little longer in a full-on fight, but they would never be able to break into the temple and take Johnis out with Witch expecting them, much less the Shataiki.

She whirled back and tore after Rosa.

"WHAT I'M SAYING IS THAT WE HAVE TO STOP AND THINK!"
Silvie cried.

Billos paced the sand behind the rocks, gearing up for battle.
She'd never seen him so eager for a fight. Darsal still sat on her
horse, eyeing both of them and deep in thought.

"But you said the books are there, right?" Billos said. "In the
city. Probably in that temple."

"It's Johnis we're after," Silvie said, "not the books."

"Johnis, of course. But it's the books that confirm we should
go after him. There's a power in those books, Silvie. Don't tell me
you didn't feel it!"

What Billos said was true. She hadn't thought too much about
the dark vision they'd all shared when touching the Books of
History with blood. Billos seemed obsessed with the books. Or
was she misreading him?

They'd approached the rocks carefully, calling in when they
were close. Billos and Darsal had embraced them with relief and
listened while Silvie hurriedly told them what had happened with
as much detail as she could cram into mere minutes.

"How did you find us?" she asked Darsal.

"Johnis's sister, Kiella, found Billos yesterday morning, and she
said she'd seen him and that Rosa was alive—a Scab, but alive. We
knew then that Johnis had gone after the Horde city and was in
trouble."

"But how did you find us?"

"Michal, the Roush. He tried to warn us off, something about Johnis learning the truth of the Horde. We've been worried sick, you know?" Darsal said. "We had a vow, and the two of you disappeared on us. Billos has been frantic! And you took the books, and now it turns out you not only took them but lost them to the Horde."

"Don't you see, Silvie?" Billos said. "It's not just Johnis who's chosen, but all four of us. He said so himself. We have to go in, just like he went to the Black Forest. We're sworn to recover the books."

"What books?" Rosa demanded. "What's all this about books? It's my son we're after!"

They all looked at her, then exchanged furtive glances. They'd already said too much in her presence.

Silvie covered for them. "The library in the temple is full of books, which the Horde seem obsessed with. If we could take them, it might give us an advantage over them. But no one can know this. And you're right: if we go in, it's for Johnis only."

Rosa looked at Billos. "You said there was a power in the books. What is that?"

"That's the power to manipulate, because the Horde is so taken by them," Billos said. "Of course, it's all about Johnis, but if we had the books, we might even be able to exchange them for Johnis. You don't think that's power?"

She seemed satisfied by his convoluted explanation.

Billos took a step closer to Silvie, pressing his point. "We entered hell and lived; I say we enter it again and bring our boy out!"

His enthusiasm was infectious. "If we had fire—"

"We do!" he cried, rushing for his saddlebag. He pulled out the fire sticks and held them up. "You think I'm a fool?" He grinned.

Now this was the Billos she knew, screaming for a fight when he wanted one, and he most certainly wanted this one.

Silvie looked at the Horde city. "You can't burn the city; it's made of mud. Besides, Johnis would likely have a fit."

"What does he care, as long as we get him out?"

She hadn't told them about the Horde girl, Karas, only that Johnis had been trapped after setting them free.

"He's taken a liking to the Horde," she said.

"Don't be ridiculous," Billos snapped.

"You can't burn the city anyway. But the temple has enough books in it to make a nice bonfire."

"Books?" Billos said, lowering his sticks. "They'll burn?"

"Of course."

"Then we can't burn the temple," Darsal said. "We'll have to burn something else to get at the Shataiki."

"Carts," Silvie said. "They have thousands of carts made of wood and straw. And I know where there are enough to put a sun in the middle of this city."

"That's it!" Billos jumped into his saddle. "It'll work."

"Then let's go," Rosa said. She and Silvie had already taken a spit bath in some of the extra lake water Darsal had brought. "Leave the rest of the water here; we can't risk losing it."

Darsal considered the suggestion, then nodded.

"Hold up. Going now is suicide," Silvie said. "They're waiting for us. Johnis is their bait, dead or alive. Fire might protect us for a while, but I'm telling you, there's no way out of the temple. We have to think this through carefully."

Darsal lifted a hand. "She's right. Slow down, Billos, or you'll get us all killed. We wait till the city's asleep before we go, but then we do go with our best plan."

"It's our vow," Billos said.

Silvie dipped her head. Honestly, she could hardly stand to wait another four hours till midnight, but she could stand the thought of losing Johnis even less.

"Agreed."

# TWENTY-THREE

Silvie stopped at the corner of a mud house to still her breathing. Crickets sang in the night; a light breeze carried the Horde stench west and rustled the thatch here and there. Many of the houses had dogs, but they seemed adequately fooled by the smelly cloaks.

The plan was a compilation of ideas Silvie had painstakingly rehearsed during the day and innovations Billos and Darsal had thrown in the mix. They would secure four cloaks with hoods—it was the only way to remain under cover even in the darkest hour.

Silvie and Billos had gone in for the cloaks and found them in two different stables on the city's outskirts. So far, so good.

Horses were out of the question. It was one thing to drive up the middle of the city unexpected, but this mission had to be executed with stealth. Their objective was the temple, and studying the city from her high vantage, Silvie had identified several primary streets that angled toward the city center. She and Rosa would go down one. Billos another. Darsal the third. Each was visible from the dunes above Thrall by the light of a thousand burning torches along the way.

How each managed to reach the temple was his or her own business, but they would meet at the stables behind the tall structure, knowing well that a hundred Shataiki eyes were likely looking for a sign of rescue. "Stay away from the main road," Silvie warned. "They'll have it watched for sure."

Getting to the temple was a task Silvie thought they could manage. The plan to get *into* the temple took a turn to the side of shaky. The plan to get *out* of the temple was hardly better than throwing a dozen ideas into the air and deciding to use the one that touched the ground first.

Still, so far, so good.

She felt Rosa breathing at her elbow. "We have to hurry."

Silvie lifted a hand. She'd tried to convince Rosa to wait behind at the boulders, but Johnis's mother would have none of it. She'd recovered most of the spunk that had gotten her taken the first time, particularly now with water at hand.

She pointed to the temple spire rising into the night sky. "The stables are on the far side," she whispered. "Stay close to the buildings."

They had come into the city from the west after an hour's hike around the outskirts. Billos was coming from the north near the main route, and Darsal from the east. They figured it would take them about three hours each to find the city center.

Silvie slid down the alley between two pale mortar buildings, whether warehouses or residences she could hardly tell—all the buildings were the same basic rectangular shape. Then they were at the back of the stables without having raised a single alarm. What's more, Billos and Darsal were waiting.

"Don't spook the horses," Silvie warned.

Darsal indicated a long row of carts along one wall. "These are all of them?"

"There are more on the other side. Quickly, exactly as planned."

Billos nodded, and they split up again. It took them an hour to position the carts, primarily because they had to move them with painstaking caution. Finding enough rope had been the single greatest challenge, and it took Darsal sneaking into a shed five houses down to get enough to tie into long strands.

Still no sign of Shataiki—maybe they'd all fled the city after the sun had gone down.

They gathered at the stable and stared out at their handiwork, which, thankfully, couldn't be seen in the darkness: two carts on either side of the door at the courtyard's edge; ropes strung to the large curved handles, then laid along the ground at forty-five degree angles. Billos and Darsal would take the far rope, Silvie and Rosa the near one.

"You're sure we won't burn the temple down?" Billos breathed.

"Only enough of it to preoccupy Witch," Silvie said. "He won't like the idea of losing the library any more than you do."

Sweat beaded Billos's face. "So light them and then pull them in."

"Light all four carts," Silvie said. "We pull only when the blaze is large enough to burn the front door. Then get your tails to the back window where we go in."

"What if the distraction doesn't take?" Darsal asked. "Witch might know exactly what we're up to."

"Then we fight our way out," Silvie said. "You have a better idea, it's not too late. I said this would be suicide, didn't I?"

"Let them come," Billos sneered. "Where would you say the missing books might be?"

"Forget the books," Rosa said. "First Johnis."

"We'd be fools not to take every opportunity to get them."

"I have no clue. There's a large room underground—I could imagine Witch hiding the books inside. If we get that far, we'll be passing through. Ready?"

A lone shriek carried through the night. Shataiki. But no sighting yet.

"Ready?" Silvie asked again.

"Let's go."

Darsal touched Billos's arm. He gripped the flint in one hand and the resin-dipped fire sticks in the other. Then Darsal was off into the night with Billos after her like a shadow.

Silvie wiped the sweat from her brow and tried to still the tremor in her fingers. "As we agreed," she whispered.

"I should go with you," Rosa said.

"Someone has to man the carts we've tied to the horses. You stay in the barn as agreed. Take the rope."

They grabbed the rope and braced for the pull.

Their wait was longer than Silvie thought it should take. Maybe Billos was having difficulty lighting the fire sticks. But then a flame ignited and took to the straw of the near cart.

She saw Billos crouched and running to the far cart. It took flame.

"Wait . . ." she said. "Wait . . ."

The flames grew, licking at the carts. A window in the temple flew open.

"Now!"

They pulled on the rope with all their might. The cart rolled slowly at first, then gained momentum and wobbled across the courtyard, spewing fire into the sky.

*What if the rope burns?*

All four carts careened toward the front doors and crashed against one another in a great burning mess.

"Ready the other carts!" Silvie ordered and ran toward the back of the redbrick house they'd escaped from earlier with Johnis.

Cries filled the night. Shrieks of Shataiki and the loud curses of Scabs yelling for water.

Silvie didn't stop to watch. She reached the side of the house, crashed through the window, and rolled to her feet inside the storage room Johnis had taken them through before.

Billos and Darsal dove through only moments after her. They scrambled to their feet.

Silvie snatched her hand up to stop them. From the hall beyond the room came grunts and yells of fire: "Water, get water!"

*It's working,* Silvie thought. But she'd guessed they might get this far. Getting out would be the real challenge. Once they went down, they would be at the mercy of Elyon. They could execute the plan perfectly and still find a trap. Witch wasn't an idiot.

"Follow me!"

She poked her head past the curtain, saw the hall was clear, and ran around the corner into the stairwell that descended to the subterranean rooms. No torches, but she didn't want to advertise their presence. She descended by feel, taking the steps two at a time, then through the curtains into the lavishly furnished room illuminated by a single oil lamp on the wall.

"This is it?" Billos asked.

"The dungeon's at the end of the hall. Grab the lamp."

*We're going to make it in,* Silvie thought.

The door at the top of the stairwell behind them slammed shut, and they spun as one.

"What was that?" Billos demanded.

Silvie took a deep breath. "That was the door to our tomb."

# TWENTY-FOUR

The screams high above woke Johnis from a dead sleep, and he sat up in his cage, wondering if he'd dreamed of Shataiki.

Then he heard shrieks, and he knew it wasn't a dream. The black bats were up in arms—why, he didn't care.

The pain on his skin had intensified slowly, but the disease still hadn't taken his mind or his muscles, which meant that he'd been down here more than one day but less than two.

A key scraped and clanked in the side door, and he stood. *It's night outside*, he thought. Surely Silvie and his mother hadn't been foolish enough to . . .

The door swung open and Billos piled in, holding a lamp high. Followed by Darsal and, finally, Silvie.

He couldn't find his voice to express either terror or relief, and honestly he wasn't sure which he should feel.

"They closed the door behind us," Silvie said, running past Billos. She snatched the key ring from his hand and tried two keys before springing the lock.

"You came back," Johnis said.

She rushed in, kissed him on the lips. "That's in case we don't make it out." Then she handed him an extra sword and pulled him stumbling from the cage.

"Nice of you to join us," Johnis said to Billos and Darsal. "Thank Elyon for little sisters."

"You think we'd leave you to run off with the books again?" Billos said, grinning. "Where are they?"

"The books? Where's Rosa?"

"Waiting," Silvie said. "Hurry! We have to go up through the library!"

"Wait, the books could be back in that room, right?" Billos ran for the door and disappeared down the hall.

"Billos!" Silvie ran after him.

"He's right, Silvie," Johnis said. "We should get the books."

"Then we'll be dead," Darsal cried, taking up Silvie's concern.

But they were already in the room. Weapons of all kinds hung on the walls around a large wooden table and reclining cushions. Johnis pulled Billos aside and hurried toward a large trunk set beneath a huge brass carving of the winged serpent, Teeleh. Why the Horde gave their images of the Shataiki a serpent's body,

Johnis had no clue. But he was sure by Karas's reaction that the missing books waited below this one.

The trunk was locked. "Billos, your blade."

Billos attacked the latch like a wolf, splintering the wood with a few hard jerks. The latch sprang open. Johnis jerked the lid up.

A candlestick in the winged serpent's image rested on either side of the trunk's red interior. And between the candlesticks . . .

Nothing.

Johnis stood back. "Gone."

"They were here," Billos said. "They had to be."

"We have to leave," Darsal snapped. "We can't find the books if we're dead."

Silvie emerged from the stairwell. "Locked. They know! Get your swords ready. We have to go out the front—it's the only other way."

She led them at a full sprint back into the cage room, then up the stairs that led into the library.

"Silvie, slow down," Johnis whispered, but she was too fast, determined not to be trapped in the dungeon again. "There's Shataiki."

Silvie threw wide the door at the top of the stairs and rushed into the library. Johnis, Billos, and Darsal slid to a stop behind her.

As one they caught their breath. The library was black with the Shataiki clinging to every square inch of wall and ceiling, glaring at them silently.

"Dear Elyon," Darsal whispered.

A few of the black beasts hissed at the use of the name.

It was as if the walls had sprouted a horrible, black, lumpy cancer.

"They can't hurt us," Johnis said, trying to believe it himself. "Not unless we go into the black forests."

"You're sure?" Darsal asked.

"Yes."

The door behind them slammed shut; and before Johnis had time to consider what that might mean, the main door swung open.

A line of Horde, all dressed in pitch black, marched in two lines, one spreading each way to encircle them. The temple guard, Johnis had learned earlier, elite assassins. Twenty of them. Or more.

Then Witch stepped in, casually, wearing a smug expression of supreme confidence. And he wasn't alone.

The large mangy black bat named Alucard, who'd tortured them once, was riding his back. The bat's two forearms snaked around Witch's neck, and its powerful legs were snug around the priest's belly. Its wings dragged on the floor behind, and its wolf-like head nestled between Witch's right shoulder and his neck, like a cat; purring comfortably.

"I assure you," the Dark Priest said, "there are more outside."

Johnis could see the main sanctuary past the door, coated in Shataiki like a bat's cave. At least twenty more Horde assassins waited there with drawn swords. The door leading outward was smoldering—Silvie must have tried to distract them with fire.

"Drop your swords."

Johnis let his clatter to the floor. The others saw what he saw, and after a moment's hesitation four swords lay on the ground. None of the Scabs made a move to retrieve them.

"The Chosen One is chosen no longer," Witch said. "I have all four of the young recruits. It seems that your luck has run out."

"Where are the books?" Billos asked. *An odd question,* Johnis thought. Yes, they were on a quest for the books, but Billos was in no position to demand them.

"Safe with me," Witch said. "The question is where the rest are."

"And that information will remain safe," Johnis said, calling the priest's bluff. "With me."

Witch walked forward, ridden by Alucard, the huge lump on his back, who slowly rubbed his furry chin against the Dark Priest's neck. His tongue flickered out and licked Witch's cheek, then eye.

"I don't think so, Chosen One," Witch said. "When all four of you are Scabs, you'll spill your secrets. Even if they could, do you think the Forest Guard will cross the desert to save four lost recruits who have betrayed them?"

*No,* Johnis thought. *They won't.*

"No, I'm afraid not," Witch said. "There's no one left to save you."

His words rang with a finality that Johnis knew was simply the truth. No Roush, no Guard, no comrades in arms. Rosa was waiting for them, but she didn't stand a chance. No one stood a chance. They really were at the end of their rope this time.

The door behind them opened. So now they would be led to the dungeon to die the slow death.

Witch froze, eyes fixed behind Johnis. Qurong? Or Martyn?

"You're wrong," a soft female voice said.

Johnis spun around. Karas stood in the doorway, dressed in a raggedy white tunic, staring at her father, the Dark Priest named Witch.

"There is one person left who can save them."

# TWENTY-FIVE

Johnis didn't know what Karas was thinking, but the thought that she would risk throwing her life away flooded him with fear.

"Karas? Please . . ."

The little Horde girl lifted up two bags, one gripped in each hand. One was lumpy, and only then did Johnis think it might contain books.

Three books.

The three missing Books of History. But even these books couldn't save them, could they?

Alucard hissed and recoiled, eyes fixed on the second bag. A bag of water. The one Johnis had brought in to douse Silvie and Rosa with.

"What do you think you're doing?" Witch demanded. "Drop it! Drop it where you stand."

Karas's eyes were on Darsal, lingering there as if something about her was especially noteworthy, though Johnis didn't know what.

"I have the dreaded water, Father," Karas said, looking at Witch. She dropped the bag of books by Billos's feet and held the water out with both hands. Billos snatched up the fallen bag and looked inside. The look on his face confirmed Johnis's suspicion. The Books of History.

Working with her small fingers, Karas opened the neck of the bag. Then she dipped one finger into the water, gasped, and brought it out.

The change on her finger was unmistakable. Gray, cracked flesh had become pink. She stared at her hand in wide wonder. Then up at Darsal again.

The Horde assassins stepped back. She'd collected the water bag from the cell where he'd dropped it several days ago, and now she intended to use the healing water as a weapon. He'd never heard of such a thing, perhaps because the forests had no inclination to save the Horde, thereby diluting their blood with converted Horde. Perhaps because there wasn't enough water to use in battle anyway.

Yet there was nothing the Horde feared as much as Elyon's water. It made a fine weapon indeed.

The sudden turn of events had frozen them all, but the guards could still kill her, Johnis realized. A thrown knife or sword could cut Karas down where she stood.

"You killed my mother," the girl said, drilling Witch with a fierce gaze that could have melted steel. "I don't want to be like you." She suddenly reached into the bag. Her hand came out cupping water. Careful not to spill a drop, she brought her hand to her face, closed her eyes, and let the water spill over the bridge of her nose.

The healing water seared her skin, sealing it as if by magic. Her small body trembled with pain. But the sensations passed, and her mouth parted in a silent cry. Tears began to seep from her eyes.

"Drop it! Kill her!" the Dark Priest screamed.

Johnis dove at Witch while all eyes were locked on the girl. He grabbed the priest's cloak and threw him to the floor. Alucard flapped for the ceiling, squawking with rage.

Johnis dragged the flailing priest into the group of four Forest fighters. "Douse him, Karas!" he yelled, foot on the priest's cloak so he couldn't stand.

She understood immediately. In one step she was over him, bag poised to douse him. But she was still fixated on the water for herself, he thought. Desperate for more.

"Get back!" Johnis cried at the Horde.

The priest threw both hands over his head. "Back! Do as he says. Back!"

No one moved.

Karas dipped her hand into the bag and splashed water over

herself, this time her head, and another palmful on her neck. And more on her chest and her shoulders. She began to tremble like a twig in the wind, weeping as she quickly doused herself and washed away the disease at the heart of the Teeleh's temple.

"It's getting on me!" the priest shrieked. "Stay back, stay back!"

Only a spot or two of water touched him, but in his mind it might well be acid burning his flesh. And perhaps it was.

Silvie had her sword at the priest's throat. "One move and you'll pray it was only water, not your own blood."

The room squirmed with a thousand Shataiki cowering back into the corners. They'd never been this close to the healing waters.

"Out of the room, all of you," Johnis snapped.

The temple guard still didn't move. Their twisted minds couldn't fathom being so soundly routed by a bag of water.

Silvie pressed her blade against Witch's neck. "Tell them."

"Get out. Out, out, out!"

They rushed out, clogging the doorway. Shataiki bats streamed out above them like a swarm fleeing their cave at dusk.

Silvie yanked the priest to his feet. "Don't think I can't sever your head with one jerk of my sword. Move!"

Johnis took the bag of water from Karas and splashed half of what remained on her back. What was once Horde had become a creature of Elyon once more.

He kissed her on her cheek. "You're the bravest little girl I know." The first moment he had the time, he would hold her tight and swing her around until she squealed with delight.

They formed a box around the priest, Johnis rushing forward with the bag of water held out threateningly. Silvie and Darsal on either side, swords at his neck. Billos behind, books in one hand, sword drawn back with the other, ready for the slightest excuse to swing.

And Karas running behind, still weeping. Some might think she was in agony, but Johnis knew. She was overcome with relief because her change wasn't simply a matter of healed skin but of a changed heart.

They plowed through a half-burned door and into the courtyard—and faced a ring of Horde gaping in disbelief. The sky swarmed with screaming Shataiki bats.

"Now, Rosa!" Silvie shouted. "Now!"

For a moment, nothing. And then three horses crashed through the stable doors, pulling a line of three carts like a train. Rosa rode the lead horse, eyes wide at the sight of so many Horde.

"Tell them to let her in," Silvie snapped.

"Let her in!" the priest cried.

Rosa didn't bother stopping the train, but pulled close enough for them all to pile on, priest included. Then she steered the horses away from the temple, onto the main road, and toward the main gates.

Silvie cut two of the carts free to lighten their load. They'd intended to use fire, Johnis saw, but with the priest aboard, they didn't have the need.

No one spoke as they rode the main street down the center of

Thrall. The priest tried once, but Johnis shut him down. Not a word. Not even a whisper.

They dumped him at the city gates with the last cart, and he watched them race away on three horses.

His cry chased them into the darkness. "He will destroy you, Chosen One!"

They stopped at the boulders, collected the hidden water, mounted the faster Guard horses, and raced toward the Middle Forest. All of them. Johnis, Silvie, Billos, Darsal, Rosa, and Karas.

And in his saddlebag Billos carried three of the seven original Books of History.

# TWENTY-SIX

"We've heard it all, but I still wonder what you think," Ciphus, high priest of the Great Romance, said. "We can't ignore what you've accomplished, despite the costs. If the decision were yours, what would it be?"

They'd spent an hour giving full account of themselves to the Council, who lined the chamber's stone seats and dressed in white tunics.

Behind Johnis sat Billos, Darsal, and Silvie on benches, having stood and given their accounts of what had happened. Silvie had passionately sworn a new allegiance to whatever love had compelled Johnis to go after his mother, because it was this love that truly separated Horde from the Forest Dwellers. Billos and Darsal had agreed with more eloquence than Johnis had expected—from

497

Billos, at least. Darsal, yes, but Billos seemed exceptionally ver-
bose in his praise of the successful mission.

Not a word spoken about the library or the Books of History,
they had all sworn.

His mother and father, Rosa and Ramos, sat next to Kiella and
Karas. The reunion of his parents alone was worth any cost he
personally could have paid, Johnis thought. They threw themselves at each other and danced like foolish children, weeping
unabashedly as hundreds gathered in stunned disbelief at seeing
Rosa alive.

On the trip back, Karas had taken to staring at Darsal, and
when Johnis asked her why, the young girl only shrugged and said
that she looked like her mother. Before her mother died.

Thomas and Rachelle sat to the Council's left, quiet mostly,
letting the other leaders of the Forest Dwellers direct the inquiry.
They were biased, Johnis knew. They alone believed he was the
Chosen One and had agreed to keep the knowledge to themselves
for now. The danger was too great.

Still, the events of the past week were unprecedented. Even
Thomas was quite sure that some kind of correction was in order.
Never before in the short history of the forests had any Guard led
them in the kind of deception that Johnis had practiced in leading the Third Fighting Group into battle and abandoning Thomas
in the Red Valley.

The Guard had nearly killed Thomas at the forest's edge, mistaking him for a Horde—only his roars of protest had stopped

them from sending arrows through his chest. He'd thrown himself into the lake and washed all traces of the desert away in a matter of minutes.

Thomas had lived, but more than a hundred fighters had not.

"For the deaths in the Third Fighting Group . . ." Johnis stopped, choked with sorrow. "For the widows and the children left behind, I should receive a flogging—one hundred lashes—or a month in prison—for each."

The room was stilled to the sound of soft breathing.

"There is no defense for my betrayal of all that I love. I would give my life for Thomas Hunter and for this Council, but I had no right to ask others to give their lives for my mother. Sentence me and be done with it. If I survive my punishment, I'll take whatever position you suggest to serve the forests."

They hadn't expected this from him, he saw, but it was how he felt. He heard a flutter of wings and turned to see Gabil and Michal perched on a long brass spear on the chamber's far end. Michal stared at him, unwavering. Johnis wondered how long they'd been watching.

"It's a just punishment," Thomas said.

Johnis turned back to the Council.

"The imprisonment, not the lashes," Thomas continued. "But there are mitigating circumstances here that should affect our judgment."

William, Thomas's lieutenant, spoke out of turn. "The Third Fighting Group knew it was going to face the Horde as they might on any other mission. How many thousands have given their lives following the commands of superiors over the last five years?"

"Following the orders of legitimate commanders," Tulas, a short, plump member said. "No sane man can excuse—"

"Let me finish," snapped William. "I am not saying that Johnis is innocent of deceiving Captain Hilgard. But 137 fighters died as any die, following orders to which end only fate or Elyon knows. This is war, not the business of civil servants."

"They wouldn't have gone if he hadn't deceived them!" Tulas said.

"Every month, more than a thousand fighters die because someone told them to go into battle! Many die on account of their commander's poor judgment. Are we to incriminate all who make poor judgments? Johnis's crime was assuming authority he did not have."

"And my husband was saved by Johnis," Rachelle said. "He sent the daughter of Qurong out into the desert looking for him. But this isn't about Thomas or the Third Fighting Group, is it? This is about the Great Romance. The love of a boy for his mother." Rachelle put her hand on her husband's knee. "Would Karas please take the center?"

Karas was dressed in a red frock made from the hibiscus flower and cotton, one that matched Kiella's. The two girls had struck an immediate bond, and Kiella was already demanding that Karas stay with them, maybe even join their family.

"Go on," Kiella whispered.

Karas stared at the Council with wide eyes, blue, as it turned out. It was so strange to think that color waited beyond the whites of all Scabs' eyes.

Kiella grabbed her hand and led her to the front, then hurried back to her seat.

Karas's arms hung by her sides. Kiella had braided her long brown hair, which was now silky smooth and clean. To match her dress she wore a hibiscus bloom behind her right ear. *We wanted to look special in honor of you, Johnis,* Kiella had informed him. *Do you like it?*

He could hardly hold back his tears. The same emotion swallowed him now, but he resolved to remain professional before the Council.

"You're a very beautiful girl, Karas," Rachelle said. "It's an honor to have you among us."

"Thank you," Karas said.

"Tell us, Johnis: what is going through your mind when you look at her?"

Johnis wasn't sure he could or should tell them how he really felt. Wasn't sure he knew fully himself, yet. It was on the morning after their escape, as they fled across the desert, that he'd seen the dramatic change in Karas, and his heart had begun to break.

"Tell us," Rachelle repeated.

He glanced over at Michal and was surprised to see the Roush dip his head.

Johnis walked over to Karas and stepped behind her. He

touched her silky hair and her pink cheek, and tears flooded his eyes. "What I feel?"

He clasped his hands behind his back and faced the Council. "I feel like Elyon must feel when he looks at me," he said. "I feel like we should open our arms to those who wish to bathe in our lakes."

Ciphus coughed. They all knew he frequently opposed the thought. The lakes were only so big, only so much water. They were chosen; the Horde was not.

"I feel like she is no different from my own sister, Kiella. And I swear to love her with every beat of my heart."

"Are a hundred fighters' deaths worth the life of this one?" Rachelle asked.

He knew he was on dangerous ground. "I would die a hundred times for Karas," he said. "Now that I know . . ."

"Know what?" Thomas demanded.

"That she, too, is chosen."

The Council broke into several exchanges, none of which had any meaning to Johnis.

Karas was looking up at him with round eyes, smiling wide enough to swallow the room. He knelt on one knee, took her hand, and kissed the backs of her fingers.

"You saved my life," he said. "Now I owe you mine."

Karas leaned forward and accepted his debt with a kiss on his forehead.

The Council had gone quiet.

"Still, it's irresistible," Rachelle said. "In any form love is truly the only healer. Even if you argue he's misguided in some of his thinking, you cannot fault Johnis for his love. Who would dare put someone like this in a deep, dark prison?"

Thomas stood. "I agree. It would be wrong to level such an unusual crime with a usual punishment. Instead of lashings or imprisonment, I say the boy should be promoted to the rank of major."

He silenced the mumbling with a raised hand.

"As a major he will report directly to me, and I will remove him from active duty until I see that he is fit to lead in a battle that requires more than his heart or mind."

"But the Third Fighting Group!" someone protested.

"Their deaths are regrettable, and we will hold another ceremony in their honor this very night. But the information that Johnis has brought us from his infiltration of the Horde city will surely save countless lives in the years to come. The fact that he himself wasn't killed was a matter of pure luck."

*Actually, the commander's words make some good sense,* Johnis thought. The only problem was that he could only share some of what he'd learned, having sworn silence about his mission.

The Council wasn't protesting.

"All in favor—"

"That's not a punishment," someone said.

"It is to him!" Thomas snapped. "All in favor, speak aye."

The room voted eleven ayes, one nay. And it was settled.

Rosa was the first to rush up to Johnis. Then the rest, slapping his back or hugging him or shaking his hand.

"How you do it, I'll never know," Silvie said, kissing his hand and winking.

"We," he said. "We did it." He reached for Darsal and pulled her close. "And Darsal. And Billos. The four of us. We can't forget that. Where's Billos?"

They looked at the bench Billos had occupied just moments ago, but it was empty.

"He was just there," Darsal said. "I could have sworn he was—"

"Where are the books?" Johnis asked, alarmed. He'd been rushed away the minute they'd returned, and he'd left the books in their care.

Darsal and Silvie looked at him with wide eyes.

"Where are the books?" he demanded.

"In his saddlebag," Darsal said. "Billos has them."

Johnis felt his heart drop into the pit of his stomach. He couldn't explain why this small piece of information disturbed him so much, but he was certain that their mission to find the seven missing Books of History had just taken a very sharp turn for the worse.

"He's going to use them," Johnis whispered. "Dear Elyon, we have to stop him!"

# TWENTY-SEVEN

Billos swung his leg over the stallion and dropped to the ground in the clearing. The sun was blazing overhead. Birds chirped in the trees. His horse snorted and lowered its head to feed on the grass.

He had to work fast. Knowing Johnis, they would be coming soon. This newly anointed major who could do no wrong. Not that he disagreed with the verdict—Johnis was certainly a worthy leader of men.

But the boy was holding something back, something about the books they'd each sworn to find. What couldn't be said in the Council's chamber was more important than what could be said. Johnis had gone to the Horde city for more than his mother.

Having freed Rosa and Silvie, he'd stayed for more than the Horde girl, as he would have them believe.

No, Johnis had gone and stayed for the Books of History.

Billos threw the saddlebag open and reached inside for the books. With trembling hands he pulled them out.

The Dark Priest had possessed the blue book before he'd stumbled into possession of the two that Johnis had lost at the massacre.

Billos hurried to the boulder at the clearing's center. He didn't know what power came with having all seven books. Nor with opening a single book.

In fact, he wasn't sure he had the courage to find out just yet.

What he did have was an insatiable need to taste the same surge of power that he'd felt when he'd touched the book with his blood.

He set the books on the stone and pulled out his knife.

His heart was hammering; sweat ran down his cheeks; his hands trembled. Inconsequential details.

The black leather book on top stared up at him, beckoning, demanding, begging.

*Touch me, Billos. Show me your blood, and I'll show you a new world.*

He sliced his finger with his knife and winced because he'd gone deeper than he'd meant to. Blood leaked from the cut.

Hooves pounded behind.

Panicked, he thrust his finger down and pressed it against the ancient leather cover.

The clearing vanished, replaced by the same darkness he'd seen before. A distorted hole erupted before him, and from the darkness the figure of a man dressed in black.

*This could be Teeleh,* he thought. Or the Dark Priest. But the figure didn't quite look like either.

The man's long arm reached out for Billos, long fingernails beckoning. A moan filled his ears, so loud Billos thought the sound might be coming from his own throat.

Then the vortex opened to another place, not as dark. A six-foot hole in this world stood right in front of him, ringed in rippling blackness. He reached out and touched the hole with a single finger. But his finger went beyond the surface into a place that was warmer than the clearing.

Billos could feel his bones shaking, but his fear didn't dim his desire. He stepped forward to the edge of the large hole.

"Billossss . . ." Someone was calling his name.

He took one last deep breath, closed his eyes, and stepped through the circle.

JOHNIS LED THE CHARGE TO THE CLEARING WITH SINKING hopes of finding Billos before it was too late.

"Billos!"

He saw the stallion through the trees. And past the stallion, Billos standing at the rock.

"Billos!"

He broke from the trees and pulled up hard. Billos stood over the boulder, hand extended to one of the Books of History bound in leather. His finger pressed against it.

Blood pooled on the cover.

The boy was shaking in his boots, like a goat hit by lightning.

Silvie and Darsal slid to a stop beside Johnis, eyes glued to the scene.

"Billos!" Johnis cried.

And then Billos disappeared, leaving behind a single flash of light that followed him into oblivion. And a bare boulder.

The birds were chirping; the horses were stamping; the breeze was blowing.

And Billos and the books were simply gone.

The three other recruits—the ones who'd sworn to find the seven missing Books of History before the Dark One could use them to wreak terrible havoc—sat on their horses and stared.

Silvie was the first to find her voice. "He's gone."

"He's gone," Johnis said.

"No!" Darsal screamed her denial. And in that one word was more meaning, more rage, more fear, more pain that Johnis had heard in such a short word.

"He is," Johnis said.

For a moment they stood in silence.

"Now what?" Silvie asked in a voice that could have come from a girl half her age.

For a while no one could answer. Then Johnis summoned the courage to tell them what they all knew was next.

"Now we find Billos."

# RENEGADE

## LOST BOOK 3

# BEGINNINGS

Our story begins in a world totally like our own, yet completely different. What once happened here in our own history seems to be repeating itself, thousands of years from now, some time beyond the year AD 4000.

But this time the future belongs to the young, to the warriors, to the lovers. To those who can follow hidden clues and find a great treasure, which will unlock the mysteries of life and wealth.

Thirteen years have passed since the lush, colored forests were turned to desert by Teeleh, the enemy of Elyon and the vilest of all creatures. Evil now rules the land and shows itself as a painful, scaly disease that covers the flesh of the Horde, who live in the desert.

The powerful green waters, once precious to Elyon, have vanished from the earth except in seven small forests surrounding seven small lakes. Those few who have chosen to follow the ways of Elyon are now called Forest Dwellers, and they bathe once daily in the powerful waters to cleanse their skin of the disease.

The number of their sworn enemy, the Horde, has grown, and the Forest Guard has been severely diminished by war, forcing Thomas, supreme commander, to lower the army's recruitment age to sixteen. One thousand young recruits have shown themselves worthy and now serve in the Forest Guard.

From among the thousand, four young fighters—Johnis, Silvie, Billos, and Darsal—were handpicked by Thomas to lead. Sent into the desert, they faced terrible danger and returned celebrated heroes.

Unbeknownst to Thomas and the Forest Dwellers, our heroes have also been chosen by the legendary white Roush, guardians of all that is good, for a greater mission, and they are forbidden to tell a soul.

Their quest is to find the seven original Books of History, which together hold the power to destroy humankind. They were given the one book in the Roush's possession and have recovered two more. They must now find the other four books before the Dark One finds them and unleashes their power to enslave humanity.

Although the full extent of the power contained in these sealed books is unknown, the four have discovered that touching them with blood creates a breach into what appears to be another reality. A breach they have been warned not to cross.

But Billos is not the kind to heed warnings. And his lust for the power contained in the books has overtaken all good sense.

# ONE

Billos swung his leg over the stallion and dropped to the ground. The sun was blazing above the clearing, birds chirping in the trees. His horse snorted and lowered its head to feed on the grass.

He had to work fast. Knowing Johnis, the self-appointed leader would be coming with Darsal and Silvie soon. Johnis, this newly anointed major who could do no wrong. Not that he disagreed with the verdict—Johnis was a worthy leader of men. But the boy was holding something back, something about the books they'd each sworn to find.

Billos threw the saddlebag open, reached inside for the three books, and hurried to the boulder at the clearing's center. He didn't know what power came with having all seven books. Nor with opening a single book. In fact, he wasn't sure he had the courage to find out just yet.

What he did have was an insatiable need to feel the same surge of power that he'd felt the first time he'd touched one of the books with his blood.

He set the books on the stone, pulled out his knife, and ran the back of a trembling hand across the sweat that ran down his right cheek. The blue leather book on top stared up at him, beckoning, demanding, begging.

*Touch me, Billos. Show me your blood, and I'll show you a new world.*

He sliced his finger, wincing because he'd gone deeper than he'd meant to. Blood swelled. Dripped.

The sound of pounding hooves reached him.

Panicked that he might be discovered too early, he thrust his finger against the ancient leather cover. In the space of one quick breath the clearing vanished, replaced by the same darkness he'd seen before.

The power was still here! *There is more raw energy than I felt a week ago when I attempted the same with the others,* he thought. Or was it just the anticipation of what he intended next?

A distorted hole erupted before him, and from the darkness emerged the figure of the man dressed in black.

*This could be Teeleh. Or the Dark Priest.*

The man's long arm reached out for Billos, fingernails beckoning. A moan filled Billos's ears, so loud he thought the sound might be coming from his own throat, louder than the thumping of his heart, which crashed like an avalanche of boulders cut from the Natalga Gap.

Then the vortex opened to another place, not as dark. A six-foot hole in this world stood right in front of him, ringed in rippling blackness. A translucent barrier distorted what lay behind.

He reached out and touched the hole with his finger. Pushed it through. His finger went beyond the veil into a place that was warmer than the clearing.

Billos could feel his bones shaking, but his fear didn't dim his desire. He inched forward.

"Billos! Billos!"

Someone was calling his name.

He closed his eyes, took one last deep breath, and stepped past the barrier.

Johnis led the charge to the clearing with sinking hopes of finding Billos before it was too late.

"Billos!"

He saw the stallion through the trees. And past the stallion, Billos standing at the rock.

"Billos!"

Johnis broke from the trees and pulled up hard. Billos stood over the boulder, hand extended to one of the Books of History bound in leather. His finger was pressed against it. Blood pooled on the cover around a deep cut. The boy shook in his boots, like a goat hit by lightning.

Silvie and Darsal pulled their horses to a stop beside Johnis, eyes glued to the scene.

"Billos!" Johnis cried.

And then Billos disappeared, leaving behind a single flash of light that followed him into oblivion. And a bare boulder.

The birds were chirping; the horses were stamping; the breeze was blowing.

Billos and the books were simply gone.

Johnis, Silvie, and Darsal sat on their horses and stared, completely dumbstruck.

Silvie was the first to find her voice. "He's gone."

"They're gone," Johnis said.

# TWO

For a long moment Darsal couldn't bring her mind to focus on what her eyes had just seen. One moment Billos had been standing over the books, finger extended, and the next he'd vanished in a flash of light.

And with him the books. But it wasn't the books that Darsal cared about now.

"Billos?"

Her voice sounded hollow in the empty clearing. She dropped to the ground and ran toward the rock, eyes scanning the trees for sight of him. Surely he hadn't actually disappeared into thin air!

"Billos! Answer me, for the sake of Elyon! This isn't funny!"

"He's gone," Johnis said. "I told you the books were dangerous. Now Billos has gone and done it, that fool!"

Darsal swung around and screamed at him, as much out of frustration at Billos as anger directed toward Johnis. "Shut up!"

Johnis swung down and approached, followed by Silvie. Both held her in a steady gaze. *The improbable events forced upon us over the last few weeks have changed us,* Darsal thought.

"Take it easy, Darsal," Johnis said. "Do I look like the enemy to you?"

"Take it easy? What do you suggest now, that I follow you to hell once again? Just head out into the desert and find Billos? He vanished before our eyes!"

"I'm not the enemy. Is that so difficult to understand? The books are gone because Billos is a fool—focus your anger at him, not me."

"Where did that imp go?" Silvie asked, blinking at the trees.

Darsal wanted to slap the girl, if for no other reason than she seemed so smug in her newfound confidence by Johnis's side. She had her man, this unlikely leader of warriors who didn't seem to know the meaning of the word *quit.* Not that Darsal resented Johnis or thought less of him than he deserved, but she felt that any attack on Billos was an attack on her.

If they knew what Billos had done for her all these years, they would understand. If Johnis was Silvie's man, then Billos was hers. In fact, much more so than these two who'd known each other less than a month. Billos was her savior, the only love she'd ever known, her life.

And now Billos was gone.

Darsal paced up to the boulder, ran her hand over the rough stone where the books had rested only a minute earlier. The surface was warm, by the books or by the sun she wasn't sure.

Johnis spit to one side. "What did I tell you? I should have taken them from him in the desert and kept them out of sight. Show Billos one ounce of trust and look what it's earned us!"

"You care more for books made of paper than you do for flesh and blood?" Darsal demanded.

"If they were just paper, Billos would still be standing here with a bloody finger on their covers."

He was right, of course. But that didn't change the fact that Billos *wasn't* standing here.

Johnis continued as if he'd read her thoughts. "I know you and Billos were . . . are . . . close. For that matter, I've risked my own life for him—"

"And he for you," she said.

"Yes, I suppose so. But you have to remember that the books must come first. We've all risked our necks for those three books, and we still have four to find."

Darsal paced, trying her best to remain calm. "For all you know, Billos has just taken the next step to *find* those blasted books! I can't believe you're taking this so lightly!"

Johnis started to nod.

"Were you the only one chosen, or was Billos also chosen?"

"All of us."

"Then quit pretending that the books are more important than he is!"

"Stop it!" Silvie cried.

Darsal grunted.

Here they stood, three new recruits to the Forest Guard—Silvie and Johnis just sixteen; Darsal seventeen—chosen for this mission that no amount of fighting or wit could accomplish.

Silvie was wearing a white cotton dress, an oddity for the fighter with short, tangled, blonde hair, who typically walked about in battle dress. She preferred to have knives strapped to her thighs.

Johnis had cleaned up as well, draped in a tunic as if he were as much a part of the council as the elder members. Even Darsal had attended the council meeting, from which all four had just come, dressed in a frock. Only Billos had turned up in battle dress.

Here they stood in a small clearing a ten-minute gallop beyond the outskirts of Middle Village, faced with a predicament that was more important than any could know—any of the hundred thousand or so Forest Dwellers who lived in the seven forests, now busying themselves with a meal or a dance or the sharpening of swords.

Or any of the millions of Horde who lived in the desert, cursing the forests and their dwellers, eating wheat cakes while they sipped wheat wine to ease the pain of their cracking skin.

Darsal walked around the stone, eyeing the bare surface. For as long as she'd known him, Billos had always been an impetuous little bulldog, getting them into as much trouble as he saved them from. She loved him; she was bound to him; she would die for him. But at the moment, she would just as soon strangle him.

His capture by the Horde had been beyond his control. But this time he'd run off without her. He'd abandoned her. She couldn't live with being abandoned by Billos. In fact, she wasn't sure she could live without him at all.

"You're right," she snapped, unable to stem her anger. "He may be a fool. But he's a fool whom I love." She rushed on, not eager to explain herself. "We have to find him! These books, this fate-of-the-world nonsense—yes, of course—but we have to find Billos!"

Johnis touched the stone and drew his hand back, rubbing his fingers. His eyes on her. "How do you search for someone who's left no tracks or scent?"

Silvie studied Darsal. "He did leave a scent. The smell of ambition—isn't that right, Darsal? He went into the books because of his thirst for power."

"And you wouldn't do the same to satisfy your thirst for revenge?"

They all knew Silvie's passion to avenge the death of her parents, who'd been killed by the Horde. She'd joined the Forest Guard as much to slay Scabs as save the forests.

"None of us is without blame," Johnis said. To Darsal: "You have my word, I'll track him to the ends of the desert if need be."

"Then you know there's only one way," she said.

Silvie frowned. "Say how?"

"Forbidden or not, dangerous as you might think, we have to match Billos's ambition or folly or whatever caused him to step past the barrier."

"Follow him?" Johnis said.

Darsal came closer, using her hands to express urgency. "You can't follow him into the desert, Johnis, because Billos didn't go into the desert. He went into the books! We have to find a book and follow him before it's too late."

"Too late for what?"

"Don't tell me you didn't see the Dark One the last time we touched the books."

"Teeleh," Silvie said, speaking about the leader of the Shataiki bats. "Or Alucard, his general."

"Or Witch," said Johnis. The Horde high priest. "But we can't just throw ourselves in because Billos did."

"Why not? You demanded that we follow you. And I doubt very much that Billos just disappeared from here to reappear with Teeleh or Witch. He's not in the desert; he's in another place altogether." She stomped for her horse, her mind clouded by her own need to find Billos. "We're wasting time!"

"Slow down," he snapped. "Even if we did agree to throw ourselves into the hole the way Billos did, we don't have a book. You can't just pluck one off the nearest 'original Books of History' tree."

Darsal spun back, started to tell him exactly what she thought of his cocky wit, then clamped her mouth and let her face grow red instead.

"He's right," Silvie said. "We have to continue the mission as if this hadn't happened. Find the books, find Billos."

"We can't just *continue* the mission!"

"Then what?"

"We have to drop everything and go after another book," Darsal cried.

"Exactly," Johnis said. "That *is* the mission."

"Now!"

"Yes, now. That's what we're doing. We're trying to get past all this emotion of yours so that we can calmly discuss the most logical next step."

"And that's what you did to find your mother?" Darsal demanded. "Fine, why don't we deceive a fighting group and get them slaughtered to find the next book. Is that the level of your commitment to Billos?"

"Enough!" Silvie stepped up, breaking their line of sight. "Both of you. You're both right: we have to find a book, and we have to do it now, but we can't run off into the desert without a plan. Think!"

She scowled at Darsal, then returned her attention to the center of the clearing. She walked around the rock.

"I can't believe they all just vanished like that. It's so . . ."

"Unnatural," Johnis said, joining her.

"Everything else we've experienced—the Roush, Teeleh, the Horde—it's all been the unseen becoming seen. But this . . ."

Johnis drew both hands through his dark hair. He was a good-looking boy with fine features and smooth skin, a poet and a writer before he'd been roped into serving with the Guard.

Billos, on the other hand, was covered in scars and had the muscle of two Johnises. A ruggedly handsome man. A true fighter who would take what was his and protect his own without so much talk.

For the moment Darsal paced and let Johnis and Silvie talk. A rustle in the trees drew her attention. She saw the fleeting white of a Roush, then the red eyes of a Shataiki bat that fled into the darkness beyond the branches.

"We see those two even though no one else can," Johnis said, looking up at the trees, "but we can't see what lies beyond the books."

"And who can see beyond?" Darsal demanded.

"Michal." Johnis nodded toward the west where Michal, one of the wise ones among the Roush, lived in the treetop village they'd visited a week earlier.

"Michal's the one who told us not to touch the books with blood," Darsal snapped.

Johnis faced her with a scowl. "You think he would lead us astray? If we go to him now?"

"There's someone else who knows even more about what is beyond what we can see." The idea came to Darsal only a moment before she spoke.

"Who?"

"Someone who may have actually gone where Billos is now."

She turned for her horse and had her foot in the stirrup before Johnis caught on.

"Thomas? That's rumor."

"And this talking won't amount to bird droppings," she snapped, swinging into her saddle.

Johnis hurried forward. "It's forbidden to tell anyone about the books! You have no idea what harm that will bring! You can't talk to Thomas about Billos!"

"No? Watch me."

Darsal kicked her mount and galloped into the forest.

# THREE

Thomas of Hunter, or Thomas Hunter, as he would say if asked, was walking the southern path that skirted the lake next to the Thrall, explaining the ins and outs of fundamental forest living to Karas when the commotion on the opposite beach caught his attention. A lead horse chased by two others, tearing up the sand. Village houses crowded the beach behind the scene.

"Is that a game?" Karas asked, watching the beasts race around the lake's perimeter.

"It's three rascals who need their hides whipped," Thomas said. "Horses aren't permitted so near the water."

"Isn't that Darsal being chased?"

He looked closer and saw that she might be right. "You can see that from here? Never mind, of course you can. I forget how dramatic the change is at first."

Johnis had brought Karas, daughter of the Horde high priest, out of the desert with him. Her painful conversion from Scab to Forest Dweller had been her doing, when she'd washed herself in lake water and had watched her skin heal before her eyes.

Johnis had risked his own life for a Scab, and in so doing delivered much more to the forests than he had anticipated. The ten-year-old girl was a gold mine of information on the Horde's political and religious machinery, and Thomas intended to hear it all.

But at the moment his mind was on her humanity, her wit, her charm, not simply her use to them. *She speaks with the intelligence of a girl much older than ten*, he thought.

Before being cleansed by the lake water, her skin had been gray and cracked, her hair matted and dark, her eyes nearly white.

Now she looked across the lake with blue eyes that peered through soft bangs lifting on angel's breath. Her skin was newborn, flawless.

"So you know her?" Karas asked in a sweet voice.

"Who?"

"The one in trouble. Darsal."

He glanced up and saw that the riders behind—Johnis and Silvie, if he wasn't mistaken—were catching Darsal. Karas was right; there was trouble.

"She's from the Southern Forest. A victim of difficult circumstance. Why do you ask?"

The girl shrugged. "I think she's a pretty woman."

"No shortage of those. You've seen Rachelle, my wife. There's a looker."

"My mother, Grace, was pretty."

"Oh? Killed by the high priest . . ." He stopped and chided himself for mentioning her mother's death so casually. "I'm sorry—"

"Don't be." Karas kept her eyes fixed on the riders, who were now rounding the lake. "We've all faced a lot of death."

True indeed. "Darsal reminds you of your mother?"

"She could be her."

"Darsal, your mother? Then she would have had you when she was seven years old, because Darsal's only seventeen."

"Of course."

Thomas squatted next to the girl—this angel who'd come to them from the Horde.

Johnis was right; she was a gift from Elyon. Though Thomas wasn't ready to extend the same sentiment to the Horde warriors who swung mallets at his men's heads.

"Johnis's father, Ramos, insists that you should live with him, but my wife and I—"

"Your wife's a very intelligent woman," Karas said

"Yes. Yes, she is. And she joins me in extending an invitation for you to live with us if you'd like."

Karas shifted her eyes and stared into his. "We'll see. But you are very kind, Commander."

Thomas playfully brushed her chin with his forefinger. "Where'd you get such a bright mind?"

"My father isn't exactly an idiot. He's deceived."

The horses pounded closer. Clearly, this was no casual social call. Thomas stood and put his hand on the girl's shoulder. "Do you mind leaving me alone with this *trouble*, as you put it? You'll find Ciphus in the Thrall."

"I'd rather not."

He looked down at her. "No?"

"I'd rather see what this trouble is all about."

"I'm sure you would. And one day, when I make you a lieutenant, I'll let you settle matters like this." He couldn't help a gentle grin. "Though what could possibly be the problem now is beyond me. Maybe I should just let you deal with them."

"Okay." Karas made no move to leave.

Darsal raced in, pulled her horse to a rearing stop, slid from her saddle, and dropped to one knee. "Requesting an audience, sir!"

Her long, dark hair was pulled back and tied, baring the scar on her left cheek. If anything, the scar accentuated her cheek's firm lines and her soft lips. A fine woman, a fierce warrior, a passionate heart.

Thomas squeezed Karas's shoulder. "Leave us," he said.

She hesitated only a moment before turning and jogging down the beach toward the Thrall.

Johnis and Silvie jumped to the ground and hurried forward. But they seemed at a loss for words. This was Darsal's show.

"What is it this time?" Thomas demanded.

"We must lead an expedition into the desert immediately, sir," Darsal said, head still bowed. She looked up at Thomas. "Billos has gone missing, and we have reason to believe that he's—"

"What she means to say," Johnis interrupted, "is that we can't find Billos. She's in love with him. You understand how that goes. Her mind is totally—"

"Silence!" Thomas had chosen the four from a thousand fighters, and despite their rather unique accomplishments in these last weeks, they were erratic, untamed, impulsive, and in general a very high-maintenance lot. If not for the half-circle birthmark on Johnis's neck, which confirmed that Elyon had chosen the boy, Thomas thought he might reconsider his choice.

"What do you mean, Billos is lost? You've all just been found, for the love of Elyon!"

"Billos is a hothead," Johnis said. "It seems he's . . . well, we don't know that he's actually missing yet, do we?"

"No, we really don't," Silvie said, eyes holding Thomas's.

Darsal stood to her feet, staring, mind clearly spinning. Quiet for the moment.

"Well?" Thomas demanded. "Is Billos missing or isn't he?"

"He's missing all right," Darsal said.

"And is it true that you are in love with him?"

She breathed deeply through her nose. "Yes. So I would know if he's missing."

"How so?"

"Billos and I are . . . very close."

"What makes you think he's not just sleeping under some wood pile?"

Darsal hesitated. "Sir, is it true that you've been to a place beyond this world?"

Thomas felt his pulse surge. A dozen distant memories flooded his mind. It had been thirteen years since he'd dreamed of Earth, thanks to the Rhambutan fruit that kept him from having *any* dreams when he slept.

"Who told you this?"

"It's well-known."

Thomas dismissed them with a hand and turned away. "Don't believe everything you hear."

"You deny it then?"

"What does this have to do with Billos?"

"Billos—" Darsal started, but again Johnis interrupted.

"Billos was talking about your . . . dreams, whatever they were, before he went missing. Darsal seems to have linked the two. Please, we are wasting his time with this, Darsal."

"And why are you trying to shut her up?" Thomas asked.

"Am I?" Johnis shot Darsal a hard glance. "I wouldn't want to do that."

"You're obviously dancing around something that has you all bothered," Thomas said. "Less than a day has passed since you came out of the desert, nearly dead, and already you're running around like frantic little rodents, sniffing for trouble. Truth be told, I'm in no mood to play games at the moment. So . . . have no fear, Johnis, I won't push for the moment. But I will know everything; you do realize that."

Silvie looked at Johnis, who stood six inches taller than her and was broader across the shoulders. His otherwise boyish features made him appear only slightly less feminine than she. Johnis's weapon was his brain, not his brawn. Silvie, despite her petite frame and delicate features, was perhaps more brawny than he. Certainly the better fighter.

*There is love between these two,* Thomas thought. He should discourage two sixteen-year-old squad leaders from pursuing their love for each other, but something about Silvie and Johnis's attraction felt right to him.

Without offering any explanation, Thomas stripped off his shirt, loosed his boots, dropped his sword, and strode to the lake's edge. He dove into the cool water and let Elyon's healing power refresh his skin. "Bathe once a day to cleanse yourself of the disease," Elyon had told them. "Until I come to save you from evil in one fell swoop, as prophesied." Thomas had heard the words himself.

He rose from the lake, threw his head back, and filled his lungs with fresh air. He turned and drilled the three fighters on the beach with a stare.

"It wasn't long ago that I could breathe Elyon's water. Do you believe that?"

He walked out of the lake without bothering to wipe the water from his skin. "Do you?"

Johnis answered, "Yes."

Thomas snatched up his shirt. "And do you believe the rest of it? That the Roush once flew overhead, protecting us from the evil Shataiki? That Elyon lived among his own? That there was no disease?"

Silvie glanced up at the treetops to their left, then gave Thomas a look that seemed to ask if he'd seen it. *What?* Thomas had no clue, because the trees were empty.

"Of course, we believe," she said.

"That there are Books of History that contain a perfect record of all that has happened?"

"Yes."

"Then you're wiser than some who've lost faith in what they can't see."

"How does this lead us to Billos?" Darsal demanded.

"You asked if it was true that I've been to a different reality," Thomas said. "If you didn't believe in what can't be seen, I wouldn't want to waste my time answering. But since you do believe—and I'm assuming that includes you, Darsal—you'll find it easier to accept the fact that I have been to a place beyond this world, as you put it."

They stared at him, waiting for more explanation.

"In fact, there are millions of people who would swear to you that I'm asleep in a hotel in Bangkok at this very moment. That I live in the histories, two thousand years ago. They could show you photographs of me in bed, where I've been sleeping for the last thirteen years."

"Thirteen years?" Darsal said. "You look quite awake to me."

"I've only slept part of one night in that reality, dreaming of the last thirteen years here. They would tell you that you yourselves are just a dream."

He shrugged into his shirt. "You, on the other hand, might tell me that my dreams of Bangkok are just that, dreams I had while asleep here. Now ask me, which reality is real?"

"Which is real?" Johnis asked.

"Both," Thomas said. "The fact that none of us can see Bangkok doesn't mean it's not real any more than the fact that we can't see fuzzy white Roush in those trees means *they* aren't there."

Darsal's face lightened a shade. "So, you're saying that it's possible for someone to step beyond this world? That Billos could easily have vanished into this dream world of yours?"

"What have you been drinking? I'm sure you'll find Billos hiding behind a wood pile, sleeping off his ride through the desert." But Thomas could tell that none of them believed it.

"Please, you're not suggesting that Billos actually *vanished* into thin air," Thomas continued.

"No," Johnis said. "It was you who suggested it."

"I was talking about me, and then only about dreams."

"Either way, it sounds as preposterous as Billos vanishing. Not that he has, mind you."

"It does," Thomas said. "But my dreams were true; I can assure you of that. Do you know what they call Elyon in that reality?"

"Billos?" Darsal suggested.

Thomas ignored her. "God."

"So you're saying you won't help us," Darsal said. She was consumed with the notion that Billos had vanished.

*And what if he has?* Thomas thought. *What if Billos has somehow crossed the breach between worlds? Impossible, of course.* Rachelle would have a fit if she knew his thoughts.

"Absolutely not. I should put you in the brink for pushing such a fool's errand. Not even an idiot would suggest that I risk warriors to find a fighter who's been lost less than an hour. None of you are idiots, which leads me to believe you're hiding something from me."

All three looked at him with unwavering eyes, like deer before the flight.

"Now your silence confirms it," he snapped. "I'm your commander; tell me what's going on."

"It's nothing," Darsal said, pulling her eyes away.

"And you're lying," Thomas said.

"What she means is that it's nothing to anyone but us," Johnis said. "A very private, personal thing. We've taken a vow not to whisper a word about it to anyone, but you have my assurance that we will deal with it."

Interesting. They were hiding more than they could say without breaking their word. That Johnis had confessed this much rather than attempt to cover up further was at least noble.

All of this confirmed Thomas's suspicion that the four were up to something beyond him, beyond all of them. Why Elyon had chosen these four scrappers was still a mystery to him, but then again, why he himself had been transported from the streets of Denver to this land was a mystery as well. He, a street fighter who'd grown up in Malaysia, elevated into such a position between worlds.

He would treat them as he would any new leaders, but there was more at work here. In time he would know it all, assuming he lived until that time.

"I trust you to keep your loyalties straight," he said.

"Of course." Johnis and Silvie dipped their heads. Darsal stared at him, still lost in her own thoughts.

"Yes?" he demanded of her.

"What? Yes . . . yes, of course."

"Then take this very private, personal thing away from me. And for the sake of Elyon, prove yourselves worthy of the faith I've placed in each of you."

Johnis swung into his saddle. "We will, sir. Rename us the Three Worthy Ones if you wish. Nothing will—"

"Three? There are *four* of you."

"Of course, it's just that there are only three here, now. Four. The Four Worthy Ones."

Thomas didn't like the far-off look in Darsal's eyes, but he didn't want to push the matter further.

"A bit juvenile, don't you think, Johnis? Instead I'll give you a charge. I want the three of you to stay together until you find Billos. Consider yourselves each other's prisoners. Don't leave the village, and don't let the other two out of your sight. Am I clear?"

"Yes, sir," Johnis replied.

Silvie mounted. "Yes, sir."

Darsal was in her saddle, turning without responding.

"Darsal?"

"Hmm? Yes, yes. Of course."

# FOUR

The first thing Billos felt was the warmth. A heat that spread from his fingertips as they entered the hole in the air, up his arm as it passed the barrier. The burning sensation intensified as his face pressed into the translucent film of power.

It occurred to him that this hole might be nothing more than the mouth of death itself. That he could and should pull back. But the sound of hooves, thundering into the clearing behind him, pushed those thoughts from his mind.

He thrust his head through, and his body effortlessly followed. He was in.

Darkness. A surge of power ripped through his body, and for a moment all he could see were the stars that ignited behind his eyes.

The heat swelled. Pain sliced through his chest, his head, his nose. So intense now that he thought blood might be streaming from his eyes and ears.

Billos cried out and threw his hands to his head. Felt his mouth spread in a scream. But the only sound he could hear was a chuckle that echoed around him in the darkness.

He'd found death.

The stars behind his eyes began to move toward him. Past him. As if he were moving through them.

Without warning the stars became a blinding explosion of light that forced him to gasp.

*This is it. This is it!*

But then the light vanished, and Billos found himself standing in a room.

A white room.

A room filled with both terror and wonder at once.

# FIVE

N ow what?" Silvie asked, pacing the hand-hewn boards that
had been strapped together to form the floor of Johnis's
house. Johnis stood at the shuttered window, staring out with his
hands on his hips, lost in thought.

Darsal sat on a stool by the table, sweating. It wasn't a hot day,
but her face felt flush, and her hands were tingling. Sitting here
after an hour of pointless discussion . . . she might as well be in
shackles, locked in a cell.

The floorboards creaked loudly each time Silvie placed her
weight on them. Evidently Johnis's father, Ramos of Middle,
didn't have the time to fix his own house.

Darsal couldn't stand this a moment longer. "Will you please
stop that?"

"Stop what?" Silvie asked.

"The boards are screaming bloody death. I'm trying to *think*!"

"Then think without being so sensitive," Silvie retorted. "I'm sorry that Billos was so selfish to leave you behind in his betrayal of us all, but you don't need to take it out on me."

In that moment Darsal wanted to reach out and slap Silvie's pretty little face. She, with her man standing pompous in the corner, loyal to the bone. But Billos was as loyal as Johnis, even if he did express that loyalty with more subtlety.

"He didn't *betray* us," Darsal snapped. "He's forcing the issue as any good leader would do."

"Forcing the issue by breaking his word," Johnis said, walking back from the window.

"And did you break your word to Thomas of Hunter in the desert this last week?"

Her accusation caught him flat-footed.

"Of course, you did. So watch what you say against Billos, both of you! As of yet he hasn't gotten anyone killed."

She stood and crossed to the same window Johnis had parked himself by. Outside the village bustled with people as the afternoon sun slipped farther into the western sky. The nightly celebration would soon sweep the beach. Song and dance and stew over blazing fires—with the Horde snatching life from them faster than they could make it, any excuse for a celebration of what remained was not only justified, but demanded.

But Darsal had no life left to celebrate. Not without Billos. He should have known better than to leave her in this fretful state. If and when she did catch up to him, she would wring his neck!

"We can't stay here," she said.

"We have to," said Johnis.

"We have to find another book."

"You talk as if it's a matter of going to market—just go out and select another book. And we can't undermine Thomas."

"You had no problem undermining him when it served your own—"

"And I was wrong!" he snapped. "We all know that now. I can't—I won't—do it again."

Darsal seethed. "We have to find another book and follow Billos. You know it's the only way!"

"For all we know Billos will pop out of thin air right here, in a few moments."

"We can't just stay here," Darsal repeated. "Elyon has given us an order. Our mission is to find the seven original books, four of which are still missing."

"All seven are missing, if you count the three with Billos," Silvie said.

Johnis sat down on the stool Darsal had vacated and crossed his arms. "We have to find the books, and we will. But we can't just run off and defy our commander, not again. Michal will come to us. Patience."

*This newfound loyalty to Thomas of Hunter will prevent Johnis from being as inventive as he'd been when searching for the first book, or his own mother*, Darsal thought. If Johnis had proven one characteristic beyond a shadow of doubt, it was his stubbornness.

But Darsal had no choice. They'd left her with none. She could wait here for Billos to magically appear, which wasn't a choice at all, or she could do what needed to be done without them. And she knew what needed to be done.

With each passing minute the conviction to follow Johnis concerned her less. Billos's betrayal stung more. And the urgency to join the only man she could ever love consumed her most. Johnis and Silvie had both betrayed their superiors. Maybe it was her turn. But fooling Johnis wouldn't be like falling off a rock.

"You asked us to follow you to the end of the earth," Darsal snapped. "And we did. You demanded we spare the Horde, and we did. Each time you were right. Now you say sit and wait. Are you right this time?"

He shifted his eyes away. "Would I have said it if I didn't think so? Based on what I know, yes, I think so. Silvie?"

Silvie shrugged. "It has to be right."

Darsal pushed herself from the wall and sighed. "You'd better be, Scrapper." She headed toward the hall. "But that doesn't mean I have to like it."

"None of us do," Johnis said. "Where are you going?"

"Please tell me waiting doesn't mean I have to hold my bladder too."

He regarded her for a moment, then nodded. "At the end of the hall. Silvie—"

"You're joking. I may be a little discouraged, but I'm not so depressed that I can't undress myself!"

Johnis blushed.

Darsal tromped down the hall, entered a small bathroom, and banged the door closed. "I'm not a child, Johnis!" she yelled.

She was moving already. With a flip of her wrist she unlatched the window, stuck her head out to check for prying eyes, and satisfied that she was in the clear, thrust herself headlong into the opening.

She coiled so that her legs followed her torso over the sill, landed on one shoulder with a soft *thud,* and rolled to her feet.

No sounds from the house, not that she could hear over her own pounding heart. She was free.

# SIX

The front of the house, where Johnis might be keeping an eye out, was to her right. So Darsal sprinted left between two other houses, then south toward the forest's edge.

Her horse. She needed the sword in its scabbard, the battle dress in its saddlebag, the water . . . dear Elyon, she couldn't forget the water!

No member of the Forest Guard wandered farther than a hundred paces from his horse—one of Thomas's standing rules in case of a sudden attack. They had tethered their horses to a feeding trough three houses south of Johnis's. No sign of pursuit. With any luck, Johnis and Silvie still didn't know she'd left them. But they would, sooner rather than later.

She grabbed a bridle from a rack next to the trough, swung

onto the saddled—always saddled—steed, and urged the beast through the gate. Several passersby gave her a casual glance, but she didn't care if they saw her go, as long as they didn't follow. That she had gone would be—maybe already was—obvious. Where she'd gone would be less so.

Darsal kicked the mount and galloped down the street, took a sharp left off the main road, and entered the forest.

A hundred thoughts crowded her mind, and only one, no matter how ludicrous it seemed, felt compelling. What was slow in coming through patience could be gotten much faster through force.

She had to make up for these last few hours of wasted time. Billos had gotten himself into terrible trouble, of that she was sure. The fact that he hadn't returned meant one of two things: Either he *couldn't* come back because he was dead, Elyon forbid, or hurt, or in some other way incapacitated. Or he didn't *want* to come back.

She moved fast, cutting back and forth every two hundred meters to slow the pursuit of even the best trackers. Not until she was a mile south and at least as far west of the village did she begin to call out for the Roush.

"Hunter!" The name of the one who'd led Silvie and Johnis to the Roush village a week earlier.

"Hunter!" She thought she heard a rustle, but no fuzzy, white, batlike creature flew in. "Hunter. Any Roush, I need you!"

The words felt stupid, not unlike those who cried out for

Elyon's salvation after a bloody battle. Save us, save us, O Elyon! And always Elyon seemed to maintain his silence.

Now she was yelling at the sky for a white creature that no one other than she, Johnis, and Silvie could see. And Billos, though Billos wasn't here to see.

"Hunter!"

"You're trying to wake the dead?"

Darsal pulled hard on the reins and spun back. A white Roush, roughly two feet in height, with wide wings and a furry, round body, perched on a branch, watching her without concern.

It had been a few days since Darsal had actually seen one of the creatures. And never before then. No one had seen the Roush since the Great Deception. Seeing a Roush now, so close, so real, still sent butterflies through her belly.

"You're alone," the Roush said.

"Are you Hunter?"

"One and the same. And you're Darsal, one of the chosen. Why are you alone?"

"Why shouldn't I be?"

"Because I was told that you were under strict orders not to leave the village."

Darsal realized her mistake then. The Roush knew what was happening, which meant that Johnis would soon know what was happening. There was no way she could make it to the Roush village without Johnis, Silvie, and even Thomas knowing exactly what she was up to.

She looked back through the trees. Still no sign of pursuit.

*You're throwing yourself off a cliff, Darsal. How far will you go for him?*

She answered herself immediately. *As far as Johnis would go to find what is precious to him.*

"Are there others around?" she asked. "Like you, I mean?"

"Roush? I can cover a flank by myself, thank you. But, yes, there are more."

"Where?"

"To the east, near the lake. Where you should be, I'm guessing. You humans always do manage to lose your way."

To the east, good.

"You're right; I should be bathing in the lake. But before I hurry back, I have a burning question."

"Then put it out."

"Put what out?"

"Your burning question. Douse it in lake water."

"I was hoping *you* could put it out. By answering it."

"Fine, fine. I'll do my best. I have been known to 'crack the wit' now and then." The Roush swept down and landed on the path, grinning at his own humor. "You do understand," the Roush said. "It's a play on words . . ."

"Yes, yes, of course. Crack the whip; crack the wit. Do you mind sitting closer, on the horse? Can you do that, or will the horse bolt?"

"No, not a problem." Hunter leapt up to the mount's rump. "You see. Not a problem; none at all."

"Hmm. The horse doesn't even know you're here?"

"Sure it does. And it could sleep like a chick with me perched on its head, for that matter. Roush are enemies of no one but Shataiki."

"Really? You could sit on its head? Show me."

Eager to demonstrate, Hunter flew around Darsal, landed with both claws between the horse's ears, and grinned. "Not bad balance, eh? I'm not scratching him, or he would bolt. Gentle as a leaf. Now, what is that question?"

Darsal wasn't sure how to go about capturing a Roush, but she'd convinced herself that she had no choice. Too much was at stake. Billos needed her.

She leaned forward as if to ask the question in a quieter voice, then shot her hands out and clamped them around the Roush's soft belly.

"What, no, that tickles! No, no!" Hunter began to cackle with laughter, loudly enough to wake the forest.

Now fully committed, Darsal tugged the animal toward her and was immediately rewarded with wings whacking at the air.

"No, no, you're killing me! I'm too ticklish!"

"Quiet!" Darsal tried to flip the bat creature around so that she could muzzle it, but its wide wings tangled with her arms, pulling her off balance. They both tumbled from the horse and landed in a heap.

Hunter squawked, alarmed. "What?"

She pounced on the creature, threw her hand over its snout,

and pulled it close. "Quiet! Be quiet. I won't hurt you, but I need you to be quiet!"

The Roush squirmed and almost broke free, forcing Darsal to clamp her arms tighter. "Stop it! You're going to get hurt. Settle down!"

Hunter settled. They were tangled on the ground, human and Roush: an odd sight, to be sure.

Darsal released its wet snout long enough to snatch a knife from her thigh and press it close to the Roush's neck.

"If you raise an alarm, I'll be forced to make my point. I'm sorry. I don't want to do this, but I need your help."

Hunter whimpered.

"We're going to get on my horse, and I'm going to have to restrain you with some rope. I won't hurt you, but I can't leave you here to turn me in."

Still no words from the talkative Hunter.

"You can speak now; just keep it down."

"Have you lost your sense?" the Roush demanded. "What are you doing?"

Darsal glanced at the trees. "You're going to help me find Teeleh."

# SEVEN

Billos stepped back, half his mind on the frightful scene in this white room, half on the thought there might be a hole in the air behind him through which he could make a quick escape.

He felt behind him: nothing but empty space. A quick glance confirmed that the gateway had closed, stranding him in this small room, roughly ten paces per side.

No sign of the books.

He closed his hands to still a shiver and tried to make sense of the strange sight before him. The stench of fire filled his nostrils. Not wood smoke, but the kind of fire that came from burning rubber trees. Only there was no fire, not that he could see.

The room was white, square, with something that made him think of water on one wall. Perfectly smooth, dark water contained in large rectangles. Square "pools" of water that did not spill, even though they were on their side.

He stared at the water, distracted from the other wonders in this room. Six similar but much smaller square pools of water were fixed to the opposite wall in two rows of three.

Billos tore his eyes from the shiny surfaces and scanned the huge, fixed monster in the room's center. What appeared to be chairs or beds or wings of some kind surrounded a large rock.

A perfectly smooth white rock with dark eyes set around the crown. Or was it a giant white mushroom? Black roots ran from the white rock-mushroom into the wing-beds.

In some ways the monster looked like a spider with six legs jutting out of a round white body. Billos blinked at the thought. He touched the knife at his waist and took another step back.

Looking at the beast, he was sure that it was indeed a massive white spider, now sleeping, but sure to waken the moment it realized that prey had fallen into its gargantuan square web.

The flat pools were its drinking source, perhaps, which left Billos as food. He'd stepped out of the green forest into a spider's white trap! But the beast wasn't moving, not twitching, not breathing that he could see. Did spiders breathe? He didn't know.

The spider-beast had a tattoo stenciled under one of its eyes. Four letters: D-E-L-L.

A name?

Why would a spider have a word on its torso? Billos straightened. So then maybe it wasn't a spider at all.

He glanced behind his shoulder again, hoping for the gateway, but saw instead what appeared to be a white door.

Without stopping to consider where the door might lead, he rushed to it, grasped the silver knob, and twisted. But the handle refused to budge.

Whirling back he let out a slow, long breath. The DELL spider—if that's what it really was—hadn't moved. Now that he was starting to think a little more clearly, Billos was quite sure this beast wasn't a spider.

Since when did spiders have doors on their webs? Since when did spiders have square webs? Since when did spiders collect water in their webs?

*When you enter a forbidden world created by the Books of History, that's when, you fool.*

So then it *could* be a spider. But there seemed to be no immediate danger, and the courage that had brought him here in the first place began to return.

*Think, Billos. Just calm down and think. First things first. You must find the way out.*

He searched the walls for another door. None. He tried the silver knob again, all the while keeping one eye on DELL. But the handle refused to budge.

So he carefully edged over to the large square pool of water on the wall. Still no movement, no sign of immediate threat. Facing the shiny dark pool, Billos reached out and touched the water's surface with his index finger.

The water didn't yield. Only then did it occur to him that this wasn't water after all. He pressed the surface with his palm. This was a cool, hard surface, like perfectly formed black glass. The kind Thomas had taught them to make from sand.

Billos spun back, heart hammering. DELL still slept. Not a sound, not a breath of air, not the slightest movement.

What would happen if he touched the beast? He gripped his knife tighter. But his reason began to return, and once again it told him that this couldn't be a spider. Spiders could sense prey from a long way off. You didn't catch a spider taking a nap or looking the other way.

For a long time Billos considered his options, which seemed particularly limited to him at the moment. Then, reaching deep for the same boldness that had served him so well on many occasions (never mind that it had also nearly cost him his life on as many), he inched forward, reaching out his knife, and touched the very edge of one of the beast's legs.

Nothing.

Billos started to let the wind out of his lungs. But then nothing became something, because at that moment the beast named DELL opened one of its eyes.

Billos leapt back, crouched for what would come next. *It is okay*, he thought. He was bred for battle. Better to die fighting than from starvation in a spider's trap.

He would take the offensive and slaughter this beast where it crouched.

# EIGHT

She'd never imagined, much less planned, the kidnapping of a Roush before, and at first handling the creature unnerved Darsal. But really it wasn't so different from handling a small, furry human with wings.

Withdrawing a length of rope from the saddlebag, she quickly tied the creature to the pommel in front of her. To any Roush or Shataiki casually observing, she hoped it would appear that Hunter was just along for the ride.

"I'm sorry, but I'm going to have to bind your snout," she said, looping the rope over the Roush's mouth.

"What? You can't mean it! It's inhuman."

"*You're* not human. And, yes, it is a bit cruel, but I can't risk you making the kinds of sounds that might draw your friends. I'm committed now."

Hunter set his jaw and sat stoically as Darsal bound his jaw shut. It ruined the casual riding-partner look, but she had no choice.

She quickly dressed in her battle clothes that were in the saddle-bag. A leather skirt, protective leg and arm shields, a breastplate. Then she swung behind Hunter and galloped into the forest, toward the lake's north end, where she dipped out of the forest long enough to fill her water bags.

Johnis and Silvie would be searching by now, informing the Roush maybe, launching a search from the sky. But Darsal was headed into the northern half of Middle Forest, which was largely uninhabited.

Time was slipping, and Billos was . . . dead? Running? In chains? Being tortured this very moment, while Darsal, the one he'd risked his very life for, sat on a horse fretting over what consequences she might face for kidnapping a furry white animal?

Hunter rode smugly in front of her, warm back against her belly. Refusing to look at her, refusing to show the slightest concern.

"We're far enough from the village; I'm going to let you talk," Darsal said, stopping below a large nanka tree that hid the sky. "Nod your head if you swear not to give an alarm."

The winged creature squared its round shoulders and sat still as if he hadn't heard.

"You're refusing to help me find Billos, the man whom I love?"

Hunter turned his green eyes up and peered into Darsal's. He finally dipped his head.

"Yes, you're refusing to help? Or yes, you're agreeing not to sound an alarm?"

"Hmmm, humm . . ."

Darsal couldn't understand, so she slipped the loop off his mouth.

"Fine. Thank you for allowing me to swallow my own spittle."

A cloud of regret and sorrow suddenly settled over Darsal, and she had to lift her face to hide her stinging eyes.

"I won't raise an alarm," Hunter said. "But you know this is a mistake. No good can come of trying to find Teeleh."

"You're afraid of him?"

"I spit on his face. I detest the air he breathes; I vomit at his sight." Hunter had gone from settled to heavy breathing in three phrases. If you hadn't abandoned your search for the books, I could see your going after that beast, but there's—"

"But I haven't abandoned the search! To find Billos I need a book. That's exactly what I'm doing: I'm going after a book."

The revelation made the Roush blink its round, green eyes. "On your own?"

"Never mind the questions; it's not your place to understand my logic. If anyone knows more about the books' whereabouts, it's the Shataiki, so—"

"What makes you say that?"

"If the Roush knew more about the books, Michal would've told us. According to Johnis, the Horde know nothing more. That leaves the Shataiki, who are obsessed with finding the books. If anyone knows more, it's them."

"You'd have to be both foolish and desperate to go after Teeleh. Besides, it's not Teeleh you want. If anyone does know more about the books—which I doubt, mind you, I sincerely doubt—it would be that other mangy one under him. Alucard."

"You're sure about that? Alucard?"

"Cut from the same rotting flesh."

Darsal's heart slammed. "Where can I find Alucard?" she asked, then swallowed.

"The Black Forest, naturally."

"It's gone! We—"

"Not that one. A forest two-days' ride north. There are seven such forests, all hidden to you humans. This one's hidden in a hole west of your Northern Forest. But I have to tell you, it's not a place you want to . . ."

Darsal kicked the horse and turned it north.

"So that's it, eh? You're just going to ignore my warning and head straight into trouble? Then why bother letting me speak, if nothing I say is more than noise to you?"

"Please, spare me the drama or I'll put the muzzle back on."

"Foolish, foolish, foolish prodigals."

"I don't have a clue what you mean."

"Humans who run off on their own and find disaster."

"I don't need to find disaster," Darsal said. "It's found me." She urged the horse into a trot. "Do I need to muzzle you?"

Hunter bounced in front of her, silent for a few beats. "No," he finally said in a heavy voice. "I suppose I'll have to come along to save your neck. But I do wish you would have let me kiss Teagan and Martin before leaving."

"Teagan and Martin? Who?"

"My two children. I have a terrible feeling they will be left fatherless."

IT TOOK THEM AN HOUR AT A FAST CLIP TO REACH THE FORest's northern border, where Darsal pulled up the horse and stared at the flat desert, stretching as far as the eye could see. Ominous, but she'd been through enough desert in the last few weeks to deal with any danger that came from the elements. Apart from the foreboding voices that kept flogging Darsal's thoughts, nothing threatened their progress.

Nothing, that is, until a horse stepped out from the trees behind them.

"Darsal?"

She spun her mount, forcing Hunter to frantically spread his wings to keep from falling. There on a brown mare that was ten times her size sat Karas, the little Horde girl who was no longer Horde.

Darsal was too stunned to speak.

"Well, well, well," Hunter crooned. "Well, well, indeed. Hello, little girl."

Karas showed no sign she'd seen or heard the Roush. But, of

course, only Billos, Johnis, Silvie, and Darsal had had their eyes opened.

"What are you doing here?" Darsal demanded. She scanned the tree line for others, but it appeared that this squat had come alone, unless she was being used as bait while they hid in the bushes. "Are you alone?"

"Yes," Karas said. "Except for the horse, that is. Do you count horses as companions?"

"People, you little fool, not horses."

Karas frowned. "You think I'm a fool?"

Darsal scanned the trees again, just to make sure there was no one else.

Eyes on Karas. "You're a fool for following me. What do you think you're doing out here by yourself?"

"Following you."

"Yes, following us," Hunter said.

"Just you remember our agreement," Darsal snapped at the Roush.

"What agreement?" Karas asked.

"Nothing. If you head back now, you'll be home before it gets dark. I suggest you get moving."

"I could take her," Hunter said. "She'd get lost on her own."

"Why would a fool who's followed this far turn back now?" the little girl on the huge horse said.

"Because following me into the desert would be even more foolish," Darsal snapped. "Because they're probably already screaming for you back at Middle. Because you have no reason to follow me in the first place!"

"Would I be here if I didn't have a reason?"

"Only if you really are a fool."

"She doesn't look like a fool to me," Hunter said.

"Shut up, Hunter," Darsal said.

"Hunter?" Karas blinked. "My name's Karas, and it's not polite to be so harsh."

Darsal set her jaw. "What reason do you have to follow me?"

Karas hesitated, then nudged her horse closer. "Does the name Grace mean anything to you?"

"I don't know, should it? I'm telling you, you'd better head back before—"

"She was my mother. My father, the high priest, killed her."

Darsal sat still. No matter how frustrated she was at the girl's presence, she didn't have the heart to tear into her the way she wanted to.

Karas continued. "She used to say that somewhere out there I had an auntie, because she had a younger sister—fifteen years younger— a long time ago. I think that I've found my mother's sister."

"Me?"

"You look like her twin."

"Don't be ridiculous. She had to be much older . . . She was a Scab."

"Weren't you listening? I said her sister was much younger. Thomas told me that when the Great Deception ruined the world thirteen years ago, families were broken up. The disease took most of their memory. But I can swear you're mother's sister because you look like my mother. Except for the scar."

Darsal didn't know how to respond to such an absurd claim. "Is this possible?" she whispered, then prodded the Roush for an answer.

"Yes. Yes, of course it's possible," Hunter said.

"Yes," Karas said.

The forest's edge stood tall and silent. Darsal couldn't accept it, not after the years of suffering following her parents' deaths.

She calmed herself and let anger creep into her tone. "Either way, you can't just walk up to people and latch yourself on to them without knowing what's happening."

"Which is what?" Karas asked.

"Which is none of your business. This is crazy. It's going to be dark in an hour!"

"Then we'll build a fire," Karas said.

Hunter offered a soft chuckle.

"No. We will not. I will, not you, because you're not coming; it's out of the question!"

Karas seemed unfazed. "I insist. I don't know what you're up to, but it looks like you're headed out into the desert. I know the desert better than you."

"We know it well enough. You just escaped the desert, for Elyon's sake! Your insolence is infuriating!"

"We? You and I? So you're saying I can come?"

"Slip of the tongue. I certainly don't mean you."

"I can help you survive danger," Karas said.

"You're a ten-year-old squat!"

"I have more water."

"She has more water," Hunter said.

Indeed, having just been healed by the lake water, she seemed especially enamored with it. Two full bags rested over her saddle.

"Where are we going?" Karas asked.

"Nowhere." Darsal turned her mount, kicked its flanks, and trotted into the desert, begging reason to catch up to the foolish little girl.

"That's it, show her who's the boss," Hunter quipped.

"Quiet."

Taking a Roush to a Black Forest to find Alucard was one thing. Taking a young girl whom Johnis had risked his life to save—whom Thomas Hunter had taken an inordinate interest in—was madness.

The way Darsal now understood her situation was that she had a two-hour head start on Johnis, who would come after her as soon as Karas returned with the news that she'd headed north. But two hours were all she needed.

"We should head west first to avoid the Horde camping in the north."

Darsal spun in her saddle and saw that Karas followed ten feet behind, undeterred.

"She's right; the Horde is camped north," Hunter said.

"You can't come! Thomas will have my head!"

567

"I hope to help you keep your head, Big Sister," Karas said.

"And stop calling me that. You don't know it's true."

"I do know. I also overheard you talking to yourself about going to the Black Forest in search of Alucard, one of the legendary Shataiki that Witch often talked about. Don't worry, you'll grow to appreciate me."

"Why do you speak like that?" Darsal demanded in frustration.

"Like what?"

"Like you're a scholar rather than a child? I thought the Horde were stupid."

"Deceived, not stupid. And I'm not Horde anymore, or didn't you notice?"

Hunter sat grinning like a monkey. "Amazing," he muttered. "For all you know, Elyon has sent her to save your skinny neck."

"Don't be stupid."

"Keep telling yourself that, you might listen," the Roush said.

Darsal took one more minute to consider her options, which were either to return with the girl or press on in the hopes of saving Billos.

She'd escaped from Johnis's house thinking that life was hers to risk. Then she'd taken Hunter by force, and now Karas was in her care. The equation had changed. But her desperation to find Billos had not. And she'd already committed herself.

Their lives, all three of them, were on Billos's head, not hers.

Darsal humphed and galloped toward the sinking sun, followed closely by the little girl who claimed she was her niece and insisted on calling her "sister."

*The world is coming apart at the seams*, she thought. *First Billos, and now Karas. They are mad, all completely mad.*

# NINE

The spider named DELL stared at Billos with glowing, pupil-less red eyes. A whole circle of them ringed its head like a crown. They hadn't actually "opened" per se, but they had come to life and were peering at him.

Still, the beast did not move.

Billos had been in tight, life-threatening situations dozens of times, and if there was one thing that had been cut into his instincts, it was the importance of seizing the advantage. He had to move now, while he had the element of surprise. Surely the beast was as stunned as he; what else explained its inaction?

Billos feigned left, then darted to his right, knife still extended. His plan was simple: disable one leg, maybe two if he had the opportunity; leave his enemy vulnerable on one side, then keep to that side.

He thrust the knife into the thigh, twisted, and ripped backward. The skin tore, bled a white fluffy substance.

Feathers.

Billos jumped back, confused by the sight. The creature had not reacted. It hadn't even flinched.

He lowered the knife and stood up. So then, it wasn't a spider, not an ant, not a beast of any kind. This was a flower, or a bush, or . . . a tree maybe. Or a weapon of some kind. Maybe a fancy buggy.

And since the wall looked like the glass Thomas insisted came from his dreams, perhaps this object also came from his dreams.

For that matter, maybe Billos had stepped into Thomas's world.

He walked forward and tentatively touched Dell's leg, then decided that his first instinct had been correct. This was a chair or a bed, not a leg. Which meant he was supposed to sit or lie on it.

For the first time since he'd crossed into this strange and terrible place, Billos grinned. A daring, fascinated grin with just a little relief.

This didn't end his troubles, of course—he still had to find a way out before he starved to death. The books were nowhere to be seen, and he didn't have the slightest idea what the contraption did or how to work it, but at least he wasn't pinned under its hungry jaws.

"So, so, so, what do we have here?" he muttered. "Tell me what surprises you hold for me, DELL. Let's make friends."

Armed with his new conclusions, Billos slowly ran his hand

over the cut he'd made. A chair. Yes, of course, how foolish of him to think this contraption was a spider.

DELL was undoubtedly a horseless buggy. Six reclining seats and a spokeless wheel in the center. He touched one of the shiny black spheres that rested at the top of each chair, saw that they were attached only by cords, and carefully lifted one up with both hands.

It was a helmet, hollowed on the inside like his own leather helmet but made of hard shell. Dark glass rounded the front to cover the eyes. One of the strange ropes he'd originally thought were roots ran between the helmet and the hub.

So then, the warrior was intended to place this helmet on for protection when he drove this buggy. It was a war machine.

Immediately Billos's pulse surged. He'd found a weapon that was far more advanced than anything he or any of the Forest Dwellers could have imagined! And if he, Billos, could find a way to operate it, perhaps find a way to return it to the forests, enter it into battle against the Horde, even . . . if he could do that, the possibilities were endless. He might single-handedly save the forests!

Each thought spun through his mind as quickly as the next, which reminded him that he was trapped in a white room without the books or food or a clue how this contraption worked. And he was here because he'd ignored the warning not to touch the books with blood.

Billos took a deep breath and walked around the machine, touching and prodding the surfaces. The central hub with all the small red lights he'd first thought were eyes was as hard as stone. But when he rapped on it with his knuckles, it sounded hollow.

So, how did one operate this beast? He rounded the whole contraption twice, looking for something to control it, like reins, though he doubted he'd find reins—this wasn't an animal. Still, there were no reins, no levers, no objects of any kind. In fact, just the smooth hub and the six seats sticking out. And the red lights that had brightened when he first touched it.

Light was coming into the room from glowing squares on the ceiling, likely some kind of glass through which the sun was shining, though Billos couldn't see past them. It made sense that the red "eyes" were just crystals reflecting light from the ceiling.

Billos sighed and was about to climb into one of the seats when he noticed a thin outline, one square foot, on the hub. He touched it, pressed lightly, felt it move.

He gasped.

The square silently slid up, revealing a row of buttons on the surface beneath. Buttons with letters on each.

How was that possible? Something unseen was making this contraption move!

Magic, then. Like the books. This weapon was even more powerful than he could imagine.

He couldn't steady the tremble in his fingers as he reached for the letters. He wasn't one who could write, like Johnis, but he knew the letters Thomas had insisted every child learn. He pushed a few and stood back.

Nothing changed. But what did he expect to change? Billos then set to work pushing buttons in every conceivable order, growing more and more frustrated as the minutes dragged on.

How many combinations could there possibly be? He tried words like *go* and *start* and *wake*, but the buggy sat dumb.

An hour stretched past, maybe two. The contraption refused to respond to his touch. Yet it had opened! There was magic inside. The weapon could be activated; he just had to learn how.

But nothing he tried seemed to work. Feeling miserably defeated, Billos tried the locked knob on the main door again, then slowly sank to his seat in the corner and stared at the silent contraption.

After what felt like a very long time, he stood and approached the weapon again, pushed a few more buttons to no avail, and decided to try something new. Moving with more deliberation now, he pushed and prodded and pulled various parts of the contraption. The seats. The ropes that ran along the sides of the seats into mesh gloves. The helmets.

Nothing happened.

He climbed into one of the seats and stuck his head into the helmet. The stench of burning rubber trees, which he'd now grown accustomed to, filled his nostrils, strong again. The helmet did nothing but darken his world.

Claustrophobia began to set in. He yanked the helmet off and sat in silence. It was useless. Nothing he tried worked. Resigned to the impossibility of his predicament, Billos leaned back and closed his eyes.

Darsal would be worried. Johnis would be furious. Silvie would be plotting his death. He'd betrayed them all, but most of all he'd betrayed Darsal.

Unless he returned with the weapon. Wasn't that justification enough to ignore Johnis's warning never to touch the books with blood?

Billos opened his eyes and stared up at the pale light. What if this really was a spider and it was playing dead, waiting for him to starve to death before it consumed him like most spiders do?

He spun out of the chair, chided himself for the absurd thought, and went back to work on the buggy. But no matter what he did, no matter what he prodded or poked or pulled, nothing happened. He was still trapped in the white room with an unresponsive weapon that provided no escape.

And now he was growing thirsty. Soon the disease would set in and crack his skin. Give him a sword and a slew of Scabs to face and he could fight to the bitter end. But in this prison he was powerless.

Billos tried to push back the panic that crowded his mind. This was it? He'd been warned, and now he was going to face the consequences.

Now motivated as much by fear as curiosity, Billos threw himself into the task of making the weapon work. For many minutes that never seemed to end, he worked feverishly, covering every square inch of the contraption, pushing every button, pulling every rope.

Nothing.

He finally retreated to the corner and dropped to his rump, breathing heavy with desperation.

"Elyon," he muttered. "Please, Elyon, I swear, I swear . . . forgive me. Deliver me from this monster that has swallowed me whole, and I'll do anything. I'll follow Johnis on this blasted mission"—he rephrased—"on this mission of yours."

Nothing happened. Naturally. Billos was now beyond himself.

"I swear, I swear." Then louder. "Help me." Then in a cry of rage. "Help me, for the sake of Elyon, help me!"

# TEN

"What do you mean 'disappeared'?" Thomas demanded. "I give you one order, to keep an eye on one person, not even an enemy at that, and you can't follow? Can you do nothing by the book?"

Johnis and Silvie had called Darsal's name after a long stretch of silence, then barged into the bathroom and found it vacant. It only took them a minute to discover that her horse was gone too.

Two hours of frantic searching through the forest had yielded nothing. When they'd finally found Gabil, the Roush who thought of himself as a great martial artist, he was no help. "Hunter would know," Gabil had said. He'd find the Roush named Hunter. And in the meantime, they'd better get their act together. Michal wasn't going to like this, not one bit.

Now the sun was nearly gone, and they had no clue where Darsal had gone.

"We're sorry, sir. And if Darsal were the enemy, our task would have been a simple one. She's far craftier than any Scab."

"Find her!" Thomas thundered.

"She took her horse, sir," Silvie said. "We have no idea which direction she headed."

"And don't tell me that Billos is still missing."

Johnis nodded. "Yes, he is."

Thomas threw out his arms and paced, eyeing them. He was showing his hard side because it was demanded—Johnis would do no different.

"I chose you four because you're all the same in ways not even *you* knew. Each of you share the character traits I find useful in battle leaders. I knew that you would butt heads at every turn—I told my wife as much when you went missing the first time. But this . . ." He shook his head. "I didn't know I was promoting four fighters who could find trouble as easily as a blind man finds the wall!"

"I understand, sir."

"Do you?"

"I think so. It must be maddening," Johnis said.

"Really? You read me like a book, little poet. My advice is to go home and wait. There's love between Darsal and Billos. Had I known how deep their bond went . . ."

Thomas turned away and took a deep breath. "They've probably run off to have some time alone from you two. Maybe you should consider doing the same."

"No."

Johnis's retort hung in the room awkwardly.

Johnis glanced at Silvie. "I mean 'no, I don't think Billos ran off for love,' not 'no, Silvie and I shouldn't consider doing that.'"

*Still awkward,* he thought, and now his face was feeling flush. "Not that we *should* run off together either, I just—"

"Save it, young man," Thomas said. "It was only a passing comment to set you at ease. I can see I failed. Though it's not a terrible idea."

Silvie seemed as flustered as Johnis was. They'd always heard that Thomas of Hunter was a romantic in his own way, a true believer in the Great Romance and completely faithful to Elyon, whom all humans, even the Horde, had once loved. But his frank advice had caught them flat-footed.

A knock sounded on Thomas's door. "Come," Thomas said.

Ramos of Middle, Johnis's father, stepped in with his younger sister, Kiella. "Well, we have the whole party here," Ramos said, grinning.

"They were just leaving," Thomas said.

"Have any of you seen Karas?" Kiella asked. "I can't find her anywhere."

Thomas looked at Johnis, then his father, incredulous. "Does losing people run in your family, Ramos?"

"Not that I know, sir."

"Find them! And do it without leaving the city. Dismissed."

# ELEVEN

The Black Forest was two days northwest, according to Hunter. A week if you went straight north and ran into the Horde who were guarding the route to the Northern Forest.

"A week?"

"If you're lucky," the Roush replied. "They'll capture you the first day, and it'll take you another six to escape, if you survive. Northwest, girl, go northwest and avoid the Horde."

"What if they've shifted west?"

"Then we're in for a fight."

The little girl's huge horse plodded over the soft desert sand to the right and just behind Darsal, who led them into the night with no intention of stopping until they reached the Black Forest. She would turn the two-day journey into one. It wouldn't take Johnis long to figure out where they were going and follow. She had to get to the book and use it without interference from him!

*But what if there is no book? What if there is a book, but you don't find it? What if there is a book and you find it, but you're killed for it, along with Karas?*

Darsal pushed the thoughts away. Great missions require great risk. She urged her mount to quicken its pace.

They traveled in silence into the early morning hours, heading for a star that Hunter had pointed out. She thought that the Roush and Karas had run out of things to say or were sulking in silence, but a glance back told her differently.

Karas was slumped over the horse's neck, with one arm draped over each side. She was small enough to lie securely. Here Darsal had been thinking that she'd effectively silenced the girl with her imposing air of authority, when all the while Karas was snoring through sweet dreams!

Darsal leaned forward and peered over Hunter's furry head. The Roush's eyes were closed. He was leaning back on Darsal, sleeping soundly.

None of this sat well with Darsal. If she was required to endure tomorrow's hot sun without the benefit of sound sleep, so should they. Her mind drifted back to the many contests Billos had talked her into after he'd rescued her from certain death at her uncle's hand when she was eight years old.

Billos was always up for a contest. Who could stay awake the longest? Who could eat the most fire ants before their throats swelled shut? Who would be the first to pull their head from the water? Who could hang from a rope tied to a branch the longest? One-handed? Three fingers? One finger? By their necks?

She smiled in the darkness. For a period she'd made it her life's ambition to break every one of his records. And she did. So convincingly that Billos had scolded her for doing nothing but practicing to beat him.

"Is your life's ambition to beat me?" he'd demanded. "Life's not just one long contest! What's your problem?"

*You,* she'd thought. *You're my problem, Billos, because I owe you my life. And I want to be like you.*

She realized then that in her attempt to please him by excelling in these feats of his, she was displeasing him. Billos was bred to be a winner; anything less only frustrated him. Though she still played his games enthusiastically after that day, she stopped practicing night and day to beat him.

Darsal reached down, untied the knot that held Hunter to the pommel, and gave him a nudge with her left arm. The Roush slowly tipped over, then toppled off the horse, a ball of fur headed to the desert floor.

He landed with a soft *thud* and, amazingly, lay still for a moment before suddenly waking and floundering for footing.

Without so much as a squawk, the Roush shook his head to clear it, stumbled forward, took flight, and settled back in his former position on the horse.

He snuggled back into Darsal's stomach, sighed deeply, and settled. Two minutes later the creature was snoring again.

Darsal was tempted to try again, but she couldn't bring herself to do it. She might have captured the Roush, but that didn't mean she couldn't like him.

"I think so too," a soft voice said to her right.

She turned to Karas, who'd woken and drawn even. Darsal returned her gaze to the gentle white sand dunes ahead. It surprised her that she was glad for the girl's company. "You think what too?"

"That it's unfair for me to sleep just because I can," Karas said.

Darsal still wasn't sure what to make of the girl. Too intelligent and witty for her own good. Brave enough to follow despite the obvious danger. But above all, Karas wanted to belong. And no wonder; her mother had been killed by her father, whom Karas had just abandoned to become a Forest Dweller. The girl had no family left.

Unless Darsal was her aunt, as the girl claimed.

"What makes you think Alucard is real?" Karas asked. "I've never seen a Shataiki, have you?"

"Yes." Was she permitted to share that?

*What does it matter now, Darsal? You've broken all the rules already.*

"Billos, Johnis, Silvie, and I can see both the Shataiki and the Roush. Our eyes have been opened."

"Really? Why?"

Darsal shrugged. "That's more than you need to know."

"I'm risking my life to help you. Doesn't that qualify me to know what I'm getting into? Maybe my eyes should be opened too."

Darsal scoffed. "You really do think that way, don't you? That everything revolves around you. You're not helping. If anything, you're a burden."

"Exactly," Karas said. "But if my eyes were opened, I could be more of a help. Think about it."

Darsal turned to her. "You think I have the power to open your eyes?"

"Then who does?" The horses plodded. "Can you see one now?"

"A Shataiki?"

"Or a Roush."

Darsal faced forward, then snuck a peek at the fur ball leaning back against her. "As a matter of fact, yes."

Karas rode silently for a dozen strides.

"If you can't open my eyes, at least tell me why *yours* are open."

Darsal considered the request. The girl might be helpful if she knew what they were looking for.

"We're on a mission to find the seven original Books of History," she said, then quickly recounted the barest overview of the quest.

"Then you're on the right path," Karas said after a pause. "Witch used to talk about the seven books. And of Alucard, who has more under his skin than anyone realizes. Or so Witch said."

"Has what under his skin?"

"I don't know. But don't you think it was a mistake to leave Johnis and Silvie behind? You're breaking the oath."

Darsal turned away. "My oath to Billos came first."

Another pause.

"Then I admire your loyalty, Sister. And I hope I can earn yours too."

THEY RODE HARD THROUGH THE NIGHT, INTO THE MORN-ing sun, then veered northwest as instructed by Hunter, whom Karas could not see. No sign of the Horde. Or of pursuit.

Darsal pushed harder.

"If you're not going to stop and sleep, maybe you should tie yourself in so you don't fall off the horse," Karas said.

"I'm fine."

"I won't be able to lift you up by myself," she persisted.

"You don't think I've gone without sleep before? Over three days once, in a contest with Billos." Her parched lips twisted at the memory of her and Billos waking side by side under a tree, arguing about who'd fallen asleep first.

"Then we should at least bathe in the water, right?"

"She's right, you know," Hunter said. "You never know when an arrow will pierce that water bag and drain its contents. Use it while you can."

So they stripped and bathed quickly.

Darsal withdrew some jerky from the saddlebag and remounted. "Let's go!"

Karas's horse was so tall that she had to jump to reach the

pommel; then she muscled her way up and swung one leg over the saddle.

Darsal led them through the desert's blazing afternoon heat, torn between anger at Karas's persistent questions and the small comfort they provided her. Questions, questions, so many questions.

*What do the Forest Dwellers eat and drink at celebrations? What's this about Thomas of Hunter coming from the Histories? What does a Roush look like? Do you really love Billos so much as to trade all the forests for him?*

"Don't be a squat. It's unfair to pass judgment cloaked in a deceptively innocent question. Who said anything about trading the forests?"

"Isn't that what you're doing?" Hunter muttered.

Karas came back with yet another question. "Is *squat* a bad word?"

"No. Not necessarily. It refers to someone's height or lack thereof. It can be used for fun or for slander."

"Which way are you using the word?"

Darsal frowned. "For fun, of course."

The two horses plodded on. Midday came and went; afternoon pulled the blazing sun inexorably toward the horizon; distant clouds turned fire red until darkness shut out all but twinkling stars.

Once again Karas fell asleep, using her mount's neck as a bed. Once again, Hunter snuggled back against Darsal's belly and started to snore softly.

Alone in the dark morning hours, Darsal finally let her emotions catch up to her. The dread she'd felt at being abandoned by Billos was now swept away by a terrible sorrow. What if she really had lost him forever? She didn't know how to live without Billos. She was meant to marry him and bear his children one day, wasn't she?

And she still would . . . She would find that boy and save his thick head. And if necessary, she would teach him a lesson or two.

Then she would marry him.

Darsal saw the first Shataiki as the western sky began to lighten. At first she thought it was a dark desert shrub on the rise ahead, silhouetted by the graying sky behind. Or a rock on the horizon, because they'd passed a rare outcropping of boulders an hour earlier.

It lifted one wing, moved a foot to its left, and she thought, *A buzzard is stalking us. What does it know that we don't?*

Then the red eyes came into focus, and Darsal pulled back on her reins. Shataiki! And not just one. A dozen or so, rising from the sand dune a hundred paces ahead.

Hunter spit to one side. Darsal hadn't noticed him waking. "Their smell ruins the desert," the Roush said. "We are close."

"Sentries?"

"Yes, but I can smell more than those fourteen. Look up."

Darsal did and saw a hundred black spots circling in the dim sky.

"How far?"

"A few miles and everything will change."

"Then it's time for you to go."

"Perhaps," Hunter said.

Karas sat up, stared around, then faced Darsal. "What's going on?"

"We're there."

"We are?" Another look. "How do you know?"

"Shataiki. Ahead and above us."

Karas craned her neck and studied the sky. "Really?"

"Really." To Hunter: "There's only one thing you can do to help us now. You don't stand a chance on your own, am I right?"

The Roush didn't admit it quickly, but he could not lie. "Yes."

"Then fly back to Middle Forest and tell Johnis where we are. I have a two-day head start—if I can't accomplish what I've come for in the two days it takes him to get here, it was never meant to be. Do you follow?"

"You want me to fly?" Karas asked. "I told you, you need sleep!"

"Not you, squat. I'm talking to Hunter. Well, Hunter? What is it?"

"You're a fool to go into the Black Forest, you realize that."

"I have some bargaining chips."

"Who's Hunter?" Karas demanded.

"The Roush who's sitting on my horse. He's been with us the whole time. Now please let me finish my business with him."

"If you wanted Johnis, why not just bring him in the first place?" Hunter asked.

"Because he wouldn't have come! And if he'd come, he might have turned us back. I couldn't take that risk. Now it's too late. He'll come. Go to him."

"Are you sure you haven't lost your mind to this desert?" Karas asked.

"Yes. Hunter, I'm waiting."

"Fine. Fine, but I don't like it." He mumbled something and hopped onto the horse's head, facing them both. "The least I can do is give you two sets of eyes."

Hunter swept his wing toward Karas and whispered. "For this one, who has ears to hear and eyes to see, let her hear and see."

Karas gasped and stared wide-eyed at Hunter. "What's that?"

"I'm Hunter, the Roush that Darsal kidnapped from Middle Forest."

Karas blinked at the furry white animal. "You're real. So cute!"

"*They're* real too," Darsal said, motioning ahead at the Shataiki who stared with red eyes. "Not so cute."

Again, Karas gasped. "Shataiki!" She grabbed a bag of water from behind her and pulled it into her lap.

"You're sure about this?" Hunter asked. "I could take her with me."

"I doubt she'd go. Besides, you can't fly with her. Go. Now. You're free; go before I change my mind."

Hunter fluttered over to Karas's horse and landed on its head. "Touch my fur, cute little girl; go on, touch it."

She reached her hand out and stroked his neck lightly, eyes sparkling with wonder.

"You see, real. It's all real, everything the Horde can't see and many Forest Dwellers don't care to see. And it's all part of the real order. Elyon's order. That's his water you have, and it's a good idea. Keep Darsal alive for me until I get back with Johnis, will you?"

"Me? I will. I swear I will!"

Then Hunter leapt off the horse, spread his wings, zoomed low over the desert sand, and winged his way south.

Darsal and Karas sat on their horses, alone, facing the Shataiki, who were unfazed by this intrusion into their domain.

"Ready?"

"For what?" Karas asked.

Darsal cast her a silent look, then nudged her horse forward.

# TWELVE

Billos awoke and found himself curled up in the corner with his cheek plastered on the hard, white floor and his saliva pooling.

He sat up, disoriented. Then he remembered where he was. Imprisoned in this white room with a useless contraption called DELL. No book, no food, no water. Abandoned by Elyon.

His desperation had grown slowly as he'd become more aware of just how confining his new environment really was. The mystery had been replaced by a predictability that offered nothing new, no matter what buttons he pushed or levers he pulled or surfaces he pried. The buggy, if indeed that's what it was, lay dormant.

There was no way out, not without a horse to kick through

the door. Maybe not even then. He'd slammed into the glass wall with his full weight and bounced back like a hollow walnut shell.

He wondered if this was hell, the place reserved for the Horde. Maybe the books were a gateway straight to hell itself. Maybe that's why Teeleh was so interested in them.

"Please, Elyon, forgive me for my hot head. I shouldn't have used the book, and I swear never to use it again if you'll save me."

But he prayed this a hundred times to no avail.

Billos pushed himself to his feet and walked around DELL again. He pushed the buttons for a few minutes, mumbling his disgust at anything so intricate and so dumb at once.

"Argh!" He slammed his hand on the lettered buttons. The glass surfaces glared black. The buggy sat like a lump. He looked around, trying his best to keep his mind but failing.

How long had it been? A day? And already he was going mad. There was nothing to do . . . but sleep.

Billos climbed into one of the seats, lay back on the cushion, and faced the glowing squares on the ceiling. Night didn't seem to come here. Not that he longed for darkness.

A shudder passed through his body. He shoved his hands into the gloves that were attached by black cords to the bed. Best he could tell, the ropes were the reins that steered the buggy, and these gloves were some kind of armor.

He pulled the battle helmet over his head and snapped the latch. Darkness swallowed him. His breathing sounded loud in his ears. The experience was rather frightful, but it was a change from the white room, and at the moment it was what he needed.

"Let's go, you haggard old beast. Do something!"

Nothing, of course.

Claustrophobia began to set in. He yanked the helmet and gloves off, rolled from the bed, and stood undecided.

He crossed to the door, kicked it with his boot, and screamed his frustration. "Open! Just open, for the love of . . ."

The door swung lazily inward.

Open?

Billos was so astonished that he stood still, unable to move. What had he done? He was free?

He threw the door open wide and stepped into a dark hallway. The door at the other end was open. He ran down the passage, feet slapping the smooth floor with each stride.

The hall opened to a larger room with a cushioned floor, unlike any he'd seen. Stuffed chairs were situated around the room in neat groupings. Against one wall stood the room's only door, this one with some letters stamped above it: EXIT.

Billos crossed to the door, heart hammering. He was free; he was going to make it. To where, he had no clue—but out. Out was what he'd needed, and out was where he was going!

He put his hand on the door and twisted. It swung easily into a dim interior. Cool air flooded his face.

Okay, okay, not the bright sunlight he'd been expecting, but he was out, right? Or was he?

The wind carried a distant voice to him. Yelling from overhead, if he wasn't mistaken.

He ran into a damp hallway with rough walls, past a curtain, into a dimly lit room with gray walls and stacks of brown containers. Stairs rose on his left, and he hurried for them.

The voices grew louder. Or voice, he should say—one gruff voice expressing enough outrage to slow Billos to a timid climb.

He nudged the door at the top, saw no immediate danger, and stepped into . . . a library of some kind?

Bookcases towered on either side of a passage that led into a great room, two stories high. A large crystalline chandelier hung from the domed ceiling.

"You betrayed them, Cutes. For that I think you deserve to die, don't you?" The voice echoed from the main room. "You think your lover boy will try to save you now? I think not."

A chill rode Billos's spine. He gripped the knife tighter and crept forward on the balls of his feet. Behind him the door clicked shut. He reached back for the doorknob.

Locked.

There would be no going back the way he'd come.

"You should be thrilled that at least one of you is going to make it out of this place alive. You know that these doors are sealed with blood. Only blood can pry them open. If not yours, then whose? Hmmm? Not mine, not a chance, Cutes."

Soft crying. Muffled, definitely muffled.

Something about that voice struck a chord deep in Billos's mind. Female. Familiar.

He stopped.

Darsal?

A dozen thoughts crashed into his mind, and he knew that he was right. Darsal was not only in this place, but her life was hanging in the balance.

And lover boy? Someone else? No, never!

But what if? He'd never even considered the possibility that Darsal might fall for another man. She'd never shown the slightest interest in anyone but him since he'd killed her uncle for habitually beating her to a pulp after her parents' deaths.

The thought of losing her to another man suddenly struck him as obscene. Billos dropped the pretense of stealth and sprinted the rest of the way.

Around him rose a round atrium bordered on all sides with bookcases. A dozen vacant tables sat in the middle. Railing ran along the perimeter, separating the bookcases from the tables.

Darsal was strapped to the railing, hands tied behind her back, mouth gagged with a brown cloth. Her eyes darted to him, spread wide with fear. Then wrinkled, begging.

In front of Darsal stood a tall man dressed in black. Black hat, black trench coat, black slacks, black boots tipped in silver. Dark hair to his shoulders, smile twisted like a snake's tail, one eyebrow arched.

"Hello, Billy." He paused. "Mind if I call you Billy? It's easier to say than this Bill*os* crap. Besides, *Bill* rhymes with *will*, and that's what we're here to fix. My will, her will, we all scream for Bill's will. Kapische?"

Billos stepped toward Darsal, who looked as if she'd been beaten before being strung up. "What's going on? Who are you? You can't do this!"

"I can't. Gee whiz, oh my gosh, I'm sorry. What's your plan? We all lie down and die? 'Cause that's what happens in about five minutes if we don't kill someone. Her. Or you. I'm not volunteering, and there's no other way out."

That was the second time the man in black had suggested that there was no way out of the library. Billos glanced around—no windows or doors that he could see.

"Name's Black," the man said. "Marsuvees Black. You, Billy Boy, and me, the Black man, and Darsal-poo here have all found ourselves trapped in a magical room that will only let us out if one of us dies. So say The Powers That Be."

Billos stared at Darsal, pushing down the confusion that throbbed through his head. Confusion that unnerved him like the rest of this crazy place. Like this—he looked back at the man called Black—this human dressed up like a Shataiki.

"The Powers That Be?" he asked.

Black forced a grin. "Evil, baby. I suggest we comply. Trust me, when we do get out of this room, the world that awaits you no less than seriously rocks. Power that will make your bones quiver like a snake's tail, baby."

The man took a breath, holding his grin. "But I'll let you make the choice. Let me kill her and walk into a new life. Or pretend you can stop me and die with her. Your choice."

Billos hesitated only a moment, filled with thoughts of power that might make his bones quiver, then regained his composure and with it his backbone. He walked toward Darsal, swiveling his knife.

The man called Marsuvees Black slipped a large silver knife from a sheath Billos hadn't seen until now and stepped up to Darsal.

"Think about this, you stupid nincompoop." The man spoke with a certain uncaring that made Billos believe he could as easily kill both Darsal and him as take a breath.

For a brief moment he considered his options. The man's eyes flashed above his curved lips, inviting or threatening or both.

"No," Billos said. Then he threw reason aside and vaulted the railing, knife extended.

"No? The boy from the land of books says no?"

"I said no!" Billos launched himself at the man in a single bound that carried him much higher than he expected with ridiculous ease.

He spun once in the air and thrust out his right foot, knowing Black could not anticipate such a precise, powerful move. Truth be told, *he* could hardly anticipate it. The air was different here.

His foot swished through the air where Black . . .

Through thin air. He'd shifted? So quickly!

Billos landed on his feet and ducked in anticipation of the blow he knew would come.

Silence filled the room. Only his heart disturbed the stillness. He whipped around to his left. No one.

To the right. No one.

No Darsal. No Black. He was alone.

Billos stood straight, breathing steadily through his nostrils, knife still ready.

"Hello?" His voice echoed softly. "Hello, hello . . ."

He'd imagined it all? He was dreaming, like Thomas of Hunter had once supposedly dreamed, unable to distinguish reality from dreams?

"Hello?" he called again.

"Hello, Billossssssss."

Billos whirled. The man in black stood between two bookcases, legs spread slightly, arms crossed, head tilted down, grinning.

"Surprised?"

Billos kept his blade out, tip trembling despite his attempt to still it.

"You did well, son. Very well, I might say." The man lowered his arms and walked out into the room, scanning the ceiling. "I had to know where your heart was, you understand. If you had made any other choice, I would have left you alone to make your way in this messed-up place. Live or die, I don't—"

"Stop!"

The man faced him. Surprised.

"How did you do that?" Billos asked. "Where did she go?"

"Nowhere. She was never here. Are your ears plugged? I set

that up to test your loyalty. You showed me that you won't turn your back on those you love."

"Which does not include you. What is this place? How did you make her appear and disappear?"

The corner of Black's mouth nudged his right cheek. "I wasn't lying about the power in this world, baby. But I need you to trust me the way I trusted you."

"Trusted me? You threatened—"

"Stop!" Black thundered. Then softer, "Stop being so dense. If I'm going to partner with you, I need to know I can trust you. Can I? Because if I can't, so help me, I'll leave you to face your own demons."

Billos felt his muscles relax some. "So none of that happened?"

"In your mind, with your body—is there a difference? It happened. I gave you a choice, and you chose her over yourself. I refuse to work with anyone who isn't completely loyal."

"I don't give my loyalty easily," Billos said. "What makes you think I care about you?"

"The fact that I'm your only way out. The fact that I can give you what you deserve. The fact, Billy-boy, that you're here for a purpose. The fact that I've been waiting for you for a long time."

So then Black was good?

The man continued. "Now and then we're all confronted with a new slice of truth, an opportunity that could change everything. The realization that the brick wall in front of us isn't solid at all, if we only have the guts to run pell-mell into it."

Billos lowered his knife.

Black smiled. "What do you think, Billy-bong?"

Billos glanced around. "I don't know . . ."

"Am I good? Or am I evil?"

He thought for a moment and gave the only answer that made any sense to him. "I don't know."

Marsuvees Black smiled, teeth white, mouth pink. "I like you, boy. We're going to get along just fine."

"Where's Darsal? The real Darsal?"

"Looking for you, I would guess."

It made sense. They would all be looking for him. Wondering what had happened to the books. Johnis would be pacing a ditch into the ground, worrying, wondering what Billos knew that they did not.

But Billos didn't know enough.

"So I suppose you'd like to know what's happening," Black said.

"Fair enough, what is happening?"

Black winked. "The million-dollar question." He interlaced his fingers and cracked his knuckles. "Or should I say the seven-book question, which makes the million-dollar question look like a piece of week-old spinach on the bottom of a boot."

"Where am I?"

Black paced to his left, eyes still on Billos. "You're here, in the good old U-S-of-A. Where three of the seven books have gone conveniently missing. Do you know what the books do, Billy? Do you mind if I call you Billy?"

"My name is Billos. And no, I'm not sure I do know what they do."

The man chuckled. But it was a friendly sound that tempted Billos to grin with him.

"Well, Billos, then let me tell you. It's high time you know why we sought your help. The books are pure transparency, baby. Reality stripped of rules except those written in the books themselves. The truth. They can make truth, and they tell it the way it is—no mincing of words. No rules except those written into the books themselves."

"What does that have to do with me disappearing into the book and waking in the white room?"

"You didn't disappear into the book. You entered the book's cover, which is a different matter, you'll see. Either way, it's all real, baby, and it's all good."

He turned his head and stared at the far wall, where Billos saw a door that he didn't remember seeing earlier.

"Well, not *all* good," Black said. "In the wrong hands, the seven books could be quite a problem."

"Why all seven books?"

"Together all seven can undo any rules written into the books." He faced Billos again, light from the windows glinting in his eyes. "Their power is limitless. Which is why we need to secure them before the Dark One gets his paws on them. And we need you to help us, Billos-baby. Not Johnny-come-lately, not Saliva, not even Dorksal, although she's a close second. We were interested in *you*."

The words made Billos dizzy for a moment. These names were nearly beyond him, but he knew Black was referring to Johnis, Silvie, and Darsal.

"Why me?"

"Who's standing here now? Johnny-come-lately? Saliva? Only you had the guts to do what needed to be done to get to where the books are. Johnis played his part, don't get me wrong. But this has always been your trip, baby."

"And who's to say that *you're* not the Dark One?" Billos asked, though he was starting to think that Black had made some good points.

The man stared at him hard, surprised. "No, no, no, boy. Don't mistake my little test with Darsal for more than that. Like I've said—to the point of making me wonder if you're thicker in the head than I was led to believe—I had to know how loyal you were."

Made sense. Right?

"Then who is the Dark One?"

"The black, nasty bat, naturally. You're going to have to choose his way. Or my way. Take your pick."

"So this is all about you finding the books," Billos said.

"Before he does. Like I said, his way or my way. You either accept the fact that you were actually meant to come here and find me for the sake of the books, which is my way. Or you believe that you betrayed the others by making off with the books and entering them; that would be the nasty way of Teeleh."

"And if I choose your way?" Billos said.

"Then you bring me the four books from your reality, which will allow us to find the last three books that are lost on Earth."

"We only had three books."

"Well, you better get those three back and then find the fourth, baby. 'Cause we need all four to find the three hidden on Earth. Where I hail from."

"And why do you need me? Go get them yourself."

"You don't know? Only those from your reality can see the books here, unless all seven are together. The three you've lost can only be found by someone from your side. By you. You see, it all comes back to you. I can clap my hands and . . ."

He clapped his hands, and a book of history materialized in his right hand.

". . . presto, I have a book. Cool, huh?"

Billos blinked. "The book's cold?"

"Expression they use here. Never mind. It's an illusion, like Darsal. Unfortunately this book isn't"—he brought his hands together again and the book vanished—"real. This, however"—he snapped his fingers and a goblet appeared in his grasp—"is real. Care for a sip?"

Black lifted the glass to his lips and drank the milky substance. "Ahhh . . . Worm sludge, they call it, but it's delicious. Take a drink." He nodded at a table to Billos's right where a similar glass goblet sat, filled to the brim with the nectar.

"It'll give you the kind of power you need to finish this task of yours."

Billos hesitated, then picked up the glass. Smelled the drink. A sweet, musky odor reached up into his nostrils and stung his eyes. He felt lightheaded and pleasant. He'd had strong grog, but nothing that smelled so delicious and none that affected the mind with a single sniff.

He took a sip. The worm sludge, as Black had called it, tasted awful, much like he imagined worm sludge would taste. But it filled him with such a feeling of . . . what was it? Confidence? Power, the man had said power.

He took another sip. On second thought it wasn't so bad at all. Warmth spread through his chest and arms. Mighty fine grog at that, this worm sludge.

Black was grinning.

"So what is it, Bill? My way or his way?"

The choice seemed clear. And although Black's approach was rather unorthodox, it was compelling.

"Naturally, I'll give you more than grog," Black said. "Clap your hands, baby."

"Now?"

"Now. Put the drink down, and clap your hands together."

Billos took one more slug, set the glass down, and clapped his hands. A bolt of energy rode up his arms. Without warning, a piece of formed steel appeared in his right fist. Like a curved knife with a handle in his palm, and a tube where the blade should be.

He was so stunned by the appearance of the strange object that he nearly dropped it. He studied it in awe. He'd done this?

"How . . . how did . . ."

Black chuckled. "You like? That's what I'm talking about, baby. Magic! I call it suhupow. Short for superhuman power."

"Suhupow," Billos repeated, staring at the weapon. "What is it?"

"It's called a gun. Pull the trigger."

He assumed the small lever under the crook of his forefinger must be the trigger, so he pulled on it.

The weapon bucked in his hand, throwing it back. *Boom!* Thunder crashed overhead.

Billos yelped, dropped the weapon, and grabbed his ears. His heart pounded. "What? What happened?"

Black chuckled and nodded at a chair next to him. "You missed me."

The chair's back had a large, splintered hole in it. He'd done that? Billos looked down at the gun. Smoke coiled from the hole on one end.

"My way or his way?" Black asked again.

"What's in it for me?"

"More power than you can imagine, Billy-boy."

Billos's lips twitched in wonder. "Your way," he said.

"Very cool." Marsuvees Black snatched up the goblet of worm sludge. "I'll drink to that. Join me?"

Billos picked up his glass, now feeling altogether intoxicated and headstrong.

Black lifted his glass. "To Billos."

Billos toasted the air. "To the books."

Black: "To grace-juice, baby!"

Billos: "To the gun!"

Black threw his head back and laughed. "Drink!"

They drained their glasses as one. Then Black threw his to the ground, where it vanished a split second before striking.

"Now, let's go rule the world!"

Billos threw his glass down and watched it disappear.

He looked up, grinning so wide it hurt. "Yes, let's rule the world . . . baby!"

# THIRTEEN

The Black Forest lay in a massive depression that could not be seen until they were upon it. Even then Darsal knew that no human besides she, Johnis, Billos, Silvie, and now Karas could see it at all.

The Shataiki parted for them as they neared. "Keep the water handy," Darsal said.

"You don't need to remind me. I know how frightened it made me just a few days ago."

They urged their horses up to the depression's lip and stared over a cliff into the abyss. Black, leafless trees covered the charred ground below. Thousands of black bats perched on the branches, looking up at them.

The forest ran a mile or so in, then dipped under a huge rock lip that stretched the depression's full width. The earth swallowed up the forest. How far underground the trees grew, Darsal couldn't tell, but according to Hunter, this forest was larger than the last, and by that measure, the underground cavern had to be massive indeed.

Evidently the black trees didn't need sunlight to grow. Only the fertile soil of death.

"We're really going to go down there?" Karas asked in a voice that trembled. Finally she was showing her youth.

"It wasn't my idea for you to come."

Karas stared at a large Shataiki bat that waddled closer and settled on the lip, staring back at her with its cherry eyes. Flies, always flies around these putrid beasts. This one looked like it had more flies than fur covering its mangy body.

And the smell . . . there were no words to describe the rotting stench that clogged their nostrils. Darsal could hardly breathe through her nose, and the idea of breathing through her mouth made her sick.

None of the Shataiki seemed surprised by their presence. It was as if they'd been long expected.

"He's waiting," the Shataiki that had come closer said in a low, scratchy voice.

Karas faced Darsal and saw that the girl's lips were quivering.

"Stay close." Darsal turned her horse onto a series of switchbacks cut from the cliff. The Shataiki watched them go. Several squawked fifty meters away, but their attention was on something they fought over, not on Darsal or Karas.

The air grew warmer and even more putrid as they descended. With each step the feeling that she had made a mistake in coming here grew, and Darsal had to work a little harder to persuade herself otherwise. But she was on a rescue mission, not unlike Johnis's mission to save his mother and the girl who rode behind her.

"Darsal?"

"Quiet, Karas."

"I'm frightened, Sister."

*So am I, Sister.* "I'm not your sister. But stay close, and keep the water closer. You're safe with me."

The path leveled at the bottom and snaked into the towering forest. Angular branches covered with moss jutted every which way in a tangled mess, blotting out the morning sun. The rancid air turned cool and damp.

Shataiki bats screeched overhead, glaring with red eyes, following them from tree to tree.

"It's dark," Karas said.

And darker yet to come. "We'll follow the eyes."

"I'm really, really frightened, Darsal. Maybe we should go back."

"We couldn't even if we wanted to. Please, just try to be brave and keep quiet."

"Can't we talk? I think it would help."

*It wouldn't hurt,* Darsal decided. And the sound of Karas's voice did cut the chatter of the Shataiki—perhaps they were trying to listen in.

"Okay, tell me about how Johnis rescued you."

So Karas told her all the details as they continued into the darkening forest, step by step. The path began to descend again when they passed under a huge overhang. Their voices sounded hollow in the cavern. To think this hole had been here the whole time, harboring a more ominous threat than all of the Horde combined!

*You do not belong here, Darsal.*

It was Billos's doing, and for a moment she hated him for his impulsive, selfish bullheadedness. She muttered under her breath.

"What?"

"Nothing."

They'd traveled into the darkness nearly an hour, giving the horses their heads, when the sound reached Darsal. She pulled up.

"Water," Karas said.

It was only a dripping sound, but now that Darsal could hear it, she could also smell the musky, dank smell of stale water.

A flame suddenly swooshed to life a hundred meters ahead, casting an orange glow in the cavern. Karas inhaled sharply.

They were at the very edge of an underground lake with a black surface. Across the water sat a wooden platform, all too familiar to Darsal. On the platform stood a solitary Shataiki, larger than the rest, and in his claw he held a large torch.

"Alucard," Karas guessed.

"Alucard."

They could see the ceiling now, hewn from the rock, jagged and dripping water from long stalactites. The drops of water fell to the lake's surface and sent out ripples—the sound they'd heard.

The path snaked around the lake, barely visible between the gnarly trees and the stagnant water. Darsal turned her horse right and forced it forward. Without trees to support them over the lake, thousands of Shataiki now perched on the trees that ran the lake's perimeter, staring with beady eyes. So many that Darsal thought the cavern's orange glow might be caused in part by the eyes, not just the torch.

Without moving, except to face them as they rounded the lake, Alucard watched them come. And then they were in the mud before the platform, eye to eye due to their being mounted on horses.

The beast stood nearly twice as tall as most Shataiki, and his skin was more than twice as mangy. Fur worn thin to reveal his skin beneath. He looked very old, if age was something that could be judged by how haggard a beast looked. His upper lip hung down on either side of his snout, like a sad hound that held a long stick supporting a flaming torch.

Only *this* hound gazed at them with furious red eyes, not dog eyes.

A centipede scurried across the bat's brow and across its upper cheek before vanishing into the beast's ear. Darsal imagined a nest inside and shivered.

"Only one of you," Alucard finally said in a low, wet voice. Saliva trailed off his snout and dripped to the ground. "And this traitor."

"I'm here on my own," Darsal said. "Armed with water—"

"Silence!" the bat snapped.

Darsal flinched.

"Does this look like your home? It's your tomb."

"Then it'll be your tomb as well," Darsal said, gathering the last reserves of her courage. She cast a quick glance to her right at Karas. The girl was shaking.

Eyes back on Alucard. "I've come to make you a deal."

That set the bat back a few moments.

"I don't make deals with my enemy," he said.

"You did with Tanis. Or was that Teeleh? You don't have the power to deal like that greater monster?"

"I could have you killed with the slightest move of my hand."

Darsal glanced at the beast's sharp, curved claws. For the last two days she'd thought about the proposition she would now voice, and however preposterous, however blasphemous, however treacherous it sounded, she saw no way around it.

But first she had to know if Alucard had one of the books.

"You can't kill me," Darsal said. "Not if you want the books."

"I'll do what pleases me in my home."

"You're not just a pawn of that bigger beast, Teeleh?" Darsal asked. "I assumed you do only what pleases him."

No response.

"You have another one of the books, safeguarding it for Teeleh, I imagine." Darsal didn't know this, of course, but she said it as if it were well-known. "I have three. But the three I have are with Billos, and Billos can only be gotten to via the book in your possession. Are you following me?"

"You've lost the books in your possession? You're even more foolish than I thought. You have nothing to bargain with."

"I do have something. I have your desire for the three books that Billos has. I can get them. But I need your book to do it."

So now it was out there. And judging by Alucard's stillness, he was interested.

"So Billos used the books. Did he open them?"

"No."

"You saw this?"

"I saw him touch the cover of one book with blood and vanish with all three." She paused. "What would have happened if he had opened a book?"

"You don't know? No, of course you don't. You're just a spoiled young warrior pretending to be important. Why he would choose you to match wits with me and the Dark One is beyond comprehension."

So Alucard knew who the Dark One was.

"Then tell me, what would happen if Billos opened a book?"

"It would depend. There were four books here: one with the Horde, one with Teeleh, one with me, and one with the Roush. Gather all four, and they would create a breach into the lesser reality where the last three books are hidden. But there is no way for him to return here with the books. Unless he has all four from this reality."

"He had only three, yet he went. I saw him."

"He's not where he might think he is."

617

Darsal pondered this but couldn't wrap her mind around the scope of these realities he suggested.

"So you've gone? You can tell me what to expect?"

"I've been to where I assume your friend went by touching the book with blood. But I would need all four books to go to Earth." Alucard slowly smiled, but offered no further explanation.

"So you need four books to go where you want to go?" Darsal questioned. "Which is different from where Billos went, because he only had three. So where has Billos gone?"

Alucard's response came slowly and carefully. "To a place of unlimited opportunity."

"Then that's what I have to offer you," Darsal said. "Three more books and yours back after I retrieve Billos's. They would have my neck for making this deal with you, and frankly I'm not sure I can offer it much longer. Any minute and I'll decide to give my life up instead of the books. Which will it be?"

"You expect me to believe that you'd give up the four books for one piece of meat?"

"He's not a piece of meat," Karas said, speaking up with a thin voice. "That's the difference between you and them. They appreciate every life; you don't."

"The traitor has stopped trembling long enough to speak," Alucard said.

"From what I gather, you're the one who turned your back on Elyon."

"Shut up, Karas," Darsal snapped.

"That would make you the traitor," the little girl said.

Alucard whipped his head back and roared, an earsplitting howl that crackled with rage.

The roar rang, then echoed. Silence filled the cavern.

"Wouldn't it?" Karas said.

Had she lost her mind?

"Do not speak that name in my home," Alucard snapped. "It makes me doubt you. Why should I agree with someone who defiles my home?"

"She's a young child; ignore her. I'm the one you're speaking to. And you can trust me because I would give my life for this 'piece of meat' named Billos."

Alucard regarded her with an expression hidden by red, pupilless eyes. The centipede slid out of his ear and disappeared into a patch of mangy black fur.

"Yes, you would die for him, wouldn't you?"

He thumped the wooden platform with his stick. Three Shataiki flew in from the side and disappeared into a hole behind the dock. Into the lair, not unlike the one Johnis had entered at Teeleh's lake.

"And I'll give you that opportunity," the beast said.

Darsal's pulse pounded, as much from the anticipation of accomplishing her first objective as from a gnawing fear.

"How many big bats like you are there?" Karas asked. The tremble was gone from her voice.

Alucard just stared at her.

"Why do you want to go where Billos has gone?"

Darsal didn't think the bat would entertain such simple questions from a little girl. "Karas . . ."

"I am Shataiki!" the beast snapped.

"And that bothers you?" Karas pushed.

"Did it bother you to be Horde?"

"No. I was too deceived. Are you saying you want to bathe in the lakes and make amends with Elyon?"

Alucard's neck stiffened, and his lips pulled back to reveal sharp, crusted fangs.

"Sorry, you didn't want me to speak Elyon's name. I forgot."

The beast's coat quivered, sending flies that Darsal hadn't noticed buzzing. "This is my home." He seemed to force each word out, one by one.

"But you don't want it to be?" Karas persisted.

For a long time Alucard just glared at her, and Karas stared back, though her shaking hands betrayed the state of her nerves. The entire forest had become deathly quiet.

When the beast spoke, his voice was nearly a growl. "Human," he said. "What I do, I do for a purpose beyond your understanding. A purpose that serves Teeleh well."

Darsal remembered something that Gabil, the Roush, had said before. That all Roush were in wonder of humans, the beings Elyon had fashioned after himself. Maybe jealous in a friendly sort of way. Now, looking at Alucard, she knew that Shataiki were also jealous. A bitter, spiteful hatred for being less than Elyon and human.

One of the three Shataiki who'd descended into the lair emerged. Darsal's horse shifted under her. The bat settled on the platform, clacked across to Alucard, and held out a leather bag.

"Take it out and put it between us."

The bat withdrew a filthy bundle. Careful so as not to touch its contents, he peeled back the dirty rags and exposed an old, green book bound in red twine. He set the half-exposed book on the wood planks. *The Stories of History.*

Darsal's fingers tingled. The fourth book. Her gateway to Billos. Her concern for any danger they had walked into fell away. It was all she could do not to slice her finger right then and there and thrust it against the ancient leather cover.

"Swear to me on your life that you will bring back all four books, and I will give you safe passage from here," Alucard said.

"I swear," Darsal said, only half-believing herself.

"If you do not, either you or Billos is mine. My choice."

"Yes."

"Then seal the oath with the book."

What did he mean?

"An oath made over the books is binding. You cannot break it and live. Did you expect me to take your unbound word?"

The revelation took some of Darsal's wind away. But now she was committed.

"Not a good idea," Karas said.

"Quiet!"

Darsal dismounted, walked to the book, placed one hand on

the cover, and swore to return all four to Alucard or forfeit her life. And Billos's, though she wasn't sure she could swear for him.

She wrapped her fingers around the book and stood. "May I?"

"Take it," Alucard said.

He stared at her for a few moments. Without another word, he turned and clacked away from them. The torchlight wavered, then snuffed out, leaving them in darkness. Surrounded by a sea of red eyes in the trees.

"What have you done?" Karas asked.

# FOURTEEN

The library led to a stone tunnel, which in turn led to a flight of rock-hewn steps, which finally ended at a trapdoor in the floor of a small cabin.

Marsuvees Black led Billos out of the cabin and down a canyon, always staying one step ahead. Turning back now and then to deliver his nuggets of truth.

"Life's what you make it, boy. A clean sheet every day."

"Do you like mustard? Keeps the mind sharp."

"They're all enemies, Billos. Don't trust them. The nicer they talk, the worse they are."

"You ever stake anyone through the heart, Bill*os*?"

Half of the comments made no sense, but all of them intrigued Billos.

To think that all along their search for the books was designed to take him through the books to this magical place where you could snap your fingers and have them filled with steel.

Billos tried it again and was immediately rewarded with a gun. He twirled it in his hand, relishing the very feel of this amazing weapon that could scare people with its bang and destroy objects some distance away with its suhupow. And to stow it you simply . . .

Billos threw the gun at the earth and watched it vanish. Amazing.

"Find me the books, and the world is yours," Black said, winking. He was both frightening and intoxicating at once. "Try snapping the fingers of your other hand."

Billos did. This time a rose appeared.

"To seduce the women, my friend."

He smelled the rose, felt it tickle his nose, then threw it into oblivion. "Ha! Is there any limit to this suhupow?"

"Not if you make it to the top. Follow me; I'll show the way."

They passed through a forested region and came out on a cliff overlooking a village. The structures were unlike any he'd ever seen. They were more square and smoother, and the roads between them were black, perfectly straight.

"Welcome to Paradise," Black said. His face twitched. "The little town that could. But that'll all change. This is where I leave."

"Leave? I don't know this place."

"Didn't stop me; shouldn't stop you. Like I said, you have to find the books on your own, then bring them to me."

"Down there?"

"Maybe they're there, maybe not. But down there is where you start. Practice. This little hole is full of conspirators who'll have you fooled the moment they open their mouths, if you let them. Think of Paradise as your final test. *Comprende?*"

"Comprende." Whatever that meant.

"Watch out for impostors. Shape-shifters. Brats who pretend to be your best friends. Conspirators, the bunch of them."

Billos walked to the edge of the cliff and studied the tiny forms of villagers walking down the main street. "Conspirators."

"Bring me the books. I need four, but I'll take three for now. See you on the dark side, baby."

"All of them are evil?" Billos asked, turning back.

But Marsuvees Black was gone. Vanished.

For a moment Billos felt alone. But just for a moment. Because then he snapped his fingers, watched a steel gun materialize in his hand, and he felt very much at peace.

He stowed the gun with a flip of his wrist, cracked his neck, faced the village below, and headed down to Paradise.

DUST BLEW OVER THE STREET THAT RAN DOWN THE MIDDLE of Paradise. Billos stopped at a sign that read, WELCOME TO PARADISE, POPULATION 545, and stared ahead in wonder. Words could hardly describe what he saw. *Suhupow, everywhere suhupow!*

The road he stood on was rock hard, perfectly formed from a

black substance that looked to have been melted and laid down in one long strip. But more stunning than this finely crafted road were the buggies that traveled on top of it. Painted in different colors with black wheels to roll over the road, they moved without horses, without any beast pulling or pushing. With suhupow and suhupow alone.

Billos felt like a child of wonder more than a warrior who'd trained his whole life to kill the Horde. What would Darsal say of Paradise? He strode down the yellow dash in the middle of the road, not bothering to wipe the crooked grin from his mouth.

Two things were now clear to him. No, three things: First, he'd made the right choice to enter the Book of History, which had, if he wasn't mistaken, taken him into history itself. Second, the mission was really about Billos's helping Marsuvees Black find the Books of History, which were invisible to all but him here in the histories. And third, this critical mission depended on his skill, his intelligence, his craftiness—his ability to defeat the enemy and find what no other man could find.

*It's your turn to follow me into hell, Johnis. Shut your flapper, Scrapper, and stay close behind. Not a peep, because I don't have time to babysit every time you cry out in fear. You too, Silvie.*

*Darsal, step up here by my side. It's our turn. It's our turn to trip, baby.*

A thought occurred to him: he wasn't dressed for the occasion. This brown tunic he'd worn from Middle Forest felt out of place. Ahead a man dressed in blue slacks and a brown hat swept dust from the sidewalk, paying him no mind. The establishment behind him had a large red sign that read SMITHER'S BARBEQUE.

On a whim, Billos snapped his fingers. The gun materialized in his hand. He shoved it into his pocket, thought of a hat, touched his head, and snapped again.

Shade covered his head. He pulled off a black, broad-rimmed hat that looked just like the one worn by Marsuvees Black. Replacing the hat, he snapped his fingers again and was immediately rewarded with black pants and a black trench coat. He was now suited for battle in the histories.

Two men sat on a bench next to the worker who swept the sidewalk. One of the buggies, a red one, rolled past him on four black wheels, purring as it swished by. It belched at him angrily, the sound of a goose honking. Billos stepped to one side and placed his hand on the gun, which was now tucked in his belt. But the machine didn't attack.

Crafty conspirators, every one of them. The Horde of the histories. He had to move among them without raising an alarm until he was ready. Practice, Black had said.

He couldn't very well just start slaying them with the gun, could he? They would likely pour out of the buildings armed with swords. Or, worse, armed with guns. Did they also have these magical weapons?

Billos had fought off the Horde in full combat, killing them with a skill he'd developed over many years, growing to be a man of seventeen. The enemies sitting on the bench and the one sweeping the porch didn't appear hostile, but Billos might prefer to face a dozen armed Scabs at the moment. At least the Horde didn't wield suhupow.

One of the men on the porch beneath the Smither's Barbeque sign faced him and tilted his hat back. Billos mistook the gesture as an aggressive move and very nearly pulled out his gun. But instead he shoved his anxiety down, lowered his head, and strode on as if at complete ease. He saw that he still wore his brown boots from the forest; they looked out of place under the black slacks. But he wasn't here to impress them with his sense of good fashion.

"Howdy, partner. Can I help you?"

Billos drilled him with a stare, walking on. "Can you? That depends."

The other man looked at him cautiously, as if measuring him for a casket, then relaxed. He considered something then dismissed it. Or was being sly.

"Well, if it's a drink you want, I'm just opening."

The two men rose, eyeing him curiously. No weapons that Billos could see. They followed the man who'd been sweeping inside, leaving Billos on the street.

He glanced around and saw that he was alone. But he wasn't so easily fooled. The enemy was undoubtedly peering at him by the dozens, lying in ambush.

Suddenly unnerved, Billos sprinted to the alley between Smither's Barbeque and the establishment next to it, All Right Convenience. Both were names that meant nothing to him.

He pulled up under the eaves, backed against the wall, and immediately chided himself for running. Such an obvious reaction was sure to put them on guard. He withdrew the gun and stared at it.

He sniffed the tube. Looked down the hole. It was a fantastic weapon that he would take with him back to the forest. They would immediately promote him to general with such a gun.

"Hello?"

Billos spun to his left, gun leveled. A young boy with blond hair stood behind the building, staring at him with round, green eyes.

"You don't need that," the boy said.

Billos lowered the barrel; no need to be too obvious. "You startled me."

"He's lying, you know."

"Who is?"

"The Dark One. Black."

So it was starting already—Billos had to tread very carefully. This boy not only knew of Marsuvees Black but was conspiring to undermine him.

"You think I don't know that?" Billos said.

"I think your mind is too full of yourself to know that," the boy said. "I think you would betray Elyon in favor of the Dark One. It wouldn't be the first time."

The boy seemed to know of his mission to retrieve the missing Books of History, which made him even more dangerous. A bead of sweat broke from Billos's brow and snaked down his temple.

"You're wrong. I would never betray Elyon. Do you know where the books are?"

The boy just stared at him, a clear sign that he knew more than he was saying.

"You're going to break his heart," he finally said. "All dressed up like the Dark One, swinging that gun around. Do you plan to kill us all?"

Billos didn't know how to respond to such direct threats, so he filled the empty space with small talk. "What's your name, boy?"

"My name?" See, even here the boy was being coy. "You can call me Samuel. You should give me the gun. The power you have didn't come from Elyon."

Billos turned away, gun cocked by his side. This small viper draped in bright colors was death. But the gun was too loud and would warn the others that the battle had started. He eased his hand closer to the knife strapped on his thigh.

"Well, Samuel, since you obviously know more than I do, you won't have trouble believing that I'm secretly working *against* the Dark One. And I would like you to help . . ."

He brought the knife around midsentence, putting his full weight into a throwing arc that would land the blade in the boy's throat and silence him before he could warn the others.

But the boy was gone.

Billos held the knife back and searched the alley. He was alone. The boy had snuck around the building while his attention was diverted. A slippery snake.

Which meant that Billos's hand was now forced. This Samuel would warn the others. Billos had to earn their trust and take the battle to them or risk an ambush. Thomas had taught them well—the best defense was often a forward attack, right down their throats.

He stowed the gun and the knife, hurried around the corner, and leapt up the steps that led into Smither's Barbeque. They might be crafty, as Black had warned, but he was craftier.

# FIFTEEN

Darsal broke from the Black Forest just behind Karas, who'd taken the lead this time despite Darsal's warning to get behind. The girl couldn't temper her desire to be out of this putrid black hole.

"There it is!" Karas cried, looking up at the cliff and beyond to the blue sky. She kicked her horse into a gallop, and Darsal followed.

The green book bound in red twine sat in her saddlebag, begging to be used, and use it she would. As soon as they cleared the danger presented by the Shataiki.

Black bats rimmed the cliff, peering down, squawking, but otherwise they presented no threat. Alucard had kept his word. The fact that he could only gain through this trade wasn't lost on

Darsal, but neither was the fact that she'd done what was necessary to follow Billos. They would work a way out of their troubles together.

Karas didn't need to urge her mount onto the switchbacks that led to the desert above them. The horse surged up the incline, leaning into each step.

Now that she had the book, Darsal had to consider what course to take with the girl. In hindsight, she might have asked the Roush to wait in the desert and escort the girl back to the forest. As it was now, she would have to send Karas back alone with all the water and clear directions.

The girl knew the desert, after all, and it had been her choice to follow.

Darsal galloped past the girl into the desert as soon as they spilled over the lip. "Go!" They rode hard for twenty minutes before she finally eased up to give the horses a rest.

"Not fun," Karas said. "This whole business is reckless."

"Welcome to life in the forests."

"Thank you for making my point. We're in the desert, not the forest."

Darsal grunted. "We'll stop in the outcropping for a proper rest," she said.

An hour later the large outcropping rose before them, and Darsal's palms began to sweat with the anticipation of cutting her finger and thrusting the blood against the book's cover.

"You're not afraid?" Karas asked, breaking a long spell of silence.

She'd already told Karas how Billos had vanished. "Like I said, life in the forests. We live with fear, little girl."

"Sounds like the Horde."

A dozen boulders towered four times the height of their horses ahead, surrounded by one or two score smaller rocks. It would make for an ideal camp; she would have to remember its location.

"I think I should come with you, Sister," Karas said.

"Don't be ridiculous."

"Why not?"

"For starters, I don't know where I'm going. For all I know, Billos vanished into oblivion. And regardless of where it is, getting back must not be easy or Billos would have done so already. We could get stuck."

"We?"

"Billos and I."

"And me?"

Darsal sighed. "It wasn't my idea for you to—"

"I don't care if it wasn't your idea!" Karas blurted. "I'm here, aren't I?"

Darsal glanced over, surprised by the emotion in Karas's voice. Tears misted the girl's eyes.

"I followed you because I saw my mother in you. And I miss my mother! Now you're just going to throw me away like a dirty rag?"

"That's not what I'm doing. If anything I'm trying to protect you!"

"Then protect my heart as well. You don't think I'm worthy to stay with you? Ask Johnis if I was helpful in saving him."

The words stung, and Darsal wasn't sure why. What was this one small girl in the grand scheme of things? It wasn't that Darsal had no heart, only that she'd learned to protect it or suffer with every blow. And in their battle with the Horde, the blows came nearly daily.

Still, she couldn't deny that there was something special about Karas.

"What good is your heart if you're dead?" she asked. "You have to get back to the forest, where Thomas can protect you."

"I'll get lost in the desert!"

"You know the desert well enough."

"I was just rescued from the desert. I hate the desert!"

"And you hate oblivion any less?" Darsal guided her horse through a wide gap between two of the largest boulders and pulled up in the shade beyond. "Look, maybe you are my niece. If so, I have an obligation to protect you. The Roush Hunter knows you're out here. Johnis is probably already on the way. They'll send out a hundred Roush to spot you from the air and take you home. Am I just stupid, or does that seem the safest for you?"

"I'm afraid to go alone. Please, Dar—"

The word caught in her throat, and Darsal looked back to see what had stopped her.

Three Scabs on horses filled the gap behind Karas. Another to her side with a long spear pressed against her neck. For a brief moment Darsal's mind went blank. Then the survival reasoning that Thomas had drilled into his Guard screamed through.

*How?* Knowing how your enemy gained the advantage they had might offer a clue as to how to undo that advantage.

*Why?* Knowing why you allowed your enemy to gain the advantage will aid you in not repeating the same mistake.

*What?* What then should you do in response to your disadvantage?

All of this, in a few scarce moments, of course, or disadvantage would become disembowelment.

The answers were painfully obvious. The wind was blowing east, which explained why the horses hadn't picked up on the Horde stench. These Scabs had probably followed their tracks and holed up here for an ambush.

As to why Darsal had been so careless: she'd been completely distracted by the book. And by Karas.

Darsal's heart thundered. What to do?

There were only four Scabs, but with Karas under the blade, the girl's chances for survival were slim. Darsal had two knives and a sword. She was already considering their use, but in the next moment the situation went from difficult to impossible.

Her horse shifted nervously under her as two more mounted Scabs stepped into the clearing from behind the boulders opposite her.

"Move and she dies," the Scab with the spear growled.

He was a massive man, with muscles that coiled around his

arms like ropes. A giant who looked like he might actually make a worthy adversary by himself.

The Scab grinned wide, exposing two shiny brass teeth.

"Come to Papa."

# SIXTEEN

Billos stepped into Smither's Barbeque, nerves strung to the snapping point, walking casually as if strolling into this establishment was something he'd done a thousand times before.

But his eyes scanned every detail, and his right hand hovered over the gun that formed a lump in his trench coat. Like the view of the village's exterior, the guts of this eatery were stunning. Glowing lamps hung from the walls, but as far as Billos could see, there were no flames. Glass. So much smooth, clear glass that Billos wondered if the histories were made from glass. Mugs, cups, lamps, windows . . . all glass.

And colors everywhere, red and blue and yellow, paintings and small statues, boxes and tables and lights; even the floor was red. All colored. The wood was carved in the most intricate and seamless fashions, curls and ovals and edges that looked sharp enough to cut meat. Almost as if they wanted him to think they were artisans rather than warriors. Crafty.

But he wouldn't be so easily fooled. Marsuvees Black was probably watching his every move at this very moment.

The man who'd invited him in for a drink stood behind a counter, drying glasses.

"What can I get you?"

Billos stared at him for a moment, checking for weapons. When he saw none that he recognized, he walked up to the counter and asked for the most common of drinks.

"Do you have blue plum wine?"

The man glanced at the other two, who were standing around a large, green table, pretending to be interested in colored balls that they struck with wood poles. It occurred to Billos that the sticks could be weapons. He would have to keep an eye on them.

"Blue plum wine, huh? No, no, I don't suppose I have any blue plum wine."

Hearing laughter in the man's tone, Billos decided that he should play the confident rabble-rouser to win their trust. Some men respected barbs more than sweet talking.

"Then what kind of grog do you have in this hole?" he demanded.

The man's eyebrow arched. "Grog? How about a light ale?"

"Ale, then!" Billos slapped his hand on the counter. He knew ale, of course, but he didn't know how putting a light inside of it might affect its taste. He'd tasted Horde ale once and had nearly thrown up. Hopefully this so-called "light ale" wasn't as bad.

"Ale," the man said, dipping his head once.

"You have no women in this village?" Billos asked, walking around the counter, looking for their hidden weapons.

"The village is full of women. All taken, I would say."

He walked up to a tall glass box, glowing red and blue with a picture of gold plates on the front. It read Jukebox and emanated the strangest music he'd ever heard. No sign of musicians.

A man began to sing from within the box, and Billos stopped. *A man is hiding in the box, singing. What kind of strategy is this?* Three men behind him now; one hidden in the box, singing to draw his attention.

Crafty, but he wouldn't let on that he was aware of their ploy.

"One ale," the server said.

Billos returned to the counter and lifted the mug of amber ale. "Thank you."

"Name's Steve," the man said, sticking out his hand.

Billos took it. "Billos," he said.

"Glad to meet you, Billy. This here's Chris and Fred."

"Bill*os*," Billos repeated, then remembered that Black had called him Billy as well. "Billy. Billy is fine." He nodded at the others, who watched him cautiously and dipped their heads.

"What brings you to Paradise?" the one called Steve asked.

Black, Billos wanted to say. "Johnis," he said instead, hoping to catch the man off guard.

"Johnny? Johnny Drake?"

"You've heard of him?" Billos asked.

"He was through here a few months ago and then disappeared. You friend or foe to Johnny?"

"Friend, of course."

"Then I suggest you find Samuel. But we don't want any trouble. We've had our share."

There was trickery afloat here. He'd already found Samuel, who was clearly the enemy. And that put Johnis and maybe the rest of them in the same camp. Like Black had said, conspirators who pretended to be your friends.

"Do you read books here?" he asked.

The man glanced at the others again, this time unsure.

"Books. Sure. Are you okay?"

"Why wouldn't I be? What kind of books, if you don't mind me asking?"

The man in the jukebox stopped singing.

"All kinds of books," Steve said. "You sure you're okay?"

Billos saw them then, all three Books of History sitting high on a bookshelf behind the counter next to some old bottles, as if they'd been there for some time.

He felt his muscles tense, then immediately removed his eyes from the shelf and forced himself to relax. This could only be the final confirmation that Black was right about Paradise. He might actually be in Teeleh's lair as it appeared in history.

Billos lifted his mug and drank deep, stilling his trembling hand. At any moment they would make their move, he was sure of it. But even as the cool nectar ran down his throat, he knew their every intention, their exact locations, and precisely how he would dispatch them.

"Think of Paradise as your test," Black had said.

In that moment a supreme confidence settled over Billos. For the average warrior, Paradise might be a test of champions, but he would show them all that for Billos of Southern, battle came as naturally as a stroll along the lake.

He loved Black, and he loved the power Black had given him, and he loved Paradise, the village in which he would prove once and for all that he was worthy of both Black and the power.

"Easy, man."

Billos drained the last of the drink and slammed the mug on the counter. He drilled Steve with a hard stare. "We can do this the easy way, or if you insist on playing coy, the hard way. But I must warn you, I'm better than all four of you put together."

The man blinked. "Four? What are you talking about?"

"The man in the jukebox. He'll be first. Give me the books, and I may let you live."

The man blinked. Crafty indeed, playing his deception to the bitter end.

"Hold on, son. You've got this all wrong. I don't know what you think you're doing here or who sent you, but it's wrong. We've had our share of trouble, but Johnny took care of that. Now . . ." Steve took a breath. "I suggest you take your black wannabe duds out of here and hit the road before someone gets hurt."

A new voice spoke behind Billos. "Everything okay, Steve?"

Billos froze. Steve glanced past him toward the door. "Morning, Jerry."

Billos slipped his hand under his trench coat, felt the cool steel at his fingertips, and spun around. A man dressed in blue stood in the open doorway. He wore a brass star on his chest and a gun on his hip. Jerry. A warrior.

Jerry's eyes shifted to Billos's hand under his trench coat. His hand reached for the gun that hung at his waist. Billos moved then, while he still had the upper hand. He jerked out the gun from which the suhupow came.

The man in blue grabbed for his own gun, and Billos threw himself to the right, pulling the lever as he moved.

*Boom!* The gun bucked in his grasp.

He saw the man spin around with the suhupow's impact; then Billos was on the ground, rolling to his right. He had to assume they would unload their own suhupow immediately, but moving would make him a hard target.

The man in the jukebox must be next. Surprisingly, he began to sing again, an odd, devious response to the obvious danger his partners were in. Surely he'd heard the loud discharge over his own crooning voice.

And this time, a woman joined in. There were *two* assassins in the box?

Billos came to one knee, pointed his gun at the jukebox, and pulled the lever four times. *Boom, boom, boom, boom!* The contraption exploded in a colorful shower of glass. Smoke coiled to the ceiling.

The man's and woman's voices caught in their throats. Both dead.

Now Billos was on his feet and running to his left. He leveled the suhupow at the two men bearing the stick-weapons and sent them both reeling back with two blasts. This left only the one behind the counter.

Steve.

Billos whirled and brought his gun to bear on the wide-eyed man, who was just now bringing a large metal weapon with twin tubes up from under the counter. A massive gun.

*Boom!* Billos sent him flying.

He held the gun steady and turned around, ready for anyone else who wanted a piece of Billos of Southern. But there was no one. His ears rang, his heart pounded, but otherwise he was surrounded by silence.

And six dead bodies, including the two in the jukebox. Dead by Billos.

"What do you make of that?" he muttered, then added, thinking of Marsuvees Black, "Baby."

A voice reached him from outside the establishment, words he couldn't make out. Other voices joined in, yelling now.

He'd awoken Paradise.

Let the fight begin.

# SEVENTEEN

COME TO PAPA."

Darsal had never encountered a Scab who seemed so cocky, but she could see why Papa was sure of himself. He was twice as big as she, had a blade against Karas's neck, and stood with five of his peers bearing down on one fighter and a child.

If Billos were here, they wouldn't have hesitated. But Billos had abandoned her, forcing her into this impossible situation.

Why hadn't Papa just killed Karas and taken up the fight with Darsal?

"Are you going to just stand there, flashing your big brass teeth, or are you going to be a man and kill us?" Darsal asked.

The Scab tilted his head, face bright and brash despite his gray eyes. "Witty are we? Good. This desert could use a lively hostage to ease the boredom."

"Just kill them as we agreed," one of the other Scabs said.

Papa shot him a stern glance. "*If* they resist, we said. This fighter hasn't touched her sword." To Darsal: "What brings you so deep into the desert with this child?"

A large Shataiki bat flapped and settled on the rock over his head.

"Him," Darsal said, looking up.

Papa followed her eyes. Faced her again. "A rock?"

"The Shataiki. You don't see it?"

"Kill them," another grunted. "No good ever came of playing with one of them. She's a viper."

"Perhaps, but even a viper can break the monotony of traveling with you, Bruntas. I would guess this one fighter could kill you with both hands tied behind her back. Care for a wager?"

"Kill the child, and you have your wager," Bruntas snapped.

Papa's grin vanished. He spit to one side. "I don't kill children."

"She's diseased!"

"She's a child!" Papa thundered.

"And you're a fool."

Papa swiveled his spear away from Karas's neck and whipped it next to his comrade's neck. "Better than a dead fool."

Darsal had never imagined, much less witnessed, a Scab defending a Forest Dweller. Either way, Papa had shown her his soft underbelly and removed his threat from Karas in one foolish move.

Darsal could attack now, but not without endangering Karas. So she kicked her horse in the flanks, driving it against Karas's mount. Before Papa could react, both horses bolted into the center of the sandy clearing.

A second Shataiki landed on the rocks above them, squawking. They were still surrounded and outnumbered, but Karas was out of reach. At least for the moment.

Papa grinned, attention back on them. "Smart," he said, fanning out with the others to form a circle of six around them. "A viper indeed."

Darsal raised both hands. "I don't want trouble."

"Then cut your own wrists, wench," the one called Bruntas growled.

There was no winning here, Darsal knew. Not without the book. The Scabs would eventually kill them both. Regardless of Papa's empathy for children, Horde law would end their lives.

"Bruntas, that is your name? I could kill you from here with a flip of my wrist. Papa knows that, but you're too stupid to realize it. Am I wrong?"

The Scab blinked. Darsal moved then, while their minds were on her words. Both hands flashing to her hip-sheaths, withdrawing a knife from each. She let them fly forward in the manner Silvie had taught her.

The blades took Bruntas and the Scab next to him in the necks. Darsal already had her sword out, spinning her horse to face the Scabs behind her. She slapped Karas's mount as she turned.

"Run for the gap!"

Karas drove her horse at the two flailing Scabs.

Darsal bolted at two others, screaming her guts out. Instead of going after both with her sword, she ducked under one of their blades and plowed her horse into theirs. Both backpedaled, snorting.

The second Scab had a spear, but the weapon was hardly more than a beating stick at this close range. Darsal struck the nearest warrior with her sword, spun it once, and drove it into the second.

"Darsal!" Karas's cry cut through the desert air.

The girl's warning told her two things: that the girl had not fled as she'd ordered, and that Papa was now bearing down on her.

She snatched the spear from the second Scab, who was now falling from his horse, twisted in her saddle, and hurled it with all her strength. She was halfway through the hurl before adjusting her sword to take out the Scab rushing her.

The blade struck him in his chest, but his momentum carried him crashing into her. They toppled to the ground as one.

She struggled to disengage the heavy, dead Scab who'd landed on top of her and finally succeeded, only to find Papa standing over her, sword extended.

"Good fight, Forest Dweller. But I'm afraid it's come to an end."

*And he is right,* Darsal thought. Her own sword lay on the sand, five paces away; her horse, which carried her other sword, had bolted across the clearing, taking the book with it.

This behemoth of a Scab had a blade inches from her throat.

"Do you know who the girl is?" Darsal asked.

"No. Should I?"

"Karas. Daughter of Witch."

Papa continued to grin, but his face suddenly appeared wooden. "Is that so? I had heard she was missing. Then I'll let Witch decide what to do with her."

"No," Karas said behind him. "You won't."

She had dismounted and was walking toward them carrying nothing but the book.

"And if you know what's good for you," she said to Papa, "you will bathe in some of the water we've brought and cleanse your mind of the disease."

"Stay back," he snapped.

Karas stopped and looked up at him. "Are you going to kill her?"

"I have to. If you really are the daughter of Witch, you know that." Then he added to make it clear, "Not that I don't *want* to kill her, mind you."

Karas tossed the Book of History toward Darsal. "Then at least let her die in peace." The book thudded to the sand, two feet away.

Darsal's mind spun through her alternatives and settled on the only course of action that made sense.

"Thank you." Slowly she reached her hand to Papa's sword. "Please, let me die with blood on the book. It's the only way I can find paradise."

"What kind of nonsense is that?" he said. But he held his blade steady.

She drew a single finger along the sword's edge, then pulled it away. "See? Blood."

Papa stared at this new ritual he'd never heard of—how could he when she'd fabricated it just now? Darsal felt her hand tremble as she reached for the book. It was going to work. *Please, Elyon, let this work . . .*

She lowered her bloody finger onto the leather cover. A hole large enough for any human to enter parted the air above her, buzzing with power. Darsal gasped. Her ears filled with the terrifying groan made by the dark, distorted figure beyond, who now beckoned her with his hand. She reached out. Touched the hole. Felt heat swim up her arm.

She was on her back, so she couldn't step in. But she didn't need to, because the gateway began to move toward her. Swallowing first her hand, then her arm. Darsal began to shake.

"Billos," she muttered.

The last thing she remembered was the sight of Karas diving through the air and grabbing her foot. Then her world went black.

# EIGHTEEN

Billos considered the two guiding objectives of this mission that Marsuvees Black had sent him on: to practice his already crafted power and to find the books.

He stood with legs spread, understanding his situation perfectly. He'd strolled into the village of Paradise with a tentative grasp of his own skill, engaged the enemy, and overcome six of them with ridiculous ease.

But then, nothing less was expected of him—he was Billos of Southern, traveler of the books, wielder of the gun, born and bred to be master of all he put his hand to. This first test had been child's play.

The voices yelled outside, nearer now. This second attack wouldn't be nearly as easy.

To get the books first or to kill them, that was the question that stalled Billos perhaps a moment too long.

Books, he decided. The books harness a way of escape. But boots were already pounding on the steps just outside.

He dove to the base of the counter and rolled behind it. Scrambling like a crab over Steve's prone body, he snatched up the long gun with twin tubes that lay beside his slain prey.

The door crashed open. "Steve!"

Billos breathed steadily, measuring his time. The books sat on the shelf above him. He would rise, unload some suhupow into the man at the door, snatch the books, and make for the back door he could see just beyond the counter. Once outside, he would regroup and plot his attack on the rest of the village.

"Get Claude!" the voice cried. "We have a shooting here! Jerry's been shot! Call the station in Delta. Get the cops up here, for goodness' sake, hurry!"

Cops. The man had named Billos's enemy. "Imposters," Black had said. But he had yet to meet someone pretending to be someone else. His mission was far from over.

The man spoke low, aiming his verbal taunting at Billos now. "Listen to me, you—"

Billos rose while the man was full of his threat. He whipped the twin-tubed firing stick at the door and jerked both levers back.

*Ba-boom!*

Twin thunder crushed his ears. The device bucked like a stallion, slamming him backward into the wall behind him. Glasses and bottles rained to the floor, crashing around him. He'd misjudged the power of this new weapon.

The assailant, however, had misjudged Billos and now lay in a heap beyond the doors as payment for his lack of respect. "Dead by Billos," he said, then spun and reached high for the books.

Rolling thunder filled the room; the wall splintered near him.

He dropped to his knees. Reinforcements had reached the door and leveled a round of suhupow at him. He was lucky to be alive!

Okay then. Bring it to Billos; Billos will bring it to you. The books would have to wait.

"Steve!" They kept calling for Steve, which probably meant that Billos had taken out an important fellow. Maybe their commander.

"Steve's dead!" he yelled, snatching a second handgun off the shelf in favor over the larger stick. "As you and all your friends will be if you don't surrender." He dropped the big gun.

Suhupow thudded against the counter in response. Their arrogance was unforgivable!

He scooped up a jar and hurled it across the room. It crashed against the far wall, and the assailant instinctively shifted his fire in the same direction.

Billos rolled into the open, firing from both guns, flinging deadly fire toward a man who stood in the door. Behind him crouched three others, but their way was blocked by the staggering body of their fallen comrade.

Dead by Billos. The enemy had now seen him and knew what they were up against.

Billos launched himself at the rear door, flung it open, and ran into an alleyway behind the establishment. He flattened his back against the wall, guns cocked by his ears, panting. Unable to hold back a smirk of intense satisfaction.

*Round one to Billos of Southern, baby.* The sense of pride and power that swelled through him was unlike any he'd ever felt. It was almost as if he'd found his purpose, here in the histories. He'd been born for this.

But the sentiment was cut short the next moment, severed by the sight of four warriors who tore around the corner of the next building, scowling, armed with suhupow guns. The wood wall behind Billos splintered when the largest of the four whipped his gun up and leveled belching fire at him. This time Billos had no surprise in his favor, and the warriors had dispensed with the trickery that had made those inside seem so unthreatening.

What did it feel like to be struck with a gun's power? The question kept Billos momentarily fixed to the ground. His vision clouded, and he blinked. The forest behind the village distorted. A new kind of suhupow?

Billos's throat suddenly felt dry. His head spun. He pressed both hands on the wall behind him for balance, dropping the guns in the process.

Had he been killed? Was this what the gun's power felt like?

A voice whispered in his ears, low and mocking. "Is that all you have, Billos? Maybe you're not as smart as you think. You puke."

Then Billos's world turned white.

# NINETEEN

I'm not saying that we aren't responsible, sir, only that I truly believe that we may be the only ones who can fix the situation."

Johnis stood next to Silvie, facing a furious commander who paced next to his wife, Rachelle, seated to his right. A single fluffy white Roush hopped along one of the rafter beams over Rachelle's head.

They were three personalities, each as distinct as the colors of Pampie fruit: Thomas the warrior, furious at those in his charge. Rachelle the lover, always ready to extend grace, though not at the expense of her wisdom. Hunter the Roush, who was desperate to make up for the embarrassment of allowing himself to be taken captive.

Thomas threw wide a dismissive hand. "Fix it? You caused it!

Every time I turn around, I find you four necks-deep in some quagmire of your own making! I simply can't believe you've lost not only Billos and Darsal but Karas of all people. What's her part in this? The next thing I know you'll have lost yourself."

"Well, sir, we think Karas might have been under the delusion that Darsal is her aunt," Johnis explained.

"Time's wasting!" the Roush cried, hopping along the rafter.

"Quiet!" Johnis snapped his frustration without thought, glancing up at the white bat.

"Pardon?" Thomas demanded.

Johnis realized his mistake immediately. Neither Thomas nor Rachelle could see the Roush, of course, and for the most part it was easy to hide the fact that he and Silvie could. However, it's not as easy when you're fighting and facing a hyperactive Roush who keeps insisting you have to leave. Even his superior, Michal, had agreed, he'd said.

Johnis closed his eyes and ground his molars. "Sorry, sir, I was only scolding myself." He walked to his right, scrambling for the right words. "You're right, we should be quiet. None of this makes sense to you, but it does to us. If you want us to become the kind of leaders who will lead our people in victory one day, you have to allow us to make our mistakes. Don't you think we're learning?"

"He's right, Thomas," Rachelle said quietly.

But Thomas was having none of it. "Mistakes, you say? And how many lives do you suggest I put in the way of your *mistakes*?"

"Point made," Silvie said. They would never forgive Johnis's indiscretion with the Third Fighting Group. As well they shouldn't.

Silvie faced Thomas. "Then let us leave alone, just the two of us. We'll take no army."

"To where?" he shouted. "Do you have some intelligence that I'm not aware of, because as I understand the situation, you don't know where they are."

"*I* know," the Roush said. "Just keep that in mind. I know exactly—"

"That's our problem," Johnis said to Thomas, this time keeping his eyes off the Roush.

"And you're my problem," Thomas said. "You're making me look like a fool. Don't forget that it was me who chose you."

"No, Thomas." Rachelle turned her head to her husband. "It wasn't you who chose him."

She was speaking of the circular birthmark on the side of his neck that marked him as Elyon's chosen one.

Thomas grunted. "Well, I'm beginning to wonder if Elyon's purpose in choosing this runt is to mortify me."

"He was a hero not two weeks ago," Rachelle said. "You don't remember the cheering?"

"And the next week he plotted to take my life! Yet here I am, giving him a secret audience in our chambers so that no one will hear that we're as foolish as he!"

"You do so because you know it's the right thing to do."

Thomas frowned, but he couldn't deny his wife's wisdom.

"Then you agree?" the Roush who'd called himself Hunter asked Thomas, knowing the man couldn't possibly hear him. "So be a leader and let them go before going makes no sense!"

"Karas could be invaluable to us," Thomas said, refusing to let the matter resolve easily.

"We were the ones who lost her," Johnis said. "You have to give us the opportunity to find her. I was the one who rescued her in the first place, for the love of Elyon! How can you deny me my right to go after her?"

"But you *are* holding something back," Rachelle said. "Aren't you, chosen one?"

How could he lie so directly to a woman who was his advocate? He couldn't. "I'm within my rights to hold back everything Elyon has told me," Johnis said, then added so as to sound more like a chosen one, "All in good time."

Thomas lowered himself into a chair next to Rachelle, crossed his legs, folded his hands over one knee, and looked at Johnis. For a few long moments he just stared at him.

"Fine," he finally said. "I'll give you my permission—for my wife's sake—to go after them, but on the condition that you tell me everything when this is over."

"Everything?"

"You can't do it," the Roush said.

Johnis glanced up at him, and this time Rachelle followed his eyes and saw nothing but an empty rafter.

Her eyes lowered and met his. *What do you see, chosen one?* But he couldn't know what she was thinking.

"What if Elyon forbids my telling you everything?"

"Elyon has put you under my authority, and I say tell me. So then Elyon has spoken, through me. Do you think I'm not his servant as well?"

The commander had a point. He'd have to sort it all out later.

"Okay, I'll tell you everything," Johnis said.

Then he swept his hand toward the door. "Don't let me hold you back. Find them. Bring them back. Alive. And don't forget your vow."

"What vow?"

"You already forget?"

"To tell you everything. It's a vow?"

"Your word to your commander is, by extension of your commission, all vow. Are you having second thoughts?"

"No. No, just looking for clarity."

"Not good," the Roush said.

Thomas lowered his arm. "Elyon knows that you could use some clarity. Now move. The sun doesn't stop, even for the chosen one."

Rachelle reached out and touched her husband's knee, smiling. She winked. "Have I told you that my blood boils when I look at you?"

"I make you angry?" he asked with a glint in his eyes.

She just winked.

TED DEKkER

"Go, go!" the Roush quipped, fluttering his wings. "Water and swords. Lots of water!"

"I hope you're right about this," Thomas said to Rachelle as Johnis and Silvie slid from the room.

"Have I ever been wrong?"

But Johnis knew that there was always a first time for everything.

# TWENTY

The blackness that swallowed Darsal when she entered the book felt like her imaginations of death, swirling and turning toward a bottomless chasm lined with charred trees and black Shataiki.

But then white light flooded her eyes, and she saw a bottom, rushing up. She crashed onto a hard surface with a loud grunt that echoed in her ears.

It took a moment for her head to clear. She pushed herself to one knee, scanned the square room, and froze solid. She was in what appeared to be a white room, at the center of which sat a lone monster, the likes of which had never crossed her imagination, much less her sight.

"What is it?"

Darsal jerked her eyes from the beast and twisted to see Karas up on one arm, staring past her.

And behind Karas . . . behind Karas the Scab, Papa, crouched, hand on his sword, staring at the beast. Two thoughts rushed through Darsal's mind: The first was that both Karas and Papa had followed her to hell or wherever this was, perhaps because they had been in contact with her when she'd touched the book with her blood. The second was that she never could have imagined feeling so relieved to have an armed Scab by her side.

She jumped to her feet and spun her eyes back over the beast. It was then that she saw Billos. Strapped onto one of the six legs, like a fly caught in a spider's web. His head was enshrouded in a black cocoon. Hands inserted in gloves.

Karas's thin voice came again. "Is he dead?"

Darsal stepped warily to her right, ready to jump back if the thing moved. Billos's chest rose and fell rapidly, she now saw. But she had no doubt that the black cocoon around his head would suffocate him if she didn't free him immediately.

She pushed aside caution for her own safety and moved closer.

"Stay back!" Papa rasped. "What foul beast is this?"

Darsal reached her hand back. "Give me your knife!"

His grasp on his sword didn't budge. He would be ready to swing at any appendage that might swipe his way.

"I'm not going to come after you, you oaf," Darsal snapped. "We have bigger problems now. Give me a blade!"

Papa slipped a long curved knife from his waist and tossed it toward her. She snatched it out of the air.

"Be careful," Karas said. "Please, Darsal, you're going to get us killed."

"You're assuming we aren't already dead."

The thing hadn't moved its legs. A flat, glassy panel against the wall showed several green and yellow lines moving across from left to right. Red eyes glared around a softly humming head with the word DELL written in block letters on one side. It was clearly alive, but nothing on its body had actually moved.

Then again, spiders sat in perfect stillness, waiting for their prey to come in close before leaping forward to sting them with poison. She would have to be careful.

"Can I have your sword?" she asked Papa without turning.

"Don't push it."

"I'm better with it than you are. Faster at least."

"As I recall, my blade was at your throat when you touched the book."

"There were four of you!" she said.

"There was only one of me."

It was hopeless. "Then get up here beside me and cover my flank."

Papa wasn't the type to show his fear. He stepped up, sword ready.

"Darsal . . ." Karas hung back. "Please, Darsal . . ."

"If it moves," Darsal whispered, "hack at the leg holding

Billos. Cut the veins." She nodded at the black ropes that ran along the hardened structure.

"Ready?"

The Scab shifted. "Ready."

Darsal held the Horde knife in her right hand and inched forward. She dove at Billos when she was within three feet, taking full advantage of the same kind of speed that the Forest Guard relied on to defeat the Horde.

With a flip of her wrist she sliced the gloves that gripped her man's hands. Still no movement. She grabbed the cocoon over his head with both hands and pulled hard, thinking at the last moment that it looked more like a strange helmet than a cocoon. It came off with surprising ease.

Billos lay still, his white face beaded with sweat, breathing hard. His eyes were wide and staring into the middle distance.

Darsal's first thought was that he had been paralyzed by this beast. But then he blinked and sat up, and she knew she'd freed him. Still concerned about a counterattack, she grabbed his arm and tugged hard, hauling him off the seatlike leg. Still dazed, Billos slid off and fell to the ground like a log. He grunted.

"What? What?"

"Hurry, Billos! Help me, Papa." With the Scab's help she dragged him away across the floor to where Karas stood watching.

"Stop it!" Billos's arms flailed, and he rolled to his feet. He stood and stared at them, clearly disoriented.

"I'm not sure he liked that," Karas said.

"Darsal? What's going on?"

She glanced at the spider thing and saw that its eyes had darkened. Still no movement.

"I don't know, Billos. You tell me."

"You . . . Where's the village?" He patted his chest and felt his head. "I'm okay?"

"No blood, if that's what you mean." But she couldn't say that he was okay, because his mind may have been compromised. He certainly didn't seem too eager to see her.

"How did I get back in here?" he demanded angrily.

"Settle down. It was you who caused this. I just followed with another book."

"I was here when you found me?"

"Are you daft, boy?" Papa said. "She said you were."

Billos was too preoccupied to give the Scab a second look. He crossed to the leg she'd freed him from and lifted the helmet.

"How did you find me?"

"I told you, the spider—"

"It's a contraption, not an animal," he snapped. "I couldn't figure out how it worked so I . . ."

He ran to the only door leading from the room and tugged on the handle. But it would not so much as budge.

"I got out," Billos said.

"Well, you weren't out just now," Papa said. "Don't tell me you don't know where we are or how we escape."

Billos faced the Desert Dweller. "Who let this thug in?"

667

"Your cursed book," Papa said. "Where are we?"

"Still in the white room, clearly." He glanced around. "I left this place; walked out that door; met a 'Marsuvees Black,' who gave me a gun; went to battle in the village of Paradise, where I clearly had the upper hand when . . ." Billos looked at Darsal. "Are we dead?"

It was a good question, but she was amazed that Billos didn't seem to be giving her a second thought.

"I risked my life to follow you," she said. "Please don't tell me all I've managed to do is follow you into death."

He looked at the spider contraption. "You're suggesting that I never left this room. Or that I left it and was returned with the magical power. Like the gun."

"What's this 'gun' business?" Papa demanded.

"A magical weapon that destroys objects from afar. You said you came with a book?"

"Yes," Darsal said.

"Then I know where it is. It's in Paradise, the village Marsuvees Black sent me to."

Darsal's mind was having difficulty keeping up with all of his disjointed comments. They seemed to be alive, which was a good thing. But they also seemed to be trapped in some kind of white prison.

"How do we get back?"

"To Paradise?" Billos asked.

"To Middle. To Thomas and Silvie and Johnis!"

He blinked. "With the books, I suppose. Not that we should go back, mind you. This is bigger than Johnis."

"We're trapped in this box with a contraption that you don't know how to work. Doesn't look so big to me."

He stared at her. "You're going to have to learn to trust me now. Once and for all."

"Is that so? The one who broke all the rules and ran off with the books? Which, I might add, are now lost. Why should I trust you?"

"Because I have the suhupow. I'm the chosen one."

She frowned, upset at finding him with this attitude after he'd put her through so much.

"You abandoned her," Karas said. "A little sensitivity would be helpful about now."

Billos could have refuted the girl. Instead he glanced at her, softened, and approached Darsal. "I'm sorry. I had to know. But it's worked out. I would have come back for you."

His words, however sketchy, filled her with warmth. She knew his heart.

"Would you? You don't have the books. We're trapped. You don't even know how to make this contraption work."

Billos smiled and touched her cheek tenderly. "Oh? Maybe that's where you're wrong."

She couldn't help but lean into him. Billos wrapped his arms around her. It was all she could do to keep her tears back. "I was so afraid," she whispered into his musky neck.

"I'm sorry; I didn't mean to leave you."

"Never again, Billos."

"I swear. Never again."

They stood in the embrace for a few seconds while she regained her composure.

"Nice, but I'm feeling no less trapped," Papa said.

Darsal pulled back. "Okay, tell me everything."

# TWENTY-ONE

Billos finished his tale and left them all staring at him incredulously. Papa was the first to speak.

"This is the most preposterous thing a man can stand to hear," he mumbled. Then louder, glaring at Billos, "You're saying that you found these books in the Black Forest under our noses? That we are blind to both the Black Forest and the books, not to mention Shataiki and Roush?"

"It's true," Karas said. "My eyes were opened as well. I saw Shataiki, I saw the Roush, and I saw the Black Forest."

"Even so, how do you know this isn't all just trickery in the mind? You say you went into the blasted village named Paradise without ever leaving this place. How do you know you ever left Middle Forest to begin with? For all we know we're still in the desert at this moment. The books are probably only making us believe we're in this white room!"

"Impossible," Darsal corrected him. "I saw Billos vanish into the books."

"Well, forgive my smallest doubt." Papa made a tiny sign between his thumb and forefinger. "Billos also believed he was in the so-called 'village of Paradise' when we saw him lying right here."

"Your mind's clogged," Karas said. "Your judgment is the least trustworthy here. I should know; I was Scab only a few days ago."

"Is that so, supposed daughter of Witch? And I should listen to a child?"

"I had the good sense to bathe in their water. Do you?"

"And now you smell like they do."

"Stop this!" Darsal snapped. To Billos: "What now?"

He tapped his fingers together and walked around the contraption. "The best I can figure, I escaped this place by donning the helmet and the gloves and speaking the right commands, not unlike a horse."

"But you didn't leave this place," Papa said. "If I'm the diseased one, why is this fact only obvious to me?"

"Because it's not that simple, Papa," Karas said. "Even if he did leave it only in his mind, he found three books there. The one we brought is probably there as well now. They're the key to our escape."

Papa waved his hand at Billos. "This fool talks as if he doesn't even want to escape! All this talk of guns and Marcudeves—"

"Marsuvees," Billos corrected.

"Whatever. Some demon who ordered you to slay common village folk."

"The enemy, armed with guns."

"Which you say they only used in defense," Papa pointed out.

"They had the books!" He gripped his head. "Why are we listening to this slug of diseased flesh? You should have killed him in the desert."

"Fine, kill me when you get your hands on one of these magical guns of yours. Until then, don't think this sword won't put you on your backside."

Billos humphed.

"Will you all stop arguing like spoiled children?" Darsal demanded.

"Yeah," Karas chimed in. "Grow up, both of you."

They all glanced at her.

Darsal walked up to the contraption and ran her hand over one of the helmets she'd mistaken for a cocoon spun from black thread. "Billos is right about the books. We need them to return. Even if there was a way to return without them, we wouldn't dare. If we return with all four books, on the other hand, all might be forgiven."

She faced Billos. "So we follow the books. As long as we agree to return the moment we find them. We're not staying in this lost Paradise of yours, no matter where it is. We have an obligation to Johnis."

Billos nodded slowly, but he didn't look convinced. "Fine."

"He doesn't mean it," Karas said.

"Shut your hole!" Billos snapped. "We should leave you as well."

Darsal felt defensive of the girl, a sentiment that surprised her some. "Easy, Billos. She's my sister. Niece, to be more precise, but she likes to call me her sister."

"Your niece? She's a Scab."

"And not long ago the Scabs and we were one," Karas said. "Or did you forget your history lessons?"

He looked from one to the other, then turned away. "Bring your niece, if that's who she really is, and bring your Scab dog; what do I care? Just keep them out of my way."

He slid up onto the same chair Darsal had rescued him from.

"So we put on the helmets and the gloves?" Darsal asked, touching another chair. "Then what?"

"Then you speak a command. 'Let's go, you haggard beast.'"

"This contraption responds to being called a haggard beast?" Papa asked, warily approaching another seat.

"Shut up and lie down." Billos grinned, then added, "Baby."

"Baby?" Papa glared. "You think I respond to insults?"

"You're acting crazy, Billos," Darsal said. "We're all under considerable stress; go easy!"

"Yes, sir. Baby."

"Why do you call us that?"

He shrugged, then pulled on his helmet. Slipped on his gloves. Spoke into the cocoon over his head. "Let's go, you haggard beast."

The contraption named DELL began to hum, and the red lights

around its crown brightened. The flat glass panel on the wall flickered and showed several lines.

Billos's body immediately arched, then slowly relaxed.

Darsal glanced at Karas, who'd climbed into a seat, then at Papa. "Seems to have worked."

"He's still here," Papa said.

"Do you have a better idea?"

The Scab grunted and pulled on his helmet.

Darsal's world went dark inside the musty-smelling headpiece. She slipped her hands into the gloves on either side, pried her eyes for a view of something besides darkness, and, seeing nothing, spoke aloud.

"Let's go, you haggard beast."

Nothing happened that she could tell. Maybe her helmet was ruined. She tried again. "Let's go, you haggard beast!"

Still nothing.

Darsal finally sat up, pulled her helmet off, and turned to the others. "What's supposed . . ."

The others were gone. Darsal faced five empty seats. Alarmed, she scanned the room, but there was no sign of them. They'd made it out and left her?

The door . . .

She flew off the seat and had crossed halfway to the door before realizing that it was ajar. She reached for the knob, threw it wide, and stared out to a dusty alley bordered by a green forest.

"Billos?"

Wind kicked up a dust devil and sent it scurrying down the alley. Darsal stepped out and looked one way, then the other.

"Billos!"

The wind slammed the door shut behind her, and she jumped.

Muffled voices reached her from down the alleyway. It took her only a moment to realize that an angry mob was prowling the streets out of her direct line of sight.

"You see them, you kill them on sight!" a voice shouted. "Spread out!"

*The villagers are responding to Billos's assault,* she thought. And if she was right, she was one of *them* the villagers were after. She had to get out of sight.

"In here!"

Darsal spun to the sound of Karas's voice. The young girl stood in the same doorway through which Darsal had exited the white room. But the space behind Karas wasn't white.

She leapt past the girl into a room with numerous shelves, each filled with supplies. Small containers made of metal and colored bags unlike any she'd ever seen. To her left stood a large cabinet made of silver with glass doors, behind which sat white containers that read MILK. The sign over the counter on her right indicated that this was a store named ALL RIGHT CONVENIENCE.

Behind the counter stood Billos, dressed in a full-length black coat and broad-rimmed black hat. He was looking down the tube of a strange contraption, something like the gun he'd described. Several similar guns rested on the counter in front of him.

Billos looked up as Karas shut the door. "Nice of you to join us." He tossed the weapon at Darsal, who caught it out of the air. "Same gun I used to teach them a lesson the first time," he said with a smirk.

"What are we doing, Billos? There's a mob headed this way!"

"Battle, baby. Point and shoot." He snatched another gun from the mantel behind him. "We're going to kill them."

"Kill who?" Karas asked.

Billos lobbed a gun at her, and she caught it clumsily.

"Kill them all," he said.

# TWENTY-TWO

This isn't good," Johnis said, staring at the dead Scabs among the boulders. "They've been tagged."

"And it's clear that they were killed by Guard."

Rather than taking the time to bury their dead, the Horde sometimes—only when it was convenient—tagged the corpses with black feathers taken from the Dambu crow to speed their delivery into the afterlife. The fact that they were tagged meant they'd been found by the Horde.

The fact that Darsal's knife was still buried in one of their necks meant that whoever had found them knew they'd been killed by members of the Forest Guard.

"This is way out of our territory," Silvie said. "They won't let it go."

Johnis scanned the horizon. "Hopefully they'll just send a scouting party. How far did you say?"

The Roush flapped to steady himself on one of the boulders. "Just past the rise. But they made it out. This killing was done after I left them."

"Do you see any tracks heading south from here?" Johnis asked.

"None. They head only in the direction of this Black Forest no one has seen. They don't see me either," Hunter said. "Does that mean I'm not real?"

Johnis wheeled his horse around and headed into the desert, north. Hunter landed between the animal's ears and repeated the same lecture he'd offered a dozen times in the last day.

"Remember—water, you have to use the water. The Shataiki are terrified of the water. And I can't go. Not alone. They'll rip my wings off and feed them to their young. We can't have any young Shataiki growing up with Roush in their bellies."

"So we've heard," Johnis said. "Isn't that them?" He nodded at the horizon.

"Where?" Hunter whirled around, saw the same black bat sitting as a mere dot on the rise ahead, and began to bounce on the horse's head. "Okay, okay. That's them, that's them."

Silvie rode stoically by Johnis's side, eyes fixed forward. Her wind-tossed tangles hung in messy but perfect symmetry. Fine features darkened by the sun betrayed her femininity, but a single glance at her ripped shoulders and you would know that this one had been born with a sword in her hands. She could easily put most men on the ground in a number of ways.

She felt Johnis's stare and looked into his eyes. He reached out his hand and took hers. Any ordinary sixteen-year-old girl facing the prospect of Teeleh's lair, as she had only a couple weeks ago, might have reacted with the same reluctance that she had then.

But Silvie was no ordinary girl. The last few weeks had re-shaped her.

She winked at him, then faced forward again.

"Okay, okay, I'll wait by the rocks. Maybe this isn't such a good idea. Maybe Thomas is right."

"Maybe," Johnis said. "We have water. We'll be okay."

"Don't think they don't learn. You lose the water and you're dead meat, as Thomas likes to say." Hunter hopped once, twice. "Okay . . ." He flapped into the air. "Remember the plan. Every detail. You have to get them back. Okay . . ."

Hunter soared low to pick up speed, then flapped south, toward the boulders where he would keep watch as long as he could, as planned.

"What details?" Silvie asked.

"Exactly." They had no details. This was entirely "ride where the horse takes you." But Hunter seemed to find comfort in having contributed to a plan, which was really no more than *Find them; get them out; water, water, water.*

Lines of black bats seemed to rise from the hazy desert as they crested the rise. Johnis pulled up. Ahead lay the hidden Black

Forest, gouged from the ground by some unseen claw. It went underground, Hunter said. Abruptly, by the looks of it, not two hundred meters ahead.

Johnis felt a shiver run down his spine despite the afternoon heat. This was the second Black Forest they'd encountered. Hunter didn't know how many there were, probably hundreds if you went far enough. All hidden from ordinary eyes.

Yet it had been here all along. Johnis wondered what would happen if a horse happened upon it. Would it fall in or walk over it as if it didn't exist? He'd have to ask the Roush.

"You ready for this?" Silvie asked.

"No. You?"

"Not really. But that's never stopped us before."

He nodded. "Douse yourself in water."

They both withdrew leather bags filled with lake water and splashed it on their faces and chests. They would keep the bags as their only weapon from here in.

"We go for the lair under the lake," Johnis said. "Let the horse have its head once we're in. Besides the water, we have only speed."

"This lair that not even Hunter can confirm," Silvie said.

"I was in Teeleh's lair and felt his presence. I assure you, each forest has a lair."

She knew that he could not be so sure, but that, too, had never stopped them.

"Then let's go," Silvie said, and kicked her horse.

# TWENTY-THREE

Billos wanted one thing and one thing only. To kill as many of these crafty, double-crossing villagers as he could turn his suhupow gun on.

It had occurred to him back in the white room that he was just a bit put out with Darsal for dragging the Scab she called Papa and the little piece of trash, Karas, into his world. In fact, he was bothered that she herself had managed to find him. He found it all oddly threatening.

And he found the way she was looking at him now even more threatening.

"Kill them all? We can't just start killing these people," Darsal said.

"Oh yes, we can. And if we don't, they'll kill us. Think of them as the Horde. Kill them all: those are our orders."

"The orders of a man we've never met," Papa said. "Who may be Teeleh for all we know."

"No one asked for your opinion, Scab. Doesn't the Horde worship Teeleh?"

Billos hurried to the front window and peeked past a drawn drape. Two uniformed warriors with silver badges on their chests were climbing out of a black-and-white buggy topped with flashing lights.

The establishment in which Billos had dispatched Steve and his jukebox warriors was only a stone's toss from here.

"Billos?"

He spun to Darsal, who was watching him with wide eyes. "What?" he snapped.

"What's happening?"

"Are you deaf? I told you what's happening! I suggest you snap out of it and make yourself useful."

"Is that what I mean to you? Just a tool to dispatch for your own purposes?"

"What are you talking about? We're in a battle. Are you blind as well?"

Her eyes glared. He'd seen this look of defiance a thousand times, and he knew that his words would do nothing to win her over.

"I'm talking about the way you look at me, as if my coming to save you means nothing. All you want to do is kill villagers. From the moment you climbed out of that chair in the white room, you've had nothing on your mind but flexing this new power of yours."

She was being about as logical as a stick of firewood. "I'm trying to save *you!*" retorted Billos.

"Is now really the time for this?" Papa asked, parting the shade next to the rear exit. Several warriors ran past the window in the direction of the establishment where Billos had slain Steve.

"Save me?" Darsal whispered harshly. "It's always me, the poor little girl who's being beaten by her uncle, that needs saving, is that it?"

"Are you saying I shouldn't have saved you back then? You'd be dead now."

"Maybe you shouldn't have. Not if you intended to make me your slave instead!"

After Darsal's parents had been killed when she was only eight, her uncle, Blaken the Blacksmith, who was too much of a coward to fight with the Guard but had proven his value by crafting metal swords, had taken her in. He used to beat her in drunken fits, but Darsal was too shy to confess her plight to anyone. Billos had witnessed such a beating late one night when he was out sneaking through the streets of Southern, looking for trouble. He had taken it upon himself to break into her room and introduce himself.

When the beatings had become unbearable six months later, Billos had arranged an accident that had put Blaken on crutches. Permanently.

"How did you suddenly become my slave?" he demanded,

flummoxed by her strained connections. "I'm trying to save us here, for the sake of Elyon!"

"No, I don't think so. I think you're trying to save your own neck for the sake of *Billos*. That's the way you've always been. It's always about Billos, isn't it?"

"I think my sister is right," Karas said.

Billos looked at the young converted Horde and suppressed the flashing impulse to level his gun at her. Why was he so bothered by these three intruders?

"And I think you're both going to get us all killed," he snapped. "This is complete nonsense! If you can't do what needs to be done, then leave."

Darsal stared at him for a moment longer, then set her jaw and averted her eyes. "Where are the books?"

Something clicked deep inside of Billos's mind with those words. Something that sounded as much like Marsuvees Black as him. *The books, Billos, she's here for the books.*

At first he didn't fully understand the significance of this suggestion, because it seemed a bit obvious. Then another thought whispered through his head. *She'll take the books and leave you powerless.* And he knew she would, to protect him, she would say.

*You know what that makes her, don't you Billy-babe?* His mind remained blank. *A traitor who will end up cutting you off at the knees and shoving her heel in your face.*

Darsal shoved her gun under her tunic and strode for the door. She grabbed the handle and pulled it open.

"What are you doing?" Billos demanded. "You'll give us away!"

She stood in the open doorway and drilled him with a glare. "Will I? They don't know me as a threat. Unlike you, I haven't killed here."

"You're dressed like a complete stranger."

"Then they'll find me a curiosity, not a threat. Now, tell me where you saw the books."

"Get back inside!" he snapped, waving his gun in her direction.

Instead she took a step outside. "An eating establishment, you said?" She looked up and down the street, then settled on a building to her right. "On the shelf above the counter. Shouldn't be hard." Back to him: "I suggest you toss the black Shataiki getup and follow me."

"She makes sense," Papa said, crossing to the front door.

"Are you mad? If Darsal looks like a complete stranger to them, you look like a monster with your diseased skin!"

"Don't be a fool," Papa shot back gruffly. "You're assuming this place has no Horde. The Horde probably rule here!"

"I didn't see any."

"Because this is a diseased village that—"

"Shut up!" Karas was following as well.

Billos waved his gun again. "Get inside, all of you."

"Or?" Darsal challenged.

"Or you'll shoot my sister, whom you supposedly love?" Karas demanded.

"I might choose you instead. Or the monster."

"No, you won't," Papa said, spitting to one side.

"Don't presume to know the way things work in this new place. All bets are off. I'd pray for the chance to kill you in the desert. Maybe Elyon would answer that prayer here, in Paradise."

"Then Paradise would be your fall," Darsal said. "You said that the suhupow makes a loud boom when it kills. This enemy of yours would come running like rats to the hole. Has this DELL-god robbed your mind as well as your heart?"

Then she walked into the street, followed promptly by Papa and Karas.

Billos stood in the All Right Convenience store dressed in black, holding his gun and at a complete loss as to what he should do.

So he began to swear bitterly under his breath.

# TWENTY-FOUR

Darsal may have never walked out into the village had she not been so perturbed with Billos. But these past few days, spent slogging through the desert on a desperate mission to save his skinny neck after he'd abandoned her, had robbed her of the grace she'd offered him for years. His dismissal of her raked on her nerves like a saw.

She marched along the sidewalk toward the building called Smither's Barbeque. Two men in strange blue costumes were entering, holding their guns up near their heads. She briefly wondered if the weapons also doubled as listening devices.

"You're just going to walk in?" Papa asked.

"Now you're afraid of being Horde?" She glanced back at the large man with flaking white skin. His leather armor, which wasn't so different from her own, might prevent their blending as much as his skin.

"I told you, you should have bathed," Karas said.

Papa grunted.

Ahead of them, the outer screened door to the eatery banged shut on its own. Two coils of wire seemed to be responsible for the closing. Darsal scanned the rest of the village. The buildings themselves were square and not so unusual looking, but the buggies were made of many colors of metal. No horses that she could see.

Tall metal poles with glass hoods perched atop; smooth black rock laid down as the main road; glass windows everywhere; strange costumes such as those worn by the two warriors who'd entered the eatery—these were the stuff of suhupow that had swept Billos off his feet and made him so power hungry.

"Keep your weapons covered," Darsal said, mounting the steps.

"How do I hide the sword?"

"Toss it. Karas, give your gun to Papa. But hide it. We want no fight."

She pushed the door open and stepped in, intending to show no concern. But the scene inside stopped her cold. One of the blue costumed warriors lay unmoving on her left, and three other bodies had been arranged side by side just beyond. Billos's little war in the eatery had left its mark.

"Hold up!"

She looked up at a warrior who was pointing a gun at her. One of the two who'd just entered. He spoke quickly into a small black box in his left hand.

"Come back, Pete; how'd you say the perp was dressed?"

The box spoke back. "Black trench coat," it said.

Karas spoke the wonder on all their minds. "Is that suhupow?"

Darsal knew it had to be. Surely no man was small enough, no matter what world, to fit into such a small box. The two warriors seemed as stunned by them as they were by the talking box. They fixed their eyes on Papa.

"No quick moves," the one said.

Darsal lifted her hands to set him at ease. "We mean no harm."

"What's with him?" the warrior asked, nodding at Papa. "Are you contagious, buddy?"

"Papa," the Scab said. "My name is Papa, not Buddy."

"Yes," Karas said. "Papa is contagious."

The man immediately lifted a hand to shield his mouth and nose. "I'm going to have to ask you to leave."

"Nonsense!" Papa boomed. "She's only making trouble. Depending on how you look at it, one of us has a skin condition, and for the sake of argument I'll accept the role. But it can't spread!"

"Then how did you get it?" Karas pushed.

Darsal glanced at the young girl. "Karas, please."

"I've always had it," Papa said.

"You turned into a Scab when evil was released from the Forbidden Circle. If you bathed in one of the lakes, you might know that."

It occurred to Darsal that crafty prodding by Karas might play to their advantage. She scanned the shelf above the counter.

On it sat four Books of History, exactly as Billos said he'd seen the three. Clearly the books ended up here when one entered them. And if he was right, only they could see them. Their way back to the forests waited for them.

Then again, these four books could also take anyone to Earth, the Earth that Alucard had traded his book for, wherever that was.

It was strange to think that at this very moment they were neither in the desert reality nor in this reality called Earth, but trapped somewhere between. In the cover. "In the skin of the worlds," as Alucard had said.

Darsal shivered. *You've made a mistake, girl. A very bad mistake that will haunt more than you.*

"Forgive them," she said to the first warrior who—evidently concluding that he was faced with imbeciles rather than killers—lowered his gun. "Karas is right. Papa is diseased, as you can clearly see. It affects his mind as well as his flesh. The physician sent us here for four books, one of which contains the cure to his disease. He said they'd be on the shelf behind the counter."

The warrior followed her glance to what he perceived was an empty shelf, then regarded her evenly. "Books, eh? Even so, this isn't exactly a clinic. What would medical books be doing here?"

"Not medical books. Books of History that mention this uncommon disease."

"Disease called what?"

"Called Teeleh," Karas said.

Darsal nodded. "Teeleh."

"And what's with the armor?" the second warrior asked, speaking for the first time.

"It protects us," Karas offered.

"Then why aren't you wearing any?"

"Teeleh is more effective in grown-ups."

The warrior seemed to be judging her words carefully. "What's the name of this physician?"

"Why do you ask so many questions?" Karas wanted to know.

"Because I think you're hiding something. Give me the name of the physician, and we'll check out your story."

"His name is Thomas of Hunter," Karas said, as if she had no doubt in the matter.

He lifted the black box and spoke into it again. "Pete, track down a doctor named Thomas Hunter and get back to me as soon as you've located him."

Darsal knew that they'd bought some time, but none of this would help them when they found no physician named Hunter.

"Without the armor, you're likely to be infected by now," Karas said.

"You really expect me to believe any of this?"

The girl shrugged. "Then you, too, can look like Papa. And smell like him. Like rotten eggs."

The man swallowed, eyes on Papa.

"At least let us look at the books," Darsal said.

"What books?"

Darsal stepped forward. "I'll show you."

"Easy now!"

"You want to see the books, I'll show you. If I go for anything but the books, feel free to level fire at me. Fair?"

He didn't answer, which she took as encouragement enough to slip past the counter and reach for the four books. In her hands they appeared perfectly natural; it struck her as odd that the warrior couldn't see them.

She faced him, four books tight between her two palms.

He looked from her hands to her eyes, lost momentarily in that gaze that clearly expressed pity for one's foolishness. She had to get one book to each of the others without interference from the warriors. Better now, quickly, before he grew difficult.

"You don't see them?" she demanded, stepping forward.

"Stop."

She stopped.

He pressed the lever on the side of the box and issued an order. "Never mind that last order, Pete. Bring the car around. I have three suspects I want you to put in custody."

"Copy that. No listing of a Hunter here anyway."

The warrior nodded and lifted his gun again. "Any of you happen to be carrying a nine-millimeter pistol?"

Darsal nonchalantly slid the books under the counter in full view of the officer. He undoubtedly saw only her setting nothing on the shelf. And when the time was right, he would see all three of them picking nothing up off the shelf before vanishing.

But first this annoyance at explaining that they had nothing to do with the slain warriors on the floor.

"Hands up where I can see them!" the man snapped.

Darsal lifted both arms.

# TWENTY-FIVE

Billos stood in the storeroom alone, fighting a terrible volley of conflicting emotions. On the one hand, he knew that Darsal was right to level her glares at him. He was the one who'd gotten them into this fix in the first place.

He'd broken ranks and abandoned her, knowing deep inside that she would follow because she was as loyal as a puppy dog—had been ever since he rescued her. And he had been as loyal to her.

But he couldn't deny the fact that he hated the way she was acting now. From the moment she'd stuck her head into his business here, liking her had been a challenge. Something was wrong with her.

*Or with you, Billos.*

Nonsense.

Still, he knew that he'd changed a little since becoming aware of the power at his fingertips. Marsuvees Black was both intoxicating and disturbing, as was all true power. Darsal stood in the way of that power. The question was whether her doing so was a good thing or a bad thing.

A low voice spoke on his left. "They're going to string you up like a straw doll."

Billos whipped his gun around and faced Marsuvees Black, who leaned against the rear wall. The black-clad man was grinning, picking his teeth with a tiny spike of wood. His big hands looked as if they could crush a face like a tomato.

Billos found his voice. "What?"

"You started out well, my man. Put four of them on their backs and returned to finish it all—not bad for a scrapper from the past."

"Six," Billos said. "The two with the sticks and balls . . ."

"That's a pool table."

"One behind the counter."

"And the counter is a bar."

"One warrior at the door."

"A cop," Black said.

"And the two singers."

Black hesitated. "That's a jukebox. It runs on electricity, not blood. Doesn't count."

"All with suhupow," Billos said.

"Bullets, my man. The gun shoots bullets." Black straightened. "The point is you got a handful, and that's just fine. But there are a couple hundred more, and I want you to kill every single one of them. Like Joshua in the battle of Jericho. Don't leave a single one of them breathing. You hearing me?"

Now it was Billos's turn to hesitate. "Yes."

"Well, you don't sound or look *Yes* to me. You look a bit like a ghost in a black costume."

Black was insulting him. Anger flared up Billos's neck. What was to say he couldn't tilt up the suhupow gun and put this thug on his back right now?

The man's hand blurred. He transformed in the blink of an eye from casual observer to warrior, clutching a gun he'd snatched off his hip. His lips twisted with each word.

"I don't think you understand who you're dealing with, sugar lips."

Another insult, no doubt. But Billos had to admit, Black would prove to be a monstrous adversary. Best to deal with his kind in kind.

"Did I threaten you, you black slug?"

A smile pulled at the edges of Black's mouth. He spun the weapon in his hand as if it were a toy, then slammed it home in the scabbard on his hip. He withdrew his hand and cracked his knuckles.

"Can I have one of those?" Billos asked.

"Slap your hip, baby. The holster will be there."

The suhupow Black brought with him was enough to make Billos's head spin. He impulsively spun his gun, poorly mimicking the man's move, and shoved it down against his hip. The gun slapped into a holster.

Billos withdrew his hand and cracked his knuckles.

"Just a tad juvenile, don't you think? I know how good it feels. Trust me, the feelings that come with true power will make your knees tremble. I can make your wildest fantasy real."

It occurred to Billos that the slight tremble now in his fingers was the result of desire. He'd never felt it so strongly.

"Or I can cut you to ribbons and feed you to the crows. Which, to be perfectly honest, happens to be *my* wildest fantasy."

"Assuming you could," Billos said, only slightly alarmed.

"And that's why I chose you."

"What is?"

"The fact that you're so full of yourself that you actually believe I won't ruin you for life. Takes a strong fool to knowingly play with me. A king. The chosen one. You, baby."

Billos wasn't sure how to take these backhanded compliments. But he did know that his fingers were still trembling.

"Are you ready to hunt?" Black asked.

The village outside had gone strangely quiet. "I was born ready."

"Then get me the books. And kill them all."

"Stop talking my ear off and I will."

"And to make up for your stupidity, I want you to bring me the imposters, Dorksel included. Share the spoils."

"How do you know they're imposters?"

He ignored the question. "Kill the big creep; bring me the two pop tarts."

Billos stared at the door. He could feel, maybe hear, a bead of sweat breaking past his temple.

"It's all about the books, baby," Black said softly. "You know she's an imposter, because she'll come between you and the books. So you choose between the power of the books and this one imposter who may mean something now but will mean nothing when you're on top. Think of it as your sacrifice, the only one I'm asking you to make for me."

The tremble in Billos's fingers was now motivated by something more than desire. Destiny and fear, all mixed into one heady, powerful emotion.

"You choose between yourself and her. Give me one or the other. The crows are waiting."

What choice did he have? Even the Roush had commanded him to retrieve the books. Well, he'd found them, hadn't he? And now Darsal was standing in his way. On the other hand, even though he didn't feel it now, he cared for Darsal. More than he'd ever admitted to her.

"Fine," Billos said. But when he turned back to face the man with his decision, Black was gone.

Billos stood still for a moment, then stripped off the black coat and hat. He withdrew his gun, cocked it up by his ear, and strode for the door.

Time to hunt.

# TWENTY-SIX

Johnis plunged into the Black Forest, gripping the horse with his knees so that both hands remained free for his water bag, his left clenching the leather seam, his right shoved into the water for the teaming Shataiki above to clearly see. Silvie's horse pounded the narrow forest trail behind him.

Without so much as a word, they'd approached the precipice that fell into the hole and headed down a path cut from the cliff. Throngs of the beasts circled and squawked on all sides, keeping just beyond the reach of any water flung their way. At the top Johnis had knocked two of them from midair with a single flick of his wet fingers. Clearly, fire wasn't the beasts' only fear; the lake water was poison to their skin—even a tiny spot of mist would kill one of these vampires. Had they known this several weeks ago, their task might have been simpler.

Still, the Shataiki dove in as close as they dared, desperate to catch one of them unaware.

"Watch your back!" Silvie cried behind him.

Johnis spun as a mangy bat veered into the thick jungle and slammed into a trunk. It fell in a heap. Killed by Silvie's water.

He whirled back and flung water in a wide arc. "Aaaargh! Stay back!"

Then to Silvie. "Douse your hair and your back!"

"What if we run out of water?"

"We'll take that risk. Douse them!"

The sound of splashing water followed immediately; she hadn't needed much encouragement. Johnis cupped cool liquid in his palm and dumped it on his head, then on his shoulders. As long as they remained wet, the bats would not touch them.

They each had three bags and were on their first. The way Johnis had explained it, one bag each for the journey in, one for the lair, the last for the escape. But they didn't know how deep the hole went or if this path really did lead to the lair. And with the dousing, the water in his bag was more than half-gone.

"You good?" he yelled.

"I'm in hell," she panted. "Alive, but not good."

"Good. Keep the extra bags wet too."

They pounded in, deeper, deeper, until the light that had peeked through twisted branches was darkened by the massive overhang they'd seen from above. The Black Forest had gone underground. They plunged ahead into pitch blackness.

"Just keep yourself wet!" Johnis yelled.

He could hear them, flapping and wheezing on every side. He could feel the wind from their wings when they swooped in close, missing him by mere inches. He could smell the putrid, sulfuric stench that stuffed his nostrils, forcing him to breathe through his mouth to keep from retching.

But he could see nothing. Fighting a fresh wave of panic, Johnis dumped more water on his head, rubbed more on his arms, splashed his face, his shoulders, his thighs.

"Johnis?"

The frantic tone in Silvie's voice betrayed her own fear.

"Are you wet?" he demanded. "Your thighs and sides, everything. Keep wet."

"I'm running out of water!"

The tip of a talon brushed Johnis's cheek, and he jerked back. The offending creature screeched, then hit a tree with a dull thump.

What if they tried suicide runs? Blasting in with claws outstretched knowing they would die on contact but killing him in the process?

*No, they are too selfish to consider anything so noble*, he decided.

"Good?" he called.

Silvie didn't respond. He could hear her breathing loudly, but she wasn't answering.

"Silvie! Are you good?"

"Don't ask such stupid questions."

They pounded deeper, deeper.

Johnis didn't know what they would find. He only knew that Darsal had come here looking for a book. The fact that they hadn't found any tracks headed back toward the forests meant she was still here somewhere, either dead or alive. Unless she had found a book and followed Billos, in which case she was somewhere else, either alive or dead.

Beyond that he could only make wild guesses, of which he'd made a hundred since the Roush Hunter had bounced up and down with the news of Darsal's betrayal.

His mount pulled up sharply and came to a stop. The air had gone strangely quiet. The musky smell of muddy water announced a change.

"We're out of the forest," Silvie said, breathing hard. "This is the lake?"

Johnis glanced up and saw them then, a hundred thousand sets of red eyes above and extending around what must be their lake.

He looked ahead and now just barely saw the dim reflection of so many eyes in the dark water. "This is it." But he couldn't see which way the path went.

He tried to force his horse left. It snorted and backed up. Right. This time it walked reluctantly forward.

"This way. How much water do you have left?"

"I'm on my second bag," Silvie said.

"Already?"

"You said keep yourself wet."

"I didn't say take a shower."

"I'm alive."

The horses kept to the darkened path, which gradually made its way around the lake. Johnis's eyes began to make out more details: the ring of leafless trees that bordered the lake; the black water, perfectly still without a breeze or a creature to move the surface; the thousands of red eyes, peering down, mostly in silence now.

And then the faint outline of a platform ahead as the path widened so that the horses could walk side by side.

"You see that?" he whispered.

"I see it," Silvie said next to him. "It looks familiar."

They'd seen another one of these platforms above Teeleh's lair. Though the Shataiki seemed to be imitating Elyon's creation of the forests and lakes, they were limited in their expression. Where Elyon's forests were circular and green, the Shataiki's were circular but black. Elyon's lakes were blue with a hint of green; Teeleh's dark and nasty. The Roush lived above the ground in the open air.

Teeleh's lair was deep underground.

"Let's pray we're right about the lair," Johnis said.

"Did you ever think you'd pray to find hell?"

He hesitated. It was madness. But then this whole business with the books had been madness from the start.

The horses stopped at the edge of the round platform. The air had grown even quieter.

"Now what?" Silvie whispered.

"Bring your water." Johnis swung off his horse, hoisted both bags of water from the saddlebag, and faced the platform, joined by Silvie.

"The horses?" she asked.

Good question. "We don't have enough water for them. Can't cover every angle, can we?"

He started to his right, following the platform's edge.

"That's a pretty important angle, wouldn't you say?" Silvie demanded, hurrying up beside him.

"Shataiki have no taste for horse meat," he said.

The form of the lair's opening loomed to his left. It reminded Johnis of the opening to the root cellars Thomas Hunter had suggested they build to store up food. Like a mouth in the ground.

He reached a trembling hand forward, felt for a handle, then pulled the door open. It creaked, not loudly, but easily heard above the still lake.

They stared into a darkness even thicker. Oily. A complete absence of light.

Silvie's cool fingers touched his elbow. Gripped him tight. "Are you sure about this?"

"Douse yourself," he said.

They both scooped fresh water over their heads.

"This feels wrong, Johnis," Silvie said.

"You want to go back then?"

Silence.

"Follow me," Johnis said and mounted the steps that led down into the lair.

# TWENTY-SEVEN

The first thing Billos saw upon exiting All Right Convenience was the empty warrior buggy sitting in front of Smither's Barbeque. Cops, Black had called them. A cop buggy.

No sign of anyone else on the streets. A face stared out from a window in the house across the street. Another person stood at the corner of a large temple-looking structure, watching him. The commoners had cleared the streets, knowing that Billos had suhupow at his fingertips. Still, it was amazing to him that there weren't more warriors crowding the streets.

It struck him in that moment that there was something amiss with this place called Paradise. It reminded him more of a staging from one of Thomas Hunter's battle schools than a fully formed village. No matter, he had his objective.

He strode for the eatery, gun held up by his right ear, ready for the slightest presentation of the enemy. He leapt up the steps and spun once to make sure he had the time he needed to do what needed doing.

Still no warriors on the street. Good.

He whirled for the door, threw it wide, and went in, gun blasting before the door had fully opened. *Boom, boom!* A beat. *Boom!*

Billos took care of where he sent his suhupow, of course. Two cops held guns on Darsal, who'd handed her weapon over to them. Their distraction by whatever threat they assumed she represented gave him the moment he needed to cut through them both.

They staggered back, clutching their chests. They slammed into the bar behind them and fell to the ground like dumped firewood.

Dead by Billos.

He swiveled the gun on the large Scab. Hesitated for only a moment. Then pulled the trigger.

The boom crashed around his ears, and Papa toppled backward. He landed with a thud that shook the whole building.

Dead by Billos.

"What?" Karas dove at the Scab's laid-out body. "Papa!"

"Papa's dead," Billos snapped. "As you will be if you don't do exactly what I say."

The power of his own dominance was nearly suffocating. Until that moment Billos wasn't sure what he would do, but feeling the gun buck in his hand and seeing the bodies drop, he now knew.

"You killed him!" Karas screamed. "Why'd you kill him?"

"Because he annoyed me. As do you. Now, kindly hand me the books and . . ."

The shelf where he'd seen the books was now bare.

Billos whirled and looked at Darsal for the first time since entering. "Where are the books?"

"You didn't take them?"

"Where are they?" he screamed.

"You tell me, O Wise Slayer of Men," she retorted, eyes fiery.

He knew her well enough to be sure she was immovable. Either she didn't know where the books were, or she had decided that the knowledge would remain with her.

"Then you'll be kind enough to walk ahead of me, out the back, before the warriors crash in and kill us all."

"I can see you've taken complete leave of your senses," she said.

"Why did you kill Papa?" Karas asked again.

Billos directed a blast of suhupow toward the shelves behind the bar. *Boom!* Glass shattered; bottles crashed to the ground.

"Move it! I'm not beyond taking a limb in this state of mind."

"Why not just kill us and be done with it?" Darsal demanded.

Billos hesitated, then spoke what he thought must be the truth. "Because I still love you."

"Love me? With a suhupow gun pointed at me?"

"You'll see. This will all make perfect sense when it's over. I'm chosen, Darsal. I was born for power, and this is the time of my making."

She refused to budge.

Billos shifted his gun so that it lined up with Karas. "Don't make me."

Darsal spit to one side, turned her back on him, and walked for the back door.

"You too." He motioned at Karas with the weapon.

"I don't know what kind of love you think this is, and I certainly don't know why Darsal ever loved anyone as mean as you," she snapped. Then she fell in behind Darsal.

Billos paraded them out of Smither's Barbeque, down the now-empty back alley, and through the store's back entrance.

"You see, now we're back to where we started," he said. "If you would have listened to me, Papa and the two cops would still be alive."

"We are listening to you," Darsal said. "And there's no doubt but that plenty of death awaits us all."

Billos searched the store for Marsuvees Black. That the man was putting him through this incredible test of loyalty, forcing Billos to betray Darsal, could only mean that what lay ahead was equally incredible.

Surely Black could have walked into the eatery and done what he wanted rather than give Billos the task. This was like battle school, and Billos was being put through the final test before being handed the sword of power.

As soon as Billos had proven himself, Black would undoubtedly give Darsal her freedom, and all would be forgiven. There was always the chance that Billos was wrong on this point, but he refused to take that slim chance seriously.

"Stop," he ordered.

Still no sign of Black.

"He wanted you to get the books for him, didn't he?" Darsal asked, turning to face him.

Billos wasn't sure what he was expected to do at this point. Maybe leave them locked up while he went after the rest of the village.

"He's after the books, Billos. For all we know, he's the Dark One. You're making a terrible mistake."

Billos had considered the possibility but refused to dwell on it. The lure of greatness was too great to be bothered by such unlikely risks. And even if it wasn't that unlikely . . . Billos had been chosen, what could he say?

"He's going to eat you up and spit you out," Darsal said.

"You're as smart as you look, peach plum."

Billos turned to face Marsuvees Black, who stood with legs spread, arms crossed, watching hard. There had been no sound of entry, but then Billos hardly expected any. The man moved in mysterious ways.

"I brought them," Billos said.

"Did you, now? Did I want the flesh alone? No. The word became flesh. I need the word. Where are the books?"

"So this is Black?" Darsal said. "Looks like the Dark One to me. A human form of Teeleh himself."

"Teeleh?" Black cocked his head and flashed Darsal a wicked grin. "Do tell."

Darsal didn't look like she was interested in backing down.

"Don't make trouble," Billos snapped at her. To Black: "The books—"

"Shut your slit. I said, 'Do tell.' Does that sound like an order to zip her yapper? Now, do . . . tell."

Billos wasn't sure what to make of Black's perturbed nature.

"Teeleh," Darsal said, "the black winged beast who leads the Shataiki, where we come from. An evil bat who despises Elyon, the creator of the Great Romance and all that is good."

"You're suggesting that I'm *not* good?" Black asked, stunned. "Me . . ."—he spread his fingers and pressed them on his chest— "not a bowl of cherries on a cool summer's eve? Not a butterfly who whistles 'Dixie' in the face of the coming storm? Not a worm dancing in a top hat with a grin as wide as the moon?" He took a calming breath. "How dare you suggest I'm not all those things. And more."

The images made no sense to Billos. More suhupow talk. The power that rolled off Black's tongue was enough to make a grown warrior surrender his sword.

"And for the record," Black continued, "where you come from is *here*. If you die here, you die. If, on the other hand, you help me retrieve the books, I'll let you live."

"Find the books yourself," Darsal said.

"Unfortunately, due to a small glitch in the system, they aren't available to me. For that I've chosen Billos. Isn't that right, O chosen one?"

Billos blinked. "Yes. That's right."

"I'm begging you, Billos." Darsal's eyes pleaded. "You're making a terrible mistake!"

"Stop it!" Billos snapped. She was going to ruin everything! Even if she was right, they were now thoroughly committed to whatever path of glory Black had chosen him for. "You're not thinking clearly."

"It's you who's lost his mind!" Karas cried.

They all looked at the young girl, who stood small to one side.

"They're waiting, Billy-baby," Black said. He nodded at the door. "Lead them outside to the back of the church. The lynching party's waiting there."

"For what?"

"For a lynching. Not you. Them."

"I thought you wanted me to kill the villagers . . ."

The muscles on Black's jaw bunched. "I've changed my mind. A grown man's got that prerogative, don't you think? Give me the books now, and I might change my mind again."

So this was Black's game. He was forcing Billos's hand.

"I don't have the books!"

A dark shadow crossed Black's face. His lips flattened. "Paradise has a history of lynching, and today's starting to feel like a history lesson."

*It's a test. And I'm no fool.* Billos faced Darsal, torn between frustration and anger. "Satisfied? Where are the books?"

"Even if I did know—"

"Outside," Black said. He snapped his fingers. "Take a look."

Billos looked from Darsal to Black, then back.

"Now you're starting to irritate me," Black said.

Billos crossed the room, put his hand on the doorknob, and pulled the door open, expecting to see a posse of cops waiting with drawn guns.

Instead he faced a windblown street, covered by sand. Black storm clouds crowded the sky so low that the instinct to crouch made him flinch. The buildings were stripped of their colors, and the glass was broken on most of them. The town had changed with the snap of Black's fingers.

But what surprised Billos the most were the villagers. Two dozen, gathered on the street facing the store. Clothes tattered. Staring hard, with slits for eyes.

Their flesh looked to be bloodied and rotting. Like human Horde, without the disease. They were half-dead, maybe all dead. Others were joining solemnly, filling the street behind.

The lynching party.

"Welcome to my world," the magic man said behind him.

Billos twisted back.

But Black was gone.

# TWENTY-EIGHT

Darsal could see the mob over Billos's shoulder, and she knew that her worst fears were about to come to pass. She glanced back with Billos and was surprised to see that the man dressed in the black trench coat was gone. He'd simply vanished.

She spun back to Billos, who was staring outside again. He stood with his back toward her and Karas, weapon pointed at the floor.

He was a handsome seventeen-year-old with dark hair and bright eyes, muscled from neck to heel, able to swing a sword through the chests of five Horde in one terrible swoop. A man of seventeen, ready to take a wife. To take Darsal as his wife.

Yet here in this crazy land of the white room where DELL played with their minds, he was a child swept away with the promise of power at whatever cost—it hardly mattered.

"Billos."

He didn't turn.

"Billos!" Karas snapped. "You big thug, listen to her!"

He whirled, angry. "It's a test, you fools!"

"And if you're wrong?" Karas demanded.

But Billos wasn't listening. "Hey!" he called out to the mob.

"Send her out," a large blond-headed one at the mob's center said. The skin on his face was peeling, revealing black flesh beneath.

A thin, wiry warrior, who looked like he might be quicker than a snake, stepped up beside the large blond. "Let me take 'em all. I can take 'em; you know I can."

"Shut up, Pete."

Another man stepped up, hands spread by his hips, as if he expected suhupow to fill them at the slightest movement. The look in his narrowed eyes put a chill in Darsal's neck. She knew their kind—warriors who lived for the love of blood more than any cause. In the Forest Guard they were called throaters: fighters who counted their value by the number of Scab throats they'd cut.

Scanning the gathering mob, Darsal saw that at least half of them looked to be throaters. They were here for vengeance, and they would not go home without their fill of blood.

"Who are you?" Billos demanded.

The leader hesitated. "Claude."

"What will you do with them?"

"We're going to string them up," the man called Claude said

matter-of-factly. "By their necks. We want to watch them twitch in the air."

The wind gusted past the door.

"What if I give you one of them?" Billos asked. "The young one?"

Darsal wasn't sure she'd heard him correctly. This was Billos, for the sake of Elyon!

"Three is better," Claude said, stepping forward. "Father, son, and all."

Darsal had no clue what he was talking about.

"The last time we just went with the one, the son, and it cost us," Claude said.

"I hear you," Billos said. "So you want to string them both up?"

"Are you deaf?" asked Claude.

Darsal had crossed the desert, traded her soul to Alucard, betrayed Thomas, all for Billos's sake. But she knew that if she didn't make a move now, they would all die. And since Billos wasn't moving with her, she would have to work alone.

She caught Karas's eye and looked to the rear exit. The young girl nodded. Darsal eased back toward the door, moving to her right as she did so, until the door frame blocked the view of the mob.

"I hear you." Billos shoved his gun into its holster. He snapped his fingers, and a glass goblet magically appeared in his hand. "I hear you, and I'll drink to that."

Amazing. Darsal briefly wondered what it felt like to have that kind of power. She bumped into the door behind her, and the questions fled. Reaching for the knob, she cracked the door soundlessly, then slipped outside, followed by Karas.

She had the presence of mind to shut the door in the face of the blowing wind before running across the back alley and into the forest behind. She rounded a crowded bunch of trees and pulled up hard.

"He's gone mad!" Karas whispered, sliding in beside her.

"Watch your tongue."

"Just because you love him doesn't mean he isn't mad. Now what?"

"We have to get the books." Darsal paced, frantic.

"Get the books and leave him?"

"If you think I would ever leave Billos, you're as mad as he is."

"So you admit he's mad? But the fact that you risked your neck to get this far is clouding your judgment."

"Was Johnis's judgment clouded when he went back for you?"

That put her back on her heels. She stared into the forest for a moment, then looked up at Darsal. "I wanted to be saved. You can't help someone who doesn't want help."

"You're assuming his desires won't change," Darsal snapped.

"What do you see in him? He's not the lovable kind."

"Zip it! What does a child know about love? There's no way this side of Teeleh's breath that I'm leaving Billos. Don't say another word of it!"

"Nice," Karas quipped. "And dangerous too."

"What is?"

"Love," Karas said.

A loud boom ripped through the air. They both started and faced the village.

"Billos?"

BILLOS RELEASED THE GOBLET, LETTING IT CRASH ON THE floorboards. He stared at the broken glass shards at his feet. The feeling of raw power that accompanied every snap of his fingers was positively intoxicating. A small part of his mind knew that he was stalling, but the greater part of his heart was so wrapped up in ambition that he couldn't bring his thoughts to focus on that corner of his thinking.

"Okay," he said, looking up. "If you—"

The words caught in his throat. Claude had lifted his long-barreled weapon and was staring at him as if *he* were the enemy.

"Cut them off behind," Claude ordered.

Four villagers broke from the mob and jogged two to each side of the building, watching Billos as they disappeared into the alley behind.

At any other time, in any battle with any of the Horde, Billos wouldn't have mistaken the move as anything but a clear threat. At the moment, however, he wasn't thinking clearly, and worse, he knew it. He couldn't make his mind work fast enough.

They were throaters. Any fool could see that much. But what

direct threat these particular throaters posed to him wasn't clear, at least not to him.

Black's order drummed through his mind. *Kill them all, every last one of them. Baby.* His guns were still in his hip holsters. But he wasn't in the business of killing them all right at this moment. He was in the business of giving them what they wanted.

He glanced over his shoulder. Saw the room was empty.

Gone? Darsal had betrayed him?

The rear door crashed open and filled with two of the four snakes who'd covered the alley. A quick glance told the story.

"They're gone!" the one on the right called. He was dressed in a blue shirt stained with something black, maybe blood from the long cut on his cheek, maybe Horde sap for all Billos knew.

But his mind was working well enough now to know that things were turning bad.

The two snakes spread out and made room for the other two. All four drilled him with piercing glares, hands spread above the butts of their weapons.

"You'll do," Claude growled.

Billos faced him, every instinct now on razor's edge. This was it, then. He'd failed in this one simple test because Darsal had betrayed him, and now instead of being the aggressor in an offensive posture, he was hopelessly surrounded by an enemy too overwhelming to even consider engaging directly.

*But you are the chosen one, Billos. And you were chosen for a reason.*

He spread his hands in a gesture of reconciliation and slowly stepped onto the boardwalk. "Okay, settle down. You want to lynch me? Fine. You can string me up and watch me twitch in the air."

Billos walked directly toward them, ignoring the trembling in his legs. He didn't know how much power waited between his fingers, or how much power Claude and the company of snakes who were poised to string him up had between theirs.

But he was about to find out.

"Why not make a sport of it, though?" he said.

The dark sky hung low overhead. Sand blew across the ground.

"Pete seems pretty eager to take me on. Let him. One-on-one. Better yet, I'll take two of you on."

Claude stared at him, no doubt taken off guard by such a bold suggestion. But he wasn't agreeing.

"Five, then," Billos said, halting ten feet from the man. "Put me in a circle with five men."

"Let's do him," one of the throaters said, stepping up. He held a sharpened stake, roughly three feet in length, in each hand. "Let's stick him."

"Back off, Roland. He's a trickster."

"But only one trickster," Billos said.

"We can take him, Dad," Pete said.

Billos glanced behind the men and calmly took in the specifics of his predicament. His fingers tingled with anticipation. Oddly enough, he felt his fear slip away, replaced only with a thirst to see just how much power Black had lit in his hands.

*The chosen one.* It had a haunting sound.

"Pete's right. This whole lynching party is a sham. I could take you all with a single sword!" Billos declared.

"Swords don't do the trick here. The only way you win is to turn the girl over to us; that's the way it goes."

The. Chosen. One.

"I don't think so, Claude." Billos held both hands out like a priest welcoming his flock. "I'll tell you what I think. I think . . ." He snapped his fingers. Cold steel filled both palms. Twin guns in addition to the one on his hip.

A bolt of adrenaline ripped down his spine, and in that single brief moment, Billos knew that he had found his calling. He regretted having ditched the black coat and hat, because in truth he was nothing less than the magic man, Marsuvees Black himself.

The. Chosen. One.

The thoughts crashed through his mind in the space of half a heartbeat, and then he was moving, faster than lightning. He dove to his right and sent two bullets, one from each gun, while he was in the air.

They struck each mark in the forehead, two of the snakes with long guns next to Claude. The long guns first, then the handguns.

Both warriors dropped like lifeless dolls, dead by Billos.

He landed on his shoulder and was twisting back for the four throaters behind him when the first bullets smacked into the dirt near his head, spraying his cheek.

Moving like a viper, he whipped around with both guns and sent the suhupow—the bullets—*boom, boom, boom, boom!*

The four throaters had their guns out, firing, running full tilt toward him, zigzagging to spoil his aim, but Billos made the appropriate adjustments on the fly. The power from his hands smashed into their foreheads and knocked them clean off their feet.

Watching it, Billos knew he was a god. Slayer of throaters. Chosen by Black to kick . . .

Something tugged at his arm. He'd been hit?

But this didn't slow Billos down. He was rolling like a log, feeling the ground around his body thump with bullets from the mob. Rolling toward the corner of the building to his right. Having eliminated the throaters, Billos had no concern of a rear attack. All he had to do was reach cover and he would win this first round.

A second tug smarted him, this one on his left leg. Then he spun past the corner, chased by the staccato beats of bullets smacking into the wood.

Billos leapt to his feet and glanced at his leg to see a flesh wound that added no concern. They'd struck him twice, but both hits were superficial. And he'd slain six of the snakes.

Thirty to go. Roughly.

"Round the back!" Claude's voice snarled. "Split up, and make sure he doesn't—"

Billos moved then before they could possibly expect a second attack. He jumped back into the open, firing as he cleared the corner, pulling the levers as fast as he could move his fingers. Faster than he could have imagined. The guns thundered in rapid succession, rolling bolts of lightning. Like drumsticks beating the low-hung clouds.

Billos was aware of each volley, each hit, each thrasher thrown from his feet. Each return shot spinning past him as he rushed directly at the mob.

There were seven long guns, and he took them out first, ending with one held by a graying woman who wore a fierce scowl. The bullet dropped her to the ground, scowl still in place.

God has spoken. Baby.

No sign of Claude, Billos realized as he cleared the corner of Smither's Barbeque. The large blond-headed leader had perhaps made his way to the back without Billos noticing.

He pulled up with his back against the side boards and glanced both directions. The street had gone quiet in the wake of his bold attack. No less than twelve of them now lay on the ground, dead by Billos.

"Kill them all," Black had said. And Billos intended to show him how easily he could do it. As easy as slicing through the Horde.

An image of Darsal skipped through his mind, then was gone. In good time she would understand. He could be wrong, misguided by his own passion to seize power, deceived, as she claimed. But he didn't want to think about that. Not now. Not when he had the rest of the village to level.

A raspy chuckle cackled through the air, stilling Billos in his boots. It came from the street around the corner, and it sounded very much like Black.

With the throaters?

Then his name, long and low. "Billieeeeeeeee . . ."

Not his name exactly, but the same name Black had called him once or twice.

"Billieeeeeeeeee . . . Olly Olly Oxen Free. Come to Papa, baby."

"You heard him."

Billos spun around and found himself staring into twin barrels only inches from his face. Holding the long gun was Claude, eyes fiery with anticipation.

Billos acted out of an instinct bred from thousands of fights in the Southern Forest as a lad, most of which he'd handily won. There was good reason he'd been selected by Thomas Hunter to lead the new recruits, and he would show it now.

He threw himself backward into a backflip, ducking beneath the weapon's line of fire and bringing his feet up in the same smooth motion.

*Boom!* The gun blast buffeted the air over his arched chest. His feet connected with Claude's arms, and he finished the full rotation before Claude's gun clattered to the ground. Now he faced a weaponless thug with round eyes.

"Dead by Billos," he said, and pulled both levers.

*Click, click.*

He blinked. The suhupow seemed to have fizzled. He jerked the levers again. *Click, click.*

"Billieeeeee . . ." Black's voice chuckled. "Come to Daddy, Billy-baby."

# TWENTY-NINE

Billos had two options: he could snap his fingers and make more suhupow, or he could trust Black and go to daddy, as the man suggested.

He dropped the guns on the ground, spun around, and walked out into the open. Black stood in the center of the street, arms and feet spread wide, grinning wickedly, trench coat whipped to one side by the gusting wind. His head was tilted down so that Billos could just see the whites of his eyes beneath the rim of his hat.

The throaters stood evenly on either side, staring at Billos, weapons lowered. Behind them the temple towered tall, nearly touching the black sky above.

"Hello, Billosssss," Black said. "Wanna trip? Wanna, wanna, baby?"

*It is a test,* Billos quickly decided. A final test to see how he would use his suhupow in the face of terrible odds.

"Do you want me to kill them all?" he called.

"Yes, Billos. Kill them all. Do it now."

So Billos snapped his fingers to fill them with steel and continue his reign of terror, to make them all dead by Billos. But this time a small glitch sidelined the plan.

This time no steel filled his hands.

He snapped again, harder.

The snaps clicked over the whistling wind.

"What's the matter, baby?" Black said. "A little low on grace-juice, are we?"

What was he saying? The suhupow was gone? Billos felt the blood drain from his face. His mind fogged. Surely . . . But he wasn't sure what he should be sure about.

Something nudged his back. Claude had retrieved his long gun and was prodding him.

"What's happening?" he asked.

"You don't know?"

"No."

"No? No, Billossssssss. You really don't know, do you? You worthless slug."

"What . . ."

"The girl is what," Black said. "I asked you to give me the girl. It was all so simple. You waltzed into town like you owned the place and laid four of them in the grave. Now they need a lynching to satisfy their lust. A life for a life, that's the way it works here. I suggested the girl. Instead you're giving them someone else. Your call, not mine."

"Who?"

Black cocked his head. "Please don't tell me this disease named idiocy has gone that far. Or are you seeing double, baby? Because I only see one of you."

Billos felt dizzy. He snapped his fingers, knowing nothing would happen. There was still a chance; there had to be. This was still a test of some kind.

But for the first time the suggestions Darsal had made spoke louder than his own confidence. There was a possibility that Black's motives were less than noble.

He looked around quickly, searching for options. Could he dodge Claude's gun again and make a run for it? But five others had now joined the large man. And those on either side of Black were spreading out to encircle him.

He faced the magic man and stepped forward. "Hold on. I thought . . . I thought we had a deal."

"Didn't your mommy tell you never to make a deal with the devil? What I give I can take. String him up!"

Behind him, Claude grunted, and something crashed into the back of Billos's head. He felt himself falling, but was out before he hit the ground.

HE CAME TO SLOWLY, TO THE SOUND OF HEAVY BREATHING and the pain of twisted joints. Light filtered past his eyes, and he saw the sky above, black and boiling, just above the nearly bare branches of a large oak that hung over him like a menacing skeleton.

Something wet dripped on his face. Sweat from the flushed face of a throater who leaned over him, pulling on a rope they'd slung over the thickest branch high above.

The full realization of what he was up against hit Billos, and he jerked his legs in a moment of panic. Pain shot down his bones. They'd tied his arms and legs back like a hog's, so that any movement from his arms only pulled his legs back behind his hips and vice versa.

"String him up," Claude said.

"Wait!" Billos cried, or tried to cry—he managed only a grunt.

They hauled him up by a rope. He left the ground facedown, arms and legs arched behind his back, barely able to hold back his screams.

The rope jerked with each pull, sending stabs of pain through his joints.

He heard the cackling then, from a porch on the back side of the temple where they'd dragged him. Black watched with arms crossed, smiling.

"Go ahead and let it all out, baby. They deserve a scream."

Billos stared into the man's eyes, set above curling lips. Black eyes that didn't appear to have any pupils. And in those dark, oily pools, Billos could see himself screaming. Clawing his way up, as if the man's eye was a tunnel into the abyss, and he, Billos, was being sucked in.

He blinked, and the image was gone. Only Black now, smiling at him with shiny white teeth and dark eyes.

"The books, Billos," Black said. "I need the books."

"I . . . I don't know . . ."

The throaters tied the rope off to one of the porch posts, leaving Billos to sway a few feet above a large circle the men formed. The rope creaked above him.

Black paced, arms still crossed. "If that's the truth, then I have no use for you; you do realize that, don't you?"

He hadn't thought of it that way. Words failed him in the face of the pain. Below, one of the villagers approached, dragging the Scab's large Horde sword. He gripped it with both hands and looked up at Billos.

"Do you know what happens to the stomach when it's sliced open in your particular position?" Black asked.

It was with those words that Billos knew his fate was sealed. How he'd missed the plain signs along the way he didn't know, but his meeting Marsuvees Black had not been a chance encounter.

Billos had been warned that entering the books was dangerous, and he was now snared by that danger. Black was the Dark One, and he'd wanted nothing but the books the whole time. Now that Billos was powerless to deliver the books, Black would simply kill him.

"I believe you," Black said. "You're a complete idiot and know nothing. Which means you have only one slim chance. Short of that, you take the long trip to the place of wailing and gnashing of teeth."

Billos's vision blurred. *What have I done?* His heart broke, nine feet from the ground, facing down at death. And all he could think was, *What have I done?*

"Darsal," he croaked.

"The name's Black," the man said. "Marsuvees Black. Cut him up!"

The throater with the sword drew it back. One cut was all it would take to spill his intestines to the ground.

Billos began to weep.

"No! Let him go."

He twisted in his ropes and looked at Darsal, who stood beyond the circle of throaters, staring up at him.

Karas, the little girl, stepped up beside Darsal. "Let him go," she said, matching Darsal's intensity.

Darsal whispered something in harsh tones, but the young girl didn't appear interested in listening. She held her ground, jaw set.

Darsal faced Black. "I'm the one you want. I know where the books are. Take me."

"We're the ones you want. We know where the books are. Take us," the young girl repeated.

"Well, well, well," Black muttered. "Lucky for you, Billy-boy, fools come in pairs." Then louder so that they could all hear: "Cut him down!"

It took only a few jerky, painful moments for Billos to reach the ground again. But it was more than enough time for the implications of what was occurring to rack his mind.

Darsal was giving herself for him. Did she think she could survive the experience? Surely she wasn't doing this out of some misguided sense called "love." He couldn't accept that. Wouldn't accept that.

Two throaters hauled Billos to his feet, where he stood shakily.

"You may leave," Black said. "If I ever see you alive again, I'll fix the problem."

Claude shoved Darsal and Karas into the circle.

"Go, Billos," Darsal said.

"Darsal?" What could he say? "You can't do this."

"Go, Billos!" she snapped. "Before you do even more damage, just go!"

"And do what? I don't know where the books are! I can't get back! And what about you? I can't let them—"

"It's too late!" she interrupted. "Do you have any suhupow in your fingers?"

He snapped his fingers. The smack of his fingers against his palm sounded stupidly weak.

"Just go," she said. Tears filled her eyes. "Please, go now, before I change my mind."

Raw horror set into Billos's chest. He couldn't go, he realized. How could he live with the knowledge that Darsal had died for him?

"I can't," he said. A knot rose into his throat. "I can't, Darsal!"

He looked down at Karas, glaring at him through silent tears. She'd been saved only a few days ago and was now returning the favor for another. But not without a struggle. A misguided fool! And now a misguided fool on his conscience.

"I suppose I could have all three of you hanged," Black said. "Romeo and Juliet and all that crap."

"Go, you fool," Karas said. "I will do what I can to save my sister. Go before her sacrifice becomes meaningless!"

Billos took a step backward, fighting waves of remorse and fear all wrapped into one terrible bundle.

Darsal added her insistence. "Go!"

He blinked, unable to hold back streams of tears. "Darsal . . ."

"Go!" she screamed.

"I think she means it," Black said.

Billos stumbled forward, through the throaters who parted for him, to the corner of the temple, powerless to stop Black or Darsal or any of them, including himself.

"Kill the little girl first," Black said behind him.

*They are both dead*, he realized. *Dead by Billos.*

And then he ran blindly into the street, wishing it was he who was dead.

# THIRTY

The stairs curved to Johnis's left as they descended, much the same as in Teeleh's lair. He guided himself by letting the tips of his right-hand fingers drag along the stones on his right, refusing to consider the makeup of the slippery, musky substance covering them.

Silvie rested her hand on his shoulder and followed close. Her breath was warm on his neck, and he drew a small amount of comfort from the human contact.

He stopped after a good twenty steps and stared ahead, trying to make something, anything, out. The odor down here was worse than above. He lifted his elbow to his nose and tried to get a few filtered draws of air without blanching, but his sleeve proved useless, so he gave up.

A sizzle on the steps below startled him. "What?"

"Water," Silvie said after a moment. "The ground doesn't like our water."

She was using more of the precious fluid and had spilled some on the stones, where it sizzled in protest.

"Don't use too much," Johnis said, resuming his descent.

The steps ended on flat ground in pitch darkness. Johnis felt his way toward a door on the right, again positioned in exactly the same place as in Teeleh's lair. They were each replicas of the same design.

He pulled the heavy door open and saw light for the first time. An orange glow ebbed and swayed in a tunnel to their right.

"It's the same as before," he said.

"You recognize it?" Her voice was thin and shaky.

Johnis took her hand. "Identical," he said. "This is his lair."

"Whose lair?"

"The prince or whatever they call him that rules this forest."

"Not Teeleh himself, then."

"I don't think so. Maybe. I think we'll know soon enough."

He led her forward, but she pulled her hand free after a few steps, preferring to keep the water bag close instead.

Johnis stopped when they saw the first worm on the tunnel wall. Ten feet long, perhaps three inches thick, sliding though its own milky mucus. He studied it for a moment, then flicked water on it.

The worm uttered a soft, alien shriek and thrashed on the

wall, skin smoking where the water had made contact. It fell to the ground with a loud splat that echoed down the tunnel.

Johnis looked at Silvie. Neither said a word. They went in, deeper.

The orange light was coming from a flame fixed to the entrance of what Johnis assumed was a library or a study, like the one in Teeleh's lair.

He stopped and nodded. "This is it."

"If Darsal's alive, she's staying quiet."

Johnis didn't want to dwell on the implications of the statement. It was bad enough that they'd seen no sign of their comrades since entering the Black Forest.

"Keep your water ready," he said, but he didn't need to. Silvie had her right hand submerged already.

They strode up to the gated entrance and found it open.

"Come in."

The voice was thin and rasped like a file on a sword. Johnis took out a dripping hand and stepped into the underground library.

The room was small, maybe ten paces square, with a bank of bookcases on his right, a short table in the center, and several stuffed chairs situated haphazardly around. A torch flame licked at the wall opposite the entrance. All very much like in Teeleh's lair.

But the tall, mangy Shataiki seated at the desk to Johnis's left was not Teeleh.

"I knew you would eventually make it," the Shataiki said.

"Alucard," Silvie whispered.

"You remember."

The bat stood. He was taller than most Shataiki by a foot or two, but shorter than Teeleh by as much. Thinner, much thinner. His mangy carcass hung off his bones like cobwebs. Vivid images of what this creature had done to them sent shivers down Johnis's spine.

"I could kill you," Johnis said.

Alucard lowered his eyes to the water bag in Johnis's hands. "Yes, I suppose you could. You're growing more clever by the day."

The bat had no fear, which could only mean he knew something they did not.

"Where's Darsal?"

"You amaze me, you humans," Alucard said. "All this way to save one lousy slab of meat? You're not fearless; I can see that by the twitching of your lips, however slight. Which means you're facing your fears. A noble thing."

"Loyalty," Johnis said. "Something you have no inkling about."

"True. I would as quickly slit Teeleh's throat as yours; he knows that. But I can't."

"Darsal," Johnis snapped. "If you can't lead me to her, you're worthless to me."

"So you come into my home with your precious water and play master."

"I have no interest in being your master."

Alucard sat down and turned back to a book on his desk. The torch cast light over an obscured title. "Your friends aren't here," the Shataiki said. "They left with a very precious possession of mine."

"One of the books," Johnis said.

"Do you know what the books can do?" Alucard asked, tracing a single black talon over the cover of the book in front of him. Then he told them, relishing his words.

"All seven and the rules which bind them are broken. Used together the original seven books can undo it all."

"For evil," Silvie said. "I wouldn't think you'd need the books to ply your trade."

"Not just evil." Alucard turned his head and stared at them with red eyes, unable to hide the smirk on his jaw. "Good always wins. You wonder why? Because it's more powerful. Evil ultimately leads to the discovery of good. Even the death of the Maker would end in some kind of good." He spat a thick wad of green mucus at the wall, where it slowly slid down to the floor.

"But all seven books used together changes that. The glory is hardly imaginable. It would change everything." Alucard slammed a fist on the desk. "Everything!"

"The Dark One seeks seven," Johnis muttered.

"The Dark One." Alucard chuckled, a phlegm-popping, raspy affair. "Unfortunately, only four of the books are here. Or should I say were here before your friends disappeared with them. A bad thing, because those four are needed to find the three books in the lesser reality."

Johnis knew he was learning more than he could hope to understand in one sitting. Being here in this underground lair was maybe not as much a consequence of Billos's indiscretion as part of their mission to find the books.

"What lesser reality?" Silvie asked.

"Open a book and find out. And it's not the place your friends went off to, not unless they have all four and opened one, in which case we're all wasting time."

A faint clicking sound ran down the tunnel behind them. Johnis focused his thoughts on the task at hand. Darsal.

"She's not here. Then why shouldn't I just kill you and leave?"

"Because I'm not as stupid as your friends," Alucard said. "You think I would just hand over my sole book out of kindness?"

"What have you done?"

"It's not me. Darsal took the book after making a binding vow on the books to return all four to me if she is able to find Billos."

Johnis felt his pulse surge. "Or?"

"She is mine," Alucard said.

"Not good," Silvie said.

The statement needed no response and received none.

"So then I should kill you."

"Then by the bond of her vow, Darsal will share my fate. Kill me, and you kill her."

True? Johnis didn't know, but the notion had a ring of authenticity to it.

Alucard continued. "You're alive because you have the water, but it won't last forever. If I were you, I'd head out now, while you still have an advantage."

Hearing Alucard speak with such reasoned skill cast him in a totally different light than the Shataiki Johnis had suffered under in Teeleh's forest or the one who'd sat upon Witch's head in the Horde city. Alucard was an enemy to be feared. And at the moment, he had spoken the truth. They had to get out of the Black Forest while they still had water. Once in the desert, they could regroup with Hunter.

Johnis stepped back. "Let's go, Silvie." To Alucard: "Just know that in the end, Elyon honors his chosen ones."

The bat cackled, unimpressed.

Johnis backed out of the library, eyes on the beast who drilled him with a red stare.

"Johnis?"

He spun at Silvie's urgent tone. The source of the clicking he'd heard earlier suddenly became apparent: dozens of worms sliding slowly toward them from deeper underground. The clicking was their popping of mucus.

This was no place for them.

"Go!"

No further encouragement needed, they ran toward the entrance together. Out into the atrium. Into darkness again. Up the stone steps, sloshing water as they stumbled forward.

Out into the open air.

"This way!" Johnis said, veering back toward the horses. The bats still ringed the lake, even more now than before. A hundred thousand, maybe two hundred thousand. A sea of red eyes peering in silence except for the odd hissing.

"Save your water . . ."

It was as far as Johnis got. He slid to a halt and stared ahead into the dim glow of red. The horses lay on their sides, butchered and stripped of flesh.

"They're dead!" Silvie cried.

An understatement.

The hissing and clicking from the trees swelled as the Shataiki became aware that their deed had been discovered. Still, not one of them moved.

"We'll never make it out on foot," Silvie said. "We don't have enough water!"

"We have to go back down," Johnis said.

Silvie stared at him. Then at her horse.

They both knew that he was right.

# THIRTY-ONE

**B**illos ran blind into the blowing wind, across the center of the town, past Smither's Barbeque, and into the alley before pulling up, panting. He spun back and tried to make sense of what was happening, but his mind wasn't working right.

His heart, on the other hand, was pumping on overload, shoving pain through his veins. Details that seemed so vague only minutes ago now sat vividly on the horizon of his mind, like statues to the dead.

He'd accepted the invitation of the Dark One to enter the books and had woken in a place in which Black gave and took powers to serve his purpose. But it was Billos's own ambition that had blinded him to the danger.

Darsal had seen what he had not. Like a child ignoring his

father's warning not to touch the fire, Billos had touched, had shoved his hand into the flames, had thrown his body onto the coals.

He paced, scrambling for a course of action that made sense, snapping his fingers uselessly. A gun still hung on his hip, but one futile pull of its lever and he knew the suhupow was gone forever. Without it he didn't stand a chance against the throaters, whose guns would still shoot this suhupow called bullets.

"Darsal . . ." Billos whimpered, hands gripped in fists. He paced, desperate to be dead, his only escape now. But Black didn't want him, not even as a sacrifice for Darsal. Only Elyon knew what atrocity was building behind that temple.

Billos lifted his chin to the black sky, let his mouth open in the face of the wind, and sank slowly to his knees. His body shook with each sob, but each cry only brought a greater sense of finality.

A lone cry drifted on the wind. It was light and too high-pitched to be Darsal. Why had the stubborn wench insisted on offering herself as well? Wasn't Darsal enough? Karas was a fool, a Scab pretending to be clean, a runt of a girl who had no business being here.

But all of that was a lie! Karas was his savior! He would worship the thought of her, give his life to save those like her. Elyon, Elyon, how foolish had he been? Billos wailed at the sky.

"Hello, Billos."

He started and jerked his head to his right. The young blondheaded boy who'd warned him about the Dark One stood in the alley, hands limp by his side. Samuel.

"Now do you believe me?" the boy asked.

Billos gripped his hair in both hands, lowered his head so that his chin rested on his chest, clenched his eyes tight, and cried to cover his shame.

"There is a way, you know," the boy said.

Billos looked up. "What? It's hopeless! They're dead already!"

"For you, I mean," Samuel said. "It might be too late for them, but there may be a way for you."

"I don't need a way!"

"That's your first mistake. You need a way more than they do."

"Black has them!" he snapped angrily. "How can you say that?"

"No. Black has you, Billos."

Whether it was the use of his name or the way that Samuel said it with such authority, Billos wasn't sure. But he knew that his whole life was somehow wrapped up in those simple words. *Black has you, Billos.*

The wind seemed to ease, quieted by the moment. Samuel stared at him with green eyes that drew him with their absolute surety.

"Do you want this?" the boy asked.

Billos pushed himself to his feet. Everything went quiet except for the thumping of his heart. The green of Samuel's eyes begged him to run, to leap into a water that would wash away the darkness Black had filled him with.

"I can give you something that makes his suhupow seem silly."

"Yes," Billos said.

Samuel's lips twisted into a tempting grin. "Are you sure?"

"Yes. Yes, show me."

"Follow me."

Samuel spun on his heels and bounded barefoot toward the forest. He glanced over his shoulder, grinning wide. "Come on!"

Billos stumbled forward, then ran after the boy. Into the forest. Following glimpses of Samuel, who raced ahead, leaping over fallen logs, crashing through the brush like a deer.

The wind was gone here, held back by the trees, replaced by the sound of Billos's feet cracking twigs and his lungs pulling at the air. There was something familiar about the trees here. A scent that seemed common to him. If he didn't know better he might have guessed that he was back in Middle Forest, racing after a Roush.

The boy was leaving him behind. "Wait!"

But there was no need for Samuel to wait, because the trees ended. Billos slid to a halt at the shore of a brilliant green lake surrounded by emerald trees.

The boy was halfway down the sandy beach, sprinting for a large rock set half in the sand, half in the water. Billos watched in amazement as Samuel launched himself up onto the rock and then catapulted himself into a beautifully arched dive.

For a moment he seemed to hang suspended, and then he plunged into the green waters with hardly a splash.

Billos stood panting from the run, waiting for the boy to reemerge, wondering if he was supposed to follow. But he knew the answer already. The lake, like the boy's eyes, begged him to run. To jump. To dive deep.

Billos ran. He tore down the shore, bounded up on the rock, and dove into the air.

The instant Billos hit the water, his body shook violently. A blue strobe exploded in his eyes, and he knew that he was going to die. That he had entered a forbidden pool, pulled by the wrong desire, and now he would pay with his life.

The warm water engulfed him. Flutters rippled through his body and erupted into a boiling heat that knocked the wind from his lungs. The shock alone might kill him.

But it was pleasure that surged through his body, not pain. Pleasure! The sensations coursed through his bones in great unrelenting waves.

Elyon.

How he was certain, he did not know. But he knew. Elyon was in this lake with him.

Billos opened his eyes. Gold light drifted by. He lost all sense of direction. The water pressed in on every inch of his body, as intense as any acid, but one that burned with pleasure instead of pain.

His violent shaking gave way to a gentle trembling as he sank into the water. He opened his mouth and laughed. He wanted more, much more. He wanted to suck the water in and drink it.

Without thinking he did that. He took a great gulp and then inhaled. The liquid hit his lungs. Billos pulled up, panicked. He tried to hack the water from his lungs, but inhaled more instead. No pain. He carefully sucked more water and breathed it out slowly. Then again, deep and hard. Out with a soft whoosh. He was breathing the water! In great heaves he was breathing the lake's intoxicating water.

Billos shrieked with laughter. He tumbled through the water, pulling his legs in close so he would roll, and then stretching them out so he thrust forward, farther into the colors surrounding him. He swam into the lake, deeper and deeper, twisting and rolling with each stroke. The power contained in this lake was far greater than anything he'd ever imagined.

*I made this, Billos.*

Billos pulled up. He whipped his body around, searching for the words' source. A giggle rippled though the water. Billos grinned stupidly and spun around.

"Elyon?" His voice was muffled, hardly a voice at all.

*Do you like it?*

The words reached into his bones, and he began to tremble again. He wasn't sure if it was an actual voice or if he was somehow imagining it.

"Yes!" Billos said. He might have spoken; he might have shouted—he didn't know. He only knew that his whole body screamed it.

Billos looked around. "Elyon?"

*Why do you doubt me, Billos?*

In that single moment the full weight of Billos's foolishness crashed in on him like a sledgehammer. He curled into a fetal position within the bowels of the lake and began to moan.

*I see you, Billos.*

*I made you.*

*I love you.*

The words washed over him, reaching into the deepest folds of his flesh, caressing each hidden synapse, flowing through every vein, as though he had been given a transfusion.

The water around his feet began to boil, and he felt the lake suck him deeper. He gasped, pulled by a powerful current. And then he was flipped over and pushed headfirst by the same current.

A dark tunnel opened directly ahead of him, like the eye of a whirlpool. He rushed into it, and the light fell away.

Pain hit him like a battering ram, and he gasped for breath. He instinctively arched his back in blind panic and reached back toward the entrance of the tunnel, straining to see it, but it had closed.

He began to scream, flailing in the water, rushing deeper into the dark tunnel. Pain raged through his body. He felt as if his flesh had been neatly filleted and packed with salt, each organ stuffed with burning coals, his bones drilled open and filled with molten lead.

Black's raspy chuckle filled his ears. Then his own laughter, as sinister as Black's, and he knew then that he had entered his own soul.

Billos involuntarily arched his back so that his head neared his heels. His spine stressed to the snapping point. He couldn't stop screaming. The tunnel gaped below him and spewed him out into soupy red water. Bloodred. He sucked at the red water, filling his spent lungs.

From deep in the lake, a moan began to fill his ears, replacing his own screams. Billos twisted, searching for the sound, but he found only thick, red blood. The moan gained volume and grew to a wail and then a scream of terrible pain.

Elyon was screaming.

Billos pressed his hands to his ears and began to scream with the other, thinking now that this was worse than the dark tunnel.

Then he was through. Out of the red, into the green of the lake, hands still pressed firmly against his ears. Billos heard the words as if they came from within his own mind.

*I love you, Billos.*

Immediately the pain was gone. Billos pulled his hands from his head and straightened. He floated, too stunned to respond.

*I choose you.*

Billos began to weep. The feeling was more intense than the pain that had racked him.

The current pulled at him again, tugging him up through the colors. His body again trembled with pleasure, and he hung limp as he sped through the water. He wanted to speak, to scream, to yell, and to tell the whole world that he was the most fortunate man in the universe. That he was loved by Elyon. Elyon himself.

*Never leave me, Billos.*

"Never! I will never leave you."

The current pushed him through the water and then above the surface not ten meters from the shore. He stood on the sandy bottom, retched a quart of water from his lungs, and straightened. For a moment he had such clarity of mind that he was sure he could understand the very fabric of space if he put his mind to it.

He was chosen.

And then a new thought mushroomed in his mind.

"Darsal."

When he spoke her name, light spilled from his lips and fell heavily to the water. He held up his hands and saw that light drifted off his fingertips. The boy's words came back.

*I can give you something that makes his suhupow seem silly.*

*Run, Billos. Run.*

Billos ran.

# THIRTY-TWO

The dark stairwell swallowed Johnis and Silvie for the second time that night, or was it still day? Either way it hardly mattered. *We are plunging into eternal darkness,* Johnis thought.

"What are we doing?" Silvie's cry echoed down the stone enclosure, battering his ears. What? Exactly what, he didn't know.

"We have to get an advantage!"

"Down here?"

Johnis reached the bottom and rushed for the door that led into the tunnel.

"Johnis!"

He spun back, and as his body turned, the water bag in his right hand slipped out. It landed with a loud slap and, before Johnis could react, splashed its contents on the stone floor. A loud hissing and sizzling filled the atrium, then slowly faded.

"What did you do?"

"I have one more."

"We won't have enough to go back!" Silvie snapped. She couldn't hide the panic in her voice, and it only pushed Johnis closer to the same.

"You don't think I know?" he shouted, then shoved his hand into his last water bag. "How many bags do you have?"

"One more. This one's almost empty. Not enough, Johnis. We'll be stranded down here."

"And not above?"

"I'd rather die fighting than be stuck in a hole!" She strode back toward the stairs.

"No! Silvie, we can't go back up. It's death!"

"And this is not?" she shouted.

"Okay." He paced, trying to think. "Okay, calm down. We have water, right? We have the blessing of Elyon. We are on a noble mission."

"Noble warriors are the first to die," she pointed out.

And so they were. Johnis lowered his voice and spoke quickly. "Okay, forget the noble part. We have water. We go in, take Alucard hostage, threatening him with only one drop of water; that's all we need. We march him out, and he leads us from the forest."

"On foot? It'll take us a day."

"Better than a day down here."

"He knows that if we kill him, Billos or Darsal will die. They have a vow."

"We don't know that they will actually die! That could be fable."

"Like the Roush are fable? Like the Shataiki are fable? Do you want to take that chance?"

"No. But he can be made to think differently."

As if in answer, a loud thump echoed down the stairwell. The outer door closed.

Metal clanged.

And now the door was sealed.

"Great," Silvie said.

Johnis turned back to the door leading in and pulled it wide. "That settles it."

Silvie hesitated, then he heard her feet moving across the wet ground.

# THIRTY-THREE

Darsal stood like a pole, refusing to look up at Karas. They'd hog-tied Karas the same way they'd tied Billos, then hoisted her up so that she hung like a bag of salt, belly down.

The girl was being brave, braver than anyone her age Darsal had met. Whether or not she really was her niece by blood, she was now a sister by a stronger bond. But even the bravest girl couldn't stop the tears that wet her pink cheeks.

Darsal had come expecting to give herself for Billos, only after convincing Karas to wait in the eatery with the books in the event she could set Billos free and would need a fast escape. But after agreeing, Karas had caught up to her at the edge of the temple and had offered a newly formed reason.

"Black wants the books," Karas had explained.

"So then get back there and guard them! Get out of here!"

"He'll take you in exchange for Billos, but you won't give him the books. So he'll kill you."

"You don't know that."

"I do, Sister. You're too principled to give him the books."

"Either way, there's nothing you can do. Now, get back!"

"I can't go back knowing that you'll die."

She had heard Billos crying out. They were running out of time!

"Please, I can't bear this!" Darsal had said. "Get back before I knock you out and drag you back."

"Then Billos will die," Karas had said. "My mind is set."

Billos had cried out again.

"Then you're a fool," Darsal had said. She had turned her back and was striding toward the temple, furious. But Karas had followed.

Now she hung like a hog to be slaughtered if Darsal didn't tell him where the books were. She had no choice. Say what she may, the young girl had grown on her.

"Okay!" Darsal snapped. "Let her down!"

"Where are the books?" Black asked.

"I'll show you."

The Dark One hesitated only a moment. He nodded at Claude.

"You sure? They killed Steve. We're owed."

Then the one named Black did something Darsal could never have predicted. His jaw snapped wide, twice as wide as she imagined possible, so that his chin slammed into his chest. Baring perfectly formed white teeth, he jerked his head forward and roared at Claude, who shrank back.

The man's jaw clacked shut. He stepped forward and lowered Karas.

"Show me," Black said.

Karas looked up at Darsal with round, apologetic eyes. Darsal marched forward, through the mob, around the corner. She scanned the village for a sign of Billos, but the weak-minded fool was nowhere to be seen.

According to Billos, Black needed them to find these books. Why, Darsal wasn't sure, but it gave her one final opportunity, however slim, to escape.

Then again, if Black kept her separated from the books, all hope was lost.

"I'm sorry, Sis," Karas said.

"Don't be."

"Keep your drums shut," Black said. "You can kiss and make up later."

Darsal led them to Smither's Barbeque and pushed the door open.

"That's far enough." The Dark One stepped past her, sauntered up to the bar, and turned around, wearing a sly grin. "Now. Come in, and keep your hands where I can see them."

She walked in, followed by Karas. Claude filled the doorway, long gun in hand. The rest stayed in the street, watching.

"Where are they?"

"You expect me to just give them to you?"

Black lifted his hand, and she watched it fill with a long gun with two barrels, stretched out toward Karas. "You expect me not to blow your little doll here all over the wall?"

He'd made his point. "How do I know you won't anyway?" she demanded.

"I'm going to count to three. One, two, thr—"

"Behind the counter."

"Get them out."

Black kept the gun on Karas, who stood too far away for Darsal to touch, no matter how well things went. And she wasn't going to leave the girl.

"Give me your assurance that you'll let us go if I give you these four, and I'll help you find the other three," she said.

"The other three? What makes you think I need your help?"

"Billos said you needed his help."

"To bring the four books to me from wherever they came. The rest was just to get his attention." The man smiled. "And for the record, the other three books aren't here. They're in the real world of Paradise. This"—he scanned the ceiling and walls—"is all a simulation of sorts. Real enough, but no flesh and blood. You're strapped in a chair at the moment, playing a game. The only way to enter the flesh-and-blood Paradise is through an open book. Unfortunately, once you do that, there's no going back. Ever."

What he was suggesting was nothing but a trick, of course. "If none of what I see is real, then neither are the books," she said. "They're useless."

"No, the books are outside all this. They're the only thing that *is* real here. Except me and your mind, that is. Which is why if I kill little Miss Muffet here, she dies. So it might as well all be real, *comprende?*"

She didn't *comprende*, whatever that meant.

"The books, if you would be so kind. Let's go on three again, shall we? One, two . . ."

The rear door crashed open. "Three."

*Boom!*

Darsal's breath caught in her throat. Billos appeared in the doorway and finished Black's threat. But the word hadn't left Billos's mouth before Black swiveled his gun and fired from both barrels.

A blast of heat swallowed her, from Billos's or Black's gun she wasn't sure at first. Light had blasted from Billos with that word, and it met the suhupow from the Dark One's gun head-on.

The light from Billos slammed into her, threatening to tear her clothes off. It rushed past her and smashed the glass from the eatery's windows like ten thousand fists.

Black stood in the face of the light for one moment, then grabbed his coat with one hand and turned into it. He spun and was gone. His last words echoed in the space he'd vacated.

"See you on the other side," he said.

The light collapsed back on Billos and winked out.

Darsal stared around, dumbfounded. The doorway where

Claude had stood was empty, as was the street beyond, she saw. Smither's Barbeque was gutted from inside out.

The light had simply and completely destroyed the darkness.

Billos stepped in, dripping wet, and stared at them.

"Well then," Karas said.

Somehow Darsal was certain that all this power would be gone when they returned to Middle Forest. The real question was whether Billos had truly changed.

A wry grin nudged his mouth. "Now, that's what I call power, baby."

Darsal strode to the counter, withdrew the four books, and plopped them on a table next to Billos—the only one left upright that she could see.

"Good to see you too," she said, looking up at Billos, who watched her with wide eyes, perhaps harboring remorse. Something had changed him, but that didn't mean she didn't have cause to be terrified by his behavior.

For the first time since entering the layer of reality that Black had insisted wasn't flesh and blood, Darsal remembered her sworn oath to Alucard. Perhaps she would soon have cause to be terrified by her behavior as well. They could probably leave this place by touching the books with blood, but then what? She didn't know.

The books were his by oath. Either the books or one of their lives.

"Let's get out of here," Billos said.

# THIRTY-FOUR

The library was empty.

Johnis and Silvie had rushed down the worm-infested tunnel and spun into Alucard's library, armed to the elbows with water, only to find the room vacated.

Silvie voiced the obvious. "He's gone."

Alucard was gone, but no fewer than a dozen shiny, thick worms slid along the walls of his lair now. The bookcase was wet with their mucus and the wall lumpy with their thick pink lengths. Johnis studied the leather-bound books in the case, ancient volumes that looked as though they hadn't been moved in a long time.

The flame on the wall spewed an oily smoke, crackling as it tongued at its own fumes. The only other sound was the soft clicking of worms sliding through their own paste in the tunnel behind them.

It occurred to Johnis that his thinking seemed to have slowed. He wondered if it had something to do with the air he and Silvie had subjected themselves to down here.

Silvie inhaled sharply, and Johnis followed her line of vision to a huge lump high on their right.

Alucard hung upside down by his feet from the corner ceiling. He was watching them with red glass globes, and his tongue was flickering at moist lips. Other than that he hung perfectly still, like a large cluster of rotten grapes.

Coiled around the beast's torso nestled a long, thick worm. Alucard's tongue reached for the mucus on the wall next to the worm, licked up a healthy portion, and withdrew the salve into his mouth.

All the while, not a word from the Shataiki. He seemed too distracted by his feeding or too smug in his confidence to react to their reappearance in his lair, which could only mean that his claim regarding Darsal's oath was indeed true.

"You've come back to kill me?" Alucard spoke around the slimy mucus in his throat, offering each word with delicacy. He followed his question with a long, low chuckle.

Silvie backed toward the desk opposite the hanging beast.

"Would you like some worm smack?" he asked, flicking his tongue out like a snake. "The blood of evil isn't red down here. Maybe if you drink, I'll give you safe passage out of my forest."

"So that we could return to burn it?"

"Burn it; I don't care anymore. This world is too restricting for me."

"And you think the world Billos and Darsal vanished to is waiting with open arms? You're condemned to hell, no matter where you go."

"I'm not interested in going where they went."

"Then what?"

Alucard closed his eyes and licked the mucus to his right with a long, slow, probing tongue. His mangy fur shivered with pleasure; a wet popping sound accompanied his swallowing.

His eyes opened red again, but he didn't answer.

"Kill him," Silvie whispered bitterly.

Johnis nearly flung the full contents of his bag at the Shataiki, knowing that something very evil had hatched behind those eyes. But there was more at stake here than Alucard's plotting.

"Darsal," he said.

"She made her choice. Our only way out is to cut the head off of this forest's power and get out while—"

"No. We can't leave without the books."

"You can't leave," Alucard said quietly from his corner. "With *or* without the books."

Johnis spun back, grabbed the gate, and slammed it shut. He shoved a bolt through the latch, effectively locking them in. "Our fate is yours," he said.

The bat chuckled. "I have all the food I need to live for a year down here. What did you have in mind?" He licked at the wall again. "It's quite delicious . . . once you get used to it."

Silvie spat to one side.

"Your water is useless now," Alucard said. "You'll see that. I promissssss."

"We have no choice!" Silvie whispered, but her voice carried all too well in the stone chamber. "He's bluffing about the vow! We have to take our chances now!"

Johnis rubbed his submerged fingers together, considering. But his mind wasn't working as quickly as it had only minutes ago. His vision shifted, showing doubles, and he blinked to clear his head.

"Maybe . . ."

Alucard was suddenly a blur, launching himself from his corner faster than Johnis could have imagined. Unless he *was* imagining it.

One moment the Shataiki hung dumb; the next he was behind Johnis with a single talon hooked around his neck, ready to slice his jugular.

"Am I a fool?" the Shataiki hissed.

A dozen options slogged through Johnis's mind. None of them were immediately useful. The creature was right: their water would only keep them alive so long. They were doomed here in this lair. The only thing they could hope for was to take this prince of darkness with them.

"And the books?" Johnis asked.

Silvie seemed to understand. "We'll have to leave the mission to Darsal and Billos," she said. Then she reached out and touched his hand. Her voice trembled when she spoke. "I love you, Johnis."

He glanced at her misted eyes. But he saw something behind her that made him start. Peering through the gate was a sea of red eyes. Not normal Shataiki, but larger beasts, like Alucard. A dozen were on each side of an even larger beast, who drilled Johnis with a glare that seemed to reach into his eyes, down his spine, and to his knees, which began to shake.

Teeleh.

Silvie saw his look and spun around. The sight of so many larger Shataiki staring with such purpose changed everything in Johnis's mind. It was as if the beasts had expected this. Or at the very least, they were taking advantage of a situation they knew could only end well for them.

"Kill me, and there are a thousand who would take my place," Alucard said.

"Kill him!" Silvie screamed, and flung a fistful of water directly at Teeleh.

The water hit his chest and sizzled. A few drops splashed onto the bat to his right; he began to tremble.

Johnis learned two things then: The first was that these Shataiki didn't die as easily as the smaller variety. The second was that Teeleh was hardly affected at all.

His mangy coat smoldered and quivered but otherwise showed no indication he'd been attacked. His eyes held steady, slicing through Johnis like bloodthirsty daggers. The Shataiki next to him was now shaking badly. *It can be killed with the water*, Johnis thought. But he didn't know how much it would take.

All the while Johnis remained still. The talon at his neck suddenly lifted from his skin, and Alucard stepped back.

"Clearer now?"

They had enough water to kill Alucard, and perhaps the bat had feared for his life to that extent. But even if they used all the water they had with them, they could never escape the lair.

Silvie was still staring at Teeleh with a mixture of disbelief and horror. The beast did not move, did not speak, did not breathe, as far as Johnis could see. It was as if he'd come only to observe and give his blessing. To what end, Johnis could not know. But he knew now that there was no good ending to this misguided journey. They'd survived once, but they would not survive twice.

"What do you want?" he asked.

*Johnis?*

The voice that spoke in his mind belonged to little Karas, whom he'd rescued. All in vain. She was now haunting him.

*Johnis!*

He turned to his left, from the direction the voice came from in his mind. In his mind's eye Karas stood, holding the four Books of History, each wrapped in red twine. She was staring with wide eyes past him at Alucard, clutching her treasure in both hands. And on either side of Karas stood Darsal and Billos, scanning the room with darting eyes.

Johnis blinked away the vision. But the sight of Karas, Darsal, and Billos remained stubbornly unchanged. Karas looked at him again. "What's . . . what's happening?"

They were real. Here. All of them. With the books.

*And this is why Teeleh is here,* Johnis realized. *For the books.*

# THIRTY-FIVE

Do your bidding," Teeleh said.

Alucard stepped around Johnis and slowly approached the trio, who stood unmoved. His wings dragged behind as he slogged forward, but Johnis knew better than to be fooled by the sluggishness of his movements.

He stopped when he was halfway to Darsal, so that they formed a triangle with Alucard at one point, Johnis and Silvie at another, and their comrades at the third.

"Give me the books," he said.

"Not exactly what I had in mind," Billos said, looking at the worms on the wall. "I think I prefer the white room with DELL."

"This isn't good," Darsal said, her eyes fixed on Alucard.

"You made a vow," the beast said.

Darsal just stared, but Johnis knew she had. They would now find out what that meant.

"You can't, Karas," he said.

"Then give me her." Alucard stretched one talon toward Darsal.

"No." The muscles in Billos's jaw bunched. "Over my dead body."

"Perhaps. But the vow was made over the books. You can't use the books to undermine that vow. They cannot help you escape me, to whom you owe your life."

The words hung between them like knives that would slash flesh before this engagement was over. The only question was, whose flesh?

Teeleh and his entourage breathed and peered from their right, undisturbed. Unflinching. Unchallenged.

Johnis looked at Darsal. The water in his fist was now nearly useless. He could slow Alucard, but to what end?

"Darsal, tell us he's lying," Silvie said.

She swallowed and shifted on her feet. "There has to be a way out," she said.

Karas gripped the books tighter. "The books—"

"Are mine!" Alucard finished.

"That wasn't the oath!" Darsal said. She'd snapped out of her indecision and glared at the beast. "The books or me, that was the deal, and you, too, are bound by that oath! Otherwise you'd have taken them already."

Her eyes switched to Johnis, and she spoke urgently. "Touch the leather skin on the books with blood and you enter a simulation between this world and another. Open these four and you enter another reality entirely. The other three books are hidden there, Johnis, sought by the Dark One."

"The Dark One?" Johnis glanced at Teeleh, who hadn't removed his stare. The beast knew all of this already.

"Marsuvees Black," Billos said. "The magic man."

It made Johnis's head spin, this business of realities. But in many ways it was like being able to see the Roush and the Black Forest here, while most of the world remained blind to them.

Beyond the skin of these books waited another reality, bristling with power.

Darsal stared at Alucard. Bitterness laced her voice. "So take your spoils!" she said, spreading out her arms. "But the books belong to them!"

"What are you saying?" Billos cried. "Not on your life. No, not a chance!"

Alucard's eyes settled on the books in Karas's arms. "Then you offer yourself in her place?" he asked Billos.

"No, he doesn't," Darsal said. "No, Billos, you aren't! That wasn't the vow I made."

"Actually, it was," Alucard said. "Either one of you. Dead."

"Stop it!" Karas cried. "Stop arguing about who will die! We don't know that he isn't lying!"

Her voiced echoed, then the room settled into silence except for the breathing that came from the Shataiki beyond the gate. Watching, ever watching.

"Then put it to the test," Alucard said.

"How?"

"Billos, do you accept the debt owed to me by Darsal?"

Darsal started to protest. "No, he—"

"Yes," Billos said.

"I accept your obligation," Alucard said. "You are now bound by the laws of the books and may not use them until you have paid your debt."

"Meaning what?" Darsal demanded, stepping forward.

"Meaning he can't use the books as long as he's alive. Unless, of course, you give me the books first."

"But . . ." She stared at Billos, then back at Alucard, lost for words.

"Show her, Billos. Open a book and see what happens."

Johnis jerked his hand from the bag and held it out without thinking of the water now dribbling to the floor. "No!"

The water hit the ground and sizzled. He'd nearly forgotten the power at his fingertips. But it wasn't enough now.

"No," he repeated. "We can't just open a book—"

"It's the only way out of here," Karas said.

She spoke the truth, and the Shataiki all seemed to know it. Then why were they standing by?

"Open the book, Billos."

He searched Darsal's eyes. They both knew that the books

might be Billos's only way to survive. If there was no way out through the books, he would be trapped here to face whatever fate the Shataiki found suitable.

"Open it," Darsal said in a thin voice.

Billos hesitated only one more moment, then reached for the green book on the stack of four in Karas's hands.

"The books have to be together to create the breach," Alucard said through dripping saliva, as if tasting a delicious fruit he'd waited his whole life to sink his teeth into. "Then the breach is accessed by any of the books until all four are gone. To return, a new breach must be created, using all four."

The breach he was talking about wasn't the same as the one that Billos had gone through. This gate opened by all four books would take them to a different place altogether: Earth.

"Are you sure this is a good idea?" Silvie asked.

Billos withdrew his knife and placed the blade on the string that bound the book. He looked at Johnis, who nodded.

The twine popped under the blade's sharp edge. Alucard held his ground. The room stilled.

"Open it," the beast said. His lips trembled with anticipation.

Billos rested one finger along the cover's edge, then lifted it open. Parchment browned with age faced them all.

But no magic. Nothing that indicated great power lay within. Not even words of another reality.

"Cut your hand. It needs blood."

Billos sliced his palm. Blood seeped from the wound.

"Put your hand on the page," Alucard said.

Billos's hand hovered above, then lowered to the open page. He let it rest there for a moment, then lifted his eyes.

"Nothing."

A coy smile twisted Alucard's lips. "You see?"

"Silvie," Johnis said. "Put your hand on the book."

"Yes, Silvie," Alucard said. "Enter the book."

Silvie glanced at the gate, then looked into Johnis's eyes. "If something happens—if I go somewhere—you'll come. Promise me."

"I promise."

She handed her water bag to Johnis, walked up to the book, cut her own palm, and unceremoniously placed her bleeding hand on the same page Billos had tried.

Only this time something did happen. This time the space where Silvie stood was suddenly spinning, as if she had become a funnel of dust, swirling in color, fading fast.

Johnis stood rooted, shocked at the sight of her transformation. The book began to suck her in.

"Do your bidding," Teeleh breathed behind them.

If Johnis had not been holding two bags, he might have been able to slow Alucard enough to prevent what happened next. The Shataiki streaked to the books with the same speed he'd shown earlier, slicing his palm with a talon as he moved.

Silvie vanished into the book just ahead of him, but Alucard reached them before Johnis could move, and he dove into the swirl that had swallowed Silvie.

The green book disappeared in a small flash of light.

Silvie and Alucard were both gone.

The sound of breathing behind the gate thickened. For a long moment no one in the room moved. The ramifications of what they'd just witnessed seeped in.

One, the books worked.

Two, a way of escape had been opened to them.

Three, where that escape would lead them was completely uncertain.

Four, Alucard had succeeded in his objective.

Five, Billos might as well be dead.

Talons grated on the gate. Johnis jerked around to see that two of the large Shataiki were opening the latch.

"Go!" he screamed, rushing forward.

"Billos?" Darsal reached for the man she loved.

Billos stepped up to Johnis, snatched both bags of water from his hands, whirled to Darsal, and kissed her on the lips.

When he pulled back, his eyes were fiery with determination. "Go!"

"Billos?"

"Go, Darsal. Never forget me."

"No!" She barged forward, grabbed one of the bags from his hands, and faced the coming Shataiki. She flung some water at them and they recoiled, smoldering. But the only cry was hers.

"I stay with you!"

"Darsal, no! Take her, Johnis!"

Johnis snatched one of the books from Karas and shoved it into Darsal's belt. "Use it!" he snapped, then turned back to Karas.

Working quickly, he popped the twine and threw the cover open as Karas did the same to the book in her hands. He sliced his palm, then hers when she hesitated.

"Ready?"

She glanced up at him with wide eyes, then Johnis shoved his palm flat on his book.

The world spun and then vanished. Johnis clenched his eyes tight, aware that he was suspended, but only for a moment before his feet felt solid ground.

Light exploded through the red in his eyelids. When he opened them again, he was standing in a desert. He blinked against a sun that hung overhead, white, blazing hot.

He was in a desert, but also on a plateau, overlooking a massive valley filled with a gray haze. Spread in the valley below was what looked to be a forest of sorts. Leafless trees of assorted shapes and sizes reached for the sky. Square, triangular, cylindrical . . .

No, not trees. This was a city. One that dwarfed the Horde city.

"Johnis?" a voice asked.

Johnis turned slowly and stared at Silvie, who was looking at him with wide eyes. She rushed up and threw her arms around his neck, rushing her words. "I was so worried . . . What took you so long? . . . I've been here for hours . . . I thought I'd been stranded!"

"Hours? It was less than a minute."

"No, no." She kissed him on the mouth. "Thank Elyon you're safe. I was sure I'd been sent to hell all alone."

Her whole body trembled against him, like a quivering puppy in his arms. He'd never seen her so upset. She pulled back, her eyes filled with tears. "I'm so afraid, Johnis. I don't know what's wrong with me."

"Shhh . . ." He kissed her forehead. "I'm here now. It's going to be okay." He glanced at the rise to their left.

Silvie followed his gaze. "I found a large placard over the hill. Big letters announcing a place named Las Vegas. But I couldn't bring myself to go any farther."

Silvie looked back into his eyes, then glanced about.

"Where are Karas and Darsal?"

# THIRTY-SIX

Darsal knew the ending of their predicament already, and she accepted it with surprising calm. They would both die in the bowels of the Black Forest. But at least she wouldn't have to live without Billos. After all she'd been through to win him back, she wasn't going to leave him, never again.

Johnis had vanished, and then a few moments later Karas as well, leaving Billos and Darsal with the last book tucked in her waist.

"Back!" Billos cried, shoving her behind him as he flung a great handful of the water toward the gates.

Teeleh had vanished during the commotion, leaving only his henchmen to attend to his interests. Two of them lay writhing, claws clacking on the stones, but otherwise silent. No screaming from this bunch. They'd evolved beyond the common shrieks of lesser Shataiki.

The gate flew wide and filled with a red-eyed beast clearly intent on reaching them. Darsal stepped up and flung the entire contents of her bag on the fellow. The Shataiki stood still, skin smoldering and melting in parts. He slowly backed out, shaking head to foot.

Billos sprang forward, slammed the gate shut, and threw the bolt home. He flicked more water on the gathered Shataiki, then even more, pushing them away.

He jumped back, face red. "You have to leave, Darsal. You know you have to leave! Now, before the water's gone. It's just a matter of time."

His words cut like knives. "I can't, Billos." Tears blurred her vision. "I won't leave you again! Not now."

She felt her back hit the wall. Wet mucus from the worms seeped past her tunic, but she didn't care.

Billos pressed in close. He glanced to see that the Shataiki were closing in on the gate again, then set his bag down and faced her. There was no way to lock the gate properly—the beasts would be in soon enough to face another round of water until it was gone. And then they would have their way.

Billos took her hands in his. "Listen to me, Darsal."

"No, I can't. I won't; you can't ask this of me!"

He grabbed her face firmly, then softened his grip. "Listen to me."

His eyes bore into hers, and for a moment she lost herself in the stare of the man who'd saved her as a child and protected her a thousand times since. This man whom she loved more than she loved her own flesh.

They could say that Billos had abandoned them for his own gain. They could say that he thought of no one but himself. That he was a bull among clay pots. More muscle than heart, more passion than brains, more sword than sense.

He would as soon kill a woman as kiss one, they could say. As soon beat her in a race as marry her.

But Darsal knew the real man bearing down on her now. This was Billos, the mad, passionate adventurer who made her laugh in times of peace and rage in times of battle. He'd given her life, and she'd made him the man he was today, faults and all.

Indeed, it was the fact that he was flawed that made her, a deeply flawed woman herself, so comfortable with him.

"You are my life, Darsal." His voice was soft but urgent. "I made my choice to—"

"You had no right," she cried.

He took a breath and started again. "I made my choice days ago, weeks ago, years ago. Those choices ended today in the lake I told you about, remember?"

He'd told her before they'd touched the books with blood in Paradise. Whatever happened there had been the stuff of mind-bending reality, whether they were seated in chairs hooked up to DELL or not. It was as real as any of this.

Billos had been changed in Elyon's lake.

"The lake gave you life! How dare you consider death now!"

Claws clacked on the gates. The bolt slid slowly back. The Shataiki were wary, but coming.

"Because this part of my life is over. There is no more for me. Except you." Billos touched her face gently, traced the scar on her cheek. He leaned forward and touched his lips to hers.

Darsal felt as though a sledgehammer was trying to force its way up her throat. Her shoulders shook in silent sobs.

He spoke through the gentle kiss. "I love you, Darsal." His breath was hot on her mouth. Musky and sweet. She longed to taste it the rest of her life. "Live so that I can die knowing I've saved you. Please, I beg you, I beg—"

"No!" Darsal cried, placing her hands on his chest and shoving him away. Then leaning into a scream, "No!"

She grabbed the water bag from him, marched up to the gate, and sent the Shataiki reeling with a huge splash. She slammed the gate, shoved the bolt down, and spun back.

"You can't do this to me . . ." But her voice faltered. Then she couldn't speak for the fist in her throat. She stood limp, shaking with terrible sobs. Darsal felt his arms pull her in, and she fell into his chest willingly. For a long moment he just held her, drawing his fingers along her back as she wept into his neck.

Behind her the gate began to rattle again. The Shataiki were coming, and this time there wasn't enough water to push them back.

The book pressed into her waist where Johnis had shoved it.

Billos spoke frantically. "You have to tell Johnis everything! The white room and Paradise were only a reflection of reality, like a game. A skin or a book's cover. But the real Paradise exists. On Earth. Marsuvees Black is the Dark One. Three of the books are hidden on Earth, but with these four all seven will be on Earth and will be visible to anyone. You have to tell Johnis."

The bolt was sliding.

"He knows! It's not a reason—"

"*I'm* the reason!" Billos shouted. Then he spoke softer, his eyes reaching beyond her to the gate. "Live for me. We'll open the book and touch it together. If I am meant to go with you, I will."

She didn't feel like she could move. The gate squealed. Billos grabbed the book from her waistband, popped the red twine, and flipped it open before her.

"For me," he said.

Darsal looked into his eyes. He was asking her to do this for him. It was the last thing she would ever do for him. But she loved him too much to deny him this one dying request.

She leaned forward and kissed him hard. Then pulled back and set her jaw. "I love you desperately, Billos of Southern. You are my chosen one."

A grin tugged gently at his right cheek. "I am, huh?"

He winked. Then he shoved his hand on the opened page.

Two thoughts crowded Darsal's mind. The first was that the Shataiki were breathing down her neck. The second was that Billos wasn't disappearing.

He suddenly grabbed her hand, sliced it open, and flattened it against the page. "And now I choose you."

Darsal made another vow then, her hand on the book. *I will avenge your death, Billos. I will wage war on all who caused you to die until the day of my own death.*

Then her world spun and blinked to black.

# THIRTY-SEVEN

Johnis and Silvie stood on the cliff, silenced by the sheer size of the hazy valley before them.

A sea of towering buildings, gray from this distance, had been built between ribbons of flat rock that crawled with horseless buggies. Whole structures looked to be as large as all of Middle under one roof. The city below would make the Horde city seem a village by comparison.

"What do you think?" Silvie asked, voice tight.

"I think I prefer the Horde."

Silvie looked at the two Books of History under his arm. "This was a mistake. We're down to two books. We don't even know if Karas and Darsal made it through. How are we supposed to find all seven books in this place cursed by Elyon?"

"You think Alucard is here?"

She didn't respond. Her hand took his and tightened. Not out of affection, he knew, but because she knew more terror now than she ever had and needed a hand of comfort. Johnis knew this because he, too, felt . . . fear. More fear than was reasonable.

"We made the right choice, Silvie." But even as he said it, doubt skipped through his mind. "We're here to find the seven books before the Dark One does. We'll do that or die trying."

"Spoken like the good old Johnis we all know so well." She said it with a bite of frustration.

"Something's wrong with us," he said. "I don't feel myself."

"Really? You just now noticed?"

He returned his attention to the valley. A dull roar rose from the city. "So . . . where are we?"

"I told you," Silvie said. "We're in hell."

# CHAOS

## LOST BOOK 4

# BEGINNINGS

Oour story begins in a world totally like our own, yet completely different. What once happened seems to be repeating itself thousands of years later.

But this time the future belongs to the young, to the warriors, to the lovers. To those who can follow hidden clues and find a great treasure which will unlock the mysteries of life and wealth.

Thirteen years have passed since the lush, Colored Forests were turned into desert by Teeleh, enemy of Elyon and vilest of all creatures. Evil now rules the land and shows itself as a painful, scaly disease that covers the flesh of the Horde living in the wasteland.

The powerful green waters, once precious to Elyon, with the exception of seven small lakes surrounded by seven small forests, have vanished from the earth. Those few who have chosen to follow the ways of Elyon are now called Forest Dwellers, bathing once daily in the powerful waters to cleanse their skin of the disease.

The number of their sworn enemy, the Horde, has grown, and the Forest Guard has been severely diminished by war, forcing Thomas, supreme commander, to lower the army's recruitment age to sixteen. A thousand young recruits have shown themselves worthy and now serve in the Forest Guard.

From among the thousand, four young fighters—Johnis, Silvie, Billos, and Darsal—have been handpicked by Thomas to lead.

Unbeknownst to Thomas and those in the forests, our four heroes have also been chosen by the legendary white Roush, guardians of all that is good, for a far greater mission, and they are forbidden to tell a soul.

Their quest is to find the seven original Books of History, which together hold the power to destroy humankind. They were given the one book in the Roush's possession and have recovered three more. They must now find the other three books before the Dark One finds them and unleashes their power to enslave humanity.

Although the full extent of the power contained in these sealed books is unknown, the four have discovered a few disturbing facts about them: They have discovered that only *four* of the seven books exist in their own reality; the other three are on Earth, made invisible until the day when all seven are united. They have discovered that they can cross to Earth using four of the books together. And they have discovered that the Dark One who seeks the seven books to enslave humanity is not in their reality but on Earth.

In keeping with their mission, Johnis and his companions have used the four books to travel to Earth, where they must now find the final three books before the Dark One does.

But Earth is not a nice place to go looking for books.

# ONE

Johnis and Silvie stood on the cliff, silenced by the sheer size of the hazy valley before them.

A sea of towering buildings, gray at this distance, had been built between ribbons of flat rock that crawled with horseless buggies. The city was constructed of structures that looked to be as large as all of Middle Forest under one roof. The entire Horde city looked like a village by comparison.

"It's called 'Las Vegas,' you say?" Johnis asked.

"That's what the sign by the road said," Silvie responded, her voice high-strung. "What do you think?"

"I think I prefer the Horde."

"It is the Horde! They've conquered the world and turned it into rock."

"You know this?" he asked, astonished. "I thought Thomas

went into the Histories, not the future. This looks more advanced than any Histories I could imagine."

Johnis glanced at the two Books of History in his hands. "We're down to our two books. We have to assume that Karas and Darsal made it through with two more. And that the three in this reality are now visible. But how do we find them? They could be scattered anywhere."

"Forget the books for now," Silvie cried. "We have to find Karas and Darsal first."

"Of course," Johnis said, pacing, "but our mission is to find all seven books, and all seven are now in this reality, visible, ready to be found. We have two; Karas and Darsal have two; that leaves the last three—only Elyon knows where—in this cursed place."

"You think Alucard is here?"

She reached for his hand and held it in her own. Not out of affection, but because after hours alone in this unnerving place she needed to be close to someone. To him.

And judging by the slight quiver in his hand, Johnis needed comfort as well.

"I'm afraid, Johnis."

"We made the right choice, Silvie." But his voice was filled with doubt. "We're here to find the seven books before the Dark One does. We'll do that or die trying."

"Spoken like the good old Johnis we all know so well."

"Something's wrong with us," he said, looking at her. "I don't feel like myself."

"Really? You just now noticed?"

Johnis returned his attention to the valley. A dull roar rose from the city. "So . . . where are we?"

"I told you," Silvie said. "We're in hell."

She tilted her head up at the sound of a distant roar. A huge white bird with fixed wings soared through the blue sky.

"Dear Elyon, look at the size of that thing." Johnis grabbed her hand and pulled her toward the boulders. They vaulted over one and came to a stop in the shade of several larger rocks. "I've seen them all day," Silvie said. "We've been spotted by now."

Johnis looked skyward. "They're birds?"

"If the buggies are ants, then maybe those monsters are birds," she said, sliding to her seat. "Either way, they can't possibly be good. If they're the enemy, which we have to assume, they can't be beaten, not by us."

His soft brown eyes searched hers, his mind spinning behind the fine features, messy brown hair, and high cheekbones. If there was one person who would remain strong in the most difficult situation, clinging to principle and all that was right, it was Johnis. He'd proven that over and over again.

"I need you, Johnis. I'm . . . I'm lost. My emotions seem to be getting the better of me."

Johnis removed his eyes from hers and looked about, dazed.

"Maybe this is what happens when you vanish from one reality and reappear in another," she said. "What if all our innards didn't come through right?"

Johnis stood, withdrew his knife, and twirled it once. Then again, twice this time. Silvie was the master with knives, but he performed the maneuver with surprising ease.

"Our bodies seem to have come through in one piece," he said.

Silvie jerked out two of her knives, flipped them into the air in perfect symmetry, caught them by their blades, and flung them at a dead log with a flip of her wrists. They plunged into the wood with scarcely a splinter to separate them.

"You haven't lost your skill," Johnis said. "You've searched these cliffs?" he asked, pointing absently at the mounds of rocks and hills.

"Every last mole hole."

"No sign of Darsal or Karas."

"Or Alucard," she said. "Or Billos."

"Time," he said, facing her.

"Clearly it's not a consistent thing."

He nodded. "I left only moments after you and appeared hours later."

"For all we know, Karas has been here for a month," Silvie said.

"And if we're in the Histories Thomas spoke about, we've gone back in time perhaps thousands of years."

Silvie retrieved her knives and slipped them into sheaths on either thigh. "None of this helps the situation."

"No, but it gives us a starting point."

"Darsal and Karas," Silvie said. If she hadn't spent so much time looking for them already, she might share some of his enthusiasm. "Like I said—"

"We have to get into that city," Johnis interrupted, looking east.

She instantly noticed the boyish look that suddenly brightened his eyes. "Not before we understand what we're getting into."

He jerked his head to face her. "No, now. While we still have a chance of finding Karas and Darsal. Before they end up in captivity . . . or worse."

"What makes you think they went into the city?"

"Where else would they go?"

"We are not going into the city without a plan that makes perfect sense to both of us," Silvie said. "We don't have the third fighting group to sacrifice this time."

It was a low blow, but he let the accusation roll off his back.

"You said you saw one of their roads over the hills?" he demanded, turning south. "How far?"

"A half-hour walk, right over the large knoll. But I don't want to rush off without feeling better about this. Not after last time. Please, we can't just walk down the road in our battle dress, climb to the top of their tallest tower, and scream for Darsal and Karas to come out of hiding."

"I do have a plan," Johnis said, with a slight grin. "Are you with me?"

"What plan?"

"Part of the plan is that you trust me. Are you with me?"

Silvie was surprised by the sudden comfort his confidence brought her. And to be perfectly honest, she did trust him. Almost as much as she loved him.

"Will we live to tell?" she demanded.

"I have no idea."

She paused, then walked past him toward the road, guessing his plan started there. "Something is definitely wrong with us."

"RIGHT OVER THE KNOLL," SILVIE HAD SAID. BUT THE ROAR from the road announced its presence loudly enough.

Johnis hurried up the last part of the hill, bent over in a crouch. Standard battle guards made of leather covered his forearms and his thighs, but he preferred a blue tunic rather than the chest protectors that many of the Forest Guard wore. A month ago this young man had never seen a sword swung in battle. Now his forearm and calf guards were scarred from head-to-head confrontation with Horde.

Seeing him scramble up the knoll ahead of her, Silvie was struck by his transformation in such a short time. His skin was darkened by the desert sun, highlighting cords of muscle in his legs and arms. He might only be sixteen, but he looked much older now—in her mind he was the best of any man she'd met.

She had opted for a dark leather skirt with thigh guards. Her blonde, tangled hair was drawn back to clear her eyes. Wide wristbands broke the line between her well-toned arms and her small hands. "Delicate," Johnis called them once. Never mind that they could wield any weapon with more power and accuracy than his, which weren't large by any unit of measure.

They both wore the same leather boots that had taken them into the Black Forest on two occasions now.

"Slow down," she'd demanded ten minutes earlier.

"I'll slow down when I can make sense of this world," he had said. "We're losing light!" And he had been right; the sun was setting.

"Don't rush into another trap."

That had slowed him some, but now he could hardly control his enthusiasm. He scrambled up the sandy slope that rose above the road and flung himself to his elbows at the top. Silvie dropped in beside him and looked at the road below.

A wide road built of black stone ran over the desert, split by a straight white dash. A building with a large black and red sign marked by the word TEXON stood on this side of the road, and two of the buggies were situated next to what looked like upright feeding troughs.

Having drunk its fill, one of the buggies pulled out onto the road to resume its journey.

"Dear Elyon," Johnis muttered.

Silvie glanced at him and saw that his jaw hung open. His eyes weren't on the feeding station, rather on the road beyond and on the speeding buggies that flew over the road on wheels that looked like they were floating.

"It's magic!" Johnis cried.

"Or worse," Silvie agreed.

"But they aren't animals. They're made out of solid material. I've never seen anything like it!"

"What did I tell you? They look dangerous."

"That's never stopped you before."

He said it without even looking at her, perhaps hardly hearing himself, but the words pulled Silvie into a different world. One in which she would be the first into battle, screaming to avenge her mother's death, urging Johnis to swing his sword.

In this world she was evidently more cautious. She wasn't sure she liked that.

Johnis watched a red buggy approach from their right, then fly past. "It's five, six, maybe seven times faster than a horse at a full gallop. Who in their right mind would walk?"

"We'll kill ourselves."

"It's their land. We do things their way, as we agreed," Johnis said. "If the Horde . . ."

One of the Horde suddenly appeared from a car and walked to a large green garbage receptacle. For the first time, Silvie saw one of history's inhabitants closely enough to make out some detail.

Long golden hair. Blue trousers that hugged the young woman's body. A pink shirt. White moccasins. But it was the woman's face and arms that made Silvie blink as she watched.

There was no trace of disease on her skin, which meant that this particular inhabitant from the Histories was not Horde.

"She's not diseased," Johnis whispered.

They watched her dispose of her garbage and climb into a brown buggy, then speed from the feeding station. Toward the city.

"It's not a Horde city!" Johnis said, pushing himself up in such a way that anyone below would have clearly seen him above the rise, had they been looking.

Silvie grabbed his shoulder and pulled him back down. "That means nothing. They could be the precursors to the Horde, just as evil. Or a different kind of Horde. For all we know, they carry their disease under their skin."

"True. But having the same skin makes blending with them all that much easier. We have to get our hands on a buggy!"

"Our battle dress doesn't blend."

"Then we change!" Johnis faced her, eyes bright. "You could wait here and cover my back. If I'm not successful, we'll try another approach."

"What is your approach?"

He remained silent for a few beats, then jumped to his feet. "Cover my back."

# TWO

Silvie raced along at Johnis's elbow, down the slope and directly toward the feeding station, aware with each step that her nerves were raw beyond reason. She felt more fear than she'd felt facing Teeleh himself.

Still Johnis strode on, as if he'd been here a dozen times.

"You're good, Johnis?" she whispered.

He didn't turn or answer. If it was the air that was affecting them, they would both feel it. So much for simple explanations.

"Johnis? Are you sure this is the best solution?"

He turned and she saw that his face was pale, not by the waning light, but for lack of blood. "I'm good," he said, but his voice trembled.

She took a small amount of comfort from their unity in despair.

He slowed to a walk, pulled his tunic straight, and headed for the stables. The sign bearing the word TEXON stuttered and came to life, glowing red and white and black. Silvie caught her breath and stopped. *Is it a warning?*

She instinctively crouched. "We've been seen!"

Johnis halted, staring up at the sign. Then plowed on.

Silvie hurried to catch him. She took his elbow, wanting to be close. He might find some comfort in showing his bravado, but she had lost her stomach for it. Ice ran through her veins, chilling her in the face of a gently hot desert breeze.

And then they were there, next to the building, with flat gray rock under their feet and a perfectly smooth glass wall before them. They could see plainly into the lighted building, where an attendant surrounded by hundreds of brightly colored boxes and tubes and bags stared back at them.

A stack of folded papers sat just inside the wall. THE LAS VEGAS HERALD. JUNE 7, 2033. Then in huge letters across the top: DROUGHT.

Johnis and Silvie stood immobilized by the wonder of such perfectly formed surroundings. The squareness and roundness of everything was breathtaking. The light was magical.

"He sees us," Silvie said, her voice cracking. "He looks like a warrior!"

Johnis began to move toward a door made of the same glass.

"Johnis, we want the buggy, not him! Don't for a minute assume he's not a throater."

"We can't just take the buggy with him watching," Johnis snapped. "Maybe he'll give it to us."

And then he was pulling the door open and stepping inside the building. Silvie released his arm and followed him past the glass door.

They stood at the entrance, side by side, facing the attendant, who didn't seem too surprised or put off by their presence. He stood taller than they did and was at least twice their weight. His head was bald and a black goatee hung off his thick chin. Tattoos ran up from each elbow and disappeared beneath a light blue shirt, then coiled up the sides of his neck and around the back of his lumpy skull.

This one had seen his share of fights. Silvie's heart pounded, but the fact that this tattooed slugger with blue eyes wasn't reaching for a sword under his counter was only a small relief.

She removed her fingers from the bone-handled knife at her waist when she saw his eyes flitter to it.

"Pardon two wearied travelers," Johnis said in his most polite voice. "We've lost our horses to the desert and need a buggy to finish our journey to the city."

The man just stared. He wore silver earrings in each lobe. No indication that he was a Scab beyond the fact that he looked to be a bit stupid.

"Can you help us?" Silvie asked. "Or are you just going to stare at us?"

She felt Johnis's elbow in her ribs.

"This look like the Excalibur?" the man asked evenly. "We got gas; we got junk food. Buy what you need and take a hike."

Johnis glanced at Silvie. Evidently encouraged by the man's nonsensical response, he stepped in and took on an air of supreme confidence.

"We would fit in at the Excalibur? How is that?"

"You're gladiators, right? So buy what you need and go die somewhere else."

"Our mission is beyond the talk of fools and commoners," Johnis said. "Not that you look like a fool or commoner—far from it."

"You deaf?" The man wasn't interested in whatever Johnis was trying to serve up. Neither was Silvie.

Johnis snatched up a rectangular package marked *Snickers*, ripped it open, and stared at the brown square exposed. He sniffed what looked to be a food bar. "We're quite hungry," he said, then shoved the food into his mouth and bit deeply.

The bald man didn't budge.

Johnis smacked his lips and took another bite. "Oh! That's simply . . . Oh, dear Elyon, this is fantastic!" And by all that Silvie could see, Johnis was truly enraptured with the brown food in his fist. "Try it!" He shoved the bar to her.

Back to the attendant: "You wouldn't happen to know about the Books of History, would you?"

Judging by the man's stone face, he was either a complete imbecile or he was so unprepared for Johnis's arrogance that he had lost track of his thoughts. He was the kind who thought with his fists.

"Johnis, I really think—"

"I thought not. If you hear anyone mention the Books of History, tell them Johnis and Silvie are alive and well and wish to meet with them. In the meantime, we need a buggy. Can you help us?"

Beat.

"What about the red one on the far side of the feeding station? It looked unused to me."

"The Chevy? It's a car, not a buggy." The man's lips twitched into a barely discernible grin. "You have no idea how close you are to a slap upside the head. And I doubt the boss would have a problem with me taking care of a couple of fruits trying to steal his little cherry while he's in LA."

"Perfect! We'll take the cherry Chevy. Have you had a go in it?"

"Look—"

"No, you look, you thick-headed fool! I'm going to throw you a bone here, but you have to go with me. We may look like fruits to you, but there's far more meat between these ears than you are used to. If you play with us, you could walk out of these stables a rich fellow. That doesn't interest you?"

Johnis had lost his mind. Silvie knew what he was trying, but she had no confidence he would succeed. She inched her hands to the blade at her side.

"Now, tell me if you've ridden the Chevy," Johnis said before the man could respond.

"The Chevy—yes."

"Good. Then making it go can't require too much intelligence. I'll make you a bet: one gold coin says I can make the Chevy go and leave you standing by your feeding trough before you can stop me."

Johnis pulled out a roughly hewn gold coin from his pocket, one of five he had on him. Thomas had instituted them as one form of currency in the forests after nuggets of the soft colorful metal had been found in the river near Middle and claimed by the Guard. The chosen had each received twenty coins upon their return from the desert with the Catalina cacti.

He flipped the coin through the air. It landed on the counter with a loud clunk, bounced once, and toppled next to the throater's hand.

The man exchanged looks with both of them, then picked up the coin. Bit it. Eyed them again. Perhaps Johnis's ploy was working after all. Thomas's words during fight school rang in Silvie's ears: "When you deal with a throater, put on the skin of a throater. They are too stupid to respect anything other than arrogance."

"Real gold," the man said, placing the coin on the counter. "You do realize that this one coin is worth more than that Chevy out there. What makes you think I shouldn't just take this from you now?"

"Because you know that something's not normal with us. We're smaller than you and have half your muscle, but we act as though we can wipe the floor with your guts. And we act that way because we know it's true. Show him, Silvie."

A dozen thoughts raced through her mind. She grabbed one out of thin air and put as much bite behind it as she could muster.

"I don't want to hurt the poor fellow," she said.

Johnis, who now stood a step ahead of her, turned back, and for the first time she saw that his face was red. "Show him. Or do you want me to show him?"

He was furious. Anger was pushing him to confront the man.

"Show him how?" she asked.

"With your knife. Cut off one of his earrings or something! Or should I do it?"

"You'd miss and rip out his cheek! Why the aggression toward me? I've done nothing!"

"Then just *show* him! We walk in here and make a simple request in good spirits, and he treats us like we're dogs!"

Silvie was right: Johnis's entire ploy had been born out of rage toward the man, not some crafty ploy to persuade him. He'd risked their necks because of his need to satisfy his anger?

"How dare you!" she snapped.

"What? How dare I what?"

"You're more interested in making a point with this fool than protecting me or finding the books."

She could see by his sudden stillness that she'd connected with him. For a moment they just stared at each other.

"Sorry," he said. Then to the tattooed man, "Sorry, she's right. If you'll just show us how to ride the Chevy, we could save you the pain of learning what a mistake it is to cross Johnis and Silvie—or any member of the Forest Guard, for that matter."

The man's face remained fixed for a moment; then a hint of smile nudged the corner of his mouth. "You guys are a real trip." The smile flattened. He flipped the coin back toward Johnis. "Out. Now."

The doorbell clanged, and a visitor walked in, eyed them once over, dropped what appeared to be two square leaves on the counter, and walked out, not bothering to give them a second glance.

"That's the feed for these steeds?" Johnis asked.

"Look, enough's enough, dude. You've done your crazy show, now hit the road before I lose my good nature. Don't push it."

But they'd already pushed it. It would be a mistake to retreat without playing this hand to the end. Regardless of why Johnis had pushed things this far, he'd been quite brave. Silvie plucked the coin from his hand and walked gracefully up to the counter, aware of the man's eyes on her as she approached him.

She smiled and held the coin up between thumb and forefinger to keep his eyes from wandering. "Answer a few questions and you can keep it. Just a few questions and we leave. It's worth your while."

She winked.

The man's blush was nearly imperceptible. Silvie set the coin before him and leaned on the counter.

"My lover is right, you know," she said, wanting to make it clear that she was taken. She withdrew her right knife and twirled it in her fingers. "We can do a few things."

814

And then, so that he would remain off balance, she whipped the blade toward Johnis with a hard flick of her wrist.

The knife flashed through the air, severed a single lock of hair next to his right ear, and thudded into a carton with the phrase *Diet Coke* printed boldly on its side.

A brown liquid spewed at the tip of the blade and pooled on the floor.

"What's your name?" Silvie asked the man.

"Ray."

"Well, Ray, I think Johnis wants to know how to make one of these car things go. Isn't that right, Johnis?"

"Yes," Johnis said, walking up to the counter. "Tell us that and you can keep the coin."

"You guys are serious? You don't know how to drive?"

"We throw knives, we kill Scabs, we put fools in their place, but we don't drive," Johnis said. "Not yet."

Ray humphed, picked up the coin, and rounded the counter. "You're both nuts."

He led them from the station, explaining that the "feed," as they called it, was actually gas, and the buggies, or more properly "cars," had motors that made them run as long as you kept the tank full of fuel. He showed them how to operate one of the upright feeding troughs, called a "pump."

Johnis took it all in with supreme confidence, though Silvie doubted he was retaining as much as he let on. Then again, he seemed completely taken by the whole business.

When they approached the red Chevy parked next to the station, his eyes stared like a spider's and his jaw remained slightly parted in dumb wonder. Silvie was more taken by his reaction to the contraption than by the car itself.

"Fantastic!" Johnis breathed, stepping lightly around the car. "Cherry Chevy. How long have they been around?"

"Chevys? You can't be serious. You guys really haven't seen a car before? You grow up in a monastery in Tibet or something?"

"Something like that." Johnis held out his hand. "How old is this one?"

"2008."

"Can I touch it?"

"Long as you don't scratch it. The boss has won his share of races in this. Modified. I'm a Harley guy, but I don't mind saying she's a beauty."

Johnis let his fingers run along the dark red skin. "Fantastic. It's like silk!" Silvie followed his example, impressed by the hard shell. She was still more fascinated by him than this cherry.

The attendant opened the doors and let them both sit inside, talking them through the "fundamentals of driving," as he called them. "Insert and turn the key to start it, like this. Put it in Drive. Most street racers are manual, but Joe likes the automatic. That's the brake to stop it. That's the gas to make it go. You steer with the wheel."

"Fantastic!" Johnis stared at the wheel in his hands, ran his fingers over the workings on the black dash, kneaded the leather-wrapped gear stick. It was enough to make Silvie jealous!

"Okay, come on, that's it. Out. I have a customer."

Johnis crawled out, then stuck his head back in and took one last long look. "Where's the key?"

"That wasn't part of the deal. You mess with this car and you'll be sorry you were ever born. In case they didn't teach you this in Tibet, knives don't do too well against shotguns."

The man left them at the door, and they headed behind the building.

"Come on," Johnis said, running back up the hill. He slid to the ground over the top of the hill and spun back on his elbows, giving him a full view of the Texon station below.

"Now what?" Silvie demanded, dropping in beside him.

"Did you feel that skin, Silvie? The smell of the leather, the smooth lines of that body—"

"It's a mechanical beast, not a woman!" she whispered.

"I *have* to have this Chevy!"

"There are hundreds—"

"No. I have to have the cherry Chevy." Johnis tried to explain, stumbling over his own words. "It's a dangerous thing, this driving . . . This is the only car I've touched . . . I know where the levers are . . . It's calling me, Silvie." Then in a stern voice, "We have priorities. We have to get to the Books of History, for the love of Elyon! We're wasting time here!"

He jumped to his feet.

"Where are you going?"

"Wait for me by the Chevy. I'll meet you there."

"No, Johnis, not without me. You can't leave me!"

"I have to get the keys! Meet me by the Chevy!"

"He has a shotgun . . ."

Johnis plunged over the slope. "What's a shotgun? I need that Chevy!"

And then he was racing down the sandy hill.

# THREE

N o change?"

"You speak as though I should know more than you. I expected more considering your power."

"The moment you stop watching the girl is the moment you become useless to me. Is this difficult to understand?"

"Forgive me," she said. "Meeting here, below the earth, among the dead in Romania, affects my judgment. No change."

He held her in a steady glare.

"And the others?" she asked.

"They'll show up eventually. When they do, I have a feeling the whole world will know about it."

"How so?"

"They're not the quiet type."

"Foolish."

"No, *chosen*," he said. "Which makes them as dangerous as they are loud."

"Then we'll just have to shut them up, won't we?"

# FOUR

Silvie crouched beside the Chevy, peering through both windows at the gas station's front entrance. The doors to the car were locked, but even if she'd found them open, she wouldn't have dared to enter the small space alone. Johnis might have found a new love in this Chevy, but to her it was still a pile of leather and metal and strange smells, finely crafted or not.

"Come on, Johnis," she muttered. Her nerves had her fidgeting like a young girl. He'd been gone too long! "Come on, come on! I knew it! He's in trouble."

She had to do something. Silvie stood and was about to run for the glass door when it slammed wide and spit Johnis out in a full sprint.

A horrendous boom shook the air, and the glass door shattered.

Johnis's feet slid on the flat concrete as he spun through his turn. Then he was pelting for her, arms pumping like batons.

The Chevy chirped like a bird, and Silvie jumped.

"Mount it!" Johnis cried. "Inside, get inside!"

Silvie jerked the lever that operated the door, flung the contraption wide, and piled in. The car had unlocked on its own?

Ray rushed from the station, bearing what appeared to be a long stick. A shotgun. If the weapon in his arm was responsible for the shattering glass, they were in trouble. Her knives were worthless in such a tiny space!

She nearly dove back out, but Johnis was there, jerking his door open. "He won't harm the Chevy!" he screamed. "You can't put a scratch on the car, can you, Ray?"

The shopkeeper used the shotgun again. Twin blasts of fire belched into the air, chased by a thundering volley. But he'd held the weapon high.

"Don't touch it!" he roared. "I'll fill your backsides so full of lead you won't be able to stand straight."

Johnis dove in and slammed the door shut. He fumbled with a small metal object, searched for the hole that Ray had pointed out earlier as being the ignition.

"I ran into some trouble," he panted.

"Really? And it doesn't look to be over."

"He won't hurt the car."

"He's coming . . ."

The man was storming toward them, shotgun cradled in his arm.

"He's coming, Johnis!"

Johnis wasn't having luck with the key, so he pulled it back and pushed at several small buttons on a black knob attached to the device's metal portion.

The car suddenly chirped again and the locks *clacked* shut.

Johnis looked at her, unable to hide his smirk. "Fantastic . . ."

A hand slammed on his window. "Out!" the tattooed man thundered. "Get out before I blast this door open!"

"He can't! He won't!" Johnis ignored the man and went back to work on the key, this time with more deliberate concentration.

Ray was cursing bitterly, but Johnis was right; he couldn't risk damaging the car. They were safe in this cocoon—for the moment. But they would face even greater danger when an overzealous Johnis got the contraption moving.

"This doesn't look good, Johnis!"

"He's a stubborn thug!"

"What were you thinking?"

The man stood outside the car, voice muted, message clear.

"You're dead meat! You can either get out now, and I might send you off with a good kick in the behind. Or you can make me go back in for the other set of keys, but if I do that, I'm going to take it out on you. You hear me?" He slammed his palm against the window to drive his point home.

Silvie felt like a small child cowering under a monster. "He's got another set of keys?"

The man whirled around and stormed off, leaving a trail of furious words behind him.

"He's got another set of keys! Stop fumbling with that thing and get us out of here!"

"I'm trying, but I can't see . . ."

She grabbed the key from him, lined it up as she saw it must go, and slid it into the hole. Without a second thought, she twisted the key as their instructor had shown them earlier.

The Chevy roared and she jerked back.

Music boomed, louder than she could bear. Not just any music, but the sound of a man screaming, as if the musician was trapped in the motor and was protesting in no uncertain terms.

"Turn it off!" She jabbed at the buttons and controls on the dash. "Stop it!"

Her knuckle must have hit something right, because the music halted as abruptly as it had begun.

Johnis sat frozen. Both hands hovering over the steering wheel, enraptured or terrified or both.

"Here he comes!" The man was running back toward them with a key dangling from his right hand.

Johnis dropped his right hand onto the shift lever and jerked it back. The Chevy started to roll.

He gripped the leather wheel, knuckles white, staring ahead like a shocked monkey.

"Faster!" she cried, seeing the man close on them, sprinting now.

CHAOS

"Careful, careful!" She jabbed her finger at the building to the right. "Watch the stable. Don't run into the hill! Watch—"

"Silence!" Johnis shouted. "I'm trying to drive the Chevy!"

The man was on top of them, banging his palm on the window, cursing obscenely in words that made no sense to Silvie— but she understood the language of his red face clearly enough.

He used the shotgun again, jolting them both.

"Faster, faster!" They were going no faster to escape this monster than if they'd taken a leisurely stroll.

"Okay, okay!" Johnis leaned back, took a quick look at the levers on the floor, then pressed one with his foot.

The Chevy stopped abruptly.

"The other one!"

The car surged forward, effectively silencing them both. Like a rock flung from a slingshot, they sped across the ground and past the stables, heading directly for the sharp incline behind the station.

It was dark, but the moon was full, and Silvie could see clearly enough the metal fencing between them and the hill.

"Stop, stop; turn, turn!"

But Johnis did not stop. He'd frozen, like a boy on his first rope swing, swaying beneath the tall trees near Middle.

"Johnis!" Silvie grabbed the wheel and jerked it hard.

The Chevy spun wildly to the right. Its wheels squealed in protest. They narrowly missed a head-on collision with the fencing and were now racing beside it.

825

"Let go; I have it!" Johnis cried. Another fence cut across their path ahead, and seeing it, he yanked the wheel as Silvie had done.

The Chevy spun again, but this time it didn't stop spinning. Johnis kept the wheel turned, forcing the car into an arc that filled the air with smoke.

The force shoved Silvie against him. "Straighten!"

Johnis flung the wheel in the opposite direction. The Chevy shot forward, this time headed for the upright pumps . . . and the red-faced attendant standing in front of the pumps.

"Stop!"

"No, no!" Having mastered the skill of turning the Chevy, Johnis opted instead for pulling the wheel to his left. They blasted by the man, who had thrown himself to the ground. Another car was entering the station, and Johnis narrowly avoided a collision.

So he could turn the thing, but could he stop it? Silvie felt her own feet instinctively smashing into the floor, wishing to slow the contraption down.

"Slow down, please! You're going to get us killed!"

"He's back there . . ."

"You're headed for a ditch! You have to stop. Stop!"

But it was too late. They slammed into a shallow ditch, bounced over the other side, and ripped through a fence she hadn't seen. Then they were on a bumpy, hard-packed dirt path instead of the flat roads of rock that the other cars seemed to prefer.

Johnis shifted his foot to the second lever and pushed. They came to a sliding halt. Dust floated past them.

Silence.

"Fantastic!"

Silvie punched his arm, furious that he'd put them in this predicament. "This isn't a child's game! Stop it with the 'fantastic' every other moment!"

"But you have to admit: it's like riding a hundred horses at once. Imagine going to battle with the Horde in one of these."

"There's no room to maneuver your sword."

"We'd use a shotgun."

They looked at each other, then twisted back for a view of the station. Sure enough, the shotgun-bearing man named Ray was already halfway across the station in a full sprint.

"Fool," Johnis said and shoved his foot on the gas lever. The Chevy spun its wheels in the dirt, then shot into the night.

Johnis managed to keep the car on the path, careening from side to side as he wrestled the wheel. But they were speeding away from the station, and that was good for Silvie.

"You can stop it if you have to, right?"

"Sure." To demonstrate, Johnis hit the brake, and the Chevy went into a slide that piled them both up on his side.

"See?"

"Does this thing not know the meaning of gentle? This whole world appears to be violent."

"Don't be ridiculous. She can glide like a feather if I tell her to."

"Now it's a she?"

Johnis took off again, this time slowly at first, then gaining speed as they bounded down the road.

"Put her on the proper road and she will glide, I can promise you that," he said breathlessly. "Fantastic, I'm telling you. Mind-blowing."

"Just drive safely. Keep your eyes on the path. Why does this one not have lamps to guide us, like the other ones?"

"Start punching buttons and you'll find them. But then we'll be seen."

He had a good point.

"They'll be coming for us, you do realize that?"

His face lost some of its boyish delight. "Yes. But we have the Chevy, and we have the night. It's a good start, Silvie."

"It could also be a good end."

# FIVE

The moon stood over them, round and bright, watching their every move. They'd brought the car to a stop a hundred yards off the dirt road in a shallow, sandy wash that protected them.

Johnis led them both in a detailed exploration of the Chevy by moonlight, and now, out of harm's way, Silvie found herself caught up in his excitement.

They'd run through a whole gamut of exercises in an attempt to find the lamps on the Chevy and succeeded in triggering everything but. The music, the rear compartment door, sticks that presumably cleaned the front window, lights that blinked orange, even a loud horn that sent Silvie diving for cover when Johnis leaned on it.

If they were going to venture onto the big road with the other Chevys, they had to use their lamps, no question. Johnis was bent over the front, looking for an exterior switch that might ignite them, when Silvie twisted the lever that moved the window cleaning sticks when pushed.

Twin lights blazed into Johnis's face.

"Ahh!" He jumped back and threw his arm over his eyes. The light reached past him and illuminated the sandy slope beyond.

Slowly Johnis lowered his arm. A broad grin split his face. "Yes! You've done it!" He twisted and stared at the far-reaching beams. "Fantastic! Look at that, will you?"

Silvie jumped out, ran to the front, and leaped into the dazzling shafts of light. "Whoo-hoo!" She grabbed his hands and they danced in a circle like children, carrying on as if they'd just heard news that the Horde had laid down their swords for good.

"What did I say?" Johnis cried.

"I don't know, what did you say?"

"I don't know, but it's fantastic."

"We made it." Silvie stared into Johnis's eyes, smiling wide with him. "You were right, my handsome warrior. We've crossed the worlds and taken the enemy's treasured Chevy from under his nose, and now we've conquered it."

"Yes, we have."

Their dancing slowed.

"I owe you my life," she said.

They were only partly serious in this mood of frivolity, but the nature of that mood was shifting quickly. They circled each other, arms stretched, hands clasped.

"I owe you *my* life," Johnis said.

Silvie felt her stomach lighten, her heart swell. The world slowed around them.

"Did you mean what you said?" Johnis asked. "To the attendant?"

The statement about him being her lover had stayed in the back of Silvie's mind, but not until now, staring into his eyes, did she understand how much she longed for the statement to be true.

"Should I have meant it?" she asked, sliding her hands up his arms.

The last of Johnis's smile faded. His boyish charm was gone, replaced by a gaze of deep longing. His eyes swallowed her, like windows into a new world—a world that could be a sanctuary of perfect peace and love.

He stepped into her arms and enfolded her in his embrace. His head tilted slightly to one side, and he pulled her to himself. His soft lips pressed lightly against hers. Then he bit her lower lip tenderly, and she felt her mind spin.

This was Johnis, the man who had led her into terrible danger, to the brink of death, alongside impossible odds, for the sake of love and loyalty—the chosen one who'd never faltered or strayed from the way of his heart.

This was the man she'd fallen madly in love with. Having that love returned now sealed her own longing. Silvie pressed against him and passionately returned his embrace. They kissed long and tenderly, hearts pounding against each other's chests.

Other sixteen-year-olds in Middle were joining in marriage, but she and Johnis had crossed worlds to find their love. And nothing could possibly be sweeter. When she pulled away from him, she half-expected the night to have passed, but the sky was still black, and the Chevy's lamps still drilled the darkness with its two beams of brilliant light.

Johnis was breathing steadily. He smiled and drew her close again. "I've dreamed of that longer than you know."

"You have?"

"From the moment I saw you fighting over the Horde ball in Middle, I wondered what it would be like to kiss you."

"Then it's not just the air here?"

"No," he said and kissed her again. "Definitely not, although the air does seem to loosen things up a bit, doesn't it?"

"Just a bit." She smiled, and they kissed yet again.

A thumping sound joined her heart, like a muted drum in the sky. The sound jerked her back to earth.

"What's that?"

They scrambled to the top of the knoll on their right and saw the source of the beating—a bird or flying car, moving across the horizon slowly, shining a light onto the road they'd traveled. Lights from cars racing toward the city stretched out along the big road beyond.

"They're looking for us!" she said. "They'll see the lamps!"

Johnis spun and raced back to the car. "How did you ignite them?"

She slid into the seat next to him and turned the lamps off. "Now what?"

"They're following the same road we did. We wait for them to pass us, then head back in the dark, join the other cars on the big road, and take the Chevy to Las Vegas."

Silvie thought about his plan, which sounded more like a vague notion than a reasoned course of action. But she felt emboldened with the taste of his lips lingering on her own.

"Assuming we survive the other Chevys and make it to this Las Vegas, then what?"

"The attendant mentioned an arena for fighters called the Excalibur. Dangerous perhaps, but I think we would fit in. We start there. And we find Darsal and Karas before the Dark One does."

"Assuming Alucard hasn't found them already."

THE BIG ROAD WAS A NIGHTMARE IN THE MAKING; SILVIE could see that much as Johnis angled the Chevy down the strip that merged with cars racing east.

He'd learned to maneuver the car fairly well on the dirt road, but his confidence was challenged by the sight ahead: not the road but the other cars.

"Lights!"

He ignited them, then pulled out onto the road. A horn blared behind as a car swerved to avoid running up their backside.

"Patience!" Johnis snapped at the passing Chevy.

"Easy, just keep us on the road. Ignore them."

"How can I? They're traveling like lightning past us. I have to speed up."

He fed the Chevy more gas, and they flew down the road. Another car blasted them, blaring a rude horn, and Johnis took his speed even higher. Cars were still passing them but not as if they were stopped. Slowly his confidence returned, and he increased their speed.

The next fifteen minutes raced by without event. The road was flat, straight as an arrow. But the moment they crested the last hill and caught their first close-up view of the city called Las Vegas, the complexity of their journey increased tenfold.

For starters, the number of cars seemed to have doubled without warning, forcing Johnis to concentrate on all sides, careful not to run into a slowing Chevy ahead yet staying in front of the impatient Chevys behind. He repeatedly braked hard, then zoomed forward with enough suddenness to tear an unprepared passenger's head from his shoulders.

"Slow down!"

A horn blared behind.

"And be run over?" Johnis muttered angrily and swerved into the space to his left, then shot past the car that had slowed before them. He shook his fist at the man as he sped by.

Two minutes later the same car drove past them, its rider glaring angrily.

"You see what happens when you lose your patience?" Silvie snapped.

"He's a menace!"

The increase in cars was made even more complicated by the sheer magnitude of the city they approached. Las Vegas was lit up like the stars, only far brighter and brimming with red, blue, and golden hues that shone like jewels.

The enormity of it all made it hard for either of them to keep their undivided attention on the Chevys around them.

The roads widened, and soon thousands of lights streamed by on all sides. The city of lights. How would they ever find this festival called "Excalibur"? But none of this prepared them for the final complexity that suddenly altered their relatively successful experience in the Histories thus far.

"Lights, everywhere lights," Johnis cried. "I can't see straight for all the lights. Now red and blue lights on top of a Chevy are riding our tail. We have to get out and find our bearings."

Silvie twisted in her seat and saw the car behind them, red and blue lights flashing on its roof. The driver . . .

She gasped.

"What?"

"He's a warrior. In uniform! He . . . he's motioning us to the side!"

"You're sure?"

A *blurp* sounded from the car, a horn of some kind, but this one didn't end. It wailed, rising and falling in a sound that sent chills down Silvie's spine.

"They're looking at us," Johnis said.

"Who is?"

"Everyone!"

And drawing aside, Silvie saw. Not unlike herding hunters pulling wide to give the archer plenty of space for a shot at the prey.

"He's after us, Johnis!" Panic swelled through her mind. "Go! Run for your life! Get us out of here!"

The Chevy surged forward. Johnis whipped the car around a white one and left it to deal with the hunter behind them. As if they needed any confirmation that they were indeed being hunted, the Chevy with flashing lights veered around the same white car and closed quickly.

"Dear Elyon, help us!" he cried and wound the motor higher.

"Faster."

"I'm going faster!"

"It's a race car; make it race!"

Johnis set his jaw the way he had heading into the Black Forest and the Horde city or a dozen other occasions when he'd thrown caution to the wind in favor of principle.

Gripping the wheel with both fists, he swerved first to the left around a third car, then all the way across to the right, racing past the Chevys as if it were now they who were standing still.

"Careful . . ." Silvie cut herself short, thinking that he was actually mastering the Chevy with surprising ease.

The hunter behind had been joined by a second, both wailing as they gave pursuit. "Never mind, go! There!" She pointed at a large green sign that read LAS VEGAS BOULEVARD.

Johnis swerved for the road under the sign and flew down the slope, blaring his own horn to warn the slowing cars to move out of his way.

An obstacle they hadn't yet seen presented itself ahead: red lights hanging over the road. A dozen Chevys had stopped under them as if facing an invisible wall.

"Johnis . . ."

"Navigate!" he cried. "We can't stop; the hunters are gaining. Find a hole, tell me . . ." His intense concentration stopped him, but she knew that he was right. They were in a Horde city from the Histories, being hounded by two warriors or hunters who undoubtedly meant to kill them.

If they were to survive and go after the books . . .

"To the right!" The opening was narrow, between two cars, and she couldn't see beyond, but it was the only gap she could see.

"Over the lip?"

"What lip?"

Johnis shot for the gap to their right, and Silvie saw Johnis's "lip" then: a thin fence bordered the road, then gave way to a cliff beyond.

"Johnis!"

But Johnis was flying faster. They cut the car on their right off, forcing its rider into a squealing brake. It was all a blur now, and Silvie threw her arms up to protect her face.

The Chevy hit a curb and launched up, nose high in the air. Then they were airborne.

"Hold on . . ."

"Dear Elyon, save us!"

They sailed ten yards and landed level with a horrendous crash, bounced once, then flew forward on spinning wheels.

They'd survived?

Unscathed, it would seem, but the car was now screaming directly for another line of cars stopped beneath a line of hanging red lights.

To this point Johnis had managed to maneuver the Chevy down the mountain and into the city without touching another car. Seeing the line, Silvie knew that would now change. She braced herself for the impact.

Johnis whipped the wheel to his left, slammed his foot on the brake, then released it and applied more gas. The Chevy went into a broad slide, then abruptly straightened, flying past the line of stopped cars.

Horns blared. The Chevy missed all but the last car, which was pulled out halfway through a right-hand turn.

"Watch it . . ."

The impact came along Silvie's door, a loud clash of metal against metal. Sparks flew. More horns blared.

And then they were through, up over a curb, clipping a tree trunk, and back on the road.

Clear.

"You okay?" Johnis asked.

"Yes. We did it?"

"We caused a ruckus. They all stopped, but they'll be after us, that's for sure."

The rising and falling horns of the warriors in pursuit wailed through the Chevy's carriage.

"By the sounds of it, a whole horde of them are after us." Silvie tried to calm the trembling in her hands but failed to.

"I think we should leave this car."

"No, no, no, we can't leave the Chevy. It's . . ." Johnis's eyes darted about, blinking at the towering lights by the road, then behind in the mirror. "You're right. You're right, we're too obvious."

Silvie settled enough to take in the lights that rose on both sides—an incredible display of reds and greens and every color of the rainbow. Massive squares the size of whole buildings were painted with moving faces and pictures.

She couldn't make sense of anything she saw. Terrifying.

"Fantastic," Johnis muttered.

Silvie twisted back and saw not one, not two, not four or six sets of flashing lights, but a dozen, racing up the empty road behind them.

"We have company."

"We have to leave the Chevy. I see it; hold tight."

Johnis whipped the car to the right through a crossroad that led to a massive pyramid structure. The sign read EXCALIBUR.

"See what?" Silvie demanded, looking back to see if the warriors had seen them make the turn.

"Excalibur. Hold on!" Johnis jerked the wheel hard, throwing her into the door. The car careened into a dark alley. They clipped a large green bin and slid to a stop. He killed the motor and extinguished the lamps.

The motor ticked in the sudden quiet. He looked at Silvie, eyes wide, face beaded with sweat.

"What do you think?"

The warriors' Chevys wailed with increasing intensity.

"I think they saw us turning," Silvie said.

They moved as one, each shoving open a door and scrambling out. The wailing from the cars in pursuit was now on top of them. Johnis grabbed her hand and pulled her into a sprint down the alley—away from their Chevy.

Toward the Excalibur.

# SIX

The Excalibur was built like a castle, with red and purple spires lit brightly against the black sky. Massive. Everything in the Histories was colossal. And as brilliant as a colored sun.

They ran side by side, their feet pounding with the roar of the city—noise, noise, everywhere noise! It was as if sun had been captured by the Horde and was now hooked into this city called Las Vegas. The burning smell was enough to make Silvie blanch, though she suspected the odor came from the cars, not the buildings.

They saved their breath, but Silvie was too astonished by the sights and sounds and smells to speak intelligently. Having been stranded in a strange world only to find company in such frightful things as warriors screaming about in Chevys and mountains of lights that flashed overhead without pause, she was a twisted knot of mangled nerves.

She grabbed Johnis's hand as they approached a flight of stairs leading into the Excalibur and pulled him to a stop, barely winded despite their fast run.

A steady river of people flowed in and out of a dozen glass doors. They stood on the landing between the Excalibur and Las Vegas Boulevard, breathing hard.

"Good night! You ever hear so many sirens?" a large redheaded man exclaimed, facing the street. "That ambulances or police?"

"Cops," said a shorter fellow wearing a sleeveless tunic and baggy shorts. "Some crash has the traffic piled up at Tropicana."

Johnis pulled Silvie forward, then released her hand and took steps two at a time. Silvie glanced back and saw no immediate threat. Their best option was to enter a crowd and lose themselves. The authorities knew the city and would quickly cut off any avenue of escape. But if they could lose themselves inside the hunter's net while they came to terms with their predicament, they stood a strong chance of slipping through that net later.

If they were to take Ray, the bald gas man, at his suggestion, they should fit in at the Excalibur. *Smart*, she agreed. But seeing Johnis rush up the steps now, she wasn't sure they would fit in. None of the other guests wore battle leather or tunics similar to their own. Boots clacked on the stone behind her, and she twisted back to see five blue-suited warriors running past a fountain fifty yards away.

"Johnis . . ." She bounded up the steps and passed him near the top. "They've seen us! Hurry!"

They spun through the doors into a world even more frightening than the one outside: hundreds of machines situated in long rows, green-clothed tables, lighted wheels. The sheer number of people and the horrendous crash of bells and gongs made her head spin.

"Excuse me."

Silvie turned to her right. A warrior in a brown shirt, bearing a club and a weapon in a waist sheath.

"Knives aren't permitted in the main casino. You'll have to take the fighter's entrance on the west side."

Silvie crouched and touched the knife on her right thigh. The warrior's demeanor changed the moment her fingers made contact with the bone handle. Had she made a mistake?

For a moment neither of them moved. And then the guard lifted a black box to his mouth and issued orders. The man waited a second, and the box spoke back to him: "On our way."

"Follow me!" Johnis whispered.

He ran over a soft red floor, woven cotton perhaps, past what he now saw were gaming tables, not so different from the more rudimentary betting cages that some of the Forest Guard played to waste their time between battles.

"Stop!"

Johnis flew through the aisles, and Silvie stayed hard on his heels. They raced the full length of one aisle before he cut sharply to his left and ran directly into a long table surrounded by eight players.

He could have stopped in time to avoid a collision, but in this state of anxiety dove over the table, landed on his hands, and rolled to his feet.

So Silvie dove as well. With all of her might, she launched herself into the air, soared ten feet, and landed on her hands as he had. She rolled to her feet and plowed into Johnis.

He staggered back a step, but his eyes were on the table. Stunned by what they'd just done with surprising ease.

"After me." He sprinted to his right, glancing up. Silvie now saw what had caused him to turn in the first place: a sign bearing a warrior dressed in fighting leathers, armed with a sword.

CLASH OF THE GLADIATORS

They'd lost the guard and whatever reinforcements had come to his aide, and they'd done so with surprising speed. But Silvie didn't have time to dwell on this small accomplishment at the moment. They were like two rats on a king's banquet table; expecting to dash around from dish to dish without being soundly smashed and fed to the dogs was the stuff of fancy.

Johnis ducked into a hallway marked by the CLASH OF THE GLADIATORS sign and slowed to a fast walk. Silvie glanced back down the aisles as they rounded the corner. Three guards raced into the aisle a hundred yards behind.

She leaped into the hall. "They're still coming!"

The hall they had entered was bordered with several white doors marked by lighted signs that made no sense to her: AUTHORIZED PERSONNEL ONLY. The hall ended at a red wall with a large picture of a stately looking fellow wearing a crown on his head.

"Find an open door." Johnis was already trying the handles.

"It's a dead end, Johnis!" She stepped across the hall and tried two of the doors—both locked.

The guard's boots pounded down the aisles.

"Johnis!" she whispered. "This is nothing! We have to get out of here!" Panic crowded her throat. They were trapped rats!

Johnis tried the other doors and found them all locked. Silvie grabbed his elbow. "We're going to have to fight them." She flipped a knife into her left palm. "If it doesn't go well, I want you to know that I love you. I always have."

The door behind them suddenly flew open, and a short, fat man with ruddy cheeks and cropped blond hair that had tinges of red in it held the door wide. He looked surprised to see them.

"Gladiators?"

Johnis hesitated only a moment, then shoved Silvie forward. "Finally!"

They hurried past the man into a dark hall that ran to a lighted door. "All participants use the west entrance, man," the fellow said after them. "Second door on your right." Then he dipped back out the door, leaving them alone.

From somewhere to their left a crowd roared. They looked to be in the innards of the building, behind the arena—this Clash of Gladiators. But for the moment they were safe.

"Did they see us?"

Silvie didn't have to answer. Muffled cries reached them from beyond the door they'd just entered. "This way! This way!"

Johnis and Silvie ran down the hall, flew into the second doorway to their right, and slid to a stop in front of a long row of uniforms.

"Dress, hurry!" Johnis dashed to the line of battle dress and quickly shrugged into a red cape.

There were three things that all Forest Dwellers held in the highest regard, things Thomas of Hunter, their supreme commander, reminded them of often: their ferocity in battle, their gentleness in love, and their enthusiasm in celebrating at the end of a long day of both.

The celebrations consisted of all forms of song, dance, and the spinning of tales. And playacting brought it all together.

"Is this for real or is it a game?" Silvie asked.

"This, or that?" Johnis indicated the crowd's roar from beyond the walls.

"That," Silvie said.

"Killing for mere sport seems a bit barbaric, but this is the Histories."

"Then this costume is ridiculous. Are we doing this to blend in or to fight? Because it won't help our fighting."

"I have no intention of fighting," Johnis said, pulling on a metal helmet. "Hurry."

Silvie threw on a cape like his, then a large metal helmet that covered her head like a gong. If they did get into a fight, the first order of business would be to ditch it.

"Good," Johnis said, looking her over. "It'll slow them down."

"And us," she said.

"Just till we get out of here."

He led her quickly through the armory. Leather and metal fighting dress. Knives and mallets and swords. Enough armor and weaponry to outfit a whole division.

Silvie snatched up a sword and spun it in her hand. A long steel blade with a handle formed from wood. Not the best craftsmanship, and the blade was duller than she liked, but the balance was decent. For the first time since entering the fireball called Las Vegas, she felt a measure of confidence.

Johnis grabbed a sword and rushed forward without bothering to scrutinize it. Silvie had spent some time showing him the finer points of swordplay, and he was improving rapidly, but the lust for battle wasn't what made Johnis great.

He tried a side door, found it open, and ducked in. Silvie followed him into what turned out to be a small white room with half a dozen stall doors and a row of white stone basins. Mirrored glass hung on one wall, reflecting them in their red capes and helmets.

"A bathroom." Johnis's voice echoed.

"Clearly."

They stood undecided for a few breaths. The guards would now be coming through the armory. They were running out of time. Only one reasonable option.

"Hide!"

Silvie was halfway to the row of stalls when the main door pushed open. A man dressed in black slacks and a black shirt with a face that looked too long for the tuft of hair perched on its crown snapped at Johnis. "Enough heaving, man, it's getting started."

Then he saw Silvie, who stood facing them both. A grin twisted his white cheeks. "Oh, I get it. Save it for later, man."

"She comes too," Johnis said.

"You wish. Let's go."

They could either play along with this dimwit or take him out and face the guard. Clearly they should do the former.

"Wait here," Johnis said to her. "I'll be right back."

"What? What are you talking about?"

He stepped closer and spoke in a hurried hush. "They're coming! We can't risk a disturbance. We have to blend. Hide in the stalls; I'll break away as soon as I can."

"Johnis!" The thought of separating from him filled her with a bone-jarring dread. "I can't!"

"You have to!"

He spun back to the man who was plastered with a knowing grin. "Okay, let's go."

She watched him walk out. The man with the long face winked. Watched the door swing shut with a *whoosh*. And all the while she could not move.

Johnis had left her.

The sound of running boots reached her from somewhere in the armory. *He was right; if we'd tried to make a run for it, we would have run into the guard.*

The sound of the cheering crowd swelled. *Johnis doesn't know what he's getting himself into!*

Rushing water swirled in the stall on the bathroom's far side. *I'm not alone.*

# SEVEN

The moment Johnis stepped into the doorway, he realized that he'd walked into a trap.

They walked onto a field similar in some ways to the stadium in Middle where they'd played with the Horde ball. Where challenges were made and fought. Bright lights lit an arena fifty yards in width. At the center rose a platform and a gallows. A circle of twenty warriors stood at attention around the platform.

The stands were filled with thousands of onlookers who'd gathered for the fight. An earsplitting roar swelled as the door behind Johnis closed. "Fight, fight, fight, fight! Kill, kill, kill, kill!" The chant rose to a crescendo.

He instinctively backed into the door, tried the handle, and found it locked. The walls that surrounded the arena rose ten feet before meeting rings of benches that ran the arena's circumference. No doors, no halls, no ladders.

This wasn't good. He'd left Silvie, knowing that the guards were looking for two people who didn't belong. Making a fuss in the bathroom would have only attracted attention. The guard had rushed past the bathroom just behind him. So his play had bought them a breath or two.

But none of this calmed his heart.

"It's a good day to die," the man said. He stepped behind a tall gate, locked it, and walked into a booth with bars.

When Johnis looked back at the platform, the warriors were spreading out in two lines. A quick glance around told him three things that were now as unbendable as the ground itself: One, the crowd was here to see someone fight. And perhaps be killed. Two, that person was him, unless his logic was failing him totally, which could be the case. He'd felt inordinately stupid since his arrival in the Histories—fast on his feet and full of passion but slow in his mind and as jittery as a trembling mouse crossing a table in broad daylight. Three, the crowd *would* see him fight and perhaps be killed because there was no avenue for escape that he could see.

A fighter dressed in black from head to foot, wearing a tight-fitting black hood, stood tall on the platform and clapped his hands three times. The crowd fell silent.

The executioner's voice rang out: "Prisoner, you have been found guilty of fleeing justice and giving aid to the enemy. As is mandated by law, you have been sentenced to death. As is also permitted by law, you may either be hanged by the neck at the gallows until dead, or you may fight to prove your innocence in mortal combat with twenty of the king's guards. Which do you choose?"

*Neither,* he tried to scream, but his throat remained closed.

"Has the cat nipped your tongue, prisoner?"

Laughter rippled through the crowd.

Johnis stepped forward, weighing his options, which were few, perhaps even nonexistent, in this death chamber. He could try to confound them and buy some time, but doing so would only give the guard more time to find him.

Or he could fight.

His limbs felt numb. This was it, then. He'd crossed the worlds to face his death in a chamber of bloodthirsty, scabless Horde—

Unless . . .

"I choose to speak to the king!" he called out.

"That is not an option."

The warriors he was to fight now stood in rows of ten on each side. The executioner motioned them forward, and they began to advance.

"Then you will have his wrath!" Johnis circled to his right. "I am his cousin, and to kill royalty is death."

His announcement stopped them cold. But not out of fear. Confusion at his audacity, more likely.

He picked up his pace, closer to the soldiers on his right and farther from those on his left. *Better to take them head-on, a few at*

*a time, than broadside, where the whole mass can club you to death.*
Silvie had learned the tactic as a child, and had also taught him.

"There's been a mistake! I am not sentenced to death. I was kidnapped on my way to the lake . . . by the Horde . . . who then forced the Chevy that was carrying the prisoner off the road and put me in his place!"

His voice echoed to silence.

"Is that so?"

"That is so! Send for the king; he'll tell you."

Johnis wasn't about to think his nonsensical little tale would earn him any more than a few seconds if the executioner had any wits, but he needed every advantage he could get. His mind spun, considering the odds of his survival in sword fight with twenty warriors.

None.

So what was he to do, kill as many as he could and then take a sword? He hadn't come to the Histories to die in an arena, mistaken for whoever they thought he was!

"You care to entertain us with your stories, is that it?" The executioner demanded, unable to hide the humor in his voice. He spread his arms to the crowd. "What is your verdict? Fight or flight?"

"Fight, fight, fight, fight! Kill, kill, kill, kill!" They'd done this before, in perfect unison. The Horde from the Histories didn't drown their prisoners as the Scabs in his world did.

They forced them into a death match for sport or hung them from the neck until dead.

Johnis tossed his sword far to one side. The crowd stilled to the snap of a twig as the blade arced gracefully through the air and landed in the dust with a dull slap.

"Then let me take any one man, give him a sword, and let me fight him bare-handed," Johnis cried. "If I win, let me go free. Or is that too much for the Horde from the Histories?"

A lone spectator yelled raw from the top of the arena. "Fight the bugger!"

"An entertainer for sure," the executioner said. "Well? Do we have a taker?"

From the far end a single warrior, twice Johnis's size in both thickness and height, stepped from the line and walked out into the open.

He ripped off his helmet with a thick, gnarled hand and dropped it into the dust. "I accept."


SILVIE CONSIDERED TEARING FROM THE BATHROOM THE moment she realized that someone else was in the stall—the party Johnis had been mistaken for.

But now she was alone, and the guard would be intensifying their search. It would be better for her to hide in one of the stalls until Johnis returned, assuming he would. The thought sent a chill down her back.

Silvie stood frozen in a moment of indecision, staring at her mirror image—a red-caped warrior with a ridiculous helmet that was suffocating her. She could hardly see in the thing! So she ripped it off.

*Move, Silvie!*

She'd taken two steps toward the nearest toilet when the far stall door flew open and a warrior dressed in a red cape stepped out, cleared his throat, and spit to one side. She knew by the widening of his eyes that he hadn't expected to see her standing here looking at him.

"Wrong bathroom," he said.

What was she to say?

"Ladies across the hall."

"Sorry."

His look of shock gave way to a thin grin that snaked over a scarred face. His head was shaven clean, but the helmet he held in his right hand was identical to hers. And he, like she, wore a red cape. He was comparable to Johnis only in his smaller size—she could see how they might be confused for one another—wearing helmets hides their features.

"I didn't know they were going to execute a lass today."

"They're not," she snapped.

"No, you just dressed up like a prisoner for the thrill of it, eh?" Now he was wearing a wicked, yellow-toothed smile that tempted her to slap him hard. Instead, she opted for keeping calm. There were still boots thudding past outside.

Another thought dawned. They'd taken Johnis, thinking he was a prisoner to be executed!

"It's all a mistake." She fought to keep her nerves under control. The man's eyes dropped to her trembling hands. Why couldn't she control herself in this place cursed by Elyon?

"Yes, of course." The man angled for the door, eyes steady on her. He smelled like too much drink mixed with a night of vomiting.

"You're a fighter. I can see it in your lovely little eyes, sweetheart. Gonna take half of them down with you, aren't you? This ain't the Dark Ages, you know: 2020 when they just played around. It's brutal out there. Why don't you let me have some fun before they kill us both?"

"Why don't you take your skinny backside out of here before I put my boot up it?" she retorted. But did she really want to leave an unconscious man on the floor for the guard to find? It would only bring more of them.

The man's grin only widened. "Passion before death and all that. It's all part of the deal, isn't it?"

Silvie suddenly realized that he wasn't intending to head out the door but was circling around to cut off her escape. She needed to distract him.

"Do they execute all prisoners here?"

"Only the ones with the red capes. Unless you manage to *kill* them all. You see, we have nothing to lose." His emphasis on the word *kill* clearly revealed his doubt that it was possible.

Johnis was in terrible trouble . . . A wave of heat spread down her neck. She nearly swatted the bald fool aside and bolted for the door then. But she had no reasonable course that would land her anywhere except in the gallows herself, in no shape to help Johnis.

"Come on, sweetie, what do you say: a kiss before the old death match?"

The door behind the skunk swung wide and filled with a guard. Silvie's line of sight was mostly blocked by the other prisoner, but she could see over his shoulder enough to know that this guard wasn't the same one who'd confronted her at the front doors.

She moved closer. "Now you're talking my language," she said. Then in a whisper, "Don't let him stop us! Kiss me . . ."

The rank-smelling man stepped up and snaked his thin arms around her. His lips smothered hers in a thick, wet kiss.

# EIGHT

The crowd sat in perfect silence, not daring to disturb the echo of those two words of invitation they longed to hear: *I accept.*

They would get their fight. And not the twenty-on-one smashing that would be over before it started, but a contest between this unorthodox runt and their Goliath.

Johnis scanned the stadium once again, hoping for an avenue of escape, but only saw doors between the seats up high, and even those were guarded.

The only advantage he might have over the huge warrior who faced him from twenty yards away was speed. One whack from the man's broadsword and Johnis would go down in a sea of blood. Helmet or not.

He lifted his helmet off his head and tossed it to one side. His opponent began to walk toward him.

The chant began like a hum, then swelled to a roar. "Vigor, Vigor, Vigor, Vigor!"

Clearly they had seen Vigor rip the heads from other prisoners' shoulders before and wanted to see the sight again. Two weeks earlier the chant from a different crowd in a different world had been in praise of him, the chosen one, who'd turned the Horde back at the Natalga Gap. The sound of it still rang in his ears: *Johnis, Johnis, Johnis, Johnis!*

"Dear Elyon, help me," he whispered. He wasn't sure if the shaking at the soles of his feet came from the crowd's roar or from his own bones, but he didn't think he'd ever felt quite so desperate as he did now.

It was one thing to face Teeleh, knowing the Roush were there to back you up. But he had no clue what kind of provision existed in the Histories.

"Vigor, Vigor, Vigor, Vigor!"

And then Vigor was lumbering for him, a large sword comfortable in his right hand. Biceps swollen the size of Johnis's whole head. Thigh muscles rippled like a stallion's flank. Worse, the man was no longer lumbering but bounding on the balls of his feet, limber and surprisingly quick.

The notion to dive for his helmet and roll into a tight protective ball entered his mind and was gone before it could be counted as more than a foolish instinct left over from his childhood. But the instinct returned stronger this time. He didn't know what to do. So he just stood still, like a twig planted firmly in the hard soil.

"Vigor, Vigor . . ." The cries softened, then faded altogether as the crowd sensed an outright pummeling—their bull would soon trample this mouse who'd spoken so bravely but now stood quivering in the dust.

Vigor uttered a grunt ten feet away, pulled back his sword (still at a full run), and swung the blade in an arc that Johnis judged would reach his neck at the peak of its momentum.

He waited a full count, then dropped into the protective ball. His body collapsed into itself and fell to the ground like a coiled spring, faster than Vigor could have anticipated.

The warrior's sword swept through empty air, and both feet reached the balled form on the ground, one right after the other. Both stopped at Johnis's midsection.

The rest of Vigor's body, however, was not so quick. It catapulted over Johnis, went airborne—feet high, head low—and sailed ten feet before gravity finally had its way with the man. Johnis watched the whole thing with his face pressed into two inches of dirt.

The *thud* of Vigor's chest and face slamming into ground.

A terrifying *crack* of bone.

The gasp from the crowd.

Johnis breathed hard, nostrils blowing at the dust. It was the only sound he heard in the wake of the mighty fall. Vigor lay still.

Johnis lifted his head and stared at the larger man's closed eyes facing him from a dozen feet away.

The eyes snapped open and stared at him.

Vigor suddenly sprang up to his feet and shook off the fall. But . . . he'd heard a crack! The man's back or his neck.

"Vigor, Vigor, Vigor, Vigor!"

Vigor rushed him.

Too late to rely on anything but raw instinct. Johnis leaped to his feet and ran away from the indestructible monster whose eyes now bulged with fury at the runt who tripped him up.

It took him only a few strides at a full sprint to feel the same surge of power he'd felt racing through the gaming hall. There was something in the air here, he'd thought then. It made him overly zealous. It made him cry. It made him dull in the head at times.

And it made him fast.

Speed might not help him fell the mighty beast named Vigor, but it would help him run away. Johnis flew straight for the line of warriors watching from behind their helmets. He could feel the red cape tug at his neck, and he shrugged out of it.

The executioner stood in his black outfit, arms crossed, atop the platform. Johnis veered to his right and headed for the far side wall. When he reached the wood planking, he angled left and ran parallel, looking back for the first time since leaving them behind.

Vigor was still sprinting toward him. But he was a good fifty yards off. He'd put that much distance on the man?

The crowd had gone quiet. A youthful, high-strung voice spoke what was on Johnis's mind, if not the crowd's. "Man, he's fast!"

Okay, so he was fast. What was he going to do, run around the arena like a chicken with its head cut off? Eventually they would tire of his running and send the rest after him.

He still had the knife strapped to his thigh, but he couldn't afford to lose it on one throw at the man bearing down on him.

Johnis feigned left then took off to his right, sprinting toward the center again, dangerously close to Vigor. Fast with the wind in his hair. Maybe twice as fast as he remembered being able to run.

He sped past the man, headed toward the platform, and veered behind, as if crossing to the far side again.

But he did not cross to the far side. Halfway down the length of the platform he turned into it, cutting as close to a right angle as his speed would allow.

He reached the platform in five streaking strides, launched himself into a dive that cleared the five-foot height, rolled across the platform, and came to his feet beside the executioner.

Before the man had a chance to recover from the brash and speedy transition from flight to fight, Johnis was behind him and had his blade at the man's neck. He slammed the back of the man's knee, dropping him off balance to his haunches.

"Call him off, or I cut your throat where you stand!" he screamed.

SILVIE LET THE BALD PRISONER KISS HER HUNGRILY AND waited patiently. He was smelly and wet and reminded her of a slug, but at the moment she would take a slug over captivity.

"Hey! There's a man and woman—"

"Can't you see we're busy here?" the man yelled, ripping his lips from hers. He spun and stared the guard down. "You have a problem with the condemned catching a moment of bliss before death?"

Presumably satisfied that the bald head didn't match the description he'd been given, the guard finally dipped his head and ducked out.

The prisoner came around, a sly grin parting his lips to reveal his smelly yellow teeth. "Now, where were we?"

Unable to tolerate the man a moment longer, Silvie slammed her right knee into the man's groin.

He gasped and doubled over in pain.

"You were begging for this." She brought her left knee up into his face. His nose cracked and he toppled to one side, out cold.

"Never mistake a woman as an opportunity for bliss."

Silvie snatched up her helmet and pulled it on as she fled the room, leaving her sword.

No guards. The crowd's roar came from up ahead. She'd pieced their predicament together well enough by now. The Horde were known to hold public executions in which prisoners were drowned. But sometimes they had sport with the prisoners before their deaths. So it was in the Histories. She and Johnis had stumbled into a public execution, and Johnis had been mistaken as the prisoner who lay unconscious behind her.

She rushed across the room that held the capes that identified prisoners as condemned. A dark passageway ran adjacent the sound of a crowd's roar. A door: locked.

*Johnis is behind this door. My lover has been led through this door to the slaughter.*

Silvie hefted the helmet off her head and tossed the useless vessel to the side. She raced along the wall, looking for another way past. It rose ten feet and cracked at the top where steel tubes crisscrossed to form girding for a large structure. An auditorium.

The crowd had grown silent. Silvie raced farther into the darkness. The passageway ended in a hallway that ran straight ahead. Green fabric covered the floor. Lights hung overhead. If she wasn't mistaken, she was headed away from the arena, but going back the way she'd come only promised to land her in a face-off with the guard. She had to find a way into the arena!

But there was no way. The crowd's roar was no longer within earshot. She was about to head back when she saw a sign indicating that the passage to her right was a DRESSING ROOM. With some luck, it was a way back to the arena.

Silvie ran up the hall, ducked into the dressing room. Mirrors. Bright lights. Jewelry. One woman sat in a chair with her legs crossed, chewing on something as she worked on her nails.

Her eyes lifted. "Yes?"

"Sorry." Silvie closed the door, now on the brink of full-fledged panic. She had to get to him. Now, while he was still alive, assuming he *was* still alive! She didn't even know if he was in *this* arena.

A crowd's roar rose farther down the hall. Silvie blinked and looked back the way she'd come. The arena was ahead of her? She'd gone in a circle, perhaps.

Heart in her throat, she rushed toward a door topped by a sign reading STAGE. Without concern for her own safety, she flung the door open and barged into a room where several people sat about, watching square tubes with moving pictures on them of a woman singing. Piles of black boxes were identified in white letters: THE CRYING SHAME.

Silvie spun to her right and saw the same woman out on a stage, singing to a huge crowd partially hidden by long, black curtains. It took her only a moment to realize that she'd stumbled into a different arena; one reserved for song, not killing.

Without bothering to judge the expressions of those in the room, she backed out, slammed the door, whirled back the way she'd come, and sprinted down the hallway. She raced past the dressing room, along the lighted hall, and was about to duck back into the dark passageway alongside the arena when she saw a shaft of light to her right.

A break in the wall she'd missed coming the other direction.

Silvie ran up to a four-inch crack and peered into a huge, brightly lit arena with a dirt floor. There, on a platform in the center, stood Johnis. He held a knife in one hand, and his other was around an executioner's neck.

"Call him off, or I cut your throat where you stand!" he screamed.

"Johnis!"

Her own scream carried through the crack and echoed into the stadium. A thousand heads turned her way and, seeing nothing, immediately returned to the spectacle on the platform.

But Johnis understood.

"Silvie! Save yourself, Silvie."

"No, don't you dare say that! Let him free! He's not who you think he is!"

A pause.

"Tell them, Silvie," Johnis cried. "Tell them we're not the prisoners they think we are."

"We're not!" she screamed through the crack in the tall wall. "We're from the future. We've come here for the Books of History. It's all a mistake!"

There was another pause.

"Tell them we're related to the king," Johnis called.

*The king?* "We're related to the king."

"Take us to your supreme commander and let us sort this whole thing out!" Johnis yelled.

Silvie held her breath, eyes pressed up against the crack to see the crowd's response.

"Let me go!" the man in black growled.

His warriors moved as one, swarming for the platform.

"Johnis!"

# NINE

To say that the sound of Silvie's voice flooded Johnis with relief would be a gross understatement. He very nearly released the man and raced for the sound of it. She was here! She'd come to save him! But then he thought about the danger she was placing herself in, and his gratuitous relief turned to horror.

Their exchange didn't produce the kind of response he'd hoped for. He had a choice now: kill the man in his hands with a jerk of his knife and face them head-on, or take the chance that this interruption would stall the planned execution.

"You're cutting me," the executioner growled.

The warriors rushed.

"Johnis!"

A whistle blew shrilly. "Take him down, boys!"

Guards were pouring in through several doors along the wall. They'd found him. Regardless of what had really happened here, he was now at their mercy, which he doubted would be very liberal.

He released the man, let the knife fall to the platform, and lifted his hands in a show of surrender. "Run, Silvie! Save yourself! Find Darsal. Find Karas. Run!"

They fell on him with a tangle of sweaty arms and sharp curses. A pair of shiny silver shackles were clamped around his wrist and tightened. They hurried him from the building and shoved him into a Chevy with lights atop it, like the ones that had first given pursuit. Johnis slouched in the back, behind a cage that separated him from the pilot.

It took them only a few minutes to reach their prison and shuffle him into a plain white holding room with a table and chairs, all made of a white material like wood, but smoother and more uniform.

Johnis had never felt as lost as he did now.

"CALL ME SERGEANT CRAMSEY," THE OFFICER SAID, OFFERing his hand and sitting across the table from Johnis. "What would your name be?"

Seated here so helplessly, Johnis considered his options with growing pessimism. Silvie was out there, completely lost without him. They had no idea where Darsal or Karas were or how to get word to them. He was no longer sure if Las Vegas really was a

Horde city from the past or some kind of mix between human and Scab.

What he did know was that he felt sick for having lost Silvie. The forlorn sound of her voice crying for him from beyond the wall made his belly rise each time he thought about it, and he couldn't get her cry out of his mind. Tears threatened to overtake his eyes. He turned away from the man, unsure if he should tell him his name.

Then again, the only way to find Silvie, Darsal, or Karas was to make his whereabouts known. Johnis faced the Cramsey. "My name is Johnis."

"Last name?"

"Just Johnis. Johnis of Middle."

"Well, Johnis Middle, seems you've gotten yourself into a bit of trouble." He flipped through a report in his hands. "Reckless driving, speeding, stolen vehicle, disrupting the peace, attempted manslaughter . . . What the heck were you thinking, boy?"

"I was thinking they wanted to execute me."

"You expect me to believe that you raced into the Excalibur with real weapons and put a blade to a man's throat because you believed someone was after you?"

Johnis looked up at a thin glass box with moving pictures. Another amazing invention from the Histories. It was all far more than he could grasp.

"What is that?"

The officer looked at the glass box. "A Net screen. The Net, the news. I don't suppose you've ever seen the Net."

He frowned and shook his head. "No, I haven't."

A box on the man's waist burped, and he lifted it to his ear. He listened, eyes flittering to the Net, then Johnis. He lifted another instrument with multiple buttons and waved it at the glass box. The Net. The picture changed to a fuzzy one of a woman on a stage. The one behind held a knife to the other's neck. The picture grew larger.

Johnis jumped to his feet. "Silvie?" How was that possible? She was in the box, or an image of her was in the box.

Silvie was on a stage, holding a singer hostage, surrounded by a dozen panicked onlookers.

"You know her?" Cramsey asked. He pressed another button, and voices spoke from the box. Johnis watch in stunned amazement.

". . . moments ago an unidentified assailant rushed in from the side of the stage and took Mira Silver, lead singer of the band The Crying Shame, hostage at knife point . . . uh . . . honestly, this is quite unprecedented. The show was being aired live, Gene. What we're seeing is live. I repeat, we are live at the Excalibur in Las Vegas, where an unknown . . ."

The sound went dead.

"You know her?"

"It's Silvie! Yes, yes, I know her." Johnis scrambled over to the Net and slapped its side. "What happened to her voice?"

As if by magic, the box spoke again, and he jumped back. Silvie was screaming now.

"You hear me? Not a hundred yards from here they took my

lover, Johnis of Middle. He was guilty of nothing but following the directives of the Roush to find the lost Books of History, three of which are in this world."

She paused, panting, eyes wide. Her strained voiced came again, wavering in fear this time.

"I realize these are extreme measures, but . . ." A close-up showed her face, tears leaking from the corners of her eyes. "You give me no choice. I know you have him. Give me Johnis, and I will let this one live."

Johnis spun to Cramsey, who was eyeing him carefully. "You have to take me to her. She'll kill her!"

No sign of concern crossed the man's face.

Johnis plopped in a chair. "Then her blood is on your head. But don't tell me I didn't warn you. Believe me when I say I know Silvie. She'd gut a hundred Scabs before one could put a blade in her. This will *not* end well!"

He knew that he was overly expressive, but his eagerness to undo what he had drawn Silvie into was overpowering.

Silvie was talking again. "I mean no harm. But don't think we can be discounted easily. My name is Silvie of Southern, and I will not rest until I have Johnis of Middle in my arms again." She caught herself, then pushed forward.

"We did not come here to cause any trouble but to save humanity before the Dark One enslaves us all. You must set him free. I beg you!"

Johnis slammed his fist on the table. "Free us!"

"Settle down, boy. If I free you now, it'll be right into the custody of the fruit farm. You want that?"

"As long as I'm with her"—he stood and shoved his finger at the box—"you may put me wherever you wish."

"Then talk her in. Tell her this is all a mistake. We can sort out the 'Books of History' business later."

Silvie was pulling her hostage backward now, her knife pressed tight against her skin. Mira Silver looked like she'd swallowed a lemon, but she wasn't a hysterical mess like others around her. The picture jerked to show the audience who'd come to watch The Crying Shame perform.

They both walked off stage, disappeared behind the curtain.

Johnis stared after Silvie, wishing her to reappear. The announcer came back on, explaining what she'd already said. Cramsey silenced the box.

"If I can see her on this box, can she see me?" Johnis demanded.

"I don't know what you two are up to, but you've just bought yourself more trouble than you can imagine."

"I have to talk to her! Can she see me?"

The door opened and another officer walked in. He glanced up at the muted Net. "You see that?"

"Yes, sir. I did."

"She has Mira Silver held up in her dressing room. The mayor wants the casino evacuated. This thing's playing on every channel on the Web." The man glanced at Johnis. "Get anywhere with him?"

"They're partners, sir. He wants to talk to her."

The superior frowned. "Mira Silver, of all people. She might as well have taken the president hostage. This doesn't look good, Jake. The news is reporting that this one made a fool of our boys on the south side."

"Then you must let me talk to her now," Johnis said. "Before she makes fools of even more of your men."

"She ain't making fools of my men. Because when she comes out, we're going to put her down."

# TEN

Silvie paced before the mirror, absently twirling both bone-handled knives by her side. The soft whirring sound was a faint reminder of her place in another world where she was Silvie of Southern, chosen from one thousand young fighters to lead. A hero, skilled with knives and, above all, Forest Guard in the service of Thomas of Hunter.

Yet here . . .

Here she was a fugitive who'd taken a singer hostage in desperation, lost from Johnis, whom she loved. Here she was a mouse among elephants, a spider in the lake, an emotional wreck with a captive who was far more at ease than she.

"You know you're toast down here," Mira said.

"Hush! I'm trying to think."

Silvie looked at the woman studying her with an even gaze. Mira looked to be in her early twenties, a dancer who could sing as well as anyone Silvie had heard in the forests. The dance moves she'd seen the performer execute were more rigid and precise than those the dancers in Southern preferred, but even in the few moments she watched through the curtains before her attack, Silvie could see that she was a master of her craft.

"I can help you think," Mira said.

"You take me for a fool who needs the help of an artist?"

"The thought had crossed my mind. Why are you dressed up like that?"

"I'm a fighter, not a dancer who prances about in a short skirt."

"A fighter who's looking for the lost Books of History," Mira said. "Right, I'd forgotten. Problem is"—she stood, against Silvie's orders, and started for the door—"no one here has any clue who this Johnis is or what the Books of History are. You're wasting your time."

"Where are you going?"

"I'm leaving."

Silvie sprang for the singer, dragged her back to her seat, and pushed her down. "I told you I'd bind you if you tried to get away."

"Ouch. Not so hard!"

"I told you: I'm a warrior not a dancer. Breaking your neck is something I could do with one hand. Don't test me."

Silvie snatched up a tubular contraption with a cord attached and wound the cord around Mira's wrists, then tied it off. "Stay!"

"Tell me about these little white, fuzzy creatures again."

She'd made the mistake of telling Mira about the Roush and the Shataiki in an attempt to gain her understanding. Her explanations had gained her only the kind of sympathy you might have for an idiot.

"The Roush," she said.

"Sounds like fun. But here, in the real world, there are no little fuzzy bats. You just have to accept that, Silvie. No Roush are coming to your rescue. Outside this room, they'll shoot you dead for what you've done. I may be your prisoner for the moment, honey, but trust me, I'm the only one around here who can help you."

"And how would you do that?" Silvie snapped. She felt like dropping to her knees and sobbing, right there in front of Mira. "They took Johnis!"

"You're in love with Johnis, and I can appreciate that. But you don't take a girl hostage for love. Not if you want to stay out of prison—and especially not a famous pop star!"

"He's not just the one I love! He's the chosen one, singled out by the Roush and by Elyon himself to recover the seven lost Books of History before the—"

"—Dark One enslaves the world," Mira finished. "Yes, I know. But you have to get a grip here, honey. They're going to crucify you out there."

"But you believe me, right?"

"Well, yes, I can help you."

"Fine. Tell me."

"For starters, you have to start communicating," Mira said.

"How?"

"There's no phone in here; you'll have to pass them a note. Tell them there's been a misunderstanding. Get some dialogue going. Turn on the Net and find out what they're saying on the news. Get a feeling for what you've done."

"What's a Net?"

Mira grinned. "Come on, don't do that."

"I'm not doing anything. Where Johnis and I come from, there is no such thing that I've heard of."

"Okay, fine. See that black box over there?" She motioned to a glass box with her chin. "You push the little green button below the screen."

Silvie walked up to the Net, keeping Mira in her peripheral view in the event this was a ploy. "How do I know this isn't some fancy weapon that will finish me off?"

"Let me turn it on, if you doubt me."

"No."

"Then push the button! It won't bite."

Silvie pushed the button. A picture filled the glass surface, and she jumped back, ready to defend against any attack.

"See, no harm. Now hand me the remote." Mira nodded at a black object on the counter. She handed the remote to her prisoner, who pressed another button.

The picture on the Net changed. A woman with dark hair was talking earnestly about what they were calling "the Mira Silver kidnapping." But what amazed Silvie even more was the smaller box to the woman's right on which the events of the kidnapping were being played out nearly identically as . . .

No, it was an actual replay of what had happened. Silvie watched herself behind Mira, crying out for all to hear her demands.

"That's us!"

"You really don't know what the Net is?"

The picture suddenly changed. An image of a prison filled the glass. Vertical bars behind which stood a man.

Johnis.

"It's . . ." Silvie took a step back, stunned at the sight. "It's Johnis." They had Johnis in a prison! "I told you!" she cried.

Mira didn't reply.

The picture of him grew until his whole face filled the screen, showing clearly his dusty cheeks, his small, smudged nose. A cut on his lip—from his fight in the arena or from torture, she couldn't tell.

Then his voice, as clear as if he were standing in that very room, was talking to her.

"Silvie . . ." He paused, glancing to his right. "I've made a deal to tell them everything I know in exchange for going on the Net, so I hope you can hear me. I saw what you did, Silvie. And I'm moved that you would put yourself in such danger for me. For us. None of them seem to have a clue about the Books of History, but I believe that when this is all over, you will be remembered as much as . . ."

He glanced off to his right and snapped at whoever was watching him on the other end. "I'll say what I want; that is what we agreed to!"

He returned his attention to the screen. "Forgive me. You will be remembered for your bravery. The Roush are watching, Silvie. History itself is watching. For all we know, Thomas Hunter is watching."

"Who?" Mira asked.

"Thomas Hunter," Silvie said absently. "Supreme commander of the Forest Guard."

"*The* Thomas Hunter?"

Silvie ignored her. She moved closer to the Net.

Johnis took a deep breath. "They've shown me the forces gathered around the Excalibur, Silvie. Chevys too many to count. 'Police cars,' they're called. Officers armed with the fire sticks. Shotguns. The only hope we have is for you to join me here, where they've given me their word they will listen to our story."

She could read the pleading lines in his face, no sign that he was saying one thing while sending a different signal.

"If they were the Horde, I would tell you to fight your way out or die trying. But I don't think they are. Stupid, yes, but not wrong in what they are doing. And Darsal, Karas, if you see me or hear me, please come to our aide. Our lives may now depend on you."

He paused again, then spoke softly.

"I love you, Silvie."

"And I love you, Johnis," she said. Tears flooded her eyes. "I love you!"

The picture changed to the announcer again. "Well, there you have it, ladies and gentleman, in this most unusual . . ."

Silvie spun to her prisoner. "Take me to him! Make me your captive and protect me. Just take me to him. It's all I ask."

A faint smile crossed Mira's mouth. "You love him."

"I do! More than you know!"

"Just like that?"

"Don't you see? He's used this invention of yours to call out to Darsal and Karas. You said this will be seen by many."

"By half the world. And you'll be lucky if they don't lock you up."

"Without Darsal and Karas our mission is lost. If they're alive, I hope they will have seen us on this Net of yours. Take me to Johnis."

Mira didn't jump and run for the door as any weaker captive might have. She studied Silvie with what could be interpreted as empathy. Mira was a true romantic at heart, likely what inspired her performances on stage.

"You're in a predicament, honey."

# ELEVEN

She stood in the main library, eyes fixed on the large screen that replayed the events half a world away in Las Vegas, Nevada. So then, he was right. They weren't the quiet type, these chosen ones.

Desire sliced through her chest. It had begun, hadn't it? The fate of so many after so much time rested in what so few would do in the next few days.

A voice spoke behind her, soft but as definite as a hammer to the forehead. "Bring them to me."

She turned casually. He was dressed in the black cape.

"The books and Johnis, as planned."

"I know my role," she snapped. "Concern yourself with yours."

"Yet you're still here."

She strode toward the door.

"Remember, Mirandaaaaa . . ." He let her name fade in a breath. She stopped at the door but did not face him. "If you fail me now, you'll be dead before they are. I don't need you."

She resisted the temptation to explain to him how wrong he was. Useless. In the seven years they'd known each other, she'd never known him to make even the slightest miscalculation in his judgment. Except this one.

"Godspeed," he said.

Oh, the irony of it all.

# TWELVE

Johnis and Silvie sat in the same jail cell, waiting for the authorities to make some sense of the psychiatrist's findings, though Silvie couldn't imagine that the results of such an absurd test could have any bearing on guilt or innocence.

The fact was, they were both guilty of all of it. They had stolen a Chevy. Fled the police. Driven recklessly. Caused a disturbance at the Excalibur. Kidnapped a world-famous pop star. And lived to tell.

This morning their faces had filled the Net screen nonstop. It was now afternoon, and already the attention had shifted to other interests, which was fine by them.

"The doctor's a charlatan!" Johnis snapped, walking the length of their ten-by-ten cell. They'd been permitted to share the cell, as negotiated by Johnis as part of Silvie's surrender.

"Agreed," Silvie said.

"Boxes and triangles and . . . bah!" Johnis dismissed the examination with a flip of his wrist.

"So we just wait?"

"What else?"

Johnis had explained his reasoning. Silvie'd been right: he'd used the Net to reach Darsal and Karas. But neither had.

"For all we know, they're dead," Silvie said.

"Then so are we."

"You don't believe that. We've been in worse predicaments. In Teeleh's lair. In the Horde city."

"Did Teeleh have shotguns? Or flying cars? Do you see Roush or the Guard rushing to our defense? We don't even have the books we came with. The authorities took everything!"

Their battle dress and the books had been confiscated, along with their knives. They now wore the white-and-brown striped slacks and smocks common among all prisoners here.

Silvie walked up to the bars and gripped them with both hands. "We have each other."

No response from Johnis. When she turned, she saw that he was nibbling on his fingernail, lost in thought.

"You forget so quickly?" Silvie demanded.

"What? What—no. Yes, we have each other. It'll have to do."

"Have to do? You threw yourself in a cage for your mother. You nearly gave up your life for Karas. But for me it'll just 'have to do'?"

"No." He gripped his hair and paced. "That's not what I meant."

The poor boy was reeling; she had no business testing his

love at such a time. But the urge to act on her emotions felt irresistible.

She closed her eyes and bit her lip. *You're as frantic as he, Silvie. Control yourself.* Then she felt his hand on her shoulder, pulling her close. Warmth filled her belly. He'd seen her disappointment and rushed to her side.

Johnis held her in his arms and spoke quickly into her ear. "I'm stronger and faster than I was before. They can't know, but there's a chance we may be superior to them." A few breaths in her ear, enough for her to realize that his embrace was for communication rather than consolation.

"Have you noticed?"

She swallowed. "Yes, but not strong enough to take them on."

"But fast enough."

"You said yourself, we don't stand a chance!"

No response. His suggestion was one of raw desperation.

A bang on the bars startled them. "Okay, love birds, I've got good news for both of you."

The guard they called "Guns" grinned at them from beyond the cage. He slapped his palm with a black stick. "The Kook says you two are not. Kooks, that is. You're as sane as I am, which, to be perfectly honest with you, ain't saying a lot."

He twitched, and nearby another guard chuckled.

"Now the bad news. Seeing as you aren't headed to the fruit farm right quick, they're going to ship you down to the main jail, where they send the hard cases." His twisted grin said it all. "If I was you, I'd think twice about this 'we're from another world' routine, 'we got no money, no kin, no guilt' junk, and start making sense."

"Back off, Guns." The detective who'd struck the deal with Johnis spoke from down the hall—Cramsey. "Open it up."

Guns sprang the latch, pulled the gate wide. Cramsey stepped up and stared at them. "Seems you have attracted attention from a friend in high places. Mira has suddenly decided to drop all kidnapping charges, and the DA has inexplicably dropped the others, paid off, if you ask me. They've made arrangements to release you. But if I see your face again, it won't go easy, you hear? And drop the stupid act. It never works." Then to someone down the hall, "They're all yours."

A woman walked into view, and Silvie felt her muscles tense. She was slightly older, perhaps in her early twenties, though she carried herself like someone who'd been around much longer.

Short, well formed, dressed in the blue trousers so many here wore, wearing shoes with high heels, which was also customary in this world, no matter how crippling they seemed. Her blouse was black; she wore a silver necklace with a large onyx pendent in the shape of a circle. Long, brown hair. Green eyes staring at them in wonder. Stern. Silvie knew this woman. She couldn't place her name, but they'd met.

For a moment neither spoke. Then the woman dipped her head enough to acknowledge a bond. "Hello, Silvie." Beat. "It's been a long time."

Johnis took a step forward. "Karas?"

"Hello, Johnis."

# THIRTEEN

As soon as Johnis said it, Silvie knew he was right. This was either Karas or her twin sister, ten years older!

"What . . . how?"

"Not here," the woman said. "I have transportation waiting." Then to Cramsey, a bite in her voice, "Bring them!"

"Of course, Ms. Longford."

Silvie exchanged a wide-eyed glance with Johnis and followed. The woman walked with clean steps, elegant despite the tall shoes, as those with privilege and authority walked.

"We came through after she did," Johnis mumbled to himself. "So long?"

Karas looked over her shoulder. "Not now."

They followed her through the station, out into the open, to a long, black car that waited at the curb. An attendant opened the door for them.

"Climb in. After you."

Silvie and Johnis slid into a richly upholstered chamber with two facing leather benches. Karas took the seat opposite them and waited for the attendant to close the door.

Silence engulfed them. Karas stared for a long time, still not smiling, and for a moment Silvie felt more alarm than relief. Then the girl's eyes flooded with tears that spilled down her cheeks. She lowered her head into one hand and sobbed quietly.

The car began to move.

"Is it really you?" Johnis asked.

Karas lifted her face and beamed through her tears. "Yes, it's me, you scrapper!" She fell forward on her knees and threw her arms around their necks, pulling them into an embrace that threatened to choke them.

"You have no idea how long I've waited for this day! Elyon, dear Elyon, I knew it would come!"

The last of Silvie's lingering doubts fell like loosed chains. Karas slid back on the leather seat and wiped her cheek with her fingers. "I could hardly believe my eyes when I played the tape last night. I'm sorry; I would have come sooner, but I was at a concert in Amsterdam. How long have you been here?"

Johnis still looked like he'd been kicked by a mule. "Two days?"

"Two days!" Karas cried, then cackled with laughter. "So, then, you think the world's turned inside out."

Johnis swallowed. "It has."

"What do you know? You've seen the lights, the cars? Well, obviously the cars—you're riding in one. And you were both on the Net. A bit overwhelming, I'm sure."

"I've mastered the Chevy," Johnis said.

She smiled wide. "So I heard." She began to cry again. "I *knew* I hadn't lost my mind. For ten years I've had to wonder if it really was all a dream. The forests, the Horde, bathing in the lakes. All of it! But it's true, isn't it?"

"True?" Silvie looked out the window. "The question is, is *this* true?" She turned back to Karas. "Are *you* true? I mean, you're real, of course, but . . . look at you!"

"You're a woman," Johnis said. There was more than a hint of wonder in his voice, and Silvie wasn't sure she wanted to share his enthusiasm. She wasn't just a woman; she was a beautiful woman of significant wealth and influence.

"How old are you?" she asked.

"Twenty-one. But I tell them all I'm twenty-four—it suits my place as an entertainment manager in this world. They have a hard enough time believing that someone in her midtwenties could have accomplished what I have. If they knew how young I really was, they'd dig even deeper than they do."

"Younger?" Johnis said. "You look old enough."

"There's so much to cover," Karas said, smiling through her tears. "I've hoped for this day for as long as I can remember. Nothing else matters. I've done it all hoping that one day I would find you. I just had no idea you would both be so . . . young still."

"We're sixteen," Silvie said. "Is that so young?"

"No. Although in the United States, sixteen isn't the age of marrying and waging war." She stopped, clearly overwhelmed. "It's so . . . refreshing to talk to someone besides my therapist about Other Earth. Did you know that Thomas Hunter was once a great hero here?"

"So, he *was* here?" Johnis asked in amazement. "This is the place from his dreams?"

"From what I can tell, Other Earth—that's what I call it—is the far future of Earth. At some point in the future here, this Earth is destroyed and everything starts over. Thomas Hunter found a way from this reality into that future."

"Then . . . can we?"

"I don't know. Not with only one book. Maybe with all four."

Karas reached into a box on the seat beside her. She carefully lifted out the brown book Johnis had used and then the green one that had brought Silvie through.

"I have the black one," Karas said, brushing her fingers over the covers as if they held the essence of her very life—which they might well.

"And Darsal?" Johnis asked.

She lifted her eyes. "I don't know."

"Then we have to find her."

Once again, tears filled Karas's eyes. "I'm sorry. I don't mean to be such a sap. So much has transpired in these last ten years. It's so good to see you."

It occurred to Silvie that, for her and Johnis, only two days had passed since they'd left their world to find themselves here, in the Histories. But Karas had survived here, in this hell, for more than ten years. She wouldn't have guessed such a thing was possible, especially for a ten-year-old. The poor girl had suffered enormously.

"So much has happened." Karas looked at the two Books of History on her lap. "I hardly know where to start."

"Tell us everything," Johnis said.

"In good time, my friend. In good time." The car slowed, then stopped. "We're here."

They exited the car behind Karas and stood before a long, tubular vehicle with fixed wings. It was one of the birds they'd seen fly overhead. Two large mouths were attached to the body, and from these mouths came a high-pitched whine that made Silvie step back.

"Ever dreamed of flying?" Karas asked, beaming.

The idea startled Silvie. "In the sky?"

"Yes, in the sky. Like a bird."

"In that thing?"

"In that thing."

Johnis's eyes were round. "Is it a Chevy?"

"No, it's a Citation 20. And it's faster than a Chevy."

"Fantastic," Johnis said.

FLYING OVER EARTH AT TWENTY THOUSAND FEET WAS AN experience that made Silvie forget all the disadvantages the Histories had presented up to this point. Neither she nor Johnis seemed to be able to hide their grins, peering out through the round windows.

"One of these contraptions would end the war with the Horde," Johnis said.

"How so?"

"You could fly over them and drop boulders without any fear of being cut down."

"Trust me, Johnis, you could drop more than rocks to end the war with the Horde," Karas said. "But you wouldn't want to kill so many others like me."

*She still has a soft spot in her heart for the Scabs,* Silvie thought, returning her attention to the clouds beneath the airplane.

They talked about the short past they'd shared, beginning with the details of Karas's rescue from the Horde City. She wanted to rehearse every detail from her memory, just to be sure she'd remembered it all as it really had happened.

Then she quickly told them about her journey through the desert with Darsal. Meeting Alucard in the Black Forest. Their escape into the cover of this world, a virtual reality that could be accessed by touching any of the seven books with blood—which is what Billos had done when he'd gone renegade on them.

"I've done it a dozen times since," Karas said. "It's like walking into a simulation of this reality. Paradise, every time. The point is, Paradise, Colorado, is real. I've been there."

"And?"

"Nothing."

"But that was before we arrived with our two books," Johnis said. "Until our books entered this reality, there were only two books here: yours and Darsal's."

Which begged the question Silvie voiced. "No sign of Darsal at all?"

Karas stared out at the blue sky. "I've searched, trust me. When all of my efforts failed, I followed this path." She motioned to the jet, meaning her life as a manager. "If I couldn't find you two or Darsal, I wanted to make sure you could find me. So I've used what skills I have to make myself highly visible. As it turned out, you managed more visibility in one day than I have in five years."

An exaggeration, but point well made.

"Darsal's never contacted me. Which means she's either dead . . ."

"Or hasn't come through yet," Johnis finished. "For all we know, she may not come through for another ten years."

"Correct. As is the case with Alucard."

"So . . . if Darsal hasn't come through yet, only our three books have come through thus far. The other three books hidden here may not even be visible yet?"

"Possibly," Karas said. "If Darsal did come through, she's clearly run into trouble, or she would have contacted me. Whoever has her book might know about me. If so, they're probably waiting for you two to surface before they expose themselves and go for all of our books at once."

The soft rush of air from the engines outside filled the cabin.

"No sign of that beast?" Silvie asked. "Alucard?"

"Signs?" Karas frowned. "Everywhere you look. What is Alucard but raw wickedness in the form of Shataiki? It's everywhere. But no, I haven't seen any Shataiki floating through the night sky."

"Then let's keep out fingers crossed," Johnis said. "With any luck, we find the seven books before he comes through."

"We have to assume he's through as well, biding his time, waiting for you two to show up," Karas said. "And we might be wise to assume the worst."

Johnis frowned. "That he has Darsal's book. That he's killed her and is biding his time."

It seemed rather pessimistic to Silvie, and she made as much clear.

"Maybe," Karas said. "But I've run through every possible scenario a thousand times over the years, and I assure you, we'd better be prepared for the worst, because I have a nasty feeling your little stunt on the Net set into motion much more than you bargained for."

Karas's speculation put a bit of a damper on the flight, but it was quickly overcome by the jet's sudden descent and frightening maneuvering over a sprawling compound of white buildings and small bodies of blue water she called "swimming pools."

They were flying over her house. A small town by all measures, nestled in the hills above the city of angels: Los Angeles. They would set down on a private airstrip, freshen up, and change into clothing more suitable than the prison smocks they currently wore.

All this according to Karas, who gave them a running commentary. Silvie wasn't entirely sure what it all meant, but she took it in wearing the same look of dumb wonder that was plastered on Johnis's face. Though she suspected by the comments he kept making that he was under the illusion he understood perfectly.

They landed, exited the airplane, and took a car to the main house. More accurately, the mansion. Towering white columns supported a huge ceiling that arched over the main atrium. Several servants greeted them, one at the front door, one in the kitchen, another near the pool area that overlooked the city below.

It was all a bit much for Silvie, but Karas glided around on her bare feet as naturally as a sparrow who'd come home to her nest.

They would eat at seven, she informed the cook—after the concert. Lobster and aged Kobe beef for the guests tonight; let's show them what the Histories have to offer.

She effortlessly ran through a stack of notes handed to her by a secretary wearing jeans and named Rick Cumberland, directing the man on a number of urgent issues, as though doing so were as natural as eating a meal.

The butler showed Sylvie and Johnis to two bedrooms where he'd laid out several outfits of new clothing as instructed by Karas. They reconvened on the patio—Johnis dressed in loose-fitting jeans with a black T-shirt, and Silvie in a black skirt with a white, sleeveless top. Johnis opted for boots. Silvie, sandals.

Karas looked them over and nodded her approval. "Not bad. You'll fit right in."

"Fit right in where?"

"I'm introducing one of my singers, Tony Montana, at a concert in the Rose Bowl. Something I foolishly agreed to do when a client wins in their respective categories at all major awards shows, which Tony did at the 12th annual VH2 Awards last week. We'll leave for the Rose Bowl by helicopter in an hour."

"A bowl?"

"A little larger than a bowl, actually," Karas laughed.

# FOURTEEN

They sat around a round table, staring out at the city, with a light breeze in their hair, the orange sun dipping to their sides, and delicacies at their fingertips. Karas, known here as Kara Longford, told them her story, and hearing it all, Silvie couldn't stop shaking her head in wonder.

She'd arrived in Nevada, as they had—why Nevada, she didn't know. A ten-year-old girl, she was lost and terrified on a highway that led to the big city of lights. She tried to be brave those first few days but couldn't stop crying.

There was no shortage of people willing to help a little girl who needed food and money, but none of them had any answers for her, and they all looked at her as if she'd lost her mind when she asked about the Horde or the Shataiki.

She took up with an old man who lived under a bridge after a week of wandering. "Scotty," he called himself, after a character from an old show called *Star Trek*. Unlike others, Scotty's eye lit up when she talked about the Horde and the Books of History. And thank Elyon, because if not for Scotty, she would have undoubtedly been committed to the fruit farm, a colloquial expression for a mental hospital.

Outside of Scotty's protective oversight, she became known as the little girl who would take your head off at the drop of a hat. A mental case, to be sure.

It wasn't until she went through therapy years later that she figured out what was wrong those first few months. Her emotions had been affected by the transition between the future and the Histories.

"Really?" Johnis shot Silvie a look of understanding.

"You've noticed?" Karas asked.

"I think it's what got us into trouble with the Chevy," Silvie said. "Johnis practically went berserk."

Johnis grinned sheepishly. "It did bring a few of our feelings to the surface."

Karas lifted an eyebrow, looking from one to the other. "Don't worry; it passes."

"We're not looking for it to pass," Silvie said. "Ever."

"I'm not talking about the love you've vowed for each other on the Net. I'm talking about the raw emotions caused by the transition between worlds. And your thinking feels a bit sluggish, right?"

"Careless. A little stupid, maybe. We're stuck with this?"

"No. The fact is, your mind isn't sluggish. Just the opposite. Your intelligence is well advanced over the average person here, so far advanced that it's struggling to compensate for the surge of emotional responses filtering through your mind. At least that's my best guess after the countless rounds of psychological testing I subjected myself to in an attempt to understand."

"But you're saying our minds will compensate soon enough?"

Karas nodded. "Have you noticed anything else?"

"Speed," Johnis said.

"Bingo . . . Sorry, just an expression. Our reflexes and strength are superior to the humans from the Histories. Not by much, but enough to pull out a few tricks now and then. Still, it's nothing compared to the advantage your minds will give you."

Karas went on to retrace her history here: How she'd soon begun compensating for her heightened emotions with a superior intellect. How she'd started using that intellect when she was thirteen to win small bets involving certain mathematical problems, then graduated to more complex problems. "Sleight of mind," she called it. Soon she was headlining as a child prodigy in her own stage show.

She studied on her own during the day and began building a small fortune performing in the evening. By the time she was fifteen, she'd exhausted the requirements of primary education and enrolled in a Web-based university program, studying entertainment business management with a secondary emphasis in language and history.

All the while, she had used every possible avenue to search for them. For Darsal. For Alucard. All to no avail.

Her plan was well formed even then. She would learn everything she could about history, never relenting in her ambition to find the companion books to the black Book of History in her possession. She would learn as many languages as she thought necessary to assist her in a global search for her friends and the books. And she would launch a career using her advanced intelligence to give her the broad access and exposure needed for her search. Rather than entertain, she would *manage* entertainers, creating both wealth and exposure through high-profile artists.

Most importantly, she would appear with her artists onstage frequently, so that she, too, would become world renowned. If Alucard was out there, and she had to assume that he was, she had to be visible enough worldwide to attract the attention of Johnis, Silvie, and Darsal before he got to them.

"So you've succeeded in all of this," Silvie said, stating what seemed to be obvious. "Well enough to spring us from jail."

"That was harder than you might guess. Fortunately, I manage the girl you kidnapped, and I'm very tight with the authorities in Las Vegas. The chief of police owes me a dozen favors. At this moment I manage fifteen of the top billing acts in the world through Global Entertainment Network, GEN."

"You'd think the warriors would own the wealth, not the artists," Johnis said, looking around the lavish setting.

She laughed. "There's plenty of money in war—always has

been, always will be. But humans will pay as much for their thrills as they will for their security. Was it any different in the forests? The first thing I noticed in Middle were the nightly celebrations."

"Like I've always said"—Johnis winked at Silvie—"'a poet is worth two fighters.' Just ask Elyon."

"There's more than one way to carve a poem," Silvie said, twirling her knife from a fold in her blouse. She slammed it into the table they were seated around.

"Nice," Karas said. "That is a ten-thousand-dollar slab of sandalwood from Indonesia you just defaced."

"The knife is from the future and will fetch you ten times that," Silvie responded.

"Touché."

"So, just how much wealth have you managed to acquire in your time here?"

"Enough to own a small country if I so choose. You once told me about the game Thomas Hunter taught you to play with the Horde ball."

"It was how we were first chosen," Silvie said.

"It's a very big game here; they call it 'football.' I own two teams. With your speed, you could both become huge stars here."

Johnis spit to one side. "Doesn't interest me."

"Please, we're not in a jungle here," Silvie chided. "Mind your manners."

"Sorry."

Karas let out a short giggle. "Brings back memories."

"Yes, sorry." He took a deep breath. "There is something I was wondering if you might help me with. Assuming it's not too much trouble. I don't want to presume upon your wealth, but—"

"Enough," Karas said. "My wealth is your wealth. What is it?"

He spoke before she'd fully finished. "A Chevy." His eyes shone like the stars. "A red Chevy."

Karas smiled. "Like the beauty you stole in Nevada? The sweet racer with the cherry paint job and souped-up engine that you tore up Las Vegas with?"

"Yes. That Chevy."

"Not a problem, my friend. I bought it as part of your get-out-of-jail package. Cost me twice what the owner had in it, but I paid every dime gladly. One day that car will go down in history. The Chevy that Johnis of Middle, world-renowned driver, first learned to drive in." She stood. "In the meantime, I have something else for you. Wait here."

Karas returned a minute later, gripping a wooden box in both hands. She set it gingerly on the table, opened it, and withdrew the black Book of History she'd harbored for all these years.

She set it next to theirs. The three books sat side by side: one brown, one green, one black.

Johnis stood and walked around the table. "We have to protect these at any cost."

"I've spared no expense doing so. I'll show you the vault before we leave. No one can know. For all we know, he's watching us at this very moment."

"Alucard?" Silvie glanced at the perimeter.

"From a satellite in the sky," Karas said. "From the stars. Unlikely, but we have to be careful."

"Then let's take a new vow," Johnis said. He dropped to one knee and placed his right hand on the black book. "To never stray from our task of finding the seven before the Dark One does."

Silvie placed her cool palm over his knuckles. Then Karas, with wide eyes, joined the ranks of the chosen.

"To never stray from our task of finding the seven before the Dark One does," they said together.

"Though far from home, to remain home in our hearts, never to betray each other or the books."

Their eyes met in solemn intent. "Though far from home, to remain home in our hearts, never to betray each other or the books."

"Until the books are found or we die."

"Until the books are found or we die."


THE HELICOPTER REMINDED SILVIE OF A FLYING BEETLE, complete with beating wings and bug eyes, and it took a little encouragement from Karas to get her inside the apparatus.

The Rose Bowl, as it turned out, was a large stadium filled to capacity with onlookers who'd come to see Tony Montana perform. Karas instructed the pilot to hover over the scene while she explained how it all worked. The lights, the long lines of cars, the sound system.

"Absurd," Silvie scoffed.

Johnis turned from the glass door. "How is this any different than our own celebrations?"

"To hear a few people sing?"

"Your mind is too consumed with war, Silvie! Our own gathering isn't so different. And the gatherings of the legends! In the end we were made to celebrate; isn't that part of the Great Romance?"

In those terms he was right, of course. But she didn't waste the opportunity to refocus his mind. "Love, my dear," she said, winking. "The Great Romance is all about love."

His face blushed. "Yes. Love."

His entire demeanor seemed to have shifted a little off center since coming to the Histories, she thought. He was more excitable than stoic.

"You think this is something? You should see Agnew take the stage when I can convince them to come out of hiding. Their concerts sell out in hours, regardless of the venue," Karas said into her mouthpiece. "Take her down, Peter."

They landed behind the stage and were ushered in by a contingent of black-suited guards awaiting their arrival. Karas acknowledged each with a nod, a shake of the hand, a smile. By all that Silvie could see, Karas was widely admired here.

They hurried into a "green" room, which was actually a dirty white room under the stadium. Tony Montana was a slight man, dressed in a black shirt and a white headband. His jeans were torn, perhaps to give the illusion that he'd just come from battle, although Silvie knew nothing could be farther from the truth. The way handlers busied themselves around him, offering him drinks and delicacies, she doubted he'd ever lifted a shovel, much less a sword.

Any doubts she had about this man the throngs had come to adore fell to the side when he turned and looked at her. His eyes were a bright blue, a complete contrast to his dark skin and black, tangled hair. He studied her with interest, simultaneously intense and innocent. But more than all of this, his face, the pouting shape of his lips, the small nose, the baby-smooth skin. Apart from his blue eyes, Tony Montana reminded her very much of Johnis.

Karas took Silvie's arm. "You see it too?"

"He looks . . ." Silvie paused, not sure she should make the comparison.

"Like Johnis," Karas said. "If I ever allow myself to fall in love, it will be with this man." She stepped up to the rock star. "Hello, Tony. I would like you to meet the two most important people in the world to me."

He kissed her cheek. "And here I thought I occupied one of those places." To Silvie, dipping his head, "A pleasure."

Tony Montana made polite conversation, but as Johnis gained confidence, they began prying with questions that seemed to genuinely engage each other. Soon they were in a deep discussion about poetry and beauty and love and all things creative.

An attendant with an earpiece approached them from a side door. "Sixty seconds, Kara."

Karas nodded. "You ready, Tony?"

"Always, my dear."

She nodded to the attendant. "Take my friends to the press box. I'll join you in a few . . ."

She stopped, slipped a thin black card from her jeans, and stared at a red light that blinked on one end.

"Kara?" Tony touched her elbow. "Everything okay?"

She blinked. Slid the card back into her pocket. "Fine." But her face had paled. "I'll meet you in the box."

They watched from the press box as Karas took the stage to the sound of cheering cries that suggested *she* was the star they'd come to see, Silvie thought. It was hard to imagine that this frail-looking woman had been a little girl trapped in Witch's dungeon only a week earlier, at least from her perspective. Yet here she was, acknowledging the roaring approval of a hundred thousand fans in the Histories.

Then Karas introduced Tony Montana, and the stadium trembled with pounding hands and feet. The lights went out, smoke rose on the stage, a single drum began to thump, and Silvie held her breath.

She wasn't ready for the thunder that followed. Lightening stuttered on the stage, blinding them. The drums pounded. Silvie grabbed Johnis's arm.

Tony leaped higher than seemed natural, his legs twisted to one side, and when his feet landed, the guitars roared. Music, the screaming variety she'd heard earlier, shook the stadium.

"Fantastic!"

She turned to see Johnis grinning from ear to ear. His delight was infectious. She had to agree: the sound of music from the Histories was, indeed, fantastic.

"Like it?"

Karas had come up behind them.

"Yes."

"Good. We have to go."

*The black card,* Silvie thought. *There's a problem.*

"What's wrong?" Johnis asked.

"I just talked to Rick. There's a woman at the house who refuses to give her name. We need to see her immediately."

"Why?"

"Because she claims to have a blue book with her. The blue Book of History."

# FIFTEEN

K aras walked with a quick, tense step. Silvie had watched her
address a hundred thousand screaming fans as casually as a
mother addressing her children before sending them off to bed.
But news of one woman who claimed to have the fourth Book of
History in her possession was enough to betray her true compass.
Whatever others thought of Kara Longford's interests in entertainment here on Earth, in truth her heart teetered on the bal-
ances of good and evil in a world far, far away.

She flung the front door to her house wide before the butler
had a chance to open it. "Where?"

"She's waiting in the atrium, my lady." He bowed.

Karas stepped out of her shoes and moved over the marble
floor in her bare feet, followed closely by Johnis and Silvie.

The woman who refused to give her name stood on the patio next to the lighted pool, her back to them. The night horizon glimmered with a million city lights. A stiff breeze whipped at the guest's loose slacks and blue blouse. Her long, black hair flowed on the wind. Silvie could only think of one name: Darsal.

They stopped ten feet from the woman, silent in the night.

"May we help you?" Karas asked.

Their guest turned and stared at them. All hope that this woman might be Darsal vanished. The resemblance went no further than her dark hair and height. No scar. Cheekbones too high. Lips thinner. Arms thin, not muscular from battle.

"Kara Longford." The woman stepped forward and extended her hand. "It's so good to finally meet you. Miranda Card."

Karas took her hand. "Miranda Card. What's this about a blue book?"

"And these"—Miranda looked at Johnis and Silvie—"are the two chosen ones: Johnis and Silvie."

"You know about us?" Johnis glanced at Silvie. "What do you know?"

"Only what Darsal told me," Miranda said. "Before she died."

"Darsal is dead?" Silvie asked. She wasn't sure what to make of the woman before them.

"Yes. I'm sorry, you have to forgive me. I never actually believed this day would come. It's all very strange to me." She smiled coyly, an expression mixed with some doubt and some intrigue. Her eyes rested on Johnis, and Silvie thought there might be some seduction behind her brown eyes as well.

They stared at her, stalled by the enormity of what the stranger named Miranda was suggesting.

"What are you trying to tell us?" Johnis asked. "That Darsal is dead, and you have her book?"

"I'm sorry, yes; I know it must come as a shock. But you have to understand that this is all a bit shocking to me as well."

"Why don't we sit?" Karas led them to a couch and two chairs that overlooked the city. "Now, perhaps you could start at the beginning. Tell us how you know Darsal and how you knew to look for us."

"Of course. Forgive me . . ." She wasn't able to wipe the faintest of grins from her face.

"No need to apologize," Silvie snapped. "Just tell us."

"I'm an American who works as the curator for a large private museum in Turkey, where Darsal first found me."

"Why was she looking for you?"

"She wasn't. She came to the library seven years ago, asking about for—"

"Seven years ago?" Silvie looked at Karas. "She's been here that long?"

"Longer," Miranda said. "She told me she'd come into this reality three years earlier on a quest to find the lost books. At first I thought she was a nutcase, you understand."

The woman withdrew a box of the white smoking sticks that

Karas called "cigarettes," lit one with a gold fire-starter, and blew smoke into the night air.

Still that slight grin.

"You find this humorous?" Silvie asked.

"I just flew five thousand miles to meet with you," Miranda said. "I think that earns me the right to express my nerves any way I wish, don't you?"

Silvie decided she didn't like this woman.

"Go on," Johnis said.

Miranda sucked on the cigarette and blew more smoke. "Let me start over. Your friend Darsal came to me in a state of desperation, suffering what I assumed were delusions of the grandest kind. End-of-the-world nonsense. The Dark One this, the lost books that. Alucard."

Johnis was on his feet. "He's here?"

"No. Not that I've seen. Sit."

He sat.

"She had a blue book that she claimed had transported her from another reality. She had to find six others and return them to the Roush. She was looking for three warriors: Karas, Johnis, and Silvie. I dismissed it all until she came to my house in the middle of the night, bleeding badly from a wound in her neck. 'A bite,' she claimed. She wouldn't let me call for medical help, so I did my best. She died the next morning on my kitchen table."

"You let her die?"

"She refused a trip to the hospital. I had no choice, trust me. Darsal wasn't the kind of woman you pushed around."

"You . . . she just died on your table and you didn't report it to the authorities?"

"I did. They cremated her body after an autopsy that confirmed she'd been bitten by an animal and perished from blood loss."

"But she gave you her blue book and told you about us," Karas said. "So why didn't you contact me sooner?"

"I can't say I truly believed her until I saw Johnis and Silvie on the Net, speaking of the books in the exact same way Darsal did. Needless to say, I was shocked. I left immediately."

"Where is it?" Karas demanded.

Miranda stared at the younger woman, dropped her smoke stick on the marble, and ground it out with a high-heeled black shoe.

"Darsal made me promise two things before she died. That I would never so much as show the book she left to any person without first confirming they had the others. And that I was to give the book to Johnis only and offer to help."

The curator from Turkey slid one leg over the other and waited for them to react.

Karas crossed her legs in similar fashion. "Then give Johnis the blue book. It's the only help we need."

Miranda smiled at her for a few long beats, then stood and crossed behind the couch. "Listen to you, refusing help from a friend who owes a debt. If Darsal was right, you already have your share of enemies, lurking out there in the night."

She ran her hand along the back cushion. A finger over Johnis's shoulder. "So beautiful and innocent, yet so naive."

"Bold for a woman standing in my house," Karas said.

"Take your hand off of him!" Silvie shouted.

Miranda continued, drawing her hand along his shoulder as she walked past. "She was very specific," she said. "According to Darsal, the presence of four books in this reality makes the final three visible. I'm assuming that to now be the case. But she also said that if the four books are brought, they can open a gateway back into the other reality. Now, you understand my reluctance to just hand over that kind of power to anyone."

"We are Johnis, Silvie, and Karas!" Johnis said. "What else do you need?"

"The books," Miranda said. "Show me the other three books, and convince me you have a plan to recover the final three, and I'll give you the fourth. I assure you it's only a matter of precaution."

Miranda might have stumbled onto Darsal's book, but she was still a seductive tramp, and the faster they satisfied her curiosity and got rid of her, the better, Silvie thought.

"Fine. Show her the books, Karas."

Johnis nodded.

Karas eyed the woman cautiously, then retreated into her mansion, to the vault that she'd shown them earlier.

Miranda leaned up against the railing and smoked another

cigarette. She stared at the mansion, ignoring them as if they didn't exist.

"I don't trust her," Silvie whispered.

"Think about it; she's playing her cards right."

"What do you mean, 'right'? She's a tramp!"

"Please, Silvie, she's sitting on what she now knows is a very powerful book. She's testing us, playing the tramp, throwing us off center."

"To what end? That's ridiculous."

"People reveal their true character when they're off center. You have to at least admire her tactics."

"Bah! I don't buy it."

Karas glided toward them, holding the wooden box. "Where is your book?" she asked.

"Show me," Miranda said, stepping up to the table.

"Are we complete imbeciles?" Johnis said. "Prove that you have the blue book."

Miranda eyed him. Smiled. She reached into her purse, pulled out an object bound in aging white cloth, and set it on the table.

Johnis unwrapped the blue Book of History and set it down gingerly. It could be a fake, but if so, it was a perfect replica. Silvie didn't think there was a way to prove the authenticity of the book without actually using it.

"Looks real."

"Of course it's real," Miranda said. "Now yours."

Johnis nodded.

Karas pulled the black, the brown, and the green Books of History out and laid them next to each other on the glass table. They stared at them in silence.

"So . . ." Miranda finally said. "Tell me how you're planning to find the other three."

"You think it's wise to discuss that in front of her?" Silvie demanded.

"Discuss what?" Johnis said. "We don't even have a plan. Admittedly, she's come off like a rude tramp." He turned to her and shrugged. "Sorry, but it's true." Back to Silvie, "But that doesn't make her wrong."

What could she say to that?

"I don't like her attitude," Karas said.

"She brought us the blue book," Johnis said. "You don't have to like her attitude. Or her hairstyle or the way she's dressed, for that matter. She makes a point. What is our next move?"

Karas sighed. "The subject of my dreams for ten years. I only know details of the mission from what Darsal shared on Other Earth, and she wasn't the most forthcoming, being so consumed with Billos. But I've also pieced together a few details from the people in Paradise, Colorado, that might help us."

"Such as?"

She sat. "I told you about the simulation called Paradise earlier, the one we entered by touching the cover of the book with blood."

"Yes."

"I dug up everything I could get my hands on about Paradise, Colorado, and I found more. It seems to be some kind of epicenter for the books, not only in the simulation, but also in reality."

"Darsal mentioned Paradise," Miranda said. "Only to say that it was the first place she searched before going to Turkey."

"And?"

"Nothing. 'A small town that refuses to grow up,' she said."

"Maybe there's a reason it refuses to grow up. Follow me here. We know that Thomas Hunter spared this world from impending disaster in 2010, roughly twenty-three years ago, right?"

"Right," Johnis said, though he couldn't possibly know this level of detail. "As you say." Better.

"What very few know is that an incident occurred in Paradise eleven years later—the year 2021. An experiment in a monastery dubbed 'Project Showdown,' in which thirty-six children were raised in a kind of utopian environment, spared from evil. But the whole thing went terribly wrong."

"How does this fit into the seven missing books?" Johnis asked.

"It's rumored that the children in the monastery had access to magical books"—she looked at Miranda—"from Turkey."

"The Books of History?"

"I think Thomas Hunter brought some Books of History into this reality," Karas said. "And among them were the books we seek."

"In Paradise?"

"It's a starting point," Karas said. "Think about it, the history of the world rests in the hands of the choices we make. My own history changed when I chose to bathe in the lake water. It's the will of men that Teeleh seeks. Paradise is made or corrupted depending on the choices of children and the evil character they shudder to think about. A priest gone bad: Marsuvees Black."

"So the quest for the books was always about saving this place, not the forests?" Silvie asked.

"Perhaps. And maybe Paradise is the epicenter. Paradise, perfection. In our history there is a number that represents perfection."

"Seven," Miranda said.

Karas nodded. "The seven lost books." She shrugged. "It's a thought anyway."

Silvie was still stuck on the suggestion that their entire mission was about saving this reality rather than saving the forests from the Horde.

"If the mission has always been about this reality," Johnis said, tracking with her, "then who is the Dark One? This 'Black' character?"

"That's the question, isn't it?"

Crickets chirped in the darkness.

"So," Miranda said, and they all looked at her. "You'll take up your search in this town of yours—Paradise, Colorado." The moon was high now, and the woman's face was pale by its light. As were her arms and hands, Silvie saw. She was a curator, who rarely saw the light of day.

Karas shook her head. "Actually, no. Not the town. I've scoured it high and low, and the monastery is gone. I'm more interested in the history of the books that destroyed Paradise." Her eyes settled on Miranda. "And those books came from Turkey."

"Oh?"

"But that's enough. We've said enough for you to know, without a shadow of a doubt, that we are who we say we are and are committed to finding the books. You can leave this book with us."

"Yes, of course. But first, Darsal insisted that I tell the chosen one something. That would be Johnis."

"We're all chosen," Silvie snapped.

"Johnis. She was quite specific. Come."

Johnis stood still, clearly unsure about the way she'd ordered him.

"Don't be afraid. Come here."

He walked up to her tentatively.

Silvie saw her move a split second before the weapon was in Miranda's hand. She whipped a gun hidden in her loose slacks like a striking snake and leveled it at his head.

"Can the chosen one dodge bullets?" Miranda asked sweetly. "I don't think so. No one moves, or he dies."

A dull thumping beat at the air then swelled to a pounding that buffeted the night.

Miranda smiled. "We're going to find out just how much power these books have. If Darsal was right, the world as we know it is about to change."

A helicopter rose over the edge of the pool—how it had remained undetected or from where it had come, Silvie didn't know, but she could see that Karas was dumbfounded.

Two warriors in black hung from either door, their weapons trained on Silvie and Karas. The flying beetle hovered ten feet from Miranda, who smiled gently.

"Do something, Silvie. Let me send at least one of you to join Darsal." And Silvie knew she would at the slightest excuse.

Miranda walked to the table, scooped up all of the books except the one she'd brought, and stepped back, maintaining her sights on Johnis.

"You can keep that blue book; it's worthless. Into the bird, baby." She waved the gun at the helicopter. "Now!"

Silvie knew she had to do something. But it was all happening too quickly, and she half-expected Karas to stop the tramp! Silvie stood rooted to the ground, her mind blank. Johnis stared, pleading for her to save him.

"Teeleh's lair," he said.

Miranda lowered her gun a few inches and pulled the trigger. A projectile tugged at Johnis's jeans, but he did not move, did not even flinch. Blood seeped from the superficial wound.

"Go on, Silvie," Miranda sneered. "Go for one of those knives in your pocket. Move, Johnis, or I go higher."

"Teeleh's lair, Silvie," he said. "Tell Karas every—"

"Silence!"

Johnis turned and walked to the helicopter.

Silvie took a step forward, her heart hammering, ready to throw herself at the woman backing to the bird.

"No, Silvie," Karas said. "Not now."

"No, Silvie," Miranda cried over the slicing blades. "Not now, not ever." She slid into the cabin, and the aircraft rose. It chopped higher into the night sky and faded into the darkness, leaving them speechless.

"We've lost the books," Karas said.

Silvie whirled on the young girl who'd grown up overnight. "The books? You have all the power in the world, and you let this tramp into your house to take Johnis?"

"Easy . . ."

"How dare you?" she screamed, trembling from head to foot. "How dare you let them take him? He's all I have!"

"Your emotions, Silvie." Karas walked up to her. "Please, I'm sorry . . ."

Silvie felt her hand move before she could stop herself. Felt the sting of her palm as it struck the older girl's cheek.

For a moment they stared at each other, Silvie breathing steadily through her rage, Karas standing white with a red cheek.

Karas stepped forward, opening her arms.

*I've lost him,* Silvie thought. *I've lost Johnis . . .*

Then she dropped her head onto Karas's shoulder and began to weep.

# SIXTEEN

Whoever Miranda Card was, she seemed to have adequate resources at her disposal, Johnis thought. He doubted any average human in the Histories had access to helicopters and jets like the one he'd been hustled into.

The two assistants that worked for the woman had strapped a muzzle over his mouth, fixed a blindfold on his head, clamped shackles on his hands and feet, and shoved him into the dark compartment in which he now lay. The whole abduction, from the time they'd left the ground at Karas's home to the time they'd switched over to the jet and taken to the air once again, had been a half hour at most. No sign of Miranda Card.

Johnis lay on his side, telling himself to remain calm. His nerves were sending fear through his system—more than he was accustomed to. He kept telling himself it was the air here, as Karas had said. He'd faced the Shataiki and felt less fear.

Then again, maybe he had reason to feel more fear now than when he'd faced Teeleh. He was in the belly of a flying beast far above the ground, being flown to the far reaches of an earth stuck in the Histories, far from anything remotely familiar to him.

And if that wasn't enough cause for alarm, there was the fact that they'd managed to hand all four books over to an enemy about whom they knew next to nothing other than her clear intent to use the books for harm. It had to be the doing of Alucard. He'd killed Darsal and then corrupted the woman who'd taken her book.

A door opened. Slammed shut. Fingers pulled the blindfold up to his forehead.

Miranda Card stood above him, expressionless except for a wicked flash in her eyes. She'd changed into a charcoal dress with thin straps over each shoulder, black lacy underclothing peeking below the hem at her knees. Instead of high heels, she wore black leather boots with dark grey socks. Black rubber straps circled her neck and wrists. A tattoo of a serpent crawled along her right shoulder.

She tugged the muzzle free and shoved a bowl of water toward him with her foot. "Drink. I don't need you dead yet."

Johnis had no appetite for water, not with this creature lording over him. She was worse than the Shataiki—at least they were inhuman beasts given to the destruction of good. But this one . . .

A human who'd turned. Like Tanis. Like the Horde. It was no wonder that the people of the Histories would come to a nasty end, as was spoken of in hushed tones around campfires—more than mere legends.

"I'm sorry your travels between the worlds had to come to such an abrupt end so soon, but I've been patient enough."

"You're bluffing; you only have three of the books," he said.

"I assure you, I have the blue book, complete with the smudge of Darsal's blood on the first page. I not only have it; I've used it to enter the simulation—Paradise—many times. I assume you know about the simulation. The skin of this world."

"I've been there once. The man in the desert."

"Oh, that—Red, one of Black's creations gone rogue. As was White. Never mind them. I have all four books now, which is the key to the final three."

"You're underestimating Karas," Johnis said. "She's probably already on a jet, chasing you down."

"Is that so? To where?"

"Turkey."

Miranda grinned, then flattened her mouth. "Turkey is where the books were collected before they went to the monastery. They disappeared again, but not to Turkey; I've exhausted my search there."

"Then where?"

Miranda walked to the door, opened it, and stepped outside. "Romania," she said, and shut him into pitch darkness once again.

THE FLIGHT LASTED FOR MANY HOURS, AND AT ONE POINT Johnis was sure they would perish. The flying contraption bounced around like a tube strapped to a stallion's rear quarters. He cried out in alarm a dozen times, begging for Elyon to take him quickly, but if anyone was listening, he neither responded nor settled the bucking ship.

It occurred to him after an hour of being thrown about that they must be under attack. Karas had found them and was giving chase! It was the only possible explanation. Surely she realized that if the jet crashed to the ground, he would go with it! But when they finally hauled him from the craft in the dead of night, no one showed any concern of having narrowly escaped disaster.

They bound him in the back of a square, black car and sped through darkness, led by another car that carried Miranda Card. "Bucharest," one of them said, when Johnis asked where they were. And then, with a chuckle, "Welcome to hell."

Johnis still had some advantages they might not know about. His speed, his strength. His superior intelligence, although according to Karas, his mind would need time to make the adjustment.

Neither his speed nor his strength offered any advantage as long as they kept him in shackles. They seemed to have taken all the necessary precautions.

The large car left the city lights behind and climbed laboriously up a winding road that quickly turned rough. Dirt rather than concrete. A light fog settled over the mountain, but the headlamps pierced it with thick chords of light. The longer they traveled, the less talking took place between the driver and his guard. Soon the only sounds were the engine's whine and crunching gravel under the wheels.

When they finally stopped and turned off the engine, the air felt heavy, or was it the silence? The fog had thinned, and he could see the colossal citadel towering over them, barely visible against the dark sky. No lights. And no windows to allow light out.

Miranda walked in ahead of him. They shoved him forward, forcing him to take small, quick steps to avoid tripping on the shackles.

He stumbled through huge wooden doors that thudded shut behind him. Miranda's hard-soled shoes echoed down the torch-lit stone hall.

"There is no escape, chosen one. Follow me." Her voice dripped with spite.

Johnis followed, his heart pounding with each clank of his chains. Down the hall, into a stairwell that curved as it fell into the ground. He stopped at the entrance to several tunnels and lifted his arm to his nose. The odor was unmistakable: Shataiki.

He'd been in Teeleh's lair. Then Alucard's lair. And now another lair, here in the Histories: Romania.

"Move!"

He obeyed. Mucus covered the walls. No worms, but they were near; all of this sludge had come from somewhere. He shivered and forced his legs to move on, toward his objective.

It was true, no matter how much fear coursed through his

veins, he was as much drawn by purpose as pushed by his enemy's demands now. He'd come to the Histories to destroy evil, not flee from it!

The thought gave him some courage, but not much.

Miranda disappeared through a gate ahead on his right. He slowed, listening. Very soft popping sounds ran up and down the tunnel. But by peering into the light cast by the wall sconces, he could see only more darkness beyond.

The iron gate rested open, and he stepped cautiously through. A couch, a desk, bookshelves mostly empty. But unlike Teeleh's or Alucard's lair, this study had a large opening in the back. Another tunnel glowed with flickering flame. Water dripped far away.

He hesitated only a moment, then headed in. The floor sloped down, deeper into the ground. For a few steady breaths, he seriously considered turning and running, but he knew that there was no escape.

So he pushed his legs on. Further. Deeper.

The tunnel opened into a large, two-story library lit by wall torches and a half-dozen candelabras rising from dark wooden tables at the center. Wrought-iron railings ran the perimeter of the second floor and opened to the large atrium in which Johnis had entered.

Thousands of books lined the shelves on either side, but the wall directly ahead was draped with red velvet swags. A single table was framed by the heavy drapes. Twin candlesticks, each forming a winged serpent, sat on the table: Teeleh's symbol.

Miranda stood before the table, her back toward him. She turned and walked to one side, giving him full view of the table. The four books lay one on top of the other—black, brown, blue, green.

"Welcome to my world," Miranda said.

Johnis looked at the woman standing like a warrior in a dress, boots, and long, stringy hair. She looked as if she might be sick.

"Your world or his world?" Johnis asked.

"Is there a difference?"

"You don't know what you've gotten yourself into."

"And I would say it's you who have no idea what you've stumbled into. If Darsal was right, you were nothing but a poet a few weeks ago, rejected by this Forest Guard of yours. Your little quest is only four weeks old, isn't that right?"

So much had happened that it felt much longer. "Yes, that's right."

"Here in the so-called Histories, the quest for the books' power is over two thousand years old." Miranda's lips twisted in a whimsical smile. "You're but the latest little blip in a very long and gruesome ordeal that's lasted centuries. Darsal stumbled into something much larger than she could possibly know. As have you. The truth is, you know nothing, little Johnis." Then much louder, even furious, "*Nothing!*"

"I know where *he* comes from!" Johnis gestured toward the candlesticks. "Who he is. What he's capable of."

Miranda chuckled and walked slowly past the table, brushing

the four books with her fingertips. "Really? Then tell me even one thing you know so well. Tell me who he is?"

"The Dark One: Alucard."

"The nasty beast, Alucard. And what do you really know about Alucard?"

"That Teeleh sent him here to deceive the likes of you, which he's done surprisingly well in such a short time."

Miranda walked back, her hands now behind her back like a lecturer. Grinning at the fool. "You see, already you're misinformed. Alucard has been here for two thousand years, sowing seeds of misery and darkness in more ways than you've imagined."

She let the statement settle.

"And although he's a nasty beast around whom a whole mythology has emerged, spawning hundreds of stories about vampires and creatures of the night and all such things, he's not this 'Dark One' Darsal went on and on about. Not in this world, anyway. For that matter, neither is Marsuvees Black. Nor Red nor White . . . nor any of the other minions."

"Who then?"

"Unfortunately, you'll never know." Miranda's eyes settled on the table, and for the first time Johnis saw a silver knife resting beside the four books. "I do believe he intends to kill you the same way he killed Darsal seven years ago."

She picked up the knife and pulled the blade out of its silver sheath. "Not with a knife; he prefers another, more intimate method that's well-known in this world."

An image of Darsal bleeding to death from a neck bite blossomed in Johnis's mind. He'd never heard of the Shataiki killing that way. Then again, until a few weeks ago, the Shataiki were hardly more than legend in a world far away.

"You cannot thwart the will of Elyon," he said with as much confidence as he could muster.

"Elyon? You haven't heard? God is dead in this world. They killed him two thousand years ago. Alucard was there."

Johnis had no clue what Miranda referred to, but it hardly mattered any longer. His task was a simple one, and he had no intention of allowing her to complicate things.

"Why did you bring me here?"

"Because I asked her to," a voice rasped from above.

Johnis jerked his head up and stared at the rafters. The diseased, batlike creature hung from the center beam, staring down with yellow eyes.

Alucard.

He hid himself among thick worms, like a mother nesting her eggs. Slowly he unfolded himself, then dropped from the ceiling and landed on the library floor next to Miranda. Eyes on Johnis.

Alucard's mangy skin was whiter than he remembered, covered with mucus now, and his eyes had turned yellow. Otherwise two thousand years hadn't changed the beast.

"Hello, Johnisssss . . ."

# SEVENTEEN

Teeleh's Lair."

Silvie paced, biting at her fingernail. "What was he thinking? We all went into Alucard's lair, but Johnis was the only one who went into Teeleh's beneath the lake. It was where he found the brown book."

"There has to be more than you've told me," Karas said. "Why else would he tell you to tell me? You have to *think*!"

"I'm trying to!" Silvie shouted. "But something about this air, this cursed world . . . I can't think straight! I thought we were supposed to be more intelligent, not less!"

"Calm down, I'm not the enemy here. And the intelligence will come; have patience. It may take a few days, a couple weeks—"

"We don't have a couple weeks!"

"Then sit down and think with me! Start at the beginning."

"Again?"

"Again!"

The night had crawled by in relentless fits of tears and threats to end it all here and now. They had to give chase, never mind that they didn't know where to—just go. They had to inform the authorities, never mind that the police would likely send them both off to the fruit farm. They had to offer money, information, cars, whatever was necessary to purchase Johnis's life back, never mind that they didn't know who to offer it to.

The eastern sky had grayed with dawn, and now even Karas was showing signs of panic, which didn't help matters. Silvie dropped onto the couch that faced Los Angeles, which was spread out like an endless gray canyon before them. Her head spun with the events of the past week. They'd gone from celebrated heroes in the forest to insignificant fruits in the Histories in a matter of days.

"It's hopeless," she said. "Look at that."

"I do," Karas said. "Nearly every day."

"Thousands and thousands of buildings. Millions of people. Cars and airplanes and endless miles of stone or concrete or asphalt or whatever you call it. Fortunes being made and lost, rock stars getting their feet kissed, ordinary people eating and dressing and dreaming. And here we sit, like two ants on the hill, thinking we must or can do something to change any of it. You don't ever feel helpless?"

"Completely," Karas said. "Try doing it for ten years . . ."

"Right." She looked at Karas. "None of them even know that there are seven Books of History that can reshape reality as they know it."

"No. But some of them wouldn't be surprised."

"Where we come from, one day's events could change everything. Are there ever earth-shattering incidents here? Wars that change everything? Outcomes that every man, woman, and child leans forward to hear?"

"Not really, no. But everyone knows it will happen one day."

"Could they imagine that it *is* happening? Right now. Today!"

"Some," she sighed. "Please, Silvie. I know you're not thinking straight. You've been uprooted; we've lost the books; Johnis is gone . . ."

"He kissed me, Karas." She felt the tears seep into her eyes and made no attempt to blink them away. "We have fallen in love. I know it's foolish for members of the Forest Guard, and I know we are only just of marrying age, but I would marry him. Nothing else matters to me anymore."

"The books . . ."

"What about you, Karas? You're twenty-one. Surely you've fallen in love."

"More than once."

"I mean, look at you! You're stunning. What's wrong with the men in the Histories? They should be lined up outside your door!"

"Well, that's not how we do things here, but they are." She

looked far off. "But I've been a little too preoccupied to entertain more than a passing interest."

Spoken like the principled little girl who'd broken ranks with the Horde at great risk to herself—almost a reprimand.

"Perhaps if I had someone like Johnis . . ."

"Don't even think about it!"

"Don't be ridiculous," Karas said, blushing. "I know when I'm beat. Unfortunately, men from our world are in short supply here."

Silvie felt bad for the girl.

"Well, I have a feeling that everything's going to change in the very near future." Silvie took a deep breath and blew it out slowly. "Okay, let's start at the beginning. What did Johnis mean, 'Teeleh's lair'? He wanted to say something that I would understand without Miranda's knowledge."

"She's after the same thing we are now: the final three books."

"Which became accessible when Johnis crossed over with the fourth book."

"Right, we've been over this." Karas stood and walked up to the railing. "Teeleh's lair . . . it's the key to the location, Silvie. Something he told you that no one else could know."

"I told you. He described it to me in the desert on the way to the Horde City. And from what I can remember, it's exactly the same as Alucard's lair except . . ."

Silvie's heart stopped. She jumped to her feet.

"What?" Karas asked.

"The poem! He said there was a poem on the wall. I don't

remember anything in Alucard's lair. That's what was unique about Teeleh's lair. He must have been trying to direct me to the poem without tipping off Miranda!"

Karas hurried over, her eyes wide. "What poem?"

"Something about a sinner, a saint, and a showdown." She blinked. "'Welcome to Paradise.'"

"It said that? 'Welcome to Paradise'?"

"Yes."

"Yes, okay, yes. So what does—"

And then Karas got it.

"Paradise. The epicenter of this showdown between saint and sinner, good and evil. You're saying that there is a lair in Paradise."

"'Welcome to Paradise,'" Silvie repeated.

"The monastery was destroyed. Flattened. I've been there. Nothing but a cabin."

"But were you looking for Teeleh's lair? Johnis must have . . ." Her voice trailed off.

Karas stared at her in silence, piecing together what she'd just learned with what she already knew.

She suddenly rushed toward the house. "Get the jet up!" she cried to one of her servants inside.

Silvie hurried behind. "To where?"

"Paradise, Colorado."

# EIGHTEEN

Alucard's tongue licked at the mucus on his fingers. He stared at Johnis like a mad doctor who'd trapped a monkey on which to run his forbidden experiments.

"The beast from hell," Johnis said. Although he meant it as an accusation, his voice came out strained.

"I have waited for this day." Alucard walked to the table, his talons clicking on the stone floor. He reached out and touched the prize Miranda had delivered.

"Four is a far cry from seven," Johnis said.

"That's where you're wrong, my friend. Finding the last three will be a simple matter now. They may be the prize locked away for centuries, but I now have the key." He faced Johnis, his lips twisted. "Surely you know where the other three are."

Johnis had his ideas, to which he'd tried to alert Silvie. But he knew more than Alucard could possibly know.

"There are only a few lairs in this reality. For all we know, the last three books are hidden here, in this very library." His eyes ran over the bookcases. Johnis wasn't positive that the books were in a lair, but they seemed to favor lairs on Other Earth.

After two thousand years, Alucard wasn't in a rush to tear the place apart, Johnis realized. If the last three books were in one of the lairs, he wasn't in any danger of someone else finding them before he did. Except for Silvie and Karas.

A chuckle echoed softly around the room. Alucard walked around him, moving easily, inspecting. "You're wondering why I didn't just kill all three of you? Are you really so foolish?"

The stench of the beast's flesh so close was enough to make Johnis temper his breathing.

"Tell him, Miranda."

"We can kill them at any time. Why would we eliminate something that could still be useful?" She spoke as if she were a disinterested peer to the Shataiki, not his servant.

*How so?* Johnis wanted to ask. But he already knew. They'd taken him in the event they needed leverage. "What makes you think Silvie and Karas won't find the books before you do?"

"Let them. It is now only a matter of time. Hours, days, it makes no difference to me." Alucard breathed heavily and continued in a soft voice that trembled with each word. "My time has come."

The worms overhead moved through their own muck, agitated.

"We have waited so long. Unlike you humans, Shataiki are born of the hive lord, the equivalent of your queen bee, only male. All we need now are the females."

Johnis shuddered. These worms were Alucard's offspring, trapped larvae, waiting for a female to somehow make them Shataiki. Or was Alucard the female? Either way, with the four books, Alucard could return to the Black Forest and bring back what he needed to turn these larvae into Shataiki. And what would happen to this world if thousands of Shataiki were set free?

"You . . . you can't do that."

"And now that you know how your little quest is going to end, I can kill you." Alucard's long, sharp talon reached around Johnis's neck from behind and drew a thin line over his exposed skin. One jerk and his head would be parted from his body. Was the beast's need to see the chosen one dead greater than his need for any leverage Johnis might give him?

Johnis didn't want to find out.

The talon bit into his skin. "Are you ready to die, chosen one?"

"You can't." He looked at Miranda's dark stare. "You don't have four of the books."

The talon at his neck hesitated.

"Don't be a fool," Miranda said.

"Am I the fool? Do you think we are that stupid?"

A tick bothered Miranda's cheek.

"You have four books on the table," Johnis said. "Three of them are genuine. One of them is a fake."

945

THE JET STREAKED FOR THE SKY, AND SILVIE GRIPPED THE armrests, her knuckles white. But once again, the flying tube of steel hung in the air as comfortably as any bird she'd seen.

She slowly released her grip. "What if we're wrong?"

"We're not," Karas said. "The books are in Teeleh's lair, wherever that is. I'm willing to stake my life on it."

"It's his life you're staking. What's all this numbers business?"

"Six of the books went missing. The number of evil, perfection divided. Three are now missing: the number that Teeleh aspires to become—perfection. Follow?"

"Not really."

"Then never mind for now. The point is, the three missing books are almost certainly hidden in the heart of darkness. Teeleh's lair."

"But what makes you think there aren't other 'hearts of darkness' here in the Histories? Why tie it directly to Teeleh?"

"Because you said it yourself, 'Welcome to Paradise.' Because the books came from our world when Thomas Hunter crossed over. They would naturally find a place consistent with that world— Teeleh's lair."

"Three books in our world; three here," Silvie said, as if it now all made perfect sense to her. "Six missing books. Evil. Perfection defiled. And if we're wrong about the lair being in Paradise?"

Karas frowned. "Then we hope Johnis has something up his sleeve besides a little extra strength."

"HE'S LYING," MIRANDA SNAPPED.

Johnis allowed himself a moment of satisfaction. "Now who's the fool?"

Alucard whipped around him and leaped to the table, where he landed on his hind legs with enough force to send a vibration through the floor. He fanned the books across the table with a flip of his wrist. "Show me!"

Miranda was already hovering over the books, the silver knife in her hand. She shoved the blue book to the side and pulled the brown book closer—sliced her finger.

Holding her eyes on Johnis, she planted her finger on the brown book's cover.

She vanished in a wink of light into this simulation they talked about, modeled after Paradise. Everyone wants a piece of Paradise.

The brown book lay still, smudged with Miranda's blood. Alucard stood by the table, breathing steadily. The worms squirmed slowly above. Johnis stood in his shackles.

A silent flash of light appeared over the book, and Miranda stood next to the table again, wearing a smirk. "Works for me."

She pushed the brown book aside and pressed her finger against the green one.

Again, a wink of light swallowed her.

Alucard grunted.

The woman reappeared. Still smiling.

"The black one," the Shataiki growled.

Miranda brushed the green book aside and pulled the black one closer. She shoved her finger against the cover.

Nothing happened.

"Cut yourself!" Alucard said.

Her finger was no longer bleeding. She snatched up the silver knife they evidently kept for this very purpose and cut her skin again. Red blood seeped from the fresh wound.

She smashed it against the cover.

But Miranda did not vanish. What Karas had told him was true: she'd made a duplicate book and hidden the original. Today her effort paid off.

Alucard snarled and rushed the ten feet to Johnis. His claw squeezed around Johnis's neck. Unable to breathe, much less scream, Johnis could only clench his eyes against the pain.

"Where is the fourth book?"

The beast's breath was hot and wet.

"Give me the book!"

"Killing him won't help us!" Miranda said. "Let him go."

Alucard held him for another five seconds, then relaxed his grip. He backhanded Johnis with enough force to throw him backward several feet.

He landed on his side, struggling for breath.

"Where is it?" Alucard repeated.

He would die before he told them. Now it was only about stalling to give Silvie more time. Johnis coughed. Blood wet the stone by his hand. Alucard had damaged his throat. He lay on the dungeon floor, broken.

Hopelessness came, like an avalanche in the night, thundering down on him from overhead. He was going to fail. This beast was far too powerful to stop!

There was only one play left for him.

"He doesn't know," Alucard said. "Kill him."

"No," Johnis gasped. "I do know!"

Miranda stooped beside him and traced his cheek with her knife. "Of course you know. Karas would tell the chosen one. You know. And we know where Silvie is headed. We don't need her; Karas will suffice. One word and Silvie will die."

"Don't . . . You can't harm her!"

"This is a waste of time," Alucard snarled. "Lock this useless slab of meat up. Cut off his leg and show it to her. If she still doesn't cooperate, kill her and work on the little runt."

"No, I can take you to the book."

"Or lead me astray." Miranda's knife lingered just beneath his jaw. "To buy your little lover more time?"

It occurred to Johnis that Miranda always spoke as if it was she, not Alucard, who should be dealt with here. As if she, not the beast, held the true power in the room. At least in her mind.

"Just tell me," she said.

"I can't. But I can take you. If you don't get the book, kill me. But leave Silvie. You have me! What can you gain by taking her now?"

*Plenty.*

Miranda smiled, drawing the knife across his cheek. Then she nicked him. "Don't flirt with the illusion that you've bought yourself more than a few more hours of life. It's all going to end soon."

She turned her back on him and spoke to Alucard. "I have reason to believe that the other three books may be in the buried monastery."

He grunted softly. "We'll see. Bring me her book."

# NINETEEN

Paradise sat in the valley directly below the helicopter. A sleepy-looking village with only one paved street that she could see.

"Hardly the kind of place you'd expect to be the epicenter of the struggle between good and evil," Silvie said.

"I think that's the point."

Since there was no place to land a jet in Paradise, they'd flown into a town named Grand Junction, then switched to the helicopter Karas had arranged.

"There's something you should know, Silvie," Karas said, staring at the town below them. "I've been debating whether to tell you because I'm afraid that they will stop at nothing to get the information from one of us if they take us. I already made a mistake in telling Johnis."

"What are you talking about?"

Karas looked at her. "My book, the one Miranda took, was a copy. Mine is hidden in Paradise. I'm sorry for not telling you sooner. But Miranda only has three books, not four."

Silvie didn't know what to think about the prospect of her trusting Johnis, but at the moment she didn't feel the need to dwell on it. There were more important matters at hand.

"Fine. It's safe, right? Probably the safest place for it right now."

"Unless Johnis—"

"He wouldn't. And Miranda may have pieced together what we have about the other three. We should test our theory first and return if we find them."

"Or we could hide my book again to protect Johnis."

"We have to see if there's a lair," Silvie snapped.

"Okay. To the canyons."

The helicopter floated over Paradise, then headed into the canyon lands to the south. A wide, white-faced gorge had been cut from the mountain. They flew down into it and pulled up near the box canyon at the end.

"Where?"

"There." Karas pointed to a cliff on her side of the helicopter where a landslide had taken down a hundred yards of the canyon wall. "They used explosives to implode a monastery built into the cliff face. A real shame. Someone went to a lot of trouble to keep this place hidden."

A small cabin had been built among the rubble, but this didn't strike Silvie as the kind of place they would find the books that had caused them so much trouble.

"Take 'er down," Karas signaled the pilot.

They landed a hundred feet from the cabin and ducked out from under the spinning blades. "Wait for us."

Karas led Silvie through an unlocked cabin door, into what looked to be a long, deserted room with two doors leading farther in. They quickly checked the two rooms: nothing obvious.

Karas switched on her battery-operated torch and ran it over the floor. "Okay, we're looking for an opening that leads below the cabin."

Silvie tried her own light. She might have been mesmerized by the contraption—fire sealed in this battery Karas referred to—but her mind was preoccupied with Johnis's absence. "How do we know the lair is here, not buried under all the rubble?"

"We don't."

"Surely Alucard would have searched this place."

"Not since all four books have been in this reality, he hasn't."

"How do you know? He could be down there right now, waiting for us."

"Turkey, maybe. Or Romania. I doubt he's here."

"Romania?"

"Never mind. Come on."

They searched the outer room first, covering every square inch on their hands and knees. The whole business was enough to soak

Silvie in sweat. All she could think about was Johnis caged in a dungeon . . . or worse.

"We're wasting time!" Silvie announced, standing. "What was that you said about Romania? This can't be the right place!"

"I'll take one room; you take the other."

The *other* was a bathroom, and it took Silvie only a few minutes to convince herself that there was nothing remotely resembling Teeleh's lair within a hundred miles of this place.

"Silvie!"

She dove for the door, slammed into its frame, and spun through, ignoring the pain that flashed up her arm.

"What is it?"

She saw what it was before Karas could answer. The wood-frame bed had been pulled to one side, and a trapdoor rose to reveal a dark tunnel beneath.

They'd actually found it?

"There's a ladder." Silvie dove for the hole and was halfway into the floor before Karas could stop her.

"Easy! I have the gun. I should lead."

Silvie hesitated as Karas dropped past her into the earth below. They were in a small tunnel that ran perpendicular to the earth's surface, not deep. It was an escape route freshly dug, not an ancient fortified tunnel like Alucard's lair.

"This isn't it," she breathed, hurrying behind Karas, who scurried forward in a crouch, her gun extended.

No response.

They rounded a bend, following the light from their battery-operated torches. The tunnel ended at another ladder heading up. Light seeped through a square trapdoor about fifty feet above their heads.

"That's it?" Silvie looked back. "We missed something! There has to be another tunnel!"

She spun and headed back, chasing the sound of her breathing now. Miranda was torturing Johnis in a land far away, while they wasted their time here beneath a cabin outside Paradise, Colorado.

"Silvie!"

She plowed on. The quicker they covered this search and left Paradise, the better. Nothing here looked like Teeleh.

"Silvie!"

She spun back. "What?"

"Do you hear that?"

Silvie heard her own wheezing. Her thumping heart. "No."

"There, listen!"

Silvie held her breath and listened. Then she heard it, a very faint, high-pitched squealing sound that sent a streak of terror down her spine.

She studied the dirt ceiling. The walls. It seemed to come at them from every direction from far away. Her eyes met Karas's, round like saucers. The squealing was louder now that they were perfectly still.

"What is that?" Silvie breathed.

"I . . . I don't know." She shoved her gun into her belt, leaned her ear close to the wall, and listened. "It's . . ." But she didn't know more.

Silvie drew her light slowly over the rough dirt walls. She walked farther down the tunnel. The sounds faded.

She walked back slowly. "It's louder here. Something's behind the walls. There has to be . . ."

Silvie suddenly saw the demarcation along the tunnel wall, rockier along a five-foot section between her and Karas. She stepped up and placed her ear between the rocks.

The squealing was now distinct, like the wailing of a million insects or lobsters, protesting their capture.

"You're right," Karas said.

"What is it?"

"I don't know." She headed back down the tunnel. "But we're going to find out."


IT TOOK THEM NEARLY AN HOUR TO DIG THROUGH THE TUN-nel wall using shovels from the helicopter. Silvie swung her spade, fighting to hold her frustration in check. It was clear that Johnis wasn't here because the earth had been undisturbed for a long time.

The books probably weren't here either. They couldn't be so for-tunate as to find them so quickly after arriving in the Histories. Then again, Karas had been searching for over ten years. She and Johnis had just shown up near the end of the search. Either way, something was here. The more they dug, the louder the squealing sounded.

"We should just use dynamite and be done with this!" Karas mumbled.

"Dynamite?" Silvie pried up on a rock, attempting to pluck it from the earth, but it remained stuck. "What's dynamite?"

The rock suddenly rolled. Not toward her, but away. Into darkness beyond.

The squealing became a faint, but much clearer, high-pitched screaming. Silvie went rigid. The sound of the boulder rolling down a slope was unmistakable. It landed far below with a dull thump.

The squealing stopped.

Karas scrambled for one of the torches. Shone it through the hole. The beam revealed nothing but darkness. And an eerie silence.

"Teeleh's lair?"

For the first time since landing in the canyon, Silvie felt a strong surge of hope. They'd certainly found something, and it could be Teeleh's lair.

Which meant the Books of History could be here. And the Books of History were their only leverage now. Johnis's life depended on what they found in this hole.

She dropped to her seat and kicked at the rocks surrounding the small hole. The wall caved as if the whole thing had been held up by a small toothpick. A small avalanche tumbled away from them.

Dust coiled.

Silvie grabbed her torch and crawled through the opening.

"What is it?" Karas asked from behind.

"A staircase. I . . . I don't know."

She eased out onto stone steps spiraling into darkness. No walls on either side or ahead that she could see. Silence.

Karas stood up beside her and played her light around. "A cavern below the old monastery. This has to be it, Silvie. Nothing else would explain this."

"Let's go." Silvie stepped gingerly around fallen rock, pushing stones aside as she descended. Fifty steps. Farther. Now a stench from below. A smell that reminded her of putrid water or . . .

She stopped. "Shataiki!" Her whisper echoed softly. She flashed her light up and saw a stone wall ahead, wet with mucus. And lying across the mucus was a large worm, perhaps a full foot in diameter. Twenty yards long.

Karas put a hand on her shoulder and held tight.

These were the same worms from Alucard's lair. Johnis had wondered if they might be larvae for the larger Shataiki, and looking at this one now, Silvie guessed he was right.

She wanted to spin, run back up the stairs, and drop fire in this hole to kill all that lived below. But Johnis . . .

Silvie clenched her jaw and stepped down, farther in.

The steps ended at the base of the wall. They were in a massive cavern, but she could only see this one wall. A single blackened wooden door hung from rusted hinges, gaping an inch or two.

"This is it." Her voice came raspy. "Is it safe?"

A stupid question, one that Karas didn't bother answering. She stepped past Silvie, her gun extended again. Still silence. So then what had done all the squealing? Karas drew the door wide with the gun's barrel.

A smaller atrium waited inside. And from this atrium several tunnels headed farther in. But the tunnel on their right was the one they should take. It was the only one with worms on the walls, slipping through their own mucus.

They held their torches on the same entrance, transfixed by the sight of two worms so close. And then the squealing came, louder than Silvie thought could have been possible from the small mouth on one of the worms, now open in a scream.

She jumped back. But other than moving its head about, the worm did nothing. No sign of threat other than this cry of protest. The halls fell quiet once more.

"They've been trapped down here," Karas said, "for Elyon knows how long. Waiting to be set free."

"By who?"

"Alucard? Maybe he couldn't do it without all seven books."

"If you're right," Silvie said, "and if he thinks he has the other four, he might be on his way now."

"So . . . we should go in."

They exchanged a look of fear, then walked forward into the tunnel.

The walls were strewn so thick with worms that they hid most of the stone. They waded through four inches of sludge covering the floor, only partially protected by their boots.

Silvie switched her torch to one hand and covered her nose

with the other. If the lair was laid out like Alucard's, the heart of the nest would be behind a set of gates, ahead on the right.

Which is where they found it. Gate locked. Empty of worms.

Their torches illuminated a study of sorts, complete with desk, a couch, and some bookcases. No dust, but plenty of worm salve. It was almost identical to the study in Alucard's lair. Slightly different furniture and arrangement, but clearly cut from the same blueprint.

"Stand back." Karas aimed the barrel of her gun at the lock, turned her head, and pulled the trigger. *Boom!*

Worms squealed. The lock lay in two. She wrestled it from the latch and opened the gate. With a screech of rusted hinges, the study opened to them.

"Are they here?" Silvie demanded.

Karas fired a stick and set the flame against an old torch mounted on the wall. The flame grew and crackled, spewing black smoke.

Orange light licked the glistening walls. Someone had carved an inscription into the rock next to the gate: *Welcome to Paradise, Population 450.*

"This is definitely what Billy wrote," Karas said.

"You mean 'Billos'?"

"No. One of the children in the monastery. It's a long story. But this is where the showdown all began. Or ended. Or is it still in full swing?"

"In my book it's still going," Silvie said. "Until we find Johnis and the books."

"So where are they?"

She turned, studying each corner. Silvie walked to the desk and pulled open one of two drawers on each side.

There, just visible in the shadows, lay an old black book. The words on its cover jumped out. Silvie gasped. Reached for the book and pulled it out. Bound in red twine exactly like the other four.

"I was right!" Karas cried. "They're here!"

But the drawer was empty. "They?"

Karas fumbled with the other drawer, yanked it open, staring inside. She reached in with both hands and pulled out two books, laying them on the desk beside Silvie's black one.

Purple and gold, bound by red twine, bearing the same name: *The Story of History.*

They'd found the three missing books.

"You know what this means?" Karas looked at her. "With the book I have hidden, we now have four. We have to collect the fourth book! We have to get down to Paradise!"

Silvie agreed. One problem: "They still have Johnis."

As one, the worms in the hall behind them began to screech.

# TWENTY

"Paradise? Why would she hide the book in Paradise, of all places? It's far too obvious."

"Not just anywhere in Paradise. You're saying you could just walk in, tear them apart, and take the books?"

"But Paradise. We've searched . . ."

"Maybe the fact that it's so obvious makes it the perfect place. Either way, you'll know soon enough."

"Tell me where."

"And minimize my value? I'll *show* you."

Miranda smiled gently, eyeing Johnis with interest. She was still dressed in the boots, the dark dress, the lace. Long, black, unkempt hair. A perfectly formed face that, apart from her betrayal, would be beautiful.

She sat beside him with her arms crossed and one leg draped over the other as the helicopter wound through the mountains, flying low. The flight from Romania had taken only a few hours aboard the orbital jet. The sun was beginning to dip in the west.

There was a strong possibility that Karas had already collected the book and, if so, Johnis was finished. But he also knew that both he and Silvie were finished anyway. His only hope was to stall Miranda long enough to give Karas time.

Time to find the last three books before Alucard could get his claws on them.

"You remind me of Darsal," Miranda said. "Both so intent, so obsessed with this mission."

"That's nice."

"She was bitter, you know. When I met her, she'd spent three years without success. She had no clue what had happened to the others. To you. But she was driven by something else entirely. Do you know what that was?"

"Billos," Johnis said.

"A man. She was in love with a man. She once told me that she blamed Elyon. It was his rules that forced Billos to give up his life."

"Billos died? She said that?"

"I suppose so. She obviously thought he was dead."

"And what did she expect to do about it?" Johnis demanded.

"That's the question, isn't it? What did she think having all seven books would do for her?"

Miranda's suggestion stunned him. This notion that Darsal might have intended to use the books for her own gain or for revenge . . . preposterous!

There had always been a strange connection between Darsal and Billos, dating back to his rescue of her when she was much younger. Clearly, whatever had happened when they'd both gone into the books had only strengthened the bond.

"Well?" Miranda pressed. "What could someone like Darsal or, for that matter, anyone do with the seven books?"

"Something in this world," Johnis said.

"Yes, this world. It's always been about this world. Even the Shataiki are about this world. They may have crossed some forbidden river, thanks to Tanis, as Alucard claims, but they've always had their sights on this world. And now they're about to repeat it, honey."

Some of what she said made sense; some it didn't. For Johnis, the matter was simple: he was here to get the books before the Dark One could. And so far he'd done that by following his heart.

"It's all about the Shataiki, and it's all about love." Miranda looked at him. "What about you, Johnis? What would you do for love?"

"Anything."

"I'm counting on it. You're just like Darsal that way." She rested her hand on his thigh. "I like that in a man."

"Take your stinking hands off me."

TED DEKKER

She leaned close. He could smell her perfume, a rich spice he didn't recognize. The scent of Shataiki lingered faintly about her.

"When I have the books, you'll change your tune, little boy. And make no mistake, I will have them."

"Don't you mean Alucard?"

"Alucard," she said slowly. "I'm sure you've figured out that it was he who killed Darsal. As he intends on killing you."

Her hand suddenly tightened like a vice above his knee. Her grip was strong, stronger than he thought possible.

She released him, lifted her hand, and slapped him with enough force to spin his head.

"Love, baby. It's all about love."

Two minutes later they settled in a field just behind a spire-tipped building Miranda called a "church," and Johnis's head was still spinning with her words. Her slap. He wasn't sure he shouldn't fear Miranda Card more than Alucard.

It was now all about timing. He would make his play, but not until they had the book. Then he would see just what this witch was made of. He had a few tricks up his sleeve himself.

"Where to?"

"To the home of Sally Drake," Johnis said.

"Let's go."

"You know where it is?"

"Like I said, I've been here in the simulation looking for clues. If you're wrong about this, I'm going to cut off your fingers. Start praying, boy."

"Hurry!"

Silvie stumbled over the stones that littered the top of the stairs. She glanced over her shoulder and saw that Karas, who carried the three Books of History, was still twenty steps behind. "Hurry!"

"This isn't a race!" Karas panted. "We have them, Silvie. You want me to lose them?"

Silvie played her light to the side. She had no idea how far it was to the bottom or if there *was* a bottom. "Just hurry; they have Johnis."

"Having the books won't help us find Johnis."

*You're wrong, Karas. The books are exactly what we need to find Johnis.* She spilled through the hole they'd punched in the tunnel.

"What we need now is the fourth book." Karas clambered up behind.

"How? How will all four help us more than three? You may have been searching for ten years, Karas, but I have more history with the books."

"With four books we could go back to the forest," Karas said.

Yes, there was that. But Johnis wasn't in the forest. He was here, in Alucard's talons.

"Of course, the fourth book. Just hurry."


JOHNIS AND MIRANDA STOOD OUTSIDE OF SALLY DRAKE'S house ten minutes later. The streets were empty except for one boy who leaned against the church, chewing on a piece of grass.

"Do you want to go in peacefully, or should I just go in, kill the tramp, and find the book on my own?"

"No need to cause a stir. Let me get the book."

"Remember: one false move and I will kill you where you stand."

He knocked on the door and waited for a few seconds.

A thin woman answered the door. "Hello?"

"Sally Drake?"

"Yes. May I help you?"

"My name is Johnis. I think you have something a friend of mine, Karas, left with you. A book. I would like the book."

She stared at him, speechless.

"Sally Drake?"

The woman blinked. "I . . . I'm sorry. For a moment there I thought you looked . . . Have we met?"

"Hurry it, please!" Miranda snapped.

Sally looked over Johnis's shoulder at Miranda. "I'm sorry, but I was told not to—"

Miranda flew past Johnis and slammed her gun against Sally's forehead. The woman dropped in a pile, unconscious.

Miranda stepped over the fallen form, muttering something about people not listening. Pulled Sally's prone body into the house.

"Get in here!"

Johnis stumbled in, dumbstruck.

"Find the book!"

She wouldn't let him out of her sight, which slowed their search some, but the house only had four rooms, including the

kitchen. Miranda found the book in the larger of the two bedrooms, under the mattress.

Black. Blood smeared on the first page. *The Story of History.*

Her eyes were fired with satisfaction. "Let's go."

"What about her? You can't just leave an innocent woman . . ."

"Innocent? She was holding one of the books, you fool! Karas
is the one who's to blame for dragging her into this. Move!"

They left Paradise behind two minutes later. The sun was setting, time was fleeting, and Johnis was running out of options.

He had to make his play, and soon. The jet that would return
them to Alucard's lair waited in a city to which they would fly in
a smaller jet.

*In the city,* he decided. At the very least he would strike in the
city.

# TWENTY-ONE

Is she okay?"

"Hurt but alive." Karas eased Silvie away from the house.

A police car with flashing lights sat in front of Sally Drake's home. They had already taken her to the hospital in Delta, twenty minutes away.

"And the book?"

"Gone."

"How do you know?"

"Because it's not where we agreed she would keep it. It's gone!" Karas yelled the last word, red faced.

"How long?"

"They came in a helicopter and were gone before anyone could talk to them. A man and a woman."

"Johnis! How long?"

"Ten minutes." Karas pressed her fingers against her temples. "This can't be happening."

"It *is* happening! They'll stop at nothing! How far could they have gone in ten minutes?"

"They were flying. They're gone."

A man dressed in a round hat and pointed boots eyed them from the sidewalk. Karas took Silvie's arm and led her across the street. The helicopter whirled in a field next to the church, ready for departure.

"We have to get out of here."

Silvie walked, numb, her mind buzzing with what they now must do. "We have to use the books."

"We only have three," Karas groaned. "We might as well have one. All we can do is enter the simulation—you know that. They're worthless!"

"Not to Alucard."

"What are you saying?"

Silvie angled for the helicopter and picked up her pace. "We have to trade the books for Johnis."

"Don't be stupid!"

Silvie whirled, furious despite the knowledge that Karas was being perfectly logical. "I'll tell you what was stupid!" She pointed a finger in Karas's face. "Going into Teeleh's lair to recover the first Book of History. Leading the Third into battle to rescue his mother. Betraying Thomas to save you from Witch! That was stupid!"

Karas's face lightened a shade.

Silvie continued, "Yet those were all things Johnis did, following his heart. Now he's in trouble, and you suggest I don't follow my heart?"

"That's not what I'm saying."

"Then what?"

"Follow your heart, but don't be stupid," Karas said. "You can't give Alucard all seven books! Your mission is to find them before the Dark One does, not to give the Dark One all seven to save your lover."

"You think I don't know the mission? I was chosen with Johnis. I was there when he went into the first lair. I was by his side when he risked his life to save you, or have you forgotten?"

"I don't see—"

"I'm saying that Johnis didn't follow perfect logic; he did what he believed was right in the face of terrible odds. And each time he ended up with a book."

"Then he was lucky."

"Luck had nothing to do with it. Johnis was chosen because he was willing to do what others were unwilling to do. It's in his heart! That is the *only* way to find the books."

It was the first time Silvie had actually thought of it in those terms, but saying it, she thought she might actually have struck on the heart of the matter.

"Think about it." She jabbed her head with a finger. "It's about the heart, not logic. The Great Romance, the fall from Elyon,

Teeleh's jealousy, the Horde, the lost books . . . all of these have to do with the heart. The only way to find the seven books is to follow your heart." She let out a long breath. "Johnis followed his. Now I will follow mine."

"But giving the books—"

"The right thing to do is to save Johnis, at all costs."

"Even if it costs the mission?"

"It's my mission to lose, not yours. Were you chosen?"

Karas looked at the helicopter, her jaw set. Silvie knew that she was wounding her friend, the only friend she had in this world at the moment. But she wasn't about to let the one man who'd repeatedly risked his life to save theirs be killed now. And yes, there was some self-serving messiness to this business. She loved Johnis. More than she loved the books, more than she loved herself.

"No," Karas said. "You were chosen. So I'll follow you. Like I followed Darsal."

"And did Darsal find the fourth book?"

"Yes."

"So then, have faith."

"Darsal also struck the deal with Alucard that put us in this mess."

Touché.

"As you say, I'm chosen. And I say we do whatever it takes to get Johnis back."

"Okay. We use the books to get Johnis back if we can. Any suggestions, chosen one?"

Silvie ignored the dig. "We get word to Miranda before she does anything foolish."

"And how do we do that?"

"The same way we got word to you. You need to get us on the Net."

"That could take some time, assuming anyone is even interested. You can't just walk up to a camera and spout off your personal messages for them to broadcast."

"Then we do something more inventive. Take someone important captive."

"Don't be ridiculous." She frowned. "You really want to do this, huh?"

"Every minute we talk takes him another minute farther from us. We have the only thing they need now. We use the books!"

Karas turned and walked toward the helicopter. "Here goes nothing."

# TWENTY-TWO

He had to move, and he had to do it quickly. And judging by the switch they'd made from the helicopter to the small jet, moving on the ground was going to be more of a problem than he'd imagined.

Miranda had shackled him before landing, his wrists separated by a short length of chain, his ankles tethered together in the same way. Then, under the cover of darkness, she'd led him across the asphalt to the waiting jet. He was supposedly stronger than most in the Histories, but he was not strong enough to break the chains—he'd tried more than once and succeeded only in bruising his wrists.

"How high are we?"

She lifted her eyes. "High enough for you to contemplate your death for three or four minutes before being smashed like a bug."

"You think I would jump shackled like this?"

"I think you would save me the hassle of disposing of your body if you jumped without a parachute."

He frowned. There were some qualities about Miranda that he found appealing, he'd decided: Her obsession with the Books of History. Her ruthlessness in pursuing what she understood to be great gain. She would have made a good leader among the Forest Guard with the right heart.

"What do you really hope to gain in all of this?" he asked.

She grinned. "You have to ask? I stand in a room below the earth with Alucard. This beast who's lived for centuries and spawned only he knows what kind of evil upon this earth. Kings and their kingdoms have risen and fallen throughout history because of him."

He hadn't thought of it in those terms.

"He has more power and more wealth than any man who has ever lived. And yet he would trade it all for seven history books bound in leather. And you ask me what I hope to gain? The question is, what do *you* hope to gain?"

"I'm doing what was asked of me."

"Of course, how silly of me. These fuzzy white bats from your world."

"Elyon."

"The one who made this mess to begin with."

He turned from her and eyed the rear compartment door again. They would fly to Alucard's lair, and with nothing left to gain from his life, she would dispose of him.

A bell sounded, and Miranda snatched her phone to her ear. Listened.

He had to get the shackles off using the key in her pocket. But even now her eyes rested on him, watching, always ready. She had two of the guns, one in each of two holsters under her arms. One wrong move and he knew she wouldn't hesitate to kill him.

She suddenly stood, spun to the Net screen that hung from the ceiling, and pressed a button. The thin box blazed to life.

There, on a stage like the one they'd seen in the Rose Bowl, stood none other than Karas. The caption below her said they were at the Pepsi Center in Denver. A Tony Montana benefit concert.

Miranda muttered a bitter curse. "They have them! They took them from under our noses!"

Johnis stood from his seat. "The books?"

Miranda whirled. "Sit!"

He remained standing, his eyes on the Net, and she spun back, momentarily preoccupied. Karas stood center stage with Tony Montana to one side. Her voice suddenly filled the box.

"So listen up, people." She stepped to one side, and Silvie walked out to the microphone. In her hand she held a stack of three books: a black one, like the one they'd retrieved from Sally Drake's home; a purple one; a gold one.

She spoke in a shrill voice, yelling, staring right at the camera. "Alucard! Listen to me, you sick monster from hell! I have them." She held up the three books. "I have the last three Books of History."

She stopped, her eyes fiery and her breathing labored. Surely she realized that millions of people were watching this. It was why she was doing it.

But what, exactly, did she have in mind? Surely not . . .

"You want them? They're yours. Give me Johnis, and you can have them. That's all I ask. Give me the man that I love, and you can have these books and wreak all the terrible havoc you want."

"She's lost her mind." Miranda laughed. "She's gone completely mad. For love!"

"You know where I am. I'll give you until daybreak. If you don't come, I'm going to burn them!"

"She's really lost her marbles this time. Totally—"

Johnis seized her momentary distraction and rushed her then, covering the carpet between them in two strides, each at the limit of the chains around his ankles.

His fingers clawed at one of the guns under her arm before she could turn. He let his momentum carry him forward, and his shoulder slammed into her back with enough force to snap her spine.

She grunted and started to rise, but he didn't wait to see what damage he'd done. Her brown bag sat on her seat, and in that bag, the Book of History she'd taken from Sally Drake's home.

He snatched it up and dove for the rear compartment door. The sign above a yellow leather pouch read PARACHUTE. But he had no clue how to use it. Taking it, however tempting, would prove useless. He was a goner, but he'd already accepted that.

Unless . . .

He tried to shove the gun into his pocket, fumbled it, shoved harder, and managed to get it in. The book . . .

He glanced back and saw that Miranda was staggering to her feet, dazed but otherwise unharmed that he could see. Frantic and completely out of options, he thrust the book into his belt. Grabbed the lever he'd watched the charter pilot shut to seal the door.

Jerked it up. The door cracked, then flung wide. Wind tugged at him with a roar. He grabbed the parachute and glanced back at Miranda, who was lifting her gun.

Johnis threw himself into the wind.

MIRANDA STARED AT THE OPEN DOOR, REFUSING TO BELIEVE that Johnis had actually jumped.

The jet had lost some altitude but wasn't leveling.

He had the book. She'd watched him shove it into his jeans before throwing himself from the aircraft. How could anyone be so committed to any idea as to throw his life away for it? If he'd jumped for love, that would be one thing. But he'd jumped for one reason only: that she would not have all seven books. Nothing else made sense.

He was protecting his mission, Elyon.

Miranda blinked. She pulled the door to the cockpit open. "Note our position. Turn around and head back to Denver."

"Ma'am, that's a good hour back the way—"

"Now!" she screamed. "Turn back now!"

JOHNIS FELL THROUGH THE DARKNESS LIKE A ROCK.

The jet zoomed away at a rapid rate, a speck against the black sky now. Air howled past his ears, tugging at his shirt. He couldn't see the ground yet, so he gripped the book at his belt and tried see past the wind.

Three minutes she'd said. How anyone could be so high as to fall for three long minutes was beyond him, but his life now depended on it.

He fell for what seemed an eternity—looking, looking, and seeing nothing. And then that nothingness darkened, and he realized he was falling through a cloud. Closer to the ground then.

The idea that he could slam into hard earth at any moment sent his heart into another fit. He'd been falling for all of a minute or two, but it felt more like an hour.

He broke out of the clouds and saw the ground below, rushing toward him. So close already? This would never work! Never! At this speed he would be flattened like a bug splattering on the Chevy's glass.

The ground was there, just there, so close but still way too far away.

Johnis shoved his right forefinger into his mouth and bit deeply into his flesh. Warm blood wet his tongue—salty and alive. With his left hand he held the book in his belt tight and held his breath. He could see the trees now, the branches, the field beneath him, screaming for him.

Then, when he was sure he'd waited too long, he thrust his

bloody finger onto the book. The gateway into the skin-world gapped suddenly, a ring of shimmering air before him. He threw himself through it, squinting against the impending crash of earth against his body.

For a moment, pure silence.

And then . . . white.

Karas had told them about how the books had been separated from them when she and Darsal had used them to enter the simulation between the worlds. Johnis had to return *now*, while the book was still in his hand.

Before he was really anywhere, before he could fully arrive at the world between the worlds, Johnis lifted his finger from the book and shoved it back down.

The reversal into darkness happened before he could see any detail in the white world he'd been heading toward. He was back again, falling through the darkness after having jumped from the airplane. But as he'd hoped, his descent had been interrupted and now started over from a distance of less than a tree's height from the ground.

Johnis was so delighted at his success that for a split second he forgot that, although it might not be as destructive as falling from the clouds, falling from ten feet was dangerous enough.

The image of his leg bones slicing up through his belly flashed in his mind. Then the ground slammed into his feet, and his flying ended in a terrible crash. Johnis stood and tested his legs and arms. No breaks. Fantastic!

He looked around at a ring of trees, tall and dark, like claws reaching to the sky. His limbs were shaking, and his heart was pounding, but he'd thrown himself from a jet and lived to tell.

More importantly, he had the book.

It took him only a minute to shoot through his shackles using the gun, imitating the way Miranda had used it. An amazing weapon.

The chains still hung from his wrists and his legs, but he was free to move unrestricted. He had to get to civilization, find a phone, and call the number Karas had given him before Miranda reached them.

*Hold on, Silvie. Hold on to the books; I'm coming.*

Johnis ran into the night, fast, faster than seemed possible.

# TWENTY-THREE

The Spartan Hotel was a veritable fortress that rose against the dark Denver skyline, a tower of glass and steel and, of course, lights. Lights were everywhere in this world.

Silvie paced in front of a window that filled an entire wall of the fortieth-floor suite Karas had whisked them away to after her announcement. The room overlooked Denver; it was an expansive suite with a separate bedroom on one side and a conference room on the other. Silvie and Karas stood in the lounge between the two, staring at the city lights.

"You're sure the message got through?"

"Trust me, if Alucard is alive, he got the message. And we know that Miranda heard of your little stunt in Las Vegas quickly enough. She's obviously on the Net. Your message was heard by the whole world, loud and clear."

"Then how long?"

"Even with our delays getting to the stadium, they couldn't have been more than an hour ahead of us."

"It's been an hour," Silvie muttered.

She flipped her bone-handled knife in her right hand for the comfort it brought her. They'd made it clear to a number of well-placed staff members at the concert that if anyone came looking for them or for the books, they would be in Karas's suite at the Spartan. Two guards from her team waited at each entrance, ready for any possible breach.

They had invited Miranda, but they wanted her to come on their terms, not her own.

"Just remember"—Karas glanced at the three books on the crystal coffee table—"no trade without Johnis."

"That's the whole point."

Karas humphed. "Don't think she won't try something."

"Which is why you have this place armed to the teeth. And we aren't exactly helpless." Silvie spun her knife into the air and caught it lightly in her palm.

"And if it's Alucard who comes?" Karas bit her fingernail. "I doubt we would be a match for him." And then she added as a muttered afterthought. "Not without a silver bullet, anyway."

"Bring him on!" Silvie snapped. "I'm sick of this whole business!" She tried to stem the tide of emotions that flooded her mind but failed miserably.

"Look at us! We started out with visions of slaughtering the

Horde to protect the forests, and that's simple enough, right? I could cut the heads off ten of the diseased Scabs and not suffer a single wound. I was Silvie! I could kill Horde! That's why I was chosen!"

She was yelling.

"But no, instead I followed Johnis into the desert and *became* a Scab!" Tears leaked down her cheek. "Instead of killing the Horde, I followed him into their city to *rescue* one! And then I followed him here, into hell itself. And he's lost." She struggled not to cry. "I'm lost, Karas."

"You love him." Karas came toward her.

"And does he love me?"

"Foolish question. Have you seen the way he looks at you?"

"But not enough to sacrifice his mission for me."

Karas stilled for a moment. "So that's it? You're angry because he seems to put this quest to save the world ahead of you?"

She didn't answer.

"You would sacrifice the mission for his sake, but you don't think he would do the same for you," Karas said. "Am I right?"

"Does it matter?"

"You said it yourself: he was chosen because of his loyalty to an idea. He doesn't distinguish his love for you from his loyalty to Elyon. To him they are one and the same."

She made sense, but it didn't ease Silvie's sadness, which she herself didn't understand. "You're right. I'm being childish."

"I doubt that's a bad thing in this situation. And I think Johnis loves you as much as he knows how to love. He's only sixteen,

Silvie. So are you. In this world people don't marry nearly so young. Give yourself time, for the sake of love!"

"Time." Silvie looked into the older girl's eyes. "Time is something the Horde never gave us."

Karas's walkie-talkie squawked. "We have an unidentified helicopter circling the roof. Just a heads-up."

JOHNIS HAD RUN THROUGH THE TREES FOR ONLY A SHORT time before stumbling upon the dirt road. And then he ran on the dirt road for about an hour before a house lit up the valley below.

He was hardly winded despite running at a full sprint for so long—at the moment this oddity was a small encouragement in the face of his predicament. But he seized it for what it was worth and ran harder. Faster. Perhaps twice the speed he could have mustered back in Middle.

He flew up the steps that led to the farmhouse, twisted the handle, and shoved the door hard without bothering to knock.

With a splinter of wood the door swung open and Johnis stood in the frame, facing a family of four seated around a table, sharing a meal.

They stared back with round eyes. The father dove for the kitchen, and judging by the scowl on his face, he wasn't running away. There was a weapon in his sight.

Johnis threw up both hands. "No harm! I just need a phone. Please, I'm no enemy!"

The man of the house swung into view, holding a long gun in his arms. Johnis's second encounter with a shotgun since coming into the Histories.

"Don't shoot!"

"Elvis!" The wife stood. "Don't you dare pull that trigger!"

The two seated boys gawked at him. "Shoot 'im, Dad!" the smaller said.

"You broke our door," Elvis said. "I have every right to shoot you where you stand."

"And I wouldn't blame you. But the truth is, I only need to make a call, and then I'll leave. Please, it's urgent."

"What's so urgent?"

"I'm lost."

"No, you ain't. Not no more."

"Please, please, I beg you. If I don't make the call, the world as you know it could be in terrible trouble!"

They stared in silence, considering his words.

"Shoot him, Dad," the older child said.

"Don't you dare," the wife snapped. "For heaven's sake, let him make his call."

"YOU'RE RIGHT," SILVIE SAID, TAKING A DEEP BREATH. STILL no sign of any approach except for the helicopter, which hadn't been reported again. "I'm just a bit emotional."

Karas offered a comforting smile. "You're doing much better

than I did. Then again, I was a ten-year-old brat dumped into Las Vegas. You should try that . . ."

A thump sounded down the hall, cutting her off. They both turned toward the door. The cell phone Karas had set down on the coffee table vibrated, loud in the sudden silence. Silvie picked it up and handed it to Karas.

"Answer it," Karas said softly, stepping toward the door.

Silvie flipped the thin black wafer open and pressed it to her ear, the way she'd seen Karas do a hundred times since their meeting. "Yes?"

Johnis's voice filled her ear. She froze. "Johnis?"

"Silvie! Thank Elyon, Silvie. You're safe?"

"I . . . oh, dear Elyon, thank you." She was trembling. "Are you okay? Yes, I'm safe, of course, I'm safe. Where are you?"

"Listen to me, Silvie. Just listen carefully. Miranda is on her way. You can't give her the books. I have one. I have Karas's book. Do you hear me? Do not give up the three books."

So he was safe then!

"I hear you. I—"

"There's more. Alucard has the other three in Romania. He's been here for over two thousand years, waiting for us. And Miranda . . . I think she may have been infected by him. I hit her with enough force to break her back. You hear what I'm saying? She's not any ordinary woman."

"Johnis, I—"

The door suddenly crashed open in front of Karas. Miranda stood in the opening, gun leveled, lips twisted.

"Not one move." Her eyes flashed to Silvie. "Drop the phone, honey."

"She's here! At the Spartan—"

The gun spit a bullet at her. She jerked and felt it slit the air by her left ear.

Miranda dove like a cat attacking a mouse. She twisted as she passed Karas, striking her jaw with her heel. Karas staggered backward, stunned by the sudden assault.

And Miranda, this woman Johnis claimed had been infected by Alucard, was already halfway to Silvie, with her gun extended.

Silvie's instincts kicked in. She threw herself back and to the right, knowing the coffee table with the three books rested there, just behind her.

She felt her body flip into the air and complete a full loop, flying farther than she'd anticipated before slamming into the window.

Two bullets punched holes in the window.

"Do you really want a fight, lover girl?" Miranda crouched between Karas and Silvie. "Because, believe me, I can. I will."

She plucked the phone from the carpet and spoke into it. "Good-bye, Johnis." The device shattered in her hand.

Silvie stood.

"You may have brought a few tricks from this other world of

yours, but I have it on excellent authority that you can't stop bullets. My aim is much better if I want it to be."

Silvie looked at Karas for direction.

"How did you get past my men?" Karas asked.

"I'll assume that was a rhetorical question." Miranda whipped out two sets of shackles and tossed one to each of them. "If you think Johnis is out of the woods yet, you don't know me well. We track every step he makes. Put the cuffs on, and I promise you'll see him again. Refuse and I'll be forced to kill you now. So sad."

Silvie blinked. She had no doubt that Miranda could and would do precisely what she said.

"We don't have all night. The helicopter is waiting."

# TWENTY-FOUR

Silvie? Silvie! Silvie, for the sake of Elyon, answer me!" Johnis screamed the last, unable to stem the fear that raged through his mind.

He could hear the miserable witch in the background. *Do you really want to fight, lover girl?*

"Fight her, Silvie! Kill her!"

Miranda answered. "Good-bye, Johnis."

*Click.*

He pulled the phone back and stared at it. Then yelled into it again. "Silvie? Silvie!"

The family of four stared at him. He slammed the phone on the counter and paced a quick circle, hands kneading his face, mumbling, "This can't be, this can't be, this can't be . . ."

"Easy, man," the farmer said. "You're not making sense."

The small one gained the courage to voice his curiosity. "Who's Alucard?"

Johnis spun to the father. "Do you have a jet?"

"A jet? No."

"I have to get to Romania, man. You have to help me get to Romania! There's a castle up in the mountains, with a dungeon. Worms larger than a grown man, a Shataiki. Alucard. He has Silvie . . ."

They just looked at him, dumbfounded. A candidate for the fruit farm. How could they understand a word he was saying with their limited knowledge?

"Then how about Denver? You've heard of the Spartan?"

"The hotel? Denver's a good two hundred miles—"

"And I need to get there. It is absolutely imperative that I get there before that witch leaves."

Miranda was probably already gone, but there was a chance that Silvie and Karas had evaded capture. Or managed to hide the three books before Miranda could get her paws on them.

"You're nuts."

"Do you have a Chevy?"

"I have a Ford truck, but if you think—"

"I'll buy it." Johnis withdrew two coins and tossed them in one palm so they clinked loudly. "These are gold. I'm told gold is very rare here. You could buy two Chevys with this gold. I'll buy your Ford, and you drive me to Denver."

The man eyed the coins skeptically. "How do I know they're real? You don't drive?"

"I do. Most excellently. But that's my offer. I buy, you drive."

THE JOURNEY TO DENVER IN THE TRUCK WAS A HAIR-RAISING affair, because Ted Blitzer insisted on "learning you how to drive proper," as he put it. The road was rough, and the car bounced like a frantic mare, wearing a blister in Johnis's right palm. He found himself yearning for a Chevy. At the very least, a good stallion.

Ted jabbered like a monkey, but Johnis's mind was on Silvie. And the books. And Alucard. And the Roush ordering him into the Black Forest to meet Teeleh. Honestly, he had difficulty remembering exactly how he'd come to this place, bucking down the road in a Ford truck, listening to Farmer Ted talk about how the government was conspiring to steal all the land from rightful owners.

A war is brewing, Ted insisted. He couldn't know how little any war meant compared to what would happen if seven ancient, leather-bound books got in the wrong hands. It could all be over in just a few hours now. In a day or two the whole world would know just how critical the words they'd heard Silvie speak from the stage at Tony Montana's concert really were.

They'd all seen her hold up three books and cry out her challenge to Alucard. The earth hung in the balance of those three books, the three in Alucard's lair, and the one inside his belt.

The farmer took over when they neared the city, and Johnis

stared ahead, pretending to listen. But his mind was gone, and his hands were sweaty, and his heart was breaking for Silvie.

Ted dropped him off in front of a towering glass building with huge red letters that spelled out SPARTAN HOTEL and left to find his brother.

The moment Johnis stepped past the double glass doors, his worst fears were confirmed. The main atrium was closed off with yellow tape, behind which a dozen police officers worked over several bodies on rolling beds.

"Silvie?" He leaped over the tape and sprinted to the first body. A white sheet covered the victim's head. "Silvie?"

He ripped off the sheet. A man.

"Hey!"

He bounded to the second body, discovered it was another male.

"Hey! Hey, you can't do that!"

As was the third victim.

He whirled to the approaching office. "Where's Silvie? And Karas?"

"Out!" The officer jabbed his flashlight at the door. "This is a crime scene, buddy."

"Please, I need to know if Karas . . . Kara Longford is one of the victims."

"Out!"

Another policeman stepped in from his right, grabbed Johnis by his arm, and escorted him past the yellow tape.

"Please," he whispered, begging. "Just tell me if there were any women among the victims. I have to know."

"Are you a relative?"

"To whom? One of the victims? How would I know unless you told me who they are?"

"Speak to OIC." The officer shoved him past the door and pulled it firmly shut behind him.

Johnis turned around, saw that several officers were watching from beyond the glass, and faced the street. He stood on the sidewalk, immobilized by indecision.

He was one among a sea of onlookers in a huge city of blazing lights, and he was alone. Lost. A dozen alternatives screamed through his mind.

He could hijack a Chevy and try to find the jet field. Foolish.

He could take an officer captive and force them to take him to Romania. Absurd.

He could stand atop the police car parked in front of him and begin to scream at the top of his lungs. Hold up the one book in his possession. Hope that the cameras would put him on the Net so that Alucard could come after him . . .

But he couldn't risk giving up the book now, not even for Silvie's sake. Could he? Alucard now had six of the books. The one in Johnis's belt was the only thing that stood between the Shataiki and—

Johnis caught his breath. The riddle in the desert pool exploded in his mind.

Beyond the blue another world is opened.
Enter if you dare.
In the west, the Dark One seeks seven
To destroy the world.

The west was this world, he knew that now—paradise gone amuck. But how would the Dark One destroy this world? By doing what the legends said he'd done once before. Release the Shataiki from the desert reality into this one. What if the seven books could create a breach between the worlds, allowing the Shataiki to physically swarm into this world, destroying it as they had after breaching the barrier between the Black Forest and the Colored Forest?

What if evil showed itself in physical form in this world as it had in his world? The sea of humanity in front of him became Horde? This was something for which Alucard would patiently wait two thousand years.

He withdrew the black book tucked in his belt. Turned it in his hands. Fanned through its blank pages. According to Karas, the *original* seven blank Books of History didn't work like the rest of the blank books.

One of the original books could take you to a simulation called Paradise.

Four books could take you from one world to the other.

All seven books could undo the rules that governed these books and create a breach for the Shataiki. Maybe worse.

Tears of desperation filled his eyes. *I'm sorry, Silvie. I don't know what to do.*

"Johnis."

He spun to his right. A woman stood on the sidewalk, her arms by her sides, heels together. She wore jeans and black boots. A red blouse hung on her thin frame. Her hair was long and dark next to skin so pale that it seemed to glow in the night.

All of this Johnis saw in a blink. But it was the scar on her cheek that his eyes settled on. His heart jumped.

"Darsal?"

Her eyes scanned the street as she hurried to his side. "Come with me."

"What . . . how's this . . . I thought—"

"You thought what they think. That I'm dead." She took his arm and guided him down the sidewalk, glancing around nervously. "Do I look dead to you?"

"What . . . what happened?"

She spoke in a rush, quickening her steps. "I just flew in from Turkey, where I've had my head buried in the caves for two weeks. And what do I see? A news story of Silvie, standing on a stage, holding up three Books of History. I got here as soon as I could."

Darsal looked at him. "You look like you've seen a ghost."

"We all thought you were dead."

"Karas made herself known. I made myself dead. They have the three books?"

"How long . . . ?"

"Ten years, just like Karas. Where are Silvie and the books?"

"But Alucard had your book!"

Darsal stopped. "You . . . you've seen him?"

"They took me."

"Miranda. To Romania." She walked again, practically dragging him now. "I had to let them have the book to complete the illusion that I was dead. I'd arranged for a doctor to confirm it, take my body, but the book left no doubt. One book by itself was no use to me anyway." She paused. "Where is Silvie?"

"They have her."

Again Darsal stopped. Fear spread through her eyes. "And the books?"

Johnis took a breath and looked at the book in his hands. It shook slightly. "Six of them."

Her eyes dropped to his hands. Then back up to his face.

She spun and began to run. "Hurry!"

Johnis gripped the book tight and ran after her. "Where?"

"They'll be coming! We can't let them have that book!"

He sprinted after her, around a corner into an alley. And then she began to run, really run, like the wind.

As did he, feeling a surge of confidence with each step.

They flew by an old drunk, who must have wondered what had been slipped into his drink. She came to a puddle and took to the air, leaping twenty feet, with Johnis in the air behind. They landed lightly and sprinted on without missing a step.

Darsal's car waited on a corner a mile from the Spartan. She vaulted over the roof, threw the door open wide, and spun in. Clearly she'd had plenty of experience.

Johnis slid in beside her and slammed his door. "It's a Chevy?"

"As a matter of fact"—she jerked the car into gear and it surged forward—"yes."

Johnis looked at her. "A good choice."

"You're the expert?"

"Granted, I'm useless in most things here, but I know a thing or two about Chevys."

"It's a bit disorienting at first. I found some clips from your episode in Vegas. You've done just fine." Darsal forced a smile.

The last ten years had made her a hard woman, he could see. Elyon only knew how she'd managed on her own for so long.

"Billos—"

"I don't want to talk about Billos," she snapped. "Only one thing matters now."

"Silvie," he said. "They have Silvie and Karas."

"The books," Darsal said. "First we lock your book so deep in a vault that no one finds it. *Ever*, if need be."

"And then?"

She stared ahead and blew out some air. "Then we go after your girlfriend."

# TWENTY-FIVE

The night air smelled of Shataiki. It was all Silvie knew for certain.

Miranda had chained their wrists and ankles, taped their mouths with gray cloth, and pulled seamless black hoods over their heads before summarily dumping them into a jet's cargo compartment.

She could hear Karas's breathing beside her, locked in darkness. And as the jet screamed down the strip and angled for the sky, her last hopes of Johnis coming to their rescue fell like a rock.

All was lost. Silvie allowed herself silent tears. Her ploy had failed miserably. She replayed the events in her mind over and over and concluded that their mistake had been in underestimating Miranda. Who could have guessed that she would have been able to overpower so many guards and catch them with the books without having to trade Johnis? Johnis's warning had come too late.

His voice echoed in her head. *I hit her with enough force to break her back. She's infected.*

Infected by Alucard? This is what gave her the strength to overcome the guards. Their only hope, however slim, now rested in the other words he'd spoken into her ear. *I have one. I have one, Silvie.*

He had a book. But one book was no advantage against Alucard.

The flight had lasted hours—how many, Silvie could not estimate. She only knew that the air was cool and quiet, which led her to believe it was night, when hands had jerked her to her feet and had pushed her from the aircraft.

They'd traveled up twisty roads for an hour and finally came to a stop—still night, as far as she could tell. Still not a word from Miranda, or anyone, for that matter. They were hustled through cool, damp air into what she guessed was a stone chamber or hall. She could tell because of the faint echo that came with each breath Karas took.

A door thumped shut behind them. Still no word.

They were led by chains down the hall into a stairwell. Down, down, feeling their way along the stone walls on either side. And she knew when the first scents of Shataiki reached past the hood that they'd entered Alucard's lair.

The floor flattened, and they slogged over wet ground. Beside her, Karas protested with a muffled cry. The odor of sulfur was strong enough to make one blanch—unlike Silvie and Johnis, Karas had been away from the Shataiki scent for ten years.

A soft popping sounded high overhead. Worms nestling in their own gook. Silvie swallowed. A hand tugged on her chain. She stopped. For several long seconds they just stood there. She could hear a flame crackling, could smell the smoke mixed with the scent of rotten eggs. Heard the worms she imagined overhead.

The sound of someone breathing. Nails clicking on the stone floor.

"Take them into the main chamber." Alucard. Silvie's blood froze in her veins. The voice was low and breathy, backed by a growl that reached into the pit of her stomach.

They were led deeper, down another flight of stone steps, wetter and slipperier than the previous one. She could hear the same squealing they'd heard below the monastery in Paradise. Worms in torment, far away.

Her desperation deepened with each step she took. They must be a hundred feet below the earth's surface now. Maybe twice that. Even if Johnis did find a way to the castle, there was no way he could save them.

She'd loved him. She'd kissed him, and she'd known with that kiss that she would marry him. If she died in the next ten minutes, she would cling to that memory, that single moment of comfort between them.

*I love you, Johnis. I love you.*

She slid, caught herself on a rail, then eased her foot to the next step. Her chain tugged.

*I love you, Johnis. I love you.*

The cry from the tormented worms grew at an alarming rate. And with the clunk of a latch and the protest of rusty hinges opening, the squealing became a scream, directly overhead.

Silvie gasped under the tape. Again someone pulled her forward.

They entered the room of screaming worms; she could smell them, hear them, feel their slime underfoot, taste their foul odor. It was a vast room, judging by the echoes off the stone walls.

A hand stopped her. The chamber fell to silence.

It occurred to her that she was panting through her nostrils. Dizzy from the hyperventilation, she tried to calm herself.

"Move," a gruff voice commanded. Hands shoved her.

She stumbled forward, tripped over a ledge, and fell headlong onto a three-foot-high riser. Karas grunted beside her. They were hoisted to their feet and clamped into brackets on the wall.

The hoods were ripped from their heads, tape from their mouths. A hooded guard with large red lumps on his face turned and walked away from them.

Silvie gazed at the chamber near the guard's torch as he slumped toward the large black door through which they had entered.

The room was perhaps one hundred feet per side. Dozens of columns bridged the span from the wet floor to the ceiling. The worms nested there: gargantuan worms that looked like white logs twisting slowly in their own mess. Thousands of them, interwoven in a blanket that looked twenty feet thicker on one end than on the other.

A sizable table engraved on all sides with Teeleh's winged serpent image sat squarely in front of the wall adjacent to them.

Larger worms clung to three of the walls, including the wall they were chained to, but the wall facing the single ornate table was free of not only worms but also their mucus. Dry stone ran from floor to ceiling. And on this wall . . .

Silvie blinked. She'd seen this. These concentric circles. Exactly like the circles on the covers of the seven Books of History.

"It's a gateway," Karas said. "They've built some kind of a gateway!"

The door slammed shut, pitching them into darkness once again.

She could hear the worms writhing in wetness. The thought that one or more might slide over them made her shiver. She tugged at her chains and was rewarded with nothing more than a rattle to break the stillness.

"Are you okay?" Karas asked.

"No. Honestly, I think I might be dead."

Silence.

"You heard him," Karas said.

Another shiver went through Silvie. "It's him."

"Alucard."

"He doesn't have all seven books," Silvie said.

"He's going to use them to open a gateway," Karas replied,

casting no confidence behind the notion that Alucard wouldn't soon have the seven if he didn't already.

"You can't know that."

"Don't you see?" Karas was whispering with urgency now. "The Books of History are a gateway to truth, to understanding, to knowledge, to history! They connect what can't be seen with what can be seen. The other world with this world—we experienced that ourselves."

"That doesn't mean he's going to use the books to connect the two worlds," Silvie said, though she wasn't so confident.

"Why else would Teeleh send him here? What can he do here that he can't do there? Teeleh intends to wipe out Earth with a virus that makes the Raison Strain virus look like a common cold."

"With Shataiki," Silvie said. "He invaded the Colored Forest exactly as the legends say. Now he will invade this world."

"With Shataiki."

# TWENTY-SIX

*Whatever Darsal has done during the ten years since the books deposited her in this world, it has brought her wealth and resourses that might be as extensive as Karas's,* Johnis thought.

She'd whisked him to the airport, where a jet waited, fueled and whining on the runway. They would make one stop in a city called New York, where she kept one of her homes; then they would cross the Atlantic for Romania.

Stopping to secure the sole book in their possession would cost them an hour, but Darsal was unwilling to risk putting all seven books in the same country, particularly Romania.

Johnis agreed. They were only two or three hours behind Miranda, if their calculations were right. Securing the book would put them into Bucharest four hours after Silvie, assuming Alucard had taken her to the same mansion he'd taken Johnis to.

"Which he has," Darsal said, spitting to one side on the runway as they boarded the jet. Alucard had done many things in his time, but none of it compared to what he intended to do now in that unholy place.

The jet flew at twice the speed of sound, faster when it climbed out of the atmosphere. This meant little to Johnis, as long as the book was safe and they reached Silvie while she was still alive.

"Tell me, Darsal," Johnis said. "Tell me everything."

She sat across from him in a black leather chair, legs and arms crossed. Her eyes diverted to the night sky over the Atlantic. "I can't."

There was enough emotion in those two words to strike fear into Johnis's heart. "You can't? Why not?"

"Because not everything can be spoken of easily, Johnis!" she snapped. "You've spent a month or two of your life frolicking about on this grand adventure. Try ten years and see if you can survive!"

She pressed her fingers together to cover her nose. Closed her eyes. "I'm sorry; that wasn't called for."

"Well . . ." *Well what, Johnis? You have no clue what horrors Darsal has suffered these past ten years.* "We've all paid a price."

She was about twenty-seven years old now, he realized. But ten years without the harsh sun had been kind to her face. Her hair was very dark next to her pale cheeks. Something about her had changed, but he couldn't put his finger on it. Her nose, perhaps? No, it was that she'd lost weight.

Karas had been a child in the other world and had grown up here without the benefit of fighting the Horde. Darsal had been a well-muscled warrior, who'd thinned out in a world without constant battle. In some ways, she was more beautiful than he remembered.

But life here had hardened her in other ways.

He wanted to ask her about Billos. About what she knew of Alucard. The books. Karas. All of it. But Darsal looked distraught, tapped out, nearly ruined.

So Johnis told her about their own journey, starting back in the forest, chasing her and Billos into the desert. Finding the Black Forest. Landing outside Las Vegas. Stealing the Chevy.

Instead of grinning at their antics, Darsal unsuccessfully fought back tears, managing only a smile or two when he described how he'd mastered the Chevy.

He told it all, hoping to remind her of home. To reconnect. And then he sat still, letting her process.

"I have something I have to tell you," she said softly, refusing to look Johnis in the eye.

"Then tell me."

"I can't. Not yet. It's too terrible."

"Will it affect our mission?"

Darsal sighed. "Is there nothing but the mission for you?"

"Yes! There's Silvie. There's getting back to Middle! There's life, because if we fail, I have a feeling there won't be any."

"Fair enough." She paused. "When I arrived in Las Vegas, I

was as lost as you. Karas was a young child then, and I had no way of contacting her. By the time I learned that the entertainment mogul was actually our Karas, I had already made the connection with Paradise and tracked the books back to Turkey and then from Turkey to Romania, where I learned that Alucard had been sowing his disease. I got too close to him and exposed myself. It was then that I decided that he and Miranda, that witch he'd taken up with, had to think I was dead."

"Sounds dangerous."

"Dangerous? Is there anything about this mission that hasn't been dangerous? I managed to pull it off—amazing what a pile of money and the right medical clinic can do for you these days."

"So what do you know about Alucard?"

"I know he plans on opening a gateway for the Shataiki. I've been in the chamber where he keeps his worms."

"The library," Johnis said.

"You've been in his dungeon?"

He told her.

"Then you know where we're going. The gateway chamber is deeper than the library you were in. That's where he'll do his deed. And that, my friend, is where we're going."

She stopped then, as if she'd come to the end of it.

"That's what you needed to tell me?" Johnis asked.

Darsal set her jaw. "This is all a bit much. We'll have time later." She reclined her seat and closed her eyes. "Get some sleep. We're going to need it."

THE NIGHT WAS STILL BLACK WHEN THEY PULLED THE CAR off the road and ran through the woods, around Alucard's mansion an hour north of Bucharest, Romania. They could see two cars parked at the front, a good indication that Miranda had brought them here, as suspected.

They both ran with silver guns firmly fixed to their hips and two long knives on each thigh. Dressed in black from head to foot, Darsal carried a few supplies in a pack at her belly, but other than that, they were going in lean.

They'd made the change on final approach into Bucharest. Darsal had given Johnis lessons on aiming and firing the guns, and she assured him that after fighting the Horde, it was child's play. Just point and shoot, and brace for a slight kick.

The stone mansion stood dark against a starry sky in the center of the clearing they faced. Asleep by all exterior indications. No lights, no smoke from chimneys, no guards, no sounds but the nearby chirping of crickets.

"Follow closely!" she whispered, breaking from the tree line.

Darsal ran in a crouch, ahead and to his right. They flew through the grass like crows from above. Crossed the hundred yards of cleared ground in a matter of seconds.

They stopped with their backs to the rear wall, listening. Nothing.

Darsal pointed to a stone well they'd passed twenty feet away. "We're going down."

"Into the well?"

But she was going already.

Darsal slipped like a cat over the lip of the well, gripped a rope hung at the center, and disappeared into the earth.

A quick tug convinced Johnis the rope would hold them both. He swung out into the well and lowered himself after her.

Down. A hundred feet. Into utter darkness.

It occurred to him that there was no scent of water. A dry well then?

"Here!" Her hands tugged at his shirt and stopped his descent. She pulled him into a tunnel built into the wall. "Water was drawn here when the well was operational. Stay close."

They hurried through the darkness, using their hands to guide them along the wall. He could hear her breathing, the sound of her boots padding on the rock. But he still could see nothing.

She stopped and put her hand on his shoulder. "Okay?"

"Okay."

"There's only one way to do this, and it won't be fun. A ventilation shaft runs down to the right just ahead. It leads to the gateway chamber. There aren't any gates to stop us."

She said it as if this alone weren't good news. "But?"

"But there are worms." She pulled something from her pack and handed it to him. "It's a raincoat with a hood. You're going to need it."

They slipped into the plastic suits, and she pulled him forward. "The more speed you hit them with, the easier it will be to get through. You don't want to get stuck in the middle. Trust me."

So. This is why she'd been coy about the details of their rescue attempt. They were going to try to slide through a nest of worms. The thought made him shudder.

He smelled the terrible scent of rotten eggs before he felt the hole open on his right. Slime on the walls confirmed they'd reached the air vent in question.

"You've done this?"

"More than once. Go on your back, feet first." She engaged her gun with a loud clank. "Go down with one gun ready."

She was serious.

But even she was hesitating. "Remember, the faster the better."

"Hold on. What can we expect past the worms?"

"A ten-foot drop into the chamber. The gateway. With any luck, Silvie."

Then she threw herself into the shaft and slid away, like a log down the mud waterfalls south of Middle.

Johnis withdrew one of his guns, chambered a round as she'd shown him, held the weapon close to his chest, pulled the hood over his head, and jumped into the slimy tube.

The worm gel was even more slippery than he'd expected. He slid down the chute like a rock, eyes clenched, breath held against the stench. Then his boots slammed into a soft body, and he was in the nest.

Squeals of protest filled his ears. He was all the way in, from head to foot, and he could feel the soft, lumpy bodies on his cheeks. And he still wasn't through!

Panicked, he gasped. A mistake. The taste of the worm gel was no less offensive than its odor. And then he was out of them, falling free. He opened his eyes for orientation, but it was dark, and gel was thick over his face.

He landed hard, rolled once, and came to his knees, the breath knocked clean out of him. The goo . . . he had to get the goo out of his eyes. The gun in his fist prevented a clean swipe of his face, but he managed to get most of the stuff off.

Johnis jumped to his feet, his gun extended in the dark.

Fire hissed loudly five feet from him, and he saw that Darsal had ignited a flare from her pack. Her hood was back, and she'd managed to avoid getting any of the mucus on her face.

Johnis glanced around the room, saw no immediate danger, and shrugged out of his plastic suit, glad to be dry. His stomach was on the verge of protesting violently, but he held it in check. Free now, he could think straight.

And see the worms on the ceiling. The huge concentric circles on one wall looked exactly like the rings on the books' covers.

"Johnis?"

He spun to the sound of Silvie's voice. She stood against the far wall next to Karas—shackled.

Johnis reached her in four long bounds, dropped his gun at her feet, and fumbled frantically with her cuffs. But the metal clasps were locked tight.

"Easy!" Darsal whispered.

"Darsal," Karas said. "I thought . . ."

"Do I look dead?"

"What . . . what happened?"

"Later. Right now we have our hands full."

"Thank Elyon," Silvie breathed. "Thank Elyon!"

Johnis grabbed her face and kissed her. She returned the kiss, and not till he pulled back did he think about the worm salve on his skin. She didn't seem to mind.

"Don't thank him too quickly." Darsal glanced about the room. "We have to destroy the gateway and get out alive."

Silvie and Karas were shackled along a wall that contained chains and metal clasps for four people. Miranda or Alucard had the keys, and the steel links were an inch thick.

"How do we get them out?"

"Not with a bullet, if that's what you're thinking. Too thick. We'll have to figure out how to get the key."

"What?" Karas cried. "Are you crazy? We have to get out of here!"

"No, we have to destroy the gateway."

"He doesn't need a gateway! He needs the books. This is all symbolic."

"Yes and no. He needs a place to gather the Shataiki that come through. He also needs a nest for the females. With Shataiki, males lay worms that females fertilize." She crossed to the wall and lit a torch. Yellow flames lapped hungrily at the air.

"A typical flame won't do much to this stuff, but get enough heat and their mucus will go up like gasoline."

"Well, then," Johnis said, "we have our way of destroying them."

"Problem is, we're in here too. Along with the books."

"Then what do you suggest?"

Darsal walked closer to them, eyeing the large black table that stood before the concentric circles formed on the wall. "I don't know. Part of me thinks we should just burn the books with this stink hole. From everything I've seen, they are as evil as Alucard."

What was she saying? Johnis glanced at Silvie.

"You can't do that," Karas said.

"Can't I?" Darsal eyed her, wearing a crooked smile. "I think I've earned the right to do whatever I need to do. The books killed Billos, didn't they?"

"You know he's dead?"

"He was left in a dungeon filled with Shataiki!" Venom laced her voice. "Of course he's dead! Either that or he's Shataiki himself." She forced a smile. "All hail the books. We should probably burn every last one."

The change in her took Johnis off guard. After ten years, she held on to a bitterness that could not be easily dismissed.

"But first we have to figure out how to get out of here." She turned her attention to the gateway. "I've been in here three times, and each time I can't help but think that there's something about the circles that look wrong. Do you see it, Silvie?"

Johnis stood by her side and looked at the gateway. The stone rings looked like they'd been melted in rather than placed. Nothing else that he could see.

"We can't stand here discussing the gateway!" Karas snapped. "Miranda could step in now, and we'd be finished."

Darsal walked closer to Silvie. Jumped up on the ledge, eyes on the rings. "At the top of the rings, the worms avoid contact."

Silvie and Johnis glanced up.

Darsal moved in that moment, when both of their eyes were diverted. She shoved Johnis's hand back and slammed a shackle over his wrist before he knew what she was doing.

It locked on contact.

Johnis moved without thought. He snatched up the gun with his free hand and spun to Darsal, who'd stepped off the ledge.

"What are you doing?" Silvie cried. "Have you lost your mind?"

"Yes, Silvie." She lifted her hands and gave Johnis a condescending smile. "I have lost my mind. I lost it with Billos in Alucard's dungeon ten years ago."

"Don't think I won't use this." Johnis kept the gun trained on her.

"Would you, Johnis? Would you really shoot one of the chosen ones? Go ahead, pull the trigger."

He lifted the barrel to the ceiling and pulled the trigger.
*Click.*

"You don't think I'd be foolish enough to give you a loaded gun, do you? After what you did to that Chevy?"

"What's the meaning of this?" Karas snapped. "You think that witch Miranda won't kill you as quickly as she kills us?"

"No, I don't think she will."

"Why not?"

"Because I am Miranda."

What? She was speaking figuratively, Johnis thought. He'd seen them both within the last twenty-four hours, and apart from their hair and their height, their frames, their eyes . . . He stopped.

"This isn't Middle, my friends. This is 2033. Masks and cosmetics have come a long way."

They stared at her, grappling with the notion that the woman they'd known as Miranda had actually been Darsal all along.

"Why?" Karas cried.

Darsal drilled her with a dark stare. "Maybe you'll understand before it's all over. Which only gives you a few minutes."

A door to their right suddenly swung open. The large Shataiki named Alucard stood in its frame, staring at them with yellowed eyes. For a long moment no one moved. No one seemed to breathe.

"Do you have it?" the beast said.

Darsal, who was Miranda, reached into her pack. Withdrew the seventh book. The black one that Karas had hidden and that Darsal had made a show of securing in New York. Her deception had run as deep as her bitterness.

She walked up to Alucard, who stepped into the room.

"The seventh book, sir."

# TWENTY-SEVEN

Flames crackled from seven lampstands that Miranda had lit around the table in front of the gateway. A thin trail of oily smoke rose from each, spreading before reaching the nest of worms writhing above. With each passing moment, their agitation seemed to increase, as though they, too, had waited an eternity for this moment.

On the table stood two finely crafted wooden candelabras holding seven colored candles, each which Darsal now lit. A silver bowl filled with water sat to one side.

All of this made sense to Silvie. Symbols from Other Earth. Colored candles on wood symbolized the Colored Forests from the legends. Water symbolized Elyon's water. But two other objects on the end of the table were less obvious to her. A framework that looked somewhat like the drowning gallows that the Horde used, and two crossed planks.

At the center, lit clearly by the wavering flame, lay the seven Books of History, side by side. The black one Michal had first given them on the left. Then the brown, the blue, the green, the purple, the golden, and another black.

Alucard stood across the room, watching Darsal quickly prepare the table. He turned with her wherever she went, as if he feared turning his back to her for even one moment. It was the way evil worked, Silvie thought. Distrusting.

So this was it? All they'd fought for came down to this moment, far below the earth, in the Romanian mountains? The search for the six missing Books of History, the love that had blossomed between Silvie and Johnis, the . . .

She swallowed at the lump gathered in her throat. "Why haven't they killed us?" she whispered.

"They're going to drown us." Karas's eyes glistened with tears. "Either that or crucify us. It's how he does it."

"You can't know that," Johnis said. "He's gloating after two thousand years of waiting; he's relishing—"

"Silence!" Alucard thundered.

The beast glared at them with yellow eyes. His mangy black coat looked like it hadn't been groomed once in the two thousand years since he'd vanished from his lair in the Black Forest— a few days ago for Silvie and Johnis, ten years for Karas and Darsal.

"How could you do this?" Johnis's voice cut through the room, heavy with bitterness. He was speaking to Darsal. "How could you betray Elyon?"

A roar crackled through the air; Alucard's wings spread wide, his jaws tilted to the ceiling. Rather than feeling any fear at his display of rage, Silvie felt some consolation in the fact that he still reacted so strongly to the name of their maker.

"And who betrayed Billos?" Darsal snapped, ignoring both Alucard's order for silence and his roar.

"You!" Johnis cried. "You're betraying him right now!"

Darsal faced him, her expression drawn and red. "Who made a mockery of the Great Romance by stealing the one love I've known for the sake of these cursed books?"

"You. You're making a mockery of the mission."

"Shut up!" she screamed. But she couldn't hold back. "If it weren't for these books, none of us would be here!" She stepped closer, jabbing the air to accentuate each point. "There would be no Shataiki or Horde. I would have died for Billos! Do you understand that? He was my life!"

"And you blame Elyon? Don't be a fool!"

"I made a vow, and Elyon help me, I'll keep it or die with Billos!"

"What can you hope to achieve by this?"

A crooked grin split her face. "You know what I hope to gain. These larvae need a female to complete their transformation into lovely black butterflies with fangs. The worms in this hall are female. Once they've been fertilized, there's no turning back."

"We begin!" Alucard snarled. He walked toward the table, and with each step his claws clacked on the stone floor.

"Please, Darsal." Johnis could beg all he liked—she didn't look interested in bending her decision to betray Elyon, Silvie thought. Embittered by her loss of the one man she was willing to die for, Darsal had sworn to wage war on the books and whoever stood in her path to do so.

"We begin!" Alucard growled again.

Darsal's fierce glare drilled Johnis for another long beat. She turned her back to them and walked to the table under Alucard's watchful gaze.

Why was the beast so attentive to her? Clearly there was some bad blood between them.

"Why him?" Karas whispered in a voice so faint that Silvie could barely hear her words. "Why is she cooperating?"

Karas's eyes were wide, and her face glistened with sweat. The thin white blouse she'd worn was now badly smudged and wet. She looked at Silvie.

"If she's waging war . . ."

"Don't, Darsal," Johnis pleaded. "You can't open the gate! They'll only destroy you."

No reaction this time.

Alucard stood over the seven books like a hawk over a nest of chicks. Saliva dribbled from pink lips and pooled on the table. Darsal stood to one side, eyes on the beast, jaw firm.

Alucard reached for a long knife, held his paw over the silver bowl with water, and slashed himself.

Blood dripped into the water.

Johnis put his free hand in Silvie's and held tight, perhaps to still the tremble in his own fingers. "He's defiling the water with blood," he whispered, citing the taboo they all knew. Silvie didn't know if the rite Alucard was performing was necessary to open the gate, but she suspected it was more a matter of mood setting for the beast after two thousand years of dreaming.

He flung the knife to one side, letting it clatter off the table and fall noisily to the floor. Facing him, Darsal picked up the black book and set it on the table directly in front of him.

The beast squeezed blood from his wound onto the cover, then pulled his claw back.

Darsal set the brown book squarely on top of the bloody black book. Now there were two books, one atop the other, joined with blood.

Again, Alucard dribbled blood onto the cover.

This was the vision that they'd seen beneath the waters at the desert oasis. All seven books aligning to create a gateway.

"Darsal . . ." Johnis didn't bother imploring this time. Just "Darsal," and it was clearly for his own remorse. *Darsal, Darsal, what have you done?*

One by one Darsal set the books on the stack as Alucard wet their covers with his blood until there was only the second black book left to set on top.

Instead of placing the book on top, Darsal held the book out to him. "This one should be yours to place, sir."

Alucard hesitated. Clearly this was not as rehearsed.

He took the book, uttering a soft growl. Held it over the sixth book with both hands. Lifted his head to the stone gateway before him.

He spoke in a low, crackling voice that filled the room. "By the power entrusted in me, for Teeleh, my master, and his precious blood, which gives life to all who despise Elyon and his waters, I call you forth . . . my bride."

Darsal eased to one side of the table, her eyes on the books.

Alucard lowered the last black book.

A flash of light cracked above the books. Silvie threw herself as low as her chains would allow her. Above them the worms began to squeal.

"Elyon, help us," Johnis breathed, gripping her hand even tighter.

The light slammed into the stone wall and ran a ring around the perimeters of the concentric circles. Alucard spread his wings, lifted his jaw, and roared, "My bride!"

The gate dissolved into light, humming with the power of a thousand lightning bolts. Silvie couldn't breathe. Her heart felt as though it had been crammed into her throat.

The first streak of black that cut through the light was a Shataiki guard, the kind that had flocked above Silvie and Johnis in the Black Forest. Roughly two and half feet of shrieking muscle, with large yellow fangs.

And then they came in a dizzying rush, dozens in the space of a few seconds, flying to the ceiling, where they hooked their claws into the squealing worms and hung, glaring with red eyes.

*It's over*, Silvie thought. *We've lost.*

But then everything changed.

Darsal moved. The smaller Shataiki were still flying through the breech, and Alucard was still glorying over his coming bride, and Darsal was moving like lightning.

She grabbed one of the wooden candlesticks and flung off the candles, rounding the table in long strides. The candlestick was now a long, sharpened stake.

Screaming at the top of her lungs, Darsal thrust the wooden stake under Alucard's raised arm. Into his heart.

An earsplitting crack from the beast's throat shook the chamber. A single, oversized Shataiki spilled out of the light and landed on the ground beyond Alucard. The female had joined her guard. And more of her guard flooded the gate.

Alucard spun about, slashing at empty air. Skin fell from his face, exposing bleached bone.

Darsal leaped over the books, snatched up the second candlestick, and descended on the still-disoriented female.

"I knew it!" Johnis cried. "I knew it!"

She sidestepped a thrust of Alucard's claw, dove for the female, and plunged the second stake into the creature's chest.

Silvie watched in disbelief as both Alucard and the female who would bring his offspring to life began to melt before them. Their flesh fell from their bodies like rotten flesh falling from an overripe fruit. Unable to hold their own weight, they fell to the ground, writhing.

Dying.

Darsal stood back, eyeing them. Silvie knew then that Darsal, chosen alongside Silvie and Johnis and Billos, had planned this all along.

Still the Shataiki flooded the chamber.

# TWENTY-EIGHT

knew it!" Johnis said. "The key, the key, hurry!"

Darsal stared at him.

"Darsal . . ."

What was she doing? She'd saved them, right? She'd planned this whole thing down to the final touches: winning Alucard's trust by giving him her book, pretending to be filled with bitterness, knowing that one day the others would come through and Alucard would have the advantage. He would beat them to the books. But she would be there to kill him, having learned precisely how to kill Shataiki in this reality.

Everything else had been lies. She'd lied to them so that Alucard wouldn't have any reason to doubt her. And she'd turned on him only when he was at his weakest, in the moment of his own glory.

She'd done it.

Hadn't she?

"Darsal," Johnis breathed. "Please, no, no, no! Tell us that you've stayed true!"

Darsal spit on Alucard, who was now a shivering blob. She crossed to the table and stood before the seven Books of Histories.

For a moment she just stood there, her back to the others.

*Stop it!* Silvie thought. *Break the connection. Shut the gateway!*

Instead, Darsal spun around, thrust both arms into the air, and screamed at the bats still swarming into the chamber.

"It's her!" Karas cried. "Darsal is the Dark One!"

So then not everything Darsal had said had been a lie. She'd intended on killing Alucard all along, but she was as bitter as she'd let on.

Darsal screamed at the ceiling, full throated, veins pronounced on her neck and arms. But now tears ran down her face. She took one long draw of air and screamed again, until Silvie thought she might tear her throat.

"Elyon!" Johnis wept. "Elyon compels you, Darsal. Elyon compels us all."

"No!" Darsal whirled to Johnis. "Elyon made the Dark One, you fool! Don't you see? I am the Dark One. The prophesy was about me! I am destined to destroy this world. I've turned my back on Elyon!"

She was right.

"I haven't turned my back on Elyon." Johnis's eyes darted to the

Shataiki filling the room. A thousand it seemed. For a moment Silvie thought she saw some white fur among them, but then it was gone.

"You may be the Dark One, but you can't deny Elyon's power," Johnis said. "Or his will to take the diseased and bathe them in his water!"

Darsal was breathing hard, her eyes fiery, desperate. But she had nothing to say.

"It doesn't matter why you did what you did any longer!" Johnis cried. "It only matters what you do right now."

Her face wrinkled. Shataiki streamed in over her head. On the ground, Alucard and his bride convulsed, then stopped moving.

The worms stopped squealing. Except for the steady beating of wings through the gateway, the room fell silent.

The Shataiki suddenly began to fall to the floor, chunks of rotting fur raining from the ceiling by the hundreds. They thudded on the stone and immediately bowed their heads to Darsal. The ground was quickly carpeted with black bats except for a large circle around Darsal and the two dead Shataiki.

Silvie blinked. Having lost one master, they were acknowledging another: Darsal.

The Dark One.

"Is Elyon so foolish?" Johnis demanded.

Darsal was out of words. Now it was tears that came from her in streams, wetting her cheeks.

"Do you think he allowed you to become this so-called Dark One without knowing it would work to his advantage?"

What was he saying?

"He knew that in this moment you would do something not even you have anticipated. That was why he chose you! He knew you would stand against evil! You will undo all that Alucard has done by saving the books."

She shook her head. "No . . ."

"You, this Dark One, will embrace Elyon's love, that same love you felt for Billos, and you will destroy evil."

"No . . ."

"Because you are not evil. Evil has just consumed you. But they . . ." Johnis pointed at the hundreds of Shataiki now on the ground, bowing to Darsal, tempting her with their service. "They are evil!"

"Nooooooo!" Darsal screamed, weeping. "Nooooooo!"

"Yes!" Johnis cried. "Yes!"

Johnis began to weep. Darsal sank to her knees.

"End it, Darsal," Johnis said. "You've killed Alucard. Now rid yourself of his evil."

She let her hands go limp by her sides, sobbing, her face tilted up, eyes closed. "I'm the Dark One," she mouthed. "I'm the Dark One."

"Fight, Darsal! Fight for Elyon." Then in a raw voice that made Silvie want to cry, "You are the chosen one!"

It was as if this truth had hit Johnis for the first time. Darsal might have convinced herself that she was the Dark One, but even being the Dark One, she was the chosen one.

Silvie suddenly felt the weight of the idea and began to cry with them. Because she, too, was the Dark One, wasn't she? They all were, as much as they were all Forest Dwellers, without Elyon's cleansing waters.

Yet they were chosen. It was up to them to follow either the one who had made them dark, or the one who had chosen each of them.

Teeleh or Elyon.

"No, no, no, no, no, no . . ." Darsal was rocking, sobbing the words.

Shataiki continued to stream into the room.

"Please, Darsal," Karas cried. "Please . . ."

Without warning, another larger Shataiki spilled through the gateway, landed next to Alucard's dead body, and flapped to steady itself.

"Darsal!" Silvie screamed.

She jerked her head up at the warning, seeing the second female. She stood shakily, staring, gathering her wits.

And then something behind her eyes snapped into place. She rushed the dead slab of meat that used to be Alucard and jerked the stake from its heart.

Screamed, red-faced.

Rushed the second female from behind.

Slammed the stake into its back, right through the rib cage, through whatever innards filled the heartless creature, and right out its chest.

She held the stake in place, resisting the attempts of the flailing beast to break free.

"Back to hell!" Darsal thundered. Then again, in a voice that cracked with emotion, "Back to hell!"

She released the stake and staggered back, breathing hard. Her heel struck her bag, and she stopped. Still Shataiki poured in through the gateway.

"Darsal . . ."

It was all Johnis needed to say. Darsal's face wrinkled with anguish for just a moment. She glanced up, saw the beasts bowing to her, and swept up her bag. Flung it sidearmed at Johnis.

"The keys!" Silvie cried. "Quick!"

Johnis frantically rummaged through the bag.

Darsal was already sprinting toward the Books of History, scattering the Shataiki gathered there. She grabbed the stack of books with both hands and tore the top three from the table with a grunt.

The light vanished immediately with a crack that echoed through the chamber. The upper halves of two Shataiki spun from the closed gateway into the room and fell to the floor, dead lumps of bleeding fur.

Darsal's sudden change of heart wasn't lost on the thousands of Shataiki gathered on the floor. They began to bob and shriek with open jaws, like begging chicks in a nest.

"Hurry!" Darsal grabbed the other four books and sprinted for them.

Johnis found the keys, freed Silvie, and was working on Karas.

Thoughts of servitude no longer in their minds, the Shataiki began to take flight around the room. First a dozen, then a hundred, then a thousand, shrieking and flapping in a river of black just below the worms.

Darsal kept one eye on the Shataiki and one on the bag as she withdrew first one, then two flares.

The bats gained courage and began to sweep down, snapping their jaws. Above them, the worms were screaming.

Darsal shoved a flare at Silvie. "Light it by ripping the cap off. It's hot enough to ignite the worms' mucus. This place will go up like a tin of gasoline."

Johnis had freed Karas, and now himself.

"Run!" Darsal jumped off the ledge and streaked for the shut door. Silvie followed hard after her. A bat brushed through her hair, and she cried out, swatting at her head.

"Light it!" Darsal slammed open the latch.

Silvie slid to a stop. She jerked the cap off the flare. It hissed and spouted red flame.

The Shataiki grew frantic. They flew every which way now, shrieking, crashing into the walls, clawing at the stone.

"Light it!" Darsal screamed again, throwing the door open.

Silvie thrust the flare against the worm salve on the wall. It sizzled but refused to light.

Shataiki had found the open door and flew out above Darsal's head now, dozens, shrieking as they disappeared.

"Go, go, go!"

Karas ran out, followed by Johnis.

Darsal snatched the flare from Silvie. "Go!"

"You—"

"Go!"

She went. Through the door.

A plume of orange flame and heat mushroomed behind her, and she spun to see Darsal tearing for the door.

The flame spread along the walls like ignited oil on water. *Whoosh!* Silvie stood like wood, stunned by how rapidly the fire consumed the room.

Shataiki, now totally aware of their impending demise, clogged the door. Behind them a huge ball of fire fell screaming from the ceiling. A burning worm.

"Go, go, go!"

Darsal tugged her. Slammed the door shut. Bats thudded into the wood. Even outside, the roaring flames were deafening.

Then they were running up the passage. Silvie was the last up the stairway into Alucard's library, where more worms crowded the ceiling. Darsal had ripped open her flare and was lighting fire to one of the wet walls behind the bookcases.

"Get out!"

No Shataiki, Silvie saw. They'd already flown out.

They waited for Darsal by the door this time, until her flame caught. The library went up like a tinderbox, chasing them out the door with heat and flames.

Darsal led them from the fortress in a full sprint. Out into the cool night air. Just in time to see a black stain winging frantically for the sky.

Shataiki screeched overhead, scattering to find safety.

Silvie spun back to the castle. Light flickered from the hallway past the door. And when she stilled her breath to listen with the others, she could hear the distant cries of burning Shataiki and igniting worms.

Alucard's lair was being consumed by hell.

# TWENTY-NINE

Johnis, Silvie, Karas, and Darsal stood on the side of the road for a long time, watching and listening to the flames. Little was said. Much was considered.

Silvie looked up at the graying eastern sky. "Morning is coming."

And for a while, nothing more was spoken.

"We did it." Johnis looked at the seven Books of History that Darsal had placed on the ground. "We have finally found the seven books."

For a few long beats they all just stared at them. Darsal's shoulders shook with a sob. She hugged herself with one arm and lifted the other hand to cover her face.

"No, Darsal." Silvie put her arm over the girl's shoulder. "You can't blame yourself."

"I . . . I . . ."

"You are chosen," Johnis said. "And you saved us all. That's all that matters now."

It was hard to imagine what kind of suffering Darsal's bitterness had caused her all these years. *She will bear that scar,* Silvie thought. But Johnis was right. They had won. They were the chosen ones, and they had recovered the seven books.

"There's still danger. The books can still be used." Karas picked up the black one and wiped Alucard's blood off its cover using a tissue from her pocket. "What now?"

"Now we have to return them," Johnis said.

A whoosh of wings disturbed the air behind Silvie, and she spun around, expecting Shataiki. But this wasn't a wad of black muscle.

It was a ball of white fur: Roush. Michal!

And hard on Michal's heels, Gabil landed a ways off, tumbled three full turns on the ground, and launched himself into a spindly but much improved karate kick.

"Hiyah!" he cried, and then landed on both feet where he managed to keep his balance. "What do you think? Was that better?"

Silvie now realized that the white streak she had seen among the flood of black Shataiki had been Michal and Gabil! They stood like two soldiers on the grass, green eyes glimmering, fur so white they looked like the marshmallows Karas had served them with coffee.

Karas rushed up to Gabil and dropped to one knee. "Thank Elyon!" She hugged the Roush. "How is Hunter?"

Gabil nearly toppled backward with her hug. "Easy, easy! My improved skills don't include protection against the hug of death! Hunter who?"

"The Roush who guards Middle?"

"Oh, *Hunter*," Gabil said. "As full of himself as always, I'm sure."

Johnis hurried up to Michal, dropped down to one knee, and bowed his head. "You have no idea how good it is to see you, Michal."

A thin grin crossed the Roush's lips. "Actually, I do."

Then they all crowded around the two furry, white bats, peppering them with questions and offering details about their close call with Alucard. And in short order, some things were finally set straight.

Yes, both realities were linked in so many ways that not even Michal had known before. Thomas of Hunter's dreams were indeed true, all of them, in both places. Teeleh's attempt to destroy the world through the disease borne in Shataiki—the Horde disease—was now foiled.

But in reality, Thomas of Hunter's greatest tests remained ahead of him. He might be a figure of history here in the Histories, but he was still the leader of the Forest Dwellers in a war that was being waged against the Horde. And things were about to get very nasty.

"Then we have to get back!" Johnis paced a tight circle. "Now!"

"You can if you wish," Michal said. "But five years will have passed when you arrive there."

"What? How's that possible?"

"I've been forbidden from allowing you to influence events there now that you know what you do."

"But five years! What's happened in five years?"

"The world has changed. You'll see."

Silvie put her hand on Johnis's arm. "How old will we be? There, I mean?"

Gabil flashed a grin. "Old enough to be blissfully married, if you so choose; no worries there, Silvie. And if you like, I could perform some of my—"

"Please, Gabil," Michal cut in. "No one wants to see you stumble through your karate moves at a wedding. Get a grip on reality, will you?"

"No." Johnis looked at Silvie and winked. "We would love to see Gabil perform at our wedding, wouldn't we, Silvie?"

She felt so buoyed by his statement that she nearly threw her arms around his neck and kissed him in front of them all.

"Yes." She returned his wink. "Yes, we would."

Michal nodded. "So I take it that you two would like to go back with the books?"

"If it's okay," Johnis said.

"Of course."

"When?"

"Now. But five years will have passed."

It was a heady idea, Silvie thought.

"Does it matter if we stay or return?" Karas eyed Darsal.

"Of course it matters. But it is your decision entirely. Wherever you live, you will have challenges, as long as evil remains unbound."

"And what about the Shataiki?" Darsal glanced above her at the gray sky.

"Yes, them. A few dozen escaped, wouldn't you say?"

"Maybe more. But they were males."

"And there are no females." Michal shrugged. "I would worry more about the others."

Karas looked up. "Others?"

A worried look crossed Darsal's face. "You're saying the rumors are true?"

"There's usually at least some truth in a rumor."

"What are you talking about?" Karas demanded.

"The vampires," Darsal said. "Alucard's been a busy beast all of these years."

Silvie listened with interest, but the greater part of her mind was on the forests. The faster she could return, be it five years or five hundred years from now, the better.

Darsal nudged a stone with her foot. "I have to know something."

"Whether or not you were the Dark One," Michal said.

Her eyes met his.

"Johnis was right," the Roush said. "You are both fallen and chosen. As are all of you. And your choices aren't finished. Do you follow?"

"Billos . . ."

"Gone. To save you. But you knew that."

She nodded gently.

"I'm proud of you, Darsal. After falling so hard, you stood. But please, try not to fall again."

She smiled.

"So it was all about this . . . these books?" Karas asked. "Paradise, the worms, the monastery. Thomas Hunter."

"Yes. And no. Yes, the lost books are now found, and this chapter is over. But as I said, Thomas has only begun to face his challenges in the forests. And here . . ." Michal glanced at the nearby forest. "Here it's all about the sinner."

The Roush said it with such a mix of passion and frustration that Silvie cringed to think what could ruffle such a stoic creature as Michal.

"Now, what will it be? Who's going, who's staying?"

Karas stepped up to Silvie and hugged her tight. "This reality is my home now. I have a world that needs some saving."

She sniffed and hugged Johnis, then Darsal.

"This place holds too many terrible memories for me," Darsal said. She was forgiven and she'd saved the day, but she was still wrestling with all of it. "I don't know what I'm going to do back in the forests without Billos, but I can't stay here."

"Then you'll be coming with us," Johnis assured her with a

slight grin. "We'll find a way to put what we now know to use, I'm sure."

Darsal offered a weak smile. "That's what concerns me."

They looked at each other in silence for a moment.

"There you have it, then." Michal waddled to where the books lay on the grass. "The books have been recovered, the quest is finished, the mission has been successful. The end."

And so it was.

Or was it?

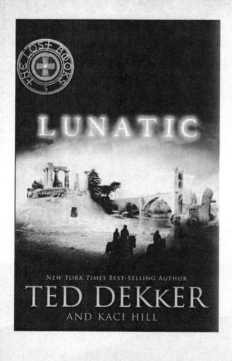

# "THIS IS THE SERIES I WAS BORN TO WRITE. DIVE DEEP."

*Ted Dekker*

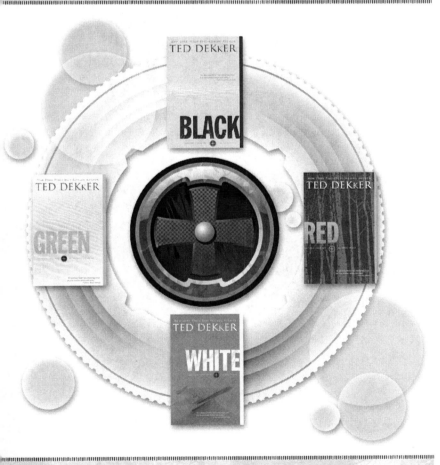

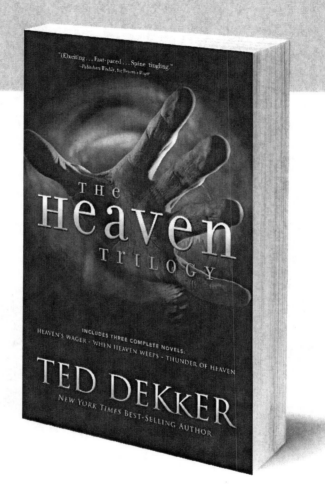

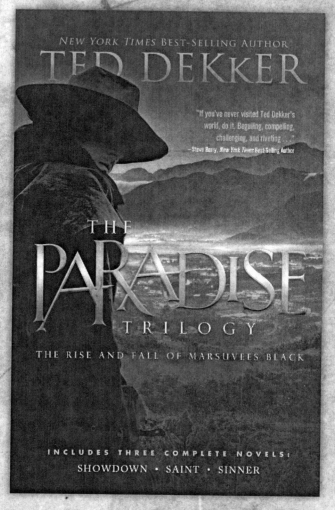

Cheryl Muhr

**Ted Dekker** is the *New York Times* best-selling author of more than 25 novels. He is known for stories that combine adrenaline-laced plots with incredible confrontations between good and evil. He lives in Texas with his wife and children.

CPSIA information can be obtained at www.ICGtesting.com
Printed in the USA
LVOW05s1454100414

380998LV00014B/19/P